RED ROCK

A CHRONICLE OF RECONSTRUCTION

SHE GAVE HIM A ROLLING-PIN AND HE SET TO WORK.

RED ROCK

A CHRONICLE OF RECONSTRUCTION

BY

THOMAS NELSON PAGE

ILLUSTRATED BY B. WEST CLINEDINST

NEW YORK
CHARLES SCRIBNER'S SONS
1903

Printed by Manhattan Press,
New York, U. S. A.

To

F. L. P.

AN OLD-FASHIONED LADY

PREFACE

The Region where the Grays and Carys lived lies too far from the centres of modern progress to be laid down on any map that will be accessible. And, as "he who maps an undiscovered country may place what boundaries he will," it need only be said, that it lies in the South, somewhere in that vague region partly in one of the old Southern States and partly in the yet vaguer land of Memory. It will be spoken of in this story, as Dr. Cary, General Legaie, and the other people who used to live there in old times, spoke of it, in warm affection, as, "the old County," or, "the Red Rock section," or just, "My country, sir."

It was a goodly land in those old times—a rolling country, lying at the foot of the blue mountain-spurs, with forests and fields; rich meadows filled with fat cattle; watered by streams, sparkling and bubbling over rocks, or winding under willows and sycamores, to where the hills melted away in the low, alluvial lands, where the sea once washed and still left its memory and its name.

The people of that section were the product of a system of which it is the fashion nowadays to have

*only words of condemnation. Every ass that passes
by kicks at the dead lion. It was an Oligarchy, they
say, which ruled and lorded it over all but those
favored ones who belonged to it. But has one ever
known the members of a Democracy to rule so justly?
If they shone in prosperity, much more they shone in
adversity; if they bore themselves haughtily in their
day of triumph, they have borne defeat with splendid
fortitude. Their old family seats, with everything
else in the world, were lost to them — their dignity
became grandeur. Their entire system crumbled and
fell about them in ruins—they remained unmoved.
They were subjected to the greatest humiliation of
modern times: their slaves were put over them—they
reconquered their section and preserved the civilization of the Anglo-Saxon.*

*No doubt the phrase "Before the war" is at times
somewhat abused. It is just possible that there is a
certain Caleb Balderstonism in the speech at times.
But for those who knew the old County as it was
then, and can contrast it with what it has become
since, no wonder it seems that even the moonlight was
richer and mellower "before the war" than it is now.
For one thing, the moonlight as well as the sunlight
shines brighter in our youth than in maturer age;
and gold and gossamer amid the rose-bowers reflect it
better than serge and crêpe amid myrtles and bays.
The great thing is not to despond even though the
brilliancy be dimmed: in the new glitter one need not
necessarily forget the old radiance. Happily, when
one of the wise men insists that it shall be forgotten,*

*and that we shall be wise also, like him, it works
automatically, and we know that he is one of those
who, as has been said, avoiding the land of romance,
"have missed the title of fool at the cost of a celes-
tial crown."*

*Why should not Miss Thomasia in her faded dress,
whom you shall meet, tell us, if she pleases, of her
"dear father," and of all her "dear cousins" to the
remotest generation; and Dr. Cary and General Legaie
quote their grandfathers as oracles, alongside the sages
of Plutarch, and say "Sir" and "Madam" at the
end of their sentences? Antiquated, you say? Provincial? Do you, young lady, observe Miss Thomasia
the next time she enters a room, or addresses a servant; and do you, good sir, polished by travel and contact with the most fashionable — second-class — society
of two continents, watch General Legaie and Dr. Cary
when they meet Miss Thomasia, or greet the apple-
woman on the corner, or the wagoner on the road.
What an air suddenly comes in with them of old
Courts and polished halls when all gentlemen bowed
low before all ladies, and wore swords to defend their
honor. What an odor, as it were, of those gardens
which Watteau painted, floats in as they enter! Do
not you attempt it. You cannot do it. You are thinking of yourself, they of others and the devoirs they
owe them. You are republican and brought up to
consider yourself "as good as any, and better than
most." Sound doctrine for the citizen, no doubt; but
it spoils the bow. Even you, Miss or Madam, for all
your silks and satins, cannot do it like Miss Thomasia.*

You are imitating the duchess you saw once, perhaps, in Hyde Park. The duchess would have imitated Miss Thomasia. You are at best an imitation; Miss Thomasia is the reality. Do not laugh at her, or call her provincial. She belongs to the realm where sincerity dwells and the heart still rules—the realm of old-time courtesy and high breeding, and you are the real provincial. It is a wide realm, though; and some day, if Heaven be good to you, you may reach it. But it must be by the highway of Sincerity and Truth. No other road leads there.

CONTENTS

xi

xiv CONTENTS

LIST OF ILLUSTRATIONS

RED ROCK

CHAPTER I

IN WHICH THERE ARE SEVERAL INTRODUCTIONS

The old Gray plantation, " Red Rock," lay at the high-est part of the rich rolling country, before it rose too ab-ruptly in the wooded foothills of the blue mountains away to the westward. As everybody in the country knew, who knew anything, it took its name from the great red stain, as big as a blanket, which appeared on the huge bowlder in the grove, beside the family grave-yard, at the far end of the Red Rock gardens. And as was equally well known, or equally well believed, which amounted almost to the same thing, that stain was the blood of the Indian chief who had slain the wife of the first Jacquelin Gray who came to this part of the world : the Jacquelin who had built the first house at Red Rock, around the fireplace of which the pres-ent mansion was erected, and whose portrait, with its pierc-ing eyes and fierce look, hung in a black frame over the mantel, and used to come down as a warning when any peril impended above the house.

The bereft husband had exacted swift retribution of the murderer, on that very rock, and the Indian's heart blood had left that deep stain in the darker granite as a perpet-ual memorial of the swift vengeance of the Jacquelin Grays.

This, at least, was what was asserted and believed by the old negroes (and, perhaps, by some of the whites, too, a little). And if the negroes did not know, who did ? So Jacquelin often pondered.

Steve Allen, who was always a reckless talker, however, used to say that the stain was nothing but a bit of red sandstone which had outcropped at the point where that huge fragment was broken off, and rolled along by a glacier thousands of years ago, far to the northward; but this view was to the other children's minds clearly untenable; for there never could have been any glacier there—glaciers, as they knew from their geographies, being confined to Switzerland, and the world having been created only six thousand years ago. The children were well grounded by their mothers and Miss Thomasia in Bible history. Besides, there was the picture of the "Indian-killer," in the black frame nailed in the wall over the fireplace in the great hall, and one could not go anywhere in the hall without his fierce eyes following you with a look so intent and piercing that Mammy Celia was wont to use it half jestingly as a threat effectual with little Jacquelin when he was refractory—that if he did not mind, the "Indian-killer" would see him and come after him. How often Mammy Celia employed it with Jacquelin, and how severe she used to be with tall, reckless Steve, because he scoffed at the story, and to tease her, threatened, with appropriate gesture, to knock the picture out of the frame, and see what was in the secret cabinet behind it! What would have happened had Steve carried out his threat, Jacquelin, as a boy, quite trembled to think; for though he admired Steve, his cousin, above all other mortals, as any small boy admires one several years his senior, who can ride wild horses and do things he cannot do, this would have been to engage in a contest with something supernatural and not mortal. Still he used to urge Steve to do it, with a certain fascinating apprehensiveness that made the chills creep up and down his back. Besides, it would have been very interesting to know whether the Indian's scalp was still in the hollow space behind the picture, and if so, whether it was still bleeding, and that red stain on the bottom of the frame was really blood.

Jacquelin Gray—the one who figures in these pages—was born while his father, and his father's cousin, Dr. Cary, of Birdwood, and Mr. Legaie were in Mexico, winning renown in those battles which helped to establish the security of the United States. He grew up to be just what most other boys of his station, stature, and blood, living on a plantation, under similar conditions, would have been. He was a hale, hearty boy, who adored his cousin, Steve Allen, because Steve was older and stronger than he; despised Blair Cary because she was a girl; disliked Wash Still, the overseer's son, partly because Steve sneered at him, and partly because the negro boys disliked him, and envied every cart-driver and stable-boy on the place. He used to drive with string "lines" two or four or six of his black boon companions, giving them the names of his father's horses in the stable; or sometimes, even the names of those steeds of which his Aunt Thomasia, a famous story-teller, told him in the hour before the candles were lighted. But if he drove the black boys in harness, it was because they let him do it, and not because he was their master. If he possessed any privileges or power, he did not know it. If anything, he thought the advantage rather on their side than on his, as they could play all the time, while he had to go to school to his Aunt Thomasia, whose bell he thought worse than any curfew; for that rang only at night, while Miss Thomasia's bell was sure to tinkle just at the moment when he was having the most beautiful time in the world. How gladly would he have exchanged places to mind the cows and ride the horses to the stable, and be free all day long; and whenever he could slip off he was with the boys, emulating them and being adored by them.

Once, indeed, his mastership appeared. Wash Still, the overseer's son, who was about Steve's age, used to bully the smaller boys, and one day when Jacquelin was playing about the blacksmith's shop, Wash, who was waiting for a horse to be shod, twisted the arm of Doan, one

of Jacquelin's sable team, until the boy whimpered.
Jacquelin never knew just how it happened, but a sudden
fulness came over him; he seized a hatchet lying by, and
made an onslaught on Wash, which came near performing
on that youngster the same operation that Wash's au-
gust namesake performed on the celebrated cherry-tree.
Jacquelin received a tremendous whipping from his father
for his vicious attack; but his defence saved his sable
companions from any further imposition than his own,
and Wash was shortly sent off by his father to school.

As to learning, Jacquelin was not very apt. It was only
when Blair Cary came over one winter and went to school
to Miss Thomasia—and he was laughed at by everyone,
particularly by Steve, because Blair, a girl several years
younger than he, could read Latin better—that Jacquelin
really tried to study. Though no one knew it, many of
the things that Jacquelin did were done in the hope that
Steve might think well of him; and whether it was riding
wild colts, with the certainty of being thrown and possibly hurt; diving into deep pools with the prospect of
being drowned, or doing anything else that he was afraid
to do, it was almost sure that it was done because of
Steve.

With some natures the mere performance of an action is
sufficient reward : that man suffers martyrdom; this one
does a great act; another lives a devoted, saint's life, impelled solely from within, and with no other idea than to
perform nobly. But these are rare natures : the Christo-
phers, à Kempises and Theresas of the world. The common herd must have some more material motive : " wine,
or sleep, or praise." That charge was led because a dark—
or blonde-haired girl was waiting somewhere ; that gate
was blown up because an army was standing by, and a
small cross might be worn on the breast for it ; that poem
was written for Lalage, or Laura, Stella, or Saccharissa.
Even the saint was crowned, because somewhere, in retired
monasteries or in distant cities, deeds were sure to be

known at last. So, now it is a big boy's praise, and later on a fair girl's favor; now the plaudits of the playground, and a few years hence salvos of artillery and the thanks of the people. And who shall say they are not worthy motives? We are but men, and only the highest win even these rewards.

Steve Allen had come to Red Rock before Jacquelin could remember—the year after Steve's father was killed in Mexico, leading his company up the heights of Cerro Gordo, and his mother died of fever far down South. Mr. Gray had brought the boy home on his mother's death; so Steve was part of Red Rock. Everybody spoiled him, particularly Miss Thomasia, who made him her especial charge and was notoriously partial to him, and old Peggy, Steve's "Momma," as she was called, who had come from the far South with him, and with her sharp eyes and sharper tongue was ready to fight the world for him.

Steve was a tall, brown-haired young fellow, as straight as a sapling, and with broad shoulders; gray eyes that could smile or flash; teeth as white as snow, and a chin that Dr. Cary used to say he must have got from his mother. He was as supple as an eel. He could turn back-somersaults like a circus man, and as he was without fear, so he was without reverence. He would tease Miss Thomasia, and play practical jokes on Mr. Gray and Dr. Cary. To show his contempt for the "Indian-Killer," he went alone and spent the night on the bloody rock, and when the other boys crept in a body to see if he were really there, he was found by the little party of scared searchers to be tranquilly asleep on the "Indian-Killer's" very grave. This and similar acts gained Steve Allen, with some, the credit of being in a sort of compact with the spirit of darkness, and several of the old negroes on the plantation began to tell of his wonderful powers, a reputation which Steve was not slow to improve; and afterward, many a strange, unearthly sound, that scared the negroes, and ghostly manifestations which went the rounds of the plantation might possibly have been traced to Steve's fertile brain.

The only persons on the place who did not get on well with Steve were Hiram Still, the manager, and his son, Wash. Between them and Steve there was declared enmity, if not open war. Steve treated Hiram with superciliousness, and Wash with open contempt. The old negroes—who remembered Steve's father, Captain Allen, Mr. Gray's cousin, and the dislike between him and Hiram —said it was " bred in the bone."

At length Steve went off to school to Dr. Maule, at " The Academy," as it was called, no further designation being needed to distinguish it, as no other academies could for a moment have entered into competition with it, and there was a temporary suspension of the supernatural manifestations on the plantation. Jacquelin missed him sorely and tried to imitate him in many things ; but he knew it was a poor imitation, for often he could not help being afraid, whilst Steve did not know what fear was. Jacquelin's knees would shake, and his teeth sometimes chatter, whilst Steve performed his most dangerous feats with mantling cheeks and dancing eyes. However, the boy kept on, and began to do things simply because he was afraid. One day he read how a great general, named Marshal Turenne, on being laughed at because his knees were shaking as he mounted his horse to go into battle, replied that if his knees knew where he was going to take them that day they would shake still more. This incident helped Jacquelin mightily, and he took his knees into many dangerous places. In time this had its effect, and as his knees began to shake less he began to grow more self-confident and conceited. He began to be very proud of himself, and to take opportunities to show his superiority over others, which developed with some rapidity the character existent somewhere in most persons : the prig.

Blair Cary gave the first, if not the final, shock to this development.

She was the daughter of Dr. Cary, Mr. Gray's cousin, who lived a few miles off across the river, at "Birdwood," perhaps the next most considerable place to Red Rock in that section. She was a slim little girl with a rather pale face, large brown eyes, and hair that was always blowing into them.

She would have given her eyes, no doubt, to have been accepted as companion by Jacquelin, who was several years her senior ; but as that young man was now aspiring to be comrade to Steve and to Blair's brother, Morris, he relegated Blair to the companionship of his small brother, Rupert, who was as much younger than Blair as she was younger than himself, and treated her with sovereign disdain. The first shock he received was when he found how much better Blair could read Latin than he could, and how much Steve thought of her on that account. After that, he actually condescended to play with her occasionally, and, sometimes, even to let her follow him about the plantation to admire his feats, whilst he tried to revenge himself on her for her superior scholastic attainments by showing her how much more a boy could do than a girl. It was all in vain. For, with this taunt for a spur, she would follow him even to the tops of trees, or the bottoms of ponds : so he determined to show his superiority by one final and supreme act. This was to climb to the roof of the "high barn," as it was called, and spring off into the top of a tree which spread its branches below. He had seen Steve do it, but had never ventured to try it himself. He had often climbed to the roof, and had fancied himself performing this feat to escape from pursuing Indians, but had never really contemplated doing it in fact, until Blair's persistent emulation, daunted by nothing that he attempted, spurred him to undertake it. So one day, after some boasting, he climbed to the peak of the roof. His heart beat so as he gazed down into the green mass far below him and saw the patches of brown earth through the leaves, that he wished

he had not been so boastful; but there was Blair behind
him, astride of the roof, her eyes fastened on him with a
somewhat defiant gaze. He thought how Steve would jeer
if he knew he had turned back. So, with a call of derision
to Blair to see what "a man could do," he set his teeth,
shut his eyes, and took the jump, and landed safely below,
among the boughs, his outstretched arms gathering them
in as he sank amidst them, until they stopped his descent
and he found a limb and climbed down, his heart bump-
ing with excitement and pride. Blair, he felt sure, was
at last "stumped." As he sprang to the ground and
looked up he saw a sight which made his heart give a
bigger bound than it had ever done in all his life. There
was little Blair on the very peak of the roof, the very
point of the gable, getting ready to follow him. Her face
was white, her lips were compressed, and her eyes were
opened so wide that he could see them even from where
he was. She was poised like a bird ready to fly.

"Blair! Blair!" he cried, waving her back. "Don't!
don't!" But Bla'r took no heed. She only settled herself for a firmer foothold, and the next second, with outstretched arms, she sprang into space. Whether it was
that his cry distracted her, or whether her hair blew into
her eyes and made her miss her step, or whether she would
have misjudged her distance anyhow, instead of reaching
the thickly leaved part where Jacquelin had landed, she
struck where the boughs were much less thick, and came
crashing through: down, down, from bough to bough,
until she landed on the lowest limb, where she stopped for
a second, and then rolled over and fell in a limp little
bundle on the ground, where she lay quite still. Jacquelin
never forgot the feeling he had at that moment. He was
sure she was dead, and that he was a murderer. In a second he was down on his knees, bending over her.

"Blair, Blair," he cried. "Dear Blair, are you hurt?"
But there was no answer. And he began to whimper in a
very unmanly fashion for one who had been so boastful a

moment before, and to pray, too, which is not so unmanly; but his wits were about him, and it came to him quite clearly that, if she were not dead, the best thing to do was to unfasten her neck-band and bathe her face. So off to the nearest water he put as hard as his legs could take him, and dipped his handkerchief in the horse-trough, and then, grabbing up a bucket near by, filled it and ran back with it. Blair was still motionless and white, but he wiped her little, scratched face and bathed it again and again, and, presently, to his inexpressible joy, she sighed and half opened her eyes and sighed again, and then, as he was still asking her how she felt, said, faintly:

"I'm all right—I did it."

In his joy Jacquelin actually kissed her. It seemed to him afterward to mark an epoch.

The next quarter of an hour was passed in getting Blair's breath back. Fortunately for her, if not for her dress, her clothes had caught here and there as she came crashing through the branches, and though the breath was knocked out of her, and she was shaken and scratched and stunned, no bones were broken, and she was not seriously hurt after all. She proposed that they should say nothing about it to anyone: she could get his Mammy to mend her clothes. But this magnanimous offer Jacquelin firmly declined. He was afraid that Blair might be hurt some way that she did not know, and he declared that he should go straight and tell it at the house.

"But I did it myself," persisted little Blair; "you were not to blame. You called to me not to do it."

"Did you hear me call? Then why did you do it?"

"Because you had done it and said I could not."

"But didn't you know you would get hurt?"

She nodded.

"I thought so."

Jacquelin looked at her long and seriously, and that moment a new idea seemed to him to enter his mind: that, after all, it might be as brave to do a dangerous thing which you are afraid to do, as if you are not at all afraid.

"Blair, you are a brick," he said ; "you are braver than any boy I know—as brave as Steve. As brave as Marshal Turenne." Which was sweet enough to Blair to make amends for all her bruises and scratches.

From that time Jacquelin made up his mind that he would never try to stump her again, but would guard her, and this sweetened to him the bitterness of having to confess when he got to the house. He did it like a man, going to his father, of whom, at heart, he was mightily afraid, and telling him the whole story alone without the least reference to Blair's part in it, taking the entire blame on himself; and it was only after he had received the punishment which was deemed due him that Blair's joint responsibility was known from her own lips.

This escapade, however, proved a little too much for the elders, and Jacquelin was sent off to school, to the Academy at Brutusville, under the learned Doctor Maule, where, still emulating Steve, who was the leader in most of the mischief that went on at that famous institution of learning, he made more reputation by the way he constructed a trap to catch one of the masters, Mr. Eliphalet Bush, than in construing the ancient language which was that gentleman's particular department.

CHAPTER II

EVERYONE knows what a seething ferment there was
for some time before the great explosion in the beginning
of the Sixties—that strange decade that changed the civilization of the country. Red Rock, like the rest of the
land, was turned from a haunt of peace into a forum.
Politics were rampant; every meeting was a lyceum; boys
became orators; young girls wore partisan badges; children used party-catchwords, which they did not understand—except one thing: that they represented "their
side." There existed an irreconcilable difference between
the two sections of the country. It could not be crushed.
Hydra-headed, it appeared after every extirpation.

One side held slavery right under the double title of the
Bible and of the Constitution. The leader of the other side
said, "If it was not wrong, then nothing was wrong"; but
declared that he would not interfere with it.

"Bosh!" said Major Legaie. "That is not a man to
condone what he thinks wrong. If he is elected, it means
the end of slavery." And so said many others. Most of
them, rather than yield, were for War. To them War was
only an episode: a pageant: a threshold to glory. Dr.
Cary, who was a Whig, was opposed to it; he had seen it,
and he took the stump in opposition to Major Legaie.

"We could whip them with pop-guns," said the fire-
eaters. Fordyce Lambly and Hurlbut Bail were two of
them.

"But will they fight with that weapon?" asked **Dr.**

11

Cary, scornfully. He never liked Lambly and Bail; he said they had no convictions. "A man with convictions may be wrong; but you know where to meet him, sir. You never know where to find these men."

"Do you know what War is?" he said in a speech, in reply to a secession-speech by Major Legaie. "War is the most terrible of all disasters, except Dishonor. I do not speak of the dangers. For every brave man must face danger as it comes, and should court glory; and death for one's Country is glorious. I speak merely of the change that War inevitably brings. War is the destruction of everything that exists. You may fail or you may win, but what exists passes, and something different takes its place. The plough-share becomes a spear, and the pruning-hook a sword; the poor may become richer, but the rich must become poorer. You are the wealthiest people in the world to-day—not in mere riches, but in wealth. You may become the poorest. No people who enter a war wealthy and content ever come out of war so. I do not say that this is an unanswerable reason for not going to war. For war may be right at any cost. But it is not to be entered on unadvisedly or lightly; but in the fear of God. It should not be undertaken from mere enthusiasm; but deliberately, with a full recognition of its cost, and resolution to support its possible and direst consequences."

When he had ended, Mr. Hurlbut Bail, a speaker from the city, who had come to the county to stir up the people, said:

"Oh! Dr. Cary is nothing but a Cassandra."

"Did Troy fall or not?" asked Dr. Cary, calmly.

This, of course, changed no one. In times of high feeling debate only fuses opinions into convictions; only fans the flames and makes the fire a conflagration.

When the war came the old Doctor flung in his lot with his friends, and his gravity, that had grown on him of late, was lighted up by the old fire; he took his place and performed his part with kindling eyes and an erecter mien.

Hurlbut Bail became an editor. This, however, was later on.

The constantly increasing public ferment and the ever-enlarging and deepening cloud did not prevent the ordinary course of life from flowing in its accustomed channels: men planned and performed; sowed and reaped; bought and sold, as in ordinary times. And as in the period before that other flood, there was marrying and giving in marriage; so now, with the cloud ever mounting up the sky, men loved and married, and made their homes as the birds paired and built their nests.

Among those who builded in that period in the Red Rock district were a young couple, both of them cousins in some degree of nearly every gentle family in the county, including the Grays and Carys. And after the blessing by old Mr. Langstaff, at St. Ann's, amid the roses and smiles of the whole neighborhood, they spent their honeymoon, as the custom was then, in being entertained from house to house, through the neighborhood. In this round of gayety they came in due order to Red Rock, where the entertainment was perhaps to be the greatest of all. The amount of preparation was almost unprecedented, and the gentry of the whole county were invited and expected. As it was a notable occasion and near the holidays, Jacquelin was permitted to come home from Dr. Maule's on the joint application of his mother, his Aunt Thomasia, and Blair Cary; and Blair was allowed to come over with her mother and father and spend the night, and was promised to be allowed to sit up as late as she pleased—a privilege not to be lightly esteemed.

Steve Allen, with a faint mustache curled above his smiling mouth, was home from the University, and so were Morris Cary and the other young fellows; and the office in the yard, blue with tobacco-smoke, was as full of young men and pipes and dogs, as the upstairs chambers in the mansion were of young girls and ribbons and muslin.

What a heaven that outer office was to Jacquelin, and

what an angel Steve was to call him " Kid " and let him adore him !

Among the company that night there were two guests who " happened in " quite unexpectedly, but who were " all the more welcome on that account," the host said graciously in greeting them.   They were two gentlemen from quite another part of the country, or, perhaps, those resident there would have said, of the world ; as they came from the North.   They had come South on business connected with a sort of traditionary claim to mineral lands lying somewhere in the range of mountains which could be seen from the Red Rock plantation.   At least, Mr. Welch, the elder of the two, came on that errand.   The younger, Mr. Lawrence Middleton, came simply for pleasure, and because Mr. Welch, his cousin, had invited him. He had just spoiled his career at college by engaging, with his chum and crony, Aurelius Thurston, in the awful crime of painting the President's gray horse a brilliant red, and being caught at it.   He was suspended for this prank, and now was spending his time, literally rusticating, seeing a little of the world, while he made up his mind whether he should study Law and accept his cousin's offer to go into his office, or whether he should engage in a manufacturing business which his family owned.   His preference was rather for the latter, which was now being managed by a man named Bolter, who had made it very successful ; but Reely Thurston intended to be a lawyer, and wanted Lawrence to go in with him ; so he was taking time to consider. This visit South had inclined him to the law.

Mr. Welch and Middleton had concluded their business in the mountains : finding the lands they were seeking to lie partly in the clouds and partly in the possession of those whom they had always heard spoken of as " squatters ;" but now found to be a population who had been there since before the Revolution, and had built villages and towns.   They were now returning home and were making their way back toward the railroad, half a day's

journey farther on. They had expected to reach Brutns-
ville, the county seat, that night; but a rain the day
before had washed away the bridges, and compelled them
to take a circuitous route by a ford higher up the river.
There, not knowing the ford, they had almost been swept
away, and would certainly have lost their vehicle but for
the timely appearance of a young countryman, who happened to come along on his way home from a political
gathering somewhere.

Their deliverer: a certain Mr. Andy Stamper, was so
small that at a distance he looked like a boy, but on nearer
view he might have been anywhere from twenty or twenty-
five to thirty, and he proved extraordinarily active and
efficient. He swam in and helped Middleton get their
buggy out of the river, and then amused Mr. Welch very
much and incensed Middleton by his comments. He had
just been to a political meeting at the Court House, he
said, where he had heard " the finest speech that ever was
made," from Major Legaie. " He gave the Yankees sut,"
and he " just wished he could get every Yankee in that
river and drown 'em—every dog-goned one !" This as he
was working up to his neck in water.

Mr. Welch could not help laughing at the look on Middleton's ruddy face.

"Now, where'd you find a Yankee'd go in that river
like me an' you—or could do it, for that matter ? " the
little fellow asked of Middleton, confidentially.

"We are Yankees," blurted out Middleton, hotly.
"And a plenty of them would." His eye flashed as he
turned to his rescuer.

The little countryman's eyes opened wide, and his jaw
fell.

"Well, I'm durned !" he said, slowly, staring in open
astonishment, and Middleton began to look gratified at
the impression he had made.

"You know, you're the first I ever seen as wan't
ashamed to own it. Why, you looks most like we all !"

Middleton flushed; but little Stamper looked so sincerely ingenuous that he suddenly burst out laughing.

After that they became very friendly, and the travellers learned much of the glories of the Grays and Carys, and of the charms of a certain Miss Delia Dove, who, Stamper declared, was as pretty as any young lady that went to the Brick Church. Stamper offered to guide them, but as he refused to take any money for what he had done, and as he said he was going to see Miss Delia Dove and could take a nearer cut through the woods to his home, Mr. Welch declined to accept his offer, and contented himself with getting him to draw a map of the roads from that point to the county seat.

"All you've got to do is to follow that map: keep the main plain road and you can't get out; but I advise you to turn in at the first plantation you come to. If you go to Red Rock you'll have a good time. They're givin' a party thar to-night. Major Legaie, he left the meetin' to go thar."

He disappeared at a gallop down a bridle-path through the woods.

Notwithstanding the young countryman's assurances and map, the two strangers had gotten "out." The plantations were large in that section and the roads leading off to them from the highway, in the dark were all alike, so that when night fell the two travellers were in a serious dilemma. They at length came to a gate and were just considering turning in at it when a carriage drove up in front of them. A horseman who had been riding behind the vehicle came forward at a trot, calling out that he would open the gate.

"I thought you fellows would have been there hours ago," he said familiarly to the two strangers as he passed, evidently mistaking them in the dusk for some of his friends. "A laggard in love is a dastard in war."

The rest of his speech was lost in the click of the gate-latch and his apostrophe to his horse. When he found that Mr. Welch was a stranger, he changed instantly. His tone became graver and more gracious.

"I beg your pardon, sir. I thought from your vehicle that you were some of these effeminate youngsters who have given up the saddle for that new four-wheeled contrivance, and are ruining both our strains of horses and of men."

Mr. Welch asked if he knew where they could find a night's lodging.

"Why, at every house in the State, sir, I hope," said Dr. Cary; for it was he. "Certainly, at the nearest one. Drive right in. We are going to our cousins', and they will be delighted to have you. You are just in good time; for there is to be quite a company there to-night." And refusing to listen for a moment to Mr. Welch's suggestion that it might not be convenient to have strangers, Dr. Cary held the gate open for them to pass through.

"Drive in, sir," he said, in a tone of gracious command. "I never heard of its being inconvenient to have a guest," and in they drove.

"A gentleman by his voice," the travellers heard him explaining a little later into the window of the carriage behind them. And then he added, 'My only doubt was his vehicle."

After a half-mile drive through the woods they entered the open fields, and from a hill afar off, on top of which shone a house lit till it gleamed like a cluster of brilliants, a chorus of dogs sent them an inquiring greeting.

They passed through a wide gate, and ascended a steep hill through a grove, and Middleton's heart sank at the idea of facing an invited company, with a wardrobe that had been under water within the last two hours. Instantly they were in a group of welcomers, gentlemen, servants, and dogs; negro boys running; dogs frisking and yelping and young men laughing about the door of the newly arrived carriage. While through it all sounded the placid voice of Dr. Cary reassuring the visitors and in-

2

viting them in.   He brought the host to them, and presented them :

"My friends, Mr. Welch and young Mr. Middleton—
my cousin and friend, Mr. Gray." It was his customary
formula in introducing.   All men were his friends.   And
Mr. Welch shortly observed how his manner changed whenever he addressed a lady or a stranger : to one he was always a courtier, to the other always a host.

As they were ushered into the hall, Middleton's blue
eyes glistened and opened wide at the scene before him.
He found himself facing several score of people clustered
about in one of the handsomest halls he ever saw, some of
whom he took in at the first glance to be remarkably
pretty girls in white and pink, and all with their eyes,
filled with curiosity, bent on the new comers.   If Middleton's ruddiness increased tenfold under these glances, it
was only what any other young man's would have done
under similar circumstances, and it was not until he had
been led off under convoy of a tall and very solemn old
servant in a blue coat with brass buttons, and shown into
a large room with mahogany furniture and a bed so high
that it had a set of steps beside it, that he was able to collect his ideas, and recall some of those to whom he had
been introduced.   What a terrible fix it was for a fellow
to be in !   He opened his portmanteau and turned to his
cousin in despair.

"Isn't this a mess ? "

" What ? "

"This ! I can never go out there.   All those girls !
Just look at these clothes !   Everything dripping !—some
of them awfully pretty, too.   That one with the dark
eyes ! "   He was down on his knees, raking in his portmanteau, and dragging the soaking garments out one by
one.   " Now, look at that."

" You need not go out.   I'll make your excuses."

"What ! Of course I'm go——"

Just then there was a knock at the door.

" Come in." Middleton finished his sentence.

The door opened slowly and the old servant entered, bearing with a solemnity that amounted almost to reverence, a waiter with decanters and an array of glasses and bowls. He was followed by the young boy who had been introduced as their host's son.

" My father understood that you had a little accident at the river, and he wishes to know if he cannot lend you something," said Jacquelin.

Mr. Welch spoke first, his eyes twinkling as he glanced at his cousin, who stood a picture of indecision and bewilderment.

" Why yes, my cousin, Mr. Middleton here, would be greatly obliged, I think. He is a little particular about first impressions, and the presence of so many charming——"

Middleton protested.

" Why, certainly, sir," Jacquelin began, then turned to Middleton—" Steve's would fit you—Steve's my cousin—he's at the University—he's just six feet. Wait, sir——" And before they could stop him, he was gone, and a few minutes later tapped on the door, with his arms full of clothes.

" Uncle Daniel's as slow as a steer, so I fetched 'em myself," he panted, with boyish impatience, as he dropped the clothes partly on a sofa and partly on the floor. " Aunt Thomasia was afraid you'd catch cold, so she made me bring these flannels. She always is afraid you'll catch cold. Steve told her if you'd take a good swig out of a bottle 'twould be worth all the flannel in the State—Steve's always teasing her." With a boy's friendliness he had established himself now as the visitors' ally.

" I'm glad you came to-night. We're going to have lots of fun. Were you at the speaking to-day ? They say the Major made the finest speech ever was heard. Some say he's better than Calhoun ever was ; just gave the Yankees the mischief ! I wish they'd come down here and try us once, don't you ?"

Mr. Welch glanced amusedly at Middleton, whose face changed ; but fortunately the boy was too much interested in the suit Middleton had just put on to notice the effect.

" I thought Steve's would fit you," he said, with that proud satisfaction in his judgment being verified which characterizes the age of thirteen, and some other ages as well.

" Steve's nineteen, and he's six feet !—You are six feet too ? I thought you were about that. I hope I'll be six feet. I like that height, don't you ? Steve's at the University, but he don't study much, I reckon. Are you at college ?—Where ? Oh ! I know. I had a cousin who went there. He and two or three other Southern fellows laid outside of the hall for one of those abolition chaps who was making a speech, to cut his ears off when he came out, and they'd have done it if he had come out that way. I reckon it's a good college, but I'm going to the University when I'm sixteen. I'm thirteen now—You thought I was older ? I wanted to go to West Point, but my father won't let me. Maybe, Rupert will go there. I go to school at the Academy—Doctor Maule's—everybody knows about him. I tell you, he knows a lot.—You have left college ? Was it too hot for you ? Were you after somebody's ears too ? What ! painted the President's horse red ! Oh ! wasn't that a good one ! I wish I'd been there. I'll tell Steve and Blair about that. Steve put a cow up in the Rotunda once. The worst thing I ever did was making Blair jump off the high barn. I don't count flinging old Eliphalet Bush in the creek, because I believe his teeth were false anyhow ! But I'll remember painting that horse. I reckon he was an abolitionist too ? "

So the boy rattled on, his guests drawing him out for the pleasure of seeing him.

" What State are you from ? Maybe, we are cousins ? " he said presently, giving the best evidence of his friendliness.

" What ! Mass—a— ! I beg your pardon."

He looked so confused that both Mr. Welch and Middle-ton took some pains to sooth him.

" Yes, of course I was not talking about you ; but I wouldn't have said anything about Massachusetts if I had known you came from there. I wouldn't like anybody to say anything about *my* State. You won't mind what I said, will you ? I think Massachusetts the best of the Northern States—anyhow——" And he left them, his cheeks still glowing from embarrassment.

This apology, sincerely given, with a certain stress on the word Northern, amused Mr. Welch, and even Middleton, to whom it presented, however, an entirely new view.

"Aren't they funny ?" asked Middleton of his cousin, after their young host had left them. " You know I be-lieve they really think it."

" Larry, you have understated it. They think they know it."

Jacquelin employed the few moments, in which he pre-ceded the visitors to the hall, in telling all he had learned, and when Mr. Welch and Middleton appeared they found themselves in the position of the most distinguished guests. The fact that they came from the North, and Jacquelin's account of his mistake, had increased the desire to show them honor. " The hospitality of the South knows no lati-tude," said Dr. Cary, in concluding a gracious half apology to Mr. Welch for Jacquelin's error ; and he proceeded deftly to name over a list of great men from Massachusetts, and to link their names with those of the men of the South whom she most delighted to honor. His dearest friend at col-lege, he said, was from New England, and unless he was mistaken, Anson Rockfield would one day be heard of. Nothing could have been more gracious or more delicately done ; and when supper was announced, Mr. Welch was taken to the table by the hostess herself, and his health was drunk before the groom's. Middleton meanwhile found himself no less honored. The artistic feat performed on the President's horse had made him a noted personage, and in consequence of this and of the freemasonry which exists among young college-men, he was soon surrounded by all the younger portion of the company, and was exchanging views with Steve Allen and the other young fellows with that exaggerated man-of-the-world air which characterizes the age and occupation of collegians.

"Where is Blair?" he asked Jacquelin, presently, who was standing by Steve, open-eyed, drinking in their wisdom as only a boy of thirteen can drink in the sapience of men of nineteen or twenty.

"Over there." Jacquelin nodded toward another part of the hall. Middleton looked, but all he saw was a little girl sitting behind a big chair, evidently trying to conceal herself, and shaking her head violently at Jacquelin, who was beckoning to her. Jacquelin ran over to her and caught her by the hand, whereupon there was a little scuffle between them behind the chair, and as Middleton watched it he caught her eye. The next second she rose, smoothed her little white frock with quite an air, and came straight across with Jacquelin to where they stood. "This is Blair, Mr. Middleton," the boy said to the astonished guest. And Miss Blair held out her hand to him with an odd mixture of the child and the lady.

"How do you do, sir?" She evidently considered him one of the ancients.

"She jump off a high barn!" Middleton's eyes opened wide.

"Blair is the champion jumper of the family," said Steve, tall and condescending, catching hold of her half-teasingly, and drawing her up close to him.

"And she is a brick," added Master Jacquelin, with mingled condescension and admiration, which brought the blushes back to the little girl's cheeks and made her look very charming. The next moment she was talking to Middleton about the episode of the painted horse; ex-

changing adventures with him, and asking him questions
about his chum, Reely Thurston and his cousin, Ruth
Welch, whom he had mentioned, as if she had known him
always.

It was a night that Middleton never forgot. So completely was he adopted by his hosts that he could scarcely
believe that he had not been one of them all his life. As
Mr. Welch said truly : they had the gift of hospitality.
Jacquelin and Blair constituted themselves young Middleton's especial hosts, and he made an engagement to visit
with them all the points which they wished to show him,
provided his cousin could accept their invitation to spend
several days there.

In the midst of their talk an old mammy in a white
apron, with a tall bandanna turban around her head,
suddenly appeared in a doorway, and dropping a curtsey
made her way over to Blair, like a ship bearing down under full sail. There was a colloquy between the two, inaudible, but none the less animated and interesting, the
old woman urging something and the little girl arguing
against it. Then Blair went across and appealed to her
mother, who, after a little demurring, came over and spoke
to the mammy, and thereon began further argument.
She was evidently taking Blair's side ; but she was not
commanding, she was rather pleading. Middleton, new to
the customs, was equally surprised and amused to hear the
tones of the old colored woman's voice :

" Well, jist a little while." Then as she turned on her
way out, she said, half audibly :

" You all gwine ruin my chile' looks, meckin' her set
up so late. How she gwine have any complexion, settin'
up all times o' night ? " As she passed out, however, many
of the ladies spoke to her, and they must have said pleasant things ; for before she reached the door she was
smiling and curtseying right and left, and carried her
head as high as a princess. As for Blair, her eyes were
dancing with joy at her victory, and when the plump

figure of the mammy disappeared she gave a little frisk of delight.

There were no more speeches that could wound the sensibilities of the guests ; but there was plenty of discussion. All the young men were ardent politicians, and Middleton, who was nothing himself, was partly amused and partly horrified at the violence of some of their sentiments. Personally, he agreed with them in the main about Slavery or, at least, about Abolitionism. He thought Slavery rather a fine thing, and recalled that his grandfather or his great-grandfather, he couldn't be certain which, had owned a number of slaves. He was conscious of some pride in this—though his cousin, Patience Welch, who was an extreme abolitionist, was always bemoaning the fact.

But he was thunderstruck to hear a young orator of sixteen or seventeen declaim about breaking up the Union, under certain circumstances, as if it were a worthless old hulk, stuck in the mud. It had never occurred to Middleton that it was possible, and he had always understood that it was not. However, he was reassured by the warmth with which others defended the Union, and the ardor with which toasts were drunk to it. Jacquelin himself was a stanch Democrat, like his father. He confided to Middleton that Blair was a Whig, because her father was one ; but that a girl did not know any better, and that she really did not know the difference between them.

The entertainment consisted of dancing—quadrilles and "the Lancers," and after awhile, the old Virginia reel. In the first, all the young people joined, and in the last, some of the old ones as well. Middleton heard Steve urging their host's sister, Miss Gray—"Cousin Thomasia" as Steve called her—a sweet patrician-faced lady, to come and dance with him, and when she smilingly refused, teasing her about Major Legaie. She gave him a little tap with her fan and sent him off with smiling eyes, which, after following the handsome boy across the hall, sad-

dened a second later as she lifted the fan close to her face
to arrange the feathers. Steve mischievously whisked
Blair off from under Jacquelin's nose and took her to the
far end of the line of laughing girls ranged across the
hall, responding to Jacquelin's earnest protest that he was
just going to dance with her himself, with a push—that
unanswerable logic of a bigger boy.

"But you did not ask me !" said Miss Blair to Jacquelin, readily taking the stronger side against her sworn
friend.

"Never mind, I'm not going to dance with you any
more," pouted Jacquelin as he turned off, his head higher
than usual, to which Miss Blair promptly replied : "I
don't care if you don't." And she held her head higher
than his, dancing through her reel apparently with double
enjoyment because of his discomfiture. Then when the
reel had been danced again and again, with double couples
and fours, to ever-quickening music and ever-increasing
mirth, until it was a maze of muslin and radiance and
laughter, there was a pause for rest. And someone near
the piano struck up a song, and this drew the crowd.
Many of the girls, and some of the young men, had pleasant voices, which made up by their natural sweetness and
simplicity for want of training, and the choruses drew
all the young people, except a few who seemed to find
it necessary to seek something—fans or glasses of water,
in the most secluded and unlikely corners, and always in
couples.

There was one song—a new one which had just been
picked up somewhere by someone and brought there, and
they were all trying to recall it—about "Dixie-land." It
seemed that Blair sang it, and there was a universal request for her to sing it ; but the little girl was shy and
wanted to run away. Finally, however, she was brought
back and, under coaxing from Steve and Jacquelin, was
persuaded ; and she stood up by the piano and with her
cheeks glowing and her child's-voice quavering at first at

the prominence given her, sang it through. Middleton had heard the song once at a minstrel-show not long before, and had thought it rather a "catchy" thing; but now, when the child sang it, he found its melody. But when the chorus came, he was astonished at the feeling it evoked. It ran:

> " Away down south in Dixie, away, away—
> In Dixie land, I ll take my stand,
> To live and die for Dixie land—
> Away, away, away down south in Dixie."

It was a burst of genuine feeling, universal, enthusiastic, that made the old walls resound. Even the young couples came from their secluded coverts to join in. It was so tremendous that Dr. Cary, who was standing near Mr. Welch, said to him, gravely:

" A gleam of the current that is dammed up ? "

" If the bank ever breaks what will happen ? " asked Mr. Welch.

" A flood."

" Then the right will survive."

" The strongest," said Dr. Cary.

The guest saw that there was deep feeling whenever any political subject was touched on, and he turned to a less dangerous theme. The walls of the hall and drawing-room were covered with pictures; scenes from the Mythology; battle-pieces; old portraits: all hung together in a sort of friendly confusion. The portraits were nearly all in rich-colored dresses: men in velvets or uniforms, ladies in satins and crinolines, representing the fashions and faces of many generations of Jacquelin-Grays. But one, the most striking figure of them all, stood alone to itself in a space just over the great fireplace. He was a man still young, clad in a hunter's garb. A dark rock loomed behind him. His rifle lay at his feet, apparently broken, and his face wore an expression of such determination that one knew at once that, whatever he had been, he had been a master. The other paintings were portraits; this was the man. To add to its distinction, while the other pictures were in frames richly gilded and carved, this was in straight black boards apparently built into the wall, as if it had been meant to stand him there and cut him off from all the rest of the world. Wherever one turned in the hall those piercing eyes followed him. Mr. Welch had been for some time observing the picture.

"An extraordinary picture. It has a singular fascination for me," he said, as his host turned to him. "One might almost fancy it allegorical, and yet, it is intensely human. An indubitable portrait? I never saw a stronger face."

His host smiled.

"Yes. It has a somewhat curious history, though whether it is exactly a portrait or not we do not know. It is, or is supposed to be, the portrait of an ancestor of mine, the first of my name who came to this country. He had been unfortunate on the other side—so the story goes—was a scholar, and had been a soldier under Cromwell and lost all his property. He fell in love with a young lady whose father was on the King's side, and married her against her parents' wishes and came over here. He built a house on this very spot when it was the frontier, and his wife was afterward murdered by the Indians, leaving him one child. It is said that he killed the Indian with his naked hands just beside a great rock that stands in the graveyard beyond the garden, a short distance from the house. He afterward had that picture painted and placed there. It is reported to be a Lely. It has always been recognized as a fine picture, and in all the successive changes it has been left there. This present house was built around the fireplace of the old one. In this way a story has grown up about the picture, that it is connected with the fortunes of the house. You know how superstitious the negroes are?"

"I am not surprised," said Mr. Welch, examining the

picture more closely. "I never saw a lonelier man. That black frame shutting it in seems to have something to do with the effect."

"The tradition has possibly had a good effect. There used to be a recess behind it that was used as a cupboard, perhaps a secret cabinet, because of this very superstition. The picture fell down once a few years ago and I found a number of old papers in there, and put some more in myself.

"Here, you can see the paint on the frame, where it fell. It was in the early summer, and one of the servants was just painting the hearth red, and a sudden gust of wind slammed a door and jarred the picture down, and it fell, getting that paint on it. You never saw anyone so frightened as that boy was. And I think my overseer was also," he laughed. "He happened to be present, settling up some matters with which I had entrusted him in the South, and although he is a remarkably sensible man—so sensible that I had given him my bonds for a very considerable amount—one for a very large amount, indeed, in case he should need them in the matter I refer to, and he had managed the affair with the greatest shrewdness, bringing my bonds back—he was as much frightened almost as the boy. You'd have thought that the fall of the picture portended my immediate death. I took advantage of the circumstance to put the papers in the cupboard, and, to ease his mind, made Still nail the picture up, so that it will never come down again, at least, in my lifetime."

"I had no idea the whites were so superstitious," said Major Welch.

"Well, I do not suppose he really believed it. But, do you know, after that they began to say that stain on it was blood? And here again."

He pointed to where three or four little foot-tracks, as of a child's bare foot, were dimly seen on the hard white floor near the hearth.

"My little boy, Rupert, was playing in the hall at the time I mention, dabbling his feet in the paint, and the same wind that blew down the picture scattered my papers, and he ran across the floor and finally stepped on one. There, you can see just where he caught it: the little heel is there, and the print of the toes is on the bond behind the picture. His mother would never allow the prints to be scoured out, and so they have remained. And now, I understand, they say the tracks are blood."

"On such slim evidence, perhaps other and weightier superstitions have been built," said Mr. Welch, smiling.

Next morning, as Mr. Welch wished to see a Southern plantation, he deferred his departure until the afternoon, and rode over the place with Mr. Gray. Middleton was taken by his young hosts to see all the things of interest about the plantation: the high barn from which Blair had jumped into the tree, the bloody rock beside which the "Indian-Killer" had been buried, and the very spot where Steve had slept that night; together with many other points, whilst Mr. Welch was taken to see the servants' quarters, the hands working and singing in the fields, and such things as interested him. The plantation surpassed any he had yet seen. It was a little world in itself—a sort of feudal domain: the great house on its lofty hill, surrounded by gardens; the broad fields stretching away in every direction, with waving grain or green pastures dotted with sheep and cattle, and all shut in and bounded by the distant woods.

During this tour Mr. Langstaff, the rector, made to Mr. Welch an observation that he thought there were evidences that the Garden of Eden was situated not far from that spot, and certainly within the limits of the State. Major Welch smiled at the old clergyman's ingenuousness, but was graver when, as they strolled through the negro quarters, he began to speak earnestly of the blessings of Slavery. He pointed out the clean cabins, each surrounded by its little yard and with its garden ; the laughing children and smiling mothers curtseying from their doors. The guest remained silent, and the old gentleman took it for assent.

"Why, sir, I have just prepared a paper which my friends think establishes incontrovertibly that Slavery is based on the Scriptures, and is, as it were, a divine institution." Mr. Welch looked up to see how the other gentlemen took this. They were all grave, except Dr. Cary, usually the gravest, around whose mouth a slight smile flickered, and in whose eyes, as they met Major Welch's, there was a little gleam of amusement.

"It is written, ' A servant of servants shall he be.' You will not deny that ? " asked the old preacher, a little of the smouldering fire of the controversialist sparkling for a moment in his face.

"Well, no, I don't think I will."

"Then that settles it."

"Well, perhaps not altogether," said Mr. Welch. "There may be an economical sin. But I do not wish to engage in a polemical controversy. I will only say that down here you do not seem to me to appreciate fully how strong the feeling of the world at present is against Slavery. It seems to me, that Slavery is doomed as much as the Stage-coach, and the Sailing vessel."

"My dear sir," declared Mr. Gray, " I cannot agree with you. We interfere with nobody ; all we demand is that they shall not interfere with us."

"It is precisely that which you cannot enforce," said Mr. Welch. "I do not wish to engage in a discussion in which neither of us could convince the other ; but I think I have not defined my position intelligibly. You interfere with everyone—with every nation—and you are only tenants at will of your system—only tenants by sufferance of the world."

"Oh ! my dear sir !" exclaimed his host, his face slightly flushed ; and then the subject was politely changed, and Mr. Welch was conscious that it was not to be opened again.

The only additional observation made was by a gentleman who had been introduced to Mr. Welch as the leading lawyer of the county, a portly man with a round face and keen eyes. " Well, as George IV. remarked, it will last my time," he said.

Before the young people had seen half the interesting places of which Jacquelin had told Middleton, they were recalled to the house. Jacquelin's face fell.

" School ! " he said in disgust.

As they returned on a road leading up to a farmhouse on a hill, they passed a somewhat rickety buggy containing a plain-looking young girl, a little older than Blair, driven by a thin-shouldered youngster of eighteen or nineteen, who returned Jacquelin's and Blair's greeting, with a surly air. Middleton thought he checked the girl for her pleasant bow. At any rate, he heard his voice in a cross tone, scolding her after they had passed.

" That's Washy Still and Virgy, the overseer's children," explained someone.

" And he's just as mean to her as he can be. She's afraid of him. I'll be bound I wouldn't be afraid of him ! " broke out Blair, her eyes growing suddenly sparkling at the idea of wrong to one of her sex. Middleton looked down at her glowing face and thought it unlikely.

On arrival at the house it proved that Jacquelin's fears were well-founded. It had been decided that he must go back to school. Jacquelin appealed to his Aunt Thomasia to intercede for him, and she did so, as she always interceded for everyone, but it was in vain. It was an age of law, and the law had to be obeyed.

As Middleton was passing from the room he occupied, to the hall, he came on Blair. She was seated in a window, almost behind the curtain and he would have passed by without seeing her but for a movement she made to screen herself entirely. Curiosity and mischief prompted

the young man to go up and peep at her. She had a
book in her hand, which she held down as if to keep out
of sight, and as he looked at her he thought she had been
crying. A glance at the book showed it was " Virgil," and
Middleton supposed, from some personal experience, that
the tears were connected with the book. So he offered to
construe her lesson for her. She let him do it, and he was
just congratulating himself that he was doing it toler-
ably well when she corrected him. At the same moment
Jacquelin came in. He too looked unusually downcast,
and Blair turned away her face, and then suddenly sprang
up and ran away.

" What's the matter ? " asked Middleton. " Can't she
read her lesson ? "

" No : she can read that well enough. You just ought
to hear her read Latin. I wish I could do it as well as
she does, that's all ! I'd make old Eliphalet open his
eyes. She's crying because I've got to go back to school
—I wish I were grown up, I bet I wouldn't go to school
any more ! I hate school, and I hate old Eliphalet, and
I hate old Maule—no, I don't quite hate him ; but I hate
school and I'm going to paint his horse blue, if he licks
the life out of me." After which explosion the youngster appeared relieved, and went off to prepare for the
inevitable.

When he rode away with Doan behind him, his last call
back was to Middleton, to be sure and remember his
promise to come back again, and to bring Reely Thurston
with him.

CHAPTER III

BOTH Larry Middleton and Mr. Welch were to visit
Red Rock again; but under circumstances little anticipated by anyone at the time the invitation to return was
given.

When Middleton came of age he turned over the manufacturing business he had inherited, to the family's agent,
Mr. Bolter, and, on leaving college, accepted the invitation of his cousin, Mr. Welch, to go in his law-office
He made only one condition: that the same invitation
should be extended to his college chum, Reely Thurston,
whom Middleton described to Mr. Welch as "at once the
roundest and squarest fellow" in his class. This was
enough for Mr. Welch, and within a few months the two
young men were at adjoining desks, professing to practise
law and really practising whatever other young gentlemen
of their age and kind are given to doing: a combination
of loafing, working, and airing themselves for the benefit
of the rest of mankind, particularly of that portion that
wears bonnets and petticoats.

Both Mr. and Mrs. Welch were glad to have Middleton
with them; for Mrs. Welch was fond of him as a near relation, and one who in personal appearance and address
was a worthy representative of the old stock from which
they had both come. And she had this further reason
for wishing to have Middleton near her: that she had long
observed his tendency to be affected unduly, as she termed

it, by his surroundings, and she meant to counteract this defect of character by her personal influence.

It was enough for Mrs. Welch to see a defect of any kind to wish to correct it, and her wish was usually but a step in advance of her action. One might see this in the broad brow above which the hair was brushed so very smoothly ; in the deep gray eyes ; in the firm mouth with its fine, even teeth ; in the strong chin, almost too strong for a woman ; and especially, in the set of her head, and the absolute straightness of her back. She was at heart a missionary : one of those intrepid and unbending spirits who have carried their principles through the world by the sheer energy of their belief. She would no more have bowed in the house of Rimmon than she would have committed theft. If she had lived in Rome, she would have died before taking a pinch of incense for Diana, unless, indeed, she had been on the other side, when she would have fed the lions with fervor. If she had been in Spain on Torquemada's side, she could have sung Te Deums at an *auto-da-fé*. As someone said of her, she would have burned like a candle. The only difficulty was that she wanted others to burn too—which they were not always so ready to do. As a girl, she had been on the eve of going out as missionary to the Sandwich Islands, when she heard the splendid oratory of one of the new apostles of abolitionism, one evening in company with Mr. Welch, then a young engineer, when her philanthropical direction changed from West to South, and she devoted herself thenceforth to the cause of the negroes— and of the young engineer.

She had great hopes of Lawrence Middleton and deplored the influence on him of the young man whom he had chosen at college as his especial friend ; and she grieved over the effect that his visit South, already described, had on him. He had come home much impressed by the charm of the life there. Indeed, he had become actually an apologist for Slavery. But Mrs. Welch did not despair.

She never despaired. It implied weakness, and so, sin.
She was urgent to have Larry Middleton accept her husband's proposal to take a place in his office, and though
she would have preferred to separate him from young
Thurston, as to whom she had misgivings, yet when he
made this condition she yielded ; for it brought Middleton
where she could influence him, and had, at least, this advantage : that it gave her two persons to work on instead
of one.

When her daughter, Ruth Welch, a young Miss with
sparkling eyes, came home in her vacations, it was natural
that she should be thrown a great deal with her cousin,
and the only singular thing was that Mrs. Welch appeared
inclined to minimize the importance of the relationship.
This, however, made little difference to the gay, fun-lov-
ing girl, who, enjoying her emancipation from school,
tyrannized over the two young sprigs of the Law to her
heart's content. She soon reduced Thurston to a condition of abject slavery which might well have called forth
the intervention of so ardent an emancipator as her
mother, and did, indeed, excite some solicitude in her
maternal bosom. Mrs. Welch was beginning to be very
anxious about him when events, suddenly crowding on
each other, gave her something widely different to think
of, and unexpectedly relieved her from this cause of care
to give her others far weightier.

Both the young men had become politicians. Middleton was a Whig, though he admitted he did not see how
Slavery could be interfered with ; while Thurston announced tenets of the opposite party, particularly when
Mrs. Welch was present.

The cloud which had been gathering so long above the
Country suddenly burst.

Middleton and Thurston were sitting in their office one
afternoon when there was a scamper outside ; the door was
flung open, and a paper thrown in—an extra still wet from
the press. Thurston seized it, his seat being nearest the

door, and gave a long whistle as his eye fell on the black headlines :

The Flag Fired on: Open Rebellion. The Union Must Be Saved At Any Cost. Etc., etc.

He sank into his seat and read rapidly the whole account, ending with the call for troops to put down the Rebellion ; while Middleton listened with a set face. When Thurston was through, he flung the paper down and sat back in his chair, thinking intently. The next moment he hammered his fist on his desk and sprang to his feet, his face white with resolve.

"By God ! I'll go."

With a single inquiring look at Middleton, he turned to the door and walked out. A moment later Middleton locked his desk and followed him. The street was already filling with people, crowding to hear the details, and the buzz of voices was growing louder.

Within a few hours the two young men were both enrolled in a company of volunteers which was being gotten up—Middleton, in right of his stature and family connections, as a Sergeant, and little Thurston as a Corporal, and were at work getting others enrolled.

As they were so engaged, Thurston's attention was arrested by a man in the crowd who was especially violent in his denunciations, and was urging everybody to enlist. His voice had a peculiar, penetrating whine. As Thurston could not remember the man among those who had signed the roll, he asked him his name.

"Leech, Jonadab Leech," he said.

When Thurston looked at the roster, the name was not on it, and the next time Leech came up in the crowd, the little Corporal called him :

"Here ; you have forgotten to put your name down."

To his surprise, Leech drew back and actually turned pale.

"What's the matter?" asked Thurston.

"I have a wife."

The little volunteer gave a sniff.

"All right—send her in your place. I guess she'd do as well."

"If he has, he's trying to get rid of her," said someone standing by, in an undertone.

"Why—ah!—my eyes are bad; I'm too near-sighted."

"Your eyes be hanged! You can see well enough to read this paper."

"I—ah!—I cannot see in the dark at all," stammered Leech as a number of the new volunteers crowded around them.

"Neither can I—neither can anybody but a cat," declared the little Corporal, and the crowd around cheered him. Leech vanished.

"Who is he?" asked Thurston, as Leech disappeared.

"He is a clerk in old Bolter's commissary."

The crowd was patriotic.

There was great excitement in the town all night: bells rang; crowds marched up and down the streets singing; stopping at the houses of those who had been opposed to ultra measures, and calling on them to put up flags to show their loyalty. The name of Jonadab Leech appeared in the papers next morning as one of the street-orators who made the most blood-thirsty speech.

Next day was Sunday. Sober second thought had succeeded the excitement of the previous day, the faces of the people showed it. The churches were overflowing. The preachers all alluded to the crisis that had come, and the tears of the congregations testified how deeply they were moved. After church, by a common impulse, everyone went to the public square to learn the news. The square was packed. Suddenly on the pole that stood above the old court-house, someone ran up the flag. At the instant that it broke forth the breeze caught it, and

it fluttered out full and straight, pointing to the southward. The effect was electric. A great cheer burst from
the crowd below. As it died down, a young man's
clear voice struck up "My Country, 'Tis of Thee," and
the next moment the whole crowd was singing and weeping.

That flag and that song made more soldiers from the old
town than all the newspapers and all the speeches, and
Larry Middleton, for having struck up the song, found himself suddenly of more note in his own home than he could
have been later if he had stormed a battery.

Loudest among the shouters was the street-orator of the
evening before, Jonadab Leech, the clerk in Bolter's commissary.

Within a week the two young men were on their way
South.

A little later, Mr. Welch, having taken time to settle
up his affairs, and also those of his cousin, Larry Middleton, went off to join the first corps of engineers from his
State, with abundance of tears from Ruth and a blessing
from his wife, whose mouth was never firmer, or her eye
clearer, than when she kissed him, and bade him God-
speed.

She replied to the astonished query of Mrs. Bolter,
"You did not cry?" with another question:

"Why should I cry, when I knew it was his duty? If
I had wept it would have been because I could not go myself to strike a blow for the freedom of the poor Afri-
can!"

"You are an unusually strong woman," said Mrs. Bolter, with a shake of her head, and, indeed, Mrs. Welch
looked it; for though Bolter had gone to Washington, he
had not gone to war, but to see about contracts.

Just at the time that the two young students from
Mr. Welch's office were in the street of their town enrolling their names as soldiers to fight for the flag of

the Union, the young men, and the elders as well, whom
Middleton had met at Red Rock a thousand miles to the
southward, were engaged in similar work—enlisting to
fight against Invasion, to fight for their State.

There had been much discussion—much dissension in
the old county, and all others like it, during the interim
since the night when Middleton and Mr. Welch had appeared unexpectedly at Red Rock among the wedding
guests. Some were for radical measures, for Secession, for
War ; others were conservative. Many were for the Union.
Matters more than once had reached a white heat in that
section, and it had looked for a long time as though an
explosion must come. Yet the cooler heads had controlled,
and when the final elections for the body that was to settle
the momentous questions at issue at last came on, the most
conservative men in the country had been selected. In our
county, Dr. Cary and Mr. Bagby, both strong Union men,
had been chosen over Major Legaie and Mr. Gray, both
ardent Democrats ; and one, the former, a hot Secession-
ist.

When they arrived at the capital to attend the session
of the Convention they found, perhaps, the most distinguished body that had sat in the State in fifty years.
In this great crisis both sides had put forward their best
men, and in face of the nearing peril the wildest grew
conservative. The body declared for Peace.

Affairs moved rapidly, however ; excitement grew ; feeling changed. Yet the more conservative prevailed.

One morning Dr. Cary received a report of a great public meeting held at the county seat, instructing him to
vote for Secession. Many of his old supporters had signed
it. He presented the resolutions at the desk, and stated
their purport fully and strongly, amid cheers from the
other side.

"Now you will vote with us ?" said one of the leaders
on that side.

"Not if every man in my county instructed me."

" Then you must resign ? "

" Not if every man in my county demanded it."

" Are you the only wise man in the county ? "

The voice trembled. Feeling was rising.

The Doctor was looking his questioner full in the eyes.

" If they signed such a paper, I should think so." And there were cheers from his side, and the vote was stayed for that day at least. Dr. Cary made an appeal for the Union that men remembered all their lives. However they disagreed with him, they were moved by him. But the magazine was being stored fuller every moment.

Then the spark fell and the explosion came.

A week after this the call for troops by the President to put down Rebellion appeared in an extra in the city where the Convention sat.

Invasion !

The whole people rose. From the time of Varrus down they had done so. The defences that conservatives like Dr. Cary had laboriously built up were swept away in an instant. The State went out with a rush.

At the announcement the population poured into the streets and public squares in a great demonstration. It was tremendous—a maelstrom—a tornado—a conflagration. Men were caught up and tossed on platforms, that appeared as if by magic from nowhere, to make speeches; bonfires were lighted and bells were rung ; but the crowd shouted louder than the ringing of the bells, for it meant War : none could now withstand it. Suddenly from some public place a gun, which had been found and run out, boomed through the dusk, and the crowd roared louder than before, and made a rush in that direction, cheering as if for a great victory.

Dr. Cary, stalking through the throng, silent and white, was recognized and lifted unresisting to a platform. After a great roar, the tumult hushed down for a moment ; for he was waiting with close-shut mouth and blazing eye, and he had the reputation of being, when he chose to exert himself, an orator. Besides, it was not yet known what he would do, and he was a power in his section.

He broke the silence with a calm voice that went everywhere. Without appearing to be strong, his voice was one of those strange instruments that filled every building with its finest tone and reached over every crowd to its farthest limit. With a gesture that, as men said afterward, seemed to sweep the horizon, he began :

"The time has passed for talking. Go home and prepare for War. For it is on us."

"Oh ! there is not going to be any war," cried someone, and a part of the crowd cheered. Dr. Cary turned on them.

"No war ? We are at war now—with the greatest power on earth : the power of universal progress. It is not the North that we shall have to fight, but the world. Go home and make ready. If we have talked like fools, we shall at least fight like men."

That night Dr. Cary walked into his lodgings alone and seated himself in the dusk. His old body-servant, Tarquin, silent and dark, brought a light and set it conveniently for him. He did not speak a word ; but his ministrations were unusually attentive and every movement expressed adherence and sympathy. Suddenly his master broke the silence :

"Tarquin, do you want to be free ?"

"Lawd Gawd !" exclaimed Tarquin, stopping quite still and gazing in amazement. "Me ! Free ?"

"If you do I will set you free, and give you money enough to live in Philadelphia."

"No, suh ; Marster, you know I don' wan' be free," said Tarquin.

"Pack my trunk. I am going home."

"When, suh ?"

"I do not know exactly ; but shortly."

Within a week Dr. Cary was back at home, working,

along with Major Legaie and the other secessionists, making preparation for equipping the companies that the county was going to send to the war.

What a revolution that week had made in the old county ! In the face of the menace of invasion, after but ten days one would scarcely have known it. All division was ended : all parties were one. It was as if the county had declared war by itself and felt the whole burden of the struggle on its shoulders. From having been one of the most quiet, peaceful and conservative corners of the universe, where a fox-hunt or an evening-party was the chief excitement of the year, and where the advent of a stranger was enough to convulse the entire community, it became suddenly a training ground and a camp, filled with bustle and preparation and the sound of arms. The haze of dust from men galloping by, hung over the highways all day long, and the cross-roads and the county seat, where the musters used to meet quarterly and where the Fourth of July celebrations were held, became scenes of almost metropolitan activity.

Men appeared to spring from the ground as in the days of Cadmus, ready for war. Red Rock and Birdwood became recruiting-stations and depots of supply. From the big estates men came ; from the small homesteads amid their orchards, and from the cabins back among the pines —all eager for war and with a new light in their eyes. Everyone was in the movement. Major Legaie was a colonel and Mr. Gray was a captain ; Dr. Cary was surgeon, and even old Mr. Langstaff, under that fire of enthusiasm, doffed his cassock for a uniform, merged his ecclesiastical title of rector in the military one of chaplain, and made amends for the pacific nature of his prescribed prayers in church, by praying before his company outside, prayers as diverse from the benignity of his nature, as the curses of Ezekiel or Jeremiah from the benediction of St. John the Aged.

Miss Thomasia, who was always trying to meet some

wants which only the sensitiveness of her own spirit apprehended, enlarged her little academy in the office at Red
Rock, so as to take in all the children of the men around
who had enlisted ; made them between their lessons pick
lint, and opened her exercises daily with the most martial
hymns she could find in the prayer-book, feeling in her simple heart that she could do God no better service than to
inculcate an undying patriotism along with undying piety.
As for Blair, she had long deserted the anti-war side, horse,
foot, and dragoons, and sewed on uniforms and picked lint ;
wore badges of palmetto, and single stars on little blue
flags sewed somewhat crookedly in the front of her frocks,
and sang " Dixie," " Maryland," and " The Bonny Blue
Flag " all the time.

Steve Allen and Morris Cary, on an hour's notice, had
left the University where all the students were flocking
into companies, and with pistols and sabres strapped about
their slender waists galloped up to the county seat together one afternoon, in a cloud of dust, having outsped
their telegrams, and, amid huzzas and the waving of handkerchiefs from the carriages lining the roadside, spurred
their sweating horses straight to the end of the line that
was drilling under Colonel Legaie in the field beside the
court-house. And so, with radiant faces and bounding
hearts were enlisted for the war. Little Andy Stamper,
the rescuer of the two visitors at the ford, was already
there in line at the far end on one of his father's two farm-
horses; and Jacquelin, on a blooded colt, was trying to keep
as near in line with him as his excited four-year-old would
permit. Even the servants, for whom some on the other
side were pledging their blood, were warmly interested,
and were acting more like clansmen than slaves.

Hiram Still, Mr. Gray's tall manager, had a sudden return of his old enemy, rheumatism, and was so drawn up
that he had to go on crutches ; but was as enthusiastic as
anyone, and lent money to help equip the companies—lent
it not to the county, it is true, but to Mr. Gray and Dr.

Cary on their joint security.   He and Andy Stamper were
not on good terms, yet he even offered to lend money to
Andy Stamper to buy a horse with.   Jacquelin, however,
spared Andy this mortification.

The boy, emancipated from school, partly because his
father was going off so shortly to the war, and partly because Dr. Maule himself had enlisted and Mr. Eliphalet
Bush, his successor, was not considered altogether sound
politically, spent his time breaking his colt to stand the
excitement of cavalry drill.   Jacquelin and Andy were
sworn friends, and hearing that Andy had applied to Hiram Still to borrow money to buy a horse with, Jacquelin
asked his father's consent to give him his colt, and was rewarded by the pick of the horses on the place, after the
carriage horses, his father's own riding horse and Steve's.
It was a proud moment for the boy when he rode the high-
mettled bay he chose, over to the old Stamper place.

Andy, in a new gray jacket, was sitting on the front
steps, polishing his scabbard and accoutrements, old Mrs.
Stamper was in her low, split-bottomed chair behind him,
knitting a yarn sock for her soldier, and Delia Dove, with
her plump cheeks glowing under her calico sun-bonnet,
which she had pushed back from her round face, was seated
on the bench in the little porch, toying with the wisteria-
vine above her, and looking down on Andy with her black
eyes softer than usual.

Andy rose to greet Jacquelin as the boy galloped up to
the gate.

"Come in, Jack.   What's up ?   Look out or he'll
git you off him.   That's the way to set him !   Ah !" as
Jacquelin swung himself down.

"Here's a present for you," said Jacquelin.

" What ? "

" This horse !"

" What !"

" Yes : he's mine : papa gave him to me this morning
and said I might give him to you.   I took the pick——"

" Well, by— " Andy was too much dazed to swear.

" Jack— " This also ended. " Now let that Hiram Still ask for s'curity. Delia, I'll lick a regiment." He faced his sweetheart, who suddenly turned and caught Jacquelin and kissed him violently, bringing the red blood to the boy's fresh face.

" If you'll do that to me I'll give him to you right now. D——d 'f I don't ! " And the little recruit looked Miss Delia Dove in the eyes and gave a shake of his head for emphasis. The girl looked for one moment as if she were going to accept his offer. Then as Andy squared himself and opened his arms wide she considered, and, with a toss of her head and a sparkle in her eyes, turned away.

That moment the latch clicked and Hiram Still's daughter, Virgy, stood beside them, shy and silent, veiled within her sun-bonnet.

" Mr. Stamper, pappy says if you'll come over to see him about that business o' yourn, maybe he can make out to help you out."

She delivered the message automatically, and, with a shy glance at Jacquelin, and another, somewhat different, at Delia Dove, retired once more within the deep recesses of her sun-bonnet.

" Well, you tell your pappy that I say I'm much obliged to him ; but I ain't got any business with him that I knows on ; 't somebody else's done helped me out." The voice was kind, though the words were sarcastic.

" Yes, sir. Good-even'." And with another shy glance and nod to each one in turn, the girl turned and went off as noiselessly as a hare.

" That girl always gives me the creeps," said Delia, when Virgy had reached a safe distance.

" How about Washy ? " asked Andy, at which Delia only sniffed disdainfully.

Jacquelin Gray was not the only one of the youngsters whose patriotic fervor was rewarded. The ladies of the neighborhood made a banner for each of the companies that went forth, and Blair Cary was selected to present the banner to the Red Rock company, which she did from the court-house balcony, with her laughing eyes sobered by excitement, her glowing face growing white and pink by turns, and her little tremulous speech, written by her father and carefully conned by heart for days, much swallowed and almost inaudible in face of the large crowd filling all the space around, and of the brave company drawn up in the road below her. But she got through it—that part about "emulating the Spartan youth who came back with his shield or on it," and all; and at the close she carried everyone away by a natural clasp of her little brown hands over her heart, as she said, " And don't you let them take it away from you, not ever," outstretching her arms to her father, who sat with moist eyes at one end of the line a little below her, with Jacquelin close beside him, his eyes like saucers for interest in, and admiration of, Blair.

"Blair, that's the best speech that ever was made," cried the boy, enthusiastically, when he saw her ; " and Steve says so, too. Don't you wish I was old enough to go ? " The little girl's cheeks glowed with pleasure.

The evening before Jacquelin's father went off, he called Jacquelin into his office, and rising, shut the door himself. They were alone, and Jacquelin was mystified. He had never before been summoned for an interview with his father unless it were for a lecture, or worse. He hastily ran over in his mind his recent acts, but he could recall nothing that merited even censure, and curiosity took the place of wonderment. Wonder came back, however, when his father, motioning him to a seat, stood before him and began to address him in an entirely new and unknown tone. He talked to him as if he were a man. Jacquelin suddenly felt all his old timidity of his father vanish, and a new spirit, as it were, rise up in his heart. His father told him that now that he was going away to the war, he might never come back ; but he left, he said, with the assurance that whatever happened, he would be worthily succeeded ; and he said that he was proud of him, and had the fullest confidence in him. He had never said anything like this to Jacquelin before, in all his life, and the boy felt a new sensation. He had no idea that his father had ever been satisfied with him, much less been proud of him. It was like opening the skies and giving him a glimpse beyond them into a new heaven. The boy suddenly rose, and flung his arms about his father's neck, and clung there, pouring out his heart to him. Then he sat down again, feeling like a shriven soul, and the father and son understood each other like two school-fellows.

Mr. Gray told Jacquelin of his will. He had left his mother everything ; but it would be the same thing as if he had left it to him and Rupert. He, as the oldest, was to have Red Rock, and Rupert the estate in the South. "I leave it to her, and I leave her to you," he said, putting his hand on the boy's shoulder. Jacquelin listened, his mind suddenly sobered and expanded to a man's measure.

"And, Jacquelin," he said, "keep the old place. Make any sacrifice to do that. Landholding is one of the safeguards of a gentry. Our people, for six generations, have never sold an acre, and I never knew a man who sold land that throve."

"I will keep it, father," said the boy, earnestly.

There were some debts, but not enough to amount to anything, his father told him ; the principal one was to Hiram Still. Still had wanted him to keep his money, and he had done so. It could be paid any time, if necessary. Still was a better man than he was given credit for. A bad manner made those who did not know him well, suspicious of him. But he was the best business man he had ever known, and he believed devoted to his interest. His father, old Mr. Still, had been overseer for Jacquelin's grandfather when Mr. Gray was a boy, and he could not forget him, and though Still was at present in poor health, **he** had contracted the disease while in their service at **the**

South, and he would be glad to have him kept in his position as long as he treated the negroes well, and cared to remain.

"And, Jacquelin, one other thing : be a father to Rupert. See that he gets an education. It is the one patrimony that no accident—not even war—can take away."

Jacquelin promised his father that he would remember his injunctions, and try faithfully to keep them, every one ; and when the two walked out, it was arm in arm like two brothers, and the old servants, looking at them, nodded their heads, and talked with pride of Jacquelin's growing resemblance to his grandfather.

Next day the companies raised in the county started off to the war, taking almost every man of serviceable age and strength, and many who were not.

When they marched away it was like a triumphal procession. The blue haze of spring lay over the woods, softening the landscape, and filling it with peace. Tears were on some cheeks, no doubt ; and many eyes were dimmed ; but kerchiefs and scarfs were waved by many who could not see, and fervent prayers went up from many hearts when the lips were too tremulous to speak.

CHAPTER IV

IN WHICH A LONG JUMP IS TAKEN

IT is not proposed to attempt any relation of that part of the lives of the people in this record which was covered by the four years of war. That period was too tremendous to be made a mere fragment of any history. "After that the deluge."

What pen could properly tell the story of those four years; what fittingly record the glory of that struggle, hopeless from the beginning, yet ever appearing to pluck success from the very abyss of impossibility, and by the sheer power of unconquerable valor to reverse the laws of nature and create the consummation it desired, in the face of insuperable force ?

It was a great formative force in every life that participated in it. It stamped itself on every face. The whole country emptied itself into it. They went into it boys, and came out of it men—striplings, and came out of it heroes. But the eye once fastened on that flaming fire would be blinded for any lesser light.

It is what took place after the war rather than what occurred during the struggle that this chronicle is concerned with.

If the part that the men played in the war must be passed over in silence as too large for this history, how much more impossible would it be to describe fitly the part that the women performed. It was a harder part to fill, yet they filled it to the brim, good measure, overflowing. It is no disparagement to the men to say that whatever courage they displayed, it was less than that which the

women showed. Wherever a Southern woman stood during those four years, there in her small person was a
garrison of the South, impregnable.

Year after year the mills of war ground steadily array
after array, and crushed province after province, and still
the ranks filled and poured with intrepid daring into the
abyss of destruction, to be ground like their predecessors
to dust ; until at the end there was nothing left to grind.
Some day the historian, annalist or novelist, may arise to tell
the mighty story, but meantime this pen must pass it by as
too great a theme, and deal with the times that come after.

One or two incidents, however, must be mentioned to
fill the break and explain what came afterward.

Colonel Gray, who had been early promoted, fell at the
head of his regiment on one of those great days which are
the milestones of history.

His body was brought home and buried in the old
graveyard at Red Rock among generations of Grays, of
whom, as old Mr. Langstaff, who had been bodily haled
back to his parish by his congregation, said to the neighbors and servants about the grave, not one was a better or
a braver man, or a truer gentleman. Colonel Gray's burial
marked one of the steps of the war in that retired neighborhood.

When it was all over, and the neighbors had gone home,
and the servants had retired to their quarters, hushed to
that vague quietude that follows the last putting away in
the earth of those who have been near to us, Jacquelin came
out of the office where he had held that last interview
with his father, and walked into his mother's room. His
shoulders were square and his figure erect. Mrs. Gray
rose from her knees as he entered, and stood before him in
her black dress, her face deadly white ; her eyes, full of
fear, fastened on his face.

"Mamma—." He stopped as if that were all he had to
say, and, perhaps, it was ; for Mrs. Gray seated herself
calmly.

" Yes, my son." The fine, sad eyes grew wistful. How like he was to his father !

—" Because, you know, there ought to be one of us in the old company, mamma," he said, quite as though he had spoken the other sentence.

" Yes, my son, I know." And the mother sighed, her heart breaking in spite of her resolve to be brave.

"—And I am the only man of the name now—and I am fifteen and a whole head taller than Andy Stamper."

" Yes, I know, my son." She had noticed it that day, and had known this would come.

" And he is one of the best soldiers in the army—*He* said so. And if—if anything happens, you have Rupert." He went on arguing, as though his mother had not agreed with him.

" Yes, my son, I know." And Mrs. Gray rose suddenly and flung herself into his arms and hugged him and clung to him, and wept on his shoulder, as though he were his father.

So the change comes : the boy in little trousers suddenly stands before the mother a man ; the little girl who was in her pinafores yesterday, to-day has stepped into full-blown womanhood ; and the children have gone ; the old has passed ; and the new is here.

General Legaie offered to make a place on his staff for Jacquelin ; but Jacquelin declined it. He wished to go into the Red Rock troop, of which Steve Allen was now Captain.

" Because, mamma, all the men are in it, and Steve has refused a majority to stay with them, and there must be one of the Grays in the old company," he said with a rise of his head.

Doan, of course, expected to go with his master ; but Mrs. Gray vetoed this ; she was afraid Doan might be killed : young men were so rash. She remembered that Doan was his mother's only son. So, by a compromise, Old Waverley was sent. He had so much judgment, she said.

The year after Jacquelin went away to the army the tide of war rolled nearer to the old county, and the next year, that which had been deemed impossible befell : it swept over it.

When the invading army had passed, the county was scarcely recognizable.

Jacquelin's career in the army was only that of many others—indeed, of many thousands of others : he went in a boy, but a boy who could ride any horse, and all day and all night; sleep on stones or in mud; and if told to go anywhere, would go as firmly and as surely among bayonets or belching guns as if it were in a garden of roses.

Being the youngest man in his company, he might naturally have been a favorite in any case ; but when he was always ready to stand an extra tour of guard-duty, or to do anything else for a comrade, it placed his popularity beyond question. They used to call him "The baby ;" but after a sharp cavalry fight on a hill-top one afternoon they stopped this. Legaie's brigade charged, and finding infantry entrenched, were retiring amid smoke and dust and bullets, when Jacquelin, missing Morris Cary, who had been near him but a moment before, suddenly turned and galloped back through the smoke. Two or three men shouted and stopped, and Steve suddenly dashed back after the boy, followed by Andy Stamper and the whole company. There was a rally with the whole Red Rock troop in the lead, Steve Allen, with little Andy Stamper close behind, shouting and sabering like mad, which changed the fortune of the day.

Poor Morris was found under his horse, past help ; but they brought his body out of the fray, and Jacquelin sent him home, with a letter which was harder to write than any charge he had ever made or was to make—harder even than to tell Dr. Cary, who was at the field hospital and who received the announcement with only a sudden tightening of the mouth and whitening of the face. After that, Andy Stamper "allowed that Jacquelin's

cradle was big enough for him" (Andy), which it certainly was, by linear measurement, at least.

Blair's letter to Jacquelin in reply was more to him
than General Legaie's mention of his name in his report.

Blair was growing up to be almost a woman now.
Women, as well as men, age rapidly amid battles, and
nearly every letter Jacquelin received from home contained something about her. "What a pretty girl Blair
has grown to be. You have no idea how we all lean on
her," his mother wrote. Or Miss Thomasia would say:
"I wish you could have heard Blair sing in church last
Sunday. Her voice has developed unspeakable sweetness.
It reminded me of her grandmother, when I can first remember her."

It was not a great while after this that Jacquelin himself went down one day, and had to be fought over, and
though he fared better than poor Morris Cary, in that the
bullet which brought him down only smashed his leg instead of finding his heart, it resulted in Steve getting both
himself and his horse shot, and Jacquelin being left in the
enemy's hands, along with Andy Stamper, who had fought
over him, like the game little bantam that he was, until a
big Irish Sergeant knocked him in the head with a carbine-
barrel and came near ending the line of the Stampers then
and there. Happily, Andy came to after a while, and was
taken along with Jacquelin and sent to Point Lookout.

Jacquelin and Andy stayed in prison a long time; Andy
because he was a hardy and untamed little warrior, of the
kind which was drawn last for exchange; and Jacquelin
partly because he was unable to travel on account of his
wound and partly because he would not accept an exchange to leave Andy.

One day, however, Andy got a letter which seriously affected him. It told him that Delia Dove was said to be
going to marry Mr. Still. Within a week little Andy,
whose constitution had hitherto appeared of iron, was in

the hospital. The doctor told Jacquelin that he though
he was seriously ill, and might die.

That night Jacquelin scribbled a line to Andy and persuaded a nurse, Miss Bush, a small woman with thin
hair, a sharp nose and a complaining voice, but gentle
eyes and a kind heart, to get it to him. It ran : "Hold
on for Delia's sake. We'll get exchanged before long."

"Who is Delia ?" asked the nurse, looking at the pape:
doubtfully. It was against orders to carry notes.

"His sweetheart."

The nurse took the note.

In a week Andy was ready to be out of the hospital.

The next morning Jacquelin and the doctor had a long
talk, and later on, Jacquelin and the nurse ; and when the
next draft for exchange came, the name of Jacquelin Gray
was on it. But Andy Stamper's was not. So the nurse
told Jacquelin. Another note was written and conveyed
by Miss Bush, and that evening, when the line of prisoners
for exchange marched out of the prison yard, Andy
Stamper, with his old blanket pulled up around his face
and a crutch under his arm, was in it. Jacquelin was
watching from a corner of the hospital window while the
line was inspected. Andy answered the questions all
right—Private in Company A, —th Cavalry ; captured at
————; wounded in leg ; and just left hospital. As the
last guard filed out behind the ragged line and the big
gate swung to, Jacquelin hobbled back to his cot and lay
with his face to the wall. The nurse came by presently
and stopping, looked down at him.

"Now you've gone and ruined your chance for ever,"
she said in the querulous tone habitual with her.

Jacquelin shut his eyes tightly, then opened them and
without a word gazed straight at the wall not a foot before
him. Suddenly the woman bent close down over him and
kissed him.

"You are a dear boy." The next instant she went
back to her duty.

An effort was made to get an exchange for Jacquelin, the principal agents being a nurse in the prison-hospital and a philanthropical friend of hers, a Mrs. Welch, through whom the nurse had secured her position; but the answer was conclusive:

"Jacquelin Gray has already been exchanged."

As for Andy, when he reached home he found the report about Miss Delia Dove to be at least premature. It was not only Mr. Washington Still, but Hiram as well, who was unpleasantly attentive to her, and Miss Delia, after the first burst of genuine delight at Andy's unexpected appearance, proceeded to use the prerogative of her sex and wring her lover's heart by pretending to be pleased by his new rival's attentions. Andy, accordingly, did not stay long at home, but accepting the renewed proffer of a loan from Hiram Still to buy a horse, was soon back with the old company, sadly wasted by this time and only kept up by the new recruits, on whom Andy looked with disdain.

When Wash Still was drafted from the dispensary department of the hospital service it was some consolation that he was at least banished from dangerous proximity to Miss Delia, but it was hard to have to accept him as a comrade, and Andy's sunburned nose was always turned up when Wash was around.

"Washy Still in place of Jacquelin Gray," he sniffed; "a dinged little 'pothecary-shop sweeper for a boy as didn't mind bullets no mo' than flies. I bet he's got pills in that pistol now! And he to be a-settin' up to Delia Dove!"

However, a few months later Andy had his reward.

So it happened, that when the end came, Andy was back with the old company, and Jacquelin was still in prison.

CHAPTER V

THE home-coming of the men who went to the war was about the same time of the year that most of them went forth. While the troops of the victorious army were parading amid the acclaims of multitudes, the remnants of that other army that had met and defeated them so often were making their way back to their dismantled homes, with everything they had fought for lost, save honor. They came home singly or in squads from northward, eastward and westward, wherever their commands happened to be when the final collapse came. And but for certain physical landmarks they would scarcely have known the old neighborhood. The blue mountains still stretched across the skyline, with the nearer spurs nestled at their feet ; the streams still ran through the little valleys between the hills, under their willows and sycamores, as they ran when Steve Allen and Jacquelin and the other boys fished and swam in them ; but the bridges were gone, and the fishing-holes were dammed with fallen trees, some of them cut down during the battles that had been fought on their banks. And the roads made by the army-wagons often turned out through the unfenced fields and the pillaged and fire-scorched forests.

Dr. Cary, now known as Major Cary, from his title as surgeon in General Legaie's brigade, and Captain Allen and Sergeant Stamper came home together as they had ridden away together through the April haze four years before. They had started from the place of their surrender with a considerable company, who had dropped off

from time to time as they had arrived at the roads which
took them their several ways, and these three were the
last to separate. When they parted, it was at the forks
where the old brick church had stood when they last
passed that way. The church had gone down in the track
of war. Nothing remained of it now except fragments of
the walls, and even these were already half hidden by the
thicket which had grown up around them. It brought
the whole situation very close home to them ; for they all
had memories of it : Dr. Cary had buried his father and
mother there, and Stamper and Delia Dove had been married in it a year before. And they did not have a great
many words to speak—perhaps, none at all at the very
last—only a "Well—Well !" with a rising inflection, and
something like a sigh ; and then, after a long pause, from
the older officer, a sudden : "Well, good-by, Steve ;
—good-by, Sergeant. We'll have to begin over again.—
God bless you—Come over and see me. Good-by." And
from each of the other two, " Good-by, Major—I will ;—
Good-by, Tarquin," to the Major's tall, gray-haired body-
servant, waiting silently, on his weary horse ; then a couple
of hard handgrips and silence ; and the horses went plash-
ing off in the mud, slow and sullen, reluctant to leave
each other. All turned once to look back ; caught each
other's glances and waved their hands ; and then rode on
through the mud, their heads sunk on their chests, and
the officer's two body-servants, old Tarquin and young
Jerry, following silently behind their masters.

The meeting at home was in the dusk.

The little group waiting on the hill-top at Dr. Cary's for
the small cavalcade as they rode up through the waning
light had been waiting and watching for days ; but there
were no words spoken at the meeting. Only, Mrs. Cary
walked out from the others and met her husband a part
of the way down the hill, and Blair followed her a moment
after.

When the doctor reached his door, walking between his

wife and daughter, an arm around each, he turned to his old servant, who was holding the horses :

"Tarquin, you are free. I present you the horse you rode home. Take the saddles off, and turn them out." And he walked into the house, shaking by the hand the servants clustered about the door.

It was only when he was inside, facing the portrait of a young boy with handsome, dark eyes, that he gave way.

The very next day Dr. Cary, to use a commercial phrase, began to "take stock."

"Taking stock" is always a serious thing to do, and it must come often into every thoughtful man's life. He is his own ledger. In all cases he must look back and measure himself by himself. Perhaps some hour brings him some question on which all must hinge. It may come unexpectedly, or he may have seen it advancing with inevitable steps. He may have brought it on himself, or he may have fought strenuously against it. It is all the same. It comes straight down upon him, a cyclone threatening to overwhelm him, and he must meet it either as a brave man or a craven. It comes, sweeps past or over him and leaves him in its track, unscathed or wounded or slain. But it comes. And this is Life. The ancients called it Fate ; we call it Providence or Chance, or the result of natural laws. But by whatever name known, it is inscrutable.

So Dr. Cary felt that soft spring morning as he stood on the front porch of the roomy and rambling old mansion, where the Carys had had their seat and had made the Birdwood hospitality celebrated for more than two hundred years, and looked across the wide lawn, once well trimmed and filled with shrubbery and flowers, now ragged and torn. His eye took in the whole scene. The wide fields, once teeming with life, stretched before him now empty and silent ; the fences were broken down or had disappeared altogether. And yet the grass was fresh and green, the trees and bushes were just bursting from bud to leaf ; the far-off mountains rose blue and tender across the newly washed sky ; the birds were flitting and singing joyously, and somewhere, around the house, a young girl's voice was singing sweeter than any of the birds.   The look on the old soldier's face was for a moment one of deep gravity, if not of dejection ; but it passed away the next instant, as Blair's song reached him and as a step sounded behind him, and a hand was laid lightly on his shoulder, followed by an even softer touch on his arm, as his wife's face rested for a moment against it.   At the caressing touch his expression changed, he looked down in her eyes and, when he spoke, it was with a new light in his own eyes and a new tone in his voice.

"Well, Bess, we'll begin all over again.   We have each other, and we have Blair, and we have—the land.   It is as much as our forefathers began with.   At least, I think we have the land—I don't suppose they'll take that away.   If they do—why, we have each other and Blair, anyhow.   If we only had the boy ! "   He turned his face away.

"He died for his country," said the mother, though her voice belied the courage of her words.

" He died like a soldier : with all his wounds before."   He looked down into his wife's eyes.

" Yes."   And she sighed deeply.

" We have to take care of what's left.   Where is Jim Sherwood ?   I have not seen him."

" He has gone."

"What ! "   The Doctor gave a whistle of amazement. " I'd almost as soon have expected Mammy Krenda and Tarquin to leave."   Jim was one of the most trusted men about the place, a sort of preacher and leader, and had married, as his third wife, Mammy Krenda's daughter, Jane.

" Yes, Jim has gone.   He went two weeks ago, and I was rather glad he went," said Mrs. Cary.   " He had never been quite the same since the Yankees came through ; you know he behaved very badly then.   He had changed more than almost anyone of them who remained. He had been preaching a good deal lately, and appeared to be stirring the others up more than I liked. There seemed to have been some influence at work among them that I could not understand. It was said that Mr. Still, Helen's manager— But I don't know," —she broke off. "I heard them one night, at the house, and went out to the church where they were, and found them in a great state of excitement. They quieted down when I appeared. That repulsive creature, Mr. Gray's Moses, was there, and I ordered him home, and gave them a talk, and the next morning Jim Sherwood was missing too, and a few days later Jane said that she had to go also. I told them they were free, but if they remained here they must observe my regulations. I put Gideon in charge and told him you would look to him to keep order till you came. And he has done so to the best of his ability, I believe. I hear that he gave Jim Sherwood to understand that he would have no more of his preaching here for the present, and that if he wanted to preach for Hiram Still he could go to Red Rock and do it, not here. And now you are here, this is the end of my stewardship, and I surrender it into your hands."

She made her husband, half-mockingly, a profound curtsey—perhaps to turn off the serious thoughts which her words called up. But the Doctor declared that, at least, one of her slaves recognized too well the blessing of servitude to such a mistress to wish for freedom, and that he declined to assume control.

"Why, Bess, we men fought a quarter of the war and you women fought three-quarters. Do you imagine we want to depose you?"

Just then a young girl came around the corner of the house, her dark eyes full of light; her hair blown back from her forehead by the morning breeze, and her hands full of jonquils and other early flowers. Her face was glowing with the exercise she has been taking, and her whole person was radiant with youth.

" The morn is breaking.   Here comes Aurora," said her father, gazing at her fondly, at which Miss Blair's cheeks glowed only the more.

It was proposed by the Doctor that they should invite to dinner such of their friends as had arrived at home and could be reached.

" Our first reunion," said Mrs. Cary, smiling, and she began to give what she called her ménu, in which, corn-bread, dried fruit, black-eyed pease, and welcome figured as the principal dishes.   She laughed at her husband's dumb amazement.

" Bess," said the Doctor, humbly, " I retract what I said a little while ago about our having fought a fourth of the war—it was the speech of a braggart."   And having fol-lowed her with his eyes, as 'she went into the house, he walked around to have a talk with his negroes.

He found a number of them congregated and evidently expecting something of the kind.

" Gideon, tell the men I wish to speak to them."
In fifteen minutes they had collected.   He called them all up, and standing on the portico of the office where he had been accustomed to speak with them, addressed a few calm words to them.

For a moment he went over the past.   They had been faithful servants, he said.   And he was glad to be able to say this to them.   Now there were to be new relations be-tween them.   He told them they were free—on which there was an audible murmur of acquiescence—and they could leave, if they pleased.   There was another murmur of satisfaction.   But if they remained they would have to work and be subject to his authority.

Upon this many of the older ones signified their assent, while some of the others turned and, looking back, called to some one in the rear of the crowd :

" Come, Brer Sherrod, you done heah de noration ; now come and gi' de 'sponse."

A low, stout negro, of middle age, whom the Doctor had

not before noticed, came forward somewhat sheepishly, but with a certain swagger in his gait. It was evidently concerted. The Doctor's mind acted quickly. At the speaker's first word, he cut him short.

"I decline to allow Jim Sherwood to be the spokesman," he said. "He does not belong here. I left him in a position of trust, and he has failed in it. Fall to the rear ; I make no terms with outsiders."

Taken by surprise at the tone of authority, the exhorter fell or was moved back, in sudden confusion, while the doctor went on :

"Gideon, I appoint you ; you have proved trustworthy. This place has supported two hundred souls in the past, and we can make it do so again. Tell them that all those who remain here and work under you, including Sherwood, shall be supported and treated fairly and paid what is proper if it takes every acre I have to do it ; the others can go and find homes elsewhere." He turned on his heel and walked into the house.

The next day there was a good force at work in the fields.

Some of those he had addressed had gone off in the night; but most of them remained, and the Doctor told Mrs. Cary he thought things would work out all right; he was ready to accept present conditions, and matters would adjust themselves.

"Time is the adjuster," he said.

CHAPTER VI

A BROKEN SOLDIER COMES HOME FROM WAR

IT was a little over two weeks or, perhaps, three, after the Confederate armies had laid down their arms and disbanded, and the rest of the men from the county had turned their faces homeward with, or without, their paroles in their pockets, that a train which had been crawling all night over the shaky track, stopped in the morning near the little station, or what remained of it, on the edge of the county, where persons bound for nearly all that region got off. A passenger was helped down by the conductor and brakeman and was laid, with his crutch and blanket, as gently as might be, on a bank a little way from the track.

"Are you all right now? Do you think you can get on? You are sure someone will come for you?" asked the train men.

"Oh! yes; I feel better already." And the young fellow stretched out his hands in the gray dawn and felt the moist earth on either side of him almost tenderly.

As the railroad men climbed back into the car they were conversing together in low tones.

"Unless his friends come before many hours they won't find him," said one of them. "I don't know but what we ought to a' brought him along, any way."

But Jacquelin Gray had more staying power than they gave him credit for, and the very touch of the soil he loved did him good. He dragged himself a little way up, stretched himself out under a tree on the grass near where they had laid him, and went to sleep like a baby. The sun came up over the dewy trees and warmed him, and he only turned and slept on, dreaming that he had escaped from prison and reached the old county too weary to go any farther; and so, lay down on a bank and waited for someone to come for him. How often he had dreamed that, and had awaked to find himself in his old cot in the hospital, maybe, with the guard peering down at him with his lantern. Suddenly a shadow fell across his face, and he woke and looked up. Yes, there was the guard, three or four of them, gazing down on him in their blue uniform.

"Jacquelin Gray. No. —. Ward ten," he muttered wearily, as he used to do in the hospital, and was closing his eyes again when he awaked fully. Two or three Federal soldiers, one of them an officer, a little fellow with blue eyes, were leaning over him, and a cavalry company was yonder at rest, in the road below him. He was free after all, back in the old county.

The Lieutenant asked him his name and how he came there, and he told them.

"Where are you going ?"

"Home !" with a little flash in his eye.

"Where is that ?"

"Above here, across the country, in the Red Rock neighborhood—beyond Brutusville."

"Why, we are going that way ourselves—we were going to give you a decent burial ; but maybe we can do you a better turn if you are not ready for immortality ; we've an ambulance along, and here's the best substitute for the honor we offered you."

The little Lieutenant was so cheery as he pressed the canteen to Jacquelin's lips that the latter could not help feeling better.

The Captain, who had remained with the company, came over, on his handsome horse, picking his way through the débris lying about.

"So he is alive after all ?" he asked as he rode up.

"Alive ? Well, if you'd seen the way he took this !"

And the Lieutenant shook his canteen up beside his ear, as if to gauge its remaining contents ; then held it to Jacquelin again.

" Have another pull ? No ? All right—when you want it. You aren't the first reb's had a swig at it."

Then he repeated to his superior, a tall, handsome fellow, what Jacquelin had told him as to his name and destination. In an instant the Captain had sprung from his horse.

" Jacquelin Gray ! Red Rock !—By Jove ! It can't be ! " He stared down at the man on the ground.

" Do you mean to say that you live at a place called ' Red Rock '—a great plantation, with a big rock by a burial-ground, and a red stain on it, said to be an Indian's blood ? "

Jacquelin nodded.

" Well by —— ! What's the matter with you ? Where have you been ? What are you dressed this way for ?—I mean an old plantation where there was a wedding—or a wedding-party, about five years ago—? " he broke out, as if it were impossible to believe it. " And—a little girl, named Blair Something, sang ? "

Jacquelin nodded.

" Yes, that's the place—Miss Blair Cary. But who are—? What do you know about—— ? "

" Well, I'm— Here, Reely, call Sergeant O'Meara ; tell him to send the ambulance here directly," interrupted the Captain. He turned back to Jacquelin.

" Don't you remember me ? I'm Middleton—Lawrence Middleton. Don't you remember? I happened in that night with Mr. Welch, and you took care of us ? I've never forgotten it."

" I remember it—you painted the horse red," said Jacquelin.

" Yes—it was really this fellow, Reely Thurston. He is the one that got me into all that trouble. And he has got me into a lot more since. But where have you been that you look like this ? "

Jacquelin told him.

By this time several of the people from the few houses in the neighborhood of the station, who had at first kept aloof from the troop of soldiers and gazed at them from a distance, had come up, seeing that they had a Confederate with them. They recognized Jacquelin and began to talk about his appearance, and to make cutting speeches as to the treatment he had undergone.

"We ain't forgot your Pa," some of them said.

"Nor you neither," said one of the women, who added that she was Andy Stamper's cousin.

They wanted Jacquelin to stay with them and let them take care of him until his mother could send for him. Captain Allen had been down to see about him, and Andy Stamper had been there several times, and had said that if he didn't hear anything from him next time, he was going North to see about him, if he had to ride his old horse there.

Jacquelin, however, was so anxious to get home that, notwithstanding the pressing invitations of his friends, he accepted the offer of the Federal officers, and, after getting a cup of coffee from Andy's cousin—who said it was the first she had had in three years—he was helped up in the ambulance and was driven off.

The company, it seemed, had come up from the city the day before and had encamped a little below the station, and was marching to Brutusville, where it was to be posted.

Julius, General Legaie's old butler, met them near the court-house and plunged out in the mud and wrung Jacquelin's hand, thanking God for his return.

The old butler was on the lookout for his master, who had not come home yet, and about whom he was beginning to be very uneasy. The General had gone South somewhere "to keep on fightin'," Julius told Jacquelin, and he invited him to come by and spend the night, and **offered** to go on himself and let his mother know he had come. The old fellow, in his best clothes—a high hat and an old blue coat with brass buttons—and with his best manners, caused much amusement to the soldiers, and Lieutenant Thurston undertook to tease him.

"You haven't any master now," he said.

The old servant looked at him.

"I ain't? Does you think I'se a free nigger?" he asked, sharply, "'Cause I ain't!"

"Yes, but I mean we've taken your master prisoner."

"You is?" He looked at him again keenly. "Nor, you ain't. It'll teck a bigger man 'n you to teck my master prisoner—And he ain' big as you nuther," he said, with a snap of his eyes. "He ain't de kind dat s'renders."

"We'll have to stand in on this together," said the little Lieutenant across to Jacquelin, as the laugh went round; and then to Julius, with a wave of his hand toward Jacquelin, "Well, what do you say to that gentleman's having surrendered?"

The old darky was quick enough, however.

"He was shot, and besides *you* never got him. I know you never got nigh enough to him in battle to shoot him."

"I think you'll have to go this alone," said Jacquelin. The Lieutenant admitted himself routed.

Late that evening Jacquelin's ambulance was toiling up the hill to Red Rock, while the troop of cavalry, sent to keep order in that section, with its tents pitched in the court-house yard under the big trees, were taking a survey of the place they had come to govern. Little Thurston, who, as they rode in, had caught sight of a plump young girl gazing at them from the open door of the old clerk's office, with mingled curiosity and defiance, declared that it was not half as bad as some places he had been in in the South. At that moment, as it happened, Miss Elizabeth Dockett, the young lady in question, daughter of Mr. Dockett, the old County Clerk, was describing to her mother the little Lieutenant as the most ridiculous and odious-looking little person in the world.

It was night when Jacquelin reached home; but so keen was the watch in those times, that the ambulance had been heard in the dark, so that when he arrived there was quite a crowd on the lawn ready to receive him, and the next moment he was in his mother's arms.

Sergeant O'Meara, who had been detailed to go on with the ambulance, took back to the court-house an account of the meeting.

"It was wurruth the drive," he said, "to see 'um whan we got there. An' if I'd been th' Gineral himself, or the Captain, they couldn't 'a' made more fuss over me. Bedad! I thought they moust tak' me for a Gineral at least; but no, ut was me native gintilitee. I was that proud of meself I almost shed tears of j'y. The only thing I lacked was some wan to say me so gran' that could appreciate me. An ould gintleman—a Docther Major Cary—a good Oirish naim, bedad!—was there to say wan of the leddies, and ivery toime a leddy cooms in, oop he gits, and bows very gran', an' the leddy bows an' passes by, an' down he sets, an' I watches him out o' the tail of me eye, an' ivery toime he gits oup, oup I gits too. An' I says:

"'I always rise for the leddies; me mither was a leddy,' an' he says, with a verra gran' bow: 'Yis,' he says, 'an' her son is a gintleman, too.' What dy'e think o' that? An' I says, 'Yis, I know he is.'"

Next morning Jacquelin was in a very softened mood. The joy of being free and at home again was tempered by memory of the past and realization of the present; but he was filled with a profound feeling which, perhaps, he himself could not have named. As he hobbled out to the front portico and gazed around on the wide fields spread out below him, with that winding ribbon of tender green, where the river ran between its borders of willows and sycamores, he renewed his resolve to follow in his father's footsteps. He would keep the place at all sacrifices. He was in this pleasant frame of mind when Hiram Still came around the house. Still had aged during the war, his voice had become more confidential.

As he came up to Jacquelin, the latter, notwithstanding his outstretched hand and warm words, had a sudden return of his old feeling of suspicion and dislike.

"Mr. Jacquelin, I swan, I am glad to see you, suh—an' to see you lookin' so well. I told yo' Ma you'd come back all right. An' I told that Yankee what brought you up last night that 'twas a shame they treated you as they done, and if you hadn't come back all right we'd 'a' come up thar an' cleaned 'em out. Yes, sir, we would that.

"I sent him off this mornin'—saw him acrost the ford myself ;" he added, lowering his voice confidentially, " because I don't like to have 'em prowling around my place—*our* place—too much. Stirs up th' niggers so you can't get no work out of 'em. And I didn't like that fellow's looks, particularly. Well, I certainly am glad to see you lookin' so well."

Jacquelin felt doubly rebuked for his unjust suspicions, and, as a compensation, told Mr. Still of his last conversation with his father, and of what his father had said of him. Still was moved almost to tears.

"Your father was the best friend I ever had in this world, Mr. Jack," he said. "I'll never—" he had to turn his face away. "You can't do no better than your father."

"No, indeed," Jacquelin agreed to that. All he wished was to do just what his father had done—He was not well ; and he should leave the management of the place to Mr. Still, just as his father had done—at least, till they knew how things stood, he added.

There was a slight return of a look which had been once or twice in Still's downcast eyes, and he raised them to take a covert glance at Jacquelin's face. Jacquelin, however, did not see it. He was really suffering greatly from his wound ; and the expression he caught on Still's face was only one of deep concern. He asked after Still's family.

Wash had gone to the city to study medicine, Still said.

"We pore folks as ain't got a fine plantation like this has got to have a trade or something."

Virgy was at home keeping house for him. She was a good big girl now—"most grown like Miss Blair," he added.

There was a slight tone in the manager's voice which somehow grated on Jacquelin a little, he did not know why. And he changed the subject rather shortly.

Some time he wished to talk to Mr. Still about that Deep-run plantation in the South, he said, as he had attended to stocking it and knew more about it than anyone else; but he did not think he was equal to it just then. Still agreed that this was right, also that the first thing for Jacquelin to do now was to take care of himself and get well.

Just then Andy Stamper came round the house, with a bucket in one hand and a bunch of flowers in the other. At sight of Jacquelin his face lit up with pleasure. Before Andy could nod to Hiram the latter had gone, with a queer look on his face, and something not unlike a slink in his gait.

The bucket Andy had brought was full of eggs, which Delia Dove, Andy said, had sent Jacquelin, and she had sent the flowers too.

"I never see anyone like her for chickens an' flowers," said Andy. "She's a good friend o' yours. I thought when I got home I wa'n't goin' to get her after all. I thought she'd 'a' sent me back to P'int Lookout," he laughed.

His expression changed after a moment.

"I see Hiram's been to see you—to wish you well? Don't know what's the reason, he kind o' cuts out whenever I come 'roun'. Looks almost like he's got some'n' ag'inst me; yet he done me a mighty good turn when I was married; he come and insisted on lendin' me some

money, not only to buy a horse with fer the ole woman :
but a horse to go back in th' army with—a whole basket-
ful of money, and he's been lendin' all aroun' the neighborhood ; an' don't seem to be in no hurry to git it back—
If you jest give him a little slip o' writin' on yo' land,
that's all. Yet, somehow, he always r'minds me of a
mink, kind of slippy-like. He don't do things all at once.
He didn't tell me he wanted no deed ; but after I was
gone, he got one from the old lady—said 'twould be all
right, and I could pay him any time ; he jest wanted it
in case he died, and she didn' know no better than to sign
it. I'm goin' to pay him off, first money I git. I never
would 'a' borrowed it 'cept I was so anxious to go back in
the army—an' to git Delia. Hiram thought he was sure
to win." The little soldier's face always lighted up when
he referred to his wife.

Jacquelin protested that he thought Still a better fellow
than Andy would admit, and added that his father had
always esteemed him highly.

"Yes, I know that ; but the Colonel didn't know him,
Mr. Jack, and he wasn't lookin' out for him. I don't like
a man I can't understand. If you know he's a liar, you
needn't b'lieve him ; but if you aint found him out yet, he
gets aroun' you. Hiram is that sort. I know he us't to
be a liar, an' I don't b'lieve folks recovers from that disease. So I'm goin' to pay him off. An' you do the same.
I tell you, he's a schemer, an' he's lookin' up."

Just then there was a light step behind them, a shadow
fell on the veranda, which, to one of them, at least, was
followed by an apparition of light—as, with a smothered
cry of, "Jacquelin!" a young girl, her hair blowing about
her brow, ran forward, and as the wounded soldier rose,
threw her arms around his neck. Blair Cary looked like
a rose as she drew back in a pretty confusion, her blushes
growing deeper every moment.

"Why, Blair, how pretty you've grown !" exclaimed
Jacquelin, thinking only of her beauty.

"Well, you talk as if you were very much surprised," and Miss Blair bridled with pretended indignation.

"Oh ! No—Of course, not. I only——"

"Oh ! yes, you do," and she tossed her pretty head with well-feigned disdain. "You are as bold with your compliments as you were with your sword."

She turned from him to Sergeant Stamper, who was regarding her with open-mouthed admiration.

"How do you do, Sergeant Stamper? How's Delia? And how are her new chickens? Tell her she isn't to keep on sending them all to me. I am going to learn to raise them for myself now."

"I daren't tell her that," said the little fellow. "You know I can't do nothin' with Delia Dove. You're the only one can do that. If I tell her that, she'd discharge me, an' sen' me 'way from the place."

"I'm glad to see she's breaking you in so well," laughed Blair.

In a short time all the soldiers from the old county who were left were back at home, together with some who were not originally from that county, but who, having nowhere better to go, and no means to go with, even if they had had, and finding themselves stranded by the receding tide, pitched their tents permanently where they had only intended to bivouac, and thus, by the simple process of staying there, became permanent residents.

The day after that on which Jacquelin arrived, General Legaie, to the delight of old Julius and of such other servants as yet remained on his place, turned up, dusty, and worn, but still serene and undispirited. He marched into his dismantled mansion with as proud a step as when he left it, and took possession of it as though it had been a castle. With him was an officer to whom the General offered the hospitalities of the house as though it had been a palace, and to whom he paid as courtly attention as if he had been a prince.

"This is Julius, Captain, of whom I have spoken to you," he said, after he had shaken hands with the old butler, and with the score of other negroes who had rushed out and gathered around him on hearing of his arrival. "Julius will attend to you, and unless he has lost some of his art you will confess that I have not exaggerated his abilities." He faced his guest and made him a low bow. "I hope, Captain, you will consider this your home as long as you wish. Julius, the Captain will stay with us for the present, and I suspect he'd like a julep." And with a wave of the hand the little General transferred the responsibility of his guest to the old butler, who stood bowing, dividing his glances between those of affection for his master and of shrewd inspection of the visitor.

The latter was a tall, spare man, rather sallow than dark, but with a piercing, black eye, and a closely shut mouth under a long, black, drooping mustache. He acknowledged the General's speech with a civil word, and Julius's bow with a nod and a look, short but keen and inquiring, and then, flinging himself into the best seat, leant his head back and half closed his eyes, while the General went out and received the negroes, who, with smiling faces, were still gathering on the news of his arrival.

During this absence the guest did not rise from his chair; but turned his head slowly from time to time, until his eyes had rested on every article in the field of his vision. He might have been making an appraisement.

The General, in fact, did not know any more of his guest than Julius knew. He had come on him only that afternoon at a fork in the road, resting, stretched out on a couple of fence-rails, while his horse nibbled and picked at the grass and leaves near by. The gray uniform, somewhat fresher than those the General was accustomed to, attracted the General's attention, and when Captain Mc-Raffle, as the stranger called himself, asked him the nearest way to Brutusville, or to some gentleman's house, the General at once invited him to his home. He had heard, he stated, that a company of Yankees had already been sent to Brutusville ; but he could show him the way to a house where gentlemen had lived in the past, and where, if he thought *he* would pass muster, one was about to live again. And with this invitation Captain McRaffle became an inmate of Thornleigh, as the General's place was called, and might have stayed there indefinitely had not unforeseen contingencies caused him to remove his quarters.

Just as the General returned from his reception on the veranda, the old butler entered with a waiter and two juleps sparkling in their glasses. At sight of them the General beamed, and even the guest's cold eyes lit up.

" On my soul ! he is the most remarkable fellow in the world," declared the General to his visitor. " Where did you get this ? "

" Well, you see, suh," said Julius, " de Yankees over yander was givin' out rations, and I thought I'd git a few, so's to be ready for you 'ginst you come."

The General smiled delightedly, and between the sips of his julep proceeded to extract from Julius all the news of the county since his last visit, a year or more before, and to give a running commentary of his own for the enlightenment of his guest, who, it must be said, appeared not quite as much interested in it all as he might have been.

All the people on the place, Julius said, had been over to the court-house already to see the soldiers, but most of them had come back. He had been there himself one day, but had returned the same evening, as he would not leave the place unguarded at night.

" The most faithful fellow that ever was on earth ; he would die for me ! " asserted the General, in a delighted aside to his guest, who received the encomium somewhat coldly, and on the first opportunity that he could do so unobserved, gave the old butler another of those looks that appeared like a flash of cold steel.

Dr. Cary had been down the day before to inquire after

the General.—"An old and valued friend of mine, the greatest surgeon in the State—ought to have been made Surgeon-General of the army," interpolated the General to his guest.

The Doctor had said the ladies were well, and were mighty anxious about the General—"Yes, sir, Miss Thomasia was very well, indeed."

"Miss Gray—a very old—I mean—ah—*dear* friend of mine—sister of Colonel Gray," the General explained to his guest. "On my word, I believe her intuitions are infallible. I never knew her at fault in her estimate of a man in my life."

The Doctor had left word asking if he would not come up to dinner next day, Julius continued:

"Bless my soul! Of course I will—and I'll take you too, Captain; they will be delighted to see you—Most charming people in the world!"

So the General annotated old Julius's bulletin, gilding everyone and everything with the gold of his own ingenuous heart.

The—ah—soldiers had left an order for him as soon as he came, to come to the court-house to swear to something, said Julius, doubtfully.

"I'll see the soldiers d—— condemned first!" bristled the General. "I shall go to pay my respects to the ladies at Red Rock and Birdwood to-morrow—the two most beautiful places in all the country, sir." This to Captain McRaffle, who received even this stirring information without undue warmth; but when their backs were turned, inspected again both the General and old Julius.

Next morning the General invited his guest to accompany him, but Captain McRaffle was not feeling well, he said, and he thought if the General would leave him, he would remain quiet. Or, perhaps, if he felt better, he might ride over to the county seat and reconnoitre a little. He always liked to know the strength of the force before him.

"A most excellent rule," the General declared, with admiration.

So the General, having given the Captain one of the two very limp shirts which "the thoughtfulness of a dear friend, Mrs. Cary, of Birdwood," had provided for him, arrayed himself in the other and set out to pay his respects to his friends in the upper end of the county, leaving his guest stretched out on a lounge.

He had not been gone long when the Captain ordered his horse and rode off in the direction of the court-house.

On arriving at the county seat the new-comer rode straight to the tavern, and dismounting, gave his horse to a servant and walked in. As he entered he gave one of those swift, keen glances, and then asked for Mrs. Witcher, the landlady. When she arrived, a languid, delicate-looking woman, the Captain was all graciousness, and, in a few moments, Mrs. Witcher was equally complacent. In fact, the new-comer had decided on the first glance that this was good enough for him, at least, till he could do better. The Captain told Mrs. Witcher that he had not had a really square meal in two months, and had not slept in a bed in six months.

"A floor, madam, or a table, so it is long enough, is all I desire. Upon my word and honor I don't think I could sleep in a bed."

But Mrs. Witcher insisted that he should try, and so the Captain condescended to make the experiment, after giving her a somewhat detailed account of his extensive family connection, and of an even larger circle of friends, which included the commanding Generals of all the armies and everybody else of note in the country besides.

"Well, this suits me," he said as he walked into the room assigned him. "Jim, who occupied this room last?" he asked the darky—whose name happened to be Paul.

"Well, I forgits the gent'man's name, he died in dis room."

"Did he? How?"

"Jes' so, suh. He died right in dat bed, 'caus I help' to lay him out."

"Well, maybe I'll die in it myself. See that the sheets are clean," said Captain McRaffle, composedly. "What are you standing there gaping at? Do you suppose I mind a man's dying? I've killed a hundred men."

"Suh !"

"Yes, two hundred—and slept in a coffin myself to boot." And the Captain turned on the negro so dark and saturnine a face that "Jim" withdrew in a hurry, and ten minutes later was informing the other negroes that there was a man in the house that had been dead and "done riz agin."

And this was the equipment with which Captain McRaffle began life as a resident of Brutusville.

CHAPTER VII

THE meeting at Birdwood was a notable occasion. It was, in a way, the outward and visible sign of the return of peace. Someone said it looked like the old St. Ann congregation risen from the dead, to which Miss Thomasia added, that the gentlemen, at least, were now all immortal, and the General, with his hand on his heart, gallantly responded that the ladies had always been so. The speech, however, left some faces grave, for there were a number of vacant places that could not be forgotten.

Jacquelin, under the excitement of his arrival, felt himself sufficiently restored and stimulated to join his mother and Aunt Thomasia, and be driven over to Birdwood, and though he suffered a good deal from the condition of the roads, yet when Blair ran forward and offered her shoulder for "his other crutch," he felt as though a bad wound might after all have some compensations.

Steve Allen was the life of the company. He had ridden over on his black horse, "Hot-Spur," that, like himself, had been wounded several times in the last campaigns, though never seriously. He spent his time teasing Blair. He declared that Jacquelin was holding on to his crutch only to excite sympathy, and that his own greatest cause for hatred of the Yankees now was either that they had not shot him instead of Jack, or had not killed Jack, and he offered to go out and let anyone shoot him immediately for one single pitying glance like those he said Blair was lavishing on Jack.

Jacquelin, with a vivid memory of the morning before,

had meant to kiss Blair on his arrival, yet when they met
he was seized with a sudden panic, and could hardly look
into her eyes. She appeared to have grown taller and
older since yesterday, as well as prettier, and when Steve,
on arriving, insolently caught and kissed her before them
all, on the plea of cousinship, Jacquelin was conscious of
a pang of consuming jealousy, and for the first time in
his life would gladly have thrashed Steve.

There was one thing that marred the occasion somewhat,
or might have done so under other circumstances. The
entire negro population, who could travel, moved by some
idea that the arrival of the Federal soldiers concerned
them, were flocking to the county seat, leaving the fields
deserted and the cabins empty.

The visitors had found the roads lined with them as they
came along. They were all civil, but what could it mean?
Some of the young men, like Steve and Jacquelin, were
much stirred up about it, and talked of organizing quietly
so as to be ready if the need should arise. Dr. Cary, however, and the older ones, opposed anything of the kind.
Any organization whatever would be viewed with great suspicion by the authorities, and might be regarded as a breach
of their parole, and was not needed. They were already
organized simply by being what they were. And, indeed,
though gaunt and weather-beaten, in their old worn uniforms they were a martial-looking set. There was not a man
there who had not looked Death in the eyes many a time,
and the stare had left something notable in every face.

It was a lovely day, and the early flowers were peeping
out as if to be sure before they came too far that winter
had gone for good. The soft haze of Spring was over the
landscape.

The one person who was wanting, to make the company
complete, was the little General. They were just discussing him, and were wondering if he had gone to Mexico;
and Steve, seated at Miss Thomasia's side, was teasing
her about him, declaring that, in his opinion, it was a

pretty widow, whose husband had been in the General's brigade and had been shot, that the General had gone South after ; when a horseman was seen riding rapidly across the open field far below, taking the ditches as he came to them. When he drew nearer he was recognized to be none other than the gallant little General himself. As he came trotting across the lawn, among the great trees, he presented a martial figure, and handkerchiefs were waved to him, and many cheers were given, so that he was quite overcome when he dismounted in the midst of a number of his old soldiers, and found himself literally taken in the arms of both the men and the ladies.

The General beamed, as he gazed around with a look that showed that he thought life might still be worth living if only he could meet occasionally such a reception as had just been given him. Others smiled too ; for it was known that the General had been an almost life-long lover and suitor of Miss Thomasia Gray, whose twenty years' failure to smile on him had in no way damped his ardor or dimmed his hope. In fact, the old soldier, in his faded gray, with his bronzed, worn, highbred face, was nearer achieving the object of his life at that moment than he had ever been in the whole twenty years of his pursuit. Had the occasion come fifteen or even ten years earlier, he might have done so ; but Miss Thomasia had reached the point when to marry appeared to her ridiculous, and the only successful rival of the shaft of Cupid is the shaft of Ridicule.

At such a meeting as this there were necessarily many serious things to be considered. One was the question of bread ; another of existence. None could look around on the wide, deserted fields and fail to take in this. Everything like civil government had disappeared. There was not a civil officer left in the State. From Governor to justices of the peace, every office had been vacated. The Birdwood meeting was the first in the county at which was had any discussion of a plan for the preservation of

order.   Even this was informal and unpremeditated ; but
when it reached the ears of Colonel Krafton, the new commander of that district, who had just arrived, it had taken
on quite another complexion, and the " Cary Conference,"
as it came to be called, was productive of some very far-
reaching consequences to certain of those who participated in it, and to the county itself.

As to some matters broached at Birdwood that day,
there was wide diversity of opinion among those present.

Dr. Cary was in favor of accepting the issues as settled
by the war ; of making friends with the high authorities—
as had already been done by some in other parts of the
State, and of other States.

" Never ! never ! " declared General Legaie, with whom
were most of the others.   " They have done their worst ;
they have invaded us, and taken our negroes from us.
Let them bear the responsibilities they have assumed."

It was easy to see, from the enthusiasm which greeted
the General, on which side the sympathy lay.

" The worst ! General Legaie ? " exclaimed Dr. Cary.
" The worst will be coming for years.   'After the sword
comes the cankerworm.'   Mark my words : the first terms
offered are always the best.   I should not be surprised
if you were to live to see negroes invested with the elec-
tive franchise."

" Impossible !   Preposterous !   Incredible ! " declared
General Legaie, his words being echoed by most of those
present.

" It seems almost impossible and quite incredible, yet
to an old man many things appear possible that are incredible," said Dr. Cary.

" We will die before such an infamy should be perpe-
trated ! " protested General Legaie, with spirit.

" The only trouble is, that dying would do no good ;
only those who know how to live can now save the Country," said the Doctor, gravely.

The old Whig looked so earnest—so imposing, as he

6

stood, tall and white, his eyes flashing under their beetling brows, that though, perhaps, few agreed with him, all were impressed, and by a common and tacit consent their position was not pressed, at least for the present. The little General even agreed to accompany Dr. Cary at some near date, to give his views, along with Dr. Cary's, to the new Commander of the district, Colonel Krafton, in order, the General stated, that the Commander might understand precisely the attitude of all persons in their county.

Steve Allen, and the other young soldiers who were there, found themselves sufficiently entertained, fighting over their battles, as though they had been the commanding generals, and laying off new campaigns in a fresh and different field ; meantime, getting their hands in, adoring and teasing their young hostess, who was related to, or connected with, most of them. They had left Blair Cary, a dimple-faced, tangle-haired romp of thirteen or fourteen, with saucy eyes, which even then, as they danced behind their dark lashes, promised the best substitute for beauty. They now found her sprung up to a slender young lady of "quite seventeen," whose demureness and new-born dignity were the more bewitching, because they were belied by her laughing glances. Mars has ever been the captive of Venus as well as her conqueror, and more than Steve Allen and Jacquelin Gray fell victims at the first fire from those "deadly batteries," as Steve afterward characterized Blair Cary's eyes, in his first poem to Belinda—published in the Brutusville *Guardian*. But they all declared they saw at once that they stood no chance with Jack Gray, whose face wore "that sickly look," as Steve called it, which, he said, "every woman thought interesting and none could resist." Over all of which nonsense, Miss Blair's dark eyes twinkled with the pleasure of a girl who is too young to comprehend it quite fully, but yet finds it wonderfully delightful. As for Jacquelin, to him she was no longer mortal : he had robed her in radiance and lifted **her among the stars.**

The older people found not less pleasure in the reunion than their juniors, and appeared to have grown young again. And while the youngsters were out on the grass at Miss Blair's feet, in more senses than one, the General and Dr. Cary and the other seniors were on the vine-covered portico, discussing grave questions of state-craft, showing precisely how and when the Confederacy might have been saved and made the greatest power on earth—together with other serious matters. The General teased himself as of old about Miss Thomasia, and the Doctor teased them both. The General had been noted formerly as a great precision-ist in matters of dress, as well as in all other matters, and now, when he stalked about the veranda, with his old uniform-coat buttoned to the chin as jauntily as ever, and with a limp bit of white showing above the collar and at the wrists, in which he evidently took much pride, the Doctor, who knew where the shirt came from, and that, like the one which he himself had on, it was made from an under-garment of one of the ladies, could not help rallying him a little. The Doctor wisely took ad-vantage of Mrs. Cary's absence from the room to do this, but had got no farther than to congratulate the General on the luxury of fresh linen and to receive from him the gallant assurance that he had felt on putting it on that morning, as a knight of old might have felt when he donned his armor prepared by virgin hands, when Mrs. Cary entered and, recognizing instantly from her husband's look of suspicious innocence and Miss Thomasia's expres-sion, that some mischief was going on, pounced on him promptly and bore him off. When he returned from the "judgment chamber," as he called it, he was under a solemn pledge not to open the subject again to the Gen-eral, which he observed to the best of his ability, though he kept Miss Thomasia on thorns, by coming as near to it as he dared with a due regard to himself in view of his wife's watchfulness.

In fact, these men were thoroughly enjoying home life

after the long interval of hardship and deprivation, and
neither the sorrow of the past nor the gloom of the present could wholly depress them. The future, fortunately,
they could not know. Then, among young people there
must be joy, if there be not death ; and fun is as natural as
grass or flowers in spring or any other outbudding of a new
and bounding life.

So, even amid the ruins, the flowers bloomed and there
were fun and gayety. Hope was easily worth all the other
spirits in Pandora's box put together.

Before the company separated they began to talk even
of a party, and, to meet the objections of old Mr. Langstaff and some others, it was agreed that it should be a
contribution-entertainment and that the proceeds should
go to the wounded soldiers and soldiers' widows, of the
county. This Steve declared was a deep-laid scheme on
the part of Jacquelin Gray. It was already decided on
when the Doctor returned to the sitting-room, after Mrs.
Cary had summoned him thence, and the question under
advisement was whether the Yankee officers at the court-
house should be invited. Steve Allen had started it.
The ladies were a unit.

" No, indeed ; not one of them should set his foot inside
the door ; not a girl would dance with one of them." On
this point Miss Blair was very emphatic, and her laughing
eyes lost their gleam of sunlight and flashed forth a sudden spark which showed deeper depths behind those dark
lashes than had appeared at any time before.

"I'll bet you do," said Steve. He stretched out his
long legs, settled himself, and looked at Blair with that
patronizing air which always exasperated her.

"I'll bet I don't ! "—with her head up, and her color
deepening a little at the bravado of using such a word.

"I'll bet my horse you'll break a set with Jack for
the Yankee captain," declared Steve.

" Don't want your old horse, he's too full of lead," said
Blair.

"Then I'll bet you his horse."

"It's a good one," said Jacquelin from his place on the lounge. "Blood-bay, with three white feet and a blaze on his nose."

"He's mine," asserted Steve with a nod of his head.

"How will you get it?" asked Blair.

"Steve knows several ways of getting horses," laughed one of the other young men.

"Shut up, you fool," telegraphed Steve with his lips, glancing quickly at Miss Thomasia, who was beaming on him with kindly eyes.

It is surprising what little things have influence. That sudden flash, with the firmer lines which came for a second in the young girl's face, did more to bind the young men to her footstool than all the fun and gayety she had shown.

The men were not so unanimous on the point touching the exclusion of the officers. Most of them agreed with the ladies, but one or two were inclined to the other side.

"Men like to fancy themselves broader and more judicial than women," said Miss Thomasia, placidly.

Jacquelin mentioned casually that Middleton was not only quite a gentlemanly fellow, but a strikingly handsome one.

"A Yankee soldier good-looking! I'll not believe that!" declared Miss Blair, promptly.

This debate created a diversion in their favor, and it was suggested and agreed to, as a compromise, that they should "wait until after a St. Ann Sunday, and see what the officers looked like. No doubt some of them would come to church, and then they could determine what they would do."

This idea was feminine, and, to offset it, it was re-declared that at present they were "unanimously opposed to regarding them in any other light than that of bitter enemies."

CHAPTER VIII

So Peace spread her white wings, extending her serenity and shedding her sweetness even in those regions where war had passed along.

Without wasting time or repining about the past, Dr. Cary and General Legaie and the other men began to pick up such of the tangled and broken threads of the old life as could be found, and to form with them the new. They mended the worn vehicles, patched up the old harness and gear, broke their war-horses to drive, and set in to live bravely and cheerfully, in as nearly the old manner as they could. They had, they believed, made the greatest fight on record. They had not only maintained, but had increased, the renown of their race for military achievement —the reputation which they most highly valued. They had been overwhelmed, not whipped ; cast down, but not destroyed. They still had the old spirit, the unconquerable spirit of their race, and, above all, they had the South.

Dr. Cary determined to use every effort to restore at once the old state of affairs, and, to this end, to offer homes and employment to all his old servants.

Accordingly, he rode down to the county seat one day to have an interview with the officers there. He went alone, because he did not know precisely how he would be received, and, besides, there was by no means general approval of his course among his friends.

He found that the ranking officer, Captain Middleton, had been summoned that morning to the city by Colonel

Krafton, the provost in command there. The next in command, however, Lieutenant Thurston, was very civil and obliging to the Doctor, and, on learning of his plans, took steps to further them.

The officer summoned all the negroes who were hanging around the village, to assemble on the court-green, told them of the Doctor's offer, and, after a short talk to them, ordered all the Doctor's old servants who were present, and had not secured employment elsewhere, to return home and go to work on the wages he had agreed the Doctor should pay. For, as he said to Middleton when he returned :

"By Gad ! Larry, I was not sure whether I was talking to Don Quixote or old Dr. Filgrave—I know he is cousin to them both, for he told me so—he is a cousin to everybody in the United States. And, besides, I was so bored with those niggers hanging around, looking pitiful, and that tall, whispering fellow, Still, who tells about the way he had to act during the war to keep the people from knowing he was on our side, that I would have ordered every nigger in the country to go with the old gentleman if he had wanted them. By the way, he is the father of the girl they say is so devilishly pretty, and he asked after you most particularly. Ah ! Larry, I am a diplomat. I have missed my calling." And, as he looked at his tall, good-looking superior, the little Lieutenant's eyes twinkled above the bowl of his pipe, which was much the shape of himself.

The engagement to furnish his negroes rations Dr. Cary was enabled to make, because on his arrival at the county seat he had fallen in with Hiram Still, who had offered to lend him a sum of money, which he said he happened to have by him. Hiram had been down to take the oath of allegiance, he told the Doctor.

"I been wonderin' to myself what I was to do with that money—and what I turned all them Confed. notes into gold and greenbacks for," he said. "Fact is, I thought myself a plum fool for doin' it ; but I says, ' Well, gold's gold, whichever way it goes.' So I either bought land or gold. But 't does look 's if Providence had somethin' to do with it, sure 'nough. I ain't got a bit o' use for it—you can take it and pay me just when it's convenient."

Still had never been a favorite with Dr. Cary, though the latter confessed that he could cite no positive ground for his dislike. When he thought of his antipathy at all, he always traced it back to two things—one that Legaie always disliked Still, the other that when Still had his attack of inflammatory rheumatism at the outbreak of the war, the symptoms were such as to baffle the Doctor's science. "That's a pretty ground for a reasonable man to found an antipathy on," reflected the Doctor.

As the Doctor and Hiram rode back together toward home, Still was so bitter in his denunciation of the Federals and of their action touching the negroes, that the Doctor actually felt it his duty to lecture him. They were all one country now, he said, and they should accept the result as determined. But Still said, "Never !" He had only taken the oath of allegiance, he declared, because he had heard he would be arrested unless he did. But he had taken it with a mental reservation. This shocked the Doctor so much that he rebuked him with sternness, on which Still explained that he did not mean exactly that, but that he had heard that if a man took an oath under threats he was absolved from it.

"There was some such legal quibble," the Doctor admitted, with a sniff, but he was " very sure that no brave man would ever take an oath for such a reason, and no honest one would ever break one." He rode off with his head very high.

When Still reached home that evening he was in uncommonly good spirits. He was pleasanter than usual to his daughter, who appeared the plainer because of the contrast that her shabby clothes presented to the showy suit which her brother wore. It was to his son, however, that

Mr. Still showed his particular good-humor. Wash had just come home for a little visit from the city, where he had been ever since his return from the army, and where he was now studying medicine. He was a tall, slim fellow, very much like his father in appearance, though in place of the rather good-tempered expression which usually sat on the latter's face, Wash's look was usually sour and discontented.

"Ah, Wash, my son, I did a good stroke of business for you to-day," said the father that evening at supper.

"What was it ? Did you buy another farm ? You'll break, buying so much land," replied his son, pleasantly.

Still put aside the ungraciousness of the reply. He was accustomed to his son's slurs.

"Yes and no." He winked at Virgy, to whom he had already confided something of his stroke of business. He glanced at the door to see that no one was listening, and dropped his voice to his confidential pitch. "I lent the Doctor a leetle money." He nodded with satisfaction.

Wash became interested ; but the next instant attempted to appear indifferent.

"How much ? What security did he give ? "

"More than he'll be able to pay for some time, and the security's all right. Aha ! I thought that would wake you up. I'll lend him some more one of these days and then we'll get the pay—with interest." He winked at his son knowingly. " When you're tryin' to ketch a shy horse, don't show him the bridle ; when you've got him, then— ! " He made a gesture of slipping on a halter. This piece of philosophy appeared to satisfy the young man and to atone for the apparent unwisdom of his father's action. He got into such a good-humor that he began to talk pleasantly with his sister and to ask her about the young men in the neighborhood.

It was striking to see how she changed at the notice her brother took of her. The listless look disappeared, and her eyes brightened and made her face appear really interesting.

Presently the young man said :

"How's Lord Jacquelin?" At the unexpected question the blood mounted to the girl's face, and after an
appealing look she dropped her eyes quickly.

When the end of the month came, Dr. Cary summoned
his hands and paid them their wages one by one, according
to his contract with Thurston, checking each name, as he
paid them, on a pay-roll he had prepared. Their reception
of the payment varied with the spirit of the men ; some
being gay and facetious ; others taking it with exaggerated
gravity. It was the first time they had ever received stipulated wages for their services, and it was an event.

The Doctor was well satisfied with the result, and went
in to make the same settlement with the house-servants.
The first he met was Mammy Krenda, and he handed her
the amount he had agreed on with Thurston as a woman's
wages. The old woman took it quietly. This was a
relief. Mrs. Cary had been opposed to his paying her
anything ; she had felt sure that the mammy would feel
offended. "Why, she is a member of the family," she
said. "We can't pay her wages." The Doctor, however, deemed himself bound by his engagement with
Thurston. He had said he would pay all wages, and he
would do so. So when the mammy took the money with
her usual curtsey, in one way the Doctor's spirits rose,
though he was conscious of a little tug at his heart, as if
the old ties had somehow been loosened. He rallied, however, at the reflection that he could satisfy his wife, at last,
that he knew human nature more profoundly than she
did—a doctrine he had secretly cherished, but had never
been entirely successful in establishing.

In this satisfactory state of mind, not wishing to sever
entirely the tie with the mammy, as the old woman still
stood waiting, he, after a moment, said kindly and with
great dignity :

"Those are your wages, mammy."

"My what, sir?" The Doctor was conscious of a certain chilling of the atmosphere. He looked out of the window to avoid her gaze.

"Your wages—I—ah—have determined—I—think it better from this time to—ah—." He had no idea it was so difficult. Why had he not got Mrs. Cary to attend to this—why had he, indeed, not taken her advice? Pshaw!—He had to face the facts; so he would do it. He summoned courage and turned and looked at the old woman. She was in the act of putting the money carefully on the corner of the table by her, and if the Doctor had difficulty in meeting her gaze, she had none in looking at him. Her eyes were fastened on him like two little shining beads. They stuck him like pins. The Doctor felt as he used to feel when a young man he went to pay his addresses to his wife—he was conscious that whenever he met Krenda she was inspecting him, searching his inmost soul—looking through and through him. He had to assert himself.

"You see, I promised the Federal officer at the courthouse to pay everyone wages," he began with an effort, looking at the old woman.

"How much does you pay *Miss Bessie?*"

"How much what?"

"*Wages.*" He had no idea one word could convey so much contempt.

"Why, nothing—of course——"

Old Krenda lifted her head.

"I'm gwine 'way."

"What!"

"I'm feared you'll charge me *bode!*" She had expanded. "I ken git a little house somewheres, I reckon—or I ken go to th' city and nuss—chillun."

"Mammy—you don't understand—" The Doctor was never in such a dilemma. If his wife would only come in! What a fool he was, not to have known that his wife knew more about it than he did.

"Won't you accept the money as a gift from me?" he said at last, desperately.

"Nor—I ain' gwine *tetch* it!" The gesture was even more final than the tone. With a sniff, she turned and walked out, leaving the Doctor feeling like a school-boy.

He rose after a few minutes and went to his wife's room to get her to make his peace. The door was shut, but he opened it. The scene within was one that remained with him through life. His wife was weeping, and the mammy and Blair were in each other's arms. The only words he heard were from the mammy.

"Ef jest my *ole marster* could come back. He'd know I didn' do it for no wages."

"Oh! mammy, *he* knows it too!"

The Doctor was never conscious of being so much alone in his life, and it took some time to make his peace.

In the same way that the old planters and landowners set in to restore the old places, the younger men also went to work. Necessity is a good spur and pride is another.

Stamper, with Delia Dove "for overseer," as he said, was already beginning to make an impression on his little place. As he had "kept her from having an overseer," he said, the best thing he could do was to "let her be one."

"Talk about th' slaves bein' free, Mr. Jack! they won't all be free long's Delia Dove's got me on her place." The little Sergeant's chuckle showed how truly he enjoyed that servitude. "She owns me, but she treats me well," he laughed.

The Stamper place, amid its locusts and apple-trees, with its hipped roof and dormer-windows, small as it was, was as old as Red Rock—at least as the new mansion, with its imposing porticoes and extended wings, built around the big fireplace of the old house—and little Andy, though being somewhat taciturn he never said anything about it, was as proud of this fact as he was of being himself rather than Hiram Still. He had got an old army wagon from somewhere and was now beginning his farming operations in earnest. It had had " U. S.," on it, but though Andy insisted that the letters stood for "*US*," not for the United States, Delia Dove had declined to ride in the vehicle as long as it had such characters stamped on it. As Mrs. Stamper was obdurate, Andy finally was forced to save her sensibilities, which he did by substituting " D " for " U." This, he said, would stand either for " Delia Stamper," or " D—d States."

Jacquelin Gray was almost the only one of the men who was not able to go to work. His wound showed a tendency to break out afresh.

Steve Allen intended to practise law as soon as matters settled themselves. As yet, however, he could not engage in any profession. He had not yet determined to take the oath of allegiance. Meantime, to the great happiness of his cousins, especially of Miss Thomasia, he deferred going to the county seat and, moved by the grassy appearance of the once beautifully cultivated fields of Red Rock, began farming. Perhaps, it was sheer pride and dislike of meeting Middleton at the court-house under circumstances so different from those under which they had met last ; perhaps it was the pleasure of being near Birdwood that kept him. It was very pleasant when his day's work was done, to don his old gray jacket, play gentleman once more, and ride across the river of an evening ; lounge on the grass under the big trees at Birdwood, and tease Blair Cary about Jacquelin, until her eyes flashed, and she let out at him, as he used to say, " like a newly bridled filly." So he hitched his war-horses, Hotspur and Kate, to ploughs and ploughed day by day, while he made his boy, Jerry, plough furrow for furrow near him, under promise of half of his share of their crop if he kept up, and of the worst " lambing " he had ever had in his life if he did not. Jerry was a long, slim, young negro, as black as tar. He was the grandson of old Peggy, Steve's mammy, and had come from the far South. Where Steve had got him during the war no one knew except Steve and Jerry themselves.

Steve said he found him hanging to a tree and cut him down because he wanted the rope; but that if he had known Jerry as well then as he did afterward, he would have left him hanging. At this explanation, Jerry always grinned, exhibiting two rows of white teeth which looked like corn from a full ear. Jerry was a drunkard, a liar, and a thief. But one thing was certain : he adored Steve, who in return for that virtue bore delinquencies which no one else in the world would have tolerated. Jerry had one other trait which recommended him to his master : he was as brave as a lion ; he would not have been afraid of the devil himself unless he had taken on the shape of Mr. Stevenson Allen, of whom alone Jerry stood in wholesome awe.

Steve's bucolic operations came somewhat suddenly to an end. One evening, after a hard day's work, he met Wash Still dressed up and driving a new buggy, turning in at Dr. Cary's gate. He was " going to consult Dr. Cary about a case," he said. Next day, as Steve was working in the field, he saw Wash driving down the hill from the manager's house with the same well-appointed rig. Steve stopped in the row and looked at him as he drove past. Just then Jerry came up. His eye followed his master's, and his face took on an expression of scorn.

"Umph ! things is tunned sort o' upside down," he grunted. " Overseer's son drivin' buggy, and gent'mens in de fiel'." Steve smiled at Jerry's use of the plural. The next moment Hiram Still rode down the hill, and turning his horse in Steve's direction came across the field.

"He sutney don' like you, Cun'l," said Jerry, " an' he don' like the Cap'n neider ;" by which last, he designated Jacquelin. Jerry always gave military titles to those he liked—the highest to Steve, of course. " He say it do him good to see you wuckin' in the fiel' like a nigger, and some day he hope to set in de gret-house and see you doin' it."

Still passed quite close to Captain Allen, and as he did so, reined in his horse, and sat looking down at Steve, as he came to the end of his row.

" We all have to come to it, at last, Captain," he said.

Whether it was his words, and the look on his face, or whether Steve had intended anyhow to do what he did, he straightened up, and shot a glance at the Manager.

" You think so ? Well, you are mistaken." He raised his hoe and stuck it in the ground up to the eye.

" There," he said to Still, in a tone of command, " take that home. That's the last time I'll ever touch a hoe as long as I live. I've brains enough to make my living by them, and if I haven't, I mean to starve !" He walked past the overseer with his head so straight, that Still began to explain that he had meant no offence. But Steve took no further notice of him.

" Jerry, you can keep on ; I'll see that you get your part of the crop."

" Nor—I ain't gwine to hit anur lick, nurr—I'll starve wid yer." And Jerry lifted his hoe and drove it into the ground ; looked at Still superciliously, and followed his master with as near an imitation of his manner and gait as he could achieve.

It was only when Steve was out of hearing, that Still's look changed. He clenched his fist, and shook it after the young man.

" I'll bring you to it yet," he growled.

That evening Steve announced his intention of beginning immediately the practice of his profession.

CHAPTER IX

MR. JONADAB LEECH TURNS UP WITH A CARPET-BAG
AND OPENS HIS BUREAU

THE young officers at the court-house meantime had fared
very well. It is true that most of the residents treated
them coldly, if civilly, and that the girls of the place, of
whom there were quite a number, turned aside whenever
they met them, and passed by with their heads held high,
and their eyes straight to the front, flashing daggers. But
this the young men were from experience more or less
used to.

Reely Thurston told Middleton that if he would leave
matters to him, he would engineer him through the campaign, and before it was over would be warbling ditties with
all the pretty girls in a way to make his cousin, Miss Ruth
Welch, green with envy. The lieutenant began by parading up and down on his very fine horse ; but the only result
he attained was to hear a plump young girl ask another in
a clear voice, evidently meant for him to hear, "What
poor Southerner," she supposed, "that little Yankee stole
that horse from !" He recognized the speaker as the
young lady he had seen looking at them from the door of
the clerk's office the morning of their arrival.

Brutusville, the county seat where they were posted, was
a pretty little straggling country village of old-fashioned
houses amid groves of fine old trees, lying along the main
road of the county, where it wound among shady slopes,
with the blue mountain range in the distance. Most of
the houses were hip-roofed and gray with age. The river—
the same stream that divided Red Rock from Birdwood—

THE GIRLS OF THE PLACE TURNED ASIDE, WHENEVER THEY MET THEM
AND PASSED BY WITH THEIR hEADS hELD HIGH.

passed near the village, broadening as it reached the more
level country and received the waters of one or two other
streams. Before the war there had been talk of establishing deep-water connections with the lower country, as
the last rapids of any extent were not far below Brutusville.
Dr. Cary, however, had humorously suggested that they
would find it easier to macadamize the river than to make
it navigable.

The county seat had suffered, like the rest of the county,
during the war ; but as it happened, the main body of the
enemy had been kept out of the place by high water, and
the fine old trees did much to conceal the scars that had
been made.

The old, brick court-house in the middle of the green,
peeping out from among the trees, with its great, classical
portico, was esteemed by the residents of the village to be,
perhaps, the most imposing structure in the world. Mr.
Dockett, the clerk—who had filled this position for nearly
forty years, with the exception of the brief period when,
fired by martial enthusiasm, he had gone off with Captain
Gray's company—told Lieutenant Thurston a day or two
after the latter's arrival, that while he had never been to
Greece or, indeed, out of the State, he had been informed
by those who had been there that the court-house was, perhaps, in some respects, more perfect than any building in
Athens. Lieutenant Thurston said he had never been to
Greece either, but he was quite sure it was. He also
added that he considered Mr. Dockett's own house a very
beautiful one, and thought that it showed evidences, in its
embellishments, of that same classical taste that Mr. Dockett
admired so much. Mr. Dockett, while accepting the compliment with due modesty, answered that if the lieutenant
wished to see a beautiful house he should see Red Rock.
And thereupon began new matter, the young officer gently
leading the old gentleman to talk of all the people and affairs of the neighborhood, including the charms of the
girls.

7

From this, it will be seen that the little Lieutenant was already laying his mines, and preparing to make good his promise to Middleton to engineer him through the campaign.

The compliment to the Dockett mansion was not without its effect on the genius who presided in that classic and comfortable abode, and, at length, Mrs. Dockett, a plump and energetic woman, had, with some prevision, though in a manner to make her beneficiaries sensible of her condescension, acceded to the young men's request to take them as boarders, and allow them to occupy a wing-room in her house.

Thus Middleton and Thurston were able to write Ruth Welch a glowing account of their "headquarters in an old colonial mansion," and of the "beautiful maiden" who sang them "songs of the South."

The songs, however, that Miss Dockett sang, though as Thurston said truly, they were in one sense sung for them, were not sung in the sense Lieutenant Thurston implied. They were hardly just the sort that Miss Ruth Welch would have approved of, and were certainly not what Mrs. Welch would have tolerated. For they were all of the most ultra-Southern spirit and tendency, and breathed the deadliest defiance to everyone and everything Northern. Miss Dockett was not pretty, except as youth and wholesomeness give beauty; but she was a cheery maiden, with blue eyes, white teeth, rosy cheeks, and a profusion of hair, and though she had no training, she possessed a pleasant voice and sang naturally and agreeably—at least to one who, like Thurston, had not too much ear for music. Thurston once had the temerity to ask for a song—for which he received a merited rebuff. Of course she would not sing for a Yankee, said the young lady, with a toss of her head and an increased elevation of her little nose, and immediately she left the room. When, however, the young officers were in their rooms, she sang all the Southern songs she knew. One, in particular, she rendered with great spirit. It had just been written. It began :

> " Oh ! I'm a good old rebel,
> Now, that's just what I am ;
> For this ' Fair land of freedom,'
> I do not care a-t all. "

Another verse ran :

> " Three hundred thousand Yankees
> Lays dead in Southern dus',
> We got three hundred thousand
> Before they conquered us ;
> They died of Southern fever,
> Of Southern steel and shot ;
> I wish they were three million,
> Instead of what we got. "

The continued iteration of this sanguinary melody float-ing in at the open window finally induced the little Lieu-tenant, in his own room one afternoon, to raise, in op-position, his own voice, which was none of the most melodious, in the strains of " The Star-Spangled Banner." But he had got no further than the second invocation to " the land of the free and the home of the brave," when there was a rush of footsteps outside, followed by a pound-ing on his door, and on his opening the door Mrs. Dock-ett bore down on him with so much fire in her eye that Reely was quite overwhelmed. And when she gave him notice that she would have no Yankee songs sung in her house, and that he must either "quit the house or quit howling," little Thurston, partly amused and partly daunted, and with the wide difference between Mrs. Dockett's fried chicken and beat-biscuit and the mess-table " truck " before his eyes, promised to adopt the latter course—" generally."

Fortunately the young officers were too much accus-tomed to such defiances to feel very serious about them, and they went on ingratiating themselves with Miss Dockett—Thurston by his fun and good-humor, and Middleton by his gentlemanly bearing and his firm management of the negroes who hung around the camp.

The peace and comfort of the young men, however, were suddenly much threatened by the arrival of a new official, not under their jurisdiction, though under Colonel Krafton, who had sent him up, specially charged with all matters relating to the negroes.

He arrived one afternoon with only a carpet-bag ; took a room in the hotel, and, as if already familiar with the ground, immediately dispatched a note to Mrs. Dockett asking quarters in her house. Even had the new-comer preferred his application as a request it might have been rejected ; but he demanded it quite as a right ; the line which he sent up by a negro servant being rather in the nature of an order than a petition to Mrs. Dockett to prepare the best room in her house for his head-quarters. It was signed "Jonadab Leech, Provost-Marshal, commanding," etc., etc. But the new official did not know Mrs. Dockett. The order raised a breeze which came near blowing the two officers, whom she had accepted and domiciled in her house, out of the quarters she had vouchsafed them. She sailed down upon them with the letter in her hand ; and, as Thurston said, with colors flying and guns ready for action. But, fortunately, little Thurston was equal to the emergency. He glanced at the paper the enraged lady showed him and requested to be allowed possession of it for a moment. When he had apparently studied it attentively, he looked up.

"I do not know that I quite comprehend. Do I understand you to insist on taking this man in ?" He was never so innocent-looking. Mrs. Dockett gasped :

"What ! ! Ta—ke in the man that wrote *that !*" She visibly expanded.

"—Because if you do, Captain Middleton and I shall have to move our quarters. I happen to know this man

personally — slightly—that is, I once had a transaction
with him as an officer which resulted unpleasantly. His
functions are entirely different from ours ; he being
charged with matters relating to the freedmen, their care
and support ; while ours are military and relate to the
government of the county and the maintenance of peace.
(He glanced at Mrs. Dockett, who was sniffing ominously.)
While we shall uphold him in all proper exercise of his
power, and recognize his authority as an officer within the
scope of his own jurisdiction, I must say that for personal
reasons his presence would be distasteful to me, and I
think I can speak for Captain Middleton (here he looked
over at his friend inquiringly), and if you contemplate
taking him in, I should prefer to remove my own quarters
back to camp."

The little Lieutenant had gathered dignity as he proceeded, and he delivered the close of his oration with
quite the manner of an orator. He had spoken so rapidly
that Mrs. Dockett had not had a moment to get in a
word. He closed with a most impressive bow, while Middleton gazed at him with mingled amusement and admiration.

Mrs. Dockett discovered the wind taken completely out
of her sails, and found herself actually forced into the
position of making a tack and having rather to offer an
apology to the ruffled little officer.

She had never dreamed of preferring this new-comer
to them, she declared. She could not but say that they
had always acted in a most gentlemanly way, so far as she
was concerned. She had, indeed, been most agreeably surprised. She had never, for a moment, dreamed of permitting this impudent upstart, whoever he was, to come into her house. Let him go to some of his colored friends.
Of course, if they wished to leave her house—they must
do so. Her head was rising again. Thurston hastened to
interpose.

Not at all—they were most charmed, etc. Only he

didn't know but she might not care to have them remain
—and they could not do so if this man came.

"He's not coming. Let him try it." And the irate
lady sailed out to deliver her broadside to the new enemy
that had borne down on her.

She had no sooner disappeared than the Lieutenant's
face fell.

"Gad! Larry, we are undone. It's that Leech who used
to live with old Bolter, and about whom they told the
story of his trying to persuade his wife to let him get a
divorce, and who shirked all through the war. Unless we
can get rid of him it's all up. We're ruined."

"Freeze him out," Middleton said, briefly. "You've
begun well."

"Freeze —— ? Freeze a snow-bank! That's his cli-
mate. He'd freeze in ——!" The little Lieutenant
named a very hot place.

Thurston had not been too soon in placing the line of
discrimination clearly between themselves and the Provost
Marshal, for the arrival of the latter in the county at once
caused a change of conditions.

On receipt of Mrs. Dockett's decisive and stinging reply
Leech immediately made application to Captain Middleton
to enforce his requisition, but, to his indignation, he was
informed that they were the only boarders, and that Mrs.
Dockett managed her own domestic affairs : which, indeed,
was no more than the truth. To revenge himself, the Provost took possession of Mr. Dockett's office, and opened
his bureau in it, crowding the old official into a back room
of the building. Here, too, however, he was doomed to disappointment and mortification ; for, on the old clerk's representation of the danger to his records, and of their value,
enforced by Mrs. Dockett's persuasive arguments, Leech
was required by Middleton to surrender possession and
take up his quarters in an unoccupied building on the other
side of the road. Here he opened his office under a flaring
sign bearing the words, "FREEDMEN'S BUREAU."

So the Provost, being baffled here, had to content him-self, as he might, at the court-house tavern, where he soon laid off a new campaign. His principal trouble there, lay in the presence of the dark, sallow Captain McRaffle, whose saturnine face scowled at him from the upper end of the table, and kept him in a state of constant irritation. The only speech the Captain ever addressed to him was to ask if he played cards, and on his saying he "never played games," he appeared to take no further interest in him. The Provost, however, kept his eye on him.

The effect of the Provost's appearance was felt immedi-ately. The news of his arrival seemed to have spread in a night, and the next day the roads were filled with negroes.

"De wud had come for 'em," they said. They "had to go to de Cap'n to git de papers out o' de buro." Only the old house-servants were left, and even they were some-what excited.

This time those who left their homes did not return so quickly. Immediately after the news of the surrender came, a good many of the negroes had gone off and estab-lished settlements to themselves. The chief settlement in the Red Rock neighborhood was known as "The Bend," from the fact that it was in a section half surrounded by a curve of the river. It was accessible from both sides of the river, and in the past had been much associated with runaway negroes.

It had always been an unsavory spot in the county, and now, the negroes congregating there, it had come into greater ill repute than ever. It was dubbed with some de-rision, "Africa." Here Jim Sherwood and Moses had built cabins, and shortly many others gathered about them. This, however, might not have amounted to much had not another matter come to light.

The Provost was summoning the negroes and enrolling them by hundreds, exciting them with stories of what the Government proposed to do for them, and telling them the most pernicious lies : that they need not work, and that the Government was going to feed them and give them all " forty acres and a mule apiece."

Even the older negroes were somewhat excited by these tales, and, finally, Mammy Krenda asked Dr. Cary if it was true that the Government was going to give them all land.

" Of course not. Who says so ? " asked the Doctor.

" I heah so," said the old woman. Even she was beginning to be afraid to tell what she had heard.

Contemporaneously with this, an unprecedented amount of lawlessness suddenly appeared : chicken-houses were robbed ; sheep and pigs and even cattle were stolen, without there being any authority to take cognizance of the thefts or any power to punish.

Andy Stamper and several others of the neighbors came over to see Dr. Cary about the matter. They had been to the court-house the day before " to see about things," Andy said, and " had found every nigger in the county piled up in front of that Leech's door."

" They're talkin' about every one of 'em gittin' forty acres and a mule, Doctor," said little Andy, with a twinkle in his eye ; but a grim look about his mouth. " The biggest men down thar are that Jim Sherwood of yours ; that trick-doctor nigger of Miss' Gray's, Moses Swift, and a tall, black nigger of General Legaie's, named Nicholas Ash. They're doin' most of the talkin'. Well, I aint got but eighty acres—jest about enough for two of 'em," added Andy, the grim lines deepening about his mouth ; " but I'm mighty sorry for them two as tries to git 'em—I told Hiram so." The twinkle had disappeared from his blue eyes, like the flash on a ripple, and the eyes were as quiet and gray as the water after the ripple had passed.

" Hiram, he's the chief adviser and friend of the new man. I thought he was hatchin' something. He was down there inside of the office — looked like a shot cat

when I come in—said he was tryin' to git some hands.
You watch him. He's a goin' over. He was at the nigger meetin'-house th' other night. I heard some white
man was there ; but I couldn't git at who 'twas till old
Weev'ly let it out."

Dr. Cary told of his conversation with Still a few days
before ; but the little Sergeant was not convinced.

" Whenever he talks, that's the time you know he ain't
goin' to do it," he said.

Still's attentions to Miss Delia Dove had not only quickened Andy's jealousy, but had sharpened his suspicion
generally, and he had followed his movements closely.

Still had quickly become assured that the two young
soldiers in command at the county seat were not the kind
for him to impress. And when the new officer came he
had at once proceeded to inspect him.

Leech was expecting him ; for though they had never
met, Still had already secretly placed himself in communication with Krafton, the Provost-Marshal in the city.

The new Provost was not pleasing to look on. He was a
man spare in figure and with a slight stoop in his shoulders
—consequent perhaps on a habit he had of keeping his gaze
on the ground. He had mild blue eyes, and a long, sallow
face, with a thin nose, bad teeth, and a chin that ended
almost in a point. He rarely showed temper. He posed
rather as a good-natured, easy-going fellow, cracking jokes
with anyone who would listen to him, and indulging in
laughter which made up in loudness what it lacked in
merriment. When he walked, it was with a peculiar, sinu-
ous motion. The lines in his face gave him so sour an expression that Steve Allen, just after he moved to the court-
house to practise law, said that Leech, from his look, must
be as great a stench in his own nostrils as in those of
other people. This speech brought Steve Leech's undying hatred, though he veiled it well enough at the moment
and simply bided his time.

The Provost-Marshal was not a prepossessing person

even to Still ; but Mrs. Gray's manager had large schemes in his mind, and the new-comer appeared a likely person to aid him in carrying them out. They soon became advisers for each other.

"You can't do nothin' with them two young men," the overseer told the Provost. "I've done gauged 'em. I know 'em as soon as I see 'em, and I tell you they don't think no more of folks like you and me than of the dirt under their feet. They're for the aristocrats."

He shortly gauged the Provost.

"When I know what a man wants, I know how to git at him," he said to his son Wash, afterward. "He wants to get up—but first he wants money—and we must let him see it. I lent him a leetle too—just to grease the skillet. When you've lent a man money you've got a halter on him."

"You're a mighty big fool to lend your money to a man you don't know anything about. You'll never get it back," observed Wash, surlily.

"Ah! Won't I? Trust me; I never lend money that I don't get it back in one shape or another—with interest too. I don't expect to get that back." He dropped his voice. "That's what I call a purchase—not a loan. Don't try to fry your chicken till you've greased the pan, my son."

"Something in that," admitted the young medical student. They were sitting on the little front porch of the overseer's house, and Hiram Still's eye took in the scene about him—the wide fields, the rich, low-grounds, the chimneys of the mansion-house peeping from the grove of great trees on its high hill a half mile away. His face lit up.

"Ah! Wash, if you trust your old pappy, you'll see some mighty changes in this here county. What'd you say if you was to see yourself some day settin' up in that big hall yonder, with, say, a pretty young lady from acrost the river, and that Steve and Mr. Jacquelin ploughin' in the furrer?"

"By G—d! I'd love it," declared Wash, decisively, his good-humor thoroughly restored.

CHAPTER X

THE PROVOST MAKES HIS FIRST MOVE

LEECH shortly determined to give the neighborhood an illustration of his power, and, striking, he struck high.

A few days after the Provost's arrival Dr. Cary received a summons to appear before him at the court-house next day. It was issued on the complaint of "the Rev. James Sherwood," and was signed, "Jonadab Leech, Provost commanding," etc.

General Legaie, who was at Birdwood when the soldier who served the summons arrived, was urgent that Dr. Cary should refuse to obey it; but the Doctor said he would go. He would obey the law. He would not, however report to Leech, but to Captain Middleton, the ranking officer. The General said if the Doctor would persist in going, he would go with him to represent him. So next morning the two old officers rode down to the Court-house together, the General very martial, and Dr. Cary very calm.

When they reached the county seat they found "the street," or road in front of "the green," which was occupied by the camp of the soldiers, filled with negroes, men and women. They had made booths of boughs in the fence-corners, where they were living like children at play, and were all in the gayest spirits, laughing and shouting and "larking" among themselves, presenting in this regard a very different state of mind from that of the two gentlemen. They were, however, respectful enough to them, and when the riders inquired where the commanding officer was, there were plenty of offers to show them, and more than enough to hold their horses. Some of them indicated that the commander was in the old store on the roadside, which appeared from the throng about it to be the centre of interest to the crowd.

"Dat ain't nuttin but the buro, sir; the ones you wants to see is up yonder at Miss' Dockett's; I knows de ones you wants to see," said Tom, one of the Doctor's old servants, with great pride.

To settle the question, the Doctor dismounted and walked in, giving his horse to the old man to hold.

The front of the store was full of negroes, packed together as thick as they could stand, and simply waiting. They made way for the Doctor and he passed through to the rear, where there was a little partition walling off a back room. The door was ajar, and inside were seated two men, one a stranger in uniform, the other, a man who sat with his back to the door, and who, at the moment that the Doctor approached, was leaning forward, talking to the Provost in a low, earnest half-whisper. As the visitor knocked the official glanced up and the other man turned quickly and looked over his shoulder. Seeing Dr. Cary he sprang to his feet. It was Hiram Still.

"I wish to see the officer in command," announced the Doctor. "Good-morning Mr. Still." His tone expressed surprise.

"I am the officer in command," said the official, shortly.

"Ah! you are not Captain Middleton? I believe he is in command."

"No, I guess not. I'm Captain *Leech*, head of the Freedmen's Bureau." His voice was thin but assertive, and he spoke as if he had been contradicted.

"Ah! It is the regular officer I wish to see."

"I'm regular enough, I guess, and if it's anything about the freedmen you'll find, I guess, I'm the one to see." He turned from the Doctor with studied indifference and motioned to his companion to resume his seat. The latter, however, came forward. He had apparently recovered somewhat from his confusion.

"This is Dr. Cary, one of the finest gentlemen in our county," he said to the officer, as if he were making a speech, and then turned to the Doctor : "Captain Leech is the gentleman to see about getting our hands back. Fact is, I am just down here about that now."

Leech had been looking at the Doctor with new interest. "So you're Dr. Cary ?" he said. "Well, I'm the one for you to see. I summoned you to appear before me to know why you turned the Rev. Mr. Sherwood out of his home." His manner was growing more and more insolent, and the Doctor stiffened. The only notice he took was to look over Leech's head.

"Ah ! I believe I will go and see Captain Middleton," he said, with dignity. "Good-morning," and he walked out, his head held somewhat higher than when he went in, leaving Leech fuming in impotent rage, and Still to give the Head of the Bureau behind his back a very different estimate of him from that which he had just declared so loudly in his presence.

"He's one of that same sort with your young men," said the manager, "only more so. What did I tell you ? See, he won't talk to *you!* He wants to talk to Captain Middleton. You trust me, I'll keep you informed. I know 'em all. Not that he ain't better than most, because he's naturally kind-hearted and would do well enough if let alone, but he can't help it. It's bred in the bone. But I'm too smart for 'em. I was too smart for 'em durin' the war, and I am still." He gave the Provost a confidential wink.

"Well, he'll find out who I am before he gets through," said Leech. "I guess he'll find I'm about as big a man as Captain Middleton." He squared back his thin shoulders and puffed out his chest. "I'll show him." He turned to the door.

"That's it—that's it," smiled Still, delightedly.

Meantime Dr. Cary had joined General Legaie, and with the single remark that it was "the commanding officer, not the commissary," that they wanted to see, they rode up the hill.

When the two gentlemen arrived at Mrs. Dockett's they found that energetic lady, trowel in hand, among her flowers, and were received by her with so much distinction that it produced immediately a great impression on her two lodgers, who, unseen, were observing them from their window.

"Gad! Larry, there's Don Quixote, and he's brought his cousin, Dr. Filgrave, along with him. He must be a lieutenant-general at least. See the way the old lady is smiling! I must learn his secret." And the little Lieutenant sprang to the mirror and rattled on as Middleton got ready for the interview which he anticipated, and the two gentlemen came slowly up the walk, bareheaded, with Mrs. Dockett, talking energetically, between them.

The next moment there was a tramp outside the door, and with that rap, which Thurston said was a model for the last trump, Mrs. Dockett herself flung open the door and announced, with a wave of her hand:

"General Legaie and Major Cary."

The two visitors were received with great respect. Middleton was at his best, and in the face of a somewhat depressing gravity on the two old officers' part, tried to give the interview a friendly turn by recalling pleasantly his visit to Red Rock before the war, and his recollection of Dr. Cary and his daughter. He ventured even to inquire after her. He supposed she was a good big girl now?

"Yes, she was almost quite grown and was enjoying very good health," said the Doctor, bowing civilly, and he proceeded forthwith to state the cause of their visit, while Thurston introduced to the General, somewhat irrelevantly, the subject of fishing.

Captain Middleton listened respectfully to all the two gentlemen had to say. He agreed with them as to the necessity of establishing some form of civil government in the counties, and believed that steps would be taken to do

so as soon as possible. Meantime he should preserve order. Matters relating to the negroes, except in the line of
preserving order, were, however, rather beyond his province, and properly under the control of an entirely distinct branch, which was just being organized, with head-
quarters for the State, in the city. He said he would go
with Dr. Cary before the Provost and see that he was
not annoyed by any frivolous charge. So he accompanied
the two gentlemen back to Leech's office and attended the
trial. It was galling enough to the two gentlemen as it
was ; and but for the presence of Middleton might have
been much more so. Leech's blue eyes snapped with
pleasure at the reappearance of the old officers, but were
filled with a vague disquiet at the presence of their companion. However, he immediately proceeded with much
importance to take up the case. The "trial" was held
in the court-house, and the Provost sat in the judge's
seat. The negroes around took in quickly that something
unusual was happening, and the court-room was thronged
with them, all filled with curiosity, and many of the older
ones wearing on their faces a preternatural solemnity.
Sherwood was present, in a black coat, his countenance
expressive of comical self-importance. Dr. Cary and General Legaie sat behind the bar, the Doctor, somewhat
paler than usual, his head up, his mouth compressed, and
his thin nostrils dilating ; the General's eyes glowing with
the fire that smouldered beneath. Middleton sat off to one
side, a little in front of the bar, a silent but observant
spectator.

The case was stated by Leech, and without the useless
formality of examining the complainant who had already
given his story, Dr. Cary was asked by the Provost, why
he had driven Sherwood off.

The Doctor rose and made his statement. When he
first stood up the compression of his lips showed the feeling under which he labored ; but the next second he had
mastered himself, and when he spoke it was with as much

respect as if he were addressing the Chief Justice. The land was his, and he claimed that he would have had the right to drive the man off had he wished to do so ; but, as a matter of fact, he had not done so—he had not done so on account of Sherwood's wife, who was the daughter of the old mammy in his family, and a valued servant. He had only deposed him from being the manager.

The Provost was manifestly a little disconcerted by this announcement. He glanced about him. The Doctor had evidently made an impression.

"Can you prove this?" he asked, sharply. The General wriggled in his chair, his hands clutching the sides, and the Doctor for a second looked a trifle more grim. He drew in a long breath.

"Well, my word has usually been taken as proof of a fact I stated," he said, slowly. "But if you desire further proof, there are several of my old servants present who will corroborate what I state. Perhaps you might be willing to accept their testimony?" He looked the Provost in the eyes, and then glanced around half humorously. "Tom!" he called to the old man who had held his horse, and who was now standing in the front row. "Will you state what occurred, to this—ah—officer?"

"Yas, suh—I'll groberate ev'y wud you say—'cus' I wuz dyah," asserted Tom, with manifest pride.

"Dat's so," called out one or two others, not to be outdone by Tom, and the tide set in for the Doctor.

The Provost, in this state of the case, declared that the charge was not sustained, and he felt it his duty to dismiss the complaint. He, however, would take this occasion to state his views on the duties of the former owners to their slaves ; and he delivered a long and somewhat rambling discourse on the subject, manifestly designed for the sable part of his audience. When he concluded, and just as he started to rise, the General sprang to his feet. The Doctor looked at him with some curiosity, perhaps not unmingled with anxiety, for the General's eyes were blazing.   With an effort, however, the General controlled himself.

"Permit me to say, Mr. Provost, that your views, like those of a good many people of your class, are more valuable to yourself than to others." He bowed low.

"Dat's so, too!" called out Tom, who was still in a corroborative mood, on which there was a guffaw from the negroes.   And with this shot, the General, after looking the Provost steadily in the eyes, turned on his heel and stalked out of the court-house, leaving Leech trying ineffectually to look as if he, as well as others, appreciated the humor of Tom's speech.

As they came out, Middleton took occasion to reopen their former conversation as to the necessity of establishing some form of civil government in the counties.   He believed, he said, that the two gentlemen might find it better to apply to the head of the bureau in this section— Colonel Krafton—rather than to attempt to secure any cooperation from Leech, who, he said, was only a subordinate, and really had little authority.

Middleton and Thurston quickly felt the beneficial effect of their civility to the old officers, in the increasing cordiality shown them by their landlady.   Mrs. Dockett gave them a full account of both visitors, their pedigrees and position, not omitting a glowing picture of the beauty and charms of the daughter of Dr. Cary, and a hint that she was bound to marry either Jacquelin Gray, the owner of Red Rock, or her cousin, Captain Stevenson Allen, who, Mrs. Dockett declared, was the finest young man in the world, and had applied to her for table-board that very day.

This was interesting, at least to Thurston, who declared that now that he was succeeding so well with Miss Dockett, it was necessary to utilize Middleton's figure.   Events, however, were moving without Thurston's agency.

An order came to Middleton from head-quarters a day or two later to go to the upper end of the county and in-

8

vestigate certain "mysterious meetings" which, it was reported, were being held in that section.

The list given of those who participated in such meetings made Middleton whistle. It contained the names of Dr. Cary, General Legaie, Captain Allen, and nearly every man of prominence in the county.

The name given him, as that of the person who could furnish him with information, was Hiram Still; and the order contained explicit directions where to meet him. He would find him at a certain hour at the house of a colored man, named Nicholas Ash.

So the Captain rode up to a small cabin situated in a little valley near the Red Rock place, and had an interview with Still, who appeared to Middleton far more mysterious than anything else he discovered on his trip. The meetings referred to, seemed to be only those social gatherings which Dr. Cary had already spoken of to the young officer. When Middleton prepared to leave, Mr. Still offered to show him a nearer way back by the ford below the old bridge that had been destroyed during the war, and as it was late in the afternoon, Middleton accepted his offer.

They were almost at the ford when an old carriage came out of the road which led down from the Red Rock plantation, and turned into the main road just before them. Still pulled up his horse, and, excusing himself from going any farther, on the ground that if Middleton followed the carriage he would be all right, turned back. All anyone had to do, he said, was to keep down the river a little, so as not to hit the sunken timbers; but not to go too far down or he would get over a ledge of rock and into deep water.

As the road was narrow and Middleton supposed that the driver knew the ford, he kept behind the carriage, and let it cross before him. One of the horses appeared to be afraid of the water, and the driver had to whip him to force him in. So when he entered the stream he was plunging, and, continuing to plunge, he got among the sunken timbers and fell.

Middleton was so close behind the carriage that he could hear the voices of two ladies inside, one of whom was apparently much alarmed, whilst the other was soothing her, and encouraging the driver. He heard her say:

"There's no danger, Cousin Thomasia. Gideon can manage them." But there was some danger, and "Cousin Thomasia" appeared to know it. The danger was that the frightened horses might turn and pull the vehicle around, upsetting it in the deep water below, and as the fallen horse struggled, Middleton dashed in on the lower side, and catching the near horse, steadied him whilst the other got up. Then, springing from his own horse, he caught the other just as he got to his feet, and held to him until they reached the farther bank, where he assisted the driver in bringing them to a stand-still, and enabled the ladies to get out and see what damage had been done.

He had taken in, even as he passed the carriage in the water, that the two occupants were an elderly lady and a young lady, the latter of whom appeared to be holding the former ; but it was after he reached the bank that he observed that the younger of the two ladies was one of the prettiest girls he had ever seen. And the next second he recognized her as Miss Cary. She evidently recognized him too. As she turned to thank him, after she had helped her companion from the carriage, the color rose to her face, appearing the deeper and more charming because of the white which had just preceded it, and which it so rapidly followed ; and there was a look in her eyes which was part shy embarrassment and part merriment. He saw that she knew him, but she did not admit it.

He began to examine busily the harness, which was old, and had been broken in several places. He had some straps on his saddle, he said, which he would get. The girl thanked him, with quiet dignity, but declined firmly.

They would not trouble him. Gideon could mend it, and she could hold the horses. She bowed to him, with grave eyes, and made a movement toward the horse, hold-

ing out her ungloved hand to catch the bridle, and saying, "Whoa, boy," in a voice which Middleton thought
might have tamed Bucephalus. Miss Thomasia, however, mildly but firmly interposed.

"No, indeed, my dear, I'll never get into that carriage
again behind those dreadful horses, unless this—this—gentleman (the word was a little difficult) stays right by their
heads. I am the greatest coward in the world," she said to
Middleton in the most confiding and friendly manner; "I
am afraid of everything." (Then to her companion again,
in a lower tone :) "It is very hard to be beholden to a
Yankee; but it is much better than having your neck
broken. And we are very much obliged to you, sir, I
assure you. Blair, my dear, let the——" She paused and
took breath.

"*Yankee*," said Middleton, in a clear voice, much
amused, as he worked diligently at a strap.

"—*Gentleman* help us. Don't be too obstinate. Nothing
distinguishes a lady more than her manner of giving in."

So, as Middleton was already at work, the girl could do
nothing but yield. He got his straps, and soon had the
breaks repaired, and, having, at Miss Thomasia's request,
held the horses while the ladies re-entered the vehicle, and
then having started them off, he stood aside and saluted as
they passed, catching, accidentally, Miss Cary's eyes, which
were once more grave. The only remark she had volunteered to him outside of the subject of the broken harness
was in praise of his horse, which was, indeed, a magnificent
animal.

A few minutes later, the young Captain galloped by the
carriage, but he did not glance in, he simply saluted as he
passed, with eyes straight to the front.

When he reached home that night Larry Middleton was
graver than usual; but little Thurston, after hearing of
the adventure, was in better spirits than he had shown for
some time. He glanced at Middleton's half-discontented
face, and burst out:

"'Oh! cast that shadow from thy brow.' It was clearly Providence. Why, Larry, after that they are obliged to invite us to dinner."

"Why, she didn't even speak to me," growled Middleton, puffing away at his pipe. "And I know she recognized me, just as clearly as I did her."

"Of course, she recognized you—recognized you as one of the enemies of her country—a hated oppressor—a despicable Yankee. Did you expect her to fall on your neck and weep? On my soul! she's a girl of spirit! Like my own adorable Elizabeth! All the same, we're as good for invitations to whatever they give as a dollar is for a doughnut."

And when a day or two later a note from Dr. Cary, in a formal handwriting and equally formal words, was brought to Captain Middleton, thanking him for his "opportune and courteous aid" to his daughter and cousin, Lieutenant Thurston declared that it was an invitation to Middleton's wedding.

CHAPTER XI

STEVE ALLEN on his removal to the county seat after his
sudden abandonment of farming, had taken up his quarters in an old building, fronting on the court-green near
the Clerk's office, and with its rear opening on a little lane
which led to two of the principal roads in the county.
From the evening of his arrival Steve took possession of
the entire village. He wore his old cavalry uniform, the
only suit he possessed, and, with his slouched hat set on
one side of his handsome head, carried himself so inde-
pendently that he was regarded with some disfavor by the
two young officers, whom he on his side treated with just
that manner which appeared to him most exasperating to
each of them. He was immediately the most popular man
in the place. He played cards with the men, and marbles
with the boys; made love to the girls, and teased the old
women; joked with the soldiers, especially with the big
Irish Sergeant, Dennis O'Meara, and fought the war over
with the officers. He boldly asserted that the Confederates had been victorious in every battle they had ever
fought, and had, as someone said, simply "worn themselves out whipping the Yankees," a line of tactics which
exasperated even little Thurston, until he one day surprised a gleam of such amused satisfaction in Steve's gray
eyes that he afterward avoided the ambuscade and enjoyed
the diversion of seeing Leech, and even Middleton, caught.

Leech had been warned in advance by Mr. Still of
Steve Allen's intention to settle at the county seat, and im-

mediately on Steve's arrival had notified him to appear before him as Provost and exhibit his parole. From that
time Steve had taken Leech as his prey. Knowing that
the Provost was not the proper officer, he did not obey the
order, and repaid Leech's insolence with burning contempt,
never failing, on occasion, to fire some shafts at him which
penetrated and stung.

General Legaie and Dr. Cary, after their experience with
Leech, determined to lose no more time than was necessary
in adopting the suggestion of Captain Middleton and
going to see the Commandant of the Freedmen's Bureau
in the city. The General, however, stipulated that he
should not be expected to do more than state his views to
the officer in command. This he was willing to do, as he
was going with Dr. Cary to the city, where the Doctor was
to see Mr. Ledger and conclude the negotiation for a loan
to re-stock his plantation.

It happened, however, that when General Legaie and
Dr. Cary called on Colonel Krafton, two other visitors from
their county had been to see that officer : Hiram Still and
Leech.

The two gentlemen were kept waiting for some time
after their names had been taken in by the sentinel before they were admitted to the Chief Provost's presence,
and every minute of that period the General grew hotter
and hotter, and walked up and down the little ante-room
with more and more dignity.

" Dr. Johnson before Lord Chesterfield," said the
Doctor, laughing at his friend's impatience and indignation.

" Dr. Johnson before a dog !" was the little General's
retort. " Why, sir, I never treated a negro in my life
as he has treated us."

At last, however, they were admitted.

The officer, a stout man with closely cropped iron-gray
hair, a lowering brow and a heavy jaw, was seated at his
desk writing. He did not look up when they entered, but

said, "Sit down," and wrote on. When he was through, he called out, and a sentinel entered.

"Send that off at once—or—wait where you are. I may have another to send." He turned to the two visitors who were still standing.

"Well?"

"I am Major Cary," that gentleman said, advancing, "And this is General Legaie." He bowed gravely.

"Oh! I know you," said the officer. He turned to his desk and searched for something.

"Oh!—I was not aware that I had had the pleasure of meeting you before," said the Doctor, brightening. "Where was it, sir? I regret that my memory has not served me better." He seated himself.

"I did not say I had met you—I said I knew you, and I do. I know you both."

"Oh! I thought I should not have forgotten," said the Doctor.

"No, nor you won't. I have a report of you, and know why you've come." He shook his head as he turned to them. "I'm Colonel Krafton, Provost of this district, and I mean to be the Provost, and you might as well understand it now as hereafter."

"Oh!" said the Doctor, rising slowly from the seat he had taken.

"I know about your conferences, and your meetings, and the terms you propose to dictate to me ; but I will show you that I am in authority here and I don't propose to be dictated to, either ; do you understand? I don't want any of your advice. When I want you I'll send for you ; do you understand?"

The Doctor, who had waited in a sort of maze for the Provost to pause, turned to his friend, whose face was perfectly white and whose usually pleasant eyes had a red rim around the irises.

"I beg your pardon, General Legaie, I thought we should find a gentleman, but——"

"I never did, Major," said the little General. "But I had no idea we should find such a dog as this." He turned to the Provost, and, with a bow, fixed his eyes on him. But that officer looked at the sentry and said :
"Open the door."
The General looked out of it, expecting a file of soldiers to arrest them, and straightened himself for the ordeal. There was none there, however. The General's countenance fell.
"I said ' dog, ' but I apologize to that animal, and say— *worm !*" He turned his eyes once more on the Provost.
"I shall be at the Brandon tavern until the evening. Do you understand that ?" he said, addressing the Provost. He stalked out, his nose high in the air, his heels ringing on the floor.
As soon as they were outside, the Doctor began to apologize to the General again ; but the latter, having blown off his steam, and fully appreciating his friend's mortification, was very handsome about it. He had at heart a sly hope that the Provost officer might consult some friend who would insist on his taking up the insult, and so give him a satisfaction which he was at that moment very eager for. None came that evening, however, and as the next day none had come, the General was forced to return home unsatisfied.
The effect of Dr. Cary's and General Legaie's interview with Colonel Krafton was shortly felt in the county.
A few days later an order came for an inquisition to be made from house to house for arms. The labor this required was so great that it was divided up. In the part of the county where General Legaie lived, the investigation was made by Middleton, who conducted himself throughout with due propriety, even declaring it, as General Legaie reported, "an unpleasant duty," and "taking in every case a gentleman's word," never touching a thing except, perhaps, where there would be an army musket or pistol. General Legaie's old duelling-

pistols, which his butler, Julius, had hidden and taken care
of all during the war, were left unmolested, and the young
officer went so far as to express, the General stated, a
"somewhat critical admiration for them," observing that
they were the first genuine duelling-pistols he had ever
seen. On this the General—though, as he declared, it required all his politeness to do so—could not but make the
offer that in case Captain Middleton should ever have
occasion to use a pair they were entirely at his service.

In the Red Rock and Birdwood neighborhood, the
people were not so fortunate. There the inquisition was
conducted by Leech—partly, perhaps, because the two
young officers did not wish to pay their first visit to Dr.
Cary's on such an errand, and partly because Leech requested to be allowed to assist in the work.

Though the other officers knew nothing of it, Leech had
two reasons for wishing to conduct the search for arms at
Dr. Cary's. He had not forgotten Dr. Cary's action and
look the day of the trial. The other reason was hatred of
Steve Allen. "I'll show him what I can smell," he said to
Still, who smiled contentedly.

"It won't do to fool with him too much, personally,"
Still warned him. "He's a dangerous man. They're all
of 'em dangerous, you hear me."

"I'll show 'em who I am, before I'm through with 'em,"
said Leech.

Thus the inquisition for arms was peculiarly grateful to
Leech.

Leech had a squad of men under his command, which
made him feel as if he were really an officer, and he gave
them orders as though he were leading them to a battle.
He intimated that they might be met with force, and asserted that, if so, he should act promptly. On riding up to
the Doctor's a Sabbatic stillness reigned over everything.

The Doctor was not at home that day, having gone to the
city to see the General in command there about the appointment of magistrates and other civil officers for the county,

and, as Mrs. Cary had a sick headache, the blinds were closed, and Blair and old Mammy Krenda were keeping every sound hushed. It was a soft, balmy afternoon, when all nature seemed to doze. The sunlight lay on the fields and grass, and the trees and shrubbery rustled softly in the summer breeze.

Flinging himself from his horse, the Provost banged on the door loudly and, without waiting for anyone to answer his summons, stalked noisily into the house with his men behind him. Both Blair and Mammy Krenda protested against his invading one particular apartment. Blair planted herself in front of the door. She was dressed in a simple white dress, and her face was almost as white as the dress.

" What's in there ?" asked Leech.

" Nothing. My mother is in there with a sick headache."

" Ah-h-h !" said Leech, derisively. He caught Blair by the arm roughly. Blair drew back, the color flaming in her cheeks, and the old negro woman stepped up in her place, bristling with anger.

The flash in the young girl's eyes as she drew herself up abashed the Provost. But he recovered himself and, pushing old Krenda roughly aside, opened the door. There he flung open the blinds and rummaged in the drawers, turning everything out on the floor, and carried off in triumph a pair of old, horseman's pistols which had belonged to the Doctor's grandfather in the Revolutionary War, and had been changed from flintlock to percussion at the outbreak of the recent hostilities.

Leech had just come out of this room when Jacquelin Gray drove up. He stopped outside for a moment to ask what the presence of the soldiers meant, and then came hobbling on his crutches into the house.

As he entered, Blair turned to him with a gesture, partly of relief and partly of apprehension.

" Oh, Jacquelin !" The rest was only a sob. The blood flushed Jacquelin's pale face, and he passed by her.

"By what authority do you commit this outrage ?" **he** asked Leech.

"By authority enough for you. By what authority do you dare to interfere with an officer in the discharge of his duty, you limping, rebel dog ? If you know what is good for you, you'll take yourself off pretty quick." Leech took in his squad with a wave of his hand, and encountering Jacquelin's blazing eyes and a certain motion of his crutch, moved a little nearer to his men, laying his hand on his pistol as he did so.

Blair made a gesture to stop Jacquelin ; but he took no heed of it. He moved on his crutches nearer to the Provost.

"I demand to know your authority, dog," he said, ignoring both Leech's threat and Blair's imploring look.

"I'll show you. Seize him and search him," said Leech, falling behind his squad and adding an epithet not necessary to be repeated.

"I am not armed ; if I were—" said Jacquelin. At Blair's gesture he stopped.

"Well, what would you do ?" Leech asked after waiting a moment for Jacquelin to proceed. "You hear what he says, Sergeant ?" He addressed the bluff, red-haired Irishman who wore a sergeant's chevrons.

"Sames to me he says nothin' at tall," said the Sergeant, who was the same man that had had charge of the ambulance in which Jacquelin had been brought home the day he arrived, and who had been a little grumpy ever since he had been put under Leech's command.

"Arrest him and if he offers any resistance, tie him securely to a tree outside," ordered Leech.

"Does Captain Middleton know of this ?" Jacquelin asked the Sergeant.

"Well, you see, it's arders from headquarrters, an' I guess the Cap'n thaught bayin' a ferrut was a little more in *his* line." The Sergeant nodded his head in the direction of Leech, who had called the other men and gone on ostentatiously with his search.

HE CARRIED OFF IN TRIUMPH A PAIR OF OLD HORSE-PISTOLS.

Just then, however, the Provost encountered a fresh enemy. If Mrs. Cary and Miss Blair deemed it more dignified and ladylike to preserve absolute silence during this invasion, Mammy Krenda had no such inconvenient views. The old woman had nursed both Mrs. Cary and her daughter. She was, indeed, what her title implied, and had all her life held the position of a member of the family. In her master's absence she considered herself responsible, and she had followed Leech from room to room, dogging his every step, and now, emboldened by Jacquelin's presence, she burst forth, pouring out on the Provost the vials of her wrath which, instead of being exhausted by use, gathered volume and virulence with every minute.

"Yaas, I know jest what sort you is," she said, mockingly: "you is the sort o' houn'-dog that ain't got sperit enough to fight even a ole hyah, let alone a coon; but comes sneakin' into folks' kitchen, tryin' to steal a scrap from chillerns' mouths when folks' backs air turned! I ain't talkin' to you all," she explained, with ready tact, to the squad of privates who showed in their countenances some appreciation of her homely, but apt illustration; "I know you all's got to do it if you' marsters tell's you to. Nor, I'm talkin' to him. I declare I'm right glad my marster ain't at home; I'm feared he'd sile his shoe kickin' yer dutty body out de do'." She stood with her arms akimbo, and her eyes half-closed in derision.

This touch, with an ill-suppressed snicker from one of the men behind, proved too much for the leader's self-control, and he turned in a rage:

"Shut up, you black hag," he snarled, angrily, "or I'll —I'll—" He paused, hunting for a threat which would appall her. "I'll tie you to a tree outside and wear out a hickory on you."

If he thought to quell the old woman by this, however, he was mistaken. He only infuriated her the more.

"You will, will you!" she hissed, straightening herself

up and walking up close to him. "Do you know what
would happen if you did? My marster would cut your
heart out o' you; but I wouldn't lef' you for him to do it!
You ain't fitten for him to tetch. De ain' nobody uver
tetched me since my mammy whipped me last; and she
died when I was twelve years ole'; an' ef you lay your
hand 'pon me I'll wear you out tell you ain't got a piece o'
skin on you as big as dat!—see?" She walked up close
to him and indicating the long, pink nail on her clawlike
little-finger, poked a black and sinewy little fist close up
under the Provost's very nose.

"Now—" she panted: "Heah me; tetch me!"

But Leech had recovered himself. He quailed before
the two blazing coals of fire that appeared ready to dart at
him, and recognizing the fact that even his men were
against him and, like Jacquelin, were secretly enjoying his
discomfiture, he angrily ordered them out of the house
and concealed as best he could his consuming inward
rage.

Incensed by Jacquelin's look of satisfaction at the old
mammy's attack, Leech took him along with him, threatening him with dire punishment for interfering with a
Union officer in the discharge of his duty; but learning
from the Sergeant that Jacquelin was "a friend of the
Captain's," he released him, assuring him of the fortunate
escape he had, and promising him very different treatment "next time." Jacquelin returned no answer whatever until at the end, when he said, looking him deep in
the eyes, "It may not be next time, you dog; but some
time will be my time."

When Dr. Cary reached home that evening, both Mrs.
Cary and Blair congratulated themselves afresh that he
had been absent during the Provost's visit. The first
mention of the man's conduct had such an effect on him
that Mrs. Cary, who had already interviewed both her
daughter and the mammy on the propriety of giving a
somewhat modified account of the visitation, felt it neces-

sary to make even yet lighter of it than she had intended. The Doctor grew very quiet, and his usually pleasant mouth shut close, bringing his chin out strongly and giving him an uncommonly stern appearance. Mrs. Cary whipped around suddenly and gave the matter a humorous turn. But the Doctor was not to be diverted ; the insolence of Leech's action to Blair, and of penetrating into his wife's chamber, had sunk in deeply, and a little later, having left his wife's sick-room, he called up the mammy. If Mrs. Cary possessed instincts and powers of self-control which enabled her to efface her sense of injury in presence of a greater danger, the old servant had no such cultivated faculty. At the first mention of the matter by the Doctor, her sense of injury rose again, her outraged pride came to the surface once more, and in the presence of him to whom she had always looked for protection her self-control gave out.

She started to tell the story lightly, as she knew her mistress wished done, but, at the first word, broke down and suddenly began to whimper and rock.

When it had all come out between sobs of rage and mortification, her master sent her away soothed with a sense of his sympathy and of the coming retribution which he would exact.

When the Doctor saw Mrs. Cary again, he was as placid as a May-morning, perhaps more placid than usual. He thought himself very clever indeed. But no man is clever enough to deceive his wife if she suspects him, and Mrs. Cary read him as though he had been an open book. As a result, before he left her room she had exacted a promise from him not under any circumstances to seek a personal interview with Leech, or even to go to the court-house for some time.

The story of the old negro woman's terrible tongue-lashing of the Provost got abroad. He had attempted to use both command and persuasion to prevent his men from telling it, but even the bribery of a free treat at a store on the roadside, which was a liberality he had never been known to display before, failed to secure the desired secrecy, and the story reached the court-house almost as quickly as he. Sergeant O'Meara related it to the camp with great gusto.

"Bedad!" said he, "the ould woman looked like wan of theyse little black game-burruds whan a dog comes around her chicks, with her fithers all oop on her back and her wings spraid, and the Liftenant—if he is a Liftenant, which I don't say he is, moind—he looked as red as a turkey-cock and didn't show much moor courege. She was a very discriminatin' person, bedad! She picked me out for a gintleman and the sutler for a dog, and bedad! she wasn't far wrong in ayether. Only you're not to say I towld you, for whan a gintleman drinks a man's whiskey it doesn't become him to tell tales on him."

Perhaps it was well for Mr. Jonadab Leech that the matter got abroad, for it gave the incident a lighter turn than it otherwise would have had. As it was, there was a storm of indignation in the county, and next day there were more of the old Confederate soldiers in the village than had been there since the war closed. In their gray uniforms, faded as they were, they looked imposing. Leech spent the day in the precincts of the camp. A deputation, with Steve Allen at their head, waited on Middleton and had a short interview with him, in which they told him that they proposed to obey the laws, but they did not propose to permit ladies to be insulted.

"For I tell you now, Captain Middleton," said Steve, "before we will allow our women to be insulted, we will kill every man of you. We are not afraid to do it." He spoke as quietly as though he were saying the most ordinary thing in the world. Middleton faced him calmly. The two men looked in each other's eyes, and recognized each other's courage.

"Your threat has no effect on me," said Middleton; "but I wish to say that before I will allow any woman to be insulted, I will kill every man in my command. Lieutenant Leech is not in my command, though in a measure subject to my authority ; but the matter shall be investigated immediately."

What occurred in the interview which took place between Middleton and Leech was not known at the time, but that night Leech sent for Still to advise him. Even the negroes were looking on him more coldly.

"I knows if he lays his han' 'pon me, I'm gwine to cut his heart out 'n him," said a tall, black young negro in the crowd as Leech passed, on his way to his office. It was evidently intended for Leech to hear. Leech had not then learned to distinguish black countenances and he did not yet know Jerry.

Still was equal to the emergency. "These quality-niggers ain't used to bein' talked to so," he explained to Leech ; "and they won't stand it from nobody but quality. They're just as stuck up as their masters, and you can't talk to 'em that way. You got to humor 'em. The way to manage 'em is through their preachers. Git Sherrod and give him a place in the commissary. He's that old hag's son-in-law, and he's a preacher. I always manage 'em through their preachers."

The result of taking Still's advice, in one way, so far surpassed Leech's highest expectation, that he could not but admit that Still was a genius. One other appointment Still suggested, and that was of a negro who had belonged to the Grays and who was believed to have as much influence with the devil as Sherwood had in the other direction. "And," as Still said, "with Jim Sherrod to attend to Heaven and Doctor Moses to manage t'other place, I think me and you can sorter manage to git along on earth.

"You've got to do with them," he added, sinking his voice almost to a whisper. "For, as I told you, you've got to work your trigger up that a-way." He waved his hand toward the North. "If you can git the money you

say you can, I can make it over and over fer you faster
than nigger-tradin'. You jest git Krafton to stand by you
and that old feller Bolter to stake us, and we're all right.

"You've got to git rid of this young Captain. One of
you's got to go some time, and the one as holds out longest
will win. 'Twon't do to let him git too strong a hold
down here.—Now this party they're gittin' up ? If they
invite your young men—you might work that string.
But you can't quarrel with him now. You say he's in
with your Mrs. Welch. Better work the nigger racket.
That's the strong card now. Git some more boxes from
Mrs. Welch and let me put 'em where they'll do most good.
Niggers loves clo'es mo' than money. Don't fall out with
your young man yet—keep in with a man till you have
got under-holt, then you can fling him."

Meantime, while this conference was going on, Middleton was in a far less complacent frame of mind. He had
just left the camp that afternoon and was on his way to
his quarters, when, at a turn in the street, he came on a
group of young gentlemen surrounding a young lady who
was dressed in a riding-habit, and was giving an animated
account of some occurrence. As soon as he turned the
corner, he was too close on them to turn back ; so he
had to pass. He instantly recognized Miss Cary, though
her back was toward him : the trim figure, abundant hair,
and musical voice were not to be forgotten.

"I don't think you need any guard, so long as you have
Mammy Krenda," laughed one of the young men.

" No, with her for the rank and file, I am just waiting
for Captain M— I mean to meet him some day, and——"

" Hush—here he is now."

"I don't care." She tossed her head.

Middleton could not help hearing what she said, or seeing the gesture that stopped her.

He passed on, touching his cap to one or two of the
young men, who returned the salute. But Miss Cary took
no more notice of him than if he had been a dog.

Thurston had reached their room a little before Middleton arrived. He was in unusually good spirits, having just relieved his mind by cursing Leech heartily to Miss Dockett, and thus re-establishing himself with that young lady, who had been turning her back on him ever since she had heard of the incident at Birdwood. In reward for this act of reparation, the young lady had condescended to tell Lieutenant Thurston of the entertainment which the young people proposed to get up ; and the little officer had made up his mind that, if possible, he and Middleton should be invited. He had just lit his pipe and was, as he said, laying out his campaign, when Middleton entered and, tossing his sword in a corner, without a word, lit a cigar, flung himself in an armchair and gazed moodily out of the window. The Lieutenant watched his friend in silence, with a more serious look on his face than usually found lodgement on that cheerful countenance. The cloud remained on Middleton's brow, but the Lieutenant's face cleared up, and presently, between the puffs of his pipe, he said :

"Larry, you need the consolations of religion."

Middleton, without taking his eyes from the distance, turned his cigar in his mouth and remained silent.

"And I'm going to make you sit under the ministrations of the pious Mr. Langstuff——"

"Foolstuff !" growled Middleton, turning his eye on him.

"—For your soul's good and your eyes' comfort," continued the Lieutenant placidly. "For they do say, Larry, that he preaches to the prettiest lot of unrepentant, stony-hearted, fair rebels that ever combined the love of Heaven with the hatred of their fellow-mortals. You are running to waste, Larry, and I must utilize you."

"Jackass !" muttered Middleton, but he looked at Thurston, who smoked solemnly.

"For they say, Larry, there's going to be a dancing-party, and we must be there, you know."

Middleton's face, which had begun to clear up, clouded again.

"What's the good of it? Not one of 'em would speak to us. I met one just now—and she looked at me—they all look at me, or *by* me—as if I were a snake!"

"As you are, Larry—a snake in the grass," interjected the little Lieutenant. "Pretty?"

"As a peach—Can't you be serious a minute?"—for Thurston's eyes were twinkling. "Every one looks as if she hated me."

"As they ought to, Larry; for you're their enemy." Thurston settled back with his pipe between his lips, and chuckled to himself. "You ought to see the way they look at me, Larry. I know you, Alexander. You're not satisfied with your success with Miss Ruth, and Miss Rockfield, and every other girl in the North, but you must conquer other worlds; and you sigh because they don't capitulate as soon as they see your advance-guard."

"Don't be an ass, Thurs!" Middleton interrupted. "You know as well as I, that I never said a word to Ruth Welch in my life—or thought of doing so. When her father was wounded so badly, it happened that I had a scratch too, and I saw something more of her than I otherwise should have done, and that is all there is about it. Besides, we are cousins, and you know how that is. Her mother would have seen me in perdition before she would have consented to anything between us; and as to Edith Rockfield——"

But the little Lieutenant did not care about Miss Rockfield. It was Miss Welch he was interested in. So he cut in, breaking into a snatch of a song:

"Sure, Kate Riley she's me cousin.
Harry, I have cousins too;
If ye like such close relations,
I have cousins close as you."

He slipped down farther in his chair, his heels up on the table, and his hands clasped above his curly head.

"If you don't stop that howling, old Mrs. Dockett will come and turn you out again," growled Middleton.

"Not me, Larry, my dear. I can warble all I like now. I'm promoted."

"Promoted! How?"

"Don't you see I sit next to the butter, now?"

"Fool!—But I'm used to being treated with a reasonable degree of civility;" Middleton went on, as if he had not been interrupted, "and I've put myself out more to be polite here than I ever did in my life, and yet, by Jove! these little vixens turn up their noses at me as if—as if— Why, they look as if they felt about me precisely as I feel about Leech!"

He looked out of the window gloomily, and his friend watched him for a moment with an amused expression in his blue eyes.

"Larry, they don't know what great men we are, do they? You know that's one of the things that has always struck me? I wonder how girls can have such a good time when they don't know me. I suppose it's the ignorance of the poor young things! But they shall know me and you, too. We'll give the girls a treat next Sunday; we'll go to church, and later to the ball."

"Church! You go to church!"

The Captain turned his head and looked at his friend with such blank amazement that the Lieutenant actually colored.

"Yes," he nodded. "You d——d Pharisee!—you think you are the only one that knows anything about church, because that little gir— cousin of yours—converted you; you're nothing but a Dissenter anyhow. But I'm a churchman, I am. I've got a prayer-book—somewhere—and I've found out all about the church here. There's an old preacher in the county, named Longstuff or Langstuff or something, and he preaches once a month at the old church eight or ten miles above here, where they say all the pretty girls in the country congregate to pray

for the salvation of Jeff Davis and the d—— nation of **the**
Yankees—poor misguided, lovely creatures that they are!
—as if we weren't certain enough of it anyhow, without
their making it a subject of their special petition. I'm going to have a look at 'em. We'll nave our trappings rubbed
up, and I'll coach your dissenting, condemned soul on the
proper church tactics, and we'll have the handsomest pair
of horses in the county and show 'em as fine a pair of true-
riding, pious young Yanks as ever charged into a pretty
girl's heart. We'll dodge Leech and go in as churchmen.
That's one place he's not likely to follow us. What do
you say? Oh, I've got a great head on me! I'll be a
general some day!"

"If you don't get it knocked off for your impudence,"
suggested Middleton.

So the equipments were burnished up; the horses were
carefully groomed; the uniforms were brushed and pressed
afresh, and when Sunday morning came, the two young officers, having dodged Leech, who had been trying all the
week to find out what was on foot, rode off, in full and dazzling panoply, like conquering young heroes, to impress, at
least, the fairer portion of their "subjects," as Thurston
called them. They were, in fact, a showy pair as they
rode along, for both men were capital horsemen, little
Thurston looking at least a foot higher on his tall bay
than when lifted only by his own short, plump legs; and
on their arrival at church, which they purposely timed to
occur after the services should have begun, they felt that
they could not have been more effective.

The contrast between them and the rest of the assemblage was striking. The grove about the church was well
filled with animals and vehicles; but all having a worn
and shabby appearance: thin horses and mules, and rickety wagons, with here and there an old carriage standing
out among them, like old gentlemen at a county gathering. A group of men under one of the trees turned and
gazed curiously at the pair as they rode up and tied their

showy horses to "swinging limbs," and then strode silently toward the church, where the sound of a chant,
not badly rendered, told that the services were already begun.

The entrance of the blue-coats created quite as much of
a sensation as they could have expected, even if the signs
of it were, perhaps, not quite as apparent as they had anticipated, and they marched to a vacant seat, feeling very
hot and by no means as effective as they had proposed to
do. Little Thurston dropped down on his knees and bowed
his head, and Middleton, with a new feeling of Thurston's
superior genius, followed his " tactics."

This was good generalship, for no one could know that
the two young reprobates were mopping their perspiring
faces and setting every button straight, instead of being
bowed in reverential devotion. No one entered their pew,
and they were left alone. Several who came in the church
after them, and might have turned to their pew, on seeing
the blue uniforms, passed by with what looked very like a
toss of the head. But what Thurston called his "straight
flush" was when he drew out his prayer-book—which he
had found "somewhere"—and began to follow the service, in a distinctly reverential voice.

As many eyes were bent on them at this as had been
directed to them when they first appeared, and Miss
Thomasia, adjusting her spectacles to satisfy herself beyond
doubt if her eyes were not deceiving her, dropped them on
the floor and cracked one of the glasses. For the idea of
a Yankee soldier using a prayer-book had never occurred
to any female member of that congregation any more than
it had that a certain distinguished being used it, popularly
supposed to be also clad in blue uniform, of sulphurous
flame. The favorable impression made by this move was
apparent to the young men, and Middleton stepped on
Thurston's toe, so heavily as almost to make him swear with
pain, trying at once to convey his admiration and to call
Thurston's attention to a very pretty young girl in the

choir, whose eyes happened to fall that way, and whom he indicated as Miss Cary. Steve Allen was with her now, singing out of the same book with her, as if he had never thrown a card or taken a drink in his life.

The self-gratulation of the two officers was, however, of brief duration. The next moment there was a heavy tread and a sabre-clatter behind them, and turning with the rest of the congregation to look, there was Leech stalking up the aisle. He made directly toward the officers, and had Middleton been at the entrance of the pew he might, perhaps, in the frame of mind into which the sight threw him, have openly refused the new-comer admittance. Thurston, however, was nearer the entrance, and nothing of the kind occurred. He simply moved down to the door of the pew, and was so deeply immersed in his devotions at that particular instant, that even the actual pressure of Leech's hand on his arm failed to arouse him, and the Provost, after standing a moment waiting for him to move, stepped into a pew behind, and sat down in the corner by himself.

The change in sentiment created by the Provost's appearance was strong enough actually to be felt by the young men, and Middleton looked in Thurston's eyes with such helpless rage in his own that the little Lieutenant almost burst out laughing, and had to drop his prayer-book and stoop for it to compose himself.

Still the congregation was mystified. It was pretty generally supposed that it was not mere piety which brought the young officers there. Some thought it was to insult them; some to show off their fine horses—some suggested that it was to watch and report on their old rector, the Rev. Mr. Langstaff, one of the best and Godliest of men, whose ardor as a Confederate was only equalled by his zeal as a Christian. But Steve Allen—speaking with the oracular wisdom of a seer, who, in addition to his prophetic power, has also been behind the scenes—declared that they had come to look at the pretty girls, and further avowed that he didn't blame them, because there were the prettiest girls in the world, right in that church, and, as for him, he was ready to walk right up, on the spot, with any one of them, from Miss Thomasia to Miss Blair, and Mr. Langstaff could settle the whole matter for them, in five minutes. Though, of course, he added, if General Legaie had any preference, he himself would waive his privilege (as having spoken first) and let the General lead the way, as he had often done before on occasion. To which proposal, made in the aisle after church, when the weekly levee was held, the General responded that he was "quite ready to lead so gallant a subaltern, if Miss—" his eye sought Miss Thomasia's placid face—"ah ! if—any lady could be found," etc.

Steve was right—he very often was, though frequently he concealed his wisdom in an envelope of nonsense.

It was conceded after the young officers had ridden away, that they had "acted decently enough, but for those odious blue uniforms," and had showed no sign beyond nudging each other when Mr. Langstaff prayed for the President of the Confederate States, with an unction only equalled by the fervor with which the entire congregation had responded "Amen"—at least, that the first two of them had showed no sign. The third, however, had proved what they were. To be sure, he had come after the others, and they had evidently tried to make it appear as if they wished to avoid recognizing him, and had gone away alone. But what did that prove ? Were they not all alike ? And even if the Provost *had* sat in a pew by himself, and did not have a uniform exactly like the others, he had never even bowed during the prayers, but had sat bolt upright throughout the whole service, staring around. And when the President was prayed for, had he not scowled and endeavored to touch his companions ? What if they had appeared to ignore him ? Might not this be all a part of their scheme ? And, as someone said, "when the hounds were all in a huddle, you could not tell a good dog from a bad one." This simile was considered good by most of the male members of the congregation ; but there were dissenters. Mrs. Gray remembered that those two young men sent Jacquelin home the day he arrived ; and the General remembered the civility of one of them in the performance of a most disagreeable duty ; Miss Thomasia recalled the closely followed prayer-book, and some of the other ladies objected to hunting similes at church.

However, when, after service, the two young officers left the church and marched straight to their horses, even without the presence of Leech to offend them—for they had clearly told him they did not wish his company— they were far less composed than their martial mien and jingling spurs might have appeared to indicate.

CHAPTER XII

THE absence of all civil government and the disorgani-
zation of the plantations were producing great inconvenience. Much thieving was going on everywhere, and there
was beginning to be an unwonted amount of lawlessness:
sheep and hogs were being stolen, and even horses and
cattle. Dr. Cary and Mr. Bagby united with some
others of the more conciliatory men in the State, to request the establishment of some form of government, and
a sort of provisional civil government was shortly established in the country. Mr. Dockett was appointed Clerk
of the county, Dr. Cary was commissioned a magistrate
in his district, and, at his solicitation, Andy Stamper was
appointed constable.

Meanwhile, Steve Allen had become the most prominent citizen of the county seat. He had taken an old
building in one corner of the court-green, and his office
soon became the most popular place of resort in the
village, for the young men. It was rumored that something other than law was practised in Steve's office, and
the lights often burned till daybreak, and shouts of
laughter came through the open windows. Stories got
abroad of poker-parties held there in the late hours of the
summer nights. Neither Middleton nor Thurston had
ever been invited there, for Steve still held himself stiffly
with the two officers, but an incident occurred which suddenly broke down the barrier.

139

Steve had never taken the oath of allegiance. This was not known at the time of his arrival at the court-house, and he had started in to practise law, and had gone on without any question as to it ever being raised, until Still notified Leech. "If you could git up a row between him and your young man, Middleton," said he, "you might get rid of one enemy, maybe two ; for, I tell you, he won't stand no foolin'. Make Middleton make him take the oath. I don't believe he'll do it—I b'lieve he'll go away first." Leech summoned Steve to exhibit his parole; and on his failing to obey, laid the matter before Middleton.

When Leech disclosed the object of his visit, Thurston was lounging in an armchair, with his pipe. He started up. Was it possible that such a flagrant violation of the law had been going on ? He gazed at the Provost blandly.

"It was and is," said Leech, sententiously. "This man never misses an opportunity to treat the Government and its representatives with contempt."

"I have heard so," said Thurston, adopting Leech's tone. "I have heard that he has even said that some of the representatives of the Government were a stench in their own nostrils."

Leech winced and glanced at Thurston ; but he was as innocent as a dove.

"It is time to make an example of him," proceeded the Lieutenant, still apparently arguing with his superior. "And I think it would be well to have him brought up at once and the most rigid oath administered to him. Why should not Lieutenant Leech administer it ? I should like to see him do it, and he might take occasion to read Captain Allen a sound homily on his duties as a citizen of this great Republic and his cause for gratitude. It might lead him to mend the error of his ways."

Nothing could have been more pleasing to Leech. He jumped at the proposal, and said he would give this young rebel a lecture that he would not soon forget, and if he refused to take the oath would clap him in jail. Middleton assented and that evening was set for the ceremony, and Middleton and Thurston said they would go down and see the oath administered.

That evening Steve was surprised to find his office-door suddenly darkened by a squad of soldiers who had come to arrest him and take him before the Provost.

" What is it for ? " Arrests by the Provost were not un-common.

" To take the oath."

There was a laugh at Steve's expense ; for it was known by his friends that he prided himself on not having yet sworn allegiance to the Government.

" Go and take your medicine, and pay me that little fiver you bet you would not take it this month," said Mc-Raffle, with a half sneer.

" I'll credit it on one of your I O U's," said Steve, dryly.

He was marched across to the Provost's office, his friends following to see the issue. Just as they arrived, Middleton and Thurston came in, looking a little sheepish when they found, as the result of their conspiracy, Steve guarded by a file of men. Leech took out a box of good cigars and offered them to the officers. He did not offer them to anyone else, but laid them on the table, and with a rap for silence, began his homily. He made it strong and long. He dwelt with particular emphasis on the beneficence of a Government that, after a wicked re-bellion, permitted rebels to return to their allegiance and receive again all the benefits of the Union—becoming, in-deed, one with her other citizens. This concluded, he tendered Steve the oath. Everyone present, perhaps, ex-pected Steve to refuse to take it. Instead of which, he took it without a word. There was a moment of breath-less silence.

" I understand then that we are, so to speak, now one?" said Steve, drawlingly.

" Ah ! yes," said Leech, turning away to try to hide his surprise from Thurston.

"Then, gentlemen, have some of *our* cigars ?" Steve took up the box, lit a cigar himself and coolly handed them around. ·

As he offered them to Thurston the little Lieutenant said :

"Captain, the honors are yours."

The next moment Steve tossed his cigar contemptuously out of the door.

"Come over to my office, gentlemen ; I have a box that a *gentleman* has sent me. I think they will have a better flavor than these. Good-evening, Lieutenant Leech. Will you join us, gentlemen ?" This was to Middleton and Thurston, and the invitation was accepted.

They adjourned to Steve's "law-office," where they proceeded to while away the hours in a manner which has sweetened, if not made, many an armistice. Fortune from the start perched herself on Steve's side as if to try and compensate him for other and greater reverses ; and at last little Thurston, having lost the best part of a month's pay, said that if Leech's cigars were not as good as Steve's, they were, at least, less expensive.

"You fellows don't know any more about poker than you do about joking," said Steve, imperturbably, as he raked in a pot. "If I'd known about this before, I wouldn't have taken that oath. I'd have done like McRaffle there. This is too easy."

"You play just as much as I do," said McRaffle, quickly.

"Yes ; but in more select company." Steve said quietly. "Not with boys."

McRaffle's cold face flushed slightly, and he started to reply, but glanced quickly round the table and reconsidered. Steve was placidly shuffling the cards.

No man likes to have his poker-game assailed, and Middleton and Thurston were no exceptions.

"You're outclassed, Captain," said Steve. "I'd be riding that whitefoot bay of yours in a week, if you played with me."

"Make a jackpot and I'll give you a chance," said Middleton, firing up.

Steve, as the winner, was not in a position to stop. The others had warmed up.

"Yes—make it a jackpot, and let that decide which is the biggest blower," laughed someone.

Steve dealt and Middleton looked pleased, as he well might. None of the others had more than a pair, and they passed out. Steve had three hearts and a pair. He was about to throw the cards down when he caught Middleton's look of content, and hesitated.

"Come in," laughed Middleton.

Steve's fingers tightened on his cards, and Middleton discarded two, showing that he held three of a kind.

"I've got you beat," he said.

"Beat? I tell you, you don't know the game," said Steve, airily. He coolly discarded his pair.

"I don't? I'll bet you a hundred dollars, I've got you beat."

Steve picked up two cards. "I'll see you and raise you," said he. "I bet you five hundred against your whitefoot horse you haven't."

"Done," said Middleton.

"Keep your horse, boy," said Steve. "I was the best poker player in my brigade." He leaned over to put his cards down. But Middleton was game and was ahead of him.

"It's a bet," he said, laying his hand on the table. There was a sigh from the others : he had three aces.

Steve laid his beside them, and there was a shout. He had drawn a flush.

"Now I'll buy the horse back from you, if you wish it ? " said Middleton.

"Thank you. I've promised him to a lady," said Steve.

Next day Steve rode his new horse to Birdwood and, with a twinkle in his eyes, offered him to Blair.

"How did you get him ? " asked the girl.

"Captured him," laughed Steve.   "Tell your friend not to play poker with me—or McRaffle," he added.

Blair's eyes flashed and she attacked Steve vigorously. She would not have him offering to present her a part of his gaming-winnings. He was becoming a scandal to the neighborhood ; leading the young men off.

"Young Larry, for instance ?" smiled Steve.   "Or Captain McRaffle ?"

"No. You know very well whom I mean," declared Blair. "Rupert thinks it fine to imitate you." The smile was still on Steve's face, and Blair paused to take breath ; then half closing her eyes as if she were sighting carefully—"And couples your name with Captain McRaffle's," she added.

A light of satisfaction came into her eyes as she saw the shaft go home. A deeper hue reddened Steve's sunbrowned face.

"Who was the young lady who bet me not long ago, against that very horse, that she would not dance with a certain Yankee Captain ? Where's her pious example ?"

Blair's face flushed. "I did wrong. But I did not expect you, Captain Allen who prides himself on his chivalry, to shelter himself behind a girl." She bowed low, and turned away in apparent disdain, enjoying the success of her shot.

Just at that moment Miss Thomasia joined them.

"What are you two quarrelling about ?" The next moment she glanced at Steve and a troubled look came into her eyes.

"Nothing. We aren't quarrelling, are we Blair ?" Steve held out his hand in sign of peace.

"Yes. Steve has just charged——"

Steve began to make signs to Blair.

"—Steve has just charged," proceeded Miss Blair, ignoring his efforts to stop her, "that all his shortcomings are due to the example set him by a woman."

"They all do it, my dear, from Adam down," said Miss Thomasia, placidly.

Her sex was to be defended even against her idol.

"There," said Blair, triumphantly to Steve.

"It's a stock phrase," said Steve. "And what I'd like to know is, did not Adam tell the truth?"

"Yes, the coward! he did. And I've no doubt he tried to keep poor Eve between him and the angel's sword. Now you, at least be as brave as he, and tell Cousin Thomasia the truth and see what she says."

Once more Steve began to signal Blair. But Miss Thomasia herself came to his rescue. Perhaps, she wanted to save him. She began to ask about Rupert. She was evidently anxious about the boy.

Whether it was because of what Blair said about Rupert, or because of the look of distress that came in Miss Thomasia's eyes at the mention of the story of Steve's playing, Steve had an interview with Captain Middleton shortly afterward, and, as a result, when he told him the dilemma in which he found himself, the horse went back into Middleton's possession, until Middleton left the county, when he became Steve's by purchase.

As time went on, a shadow began to fall between Jacquelin and the sun. Steve was in love with Blair. Steve was always with her; his name was always on her lips, and hers frequently on his. She rode his horse : and he often came to Red Rock with her. And as Jacquelin watched, he knew he had no chance. It cut deeper than anyone ever knew ; but Jacquelin fought it out and won. He would not let it come between him and Steve. Steve had always been like a brother. He would still love Blair. This was not forbidden him. Not every knight always won his great love. It was the loyalty, not the success, that was knightly. If she loved Steve, he could make her happier than Jacquelin himself ever could have done. And Jacquelin, if God gave him power, would rejoice with them in time.

The preparations for the contemplated entertainment

10

for the benefit of the poor wounded Confederate soldiers
in the county were already begun. It was to be given at
Red Rock, and the managers waited only for Jacquelin
to recover somewhat from a set-back he had had after
his meeting with Leech at Dr. Cary's. Blair Cary had
offers from at least a dozen escorts; but Steve was the
fortunate contestant. Miss Dockett was so much interested in her preparations that the two lodgers caught
the fever, and found themselves in the position of admirers and part advisers as to a costume for an entertainment to which they were not considered good enough
to be invited. Little Thurston had to purchase a part
of it in the city, where he went on a visit, and, truth
to tell, finding that the small amount entrusted to him
—which was all that could be got together even by
Mrs. Dockett's diligence, stimulated by her natural pride
in her daughter's first ball—was not sufficient to purchase
material as fine as he thought suited to adorn the plump
person of a young lady who had condescended to warble
with him, he added to it a small sum from his own by no
means over-plethoric pocket, and then lied about it afterward like a trooper and a gentleman.

"Well, I always heard a Yankee was a good hand at a
bargain," declared Mrs. Dockett; "but you are the best I
ever knew." And this was Thurston's reward.

The officers had given up hope of being invited to the
assembly, when one evening two formal notes, requesting
their company, were brought by Steve's boy Jerry. They
were signed simply, "The Committee."

"And now," said Middleton, "we're in a bigger hole
than before; for it's for the benefit of the rebels; and if
that gets out— But, perhaps it will not?"

"Gets out? Of course it will get out. Everything one
doesn't want to get out, gets out; but yet we must go.
Does not our high sense of duty require us to sacrifice our
personal prejudices so far as to keep an eye on this first
large assemblage of rebels?"

"Reely, you're a genius," said Middleton, in open admiration.

"Of course I am," was the Lieutenant's modest reply.

Formal notes of acceptance were sent, and the two young officers were soon as busy as anyone making their preparations for their "summer campaign," as Thurston called it. Both ordered new boots, and Thurston a whole suit, for the occasion. Thurston, in the seclusion of their room, drilled Middleton sedulously in the Old Virginia reel, so as to astonish the native and, as he profanely termed it, "make sure of the capture of the fish Middleton had found in the ford."

An evening or two later, the mail was brought in, and in it were two official letters for Middleton. As he read them, his face fell, and he flung them across to Thurston, who, as he glanced at them, gave an ejaculation hardly consistent with the high-church principles he so proudly vaunted.

One was an order forbidding, for the present, all public gatherings at night, under any guise whatever, except in churches; the other forbade the wearing of any Confederate uniform or garment forming part of a uniform, or, at least (as persons might not have any other clothes whatever), brass buttons, braid, chevrons, etc., which were the insignia of a uniform. These were to be cut off or covered. These were general orders, and the officers in command stationed throughout the country were directed to see them enforced.

"This comes of having a d—d tailor for President," said the little Lieutenant. "I always did hate 'em ; and to think I've ordered a new uniform for it too ! Your wedding, Larry, will not come off as soon as I anticipated. Well, there's one consolation ; one tailor will have to wait some time."

This view appeared to please the Lieutenant so much that, as he glanced over the orders again, he began to whistle, while the Captain looked on despondently. The whistling grew louder as Thurston read on, and he suddenly bounced up.

" I've got it, Larry.   Are you a Mason ? "

" No.   Why ? "

" Oh !   Nothing—I was just thinking of that old Masonic
lodge where the chaplain preached and Leech led in prayer.
You issue your orders—and leave me to manage it: this
tailoring part is what's going to play the deuce.   I can
settle the other—I'm a churchman—I ought to have been
a bishop."

As Thurston foresaw, it was the order touching the uniforms which gave the greatest offence, and in the indignation which this aroused, the other was almost lost sight of.
It was intended to show the negroes, the old residents said,
that the Southerners were completely in subjection to the
Federal authorities.   Which view gained some ground
from the fact that the orders were issued by Leech, who
appeared to be charged with their enforcement.

The next day there was a storm in the county.

The little General made old Julius burnish up his buttons until they shone like gold, and then rode into the village to interview the officer in command.   He was stopped
on the street by Leech, and was ordered to cut them off
immediately if he did not wish him to do it for him, on
which the gallant old Confederate stated to that functionary
as placidly as he might have returned an answer to Miss
Thomasia on the subject of roses, that if Leech so much as
attempted to lay his hand on him, he would kill him immediately ; and the look in his eyes was so resolute and
so piercing that Leech, who supposed from this that he
was fully armed, slunk away to secure a squad of soldiers
to enforce his order.   The General rode serenely on to
find Middleton.   No one was present at the interview.
But it became known afterward that the General had
begun by an intimation that he was ready to renew his
polite offer of the pair of duelling pistols to Captain
Middleton, if the Captain wished to give a gentleman who
found himself temporarily in a somewhat embarrassing
position, a gentleman's satisfaction ; and that he had come

away, not, indeed, with this satisfaction, but, at least, with renewed esteem for the young men, whom he continued to speak of as " most gentlemanly young fellows " ; and he covered his buttons with cloth.

Steve Allen let Miss Thomasia cover his with crêpe, and having led Leech into questioning him as to the reason for this, said that it was mourning because a certain cowardly hound had only barked at Mammy Krenda one day, instead of attempting to touch her, and giving her the opportunity to cut the skin from him. Dr. Cary found his buttons cut off by Mrs. Cary and Miss Blair— " to prevent," Blair said, " their being defiled by sacrilegious hands."

Jacquelin Gray was at this time confined to his lounge, by his wound ; but it had this drop of consolation for his mother and Aunt Thomasia, that so long as he stayed there he could not be subjected to what others underwent. They reckoned, however, without their host.

One afternoon Leech rode into the Red Rock yard with a squad of soldiers at his back, and riding across the grass to the very door, dismounted and stamped up the steps, and, without waiting for an answer to his loud rap, stalked into the hall, with his men behind him. Where he had come from no one knew ; for he had ridden in the back way. It transpired afterwards that he had stopped for a minute at the overseer's house.

At the moment Leech appeared in the hall, Jacquelin was lying on his lounge, with Blair Cary and Rupert sitting beside him, and the first he knew of the Provost's presence was when Blair, with an exclamation, sprang to her feet. He turned and faced Leech as he entered the hall. The Provost appeared dazed by the scene before him ; for scores of eyes were fastened on him from the walls, and he stood for a moment rooted to the spot, with his gaze fixed on the face of the " Indian-killer " over the big fireplace. That strange embodiment of fierce resolve seemed almost to appal him. The next instant, with a gesture, he came forward to where Jacquelin lay. At the same moment Blair retired to seek Mrs. Gray and Miss Thomasia. Leech's eyes followed her as she went out.

"Well, sir, what do you want?" Jacquelin asked, haughtily.

"Take off your coat."

It was the form of order given to negroes when they were to be thrashed. Jacquelin's face flushed.

"What for?"

"Because if you don't, I'll take it off for you. I mean to cut these buttons off."

"You can cut them off." Jacquelin had grown quiet, and his face was white. Rupert drew nearer to him, his cheeks flushed and his breath coming quickly.

"I guess I can," sneered the Provost. He came up to the lounge, pushing Rupert aside, who interposed between them. He leaned over and cut the buttons from the jacket, one by one.

"I'll send these to my girl," he said, tauntingly—"Unless you want them for yours," he added, with a meaning laugh. Jacquelin controlled himself to speak quietly.

"Tell your master that some day I will call him to account for this outrage."

"Young puppies bark, but don't bite," sneered the Provost.

In an instant Rupert was on him, and, boy as he was, he struck the Provost a blow which, taking him unawares, staggered him. Leech recovered himself, however, and seizing the boy, slapped him furiously several times. Jacquelin was on his feet in a moment. He sprang toward the Provost, but the men interposed, and he sank back on his lounge, breathless and white.

"Hound, for that I will some day make a negro whip you within an inch of your life," he said, beside himself.

Leech grinned in triumph and, walking up, leant over him officiously, as though to see if there were still any buttons left.

As he did so, Jacquelin raised himself and slapped him across the face. Leech with an oath sprang back and jerked out a pistol ; and possibly but for an accident which gave time for the intervention of his men, Jacquelin Gray's career would have ended then.

He looked so cool, however, and withal so handsome and intrepid as he lay back and gazed into Leech's eyes, denouncing him fiercely and daring him to shoot, that Leech hesitated and turned toward his men for encouragement. As he did so, the door opened hastily and a curious thing happened. The great full-length portrait over the big fireplace, loosened, perhaps, by the scuffle with Rupert, or by the jar of the door as Mrs. Gray and Miss Thomasia, entered, slipped in its frame and at the moment that Leech turned, fell forward, sending the Provost staggering back among his startled men. When Leech recovered, his men interfered. They were not ready to see a man murdered before his mother. Baffled in this, the Provost determined on another revenge. He swore he would have Jacquelin hanged, and made his men take him out and put him on a horse. Jacquelin was unable to sit in the saddle, and fell off in a faint. At this moment Hiram Still, whom Mrs. Gray had summoned, came up and interposed. At first, the Provost was not amenable even to Still's expostulations ; but at length he pressed a wagon and had Jacquelin put in it, and hauled him off to the court-house, to jail, still swearing he would have him hanged. Mrs. Gray, having sent off by Blair in hot haste for Dr. Cary to follow her, directed Still to replace the picture, 'ordered her carriage, and, without waiting, set out for the court-house, accompanied by Miss Thomasia and Rupert.

They had hardly left when Still went into the house to set the picture back in its place. It was surrounded by a group of curious, half-frightened servants who, with awe, alternately gazed on it and on the yawning hole in the wall, making comments, full of foreboding. Still sent them all off except Doan, whom he kept to help him set the picture back in place. It was necessary to get up on a chair and lean half way in the hole and examine the sides where the nails were to be driven, and this Still did himself, making an examination of the entire recess, even moving a number of bundles of old papers.

"Ah!" he said, with a deep inspiration, as he ran his eye over one bundle, which he laid off to one side. He sent Doan out to get him some long nails, for, as he explained, he meant now to nail the picture up to stand till judgment day. The negro went with a mutter, half timid, half jest, that he wouldn't stay in that hole by himself not for the whole Red Rock plantation and every mule on it. While he was absent Still was not idle. Doan had no sooner disappeared than the manager seized the bundle of papers he had laid to one side, and, hastily cutting the string which bound it, extracted several papers.

"I thought I remembered which one it was in," he murmured. "I didn't know when it was put in here as I'd ever git hold of it again." He held the papers up so as to get the light over his shoulder on them.

"Yes, that's the big bond with the paint on it, payable to me. I thought 'twa'n't cancelled."

He was so busy with the papers that he did not see the faces, outside the window, pressed against the pane, or hear Doan enter, and did not know he had returned until his shadow fell across the hearth. He slipped the papers in his pocket so hastily that one of them fell out and would have fluttered down on the floor had he not caught it. He turned on the negro :

"How did you come in, fool?" he asked, with a start, as he rammed the paper back in his pocket.

"I come in by de do'," said Doan, sullenly.

The portrait was soon nailed back, this time Still driving the nails in to make sure they wouldn't come out again.

Meanwhile the ladies were making their way to the court-house. It was quite dusk when they reached the

county seat and, to their surprise, the wagon had not
yet arrived. Miss Thomasia was in great distress over
it, and was sure that Leech had executed his threat
against Jacquelin. But Mrs. Cary, though much disturbed,
thought that more probably they had taken another road
and had travelled more slowly. This, indeed, proved to
be the case, and some hours later, Leech and his prisoner
turned up.

Mrs. Gray had not been idle. On reaching the court-
house she sent at once for General Legaie, and drove to
Mrs. Dockett's, where she knew the commanding officer
had his quarters. There she found the family at supper,
and it may be safely asserted that no meal was ever more
unceremoniously interrupted. Mrs. Dockett no sooner
heard Mrs. Gray's name, than she left the table and went
to receive her, and having in the first two minutes learned
the cause of her visit, she swept back into the dining-
room and swooped down on the two young officers, with a
volubility which, at least, terminated the meal, and looked
for a little while as if it would also terminate the relation
of hostess and guest. She announced that Leech had
broken into Mrs. Gray's house, assaulted her son, and
finally dragged him from his dying bed and, no doubt, had
murdered him in the woods. And she summoned the two
officers to assert immediately their authority and execute
summary justice on the Provost, if they ever wished to eat
another meal under her roof. Not that Mrs. Dockett
really took the view that Miss Thomasia took, for outside,
she had already reassured Mrs. Gray, giving her calmly
most excellent reasons to show that Leech would never
dare to injure her son. But she felt that she had a warrant for this lurid picture in Miss Thomasia's forebodings,
and she could not resist the pleasure of presenting it in
all its blackness. Fortunately, Middleton, with his quiet
manner, could, when he chose, be impressive enough.
He listened to Mrs. Gray's statement calmly; was very
grave, but very polite to her, and though he did not

promise to release her son, or indicate what would be done in the matter, he assured her that Jacquelin should have proper treatment on his arrival, and promised that she should have access to him.

Suddenly Rupert, who had been crying on the way down whenever he could do so unobserved, stepped forward from behind his mother, where he had been standing.

"I struck him first, and I am the one to hang, not my brother." His face which had been red when he began, paled suddenly, and his lip quivered a little; but his head was held straight and his eyes were steady and were filled with light.

Mrs. Gray started to speak; but her voice trembled and failed her, and she could only hold out her hand to the boy. Middleton's eyes softened.

"No one will be hanged," he said. Then added, gravely : "But you shouldn't have struck him."

"He called my brother a puppy," said the boy, defiantly, his eyes flashing, "and I'll let no one do that—not you, nor anyone."

That night Thurston said to Middleton :

"Gad, Larry, I said I ought to be a bishop, but you ought to be one—the way you preached to that boy, and I'd give a thousand dollars for him."

"I wish you were Captain," growled Middleton.

"He looked like a little game-cock, didn't he ? "

When the prisoner arrived, about midnight, under his guard, everything was found ready for his reception, and his mother was detailed to nurse him, to which, probably, was due the failure of Leech's and one other's plan.

CHAPTER XIII

THE roughness of the treatment Jacquelin had received
at Leech's hands caused his wound to break out afresh, and
for a time he was seriously ill. But he had some compensations. Every girl in the neighborhood deemed him her
especial favorite and charge. And from time to time, in
the door walked, floated, or entered somehow, a goddess ;
and with her came heaven. Her entrance was always a
miracle ; she lit up the room, radiance took the place of
gloom ; the racked nerves found a sudden anodyne, and in
the mere joy of her presence, Jacquelin forgot that he was
crippled. She read to him, sat by him, soothed him,
talked with him, sympathized with him, turned darkness
into light, and pain, at least, into fortitude. How divinely
tender her eyes could grow as some sudden paroxysm
wrung his nerves, and brought a flush to his wan cheek !
How solicitous was her voice ! How soft her touch ! And
how much she knew ! As much as Aunt Thomasia ! How
could a young girl have read so much ! It stimulated
Jacquelin, and he began to emulate her, as in old days,
until reading became a habit.

Under these influences Jacquelin actually began to get
well.

Middleton passed by one evening and saw the young girl
sitting on the rose-bowered veranda, by Jacquelin's lounge,
reading to him. The soft cadences of a charming voice
were borne to him murmurously. A strange pang of loneliness shot through him. That far-away visit in the past
seemed to rise up before him, and the long years were sud-

denly obliterated. He was back, a visitor at a beautiful old country - place, where joy and hospitality reigned. Jacquelin was a handsome, bright-faced boy again, and Blair was a little girl, with those wonderful eyes and confiding ways. Middleton wondered if he should suddenly turn and walk in on them, with a reminder of that old time, how they would receive him. He was half-minded to do it, and actually paused. He would go in and say, "Here, the war is over—let's be friends." But suddenly a man passed him and glanced up in his face and saluted. It was Leech, and Middleton saw him look across to where the invalid and his fair young nurse sat on the shaded veranda, and knew what his thoughts were. The spell was broken. Middleton stepped down from romance to the hard ground of reality, and passed on to give his orders for the evening.

Jacquelin's arrest and illness had come near breaking up the entertainment (a name which had been substituted for ball, to meet the scruples of Miss Thomasia and some other pious ladies). But this Jacquelin would on no account hear of. Besides, after the order forbidding public gatherings at night, it would look like truckling. As, however, in the family's absence, the assembly could not be held at Red Rock, it was decided to have it at the courthouse, where Jacquelin now was. This concession was made ; the largest and best building there for such an entertainment was one used as a Masonic hall, and occasionally as a place for religious services. This hall was selected. Who was responsible for its selection was not actually known. Thurston told Middleton that when he said he ought to have been a bishop, he placed his abilities far too low—that really he ought to have been a pope. But he did not appear in the matter at all except to meet the objections raised by Leech, and to silence that official by an allusion to his recent pious ministrations in that building. Steve Allen was the chief advocate of the hall, and took the lead in its selection and also in its defence ;

for some objection was made by others than Leech to having a party in this building, and on very different grounds.
Miss Thomasia and some others who were not entirely satisfied anyhow about dancing, thought that it was certainly
more likely to be wrong in a room which had been sometimes used, however rarely, for religious services, and it
took some skill to overrule their objections. Thurston
said to Mrs. Dockett that it had never been consecrated.
" So far from it," said Mrs. Dockett, " it has been dese-
crated." (The last service held in it had been held by a
Union chaplain, who had come up from town and preached
in it to the soldiers, with Leech on the front bench.)

Miss Thomasia, being for once in accord with both
Thurston and Steve, gave in, and actually lent her aid and
counsel, at least so far as related to the embellishment of
the hall, and of some who were to attend there. She ventured her advice to Steve in only one matter relating to
the outside. Having found him at work one evening,
making a short rustic bench to be placed under one of the
trees in the yard, she said she hoped he did not intend that
for two people, and that young man scandalously replied
that he was making it short on purpose for her and the
General ; and, in the face of her offended dignity, impu-
dently added that the General had engaged him to do it,
and had given him the measurements.

" Steve Allen, I am too old for you to talk to me so,"
said Miss Thomasia.

" 'Taint me, Cousin Thomasia ; 'tis the General," persisted Steve, and then, as the little faded lady still remained grave and dignified, he straightened up and glanced
at her. Stepping to her side, he slipped his arm round
her, like a big stalwart son, and, looking down in her
face with kindly eyes, said, tenderly :

" Cousin Thomasia, there aren't any of 'em like you nowadays. They don't make 'em so any more. The mould's
broken." He seated the little lady gently on the bench,
pleased and mollified, and flung himself on the grass at her

feet, and the two had a long, confidential talk, from which both derived much comfort, and Steve much profit (he said). At least, he learned something new, and when as the dew began to fall Miss Thomasia rose, it was with a better insight into the nature of the reckless young fellow ; and Steve, on his part, had a new feeling for Miss Thomasia, and led her in with a new tenderness. For Miss Thomasia had told the young man, what she had never admitted to a soul in all her life—that the reason the General, or anyone else, had never won her was that long ago her heart had been given to another—" the handsomest, most brilliant man I ever saw," she said—who had loved her, she believed, with all his soul, but had not been strong enough to resist, even for her sake, the temptation of two besetting sins—drink and gambling—and she had obeyed her father, and given him up.

Steve was lying full length on his back at her feet, his face turned to her, and his clasped hands under his head.

" Cousin Thomasia, who was he, and what became of him ? " he asked, gently.

" He was your father, Steve, and you might have been—" The voice was so low that the young man did not catch the last word. He unclasped his hands, and placed one forearm quickly across his face, and lay quite still for a minute or two. Then he moved it. Miss Thomasia was sitting quite motionless, her eyes in her lap, and with the fading light of the evening sky slanting under the trees and resting on her face and soft, silvered hair. She sighed so softly it might have been only breathing.

" I never knew it," said Steve, gently ; " but I might have known."

He rose slowly, and leaning over her, kissed her tenderly, and she laid her head on his shoulder.

" Yes, Steve, now you know."

And Steve said, yes, and kissed her again like a son.

" Cousin Thomasia," he said, presently, " I will not say I will never drink again ; but I will promise you not to gamble again, and I will not drink to excess any more."

"Oh ! Steve, if you knew how I have prayed for you ! " said the little lady, softly.

"Well, maybe, Cousin Thomasia, this is in answer to it," said Steve, half seriously.

There was as much preparation for the entertainment as there had ever been in the old times for the greatest ball given at Red Rock or Birdwood. Some of the guests from distant neighborhoods came several days before- hand to be in time, or to help superintend, and stayed at the houses of their friends near the county seat. Even the General's bachelor establishment was transformed for the occasion into a nest of doves, who, it was said, put up more little knick-knacks than he had ever seen, and made the old fellow more comfortable than he had ever been before in all his life.

Thus the little village, which for some time had been hardly more than a camp, over-run with negro camp-fol- lowers, suddenly took on a new air and freshened up, with young girls in cool dresses and big hats on the streets, or making pleasant groups under the trees in the yards on the slopes outside the hamlet, from which laughter and singing to the music of guitars floated down to the village below. The negroes themselves joined in, and readily fell into old habits, putting themselves in the way of the visitors, whom they overwhelmed with compliments, and claims, and offers of service.

Amid this, Middleton and Thurston went in and out quietly, attending to their duties, drilling and inspecting and keeping their eyes open, less for treason than for the pretty girls who had come suddenly upon them like flowers after a spring rain. They met a few of them casu- ally, either through Steve Allen or Mrs. Dockett, whose house was filled with them ; but the new-comers treated them with such undeniable coolness that there was little encouragement to prosecute the acquaintance. Even plump Miss Dockett stiffened perceptibly, and treated Lieutenant Thurston with more severity than she had ever exhibited since he had made those wonderful bargains.

Only one man in the whole village appeared absolutely out of humor over the stir and preparations, and that was Leech. The plan which he and Still had laid down to prevent the assembly having failed, Leech determined to break it up, at all hazards. Still was in constant, if secret, conference with him. They had told Sherwood and Moses that they could prevent it. If it were held in spite of them, it would prove that they were less powerful than they pretended to be.

Leech would go to town and obtain a peremptory order forbidding this very meeting.

"Have it made out so you can give it, yourself," counselled Still. "Wait till the last minute and then spring it on 'em. We'll show 'em we're not to be treated as they please. They don't know me yet, but they soon will. I've got that as will make some of 'em wince. I'll show 'em who Hiram Still is." He tapped his pocket significantly.

So it was decided, and Leech went off to the city to use his influence with Colonel Krafton, while Still was to prepare a foundation for his interference, through the negro leaders, Sherwood, Moses, and Nicholas Ash.

That evening there was a little more stir among the negroes about the court-house than had been observed before. Sherwood and Moses were there, sent down by Still, and that night they held a meeting—a religious meeting it was called—at which there was some singing and praying, and much speaking or preaching—the two preachers being Sherwood and Moses. They could be heard all over the village, and at length their shouting and excitement reached such a pitch and attracted so much attention that some of the residents walked down to the place where they were congregated, to look into the matter. Moses was speaking at the moment, mounted on an impromptu platform, swaying his body back and forth, and pouring forth a doctrine as voluble in words as it was violent in sound and gesture, whilst his audience surged around him, swaying and shouting, and exciting themselves into a sort of wild frenzy. The white men who had gathered, listened silently and sullenly to the sounds rising in unison with the speaker's voice. Some were of the opinion that he ought to be stopped at once and the meeting broken up, and there were plenty of offers to do it. A more prudent head, however, had adopted another course. Dr. Cary, who happened to be in the village that night, hearing what was going on, and knowing what might occur at any moment, called on the officer in command, and stated to him the danger of a collision. Captain Middleton walked down to the meeting with him to make his own observation. Only a few moments sufficed. The violence of the speaker, who was now dancing back and forth ; the excitement of the dusky crowd pressing about him ; the gathering of white men on the edge of the throng, speaking in low, earnest tones, their eyes turned to the speaker, suggested prompt measures.

"Don't de Book say, as we shall inherit the uth ?" cried the speaker, and his audience moaned and swayed and shouted in assent.

"An' ain't de harvest white fur de laborer ?"

"Yas—yas," shouted the audience. "White fur de laborer !"

"Unless you stop them, Captain, we shall ; for we know that it is necessary and that it will be a kindness to them," said the Doctor, quietly ; and the officer recognizing the necessity, though he little understood the Doctor's full meaning, assented promptly. He pushed his way through the throng, followed by the Doctor. He stopped the speaker and mounted the platform, and in a few words forbade any further speaking and ordered the crowd to disperse, which it did almost immediately, dissolving like magic before the officer's order. Then he turned to the speaker, and with a sharp reprimand for his action commanded him to leave the village. The trick-doctor cringed, and with a whine of acquiescence bowed himself off.

11

CHAPTER XIV

LEECH SECURES AN ORDER AND LOSES IT

WHEN Leech returned from the city, next day, he was in such good spirits that Steve and Thurston both arrived at a similar conclusion, and decided that there was some mischief brewing. Steve called Jerry and had a talk with him.

About sunset Leech mounted his horse at his stable and rode out of the village through a back lane. He was to meet Still that night at Nicholas Ash's. Still and his son met him according to appointment, and the details of their plan were arranged.

Leech found that he had an ally stronger than he had dreamed of. Still showed him that he was a much richer man than he had ever admitted. He not only held the bonds of Dr. Cary, given for the money he had lent the Doctor, and a bond of his late employer, Mr. Gray, of which Leech already knew; but he held another bond of Mr. Gray for an amount large enough to swallow up his entire estate. Leech could scarcely believe his eyes. Mrs. Gray did not know of its existence; but the bond was undoubtedly genuine. Mrs. Gray herself, Still said, would admit that. He had a satisfactory explanation for her ignorance, as well as for the fact that he had never before mentioned to Leech that he held so large a claim against the Gray estate. He had made the money by negro-trading quietly, before the war, and had lent it to Mr. Gray to stock a plantation, which he, as Mr. Gray's agent, had bought for him in the far South. And he had not mentioned it to Mrs. Gray or anyone else for a very simple reason. He had promised Mr. Gray that he would never trouble Mrs. Gray about the bonds during her life.

Leech did not believe this ; but there were the bonds— one a small one, and one a very big one, and Still had of late hinted several times at something that he was storing up for the proper moment.

" I told you I didn't care if you killed that young Jacquelin that night," he laughed. " Why didn't you do it ? I must say I never allowed that he'd git thar alive."

" Neither did I," suggested Leech. " And I believe it did him good."

" I don't know about that," said Still, enigmatically ; " but I wouldn't 'a' shed no tears over him. But if you do as I tell you, we'll git even and have a leetle somethin' to spare. You just work Krafton and get your friends to back you, and you and me'll own this county. I'll see that Moses is there on time, if he don't have an inch of skin left on him."

A rumor had meantime got abroad at the county seat that an order had been secured by Leech forbidding the assembly, and that though Middleton knew nothing of it as yet, Leech would spring it at the proper time and try to prevent the assembly. There was much excitement over it. A number of young men dropped in at Steve Allen's office to ascertain the truth of the report, and there was a rather general expression of opinion that the ball would take place whether Leech had such an order or not.

" Go and ask Middleton, directly," advised Jacquelin, and Steve did so. Middleton said he had no knowledge on the subject, and knew of no one to whom such an order should be addressed except himself.

Jerry, who was lounging sleepily not far from Leech's office, was called in by Steve and interrogated again with sundry forcible intimations of what would happen in case he should be deceiving him. But Jerry was firm. He reiterated again and again his fervent wish for a speedy dissolution and a perpetual condemnation of the most lurid character, if every word he had spoken were not more than true. Leech, he declared, had the paper in his pocket, and had read it to Sherwood and Moses and Nicholas in his back office, and was going to deliver it to Captain Middleton next day, the day set for the entertainment.

"I lies to urrers ; but the Cun'l knows I wouldn' lie to him," protested Jerry, in final asseveration.

"That's so—he knows better," said Steve ; and Jerry, with a grin, went back to his post in sight of Leech's back door.

Steve, with a new light in his face, went up to Mrs. Dockett's and had a little talk with Miss Dockett and one or two of the young ladies there, and in ten minutes, with locked doors, they were busy sewing for life. It must have been something very amusing they were engaged in, to judge from the laughter that floated down from their windows.

That night Hiram Still, with his son, was on his way back to Red Rock from his meeting with Leech, while Leech was riding back to the court-house.

It was about ten o'clock and the moon was covered by clouds ; Leech was riding along, thinking of the plans he had formed and the manner of publishing his order, and of the effect it would have in establishing his position in the county. He had got within a mile or two of the village when, in a little "bottom" in a lonely piece of woods, just before reaching a fork in the road, there was an owl-hoot behind him, and another, as if in response, a little ahead of him. The next moment his horse started violently, as a dark object which Leech had noticed when still at a distance from it, but thought merely a bush, moved out into the road immediately before him. His heart jumped into his throat, for it was not like anything earthly. In the darkness, it looked as much like a small elephant with a howdah on it, as anything else ; but he did not have time to think much about it, for the next instant it was close on him right across the road, a huge muffled figure on a high, shapeless beast. Leech's horse snorted and wheeled. Another figure was behind him, closing in on him. Leech pulled in his frightened horse; for somewhere about the middle of the dark figure lowering above him there was a momentary flash of steel. Leech thought of his own pistol, but the great figure moved closer to him, very close to him, and stopped. Not a word was said. The figure simply sat in front of him, silent and motionless, while the other moved up on the other side and did the same. Leech's tongue was sticking to his mouth. The stillness and silence were more awful than any words could have been. He tried to speak, but his lips could scarcely frame the words. Presently he managed to falter :

" What do you want ? "

There was no answer, and again the silence became worse than ever. The voices of the katydids sounded far and near.

" Who are you ? "

There was not a word. Only the figures pressed closer to him.

" What—what do you want ? "

Silence and the katydids in the woods.

" Let me go by. I have no money."

There was no answer, and for a moment no motion, only the gleam of steel again. Then the two figures, pressing close against the Provost, silently turned his horse around and moved slowly off into the woods, without a word, with him between them.

He tried to pull up his reins ; they were held on either side, and an arm was thrown around him.

" Where are you going ? " faltered Leech.

They moved on without a word.

" Wait—I will—I will give——"

A bag or something was suddenly thrown over his head and pressed down to his elbows, which at the same moment were pinioned to his side, and his pistol was taken.

He was afraid to cry out, and perhaps could not have done so even had he tried.

The next instant a hand was put into his breast pocket and his pocket-book and all his papers were taken out ; he was conscious of a match being struck and a light made, and that his papers were being looked over. He thought he heard one of his captors say, " Ah ! " and the next moment the papers and pocket-book were put back in his pocket, and the light was extinguished ; the bag was drawn from over his head, and his captors rode off through the woods. When he tried to move he discovered that his horse was tied to a bush and he had to dismount to untie him. His pistol was lying at the foot of the sapling. Long before he had finished loosing his horse, the sound of his two waylayers had died out.

As the Provost entered the village the sour expression on his face deepened. The clouds had disappeared and the summer night was perfect ; the village lay before him, a picture of peace ; the glint of white beneath the court-house trees being just enough to suggest that the tents there were hidden. The streets were filled with a careless throng, and all the sounds were those of merriment : laughter and shouting, and the twang of banjos. There was never an unlikelier field for such a plan as the Provost had in mind.

He rode through like a shadow, silencing the negroes and scowling at the whites, and as soon as he had put up his horse, he called on Captain Middleton. It was not a long interview, but it was a stormy one, and when the Provost came out of the Captain's office he had thrown down the gauntlet and there was an open breach between them. He had complained to Middleton of being beset by highwaymen and robbed of his order, and Middleton had told him plainly he did not believe a word he said.

" How did you get such an order ? If there was such an order, why was it not addressed to me ? " he asked.

Leech said that he declined to be interrogated, but he would soon show him that he had authority.

" Then you will have to bring some better evidence than your own word," said Middleton, coldly.

Leech fired up and attempted a bolder tone than he had ever dared use before with Middleton, and actually forbade the meeting the following night. The young Captain, however, gave him to understand that he himself was the commandant there and that for another word, order or no order, he would place him under arrest, which step at that moment would have so interfered with Leech's plans that he had not ventured to push the matter further.

Next night the long-talked-of entertainment came off duly, and Miss Blair Cary and Miss Elizabeth Dockett and the other girls who had waited so long, showed their little plain, sweet, white and pink dresses which they had made themselves, and their prettier white throats and pink faces, and lovely flashing eyes which God had made ; and danced with their gray-jacketed escorts, their little feet slipped in their little slippers, many of which were high-heeled and faded with age, having belonged to their mothers, and grandmothers—even great-grandmothers—and enjoyed it all as much as ever the former wearers of the slippers did in their full glory of satin and lace. For of such is the Kingdom of Youth.

The Yankee officers attended, very dignified, and were treated politely, but not warmly, of course, only just so civilly as to show that Southerners knew what was due to guests even when they were enemies ; but not so warmly as to let them forget that they were foes.

This, however, made little difference to the young men, for the civility which it was felt was " their due as guests" was sufficient to make a marked contrast with a past in which not a soul in petticoats had noticed them, and the girls were pretty enough to satisfy them at first, even if there was no other privilege conferred than merely that primal right of the cat in the proverb. Everyone, however, meant to be civil, and for the time, at least, at peace.

But there was more than this ; the night was perfect ; the breath of flowers and shrubbery came in through the open windows ; the moon was almost at her full, and her soft light was lying on the grass, mantling the trees, and filling the night with that amber mellowness which sometimes comes in summer, and seems to bring a special peacefulness.

The camp lay hidden in the distance, and the throng in the streets hung on the fences, listening to the music, or laughed and danced in full sympathy with the occasion.

Steve Allen constituted himself the especial host of the two officers. It was by him that Middleton and Thurston were introduced to most of the girls, and to the older ladies, who sat at the end of the room farthest from the music, their eyes, filled with light, following their daughters or others whose success was near to their hearts, or, like Miss Thomasia, beaming a benediction on the whole throng of happy dancers.

Still, an hour after the dancing began, the one person whom Middleton particularly wished to meet had not appeared, and Middleton, who had been planning for a week what he should say to Miss Cary, found himself with a vague feeling of dissatisfaction. Little Thurston was capering around as if to the manner born ; perspiring at every pore ; paying attention to half the girls in the room, and casting glances at Miss Dockett languishing enough, as Middleton said, to lay the foundation for a breach of promise suit. But Middleton could not get into the spirit of the occasion. He asked a number of girls to dance, but they were all "engaged," and politely showed their cards. So Middleton fell back. General Legaie, and the other older gentlemen courteously drew him into their conversation, and the General rallied him, with an old bachelor's license, on not dancing, declaring that the sight of such girls was the true fountain of youth ; but the young Captain was not in the mood for fun. A vague feeling of unrest was on him. The order that Leech had mentioned ; the Pro-

vost's positive manner ; the warning that he had given ;
the covert threat he had dared to employ, all began to
recur to Middleton and worry him.   He felt that he would
be responsible if any trouble should occur.   He went out
and walked through the village.   A light was shining under
the door of Leech's office ; but all was as it had been: good-
humor everywhere.   The moonlight soothed him and the
pleasant greetings as he passed served to restore his good-
humor, and he returned to the ball.   As he did so an old
high-backed carriage, which he thought he recognized,
made its way slowly past him.   The driver was explaining
to someone who walked beside him the cause of his delay.

"Dat fool hoss—you can't git him in de water to save
your life.   He'll breck ev'ything to pieces fust.   But my
young Mistis, she's dyah now, an' she's de queen on 'em all,
I tell you.   You go dyah an' look at her th'oo de winder,"
he wound up with a proud laugh.

As Middleton re-entered the ball-room there was quite a
group near the door surrounding someone who was the
centre of attraction, and whom Captain Allen was teasing.

"Oh! You'll dance with him.   He left because you
had not come, but I have sent for him.   He's saved a set
expressly for you."

"I won't.   He has done no such thing, and I won't
dance with you either, unless you go away and let me
alone."   The voice was a charming one.

"I'll bet you do.   I understand why you made old
Gideon drive you up the stream that evening ; but you
can't expect him to be mooning on the bank of every creek
in the county, you know——"

"That settles it for you, Steve," said the voice over behind the heads.   "Jack, I have the seventh dance with
you as well as the first and fourth," she called to Jacquelin
who was seated against the wall, his crutches beside him.

"Jack never was any hand at arithmetic, and besides
he can't dance," declared Allen, as his friend professed his
gratitude.

Just then Allen caught sight of Middleton, over the heads of the others.

"Ah! here—Captain Middleton, I want to present you to my cousin, Miss Blair Cary, who wishes to know how you happened not to be—" He caught his cousin's eye, and changed his speech "—who has a question to ask you. Captain Middleton—Miss Cary." The others made way for Middleton, and he stepped forward and bowed low.

She was all in white, and was blazing with brass buttons. They were her only ornaments, except a single old jewel consisting of a ruby surrounded by diamonds. She wore bracelets of the buttons on her arms, and a necklace of larger ones on a band around her white throat. A broad belt of them girdled her little waist.

As Middleton bowed, he caught her eye and the same look of mingled defiance and amusement which he remembered so well at the ford. He hardly knew whether to laugh or be grave, and was conscious that he was growing red, as her look changed into one of triumph. He remained grave, however, and rallied enough to ask her for a dance. She bowed. They were all engaged.

"I have the seventh—to sit out, I believe?" said Jacquelin Gray maliciously, from his seat, for Steve's benefit. Miss Blair looked at her card;—then to Jacquelin:

"You only *believe?* As you have forgotten so far as to have a doubt about it, the seventh is *not* engaged," said the young coquette, with a curtsey. She turned. "I will give it to you, Captain Middleton." She looked at Jacquelin and with a little—only the least little toss of the head, took the arm of a young man who had just claimed his set, and bowing to Middleton moved off, leaving both Steve and Jacquelin looking a trifle blank.

"That girl's the most unaccountable creature that ever was on earth," growled Jacquelin. "I'll be hanged if I'll be treated so!" He looked across the room after her floating form.

"Go slow, old man, go slow," said Steve. "You'll be

treated that way and come again for more.   And you
know you will."

Jacquelin growled.   He knew in his heart it was true.

Middleton thought that the seventh set would never
come, but, like everything else in life, it came at last, and
though there were three claimants for it, the one who
was the final judge decided for Middleton and walked
off with him, calmly leaving both the other aspirants
fuming and scowling.

"You can't fight him Jack," said Steve with a laugh to
his cousin, who was muttering to himself, "because I'd
first have to fight you, you know."

Having thus punished both her admirers, Miss Cary
declined to dance—whether to keep her word ; to avoid
pleasing too much the young Federal Captain, or to soothe
the ruffled spirits of his unsuccessful competitors, who may
tell ?   For no one can thread the mazes of a girl's caprice.

But this made little difference to Middleton.   They
strolled outside and found a seat.   The moonlight appeared to Middleton more charming than he ever remembered it, and he discovered something which he had
never known before.   He wanted to please this girl as he
never recalled having wanted to please any other, and he
was conscious that it was a difficult, if not an impossible
task.   It was as though he lay in face of a foe, one who
appeared at the outset stronger than he.   Yet she did not
appear to be attempting anything.   She was simply in
opposition to him, that was all.   She appeared so unaf-
fected and simple that, remembering what he had just
seen of her coquetry, he wondered if she could be as
natural as she seemed to be.   Her gaze was so direct, her
voice so placid, her manner so self-possessed, that he felt
she had the advantage of him.   And all the time he
wanted to please her.

In the course of their conversation she spoke of her
brother.

Middleton had not remembered that she had a brother.

"Where is he ?" he asked.

"He was killed." She spoke very quietly.

"Oh !" he said, softly. "I beg your pardon."

"He was killed at Jacquelin Gray's side, and Jacquelin brought his body out under fire—just as Steve afterward tried to bring Jack." She sighed deeply, and her eyes seemed to say, "You can understand now ?"

Middleton had a strange sensation. He had never before looked in the eyes of a woman whose brother had been killed, possibly by his command. He hated Jacquelin, but in a way he was grateful to him too ; for it was the first time Miss Cary had softened at all.

"I believe that all your men went in the army," he said, feeling about for a new subject.

"Of course."

"And some of your ladies ?" he smiled.

"All of them." Up went her head again.

"I wonder that you were ever conquered ?"

"Conquered ! We were not conquered." She looked it, as she stood there in the moonlight. Middleton had a sudden thrill that it would be worth his life to win such a girl, and she had never given him even one friendly glance. He could not help thinking,

"What would Thurston say ?"

A partner came and claimed his set, and Middleton was left outside. He sat for a moment thinking how lonely her departure had made the place. He had never felt this way about any other girl. Just then a strange sound, like distant shouting, came through the stillness. Middleton rose and strolled down to the gate. There were fewer people in the street. A man came hurrying along and spoke to another. His voice was so excited that it arrested Middleton's attention, and he caught the last of his sentence.

"It ought to be broke up at once. Go in there and call Captain Allen and McRaffle out."

"What's that ?" asked Middleton, walking out of the gate, and up to him

" A nigger-meetin' down yonder," answered the man,
sullenly.   " If it ain't broken up there'll be trouble.
Leech started it by reading a paper he had, tellin' 'em the
Gov'ment wants the party broke up, and then he put
Sherrod up, and now that yaller nigger, Dr. Moses, is up.
Leech's been givin' 'em liquor, and unless it's stopped
there'll be the devil to pay."

" I'll see about it," said Middleton.   He walked rapidly
down in the direction the man had indicated.   He was
sensible, as he passed along, of some change, and, presently,
the distant sound of a man speaking at the top of his voice
came to him, followed shortly by a roar of applause.   He
hurried on and passed a group of half a dozen white men,
some of whom were advocating sending for " reinforce-
ments," as they said, while others were insisting that they
should go right in on them at once.   All were united as
to one thing : that the meeting ought to be stopped.

" If we don't," said one, " there'll be trouble, and we
might's well do it at once.   I can do it by myself."

Some one said something about " the Yankee officers."

" Yankees be blanked ! " said the other.   " Wasn't it
that scoundrel Leech as started it all ?   He's been workin'
it up all day.   I got wind of it up at home ; — that's the
reason I come down.   We've got to do it ourselves."   It
was Andy Stamper.

Just then they saw Middleton and followed him, offering
their advice and services.   All they wanted was authority.

When Middleton arrived, he agreed with them that the
speaking ought to be stopped at once.   He had never seen
such a sight.   The entire negro population of the place
appeared to be packed there, moaning and singing, hug-
ging each other and shouting, whilst Moses, the negro he
had ordered to leave town, was on the platform, tossing
his arms in a sort of frenzy and calling on them to rise
and prove they were the chosen people.   " God had
brought their enemies all together in one place," he cried,
" and all that was needed was for Samson to arise and

prove his strength.　Their deliverer was at hand.　" Ain't
you heah dat de wud done come from de New Jerusalem,
an' ain't my name Moses—Moses ?　Moses is my name !" he
shouted, intoning the words in a sort of wild frenzy.　The
shout that greeted him proved the danger of his course.

"D—n him, I'll stop his mouth," said one of the young
men, pushing his way through the throng, but Middleton
was before him.　He forced his way, followed by the
others, through the crowd which gave way before him
at his command, and, when still some yards away from the
platform, he ordered the speaker to cease.　But Moses was
either too drunk or too excited to heed, and went on
shouting his singsong.

"I'll lead you to de burnin' bush," he cried.　"I'll
give you de promise lan'."　As it happened, a man
standing in the crowd had a carriage-whip in his hand.
The Captain snatched it from him and sprang on the platform, and the next instant was raining on the would-be
prophet and leader such a thrashing as he had never had
in his life.　The effect was miraculous.　The first lash of
the heavy whip took the preacher by surprise and dazed
him ; the second recalled him to himself and stripped his
prophetic character from him, leaving him nothing but a
whining, miserable creature, who was trying to deceive and
mislead others as miserable and more ignorant than himself.

As the Captain laid the blows on fast and thick, Moses
cringed and finally broke and fled from the platform, followed by the jeers and shouts of the crowd who had just
been ready to follow him in any violence, if, indeed, he
would have had the courage to lead them.　And when the
irate officer appeared ready to turn his whip on them, and
did accompany his peremptory order that they should disperse at once, with a few contemptuous lashes at those
nearest him, they broke and ran with as much good-humor
as they had shown an hour previously, when they were dancing and shuffling in the street, before Leech and his agents
got hold of them.

CHAPTER XV

THE next day there was much stir in the county, at least
about the court-house, and it was known that Middleton
had summoned Leech before him and had had an interview
with him, which rumor said was stormy, and that it had
ended by the Provost being sent to his room, it was said,
under arrest.

So much was certain, Middleton after this took charge
of matters which up to this time Leech had been attending
to, and Leech remained out of sight until he left the place,
which he did two days later. One of the first steps Middleton took was to summon the negroes before him and
give them a talk. And he closed his speech by a warning
that they should keep order wherever they were, declaring,
that if there were any repetition of Moses's performance
of the previous night the offender would not escape so
easily.

The effect of his act was admirable. By nightfall nearly
every negro who was not employed about the county seat
had left, and within two days many of them were at work,
back at their old homes.

Middleton found himself suddenly as popular as he had
formerly been unpopular, receiving visits and invitations
from half the gentlemen in the place, so that Thurston
said it was just the old story: he set the triggers and
worked everything, and Middleton just walked in and
took the game.

" **Here** I have been working like a nigger," he said to

Middleton, "watching around and following that fellow
Leech in all his rascality; displaying the most consummate
qualities of leadership, and singing my head off, and you
happen to come along, pick up a driver's whip and let into
a drunken rascal, talk a lot of rot next morning, and in
five minutes do what I with all my genius haven't been
able to do in as many months.   It's the old story, Larry,
it's fate !   What did I tell you ?   Long legs are worth
more to a man than a long head.   But, Larry, look out
for Leech.   He's a blood-sucker.   Tra-la ; I have an engagement.   Might as well get some of the good of your
glory, old man, while it lasts, you know.   Beauty fadeth
as a flower."   And leaving Middleton over his report, the
cheery little Lieutenant went off to have a ride with Miss
Dockett, who, in view of certain professions of his and proceedings of his Captain's the night before, had honored
him so far as to vouchsafe him that privilege.

Reely Thurston's half humorous warning to his friend
was not without foundation, as both he and Middleton
knew, and within a week the Captain was up to his ears in
reports and correspondence relative to his conduct in the
county.

The quietness of everything around him was a fact to
which he pointed with pride ; the restoration of order
throughout the county was a proof of the wisdom of
his course.   Crime had diminished ; order had been restored ; good feeling had grown up ; the negroes had returned to work, and were getting regular wages.   They
were already beginning to save a little and some were buying land.   The whites had accepted the status of affairs
in good faith and were, he believed, turning all their
energies to meet the exigencies of the time in the best way
they could.   In a word, peace was fully restored in the
territory under his command.   He congratulated himself
that he was able to state a condition of affairs so entirely
in accord with the observation of the commander-in-chief
of the armies, who about that time visited the State and

made a similar report on it. Even Reely Thurston commended Middleton's report, and confided to Miss Dockett, who was beginning to receive such confidences more graciously of late, that "Larry had somewhere, in that high head of his, a deuced lot of brains," a compliment which the young Captain would have taken more gratefully from him than from any other soul on earth.

Another cause of content was just then beginning to have its effect on Middleton. Miss Cary was beginning to treat him with some degree of Christian charity, and actually condescended to take a ride with him on horseback, and when he proved himself sufficiently appreciative of this honor, took another.

So things went, and before the summer evenings were over, the young Captain had ridden to the point where he had given Blair Cary all the confidences which a young man in his twenties is likely to give the prettiest girl in his circle of acquaintance, especially when she is the only one whose eyes soften a little at the recital, and who responds a bit by giving just a little of her own. Not that Miss Cary for a moment allowed Middleton to forget that on the one great subject always present, the world stretched between them. They were enemies. Between them there was never more than a truce. She would be his friend while it lasted ; but never more. That was all ! Her skirmish-line, so to speak, exchanged courtesies with his ; but, on the first suggestion of a signal, sprang to her rifle-pits.

She always wore, when she rode, a gray cap, which Middleton, without asking any questions, knew had been her brother's. It was a badge, and the young man recognized it as such. She still wore her brass buttons, and would never give him one of them. One afternoon, as they were returning from a ride in which he had told her all about Ruth Welch, dwelling somewhat on their cousinship, they stopped at the ford where he had gone to Blair's rescue the day her horse fell, and he asked her casually if she would give him one of the buttons to save

12

his life. She quietly said "No," and he believed her. Yet this made little difference to the young man. He was not in love with her, he was sure. He only enjoyed her. And the summer evenings which he spent at Birdwood, or riding with her through the arching woods, were the pleasantest he had ever known. As they watered their horses at the ford that afternoon no less than four other couples came riding up on their way home, and there was quite a little levee held in the limpid stream, Middleton finding himself taken into the talk and raillery quite as a member of the circle. The far-off call of ploughmen to their teams in the low-grounds of Red Rock and the distant lowing of cattle in the pastures came muffled on the soft air, while a woodlark in the woods along the waterside sang its brilliant song to its tardy mate with a triumph born only of security and peace. As Captain Middleton looked at the faded gray coats and his blue one, the numbers doubled by the reflection in the placid stream, and listened to the laughter about him, he could not but think what a picture and proof of peace it was. And Miss Cary was the prettiest girl in the party.

Suddenly one of the horses became restive, and slashed away at the nearest horse to him. Blair, in pulling her horse out of the way, got under an overhanging bough and her cap was knocked from her head into the water. She gave a little cry of dismay as it floated down the stream, and at her call more than one of the young men turned his horse to recover the cap ; but Middleton was nearest, and he spurred straight into the deep water below the ledge and swam for the cap, reaching it just before the others got it. He was pleased at the applause he received when he returned.

Miss Cary only said "thank you," as she might have said it if he had picked the cap from the floor.

Not all the county people, however, acquiesced so entirely in receiving Middleton on so friendly a basis; some did not see why a Yankee officer should be taken up as a friend.

There was one young man who did not appreciate at least Middleton's mode of exhibiting his friendliness. Steve and Middleton had become very good friends ; but Jacquelin Gray, as jealous as Othello, grew more and more reserved toward the young officer, and began to give himself many airs about his attentions to Blair Cary. If anything, this only incited Blair to show Middleton greater favor, and at last the young lady gave Jacquelin to understand that she intended to do just as she pleased and did not propose to be held accountable by him for anything whatever.

The evening of the ride on which Blair lost her cap and Middleton recovered it for her, Jacquelin had driven over "to see the doctor," he said, and found her gone off with Middleton. As Dr. Cary was away, visiting his patients, which Jacquelin might have known, and Mrs. Cary was confined to her room that day, Jacquelin was left to himself and had plenty of time as he sat on the porch all alone, to chew the cud of bitter fancy, and reflect on the caprices of a part of the human race. He was not much consoled when Mammy Krenda came out and, with kindly sympathy, said :

"You too late—you better make haste an' git off dem crutches, honey, and git 'pon horseback. Crutches can't keep up with horses." She disappeared within and Jacquelin was left in a flame of jealousy. By the time Blair arrived he was in just the state of mind to make a fool of himself. When Jacquelin began the interview, he, perhaps, had no idea of going as far as his heat carried him ; but unhappily he lost his head—or as much of a head as a man can have who is deeply in love and, having gone to see his sweetheart, finds her off riding with a rival.

It was quite dusk when the riders rode slowly up the avenue. They stopped at the gate, and Jacquelin could hear Blair's cordial invitation to her companion to come in and take supper with them. Middleton declined.

"But I'm afraid you will catch cold, riding so far in wet clothes," she urged. He, however, had to return immediately, he declared, and after a few more words he galloped off, while Blair came on to the house.

"Why, Jacquelin! You here all by yourself!" she exclaimed. She bent over him quickly to prevent his rising for her. Had Jacquelin been cool enough to note her voice it might have saved him; but he was not even looking at her. His manner hauled her up short, and the next instant hers had changed. She seated herself and tried for a few moments to be light and divert him. She told of the episode at the ford. Jacquelin, however, was not to be diverted, and, taking the silence which presently fell on her for a confession, he began to assume a bolder tone, and proceeded to take her to task for her conduct.

"It was an outrage—an outrage on—Steve. It was shameful," he said, "that with such a man as Steve offering his heart to her, she should be boldly encouraging a Yankee officer, so that everybody in the county was talking about it." It was when he said it was an outrage on Steve that the explosion came. Blair was on her feet in a second.

"Jacquelin!" she exclaimed, with a gasp. The next second she had found her voice. He had never seen her as she became. It was a new Blair standing above him, tall and straight in the dusk, her frame trembling, her voice vibrating. She positively flamed with indignation, not because of the charge, but against him for making it.

"Whose business is it?" she asked him, with glowing cheeks and flashing eyes. If her father and mother did not object, had he a right to interfere? If Steve were not satisfied, could not he take care of himself? Who had given him such a right? And before Jacquelin could recover from his surprise, she had burst into tears and rushed into the house.

Jacquelin drove home in black despair. He had been put wholly in the wrong, and yet he felt that he had had right originally on his side. His whole past appeared suddenly rooted up; his whole future destroyed by this newcomer, this hostile interloper. How he would love to have some cause of personal quarrel with him ! How gladly he would put it all to the test of one meeting. Yet what had Middleton done but win fairly ! and he had been a gentleman always. Jacquelin was forced to admit this. But oh ! if he only had a just cause of quarrel ! Let him look out hereafter. But—if he were to meet him and he should fall, what would be the consequence ? He would only have ruined Blair's happiness and have destroyed his only hope. He almost ground his teeth at his helplessness as he drove home through the dusk. He did not know that at that moment Blair Cary, with locked door, was sobbing in her little white-curtained room, her anger no longer turned against him, but against herself.

When Jacquelin awoke the next morning it was with a sinking at the heart. Blair was lost to him forever. Daylight, however, is a great restorer of courage, and, little by little, his spirits revived, until by evening he began to consider himself a most ill-used person, and to fancy Blair suing for pardon. He even found himself nursing an idea that she would write a note ; but instead of that, he heard that Middleton had been up to see her again, and once more his heart sank and his anger rose. He would show her that he was not to be trampled on and insulted as she had done.

When Middleton arrived at the court-house the afternoon of his ride, he found an order transferring his company to a frontier post in the far Northwest. They were to leave immediately.

The same train by which the old company was to go was to bring its successor.

The afternoon before his company left, Middleton rode up to Birdwood. He had given no one any notice, and he arrived unexpectedly. No one was in sight. The lawn appeared as deserted as if it were in the heart of a wilderness. The trees were as quiet as if Nature herself were asleep, and the sound of a dove cooing far down in the grove only intensified the quietude. Tying his horse,

Middleton walked up through the grove. As he passed along he happened to cast his eyes in the direction of the little double building, which was off to one side at some distance back of the dwelling, and seeing the old mammy enter one of the doors he turned that way, thinking that she might come out, and he would ask if the family were at home. He stopped in front of the nearest door and looked in. It was the kitchen, and he was facing, not the mammy—who as a matter of fact, had entered another door—but Miss Cary herself. She was dressed in a white dress, and her skirt was turned back and pinned about her slender waist; her sleeves were rolled up, showing her round, white arms. She was busy with a bread-tray. Middleton would have drawn back, but Blair looked up and their eyes met. There was a moment of half embarrassment, and Middleton was about to draw back and apologize for his intrusion, but before he could do so she came forward, smiling.

"Won't you come in ?" she said, "or will you walk into the house ? " The color had mounted to her cheeks, and the half mocking smile had still a little embarrassment in it ; but Middleton thought she had never looked so charming. His heart gave a bound.

"Can you doubt what I will do ? " He stepped over the high threshold. "Even if I be but scullion——"

"You must have been taking lessons from the General. Here—no one was ever allowed in here who would not work." She gave him a rolling-pin, and he set to work with it industriously.

"This comes of your doing," she said, still smiling. "I am the only cook left. Why don't you detail me one ? If you were worth a button you would."

"How would I do ?" hazarded Middleton. "I'm a pretty good cook."

"Aunt Betty wouldn't have let you come into the kitchen if you handled your rolling-pin that way. Let me show you."

"Which is the best argument yet for the change of cooks," said Middleton, guilefully holding the rolling-pin more and more awkwardly, for the very pleasure of being set right by her. "Now, don't you think I am worth a button?"

"No, but you may learn."

"Unfortunately, I am going away."

"Are you?—When are you coming back?"—A polite little tone coming into her voice.

"Never." He tried to say it as indifferently as he had said it in practising when he rode up, which he liked better than the tragic "NEVER!" which he had first proposed to himself; and all the time he was watching her out of the tail of his eye. She said nothing, and he felt a little disappointed.

"We are ordered away—" he began. She was busying herself about something. But he was sure she had heard. "—to the Northwest to keep the Indians down," he proceeded.

"Oh!" She turned quickly toward him, and their eyes met.

"Well, I hope you'll be as successful and find your task as pleasant there as you have here." Her head had gone up, as it did on the veranda the night of the ball.

"I do not appear to have been particularly successful here," Middleton began, banteringly, then walked over to her side. "Miss Cary, do you think I have really enjoyed my task here?"

"Why—yes," she began; then she glanced up and found him grave. "I don't know—I thought——"

"No," said Middleton, "you did not."

Just at that moment a shadow fell across the light, and Mammy Krenda stood in the door.

"Well—I declare!" she exclaimed, with well-feigned astonishment. "What in the worl' air you doin' in this kitchen?"

They both thought she was addressing Middleton, and

he began to stammer a reply; but it was her young mistress whose presence there appeared to scandalize the old woman.

"Don't you know you ain' got no business in heah? I can't turn my back to git nothin', but what you come interferin' wid my things. Go right in de house dis minute and put yo' nice clo'es on. I air really ashamed o' you to let a gent—a—anybody see you dat way." She was pushing Blair out gently. "I don' know what she air doin' in heah," she said to Middleton, addressing him for the first time, and with some disdain in her manner, as if she wished him to understand that he had no business there either.

As Blair passed him on her way out she said to him in a whisper, with a low laugh:

"That's a yarn. I do nearly all the cooking since our cook went off, but she thinks it's beneath my dignity to be caught at it."

They did not go into the house, but walked over through the grove and sat down on the grass on the farther slope overlooking the rolling lands, with the blue spurs in the distance. There Middleton threw himself at Blair's feet. He had made up his mind to stake all before he left. As the old mammy passed from the kitchen to the house she made a little detour and cast a glance through the grove. The glint of a white dress through the trees caught her eye, and she gave a little sniff as she went on.

An hour later, Middleton, his face as grave as it had ever been in battle, mounted his horse and rode away without returning to the house, and Blair Cary walked back through the grove alone. She turned across to the smaller house which the old mammy occupied. It was empty, and she entered and flung herself on the snowy counterpaned bed.

The old woman came in a moment later. She gave the girl a swift glance, and, turning to the window, dropped the white curtain to shut out the slanting afternoon sun.

"'Taint no use to 'sturb yo'self, honey; he ain' gone,"

she said, sympathizingly. "He comin' back jest so sho' as I live."

"He *has* gone," said Blair, suddenly, with some vehemence. "I have sent him away. I wish he had never come." But was she thinking of Middleton?

The old woman had turned and was looking down at her from where she stood.

"An' I glad you is," she said. "I ain't like Yankees, no way. Dat deah Leech man——"

"Mammy," said Blair, rising, "I do not wish you to speak so of a gentleman—who—who has been our guest."

"Yes, honey, dat's so," said the old woman, simply, without the least surprise. "Mammy, won't say no more about him. What I got to do wid abusin' a gent'man, no-how!"

"Oh! Mammy!" said the girl, throwing her arms about her, and the old woman only said:

"Yes, honey—yes—yes. But don't you pester yoreself. 'T'll all come right."

Next evening the news that Middleton and his company were ordered away was known. Jacquelin was conscious of his heart giving a bound of joy. He would be only cool and chilling to Blair and show her by his manner how disapprovingly he regarded her conduct. After a little, this mood changed and he began to think it would be more manly to be only very dignified and yet show her that he was above harboring little feelings. He would be generous and forgive her. When, however, he met Blair, she was so far from showing any contrition, that she was actually savage to him; so that instead of having an opportunity to display his lofty feelings, Jacquelin found himself thrown into a situation of the strongest hostility to her, and after a lifetime of friendship they scarcely spoke. Their friends tried to patch up the quarrel, but in vain. Jacquelin felt himself now really aggrieved, and Blair declined to allow even the mention of him. Her severity toward him was almost incomprehensible.

CHAPTER XVI

THE NEW TROOP MEETS THE ENEMY

THE difference between the old company and the new one which came in its place, was marked in many ways besides color, and the latter had not been in the county an hour before the people knew that the struggle was on, and set themselves to prepare for it.

The evening of the arrival of the new company, Jerry entered Captain Allen's office somewhat hastily, and busied himself with suspicious industry. Presently Steve looked at him amusedly.

"Well, what do you want now?—grandmother dead again? If you get drunk I'll thrash you within an inch of your life."

Jerry giggled.

"Done sent a company o' niggers heah," he announced, with something very like a grin as he cut his eyes at his master.

"Negroes—hey?" Steve's expression did not change a particle, and Jerry looked disappointed. If anything, there was a little more light in Steve's eyes, but they were gazing out of the window, and Jerry could not see them.

"Leech back?" asked Mr. Allen, indifferently.

"Don' know, suh—I'll fine out." The look on Jerry's face once more became pleasant.

Just then the sound of a distant bugle came in at the window, and Steve rose and walked to the door of his office. The doors of several other offices were filled about the same moment. Steve walked down to the fence in front of the court green, and stood leaning against it listlessly, watching

186

as the company came up the road, with bugle blowing, dust
rising, and a crowd of young negroes running beside them.

"Halt!" The Captain, a stout, red-faced man, turned
his horse, and waved his sword to the negroes in the road.
"Pull that fence down." He indicated the panel where
Steve stood, adding a string of oaths to stir the negroes
from their dulness. A dozen men jumped toward the
fence. Steve never budged an inch. With his arms resting on the rail, he looked the Captain in the eye calmly,
then looked at the negroes before him, and kept his place.
Except for a slight dilatation of the nostrils he might not
have known that there was a soldier within a hundred
miles. The men hesitated a second, then, just as the Captain began to swear again, ran to the next panel and tore
it down even with the ground, dragging the posts out of
their holes, and making a wide breach through which the
company passed into the court-yard to the old camp which
Middleton's company had occupied.

As Steve turned away he said to a man near him :
"Seventy-nine negroes, and three white men. We can
manage them. Jerry, saddle my horse, and find out when
Leech is coming back—and where Captain McRaffle is."

"Yes, suh," and Jerry, with a shrewd look, disappeared.

When Jerry returned, his master was writing, and as he
did not look up, Jerry went into the inner room, and
shortly brought out a pair of saddle-bags, and a pair of
pistols.

Steve had just finished his letters, and was sealing them.
Jerry gave his report.

"Nor, suh, he ain' come yet ; but dee's 'spectin' of him,
de Cap'n says. Cap'n McRaffle, he's away, too."

"I thought as much. Take this letter over to the General. These two are for Mr. Hurley and Mr. Garden. If
I'm not here, come up to Dr. Cary's to-morrow morning."

"Yes, suh—yo' horse is in de stable. I'll take de saddle
bags over dyah."

Steve buckled one pistol on under his coat, put the other

in his saddle-bags, and went out. He sauntered across to where the company was pitching camp. The throng of negroes was already increasing. A tall, black sergeant, with great pompousness, was superintending the placing of the lines, cursing and damning his men, with much importance, for the benefit of the crowd around. Sweeping the crowd aside, Steve walked right up to him.

"Boy, where's your Captain ?" The Sergeant turned and faced him. Perhaps, had Steve been ten feet off the soldier might have been insolent ; but Captain Allen was close up to him, and there was that about him, and the tone of command in which he spoke, which demanded obedience. The Sergeant instinctively pointed to the other side of the camp.

"Go and tell him that Captain Allen wishes to speak to him. Go on." Impelled by the tone of authority, the imperative gesture, and the evident impression made on the crowd, the Sergeant moved off, with Steve at his heels.

"Dat's one o' my young marsters—he wuz a gret soldier," said one of the old negroes just outside the camp to a squad near him.

Steve and the Sergeant found the Captain sitting against a tree smoking. He was a heavy-looking man, with a red face. Steve took in the familiarity with which the Sergeant addressed him, and governed himself accordingly.

"Here, boy—" Steve gave the negro a five-dollar note, not the less coolly because it was his last ; thanked him as he would have done any other servant, only, perhaps, with a little more condescension, and addressed himself to the officer.

"Captain, I am Captain Allen, and I have come to have an understanding with you at the outset."

Perhaps, his very assurance stood him in stead. Had he been a victor dictating terms he could not have done it more coolly.

"You have seventy-nine men and three officers—I have ten times as many."

"Major Leech—told me—" began the Captain.

"Your Major Leech is a liar, and a coward, and you will find it so. We propose to obey the laws, but we do not mean to be governed by negroes, and if you attempt it you will commit a great mistake." He walked back through the camp inspecting the horses, leaving the other to wonder who and what he could be.

Ten minutes later the officer had called a guard, but Steve was already riding out the back lane toward the upper part of the county.

Leech arrived on the next train after that which brought the new troops. He opened a law office in a part of the building occupied by his commissary, and announced himself as a practitioner of the law, as well as the Provost of the county.

He had evidently strengthened his hands during his absence. Krafton, who appeared now to be the chief authority in the State, was in constant communication with him.

Leech boasted openly that he had had Middleton's company removed, and he began to exercise new functions. The new company seemed to be under his authority.

Within a few weeks Dr. Cary and the other civil officers in the county received notices from Leech vacating their commissions on the ground, among others, that they had exceeded their powers. Still was appointed Justice of the Peace in place of Dr. Cary, and Nicholas Ash was made Constable. Their services were not in immediate requisition, however, as, for the time being, Leech appeared to prefer to exercise his military, rather than his civil, powers. He began, forthwith, to send out the soldiers in squads on tours throughout the county, partly to distribute rations, and partly to patrol the country.

They had not been at this business long when they began bullying and tyrannizing over the people and terrorizing them as far as possible. At first, they devoted their energies principally to the whites, and the negroes were both impressed and affected by their power and insolence

But after more than one of the marauders were shot, they began to go in large parties, and soon turned their energies against the negroes as well as against the former masters, and were quickly almost as obnoxious to the blacks as to the whites. Their action caused intense excitement in the county.

Steve Allen had almost abandoned his law practice, or at least his office, and spent his time visiting about in the adjoining counties. Leech took it as a sign of timidity and breathed the freer that the insolent young lawyer was away.

"I mean to drive him and that Jacquelin Gray out of the county," he boasted to Still. "I'll make it too hot for him."

"Wish you could," answered Still, devoutly. "But don't you go too fast. They ain't the sort to drive easy. They was taken up late. And if you push 'em too hard there'll be trouble."

Leech sneered. He wished Allen would do something so he might get his hand on him.

"You don't mean nothin' to *you?* 'Cause if he got his hand on you first——"

"No—I ain't afraid of him. He ain't such a fool as to do anything to me. I am the Government of the United States!" The Provost puffed out his bosom, and with a look of satisfaction glanced at himself in a mirror.

"He ain't afeared of the Gov'ment or nothin' else. I wish he was," declared Still, sincerely.

"Well, he'd better be," asserted Leech. "As soon as I get things straight, I mean to make him give an account of himself."

Someone soon gave an account of himself. A considerable party of the men of the negro troop, under command of a sergeant, was "raiding," one afternoon, in the upper end of the county, when an incident occurred which had a signal effect on both the company and the county. They had already "raided" several places on their tour and were on their way home, their saddle-bows

ornamented with the trophies of their rapacity: from sheep
to ladies' bonnets, when toward sunset they stopped near
the edge of the Red Rock plantation, at a roadside store,
of which Mr. Andy Stamper had recently become the owner.
Mr. Stamper was absent, and the store was in charge
of his agent, an old soldier named Michael.

The men demanded liquor.   They took all they wanted,
and called in a number of negroes and made them
drunk also.   Old Waverley, who had come to the store
to make some little purchases, was sitting on a block,
smoking.   Him they tried to induce to drink too, and
when he declined, they hustled him a good deal and
finally kicked him out into the road.   He was a "worthless old fool who didn't deserve to be free," they said.
Then in their drunken folly they began to talk of going
to Red Rock and ordering supper before returning to
camp.   It would be a fine thing to take possession of that
big house and have supper, and they would raid Stamper's
also on the way.   They knew all about both places, and
declared that they ought both to be burnt down.   Meantime, they demanded more liquor, which the storekeeper
seemed suddenly ready to furnish.   He made a sign to old
Waverley, and the latter slipped off and took a path
through the woods.   The nearest place was a little homestead on the roadside, belonging to a man named Deals;
but there was no one there but a woman; her husband
had gone up to Mr. Stamper's, she told Waverley.   So
warning her as to the squad of negroes, the old man set
out as hard as he could for home.   Before he was through
the woods, however, he met Rupert, riding down to the
store on his colt, a handsome gray, and to him he gave
notice, telling him that the store-keeper was doing what
he could to hold the men there.   Rupert wheeled his
horse, and was off like a shot, and when Waverley
emerged from the woods, he saw the boy a half mile away,
dashing up—not to Red Rock; but to the Stamper place,
which stood out, off to one side, clear on its little hill, a

straight column of smoke going up in the still evening air. It seemed to the old man that there were a number of horses standing about in the yard, and it occurred to him to wonder if the soldiers could possibly have gotten there already. If so, his young master would be in danger of being hurt. But if the horsemen were soldiers they did not remain long; for in a few minutes Waverley saw a number of men mount and the whole party ride rapidly away down the hill, with Rupert on his gray colt among them. Waverley caught one more glimpse of the riders as they disappeared at a gallop in the wood, going in the direction of the store, and then he hurried on to Red Rock, where he found everything quiet.

Jacquelin was ill in bed that day, and Steve Allen had left the house about noon. Rupert had gone to the store for the mail. Waverley did not tell anything about having seen Rupert go off with the men from Stamper's; but he turned and hurried back to the store, thinking now only of Rupert. He had not gone far when he heard a shot or two fired, and then on a sudden a dozen or more. The old fellow broke into a run. When he reached the edge of the woods from which he could see the Deals's homestead he stopped appalled.

A half dozen negroes lay on the ground dead or dying, and a half dozen young white men, among them Captain McRaffle, were engaged either reloading their pistols or talking. Rupert was sitting on his horse at a little distance.

The little company of men Waverley had seen were a few who had gathered together on hearing of the raid that was taking place in the neighborhood that day. They too had heard of the contemplated visit to Red Rock and the Stamper place; for Jerry had got from someone that morning a hint that a descent was to be made on these places.

Shortly after Waverley had left the store the squad of soldiers had started for Red Rock; but, thinking to make

a clean sweep as they went, they had stopped at the little
house on the way, where Waverley had warned the woman
and where there was a well, to take another drink. They
were engaged in the pleasant amusement of looting this
place, shooting chickens, etc., when the company that
Waverley had seen ride off from Stamper's came upon them.
It was well for Mrs. Deals that the young men arrived when
they did, for the troopers were tired of merely destroying
property, and just as the white men rode up they had
seized her. Her scream hastened the rescuing party.
No one knew for a long time who composed the party ;
for in five minutes every one of the raiders was stretched on
the ground, and the two or three neighborhood-negroes
who were with them were sworn to secrecy under threats
which they feared too much to wish to break their oaths.

There was excitement enough in the county that night,
and when the news reached the court-house, which, owing
to the picketing of the roads, it did not do till next morning, the citizens were prepared for the consequences. The
comrades of the dead men swore they would burn the village and carry fire and sword through the county ; but it
was too grave a matter to be carried through too heed-
lessly. The officers suddenly awoke to the gravity of the
situation, which was well for them. They were, no doubt,
aided in doing so by the appearance of two or three
hundred grave - looking men who were riding into town
by every road that led to it, silent and dusty and
grim. They were of every age and condition, and they
lacked just order enough not to appear marching troops ;
but showed enough to seem one body. They were all serious and silent, and with that something in their deliberate
movements which, whether it be mere resolution or des-
peration, impresses all who behold it. The negroes about
the village who had been in a flurry of excitement since
the news came and had been crowding about the camp
shouting and yelling, suddenly settled down and melted
out of sight, and even the soldiers quieted at the appear-
13

ance of that steadily increasing force of resolute and orderly men gathered along the fences, facing the camp.
General Legaie and Dr. Cary were their spokesmen,
and they held an interview with the Captain, in which
they gave him to understand certain things : They would
obey his orders, they said, if he sent them by a single
messenger ; but if armed bodies of negroes continued to
ravage the country they would not be responsible for the
consequences.

Leech was not to be found that afternoon. He had
"gone to the city." Jerry learned afterward and told
Captain Allen that he did not go until that night, and that
when the crowd was there he was hidden at Hiram Still's.

An investigation of the outbreak was held, and as a consequence Captain McRaffle and several young men left the
county, among them Rupert Gray, who was sent off to
school to an academy which was not known to the neighbors generally. Another result was that the old county
got a bad name with those who were controlling the destiny of the State, which clung to it for many years. Andy
Stamper was arrested for the affair, and was taken, handcuffed, by Leech and thrown in jail. Fortunately for him,
however, it was shown that he was absent from the county
that day, and he was discharged. All of these things,
however, at the time were little cared for by the residents
there, for the negro troop was removed and two white
companies were sent in its place. The disorder breaking
out wherever negro troops were stationed had attracted
attention and caused the substitution of white soldiers.

CHAPTER XVII

JACQUELIN GRAY GOES ON A LONG VOYAGE AND RED ROCK PASSES OUT OF HIS HANDS

JACQUELIN had never recovered from the rough handling which he had received that night from Leech. His wound had broken out afresh and he was now confined to his bed all the time. There was one cause which, perhaps, more than all the rest, weighed him down, and that, certainly, Dr. Cary did not know, though, no doubt, Mrs. Cary and Mrs. Gray knew. It was a secret wound, deeper than that which Dr. Cary was treating. He had never been the same since the evening of his misunderstanding with Blair Cary. The affair in which the negro soldiers were killed, and Rupert's and Steve's part in it, with the necessity of sending Rupert away, and the consequences which followed, seemed to be the finishing stroke, and it appeared to be only a question of a few months with Jacquelin.

One other reason for his anxiety Dr. Cary had. Reports of threats made by Leech came to the Doctor. "Another arrest, and he will go," said Dr. Cary. "We must get him away. Send him first to a city where he can have better surgical treatment than he is able to receive in the country. Then, when he is fit for it, put him on a sailing vessel and send him around the world." How cleverly he had managed it, thought the Doctor!

Mrs. Gray also had her own reasons for wishing to get Jacquelin away, though they were not mainly what Dr. Cary thought. With a keener insight than the good Doctor had, she had seen Blair Cary's change and its effect on Jacquelin. And she eagerly sought to carry out the Doctor's suggestions. The chief difficulty in the way was

want of funds. The demands of the plantation, according
to Mr. Still's account, had been enough of late to consume
everything that was made on it. The negroes had to be
supported whether they worked or not, and the estate was
running behind.

The Doctor felt certain he could manage the matter of
means. Hiram Still had just offered to lend him a further
sum. Indeed, Still had himself brought up the matter of
Jacquelin's health, and had even asked the Doctor if he did
not think a long visit somewhere might do Jacquelin good.

"He is a strange mixture, that man Still. He is undoubtedly a very kind-hearted man," asserted the Doctor.

Mrs. Gray did not altogether agree with her cousin in
his estimate of Still; she had her own opinion of him;
but she was somewhat mollified by hearing of his interest
in Jacquelin's welfare. She could not, however, allow her
cousin to borrow money in his own name on her account,
but, in the face of Jacquelin's steady decline, she finally
yielded and bowed her pride so far as to permit the Doctor
to borrow it for her, only stipulating that the plate and
pictures in the house should be pledged to secure it. This
would relieve her partly from personal obligations to Still.
One other stipulation she made : that Jacquelin was not to
know of the loan.

When the Doctor applied to Still he obtained the loan
without difficulty, and Still, having taken an assignment
of the plate and pictures, agreed without hesitation to his
condition of silence, even expressing the deepest interest
in Jacquelin's welfare, and reiterating his protestations of
friendship for him and Mrs. Gray.

"It is the most curious thing," said the Doctor to Mrs.
Cary, afterward : "I never apply to that man without
his doing what I ask. I always expect to be refused. I
am always surprised—and yet my suspicion is not relieved
—I do not know why it is. I think I must be a very suspicious man."

Mrs. Cary's mouth shut closely. But she would not add

to her husband's worries by a suggestion, the very idea of
which she thought was an indignity.

"I wish you had not applied to him," she said. "I
do not want to be under any obligations to him whatever.
I do not think Helen should have asked it of you."

"Oh! my dear!" said the Doctor. "She didn't ask it
of me, I offered it to her."

"I cannot bear him," declared Mrs. Cary, with the tone
of one who delivers a convincing argument. "And the
son is more intolerable than the father. It requires all my
politeness to prevent my asking him out of the house whenever he comes. He comes here entirely too often."

"My dear, he is a young doctor who is trying to practise
his profession, and needs advice," expostulated the old
doctor, but Mrs. Cary was not to be convinced.

"A young doctor, indeed! a young—" The rest of the
sentence was lost as she went out with her head in the air.

When the matter of removing Jacquelin was broached to
him, a new and unexpected difficulty arose. He refused
to go. The idea of his getting better treatment than Dr.
Cary was able to give was, he said, all nonsense, and they
could not stand the expense of such a plan as was proposed.
In this emergency his mother was forced to bow her pride.
She summoned Blair Cary as an ally. Blair yielded so far
as to add an expression of her views to the mother's, because she did not know how to refuse; but, with a woman's finesse, she kept herself within limitations, which
Jacquelin, at least, would understand. She came over on
a visit, and went in to see him, and took occasion to say
that she thought he ought to go to the city. It was a
very prim and stiff little speech that she made. Jacquelin's face showed the first tinge of color that had been on it
for months, as he turned his eyes to her almost eagerly.
So impassive, though, was she, that the tinge faded out.

"Do you ask me to go?"

"No—I have nothing to do with it. I only think you
ought to do what your mother wishes." The mouth was

closer than usual. There was a little deeper color in her face now.

"Oh ! it was only a moral idea you wished to inculcate ? "

" If you choose to call it so." The mouth drew closer.

"Well—will you ask me ? "

" I don't mind doing it—for your mother." It was no accident that a woman was chosen to be the oracle at Delphi. Jacquelin could make no more of the face before him than if he had never seen it before, and he had studied it for years.

Jacquelin agreed to go to the hospital. So he was sent off to the city, where an operation was performed to remove some of the splintered bone and relieve him. And as soon as he was well enough he was sent off on a sailing vessel trading to China. He thus escaped the increasing afflictions that were coming on the county, and his mother, who would have torn out her heart for him, for fear he would come home if he knew the state of affairs, kept everything from him, and bore her burdens alone.

The burdens were heavy.

The next few years which passed brought more changes to the old county than any years of the war. The war had destroyed the Institution of slavery ; the years of the carpet-bagger's domination well-nigh destroyed the South. As Miss Thomasia said, sighing, it was the fulfilment of the old prophecy : " After the sword shall come the canker-worm." And the Doctor's speech was recalled by some : " You ask for war, but you do not know what it is. A fool can start a conflagration, but the Sanhedrim cannot stop it. War is never done. It leaves its baleful seed for generations."

Dr. Cary, when he uttered this statement, had little idea how true it was.

Events had proved that although the people were impoverished, their spirit was not broken. Unhappily, the power was in the hands of those who did not understand them, and Leech and his fellows had their ear. It was deemed proper to put them in absolute control. Leech wrote the authorities that he and his party must have power to preserve the Union; he wrote to Mrs. Welch that they must have it to preserve the poor freedmen. The authorities promised it, and kept the promise. It was insanity.

One provision gave the ballot to the former slave, just as it was taken from the former master. An act was so shrewdly framed that, while it appeared simply to be intended to secure loyalty to the Union, it was aimed to strike from the rolls of citizenship almost the entire white population of the South; that is, all who would not swear they had never given aid or comfort to the Confederacy. It was so all-embracing that it came to be known as the " ironclad " oath.

" It is the greatest Revolution since the time of Poland," said Dr. Cary, his nostrils dilating with ire. " They have thrown down the man of intelligence, character, and property, and have set up the slave and the miscreant. ' Syria is confederate with Ephraim.' More is yet to come."

" It is the salvation of the Union," wrote Leech to Mrs. Welch, who was the head of an organization that sent boxes of clothes to the negroes through Leech. Leech was beginning to think himself the Union.

While General Legaie and Steve Allen were discussing constitutional rights and privileges, and declaring that they would never yield assent to any measures of the kind proposed, a more arbitrary act than these was committed: the State itself was suddenly swept out of existence, and a military government was substituted in its place; the very name of the State on which those gentlemen and their ancestors had prided themselves for generations was extinguished and lost in that of " Military District, Number ——." The old State, with all others like it, ceased to be.

Colonel Krafton was the chief authority in that part of the State, and Major Leech, as he was now called, was his representative in the county. And between them they had the enforcement of all the measures that were adopted.

When their hands were deemed strong enough, it was determined to give them the form of popular government.

It was an easy process ; for the whites had been disfranchised, and only the negroes and those who had taken the
ironclad oath could vote.

At the first election that was held under the new system,
the spectacle was a curious one. Krafton was the candidate
for governor. Most of the disfranchised whites stayed
away, haughtily or sullenly, from the polls, where ballots
were cast under a guard of soldiers. But others went to
see the strange sight, and to vent their derision on the de
tested officials who were in charge. Dr. Cary and General
Legaie, with most men of their age and stamp, remained
at home in haughty and impotent indignation.

" Why should I go to see my former wagon-driver standing for the seat my grandfather resigned from the United
States Senate to take ? " asked General Legaie, proudly.

Steve Allen and Andy Stamper, however, and many of
the young men were on hand.

Leech and Nicholas Ash were the candidates for the Legislature, and Steve went to the poll where he thought it
likely Leech would be. Steve had become a leader among
the whites. Both men knew that it was now a fight to the
finish between them, and both always acted in full consciousness of the fact. Leech counted on his power, and
the force he could always summon to his aid, to hold Steve
in check until he should have committed some rashness
which would enable him to destroy him. Steve was conscious that Leech was personally afraid of him, and he
relied on this fact—taking every occasion to assert himself—as the master of a treacherous animal keeps ever
facing him, holding him with the spell of an unflinching
eye.

The negroes were led in lines to cast their votes.

It was a notable thing that in all the county there was
not an angry word that day between a white man and a
negro. Leech, in a letter to Mrs. Welch describing the

occasion, declared that the quietness with which the election passed off was due wholly to the presence of the soldiery, and he was very eloquent in his denunciation of the desperadoes who surrounded him, and who were held at bay only by fear of the bayonets about them. But this was not true. The situation was too novel not to be interesting, and there was feeling, but it was suppressed. It was a strange sight, the polls guarded by soldiers; the men who had controlled the country standing by, disfranchised, and the lines of blacks who had just been slaves, and not one in one hundred of whom could read their ballots, voting on questions which were to decide the fate of the State. There were many gibes flung at the new voters by the disfranchised spectators, but they were mainly good-natured.

"Whom are you voting for, Uncle Gideon?" asked Steve of one of the old Red Rock negroes.

"Marse Steve, you know who I votin' for better'n I does myself."

To another:

"Whom are you voting for?"

"Gi' me a little tobacker, Marse Steve, an' I'll tell you." And when it was given, he turned to the crowd: "Who is I votin' for? I done forgit. Oh! yes—old Mr. Linkum—ain' dat he name?"

"Well, he's a good one to vote for—he's dead," said Steve.

"Hi! is he? When did he die?" protested the old man in unfeigned astonishment.

"You ain' votin' for him — you'se votin' for Mist' Grant," explained another younger negro, indignant at the old man's ignorance.

"Is I? Who's he? He's one I ain' never heard on. Marse Steve, I don' know who I votin' for—I jis know I votin', dat's all."

This raised a laugh at Steve's expense which was led by Leech, and to atone for it the old servant added:

"I done forgit de gent'man's name."

"The gentlemen you are voting for are Leech and Nicholas Ash," said Steve.

"Marse Steve, you know dey ain' no gent'mens," said the old fellow, undisturbed by the fact that Leech was present.

"Uncle Tom, you know something, anyhow," said Steve, enjoying the Provost's discomfiture.

The only white man of any note in the upper end of the county who took the new "ironclad" oath was Hiram Still. Andy Stamper met him after Hiram had voted. Still tried to dodge him.

"Don't run, Hiram," said the little Sergeant, contemptuously, "I ain't a going to hurt ye. The war's over. If I had known at the time you was givin' the Yanks information, I might 'a' done it once—and I would advise you, Hiram, never to give 'em too much information about *me* now. You've already giv' 'em too much once about me. See there?" He stretched out his arm and showed a purple mark on his wrist. It was the scar that had been left by the handcuff when he was arrested for the riot at Deal's. "It won't come out. You understand?" The little fellow's eyes shot at the renegade so piercing a glance that Still cowered and muttered that he had nothing to do with him one way or another.

"Maybe, if you didn't give no aid and comfort to the rebels you'd like to give me back that little piece of paper you took from my old mother to secure the price of that horse you let me have to go back in the army?" drawled Stamper, while one or two onlookers laughed.

The renegade made his escape as quickly as possible.

Still's reply to the contempt that was visited on him was to bring suit on the bonds he held. Leech was his counsel. One of the first suits was against Andy Stamper. Andy was promptly sold out under the deed which had been given during the war; the place was bought by Still, and Andy and Delia rented another little house. This was only the beginning, however.

When Still flung away his mask, he went as far as he dared. It was now open war, and he had thrown in his fortune with the other side.

Dr. Cary received a note one morning from Mrs. Gray asking him to come and see her immediately. He found her in a state of agitation very unusual with her. She had the night before received a letter from Still, stating that he was a creditor of her husband's estate and held his bonds for over fifty thousand dollars. Mrs. Gray had known that there were some outstanding debts of her husband due him, though she had supposed they were nearly paid off—but fifty thousand dollars! It would take the whole estate !

"Why, it is incredible," declared the Doctor. "Quite incredible ! The man is crazy. You need give yourself no uneasiness whatever about it. I will see him and clear up the whole matter."

Yet, even as the Doctor spoke, he recalled certain hints of Still's, dropped from time to time, recently, as to balances due by his former employer on old accounts connected with his Southern estate, and Mr. Gray was a very easy man, thought the Doctor, who believed himself one of the keenest and most methodical of men.

Women love to have encouragement from men, even though they may feel the reverse of what they are told to believe. So Mrs. Gray and Miss Thomasia were more comforted than they could have found ground for.

When Dr. Cary did look into the matter, to his amazement he found that the bonds were in existence. Still gave the account of them which he had already given to Leech, and produced some corroborative evidence in the shape of letters relating to the transaction of buying and stocking the sugar plantation. There was hope for awhile that the writers of the letters might be able to throw some light on the matter, but, on investigation, it turned out that they were without exception dead, and Mrs. Gray herself, on seeing the big bond, pronounced it genuine, and declared that she remembered her husband once spoke of it, though she thought he had told her it was all settled. She hunted all through his papers, but though she found other bonds of his which he had taken in she could find no record of this big one. Jacquelin was written to, but in his reply he said that no matter what the cost, he wanted his father's debts paid. So no defence was made to the suit which Still had instituted by Leech as his counsel, and judgment was obtained by default. And soon afterward the Red Rock place, with everything on it, was sold under this judgment and was bought in by Still for less than the amount of his claim.

Jacquelin was still abroad and Mrs. Gray purposely kept him in ignorance of what was going on; for her chief anxiety at this time was to prevent Jacquelin from returning home until all this matter was ended. He had written that his health was steadily improving.

Mrs. Gray did not remain at Red Rock twenty-four hours after Still became its owner. She and Miss Thomasia moved next day to Dr. Cary's, where they were offered a home. She congratulated herself anew that morning that Jacquelin was yet absent.

Mrs. Gray and Miss Thomasia walked out with their heads up, bidding good-by to their old servants, who had assembled outside of the house, their faces full of concern and sorrow.

There was hardly a negro on the place who was not there. However they might follow Still in politics, they had not yet learned to forget the old ties that bound them in other matters to their old masters, and they were profoundly affected by this step, which they could all appreciate.

"I drives you away, my mistis," said the driver, old Waverley. "I prays Gord I may live to drive you back."

"Not me, Waverley; but, maybe, this boy," said Mrs. Gray, laying her hand on Rupert's shoulder.

"Yes'm, we heah him say he comin' back," said the old driver, with pride. "Gord knows we hopes so."

Just then Hiram Still, accompanied by Leech, rode up into the yard. He had evidently kept himself informed as to Mrs. Gray's movements. He rode across the grass and gave orders to the negroes to clear away. Mrs. Gray took not the least notice of him, but, outraged by his insolence, Rupert suddenly sprang forward and denounced him passionately. His mother checked him : " Rupert, my son." But the boy was wild with anger. " We are coming back some day," he cried to Still. " You have robbed us ; but wait till my brother returns."

Both Still and Leech laughed, and Still ostentatiously ordered the negroes off. Still moved in that afternoon.

Before Still had been installed in his new mansion twenty-four hours he repented of his indiscretion, if not of his insolence. He was absent a part of the evening, and on his return he heard that Captain Allen had been to see him. The face of the servant who gave the message told more than the words he delivered.

" What did he want ? " Still asked, sharply.

" He say he want to see you, and he want to see you pussonally." The negro looked significant.

" Well, he knows where to find me."

" Yes, he say he *gwine* fine you—dat's huccome he come, an' he gwine *keep on* till he do fine you." Still's heart sank.

" I don't know what he wants with me," he growled, as he turned away and went into the house. The great hall filled with pictures had never looked so big or so dark. The eyes fastened on him from the walls seemed to search him. Those of the " Indian-Killer" pierced him wherever he went.

"Curse them ; they are all alike," he growled. " I wish I had let them have the d——d rubbish. I would, but for having to take that one down."

Poor Virgy, who had been given the room that had formerly been Jacquelin's, came toward him. She was scared and lonely in her new surroundings, and had been crying.

This increased her father's ill-humor. He inquired if she had seen Captain Allen. She had, but he had only bowed to her; all he had said was to the servant.

" Did he seem excited ? " Still asked.

" No, he only looked quiet. He looked like one of those pictures up there." It was an unlucky illustration. Her father broke out on her so severely that she ran to her own room weeping. It was only of late that he had begun to be so harsh.

Still, left alone, sat down and without delay wrote a letter to Captain Allen, expressing regret that he had been away when he called. He also wrote a letter to Dr. Cary, which he sent out that night, apologizing to Mrs. Gray and calling heaven to witness that he had not meant to offend her, and did not even know she was on the place when he rode up. He did not wait for replies. The next morning before daylight he left for the city.

" I would not mind one of them," he complained to his counsel, Leech. " I'm as good a man as any one of 'em ; but you don't know 'em. They stick together like Indians, and if one of 'em got hurt, the whole tribe would come down on me like hornets."

" Wait till we get ready for 'em," counselled Leech. " We'll bring their pride down. We'll be more than a match for the whole tribe. Wait till I get in the Legislature ; I'll pass some laws that will settle 'em." His blue eyes were glistening and he was opening his hands and shutting them tightly in a way he had, as if he were crushing something in his palms.

" That's it—that's it," said Still, eagerly.

CHAPTER XVIII

WHEN Leech arrived at the capital in the capacity of
statesman he found the field even better than he had anticipated. It was a strange assembly that was gathered together to reconstruct and make laws for a great State after
years of revolution. The large majority were negroes who,
a few years before, had been barbers, porters in hotels,
cart-drivers, or body-servants, with a few new-comers to the
State, like Leech himself : nomadic adventurers, who, on
account of the smallness of their personal belongings, were
termed " carpet-baggers." Besides these, a few whites
who, in hope of gain, had allied themselves with the new-
comers ; and a small sprinkling of the old residents, who
had either been Union men or had had their disabilities removed, and represented constituencies where there were
few negroes. They were as distinguishable as statues in
the midst of a mob. But the multitude of negroes who
crowded the Assembly halls gave the majority an appearance of being overwhelming. They filled the porticos and
vestibules, and thronged the corridors and galleries in a
dense mass, revelling in their newly acquired privileges.
The air was heavy with the smoke of bad cigars, which,
however, was not wholly without use, as the scent of the
tobacco served at least one good purpose ; the floors were
slippery with tobacco-juice. The crowd was loud, pom-
pous, and good-natured. Leech looked with curiosity on
the curious spectacle. He had had no idea what a use-
ful band of coadjutors he would have. He took a survey

of the field and made his calculations quickly and with shrewdness. He would be a leader.

"Looks like a corn-shuckin'," said Still, who had accompanied his friend to the capital to see him take his seat. "A good head-man could get a heap of corn shucked."

"Does look a little like a checker-board," assented Leech, "and I mean to be one of the kings. It's keep ahead or get run over in this crowd, and I'm smart as any of 'em. There's a good cow to milk, and the one as milks her first will get the cream." His metaphors were becoming bucolic, as befitted a man who was beginning to set up as a planter.

"The cream's in the drippin's," corrected Still.

"Not of this cow," said Leech.

Leech soon came to be regarded as quite a financier. He talked learnedly of bonds and debentures, of per cents. and guarantees, and dividends, of which more than half the body did not even know the meaning. Once, when he was speaking of the thousands of "bonds" he would put on a railway to the mile, one of his confrères asked what he would put in so many barns.

"Ain't you heah him say he's gwine have a million o' stock?" asked another colored statesman, contemptuously. The answer was satisfactory.

The amount of spoil which in time was found to be divided was something of which not even Leech himself, at first, had any idea. The railways, the public printing, insurance, and all internal improvements, were fertile fields for the exercise of his genius. He was shortly an undisputed power. He followed his simple rule : he led. When someone offered a resolution to put down new matting in the Assembly hall, Leech amended to substitute Brussels carpet. To prove his liberality he added mahogany furniture, and handsome pier-glasses. The bills went up into the scores of thousands ; but that was nothing. As Leech said, *they* did not pay them. If rumors were true, **not** only did Leech not pay the bills, he partly received their proceeds. His aspirations were growing every day. He had no trouble in carrying his measures through. He turned his committee-room—or one of his rooms, for he had several—into a saloon, where he kept whiskey, champagne, and cigars always free for those who were on his side. "Leech's bar" became a State institution. It was open night and day for the whole eight years of his service. He said he found it cheaper than direct payment, and then he lumped all the costs in one item and had them paid by one appropriation bill, as "sundries." Why should he pay, he asked, for expenditures which were for the public benefit? And, indeed, why? As for himself, he boasted with great pride when the matter came up at a later time, that he never touched a drop.

He had "found the very field for his genius." He boasted to Still : "I always knew I had sense. Old Krafton thinks he's running the party. But I'm a doin' it. Some day he'll wake up and find I'm not only a doin' that, but a runnin' the State too. I mean to be governor." His blue eyes twinkled pleasantly.

"Don't wake him up too soon," counselled Still.

One of the statesman's acts was to obtain a charter for a railway to run from the capital up through his county to the mountains. Among the incorporators were himself, Hiram Still, Still's son, and Mr. Bolter.

"How will you build this road?" asked Mr. Haskelton, an old gentleman who had been a Union man always—one of the few old residents of the State in the body.

"Oh! we'll manage that," declared Leech, lightly. "We are going to teach you old moss-backs a few things." And they did. He had an act passed making the State guarantee the bonds. The old resident raised a question as to the danger to the credit of the State if it should go into the business of endorsing private enterprises.

"The credit of the State!" Leech exclaimed. "What is the credit of the State to us? As long as the bonds sell she has credit, hasn't she?"

14

This argument was unanswerable.

"But how will you pay these bonds?" urged Mr. Haskelton.

"I will tell you how we will pay them; we will pay them by taxes," replied Leech.

"Ay-yi! Dat's it!" shouted the dusky throng about him.

"Someone has to pay those taxes."

"Yes, but who?" Leech turned to his associates who were hanging on his words. "Do you pay them?"

"Nor, dat we don't," shouted Nicholas Ash.

"No, the white people pay them—and we mean to make them pay them," declared Leech.

This declaration was received with an outburst of applause, not unmingled with laughter, for his audience had some appreciation of humor.

"Lands will only stand so much tax," insisted his interlocutor; "if you raise taxes beyond this point you will defeat your own purpose, for the lands will be forfeited. We cannot pay them. We are already flat on our backs."

"That's where we want you," retorted Leech, and there was a roar of approval.

The old gentleman remained calm.

"Then what will you do?" he persisted.

"Then we will take them ourselves," asserted Leech, boldly. He looked around on the dusky throng behind him, and up at the gallery, black with faces. "We will make the State give them as homes to the people who are really entitled to them. They know how to work them." A great shout of applause went up from floor and gallery. Only the old gentleman, gray and pallid, with burning eyes stood unmoved amid the tumult.

"You cannot do this. It will be robbery."

The crowd, somewhat disturbed by his earnestness, looked at Leech to hear how he would meet this fact. He was equal to the emergency.

"Robbery, is it?" he shouted, waving his arms, and

advancing down the aisle. "Then it is only paying robbery for robbery. You have been the robbers ! You robbed the Indians of these lands, to start with. You went to Africa and stole these free colored people from their happy homes and made them slaves. You robbed them of their freedom, and you have robbed them ever since of their wages. Now you say we cannot pay them a little of what you owe them ? We will do it, and do it by law. We have the majority and by — ! we will make the laws. If you white gentlemen cannot pay the taxes on your homes, we'll put some colored ones there to get the benefit." He shook his hand violently in the vehemence of his speech. And again the crowd roared.

"Don't shake your finger in my face," said the old man so quietly that only Leech heard it. He backed off.

He became an undisputed leader. "By — ! I had no idea I was such an orator," he said to Still, smiling.

"I haven't made such a speech as that since just before the war. I made that old coon admit he was flat on his back."

"A coon fights better on his back 'n' any other way," warned Still.

"I'll put some hunters on this coon that will keep him quiet enough," said Leech. "I'll arm a hundred thousand niggers."

Leech made good his promises. The expenditures went up beyond belief. But to meet the expenses taxes were laid until they rose to double, quadruple, and, in some parts of the State, ten times what they had been. Meantime he had been in communication with Mr. Bolter, who had come down and paid him and Still a flying visit, and a part of the bonds of his railroad were "placed."

The taxes, as was predicted, went far beyond the ability of the landowners to pay them, and vast numbers of plantations throughout the State were forfeited. To meet this exigency, Leech was as good as his word. A measure was introduced and a Land Commission was appointed to take charge of such forfeited lands and sell them to his followers on long terms, of fifteen to twenty years. Leech was a member of the general Commission and Still was appointed agent of the Board in his section of the State. Still was a very active commissioner—"efficient," the Commission called him.

Several places were sold which shortly were resold to Leech and Still. Leech added to a place he bought on the edge of Brutusville, adjoining General Legaie's, the plantations of two old gentlemen near him. Sherwood had bought one and Moses the other. Leech gave them "a fair advance." He said it was "all square." He was now waiting for General Legaie's place.

Leech built himself a large house, and furnished it with furniture richer than that in any other house in the county. It was rumored that he was preparing his house for Virgy Still.

Nicholas Ash bought a plantation and a buggy and began to drive fast horses. Many of their fellow-lawmakers bloomed out in the same way. They were the only ones who now rode in carriages. Their proceedings did not affect themselves only. They reached Dr. Cary and General Legaie and the old proprietors on their plantations, quite as directly, though in the opposite way. The spoils that Leech, Still, Governor Krafton and their followers received, someone else paid. And just when they were needed most, the negroes abandoned the fields. No one could expect statesmen to work. Cattle, jewels, and plate were sold as long as they lasted, to meet the piled-up taxes; but in time there was nothing left to sell, and the plantations began to go. In the Red Rock neighborhood, rumors were abroad as to the destiny of the various places. A deeper gravity settled on Dr. Cary's serious face, and General Legaie's lively countenance was taking on an expression not far from grim. It was less the financial ruin that was overwhelming them than the dishonor to the State. It was a stab in their bosoms.

Mr. Ledger was making inquiries as to the possibility of their reducing shortly their indebtedness to him, and the Doctor was forced to write him a frank statement of affairs. He had never worked so hard in his life, he wrote; he had never had so much practice ; but he could collect nothing, and it was all he could do to meet his taxes.

"Why don't you collect your bills ?" naturally inquired Mr. Ledger.

"Collect my bills ?" replied the Doctor. "How can I press my neighbors who are as poor, and poorer, than I am?"

However, inspired by Mr. Ledger's application, the Doctor did try to collect some of the money due him. He did not send out his bills. He had never done that in his life. Instead, he rode around on a collecting-tour. He was successful in getting some money ; for he applied first to such of his debtors as were thriftiest. Andy Stamper, who had just returned from town where he had been selling sumac, chickens, and other produce, paid him with thanks the whole of his bill, and only expressed surprise that it was so small. "Why I thought, Doctor, 'twould be three or four times that ?" said Andy. "I've kept a sort of account of the times you've been to my house, and seems to me 't ought to be ?"

"No, sir, that's all I have against you," said the Doctor, placidly ; replying earnestly to Andy's voluble thanks. "I am very much obliged to you." He did not tell Andy that he had divided his accounts by three and had had hard work to bring himself to apply for anything.

This and one or two other instances in the beginning of his tour quite relieved the Doctor ; for they showed that, at least, some of his neighbors had some money. So he rode on. He soon found, however, that he had gleaned the richest places first. On his way home he applied to others of his patients with far different results. Not only was the account he received very sorrowful ; but the tale of poverty that several of them told was so moving that the Doctor, instead of receiving anything from them, distributed amongst them what he had already collected, saying they were poorer than himself. So when he reached home that evening he had no more than when he rode away.

"Well, Bess," he said, "it is the first time I ever dunned a debtor, and it is the last." Mrs. Cary looked at him with the expression in her eyes with which a mother looks at a child.

"I think it is just as well," she said, smiling.

"You must go and see old Mrs. Bellows," he said. "She is in great trouble for fear they'll sell her place."

Blair Cary, like her mother, watched with constant anxiety the change in her father. His hair was becoming white, and his face was growing more worn.

At length, a plan which she had been forming for some time took definite shape. She announced her intention of applying for one of the common schools which had been opened in the neighborhood. When she first proposed the plan, it was received as if she were crazy—but her father and mother soon found that they no longer had a child to deal with, but a woman of sense and force of character. The reasons she gave were so clear and unanswerable that at length she overcame all objections and obtained the consent of all the members of the family except Mammy Krenda. The only point on which her father stood out for was that she should not apply for one of the schools under the new county-managers. A compromise was effected and she became the teacher of the school that had been built by the old residents. The Mammy still stood out. The idea of "her child" teaching a common school outraged the old woman's sense of propriety, and threw her into a state of violent agitation. She finally yielded, but only on condition that she might accompany her mistress to the school every day.

This she did, and when Miss Blair secured the little school at the fork in the road not far from their big gate, the old mammy was to be seen every day, sitting in a corner grim and a little supercilious, knitting busily, while her eyes ever and anon wandered over the classes before her, transfixing the individual who was receiving her mistress's attention with so sharp a glance that the luckless wight was often disconcerted thereby.

As old Mr. Haskelton had said, the old residents were flat on their backs. Leech was of this opinion when he passed his measures. But remembering Still's warning, to make sure, as the troops had been withdrawn from the county, he put through a bill to organize a State militia, under which large numbers of the negroes in the old county and throughout the State were formed in companies.

He had other plans hatching which he thought they would subserve.

CHAPTER XIX

HIRAM STILL COLLECTS HIS DEBTS

THE old Doctor had become the general adviser of his neighbors. There was that in his calm face and quiet manner which somehow soothed and sent them away with a feeling of being sympathized with, even when no practical aid was rendered. "I believe more people consults the old Doctor than does Mr. Bagby and General Legaie together," said Andy Stamper; "and he don't know any more about the way to do business these days than my baby. To be sure, they all seem to be helped somehow by goin'."

It was soon a problem whether the Doctor could keep his own place from falling into the hands of the Commission. He had often wondered why it had not been listed, for he had not been able to keep the taxes down. Though he did not know, however, Hiram Still did.

All this while Blair had some secret on her mind. She was always working. She would be up before sunrise, looking after her chickens; and in the afternoons, when she came from school, and all day in the summer, she would be busy about the kitchen or in some shaded spot, back among the fruit trees, where kettles were hung over fires, and Mrs. Cary at times gave advice, and Mammy Krenda moved about with her arms full of dry wood, in a mist of blue smoke. Sometimes Steve Allen lounged in the shade, at the edge of the cloud, giving Blair what he termed his legal advice, and teasing Mammy Krenda into threats of setting him on fire "before his time." "Making preserves and pickles," was all the answer the Doctor got to his inquiries. Yet for all Miss Blair's work

there did not seem to be any increase in the preserves that
came to the table, and when her father inquired once if
all her preserves and pickles were spoilt, though she went
with a laugh and a blush and brought him some, he saw
no increase in them afterward. She appeared suddenly to
have a great many dealings with Mr. and Mrs. Stamper,
and several times Andy Stamper's wagon came in the Doctor's absence and took away loads of jars which were
transported to the railroad, and when the Doctor accidentally met Andy and inquired of him as to his load and its
destination, Andy gave a very shuffling and cloudy reply
about some preserves his wife and some of her friends
were sending to town. Indeed, when the Doctor reached
home on that occasion, he spoke of it, declaring that Mrs.
Stamper was a very remarkable young woman ; she actually sent off wagon-loads of preserves. He asked Blair
teasingly how it was that Mrs. Stamper could do this while
they could hardly get enough for the table. Blair only
laughed and made a warning sign to Mammy Krenda,
who was sniffing ominously and had to leave the room.

At length the secret came out. One day the Doctor
came home worn out. The taxes were due again. Blair
left the room, and returning, placed a roll of money in
his hands. It was her salary which she had saved, together with the proceeds of the kettle in the orchard.

"That will help you, papa," she said, as she threw her
arms round his neck. "These are my preserves."

The old gentleman was too moved to speak before she
had run out of the room. After a little he went to find
his wife. That was the sanctuary he always sought, in joy
and sorrow.

"I reckon now he know de Stampers ain' de on'ies'
ones kin meck preserves," said Mammy Krenda, with a sniff.

That very evening old Mrs. Bellows came to see the
Doctor. Mrs. Bellows was the aunt of Delia Dove. Her
husband had been a blacksmith, and had died the year
after the war. They owned a little place near the fork

in the road, just on the edge of the Birdwood plantation, where her husband had in old times made a good living. The house was a little cottage set back amid apple and peach trees some hundreds of yards from the shop. Since her husband's death, Andy Stamper and Delia Dove had helped her; but now, since Andy had been turned out of his old home and was paying for another, the times had grown so hard that it was not a great deal they could do. Andy thought they'd better let this place go and that she should come and live with them, but the old woman had refused, and now her place among many others had been forfeited and was on the list of those advertised for sale. And Mrs. Bellows came to Dr. Cary. Still had his eye on her home, and intended to buy it for the Commission. Andy had heard that Nicholas Ash wanted it, and that Still had promised it to him—"just out of spite to Andy and Delia," the old woman said. She was in a great state of excitement.

"I been tellin' Andy 'twant no use to be fightin' Still," she wailed; "he's too smart for him. If he could git hold o' Red Rock, Andy might 'a' known he could beat *him*."

Dr. Cary sat in deep reflection for a moment. He had a pang as he thought of the money he had made Andy pay. The sum saved by Blair was only a small part of the taxes due on Birdwood, but was enough to pay all the back taxes and redemption fees on Mrs. Bellows's place. It looked like Providence. The Doctor sent her away comforted. Still's plans with regard to the Bellows place soon became an assured fact. He boasted of what he would do. He would show Andy Stamper who he was. The fact that it would be Delia Dove's was enough for him, and it became known throughout the county that the Commission would take it. When the day of sale came, little Andy was on hand at the county seat. Still was there too, and so was Nicholas Ash. Still tried to find out why Andy came. He knew he did not have the money to redeem the place. He thought it was to pick a quarrel with him; but Andy's face was inscrutable.

Under the formality of the law, a party interested could redeem the land at any time before it was sold, paying the amount due to the clerk, with interest and fees. Still examined the list just before the crying began. The Bellows place was still on it. So the auction began. Andy was closeted with old Mr. Dockett, whose duty it was, as clerk, to receive the redemption money; but when the sale started, he came out and sauntered up into the crowd. Several places belonging to persons whose names began with A, were put up and knocked down to "Hiram Still, Commissioner," and as each one went to him there were groans and hoots, and counterbalancing cheers from the negroes. At length the Bellows place was reached. The amount of taxes for the several years for which it was delinquent was stated, and the sheriff, a creature of Leech's, offered the place. There was a dead silence throughout the crowd, for it was known that it was between Still and Stamper. Still was the only bidder. The crowd looked at Stamper, but he never stirred. He looked the most indifferent man on the ground. Still, on the other side of the crowd, whispered with Ash and made a sign to the sheriff, and the latter, having made his preliminary notice, announced:

"And there being no other bid than that of the Commissioner, I knock this place also down to ——"

There was a movement, and a voice interrupted him.

"No, you don't. That place has been redeemed." Andy spoke quietly, but with a sudden blaze in his eyes. He held up the certificate of payment, gripped in his hand, and looked across at Hiram Still.

There was a moment's pause, and then cheer after cheer broke out from the crowd of whites; and the long, pent-up feeling against Still burst forth so vehemently that he turned and pushed deep into the middle of the throng of blacks about him, and soon left the ground.

The excitement and anxiety, however, proved too much for old Mrs. Bellows, and she died suddenly a few nights later.

"One more notch on the score against Hiram and Major Leech," said Andy Stamper, grimly, as he turned the key in the door of the empty house, and, taking it out, put it in his pocket.

Andy's wife, as the old woman's heir, was the owner of the place; but a few days after Mrs. Bellows's death Andy rode up to Dr. Cary's door.

Delia had sent him over, he said (he always laid the credit of such things on Delia, he was simply clay in the potter's hands).—Delia had sent him to say that the place belonged to Miss Blair. "She had found out where the money came from which bought it back, and she wan't goin' to take it. She couldn't take care of the place anyhow— 'twas all she could do to keep the place they had now; and she would not have this one if she was to pay taxes on it. All she wanted, was to beat Hiram. So if Miss Blair wouldn't take it, she s'posed Nicholas Ash would git it next year, after all."

Andy pulled out a deed, made in due form to Miss Blair Cary, and delivered it to the Doctor, meeting every objection which the Doctor raised, with a reason so cogent that it really looked as if he were simply trying to shield Delia Dove from some overwhelming calamity. So the Doctor finally agreed to hold the place for his daughter, though only as security for the sum advanced, and with the stipulation that Andy should at any time have the privilege of redeeming it. It was well for Dr. Cary that he had placed his money as he did.

A few days after this sale at the county seat, Dr. Cary received a letter from Mr. Ledger, telling him that the condition of affairs had become so gloomy that his correspondents in the North were notifying him that they could not continue their advances to him at present, and as the notes given him by Dr. Cary and General Legaie, which had already been renewed several times, were about to fall due again, he found himself under the disagreeable necessity of asking that they would arrange to pay them at their next maturity. General Legaie, who had received a similar letter, rode up to see Dr. Cary next morning, and the following day they went to the city together. They rode on horseback, as they had no money to pay even the small sum necessary for the railway fares.

When the Doctor and General Legaie called on Mr. Ledger he was at the moment talking to a youngish, vigorous-looking man, whose new clothes and alert speech gave him almost a foreign air beside the stately manner of the two old gentlemen. Mr. Clough, the stranger, rose to go, but both Dr. Cary and General Legaie begged him to remain, declaring that they had " no secrets to discuss," and that they should themselves leave if he did so, as he had been there first.

They had exhausted every resource in their power to raise the means to pay Mr. Ledger, they said. And now they had come to him with a proposition. They looked at each other for support. It manifestly cost an effort to make it. They proposed that he should take, at a proper valuation, so much of their lands as would meet his debt. A sigh followed the proposal. It was evidently a relief to have got it out.

"It is good land, and not an acre has ever been sold from the original grant," said Dr. Cary. It manifestly added to the value of the terms offered.

" My dear sirs, what would I do with your lands ? " said Mr. Ledger. " I already have the security of the lands in addition to your personal obligation. My advice to you is to try and sell them—or, at least, so much of them as will enable you to discharge your debts. There are one or two men up in your section who have plenty of money.—This man Leech—and that man Still—they are land-buyers. Why don't you sell to them ? "

" What ! " exclaimed both Dr. Cary and General Legaie,

in one breath. "Sell our old family places to that man Leech ? "

"My dear sirs, it will come to this, I fear—or worse. My correspondents are all calling in their loans. I know that Mr. Still would not be averse to buying a part of your place or, indeed, all of it, Doctor ; and I think Leech would like to have yours, General."

The two old gentlemen stiffened.

"Why, that man Leech is a thief !" said the little General, with the air of one making a revelation. "He could not pay me a dollar that had not been stolen, and that fellow Still, he's a harpy, sir."

"Yes, I know, but I tell you frankly, gentlemen, it is your only chance. They mean to tax your land until you will find it impossible to hold on to it."

"In that case we should not wish to put it off even on those men," said the Doctor with dignity, rising. " I shall see if I cannot raise the money elsewhere to relieve you. Meantime I shall hold on to the old place as long as I can. I must make one more effort." And the two old gentlemen bowed themselves out!

"A very striking-looking pair," said the stranger, "but they don't seem to have much business in them."

"No," said Mr. Ledger, "they haven't. They are about as able to cope with the present as two babies." He sat in deep abstraction for a minute and then broke out suddenly : "But I'll tell you what : if you up yonder would just hold off they could clean up that pen on the hill in fifteen minutes. And I believe it would be the best thing for you to have them do it." His eyes blazed with a light that gave his visitor a new idea of him.

In consequence of this talk, Mr. Clough, when he had concluded his business, went for amusement to observe the proceedings of the State Legislature which was in session. It was undoubtedly strange to see laws being enacted by a body composed of blacks who but a few years before had been slaves, and he went away with a curious sense of the

incongruity of the thing. But it was only amusing to him.
They appeared good-natured and rather like big children
playing at something which grown people do. His only
trouble was the two old gentlemen.

"Of course it is all nonsense, those slaves being legisla-
tors," he admitted to Major Welch, on his arrival at home,
and to his father-in-law, Senator Rockfield. "But they
are led by white men who know their business. The fact
is, they appear to know it so well that I advise calling in
all the debts at once."

What simply amused this casual visitor, however, was a
stab in the heart of the two old gentlemen he had met.

Dr. Cary and General Legaie returned home without being able to raise anywhere the money that was due.

In reply to the letter announcing this, Dr. Cary received a letter from Mr. Ledger, informing him that he had
just had an offer from someone to take up the Doctor's
notes, and he had felt it his duty to notify him before he
assigned them. The person who had made the offer had
insisted that his name should not be known at present,
but he had intimated that it was with friendly intentions
toward Dr. Cary, though Mr. Ledger stated, he would not
like the Doctor to rely too much on this intimation. He
would much prefer that Dr. Cary should take up the notes
himself, and he would not for a moment urge him if it
were not that he himself was absolutely obliged to have
the money to meet his obligations.

To this letter the Doctor replied promptly. Mr. Ledger
must accept the offer from his unnamed correspondent if it
were a mere business transaction, and the Doctor only asked
that he would do so without in any way laying him under
any obligation to the person referred to, for a pretended
kindness.

"The old Doctor evidently knows his man," was Mr.
Ledger's reflection.

The next day Hiram Still held Dr. Cary's notes secured by deed of trust on the whole Birdwood estate.

Still was sitting in the big hall at Red Rock on his return home, and he took out the notes and laid them on the table before his son.

"Ah ! Dr. Wash," he said, with a gleam in his eyes; "things is comin' roun'. Now you've got it all your own way. With them cards in your hand if you can't win the game, you ain't as good a player as yer pappy. I don't want nothin' for myself, I just want 'em to know who I am—that's all. And with you over yonder at the old Doctor's, and Virgy in Congress or maybe even in the Governor's house down yonder, I reckon they'll begin to find out who Hiram Still is."

The son was evidently pleased at the prospect spread out before him, and his countenance relaxed.

"'Twon't do to let Leech get too far ahead—I'm always telling you so." Young Still was beginning to show some jealousy of Leech of late.

"Ahead ? He ain't ahead. He just thinks he is." The speaker's voice changed. "What's the matter with Virgy these days ? I've done set her up in the biggest house in the county, and brought the man who's goin' to be one of the biggest men in the State to want her to marry him, and she won't have nothin' to do with him. It clean beats my time. I don't know what's got into her. She ain't never been the same since I brought her here. Looks like these pictures round here sort o' freezes her up."

As he glanced around Hiram Still looked as if he were freezing up a little himself.

"She's a fool," said the brother, amiably.

"I thought maybe she's been kind o' ailin' an' I'd git the old Doctor to come and see her. Say what you please, he have a kind o' way with him women folks seems to like. But she won't hear of it."

"She's just a fool. Let her alone for awhile, anyhow." His father looked at him keenly.

"Well, you go ahead—and as soon as you've got your

filly safe, we'll take up t'other horse—time enough. Thar's the bridle." He touched the notes on the table and winked at his son.

Dr. Still, armed with the assurance which the possession of Dr. Cary's notes gave, drove over to Birdwood the very next evening in a double buggy. He was met by Dr. Cary, who treated him with his usual graciousness, and who so promptly assumed that the visit was merely a professional one that the caller never found the opportunity to undeceive him.

When Washington Still arrived at home that night his father was watching for him with eagerness. He met him as the buggy drove up into the yard; but Wash's face was sphinx-like. It was not until nearly bedtime, when the father had reinforced his courage with several drinks of whiskey, that he got courage to open the subject directly.

"Well, what news?" he asked, with an attempt at joviality.

"None," said Wash, shortly.

"How'd you come out?"

"Same way I went in." This was not encouraging, but another glass added to Mr. Still's spirit.

"How was she lookin'?"

"Didn't see her.—Didn't see anybody but the old Doctor; never do see anybody but him—and the old nigger that opens the door. He thought I'd come over to consult him about that sick nigger down at the mill, so I let him think so. I wish the d—d nigger would die!"

"And you didn't even ask for her?"

The young man shifted in his chair.

"What's the use! That old fool's got a way with him. You know how it is. If he wa'n't so d—d polite!"

"Ah! Washy, you're skeered," said the father, fondly. "You can't bridle a filly if you're afeard to go in, boy. If you don't git up the grit I'll go over thar myself, first thing you know. Why don't you write her a letter?"

15

"What's the good! I know'm. She wouldn't **look at** me. She's for *Lord* Jacquelin or Captain Steve **Allen**."

"She wouldn't!" Still rose from his chair in the intensity of his feeling. "By —— she shall! I'll make her."

"Make her! You think she's Virgy? She ain't."

A day or two later a letter from Dr. Still was brought to Birdwood by a messenger. Dr. Cary received it. It was on tinted paper and was for Blair. That afternoon another messenger bore back the same letter unopened, together with one from Dr. Cary, to the effect that his daughter was not accustomed to receive letters from young men, and that such a correspondence would not be agreeable to him.

Dr. Still was waiting with impatience for a reply to his missive. He was not especially sanguine. Even his father's hope could not reassure him. When he looked at the letter his countenance fell. He had not expected this. It was a complete overthrow. It not only was a total destruction of his hopes respecting Miss Cary, but it appeared to expose a great gulf fixed between him and all his social hopes. He had not known till then how much he had built on them. In an instant his feeling changed. He was enraged with Blair, enraged with Dr. Cary, enraged with Jacquelin Gray and Captain Allen, and enraged with his father who had counselled him to take the step. He took the letter to his father, and threw it on the table before him.

"Read that."

Hiram Still took up the letter and, putting on his glasses, read it laboriously. His face turned as red as his son's had turned white. He slammed the letter on the table and hammered his clenched fist down on it.

"You ain't good enough for 'em! Well, I'll show 'em. I'll turn 'em out in the road and make their place a nigger settlement. I'll show 'em who they're turnin' their noses up at. I'll show 'em who Hiram Still is. I'll make Leech Governor, and turn him loose on 'em, if it

takes every cent I've got in the world." He filled his
glass. " We'll show 'em yet who we are. When I'm settin'
up here and you're settin' up thar they'll begin to think
maybe after all they've made a little mistake."

Still was as good as his word. Within a day or two, Dr.
Cary received a letter from him asking the payment of his
obligations which he held. He assigned the necessity he
was under to raise a large sum of money himself.

The Doctor wrote in reply that it was quite impossible
for him to raise the money to pay the debts, and begged
that Still would without delay take the necessary steps to
close the matter up, assuring him that he should not only
not throw any obstacle in his way, but would further his
object as far as lay in his power.

Steve urged the Doctor to make a fight, declaring that
he could defer the sale for at least two years, maybe more,
and times might change ; but Dr. Cary declined.

"What can I do ? I owe a debt and I cannot pay it. I
might as well save the man the mortification of telling a
multitude of unnecessary lies."

So in a little while Still, through Leech, his counsel,
had subjected the Doctor's property to his debts and was in
possession of Birdwood as well as Red Rock.

Mrs. Cary and Blair left their roses and jonquils and with
the Doctor moved to the old Bellows place, where they
were as happy as they had ever been in the days of their
greatest prosperity. Old Tarquin, who accompanied them,
observed his master closely and followed his example, carrying his head as high as if he still walked the big halls
and polished floors of Birdwood. Mammy Krenda alone
was unhappy. She could not reconcile herself to the
change. The idea of "dat nigger-trader an' overseer
ownin' her old marster's place, an' o' her young mistis
havin' to live in de blacksmiff' house," was more than the
old woman could bear.

CHAPTER XX

LEECH LOOKS HIGHER AND GETS A FALL

MAJOR LEECH was now one of the leading men in the State. No one had been so successful in his measures. He boasted openly that he owned his own county. Carried it in his breeches pocket, he said.

Hiram Still had become the largest property-holder in the county. "I don't know so much about these here paper stocks," he said to his son. "But I know good land, and when you've got land you've got it, and everybody knows you've got it."

It was understood now that Leech was courting Still's daughter, and it began to be rumored that reinforced by this alliance, after the next election he would probably be the leader in the State. He was spoken of as a possible candidate for the Governorship, the election for which was to come off the following year.

The people were now as flat on their backs as even Leech could wish.

Fortunately there is a law by which conditions through their very excess are sometimes rectified. Absolute success often bears in it the seeds of its own destruction. With the power to make such laws as they wanted, and to gild all their acts with the tinsel of apparent authority, Leech and his associates had been so successful that they had lost all reckoning of opposition, and in their security had begun to quarrel among themselves.

The present Governor, Krafton, was a candidate for re-election, and his city organ declared that Leech was pledged to him. He had "made Leech," it said. "Leech

was bound to him by every tie of gratitude and honor."
Leech in private sneered at the idea. " Does he think I'm
bound to him for life ? Ain't he rich enough ? Does he
want to keep all the pie for himself ? Why don't he pay
that rent to the State for the railroad him and his crowd
leased ? He talk about beatin' me ! I'll show him. You
wait until after next session and all h—l can't beat me,"
he said to Hiram Still. He did not say this to the Governor. But perhaps even counting this Leech did not
count all the forces against him. Emboldened by the
quietude which had existed so long, Leech moved more
openly. He believed he was strong enough now for anything. Success was at length turning even Still's head.

" You got to keep yourself before the people, and do it
all the time. If you don't they'll forgit you, and somebody else will reap your harvest," Still explained to his
ally.

"Anybody as reaps for me is welcome to all he gets,"
said Leech.

The campaign opened, and soon Leech was as prominent as he could have wished. However prostrate the
people were, they were not ready to have Leech for the
Governor of the State, and they so declared. At a public
meeting that was held, Steve Allen in a speech declared
that " Krafton is a robber ; but Leech is a thief."

Both Leech and Still were sensible of the stir ; but they
did not heed it. Leech was daily strengthening himself.

When the rumor started that the whites were rousing
up and were beginning to think of organizing in opposition, Leech only laughed.

"Kick, will they ? " said he. "I want 'em to kick.
I'm fixed for 'em now. I've got the power I want behind
me now, and the more they kick the more they'll git the
rowels. I guess you're beginning to find out I'm pretty
well seated ? " he added triumphantly to Still. Still could
not but admit that it was so.

"Fact is, things're goin' almost too smooth," he said.

" You're hard to please," growled Leech.

" No ; but you know, sometimes I'm most afeered I'll wake up and find it a dream. Here I am settin' up, a gen- tleman here in this big house that I used to stand over yonder on the hill in the blazin' sun and just look at, and wonder if I ever would have one even as good as the one I was then in as my own ; and yonder are you, one of the big men in the State, and maybe will be Governor some day, who knows ? " Leech accepted the compliment with becoming condescension.

" That was a great stroke of yours to git the State to endorse the bonds and then git your man Bolter down here to put up that money. If this thing keeps up we soon won't have to ask nobody any odds," pursued Still.

" I don't ask any of 'em any odds now. When I get my militia fully organized, I'm going to make a move that will make things crack. And old Krafton will come down too. He thinks he's driving, and he's just holding the end of the reins."

" I don't count so much on your militia as I do on your friends. I know these people, and I tell you, you can't keep 'em down with niggers. If you try that you'll have a bust up 't will blow you—somewhere you won't want to be," cautioned Still. " I never was so much in favor of that militia business as you was. Comes to a fight, the whites will beat every time—and it costs too much. My taxes this year'll be——"

Leech frowned.

" Your taxes ! If it hadn't been for high taxes I'd like to know where you'd been. You're always talkin' about knowin' these people. You're afraid of 'em. I'm not. I suppose it's natural ; we've whipped you."

There was a sudden lower in Still's eye at the sneer.

" You're always talkin' about havin' whipped us. *You* ain't whipped us so much," he growled. " If you ain't afraid of 'em, whyn't you take up what Steve Allen said to you t'other day when he told you he'd be Governor before

you was, and called you—ur worse than Krafton? He's
given you chances enough."

"You wait, and you'll see how I'll take it up. I'll take
him up. I've got the government behind me, and when
I'm Governor and get a judge such as I want, you'll see
things working even enough."

"Well, 'twon't do for us to quarrel, Major. We're like
two steers yoked together," Still said, conciliatorily. "Only
don't go too fast at first—or you may break your team down
before you git anywhere near where you want to go."

When Still was alone with his son after this interview
he told him that Leech was in danger of ruining everything.

"He's gittin' sp'iled. We must keep the brakes on him
or he'll bust the wagon all to pieces. If he gits up too fast
he won't remember me and you," observed Mr. Still.
"Where would I be now if I hadn't gone a little keerful?"

"Careful," corrected his son, superciliously.

"Well, careful, then; I can't keep up with your book
learnin'. But I know a few things, and he's about to make
a fool of himself. He wants to break with old Krafton before it's time, and I ain't sure he's strong enough yet to do
it. We may have to call on Krafton yet, and 'twon't do to
let him go till we get Leech settled. He's goin' too fast
with his niggers. We've got to keep the brakes on
him."

Leech soon perfected the organization of his negroes.
The League furnished the nucleus. He had quite an army
enrolled. At first they drilled without arms, or with only
the old muskets which had come down from the war; but
in a little time a consignment of new rifles came from
somewhere, and at their next drill the bands appeared
armed and equipped with new army muskets and ammunition. Nicholas Ash was captain of one company, and
another was under command of Sherwood. Leech was
Colonel and commanding officer in the county. Under
the law, Krafton, as Governor, had the power to accept or

refuse any company that organized and offered itself. **The** effect of the new organization on the negroes was immediately felt. They became insolent and swaggering. The fields were absolutely abandoned. Should they handle hoes when they could carry guns! Should they plough when they were the State guard!

When Leech's new companies drilled, the roadsides were lined with their admirers. They filled the streets and took possession of the sidewalks, yelling, and hustling out of their way any who might be on them. Ladies walking on the street were met and shoved off into the mud. In a little while, whenever the militia were out, the whites disappeared almost wholly from the streets. But the men were to be found gathered together at some central place, quiet, and apparently without any object, but grim and earnest. Steve Allen was likely to be among them.

Steve organized a company and offered its services to the Governor, asking to be commissioned and armed. Only negro companies were being commissioned. The Governor referred him to Leech, who was, he said, the Commandant in that section. The next time Steve met Leech he said :

"Major Leech, your man Krafton says if you'll recommend it he'll commission a company I have." Leech hemmed and stammered a little.

"No need to be in a hurry about it, Major," said Steve, enjoying his embarrassment. "When you want 'em let me know. I'll have 'em ready," and he passed on with cheery insolence, leaving the carpet-bagger with an ugly look in his pale blue eyes.

Leech conferred with Still, who counselled that they should move with deliberation. Leech had grown impatient. He thought himself strong enough now to overawe the whites. Night meetings were being held everywhere, at which Leech addressed his followers. Their response was almost an outbreak.

A number of acts were committed that incensed the people greatly. Andy Stamper, with his wagon full of chickens and eggs, was coming along the road when he met one of the companies, followed by the crowd of negroes that usually attended the drills. In a few minutes the wagon was thrown down a bank and upset, the eggs were all smashed, and little Andy, fighting desperately with his whip, was knocked senseless and left on the roadside, unconscious. He said afterward it served him right for being such a fool as to go without his pistol, and that if he had had it he would have whipped the whole company. Mrs. Cary and Blair and Miss Thomasia came near having a similar experience. They were stopped on the road in their old carriage, and nothing but Mrs. Cary's spirit and old Gideon's presence of mind saved them perhaps from worse usage. Mrs. Cary, however, stepped out and stood beside her horses commanding that they should not be touched, while the old driver, standing up in the boot of the carriage, talked so defiantly and looked so belligerent that he preserved his mistresses from anything worse than being turned out rudely into the woods and very much frightened.

These things caused much excitement.

The first movement in the campaign was a great meeting that was held at the county seat. The negroes were summoned from several counties round, and there was to be a great muster of Leech's "new militia." It was a grave time in the county. All such assemblages were serious now, more for what might happen than for anything that had ever happened yet. But this one was especially serious. It was rumored that Leech would launch himself as a candidate for Governor, and would outline his policy. The presence of his militia was held to be a part of his plan to overawe any opposition that might arise. So strong was the tension that many of the women and children were sent out of the village, and those that remained kept their houses.

When the day for the meeting at the county seat came, nearly the entire male population of the county, white and colored, were present, and the negro companies were out in force, marching and parading up and down in the same field in which the white troops had paraded just before going off to the war. Many remarked on it that day. It served to emphasize the change that a few years had brought. When the parade was over, the companies took possession of the court green, and were allowed to break ranks preparatory to being called under arms again, when they were to be addressed on the issues of the campaign. The negroes, with a few white men among them—so few as not to make the slightest impression in the great dusky throng—were assembled on the court green. The whites were outside.

There was gravity, but good-humor.

Steve Allen, particularly, appeared to be in high spirits. To see the way the crowd was divided it might have looked as if they were hostile troops. Only, the whites apparently had no arms. But they had almost the formation of soldiery waiting at rest. Steve sauntered up into the crowd of negroes and made his way to where Leech stood well surrounded, talking to some of the leaders.

"Well, Colonel, how goes it? You seem to have a good many troops to-day. We heard you were going to have a muster, and we came down to see the drill."

The speech was received good-temperedly by the negroes, many of whom Steve spoke to by name good-humoredly.

Leech did not appreciate the jest, and moved off with a scowl. The young man, however, was not to be shaken off so. He followed the other to the edge of the crowd, and there his manner changed.

"Mr. Leech," he said, slowly, with sudden seriousness and with that deep intonation which always called up to Leech that night in the woods when he had been waylaid and kidnapped. "Mr. Leech, you are on trial to-day. Don't make a false step. You are the controlling spirit of these negroes. They await but your word. So do we. If a hand is lifted you will never be Governor. We have stood

all we propose to stand. You are standing on a powder
magazine. I give you warning."

He turned off and walked back to his own crowd.

It was the boldest speech that had been made to Leech
in a long time. His whole battalion of guards were on the
grounds, and a sign from him would have lodged Steve in
the jail, which frowned behind the old brick clerk's office.
He had a mind to order his arrest ; but as he glanced at
him there was a gleam in Steve's gray eyes which restrained
him. They were fixed on him steadily, and the men behind him suddenly seemed to have taken on something like
order. Until that moment Leech had no idea what a force
it was. There were men of all classes in the ranks. He
seemed suddenly the focus of all eyes. They were fastened
on him with a cold hostility that made him shiver. He
had a sudden catching at the heart. He sent for Still and
had a conference with him. Still advised a pacific course.
" Too many of 'em," he said. " And they are ready for
you."

Leech adopted Still's advice. In the face of Steve's
menace and that crowd of grim-looking men he quailed.
His name was put forward, and many promises were made
for him, revolutionary enough, but it was not by himself.
Nicholas Ash, after a long conference with Leech and Still,
was the chief speaker of the occasion, and Leech kept himself in the background all day.

The policy laid down by Nicholas Ash, even after his
caution from Leech and Still, was bad enough. " They
say the taxes are too high," declared the negro statesman.
" I tell you, and Colonel Leech tells you, they ain't high
enough, and when he's Governor they'll be higher yet. We
are goin' to raise 'em—yes, we are goin' to raise 'em till we
bankrupt 'em every one, and then the land will go to the
ones as ought to have it, and if anybody interferes with
you, you've got guns and you know how to use 'em."
Tumultuous applause greeted this exposition of Leech's
principles. Only the earnest counsel of Dr. Cary and some

of the older and cooler heads kept the younger men quiet. But the day passed off quietly. The only exception was an altercation between Captain McRaffle and a negro. Leech's name had been suggested for the Governorship, and had taken well. So he was satisfied. That night the negroes paraded in companies through the village, keeping step to a sort of chant about raising taxes and getting the lands and driving out the whites.

As Dr. Cary rode home that evening on his old horse, Still and Leech passed him in a new buggy drawn by a pair of fine horses which young Dr. Still had just got. Both men spoke to Dr. Cary, but the Doctor had turned his head away so as not to see them. It was the nearest his heart would let him come to cutting a man direct.

Next night after dark there was a meeting, at which were present nearly all the men whose names have appeared in this chronicle, except Dr. Cary and one or two of the older gentlemen, and a number more besides.

The place selected for the meeting was the old hospital, a rambling, stone house with wings, and extensive cellars under it. It was in a cleft between two hills, surrounded by a dense grove, which made it at all times somewhat gloomy. It had been used as a field-hospital in a battle fought near by, and on this account had always borne a bad name among the negroes, who told grewsome tales of the legs and arms hacked off there and flung out of the windows, and of the ghostly scenes enacted there now after nightfall, and gave it a wide berth.

After the war, a cyclone had blown down or twisted off many of the trees around the mansion, and had taken the roof off a part of the building and blown in one of the wings, killing several of the persons who then occupied it, which casualty the superstition of the negroes readily set down to avenging wrath. The rest of the house had stood the storm ; but since that time the building had never been repaired and had sunk into a state of mournful dilapidation, and few negroes in the county could have been in-

duced to go there even in daylight. The fields had sprung
up in dense pines, and the roads leading out to the highways had grown up and were now hardly distinguishable.
It had escaped even the rapacious clutch of Land Commissioner Still.

The night after the speaking at the court-house there
was a meeting of ghostly riders at this old place, which had
any of the negroes around seen, they would have had some
grounds for thinking the tales told of the dead coming
back from their graves true.

Pickets, with men and horses heavily shrouded, were
posted at every outlet from the plantation, and the riders
rode for some distance in the beds of streams, so that when
the hoof-tracks reached certain points, they seemed suddenly to disappear from the earth.

Rumors had already come from other sections of a new
force that had arisen, a force composed of ghostly night-
riders. It was known as the "Invisible Empire," and the
negroes had already been in a tremor of subdued excitement;
but up to this time this county had been so quiet, and
Leech had been so supreme, that they had not taken in
that the Ku Klux might reach there.

After the muster of Leech's militia at the county seat the
companies had been dismissed and the members had strag-
gled to their homes, taking with them their arms and accoutrements, with all the pride and pomp of newly decorated children. But their triumph was short-lived.

In the dead of night, when the cabins and settlements
were wrapped in slumber, came a visitation, passing
through the county from settlement to settlement and
from cabin to cabin, in silence, but with a thoroughness that
showed the most perfect organization. When morning
dawned every gun and every round of ammunition which
had been issued throughout the county, except those at the
county seat, and some few score that had been conveyed to
other places than the homes of the men who had them,
had been taken away.

In most cases the seizure was accomplished quietly, the surprise being so complete as to prevent wholly any resistance. All that the dejected warriors could tell next day was that there had been a noise outside, the door had been opened; the yard had been found full of awful forms wrapped like ghosts in winding-sheets, some of whom had entered the houses, picked up the guns and ammunition, and without a word walked out and disappeared.

In other instances, the seizure had not been so easily effected, and in some few places there had been force exerted and violence used. But in every case the guns had been taken either peaceably or by force, and the man who had resisted had only called down on his head severity. One man only had been seriously hurt. It was the man with whom McRaffle had had the difficulty.

The whites had not been wholly exempt.

Leech had spent the night at Hiram Still's. They had talked over the events of the meeting and the whole situation. Ash's speech proposing Leech for Governor had taken well with the negroes, and for the whites they did not care. The whites had evidently been overawed. This was Leech's interpretation of their quietude. Leech was triumphant. It was the justification of his plan in arming his followers. He laid off his future plans when he should have fuller powers. His only regret was that he had not had Steve Allen arrested for threatening him. But that would come before long.

"D—n him! I wish he was dead," he growled.

"Go slow, Colonel; if wishes could kill, he'd 'a' been dead long ago—and maybe so would you," laughed Still.

"What a —— unpleasant laugh you have," frowned Leech. He did not often allow himself the luxury of a frown; but he found it effective with Still.

Next morning Leech was aroused by his host calling to him hastily to get up. Still was as white as death.

"What is it?" demanded Leech.

"Get up and come out quick. Hell's broke loose."

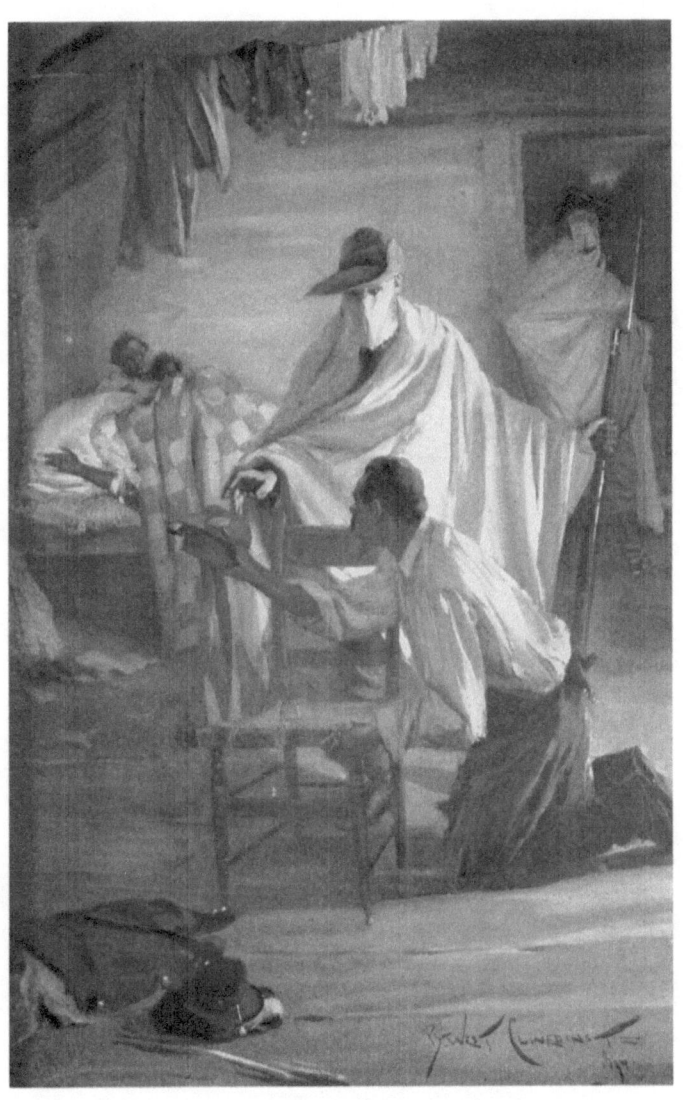

KU KLUX—"AWFUL FORMS WRAPPED LIKE GHOSTS IN WINDING-SHEETS."

he flatly charged him with treachery in announcing himself a candidate in opposition to him, and declined to interfere unless Leech at once retired.

In this dilemma Leech promptly denied that he had ever announced himself as a candidate.

Well, he allowed Nicholas Ash to do it, which amounted to the same thing, the Governor asserted.

Leech repudiated any responsibility for Ash's action, and denied absolutely that he had any idea whatever of running against the Governor, for whom he asseverated the greatest friendship.

Thus the matter was ostensibly patched up, and Leech and Still received some assurance that action would be taken. When, however, they left the presence of the Governor, it was to take a room and hold a private conference at which it was decided that their only hope lay in securing immediately the backing of those powers on whose support the Governor himself relied to be sustained.

"I know him," whispered Still. "You didn't fool him. He ain't never goin' to help you. May look like he's standin' by you ; but he ain't. We've got to go up yonder. Bolter's obliged to stand by us. He's too deep in." He chucked his thumb over his shoulder in the direction in which his noon-shadow was pointing. Leech agreed with him, and instead of returning home, the two paid a somewhat extended visit to the seat of government, where they posed as patriots and advocates of law and order, and were admitted to conferences with the most potent men in the councils of the nation, before whom they laid their case.

When Leech came out, Still pointed him to a picture drawn with red chalk on the floor of the portico, a fairly good representation of the "Indian-killer." There were also three crosses cut in the bark of one of the trees in front of the door.

"What does that mean?"

"Means some rascals are trying to scare you : we'll scare them."

But Still was not reassured. Anything relating to the "Indian-killer" always discomposed him. He had to take several drinks to bring back his courage—and when about breakfast-time the news began to come to them of the visitation that had been made through the county during the night, Leech, too, began to look pale.

By mid-day they knew the full extent and completeness of the stroke. A new and unknown force had suddenly arisen. The negroes were paralyzed with terror. Many of them believed that the riders were really supernatural, and they told, with ashy faces, of the marvellous things they had done. Some of them had said that they had just come from hell to warn them, and they had drunk bucketfuls of water, which the negroes could hear "sizzling" as it ran down their throats.

By dusk both Leech and Still had disappeared. They saw that the organization of the negroes was wholly destroyed, and unless something were done, and done immediately, they would be stampeded beyond hope. They hurried off to the city to lay their grievances before the Governor, and claim the aid of the full power of the Executive.

They found the Governor much exercised, indeed, about the attack on his militia ; but to their consternation he was even more enraged against themselves by the announcement of Leech's prospective candidacy in opposition to him. He declared that he had aided Leech in all his schemes, with the express understanding that the latter should give him his unqualified support for re-election, and

CHAPTER XXI

DR. CARY MEETS AN OLD COLLEGE MATE AND LEARNS THAT THE ATHENIANS ALSO PRACTISE HOSPITALITY

THE Ku Klux raid, as it was called, created a great commotion, not only in our county but in other quarters as well. There had been in other sections growlings and threatenings, altercations, collisions, and outbreaks of more or less magnitude, but no outbreak so systematic, so extensive, and so threatening as this had hitherto occurred, and it caused a sensation. It was talked about as "a new rebellion," calling for the suspension of the writs of privilege and the exercise of the strongest powers of the Government.

When therefore Leech and Still appeared at the national capital, as suitors appealing for aid to maintain the laws and even to secure their lives, they found open ears and ready sympathizers. They were met by Mr. Bolter, who mainly had taken the bonds of their new railway, which was not yet built, and who was known as a wealthy capitalist. Thus they appeared as men of substance and standing, well introduced, and as they spoke with doubtful endorsement of the Governor they were even regarded as more than commonly conservative, and their tale was given unbounded credit.

When they returned home it was with the conviction that their mission had been completely successful ; they had not only secured the immediate object of their visit, and obtained the promise of the strongest backing that could be given against their enemies, but they had gained even a more important victory. They had instilled doubts as to both the sincerity and the wisdom of the Governor; had, as Still said, "loosed a lynch-pin for him," and had established themselves as the true and proper persons to be consulted and supported. Thus they had secured, as they hoped, the future control of the State. They were in an ecstasy, and when a little later the new judge was appointed, and proved to be Hurlbut Bail, the man Bolter had recommended against one the Governor had backed, they felt themselves to be masters of the situation.

When the mission of Leech and Still became known in the old county it created grave concern. A meeting was held and Dr. Cary and General Legaie, with one or two others of the highest standing, were appointed a committee to go on and lay their side of the case before the authorities and see what they could do to counteract the effect of the work of Leech and his associates.

It was the first time Dr. Cary and General Legaie had been to the national capital or, indeed, out of the State, since the war, and they were astonished to see what progress had been made in that brief period.

They found themselves, on merely crossing a river, suddenly landed in a city as wholly different from anything they had seen since the war as if it had been a foreign capital. The handsome streets and busy thoroughfares filled with well-dressed throngs; gay with flashing equipages, and all the insignia of wealth, appeared all the more brilliant from the sudden contrast. As the party walked through the city they appeared to themselves to be almost the poorest persons they saw, at least among the whites. The city was full of negroes at this time. These seemed to represent mainly the two extremes of prosperity and poverty. The gentlemen could not walk on the street without being applied to by some old man or woman who was in want, and who, as long as the visitors had anything to give, needed only to ask to be assisted.

"We are like lost souls on the banks of the Styx," said Dr. Cary. "I feel as much a stranger as if I were on

another planet. And to think that our grandfathers helped
to make this nation!"

"To think that we ever surrendered!" exclaimed General Legaie, with a flash in his eye.

They took lodgings at a little boarding-house, and called
next day in a body on the Head of the Nation, but were
unable to see him; then they waited on one after another
of several high officers of the Government whom they
believed to be dominant in the national councils. Some
they failed to get access to; others heard them civilly, but
with undisguised coldness. At one place they were treated
rudely by a negro door-keeper, whose manner was so insolent that the General turned on him sharply with a word
and a gesture that sent him bouncing inside the door.
After this interview, as Dr. Cary was making his way back
to his boarding-house, he met one of his old servants. The
negro was undisguisedly glad to see him. He wrung his
hand again and again.

"You's de fust frien', master, I's seen since I been
heah!" he said.

"You are the first friend, John, I have seen," said the
Doctor, smiling. He put his hand in his pocket and gave
the old man a bank-note.

As the Doctor was engaged in this colloquy he was
observed with kindly interest or amusement by many
passers-by—among them, by an elderly and handsomely
dressed couple, accompanied by a very pretty girl, who
were strolling along, and loitered for a moment within
earshot to observe the two strangers.

"What a picturesque figure!" said the lady as they
passed on.

"Which one?"

"Well, both. I almost thought of them as one. I
wish, Alice, you could have got a sketch of them as they
stood."

" He is a Southerner—from his voice," said her husband,
who was Judge Rockfield, one of the ablest and most noted

men at that time in public life ; one of the wisest in council, and who, though his conservatism in that period of
fierce passion kept him from being as prominent as some
who were more violent and more radical, yet was esteemed
one of the ablest and soundest men in the country.
He was a Senator from his State, and the owner of one of
the leading and most powerful journals in the country.

Dr. Cary, having given the old negro his address, took a
street-car to try to overhaul his friends. It was quite full,
and the Doctor secured the last vacant seat. A few blocks
farther on, several persons boarded the car, among them
the elderly gentleman and his wife and daughter, already
mentioned, and another lady. The Doctor rose instantly.

"Will you take my seat, madam ? " he said to the nearest lady, with a bow. The other ladies were still left
standing, though there were many men seated ; but the
next second a young fellow farther down the car rose, and
gave up his seat. As he took his stand the Doctor caught
his eye.

" 'The Athenians praise hospitality, the Lacedemonians
practise it,' " he said in a distinct voice that went through
the car, and with a bow to the young fellow which
brought a blush of pride to his pleasant face.

The next moment the gentleman who had entered with
his wife touched the Doctor on his arm.

"I beg your pardon: is your name Cary ? "

"Yes, sir."

" Can this be John Cary of Birdwood ? "

"Yes, sir."

" Don't you remember Anson Rockfield ? "

"Why, Rockfield, my old college-mate ! " exclaimed the
Doctor. The two men grasped each other's hands with a
warmth which drew to them the attention and interest of
the whole car. " Rockfield, you see I am still quoting
Plutarch," said the Doctor.

"And still practising his principles," said the Senator,
smiling, as he presented him to his wife.

"My dear, this is the man to whom you are indebted
for whatever is good in me. But for him I should have
gone to the d—l years before you knew me."

"He gives me far too much credit, madam, and himself
far too little," said the Doctor. "I am sure that ever to
have been able to win the prizes he has won he must have
been always worthy, as worthy as a man can be of a
woman." He bowed low to Mrs. Rockfield.

Senator Rockfield urged the Doctor to come at once to
his house and be his guest while in the city, an invitation
which his wife promptly seconded with much graciousness.

"Let us show you that some of the Athenians practise
as well as praise hospitality," she said, smiling.

Thanking them, the Doctor excused himself from accepting the invitation, but said that with Mrs. Rockfield's permission he would call and pay his respects, and he did so
that evening.

As a result of this meeting an audience was arranged for
him and his friends next day with the President, who
heard them with great civility, though he gave them no
assurance that he would accept their views, and furnished
no clew to lead them to think they had made any impression at all. They came away, therefore, somewhat downcast.

Before the Southerners left for home, Senator Rockfield
called on Dr. Cary and, taking him aside, had a long talk
with him, explaining somewhat the situation and the part
he had felt himself compelled to take. He wound up,
however, with an appeal that Dr. Cary would not permit
political differences to divide them and would allow him
to render him personally any assistance that his situation
might call for.

"I am rich now, Cary," he said; "while you have suffered reverses and may have found your means impaired
and yourself at times even cramped. (The Doctor thought
how little he knew of the real facts.) "It is the fortune
of war, and I want you to allow me to help you. I sup-

pose you must have lost a good deal ? " he said, interrogatively.

A change passed over the old Doctor's face. Reminiscence, pain, resolution were all at work, and the pleasant light which had been there did not return, but in its place was rather the shade of deepened fortitude.

"No," he said, quietly. " ' War cannot plunder Virtue.' I have learned that a quiet mind is richer than a crown."

" Still, I know that the war must have injured you some," urged the Senator. " We were chums in old times and I want it to be so now. I have never forgotten what you were to me, and what I told my wife of your influence on me was less than the fact. Why, Cary, I even learnt my politics from you," he said, with a twinkle in his eye.

Dr. Cary thanked him, but was firm. He could think of nothing he could do for him.

" Except this : think of us as men. Come down and see for yourself."

" Still practising Plutarch," said the Senator. " Well, the time may come, even if it has not come yet, and I want you to promise me that when it does, you will call on me—either for yourself or any friend of yours. It will be a favor to me, Cary," he added, with a new tone in his voice, seeing the look on the Doctor's face. " Somehow, you have turned back the dial, and taken me back to the time when we were young and fresh, and full of high hopes and—yes—aspirations, and I had not found out how d—d mean and sordid the world is. It will be a favor to me."

" All right, I will," said the Doctor, " if my friends need it." And the two friends shook hands.

So the Commission from the old county returned home.

Captain Allen of late spent more and more of his time at Dr. Cary's. His attitude toward Blair was one of gallantry mingled with protection and homage ; but that was his attitude toward every girl ; so Blair was under no delusion about it, and between them was always waged a warfare that was half pleasantry. To Mammy Krenda, however, the young man's relation to her mistress meant much more. No one ever looked at Blair that the old mammy did not instantly interpret it as a confession and a declaration, and having done this she instantly formed her judgment, and took her stand. She had divined the ambition of Dr. Still long before that aspiring young man dispatched to Miss Blair that tinted note which was the real if not the immediate cause of the Carys' removal from Birdwood to the Bellows cottage. And during those preliminary visits which the young physician had made to the old one, the old woman had with her sharp eyes penetrated his assumed disguise and made him shiver. Dr. Still knew that though Dr. Cary was taking him at his word and believed he really came so often to talk of medicine and seek advice, yet the old mammy discerned his real object, and despised him.

In Captain Allen's case it was different. Though the old woman and he were ostensibly always at war and never were together without his teasing her and her firing a shot in return at him, yet, at heart, she adored him. His distinguished appearance and his leading position, taken with his cordial and real friendliness toward herself, made him a favorite with her—and the speech he had made to Middleton on her account and his hostility to Leech made her his slave.

Her manner to him was always capricious and fault-finding, as became the jealous guardian of Miss Blair; but "old Argos," as Captain Allen called her, was his warm ally and he knew it. She took too many occasions to promote his and Blair's wishes, as she understood them, for him to doubt it, and, possibly, it was as much due to her misapprehension as to anything else, that Steve was drawn on to do what, but for Blair's good sense, might have imperilled both his happiness and hers.

Since the stir created by the Ku Klux raid, Captain Allen had exercised more precaution than he was accus-

tomed to do. All sorts of rumors were afloat as to
what the Government had promised on the instigation of
Leech and Still. Captain Allen's name was mentioned in
all of them. Steve, in consequence, had of late been at
the court-house less continuously than usual. And from
equally natural causes, he had been much more at Dr.
Cary's. To Mammy Krenda's innuendoes, he laughingly
replied that it was healthier near the mountains—to which
the old woman retorted that she knew what mountains he
was trying to climb.

One afternoon he rode up to Dr. Cary's a little earlier
than usual, and, finding the family absent, turned his
horse out in the yard and lounged on the porch, awaiting
their arrival. He had not been there long when Mammy
Krenda appeared. Steve watched her for a moment with
amusement. He knew she had come out to talk to him.

"What are you prowling about here for, you old Ku
Klux witch, you?" he asked, with a twinkle in his eye.

Mammy Krenda gave a sniff.

"Ku Klux! Ku Klux!! If prowlin' meeks Ku Klux,
I wonder what you wuz doin' last night? An' what you
doin' now?"

"Jerry's been around, the drunken rascal!" thought
Steve to himself. He knew Jerry was courting a grand-
daughter of old Krenda's.

"How's Jerry coming on with his courting?" he asked,
irrelevantly.

"N'em mind about Jerry," said the old mammy.
"Jerry know mo' 'bout co'tin' than some other folks."

This was interesting, and Steve, seeing that she had
something on her mind, gave her a lead. He learned that
the old woman thought her " chile " was not well—that she
was " pesterin' herself mightily " about something, and,
what was more astonishing, that Mammy Krenda held that
he himself was in a measure responsible for it.

A little deft handling and a delicate cross-examination
soon satisfied Steve that Jacquelin stood no chance. He

hinted as to Middleton. Mammy Krenda threw up her head. "She ain' gwine marry no Yankee come pokin' in folks' kitchen."

That disposed of it so far as Middleton was concerned.

"How about McRaffle ? He's always hanging around?" laughed Steve.

Krenda gave a sniff and started on.

"Dat man what been in a coffin ! Jes' soon marry a lizard ! You know she ain' go' marry dat man ! She wouldn' look at him !"

"Well, who is it ?" demanded Steve.

The old woman turned and faced him ; gave him a penetrating glance, and, with a toss of her turbaned-head, walked into the house.

Steve sat on the porch for some time in deep reflection, and then rising, walked across the grass, saddled his horse and rode quietly away. All the past came before him and all the present too. Could it be possible that he had been the cause of Middleton's repulse and of Jacquelin's failure ? It had never occurred to him. Yet, this was undoubtedly the old mammy's theory. She had as good as told him that he was the cause of Blair's disquietude, and in the light of her revelation it all seemed reasonable enough. This was the secret of her attitude toward Jacquelin. If she cared for him, it was his duty to marry her. And where could he ever find her superior ? Who was so good and fine ? Such were his reflections.

So one evening when he was with Blair, he suddenly began to speak to her as he had never done before. Blair was not looking at him, and she answered lightly. But Steve did not respond so. He had grown serious. Blair looked at him quickly ; her smile died out, and the color flushed her face. Could Steve be in earnest ? She gazed at him curiously ; but unhesitatingly ; only a look almost of sorrow came into her eyes. Steve went on and said all he had planned. When he had finished, Blair suddenly sat down by him and put her hand over his. She was perfectly composed and her eyes looked frankly into his.

"No, Steve—you are mistaken," she said, quietly. "You have misunderstood your feelings. You do not love me—at least, you are not in love with me. You love me I believe, devotedly, and I thank God for it every day of my life; as I love you as a sister—but you are not in love with me. You would help me, relieve me, spare me trouble and anxiety, save me from Captain—M—Middleton—and you see no reason why we should not marry. But there is one reason. You are not in love with me and I am not in love with you." She was speaking so gravely and her eyes were looking into his so frankly and with such true friendliness that Steve, though feeling somewhat flat at his repulse, could not deny what she said.

"I know the difference," she went on, quietly. She paused and reflected and, to Steve's surprise, suddenly changed and choked up. "I have had men in love with me—and—" Her voice faltered. She looked down, put her hand to her eyes and with a cry of, "Oh! Steve!" buried her face against his shoulder. "I seem to curse everyone that loves me."

In an instant Steve's strong arm was around her and he was comforting her like an older brother. His sympathy opened the girl's heart, and drew out the secret of her unhappiness as nothing else could have done. Blair had revealed her feelings to him as she had hardly before revealed them even to herself. It was the old story of misunderstanding, and high spirit; stung pride, hot words, and vain regret—regret not for herself; but only for others. Her unhappiness was that she had brought sorrow to others. It was because of her that Jacquelin had left home, and that his mother was dying of a broken heart. Steve tried to comfort her. She was all wrong, he assured her—she took a wholly erroneous view of the matter. But it was not a success. Jacquelin, she knew, had incurred Leech's personal hatred on her account, and that was the primary cause of his exile. All the other trouble had flowed from it; his mother's decline was owing to her repining for Jacquelin and her anxiety about Rupert, who, cut off from his mother's care and influence, was beginning to show symptoms of wildness. All these Blair traced back to her folly.

Steve, having failed in his effort to comfort her by argument, took another method and boldly assailed her whole idea as unreasonable and morbid. He threatened to write to Jacquelin and fetch him home, and he would have Rupert back at once, and keep him straight too, and if Leech molested him, he would have him to settle with.

The effect of this was just what Steve had anticipated. Blair suddenly took the opposite tack ; but in the battle that ensued she showed that she had recovered at least a part of her spirit.

Steve that evening sent Jacquelin a letter intended to meet him on the arrival of his vessel, telling him of his mother's declining health and urging him to hasten home. He also wrote to the head of the school where Rupert was.

CHAPTER XXII

WHEN Jacqu lin Gray returned home, his arrival was
wholly unexpected. His ship had reached port only a
few days before and he had planned to take his friends by
surprise, and, without giving any notice, had at once started
for home. He would hardly have been known for the
same man : in place of the pallid and almost bed-ridden
invalid who had been borne away on a stretcher a year
or two back, appeared a vigorous, weather-browned man,
almost as stalwart as Steve himself. The first to recognize
him was Waverley, who had been sent to the railroad by
Mrs. Gray to try and get news of him.

"Well b'fo' de Lord !" exclaimed the old man, "ef dat
ain't !—" He paused and took another scrutinizing look,
and, with a bound forward, broke out again. "Marse
Jack, you done riz f'um de dead. Ef I didn' think 'twas
my ole marster—er de Injun-Killer. Bless de Lord !—
you's jest in time. My mistis sen' me down fur a letter—
she say she 'bleeged to have a letter to-day. But dis de
bes' letter could 'a' come in dis wull fur her. Yas, suh,
she'll git well now." He took in the whole crowd confidentially. He was wringing Jacquelin's hand in an ecstasy
of joy, and the welcome of the others was not less warm, if
less voluble. Under it all, however, was something that
struck Jacquelin and went to his heart—something plain-
tive—different from what he had expected. The negroes
too had changed. The hearty laughter had given place to
something that had the sound of bravado in it. The shin-

252

ing teeth were not seen as of old. Old Waverley's words
sent a chill through him. What could they mean ?

How was his mother ? And aunt—and all the others ?
—at Birdwood and everywhere ? he asked.

His mistress had been " mighty po'ly, mighty po'ly indeed," the old servant said. " Been jes' pinin' fur you to
git back. What meck you stay so long, Marse Jack ? Hit
must be a long ways 'roun de wull ? But she'll be all
right now. De Doctor say you de bes' physic she could
git. All de others is well."

" And all at Birdwood ? " asked Jacquelin.

" 'Tain't Budwood you's axin' 'bout. Washy Still, he's
at Budwood. Dem you want know 'bout is at Mis' Bel-
lers ! Washy Still thought he wuz gwine git one o' dem
whar wuz at Budwood ; but he ain't do it. Rich or no
rich, dee tun up dey nose at him—and all he git wuz de
nest arter de bud done fly. Dee look higher'n him I
knows. But I mighty glad you come. Marse Steve, he's
dyah. He's a big man now. You's done stay away too
long. He's one o' de leaders."

What could this mean ?

As Jacquelin drove homeward with the old man he discovered what it meant ; for Waverley was not one to take
the edge from a blow. He had a sympathetic heart and
he made the most of it.

" Marse Jack, de debble is done broke loose, sho ! " he
wound up. " De overseer is in de gret house, and de
gent'man's in de blacksmiff shop. I wonders sometimes
dat old Injun-Killer don' come down out de picture sho
'nough—like so many o' dem dead folks what comin' out
dey graves."

" What's that ? " asked Jacquelin.

" Dat's what dee tells me," protested Waverley. " De
woods and roads is full on 'em at night. An' you can't git
a nigger to stir out by hisself arter dark. I b'lieves it,
and so does plenty o' urrs." He gave a little nervous
laugh.

"What nonsense is this?" demanded Jacquelin.

"'Tain' no nonsense, Marse Jack. 'Tis de fatal truf—Since sich doin's been goin' on, de graves won' hole 'em. De's some knows 'tain' no nonsense Dee done been to de house o' several o' dese sarsy niggers whar done got dee heads turned and gin 'em warnin' an' a leetle tetch o' what's comin' to 'em. Dee went to Moses' house turr night an' gin him warnin'. Moses wa'nt dyah; but dee done lef him de wud—cut three cross marks in de tree right side he do '; an' he wife say dee leetle mo' drink de well dry. One on 'em say he shot in de battle nigh heah and was cut up in de ole horspittle, and dat he jes come from torment to gi' Moses an' Sherrod an' Nicholas Ash warnin'. Dee say he drink six water-bucketfuls and hit run down he guzzle sizzlin' jes like po'in' 't on hot stove. Moses say he don' mine 'em; but I tell you he better!" A sudden gleam of shrewdness crossed the old fellow's face.

"Things had done got pretty bad, Marse Jack," the old man went on, confidentially. "Hiram Still and Cun'l Leech, dee owned ev'y thing, and ef you didn't do what dee say you couldn' turn roun'. Hiram, he turn' me out my shop jes soon as he got our place; an' soon as he fine he couldn't git my young mistis, he turn' de Doctor out. Look like he and dat urr man, Leech, sutney is got a grudge 'ginst all o' we all. Dee done put dee cross marks 'ginst Hiram too. Some say 'twas de Injun-Killer. Leech say he don' mine 'em—he's gwine to be gov'ner an' he say he'll know how to settle 'em; but Hiram, sence he fine dat mark on de porch and on de tree, he walks right smart lighter'n he did."

As they neared the county seat they met a body of negroes marching. The officers yelled at them to get out of the way, and old Waverley pulled out to one side. "What are they?" asked Jacquelin.

"Dem's Cun'l Leech's soldiers," said Waverley— "dem's de mellish. When you meets dem you got to git out 'n de way, I tell you."

The change in the aspect of the county in the few years of his absence impressed Jacquelin. It seemed to him greater even than that which had taken place during the war. The fields were more grown up ; the houses more dilapidated. But as much as these warned him, Jacquelin was not prepared for the change which on his arrival at Dr. Cary's he found had taken place.

His mother's appearance struck a chill to his heart. His mother had become an old woman. She had kept everything from him that could disturb him. He was shocked at the change which illness had made in her, and all he could do was to try and conceal his anguish.

He sought Dr. Cary and had a long talk with him ; but the Doctor could not hold out any hope. It was simply a general breakdown, he told him : the effect of years of anxiety. " You cannot transplant old trees," he said, sadly. Jacquelin ground his teeth in speechless self-reproach.

" Ah ! my dear Jacquelin, there are some things that even you could not have changed," said the Doctor, with a deep sigh.

As Jacquelin looked at him the expression on the old physician's face went to his heart.

" Yes, I know," he said, softly. " Ah ! well, we'll pull through."

" You young men, perhaps ; not we old ones. We are too broken to weather the storm. Your father was the fortunate one."

As the young man went out from this interview he met Blair. She had just come in from her school ; her cheeks were all aglow and she gave him a warm handclasp—and her eyes, after the first glance into his, fell. He was sure from what he had heard that she was engaged to Steve, and he had rehearsed a hundred times how he should meet her. Now like a puff of wind went all his strong resolutions. It was as though he had opened a door toward the sunrise. A fresh sense of her charm came over him as though he had just discovered her. Her presence appeared to him to fill all the place. She had grown in beauty since he went away. She was blushing and laughing and running away from Steve, who had met her outside and told her of Jacquelin's arrival, and was calling to her through the door to come back ; but after shaking hands with Jacquelin she sped on upstairs, with a little side glance at him as she ran up. She had never appeared so beautiful to Jacquelin. and his heart leaped up in him at her charm. It was the vision that had gone with him all around the globe. He followed her with his eyes. As she turned at the top of the stairs his heart sank ; for, leaning down over the banisters, she gave Steve a glance so full of meaning that Jacquelin took it all in in an instant.

"I'm going to tell him," called Steve, teasingly.

"No, you promised me you would not, Steve," and she was gone.

Jacquelin turned to the door.

Steve called him :

"Jack, Jack, come here."

But Jacquelin could not stand seeing him at that moment. He wanted to be alone, and he went out to meet the full realization of it all by himself.

Jacquelin made up his mind at once. Although Doctor and Mrs. Cary pressed him to stay with them, he felt that he could not live in the house with Blair. How could he sit by and see her and Steve day by day! Steve was as a brother to him, and Blair, from her manner, meant to be a sister ; but he could not endure it. He declared his intention of starting at once to practise law. Steve offered him a partnership, meeting Jacquelin's objection that it would not be fair, with the statement that he would make Jacquelin do all the work, as he proposed to be a statesman.

So, as the Doctor had said that a change and occupation in household duties might possibly do Mrs. Gray good, Jacquelin rented a small farm between the Carys' and the old hospital-place on the river, and they moved there. His

mother and Miss Thomasia furnished it with the assistance
of Mrs. Cary, and Blair, and other neighbors ; the old
pieces of furniture and other odds and ends giving, as
Miss Thomasia said, "a distinction which even the meanness of the structure itself could not impair. For, my
dear," she said to Blair, who was visiting them the evening after they had made their exodus from Dr. Cary's
to their new home, "I have often heard my grandfather
say that nothing characterized gentle-people more than dignity under misfortune." And she smoothed down her
faded dress and resumed her knitting with an air which
Blair in vain tried to reproduce to her father on her return.

Jacquelin was vaguely conscious that a change had come,
not only over the old county since he left it, but over his
friends also. Not merely had the places gone down, but
the people themselves were somewhat changed. They
looked downcast ; their tone, formerly jovial and cheery,
had a tinge of bitterness. In those few years a difference
between him and them had grown up. He did not analyze
it, but it was enough to disquiet him. Had his point of
view changed ? He saw defects which he thought he
could remedy. Those he was with, apparently saw none.
They simply plodded on, as though oblivious of the facts.
It made him unhappy. He determined to use his enlarged
view, as he deemed it, to instruct and aid those who
lacked his advantages. It seemed to him that, in his travels,
his horizon had widened. On the high seas or in a foreign land, it had been the flag of the nation that he wanted
to see. He had begun to realize the idea of a great nation
that should be known and respected wherever a ship could
sail or a traveller could penetrate ; of a re-united country
in which the people of both sides, retaining all the best
of both sides, should vie with each other in building up
the nation, and should equally receive all its benefits. He
had pondered much on this, and he thought he had discovered the way to accomplish it, in a complete acceptance of
the new situation.

17

It was a great blow to Jacquelin to find on his return
what extraordinary changes had taken place in the county:
Still, occupying not only his old home, but Dr. Cary's;
Leech the supreme power in all public matters in the
county; Nicholas Ash driving a carriage, with money that
must have been stolen; and almost the entire gentry of the
State either turned out of their homes or just holding on,
while those whom he had left half-amused children playing
at the game of freedmen, were parading around the country in all the bravery and insolence of an armed mob. All
this was a shock to him. He spoke of his views to Dr.
Cary. The Doctor was the person who had first suggested
the idea to his mind, and was the one who, he felt, was the
soundest and safest guide to follow. In the little that he
had seen of him since his return he had found him, as he
knew he would be, precisely the same he had always been,
absolutely calm and unruffled. To his astonishment the
Doctor shook his head.

"It is Utopian. I thought so myself formerly and, as you
may remember, incurred much animadversion and some
obloquy. I did not care a button about that. But I am
not sure that General Legaie and those who agreed with
him, whose action I at that time thought the height of
folly, were not nearer right than I was. I am sure my
principle was correct, and, perhaps, had they yielded and
gone in with us at the beginning it might have been different; but I am not certain as to it now." He bowed his
head in deep and painful reflection.

"It is now *vae victis*, and the only hope is in resistance,"
he proceeded, sadly. "Yielding is esteemed simply a confession of cowardice. The miscreants who rule us know
no restraint except fear. You will be astonished when I
tell you that the last few years have almost overthrown the
views I have held for a lifetime. I am nearer agreeing
with Legaie than I ever was in my whole life." The old
fellow shook his head in deep despondency over this fatal
declension.

Jacquelin did not agree with him. He had all a young man's confidence. He determined that he would effect his ends by law. He shortly had an illustration of what the Doctor meant.

Mrs. Gray was failing steadily. The strain she had undergone had been too much for her. She had lived only until Jacquelin's return.

To the end, all her heart was on her old home. In those last days she went back constantly to the time when she had come as a bride to her home adorned with all that love and forethought could devise. The war and the long years of struggle seemed to have been blotted out and her memory appeared only to retain and to dwell on every scene of the old life. One of her constant thoughts was : If she could only have lain at the old home, at her husband's side ! So, she passed quietly away. In the watches of the last night, when no one was with her but Jacquelin, after she had talked to him of Rupert and confided him to his care, she asked Jacquelin if he thought she might ever be taken home. His father and she had picked out the spot under one of the great trees.

"Mother," said Jacquelin, kneeling beside her and holding one of her thin, transparent hands in his, "if I live and God is good to me, you shall lie there."

He had consulted General Legaie and Steve on the subject, and they both had thought that the burying-ground had not been conveyed in the deed to Still, though Leech, to whom, as counsel for Still, they had broached the matter, asserted that it had been included.

The day Mrs. Gray died, Dr. Cary wrote a note to Still on Jacquelin's behalf, though without his knowledge, indicating his cousin's wish to bury his mother beside his father, and saying that it would not be held to affect any question of ownership at issue between them.

To this Still replied that while he should be "very glad to do anything that Dr. Cary or *any member of his family* asked for *themselves,*" he would not permit any *outsider* to

be buried on his place, especially one who had insulted
him; that he did not acknowledge that any question existed as to his title; and that he was prepared to show that,
if so, it was unfounded. He added that he was " going to
remove the tomb-stones, cut down the trees, clear up the
place, and get rid of the old grave-yard altogether."

A part of the letter was evidently written by a lawyer.

Dr. Cary felt that he could not withhold this notification
from Jacquelin. Before doing so, however, he consulted
General Legaie. The little General's eyes snapped as he
read the letter. " Ah ! if he were only a gentleman ! " he
sighed. The next moment he broke out. " I'll lay my
riding-whip across the dog's shoulders ! That's what I'll
do." The Doctor tried to soothe him. He would show
the letter to Jacquelin, he said. The General protested.
" My dear sir, if you do, there will be trouble. Young
men are so rash. They have not the calm deliberation that
we have." The Doctor, recalling his conversation with
Jacquelin, said he thought he could rely on his wisdom.
" If he sees that letter there will be trouble," asserted the
General, " or he is not the nephew of his—ahem ! not the
son of his father." However, the Doctor was firm. So he
broke the matter to Jacquelin. To their surprise, Jacquelin
took it very quietly ; he did not say anything nor appear
to mind it a great deal. The General's countenance fell.
" Young men have changed since my day," he said, sadly.

So Mrs. Gray was buried in what had been a part of the
church-yard of the old brick-church, and Jacquelin, walking with his arm around Rupert, was as quiet as Miss
Thomasia.

That afternoon he excused himself from the further attendance of his friends, left his aunt and Rupert and
walked out alone. He went first to the house of his neighbor, Stamper. Him Jacquelin told of his purpose. Stamper
wished to accompany him ; but he would not permit that.
" Have you got a pistol ? " asked Stamper. No, he was
not armed, he said ; he only wanted his friend to know,

"in case anything should happen." Then he walked away in the direction of Red Rock, leaving little Stamper leaning on the bars looking after him rather wistfully until he had disappeared.

He had not been gone long when Stamper started after him. "If he gets hold of him, I'm afeared he'll kill him," he muttered as he hurried along.

It was after sunset, and Hiram Still was sitting alone in the hall at Red Rock, by a table in the drawers of which he kept his papers. He never liked to sit in the dark, and had just called for a light. He was waiting for it. He was not in a good humor, for he had had something of a quarrel with Leech, and his son Wash had taken the latter's side. The young doctor was always taking sides against him these days. They had made him write Dr. Cary that he was going to clear up the grave-yard, and he was not at all sure that it was a good thing to do; he had always heard that it was bad luck to break up a grave-yard, and now they had left him alone in the house. Even the drink of whiskey he had taken had not restored his good spirits.

Why did not the light come? He roared an oath toward the open door. "D——n the lazy niggers!"

Suddenly there was a step, or something like a step, near him—he was not sure about it, for he must have been dozing—and he looked up. His heart jumped into his throat. Before him in the hall stood, tall and gray, the "Indian-killer," his eyes blazing like coals of fire.

"Good God!" he gasped.

No, it was speaking—it was a man. But it was almost as bad. Still had not seen Jacquelin before in two years. And he had never noticed how like the "Indian-killer" he was. What did he want?

"I have come to see you about the grave-yard," said Jacquelin. The voice was his father's. It smote Still like a voice from the dead.

Still wanted to apologize to him; but he could not speak,

his throat was dry.   There was a pistol in the drawer before him and he pulled the drawer open and put his hand
on it.   The cold steel recalled him to himself and he drew
it toward him, his courage reviving.   Jacquelin must
have heard the sound ; he was right over him.

"If you attempt to draw that pistol on me," he said,
quietly, " I will kill you right where you sit."

Whether it was the man's unstrung condition, or whether
it was Jacquelin's resemblance to the fierce Indian-killer,
as he stood there in the dusk with his eyes burning, his
strong hands twitching, or whether it was his unexpected
stalwartness and fierceness as he towered above the overseer, the latter sank back with a whine.

A negro entered at a side door with a light, but stood
still, amazed at the scene, muttering to himself : " Good
Lordy ! "

Jacquelin went on speaking.   He told Still that if he
cut down so much as a bush in that grave-yard until he had
a decision of court authorizing him to do so, he would kill
him, even if he had the whole Government of the United
States around him.

"Now, I have come here to tell you this," he said, in
the same quiet, strange voice, "and I have come to tell
you one thing more, that you will not be in this place
always.   We are coming back here, the living and the
dead."

Still turned even more livid than before.   " What do you
mean ? " he gasped.

" What I say, we are coming back."   He swept his eye
around the hall, turned on his heel, and walked toward
the picture over the fireplace.   Just then a gust of wind
blew out the lamp the negro held, leaving the hall in
gloom.   When the servant came back with a light, according to the story that he told, Still was raving like a mad-
man, and he drank whiskey and raved all night.

Neither Still nor Jacquelin ever spoke of the interview ;
but a story got abroad in the neighborhood that the old

BEFORE HIM STOOD, TALL AND GRAY, THE INDIAN-KILLER.

Indian-killer had appeared to Still the night of Mrs. Gray's burial and threatened him with death if he should ever touch the grave-yard. Still said he had never meant to touch it anyhow, and that Leech had made him put it in the letter for a joke. It was, however, a dear joke.

For a time there was quite a coolness between the friends ; but they had too much in common to be able to afford to quarrel, so it was made up.

CHAPTER XXIII

OTHER changes than those already recorded had taken place in the years that had passed since the day when Middleton and Thurston, on their way to take command of a part of the conquered land, had found Jacquelin Gray outstretched under a tree at the little country station in the Red Rock County. In this period Middleton had won promotion in the West, and a wound which had necessitated a long leave of absence and a tour abroad ; and finally, his retirement from the service. Reely Thurston, who was now a Captain himself, declared that Middleton's wound was received in the South and not in the West, and that if such wounds were to be recognized, he himself ought to have been sent abroad. The jolly little officer, however, if he wished to boast of wounds of this nature, might have cited a later one ; for he had for some time been a devoted admirer of Miss Ruth Welch, who had grown from a romping girl to a lively and very handsome young lady, and had, as Reely said of her, the warmest heart toward all mankind, except a man in love with her, and the coldest toward him, of any girl in the world. However this might be, she had turned a very stony heart toward Thurston in common with a number of others, and after a season or two at fashionable summer-resorts was finding, or thinking she was finding, all men insipid and life very commonplace and hollow. She declared that she liked Thurston better than any other man except her father and a half dozen or more others, all of whom labored under the sole disadvantage of being married, and she finally, as the price of the continuance of this somewhat measurable state of feeling, bound the Captain by the most solemn pledges never to so much as hint at any desire on his part for a higher degree of affection.

The little soldier would have sworn by all the gods, higher and lower, to anything that Ruth Welch proposed, for the privilege of being her slave ; but he could no more have stopped bringing up the forbidden subject when in her presence, than he could have sealed up the breath in his plump and manly bosom. He was always like a cat that in sight of cream, though knowing he is on his good behavior, yet, with invincible longing, licks his chops.

No doubt the game had additional zest for Captain Thurston from the disapproval with which Mrs. Welch always regarded him. He never approached Miss Ruth without that lady fluttering around with the semi-comical distress of an anxious hen that cannot see even the house-dog approach her chick, without ruffling her feathers and showing fight.

This had thrown Thurston into a state of rather chronic opposition to the good lady, and he revenged himself for the loss of the daughter, by a habit of apparently espousing whatever the mother disapproved of, who on her part, lived in a constant effort to prove him in the wrong.

He had even ventured to express open skepticism as to the wisdom of the steps Mrs. Welch and her Aid Society had been taking in their philanthropic efforts on behalf of the freedmen ; giving expression to the heretical doctrine that in the main the negroes had been humanely treated before the war, and that the question should be dealt with now from an economical rather than from a sentimental standpoint. He gave it as his opinion that the people down there knew more about the Negro, and the questions arising out of the new conditions, than those who were undertaking to settle those questions, from a distance, and that, if let alone, the questions would settle themselves. While as to Leech, the correspondent of Mrs. Welch's society, he declared that he would not believe anything he said.

Nothing could have scandalized Mrs. Welch more than such an utterance. And it is probable that this attitude on Thurston's part did as much as her real philanthropy to establish her in the extreme views she held.

For some time past there had been appearing in the *Censor*, the chief paper in the city where the Welches lived, a series of letters giving a dreadful, and, what Mrs. Welch considered, a powerful account of the outrages that were taking place in the South. According to the writer, the entire native white population were engaged in nothing but the systematic murder and mutilation of unoffending negroes and Northern settlers, who on their side were wholly without blame and received this persecution with the most Christian and uncomplaining humility.

The author's name was not given, because, it was stated in the letters, if it were known, he would at once be murdered. Indeed, it was declared that the letters were not written for publication at all, but were sent to a philanthropic organization composed of the best and most benevolent ladies in the country, who would vouch for the high standing of the noble Christian gentleman from whose pen the accounts emanated. As the letters were from the very section—indeed, from the very neighborhood which Thurston always cited as an evidence of the beneficent effect of his theory of moderation—Mrs. Welch, who was the head of the organization to which Leech had written them, saved them for the purpose of confounding and, once for all, disposing of Captain Thurston's arguments, together with himself.

So one morning when Thurston was calling on Ruth Mrs. Welch brought in the whole batch of papers and plumped them down before him with a triumphant air.

"Now, you read every word before you express an opinion," she said, decisively.

While Thurston read, Mrs. Welch, who was enjoying her triumph, annotated each letter with running comments. These impressed Ruth greatly, but Thurston wilily kept his face from giving the slightest clew to his thoughts. When he was through reading, Mrs. Welch drew a long breath of exultation.

"Well, what do you say to that?"

"I don't believe it!" said Thurston, calmly.

"What!" Mrs. Welch was lifted out of her chair by astonishment.

"The writer of that is Jonadab Leech, one of the most unmitigated——"

"Captain Thurston! You do not know what you are talking about!" exclaimed Mrs. Welch.

"Do you mean to say Leech is not the writer of those letters?"

"No, I did not say that," said Mrs. Welch, who would have cut out her tongue before she would have uttered a falsehood.

"I would not believe Leech on oath," said the Captain, blandly.

"Oh, well, if that's the stand you take, there's no use reasoning with you." And with a gesture expressive both of pity and sorrow that she must wash her hands of him completely and forever, Mrs. Welch gathered up her papers and indignantly swept from the room.

When Thurston went away that day he had entrusted Ruth with an apology for Mrs. Welch capable of being expanded, as circumstances might require, to an unlimited degree; for Ruth had explained to him how dear to her mother's heart her charities were. But he had also given Ruth such sound reasons for his views regarding the people in the region where he had been stationed that, however her principles remained steadfast, the sympathies of the girl had gone out to those whom he described as in such incredible difficulties.

"Ask Larry about Miss Blair Cary," he said. "Ask

him which is the better man, Dr. Cary or Jonadab Leech, and which he'd believe first, that Steve Allen, who is spoken of as such a ruffian, or Hiram Still, the martyr."

"And how about Miss Dockett?" Ruth's eyes twinkled.

"Miss Dockett?—Who is Miss Dockett?" The little Captain's face wore so comical an expression of counterfeit innocence and sheepish guilt that the girl burst out laughing.

"Have you been in love with so many Miss Docketts that you can't remember which one lived down there?"

"No—oh, the girl I am in love with? Miss Ruth—ah, Dockett wasn't the name. It began with Wel—." He looked at Ruth with so languishing an expression that she held up a warning finger.

"Remember."

He pretended to misunderstand her.

"Certainly I remember—Ruth Welch."

Ruth gathered up her things to leave.

"Please don't go.—Now that just slipped out. I swear I'll not say another word on the subject as long as I live, if you'll just sit down."

"I can't trust you."

"Yes, you can, I swear it; and I'll tell you all about Miss Dockett and—Steve Allen."

This was too much for Ruth, and she reseated herself with impressive condescension.

Miss Welch was greatly interested for other reasons. Her father's health had not been very good of late, and he had been thinking of getting a winter home in the South, where he could be most of the time out of doors, as an old wound in his chest still troubled him sometimes, and the doctors said he must not for the present spend another winter in the North. He had been in correspondence with this very Mr. Still, who was spoken of so highly in those letters, about a place just where this trouble was.

Besides, a short time before this conversation of Ruth's

with Thurston, Major Welch had received a letter from Middleton, who was still abroad, asking him to look into his affairs. He had always enjoyed a large income, but of late it had, he stated, fallen off, owing, as Mr. Bolter, his agent, explained, to temporary complications growing out of extensive investments Bolter had made for him on joint account with himself in Southern enterprises. These investments, Mr. Bolter assured him, were perfectly safe and would yield in a short time immense profits, being guaranteed by the State, and managed by the strongest and most successful men down there, who were themselves deeply interested in the schemes. It had happened, that the very names Bolter had given as a guarantee of the security of his investment, had aroused Middleton's anxiety, and though he had no reason, he said, to doubt Bolter, he did doubt Leech and Still, the men Bolter had mentioned.

Major Welch had made an investigation. And it had shown him that the investments referred to were so extensive as to involve a considerable part of his cousin's estate.

Bolter gave Major Welch what struck the latter quite as an "audience," though, when he learned the Major's business, he suddenly unbent and became much more confidential, explaining everything with promptness and clearness. Bolter was a strong-looking, stout man, with a round head and a strong face. His brow was rather low, but his eyes were keen and his mouth firm. As he sat in his inner business office, with his clerks in outer pens, he looked the picture of a successful, self-contained man.

"Why, they fight a railroad coming into their country as if it were a public enemy," he said to Major Welch.

"Then they must be pretty formidable antagonists."

"And I have gotten letters warning me and denouncing the men who have planned and worked up the matter—and who would carry it through if they were allowed to do so —as though they were thieves."

He rang a bell and sent for the letters. Among them was one from Dr. Cary and another from General Legaie. Though strangers, they said they wrote to him as one reported to be interested, and protested against the scheme of Still and Leech, who were destroying the State and pillaging the people. They contrasted the condition of the State before the war and at the present time. Dr. Cary's letter stated that "for purposes of identification" he would say that both his father and grandfather had been Governors of the State. General Legaie's letter was signed "Late General, C. S. A."

"What are you going to do with such people!" exclaimed Mr. Bolter. "They abuse those men as if they were pickpockets, and they are the richest and most influential men in that county, and Leech will, without doubt, be the next Governor." He handed Major Welch a newspaper containing a glowing account of Leech's services to the Commonwealth, and a positive assertion that he would be the next Governor of the State.

"What did you write them in reply?" asked Major Welch, who was taking another glance at the letters.

"Why, I wrote them that I believed I was capable of conducting my own affairs," said the capitalist, with satisfaction, running his hands deep in his pockets; "and if they would stop thinking about their grandfathers and the times before the war, and think a little more about their children and the present, it would be money in their pockets."

"And what did they reply to that?"

"Ah—why, I don't believe I ever got any reply to that. I suppose the moss had covered them by that time," he laughed. Major Welch looked thoughtful, and the capitalist changed his tone.

"In fact I had already made the investments, and I had to see them through. Major Leech is very friendly to me. It was through him we were induced to go into the enterprise—through him—and because of the opportunities it offered, at the same time that it was made perfectly safe by the guarantee of both the counties and the States. He

used to be in my—in our—employ, and he is a very shrewd
fellow, Leech is. That was the way we came to go in, and
it doesn't do to swap horses in the stream."

"Mrs. Welch thinks very highly of him," said Major
Welch, meditatively. "She has had some correspondence with him on behalf of her charitable society for
the freedmen, and she has been much impressed by
him."

"My only question was whether he was not a little too
philanthropic," said Bolter, significantly. "But since I
have come to find out, I guess he has used his philanthropy
pretty discreetly. He's a very shrewd fellow." His smile
and manner grated on the Major somewhat.

"Perhaps he is too shrewd ?" he suggested, dryly.

"Oh, no, not for me. I have made it a rule in life to
treat every man as a rascal——"

"Oh !" A shadow crossed the Major's brow, which
Bolter was quick to catch.

"Until I found out differently."

"I should think the other would have been rather inconvenient." Major Welch changed the subject. "But Captain Middleton had some sort of trouble with this man, and
has always had a dislike for him. And I think I shall go
South and look into matters there."

"Oh, well, that's nothing," broke in Bolter, hotly.
"What does Middleton know about business ? That's his
trouble. These military officers don't understand the word.
They are always stickling for their d—d dignity, and think
if a man ain't willing to wipe up the floor for 'em he's
bound to be a rascal."

It was as much the sudden insolence in the capitalist's
tone, as his words that offended Major Welch. He rose to
his feet.

"I am not aware, that being officers, and having risked
their lives to save their country, necessarily makes men
either more narrow or greater fools than those who stayed
at home," he said, coldly.

The other, after a sharp glance at him, was on his feet in an instant, his whole manner changed.

"My dear sir. You have misunderstood me. I assure you you have." And he proceeded to smooth the Major down with equal shrewdness and success; delivering a most warm and eloquent eulogy on patriotism in general, and on that of Captain Lawrence Middleton in particular. Truth to tell, it was not hard to do, as the Major was one of the most placable of men, except where a principle was involved; then he was rock.

Bolter wound up by making Major Welch an offer, which the latter could not but consider handsome, to go South and represent his interests as well as Middleton's.

"If he is going there he better be on my side than against me, and his hands would be tied then anyway," reflected Bolter.

"You will find our interests identical," he said, seeing the Major's hesitation. "We are both in the same boat. And you will find that I have done by Mr. Middleton just what I have done for myself. And I have taken every precaution, of that you may be sure. And we are bound to win. We have the most successful men in the State with us, bound up by interest, and also as tight as paper can bind them. We have the law with us, the men who make, and the men who construe the law, and against us, only a few old mossbacks and soreheads. If they can beat that combination I should like to see them do it."

The only doubt in Major Welch's mind as to the propriety of a move to the South was on account of his daughter.

The condition of affairs there made no difference to Major Welch himself—for he felt that he had the Union behind him—and he knew it made none to Mrs. Welch. She had been working her hands off for two years to send things to the negroes through these men, Still and Leech. But with Ruth, who was the apple of her father's eye, it might be another matter.

But when the subject was broached to Ruth, and she chimed in and sketched, with real enthusiasm, the delights of living in the South, in the country—the real country— amid palm and orange groves, the Major's mind was set at rest. He only cautioned her against building her air-castles too high, as he knew there were no orange-groves where they were going, and though there might be palms, he doubted if they were of the material sort, or very easy to obtain.

Ruth's ardor, however, was not to be damped just then.

"Why, the South is the land of Romance, Papa."

"It will be if you are there," smiled her father.

It is said that curiosity is a potent motive with what used to be called the gentler, and, occasionally, even the weaker sex, a distinction that for some time has been passing, if it has not altogether passed, away. But far be it from the writer even to appear to give adherence to such a doctrine by anything that he may set down in this veracious chronicle. He does not recollect ever to have heard this remark made by any of the thousands of women whom he has known, personally, or through books with which the press teems, and he feels sure that had it been true it would not have escaped their acute observation. In recording, therefore, the move of the Welches to the South he is simply reporting facts.

On the occasion of the discussion between Mrs. Welch and Captain Thurston, Mrs. Welch was left by that gentleman in what, in a weaker woman, might have been deemed a state of exasperation. After all the trouble she had taken to secure the evidence to confound and annihilate that young man, he had with a breath undermined her foundation, or, rather, had shown that her imposing fabric had no foundation whatever. He knew Leech, and she did not. She would now go and satisfy herself by personal knowledge that she was right and he wrong—as she well knew to be the case, anyhow. So, many people start out on a quest for information, not to test, but to prove,

18

their opinions. Thus, when Major Welch came with the statement of the offer he had received, Mrs. Welch truthfully declared that she in some sort saw in it the hand of Providence. This was strengthened by a conversation with Miss Ruth, who quoted Thurston's opinion of Leech.

" Captain Thurston, my dear ! " said Mrs. Welch. " So light and frivolous a person as Captain Thurston is really incapable of forming a just opinion of such a man as Mr. Leech, whose letters breathe a spirit of the truest Christian humility, as well as the most exalted courage under circumstances which might well make even a strong man quail. I hope you will not quote Captain Thurston to me again. You know what my opinion of him has always been. I never could understand what your father's and Lawrence Middleton's infatuation for him was. Besides, you know that Captain Thurston was in love with some girl down in that country, and when a man is in love he is absolutely irresponsible. Love makes a man a fool about everything."

Thus Mrs. Welch, so to speak, shot at, even if she did not kill, two birds with one stone. If she did not kill this second bird it was not her fault, as the glance which she gave Ruth showed. Ruth's face did not wholly satisfy her, for she added :

" Besides that, Mr. Bolter has been down there and he tells me that he thinks very highly of Major Leech."

" Oh, Mr. Bolter ! I don't like Mr. Bolter, and neither do you," began Miss Ruth.

" My dear, that is very unreasonable ; what possible cause can you have to dislike Mr. Bolter, for you do not know him at all ? "

" I have met him. He did not go into the army ; but stayed at home and made money. Papa does not like him either."

" Don't you see how illogical that is. We cannot dislike everyone who did not go into the army."

" No, I know that." Ruth pondered a moment and then broke out, laughing : " Why, mamma, I have given two reasons for not liking Mr. Bolter, and you did not give any for disliking Captain Thurston."

" That is different," replied Mrs. Welch, gravely, though she did not explain precisely how, and perhaps Ruth did not see it.

" Mamma," burst out Ruth, warmly, her face glowing, " I believe in a man's fighting for what he believes right. If I had been a man when the war broke out I should have gone into it, and if I had lived at the South I should have fought for the South."

" Ruth ! " exclaimed her mother, deeply shocked.

" I would, mamma, I know I would, and you would too ; for I know how much trouble you took to get an exchange for that young boy, Mr. Jacquelin or something, that Miss Bush, the nurse, was interested in."

" Ruth, I hope I shall never hear you say that again," protested Mrs. Welch, warmly. " You do not understand."

" I think I do—I won't say it again—but I have wanted to say it for a long time, and I feel so much better for having said it, mamma."

So the conversation ended.

It was decided that Major Welch and Ruth should go ahead and select a place which they could rent until they should find one that exactly suited them, and then Mrs. Welch, as soon as she could finish packing the furniture and other things which they would want, should follow them.

A week later, Ruth and her father found themselves in the old county and almost at their journey's end, in a region which though as far as possible from Ruth's conception of palm and orange groves, was to the girl, shut up as she had been all her life in a city, not a whit less romantic and strange.

It was far wilder than she had supposed it would be. The land lay fallow, or was cultivated only in patches ; the woods were forests and seemed to stretch interminably, the fields were growing up in bushes and briars. And yet the birds flitted and sang in every thicket, and over every-thing rested an air of peace that sank into Ruth's soul, as she jolted along in a little rickety wagon which they had hired at the station, and filled her with a sense of novelty and content. She was already beginning to feel something of the charm of which her cousin, Larry Middleton, and Captain Thurston were always talking. Some time, per-haps, she would see Blair Cary, about whom Reely Thur-ston was always hinting in connection with Larry Middle-ton ; and she tried to picture to herself what she would be like—small and dark and very vivacious, or else no doubt, haughty. She was sure she should not like her.

On her father, however, the same surroundings that pleased Miss Ruth had a very different effect. Major Welch had always carried in his mind the picture of this section as he remembered it the first time he rode through it, when it was filled with fine plantations and pleasant homesteads, and where, even during the war, the battle in which he had been wounded had been fought amid orchards and rolling fields and pastures.

At length, at the top of the hill they came to a fork, but though there was an open field between the roads, such as Major Welch remembered, there was no church there ; in the open field was only a great thicket, an acre or more in extent, and the field behind it was nothing but a wilder-ness.

" We've missed the road, just as I supposed," said Major Welch. " We ought to have kept nearer to the river, and I will take this road and strike the other somewhere down this way. I thought this country looked very different— and yet— ? " He gazed all around him, at the open fields filled with bushes and briars, the rolling hills beyond, and the rampart of blue spurs across the background.

" No, we must have crossed Twist Creek lower down that day." He turned into the road leading off from that they had been travelling, and drove on. This way, however, the country appeared even wilder, and they had driven two or three miles before they saw anyone. Finally they came on a man walking along, just where a footpath left the road and turned across the old field. He was a small, sallow fellow, very shabbily dressed, the only notice-able thing about him being his eyes, which were both keen and good-humored. Major Welch stopped him and in-quired as to their way.

"Where do you want to go?" asked the man, politely.

"I want to go to Mr. Hiram Still's," said the Major.

The countryman gave him a quick glance.

"Well, you can't git there this way," he said, his tone changed a little; "the bridge is down, on this road and nobody don't travel it much now—you'll have to go back to Old Brick Church and take the other road. There's a new bridge on that road, but it's sort o' rickety since these freshes, and you have to take to the old ford again. One of Hiram's and Jonadab's jobs," he explained, with a note of hostility in his voice. Then, in a more friendly tone, he added: "The water's up still from last night's rain, and the ford ain't the best no time, so you better not try it unless you have somebody as knows it to set you right. I would go myself, but——" He hesitated, a little embar-rassed—and the Major at once protested.

"No, indeed! Just tell me where is Old Brick Church."

"That fork back yonder where you turned is what's called Old Brick Church," said the man; "that's where it used to stand."

"What has become of the church?"

"Pulled down during the war."

"Why don't they rebuild it?" asked the Major, a little testily over the man's manner.

"Well, I s'pose they think it's cheaper to leave it down," said the man, dryly.

"Is there any place where we could spend the night?" the Major asked, with a glance up at the sunset sky.

"Oh, Hiram Still, he's got a big house. He'll take you in, if he gits a chance," he said, half grimly.

"But I mean, if we get overtaken by night this side the river? You tell me the bridge is shaky and the ford filled up now. I have my daughter along and don't want to take any chances."

"Oh, papa, the idea! As if I couldn't go anywhere you went," put in Ruth, suddenly.

At the Major's mention of his daughter, the man's manner changed.

"There's Doct'r Cary's," he said, with a return of his first friendly tone. "They take everyone in. You just turn and go back by Old Brick Church, and keep the main, plain road till you pass two forks on your left and three on your right, then turn in at the third you come to on your left, and go down a hill and up another, and you're right there." The Major and Ruth were both laughing; their director, however, remained grave.

"Ain't no fences nor gates to stop you. Just keep the main, plain road, like I tell you, and you can't git out."

"I can't? Well, I'll see," said the Major, and after an inquiring look at the man, he turned and drove back.

"What bright eyes he has," said Ruth, but her father was pondering.

"It's a most curious thing; but that man's face and voice were both familiar to me," said he, presently. "Quite as if I had seen them before in a dream. Did you observe how his whole manner changed as soon as I mentioned Still's name? They are a most intractable people."

"But I'm sure he was very civil," defended Ruth.

"Civility costs nothing and often means nothing. Ah, well, we shall see." And the Major drove on.

As they passed by the fork again, both travellers looked curiously across at the great clump of trees rising out of the bushes and briars. The notes of a dove cooing in the soft light came from somewhere in the brake. They made out a gleam of white among the bushes, but neither of them spoke. Major Welch was recalling a night he had spent in that churchyard amid the dead and the dying.

Ruth was thinking of the description Middleton had given of the handsome mansion and grounds of Dr. Cary, and was wondering if this Dr. Cary could be the same.

CHAPTER XXIV

THE TRAVELLERS ARE ENTERTAINED IN A FARM-HOUSE

THE sun had already set some little time and the dusk was falling when they came to a track turning off from the "main, plain road," which they agreed must be that described to them as leading to Dr. Cary's. They turned in, and after passing through a skirt of woods came out into a field, beyond which, at a little distance, they saw a light. They drove on; but as they mounted the hill from which the light had shone Ruth's heart sank, for, as well as they could tell through the gathering dusk, there was no house there at all, or if there was, it was hidden by the trees around it. On reaching the crest, however, they saw the light again, which came from a small cottage at the far side of the orchard, that looked like a little farm-house.

"Well, we've missed Dr. Cary's after all," said Major Welch.

It was too late now, however, to retrace their steps; so Major Welch, with renewed objurgations at the stupidity of people who could not give a straight direction, determined to let Dr. Cary's go, and ask accommodation there. Accordingly, they picked their way through the orchard and drove up to the open door from which the light was shining.

At the Major's halloo a tall form descended the low steps and came to them. Major Welch stated their case as belated travellers.

Ruth's heart was instantly warmed by the cordial response:

" Get right out, sir—glad to have you.

" Ah, my dear—here are a lady and gentleman who want
to spend the night." This to a slender figure who had come
out of the house and joined them. " My daughter, madam;
my daughter, sir."

" Good-evening," said the girl, and Ruth, who had been
wondering at the softness of these farmer-voices, recollected
herself just in time to take the hand which she found held
out to her in the darkness in instinctive friendliness.

" I am Major Welch," said that gentleman, not to be
behind his host in politeness.   " And this is my daughter."

" We are glad to see you," repeated the young girl simply to Ruth in her charming voice, as if the introduction
required a little more formal greeting.

" Ah ! Major, glad to see you," said the host, heartily.
" Are you any relation to my old friend, General Welch
of Columbia, who was with Johnson ? "

" I don't think so," said Major Welch.

" Ah ! I knew a Major Welch in the Artillery, and another in the Sixth Georgia, I think," hazarded the host.
" Are you either of those ? "

" No," said the Major, with a laugh, " I was not.   I
was on the other side—I was in the Engineer Corps under
Grant."

" Oh !" said the host, in such undisguised surprise that
Ruth could feel herself grow hot, and was sensible, even in
the darkness, of a change in her father's attitude.

" Perhaps it may not be agree——I mean, convenient,
for you to take us in to-night ?" said Major Welch, rather
stiffly.

" Oh, my dear sir," protested the other, " the war is
over, isn't it ? Of course it's convenient. My wife is
away just now, but, of course, it is always convenient to
take in wayfarers." And he led the horse off, while his
daughter, whose quiet " Won't you walk in ?" soothed
Ruth's ruffled spirit, conducted them into the house.

When Ruth entered she had not the slightest idea as to

either the name or appearance of their hosts. They had
evidently assumed that the travellers knew who they were
when they applied to spend the night, and it had been too
dark outside for Ruth to see their faces. She only knew
that they had rich voices and cordial, simple manners,
such as even the plainest farmers appeared to have in this
strange land, and she had a mystified feeling. As she
entered the door her mystification only increased. The
room into which she was conducted from the little veranda was a sitting or living room, lower in pitch than almost any room Ruth had ever been in, while its appointments appeared curiously incongruous to her eyes, dazzled
as they were from coming in suddenly from the darkness.
Ruth took in this rather than observed it as she became
accustomed to the light, for the first glance of the two
girls was at each other. Ruth found herself astonished
at the appearance of her hostess. Her face was so refined
and her figure so slim that it occurred to Ruth that she
might be an invalid. Her dress was simple to plainness,
plainer than Ruth had ever seen the youngest girl wear,
and her breast-pin was nothing but a brass button, such
as soldiers wear on their coats; yet her manners were as
composed and gracious as if she had been a lady and in
society for years.

"Why, she looks like a lady," thought the girl, with a
new feeling of shyness coming over her, and she stole a
glance around her for something which would enable her
to decide her hosts' real position. The appointments of
the room, however, only mystified her the more. A plain,
white board bookcase filled with old books stood on one
side, with a gun resting in the corner, against it; two or
three portraits of bewigged personages in dingy frames,
and as many profile portraits in pastel hung on the walls,
with a stained print or two, and a number of photographs of
soldiers in uniform among them. A mahogany table with
carved legs stood in the centre of the room, piled with
books, and the chairs were a mixture of home-made split-

bottomed ones and old-fashioned, straight-backed arm-chairs.

"How curious these farmers are," thought Ruth; but she did not have a great deal of time for reflection, for the next instant her hostess, who had been talking to her father, was asking if she would not "take her things off" in so pleasant a voice, that before hat and coat were removed all constraint was gone and Ruth found herself completely at home. Then her hostess excused herself and went out for a moment. Ruth took advantage of her absence to whisper to her father, with genuine enthusiasm, "Isn't she pretty, father? What are they?"

"I don't know, but I suspect—" Just what it was that he suspected Ruth did not learn, for at that moment their host stepped in at the door, and laying his old worn hat on a table, made them another little speech, as if being under his roof required a new welcome. Major Welch began to apologize for running in on them so unceremoniously, but the farmer assured him that an apology was quite unnecessary, and that they were always glad to welcome travellers who came.

"We are told to entertain strangers, you know; for thereby, they say, some have entertained angels unawares, and though we cannot exactly say that we have ever done this yet," he added, with a twinkle in his eye, "we may be beginning it now—who knows?" He made Ruth a bow with an old-fashioned graciousness which set her to blushing.

"What a beautiful nose he has, finer even than my father's," she thought.

Just then the young hostess returned, and the next moment an old negro woman in a white kerchief stood in the door dropping courtesies as though she were in a play. Ruth was shown up a narrow little flight of stairs to a room so close under the sloping roof that it was only in the middle of it that she could stand upright. Everything, however, was spotlessly clean, and the white hangings, plain and simple as they were, and the little knick-knacks arranged about, made it dainty. The girl picked up one of the books idly. It was an old copy of " The Vicar of Wakefield." As she replaced the book, she observed that where it lay it covered a patch.

At supper they were waited on by the old negro woman she had seen before, whom both their host and hostess called " Mammy," and treated not so much as a servant, as if she were one of the family; and though the china was old and cracked, and mostly of odd pieces, the young hostess presided with an ease which filled Ruth with astonishment. " Why, she could not do it better if she had lived in a city all her life, and she is not a bit embarrassed by us," she thought to herself. She observed that the only two pretty and sound cups were given to her and her father. The one she had was so dainty and unusual that she could not help looking at it closely, and was a little taken aback, on glancing up, to find her hostess's eyes resting on her. The smile that came into them, however, reassured Ruth, and she ventured to say, half apologetically, that she was admiring the cup.

" Yes, it is pretty, isn't it?" assented the other girl. " It has quite a history; you must get my father to tell it to you. There used to be a set of them."

" It was a set which was presented to one of my ancestors by Charles the Second," said the father thus appealed to, much as if he had said, " It is a set that was given me yesterday by a neighbor." Ruth looked at him with wide-open eyes and a little uncomfortable feeling that he should tell her such a falsehood. His face, however, wore the same calm look. " If you inspect closely, you can still make out the C. R. on it, though it is almost obliterated. My ancestor was with his father at Carisbrooke," he added, casually, and Ruth, glancing at her father, saw that it was true, and at the same moment took in also the fact that they had reached the place they had been looking for; and that this farmer, as she had supposed him

to be, was none other than Dr. Cary, and the young girl
whom she had been patronizing, was Larry Middleton's
Blair Cary, a lady like herself. How could she have
made the mistake! As she looked at her host again, the
thoughtful, self-contained face, the high-bred air, the
slightly aquiline nose, the deep eyes, and the calm mouth
and the pointed beard made a perfect Vandyke portrait.
Even the unstarched, loose collar and turned-back cuffs
added to the impression. Ruth seemed to have been suddenly carried back over two hundred years to find herself
in presence of an old patrician. She blushed with confusion over her stupidity, and devoutly hoped within herself
that no one had noticed her mistake.

After supper, Major Welch and Dr. Cary, who had renewed their old acquaintance, fell to talking of the war,
and Ruth was astonished to find how differently their host
looked at things from the way in which all the people she
had ever known regarded them. It was strange to the girl
to hear her people referred to as "the Yankees" or "the
enemy"; and the other side, which she had always heard
spoken of as "rebels," mentioned with pride as "the
Confederates" or "our men." After a little, she heard
her father ask about the man he had come South to see—
Mr. Hiram Still. "Do you know him?" he asked their
host.

"Oh, yes, sir, I know him. We all know him. He
was overseer for one of my friends and connections, who
was, perhaps, the wealthiest man in this section before the
war, Mr. Gray, of Red Rock, the place where you spent
the night you spoke of. Colonel Gray was killed at Shiloh,
and his property all went to pay his debts afterward. He
had some heavy indorsements, and it turned out that he
owed a great deal of money to Still for negroes he had
bought to stock a large plantation he had in one of the
other States—at least, the overseer gave this explanation,
and produced the bonds, which proved to be genuine,
though at first it was thought they must be forged.

I suppose it was all right, though some people thought not, and it seems hard to have that fellow living in Gray's house."

"But he bought it, did he not?" asked Major Welch.

"Oh, yes, sir, he bought it—bought it at a forced sale," said Dr. Cary, slowly. "But I don't know—to see that fellow living up there looks very strange. There are some things so opposed to the customary course of events that the mind refuses to accept them."

"Still lives somewhat lower down, I believe?" said Major Welch.

"No, sir, he is not very far off," said Dr. Cary. "He is just across the river a few miles. Do you know him?"

"No, I do not. Not personally, that is. What sort of a man is he?"

"Well, sir, he does not stand very well," answered Dr. Cary, deliberately.

"Ah! Why, if I may ask?" Major Welch was stiffening a little.

"Well, he went off to the radicals," said Dr. Cary, slowly, and Ruth was amused at the look on her father's face.

"But surely a man may be a republican and not be utterly bad?" said Major Welch.

"Yes, I suppose so, elsewhere," admitted the other, doubtfully. "In fact, I have known one or two gentlemen who were—who thought it best to accept everything, and begin anew—I did myself at first. But I soon found it impossible. It does not prove efficacious down here. You see—But, perhaps, you are one yourself, sir?" very politely.

"I am," said Major Welch, and Ruth could see him stiffen.

"Ah!" Their host leaned a little back. "Well, I beg your pardon. Perhaps, we will not discuss politics," he said, with great courtesy. "We should only disagree and —you are my guest."

"But surely we can talk politics without becoming—ah—We have been discussing the war?" said Major Welch.

"Ah, my dear sir, that is very different," said Dr. Cary. "May I ask, have you any official—ah—? Do you expect to stay among us?"

"Do you mean, am I a carpetbagger?" asked Major Welch, with a smile. But the other was serious.

"I would not insult you under my roof by asking you that question," he said, gravely. "I mean are you thinking of settling among us as a gentleman?"

"Well, I can hardly say yet—but, perhaps, I am—thinking of it," said Major Welch. "At least, that is one reason why I asked you about that man, Still."

"Oh, well, of course, if you ask as my guest, I will take pleasure in giving you any information you may wish."

"Is he a gentleman?" interrupted Major Welch.

"Oh, no—certainly not that, sir. He is hand in glove with the carpetbaggers, and the leader of the negroes about here. He and a carpetbagger named Leech, and a negro preacher or exhorter named Sherwood, who, by the way, was one of my own negroes, and a negro named Ash, who belonged to my friend General Legaie, and a sort of trick-doctor named Moses, whom I once saved from hanging, are the worst men in this section."

Major Welch had listened in silence, and now he changed the subject; for from the reference to Leech he began to think more and more that it was only prejudice which made these men objects of such narrow dislike.

When Ruth went up to bed she was in a sort of maze. The old negro woman whom she had seen downstairs came up to wait on her, and Miss Welch was soon enlightened as to several things. One was, that Dr. Cary's family was one of the greatest in the State—perhaps, in the old woman's estimation, the greatest—except, of course, Mrs. Cary's, to which Mammy Krenda gave rather the pre-eminence as she herself had always belonged to that family and had nursed Mrs. Cary and Miss Blair, her daughter. According to her they had been very rich, but had lost everything, first by the war, and then, by the wickedness of someone, against whom the old woman was especially bitter. "He ain' nuttin' but a low-down nigger-trader, nohow," she declared, savagely. "He done cheat ev'ybody out der home, he and dat Leech together, an' now dey think dey got ev'ything der own way, but dey'll see. Dey's dem as knows how to deal wid 'em. An' ef dee ever lay dee han's pon me, dee'll fine out. We ain' gwine live in blacksmiff shop always. Dem's stirrin' what dee ain' know 'bout, an' some day dee'll heah 'em comin' for 'em to judgment."

"Ken I help you do anything?" she asked, presently.

"No, I thank you," said Ruth, stiffly. "Good-night."

"Good-night," and she went.

"Why, she don't like us as much as she does them!" said the girl to herself, filled with amazement at this revolution of all her ideas. "Well, Larry's right. Miss Cary is charming," she reflected.

As she dropped off to sleep she could hear the hum of voices below, where Dr. Cary and her father were keeping up their discussion of the war. And as she was still trying to make out what they were saying, the sun came streaming into her room through a broken shutter and woke her up.

CHAPTER XXV

THE TRICK-DOCTOR

RUTH WELCH on awaking, still, perhaps, had some little feeling about what she understood to be her hosts' attitude on the question of Northerners, but when on coming downstairs she was greeted on the veranda by her young hostess, who presented her with a handful of dewy roses, and looked as sweet as any one of them, or all of them put together, her resentment vanished, and, as she expressed it to her mother afterward, she "went over to the enemy bag and baggage." As she looked out through the orchard and across over the fields, glowing after the last night's rain, there came to Ruth for the first time that tender feeling which comes to dwellers in the country, almost like a sweet odor, and compensates them for so much besides, and which has made so many a poet, whether he has written or not. Her hostess took her around the yard to show her her rosebushes, particularly one which she said had come from one which had always been her mother's favorite at their old home.

"We have not always lived here?" Her voice had a little interrogation in it as she looked at Ruth, much as if she had said, "You know?" And just as if she had said it, Ruth answered, softly, "Yes, I know."

"It was almost entirely destroyed once during the war when a regiment of cavalry camped in the yard," continued the young hostess, "and we thought it gone; but to our delight a little sprig put up next spring, and some day I hope this may be almost as good as the old one." She sighed, and her eyes rested on the horizon far away.

Ruth saw that the roses she had given her had come from that bush, and she would have liked to stretch out her arms and take her into a bond of hearty friendship.

Just then Major Welch appeared, and a moment later, breakfast was announced. When they went into the little plain dining-room there were other roses in an old blue bowl on the table, and Ruth saw that they not only made the table sweet, but were arranged deftly to hide the cracks and chipped places in the bowl. She was wondering where Dr. Cary could be, when his daughter apologized for his absence, explaining that he had been called up in the night to go and see a sick woman, and then, in his name, invited them to remain as their guests as long as might be convenient to them. They " might find it pleasanter than to stay at Mr. Still's ? " This hospitality the travellers could not accept, but Ruth appreciated it now, and she would have appreciated it yet more could she have known that her young hostess, sitting before her so dainty and fresh, had cooked their breakfast that morning. When they left after breakfast, Miss Cary came out to their vehicle, giving them full directions as to their road. Had her father been at home, she said, he would have taken pleasure in conducting them himself as far as the river. Uncle Tarquin would tell them about the ford.

The horse was held by an old colored man, of a dark mahogany hue, with bushy gray hair, and short gray whiskers. On the approach of the visitors he took off his hat and greeted them with an air as dignified as Dr. Cary's could have been. As he took leave of them, he might have been a host bidding his guests good-by, and he seconded his mistress's invitation to them to come again.

When they drove off, Ruth somehow felt as if she were parting from an old friend. Her little hostess's patched table-cover and darned dress, and cracked china hidden by the roses, all seemed to come before her, and Ruth glanced at her father with something very like tears in her eyes. They had been in her heart all the morning. Major Welch, however, did not observe it. The fresh, balmy air filled his lungs like a draught of new life, and he felt an interest in the country about him, and a right to criticise it. It had been rich enough before the war, he said, and might be made so now if the people would but give up their prejudices and go to work. He added many other criticisms, abstractly wise and sensible enough. Ruth listened in silence.

As the travellers drove along they passed a small house, just off the road, hardly more than a double cabin, but it was set back amid fruit-trees, sheltered by one great oak, and there was an air of quietude and peace about it which went to Ruth's soul. A lady in black, with a white cap on her gray hair, and a white kerchief on her shoulders, was sitting out on the little veranda, knitting, and Ruth was sure that as they drove by she bowed to them.

The sense of peace was still on the girl when they came on a country store, at a fork in the road a mile below. There was a well, off to one side, and a small group of ne-groes stood around it, two or three of them with mus-kets in their hands, and one with a hare hung at his waist. Another, who stood with his back to the road and had a twisted stick in his hand, and an old army haversack over his shoulder, was, at the moment the wagon drew up, talking loudly and with vehement gesticulation ; and, as Major Welch stopped to ask a question, Ruth caught the end of what this man was saying :

"I'm jest as good as any white man, and I'm goin' to show 'em so. I'm goin' to marry a white 'ooman and meck white folks wait on me. When I puts my mark agin a man he's gone, whether he's a man or a 'ooman, and I'se done set it now in a gum-tree."

His hearers were manifestly much impressed by him. An exclamation of approval went round among them.

The little wagon stopping attracted attention, and the speaker turned, and then, quickly, as if to make amends for his loud speech, pulled off his hat and came toward the vehicle with a curious, cringing motion.

"My master; my mistis," he said, bowing lower with each step until his knee almost touched the ground. He was a somewhat strongly built, dark mulatto, perhaps a little past middle age and of medium height, and, as he came up to the vehicle, Ruth thought she had never seen so grotesque a figure, and she took in by an instinct that this was the trick-doctor of whom Dr. Cary had spoken. His chin stuck so far forward that the lower teeth were much outside of the upper, or, at least, the lower jaw was; for the teeth looked as though they had been ground down, and his gums, as he grinned, showed as blue on the edges as if he had painted them. His nose was so short and the upper part of his face receded so much that the nostrils were un-usually wide, and gave an appearance of a black circle in his yellow countenance. His forehead was so low that he had evidently shaved a band across it, and the band ran around over the top of his flat head, leaving a tuft of coarse hair right in the middle, and on either side of it were cer-tain lines which looked as if they had been tattooed. Im-mediately under these were a pair of little furtive eyes which looked in quite different directions, and yet moved so quickly at times that it almost seemed as if they were both focussed on the same object. Large brass earrings were in his ears, and about his throat was a necklace of blue and white beads.

Major Welch, having asked his question, drove on, the mulatto bowing low at each step as he backed away with that curious motion toward his companions by the well; and Ruth, who had been sitting very close to her fa-ther, fascinated by the negro's gaze and strange appear-ance, could hardly wait to get out of hearing before she whispered: "Oh, father, did you ever see such a repulsive-looking creature in all your life?"

The Major admitted that he was an ugly fellow, and then, as a loud guffaw came to them from the rear, added, with that reasonable sense of justice which men possess and are pleased to call wisdom, that he seemed to be very civil and was, no doubt, a harmless good-natured creature.

"I don't know," said Ruth, doubtfully. "I only hope I shall never set eyes on him again. I should die if I were to meet him alone."

"Oh, nonsense!" said her father, reassuringly. "They are the most good-natured, civil poor creatures in the world. I used to see them during the war."

The Major was still contesting Dr Cary's prejudices.

CHAPTER XXVI

MAJOR WELCH AND RUTH BECOME RESIDENTS

IT was yet early in the day, when the travellers drove up to Red Rock, and though there were certain things which showed that the place was not kept up as it had formerly been, it was far handsomer, and appeared to be more extensively cultivated, than any plantation they had yet seen. A long line of barns and stables lay at some little distance behind the mansion, half screened by the hill, and off to one side stretched a large garden with shrubbery, apparently somewhat neglected, at the far end of which was a grove or great thicket of evergreens and other trees.

A tall man with a slight stoop in his shoulders came down the broad steps, and advanced to meet them as they drove up.

"Is this Colonel Welch ? " he asked.

"Well, not exactly, but Major Welch," said that gentleman, pleasantly, wondering how he could know him, "and you are—Mr. Still ? "

"Yes, sir, I'm the gentleman : I'm Mr. Still—Colonel Still, some of 'em calls me ; but I'm like yourself, Colonel, I don't care for titles. The madam, I suppose, sir ? " he smiled, as he handed Ruth down.

"No, my daughter, Miss Welch," said the Major, a little stiffly, to Ruth's amusement.

"Ah ! I thought she was a leetle young for you, Colonel ; but sometimes we old fellows get a chance at a fresh covey and we most always try to pick a young bird. We're real glad to see you, ma'am, and to have the honor of entertainin' so fine a young lady in our humble home. My son Wash, the Doctor, ain't at home this mornin', but he'll be back to-night, and he'll know how to make you have a good time. He's had advantages his daddy never had," he explained.

There was something almost pathetic, Major Welch thought, in this allusion to his son, and his recognition of his own failure to measure up to his standard. It made Major Welch overlook his vulgarity and his attempt to be familiar. And the Major decided anew that Hiram Still was not half as black as he had been painted, and that the opposition to him which he had discovered was nothing but prejudice.

As they entered the house, both Major Welch and Ruth stopped on the threshold, with an exclamation. Before them stretched one of the most striking halls Ruth had ever seen. At the other end was an open door with a glimpse of green fields and blue hills in the distance; but it was the hall itself that took Ruth's eye. And it was the picture of the man in the space just over the great fireplace that caught Major Welch. The "Indian-killer" again stood before him. Clad in his hunter's garb, with the dark rock behind him, his broken rifle at his feet, his cap on the back of his head, and his yellow hair pushed from under it, his eyes fastened on Major Welch with so calm and yet so intense a look that Major Welch was almost startled. That figure had suddenly obliterated the years. It brought back to him vividly the whole of his former visit.

Ruth, impressed by the expression of her father's face, and intensely struck by the picture, pressed forward to her father's side, almost holding her breath.

"I see you're like most folks, ma'am; you're taken first thing with that picture," said Still; then added, with a half laugh, "and it's the only picture in the batch I don't really like. But I jist mortally dislikes that, and I'd give it to anybody who'd take it down from thar, and save me harmless."

He went off into a half reverie. The Major was examining the frame curiously. He put his finger on a dim,

red smear on the bottom of the frame. Memory was bring‹
ing back a long train of recollections. Hardly more than
ten years before, he had stood on that same spot and done
the same thing. This hall was thronged with a gay and
happy and high bred company. He himself was an honored
guest. His gracious host was standing beside him, telling
him the story. He remembered it all. Now—they were
all gone. It was as if a flood had swept over them.
These inanimate things alone had survived. He ran his
hand along the frame.

The voice of his host broke in on his reflections.

"That thar red paint I see you lookin' at, got on the
frame one day the picture fell down before the war. A
nigger was paintin' the hairth right below it; it wa'n't
nailed then—and a gust of wind come up sudden and
banged a door and the picture dropped right down in the
paint. Mr. Gray, who used to own this place, was a settin'
right by the winder where his secretary used to stand, and
I had jest come back from the South the day befo' and was
talkin' to Mr. Gray about it in the hall here that minute.
'Well,' says I to him, 'if I was you, I'd be sort o' skeered
to see that happen'; — because thar's a story about it, that
whenever it comes down the old fellow in the graveyard
gits up, and something's goin to happen to the man as lives
here. 'No,' he says, 'Hiram (he always called me Hiram),
I'm not superstitious; but if anything should happen, I
have confidence in you to know you'd still be faithful—a
faithful friend to my wife and boys,' he says, in them very
words. And I says to him, 'Mr. Gray, I promise you I
will, faithful. And that's what I've done, Major, I've
kept my word and yet, see how they treat me! So after I
got the place I nailed the picture in the wall—or rather
just before that," he said in his former natural voice, "and
it ain't been down since, an' it ain't comin' down neither."

"But does that keep him from coming on his horse as
they say? Has he ever been seen since you nailed the
frame to the wall?" Ruth asked.

"Well, ma'am, I can only tell you that I ain't never seen him," said their host, with a faint, little smile. "Some says he's still ridin', and every time they hears a horse nicker at night around here they say that's him ; but I can't say as I believes it."

"Of course you cannot," said the Major, a little abruptly, "for you know it isn't he ; you have too much sense. A good head and a good conscience never see apparitions." The Major was still thinking of the past.

"How like he is to a picture I saw at Dr. Cary's, that they said was of a young Mr. Gray who still lives about here," said Ruth, recurring to the picture. She turned and was surprised to see what a change had come over her host's face. He suddenly changed the subject.

"Well, I'm glad you've come down, Colonel. Only I'm sorry I didn't know just when you were coming. I'd have sent my carriage for you. I've been lookin' out for you, and I've got the prettiest place in the country for you," he said. He nodded over in the direction of the garden. "I want to take you to see it. It will just suit you. The house ain't big, but the land's as rich as low grounds.

"And you're the very sort of a man we want here, Major. Your name will be worth a heap to us. Between ourselves, you can conjure with a Gover'ment title like a trick-doctor. Now, this fall, if you just go in with us—How would you like to go to the Legislature?" he asked, his voice lowered the least bit, and interrupting himself in a way he had.

"Not at all," said Major Welch. "No politics for me. Why, I'm not eligible—even if I settle here. I suppose there are some requirements in the way of residence and so forth?"

"Oh ! requirements ain't nothin'. We've got the Legislature, you see, and we—There's some several been elected ain't been here as long as you'll been when the election comes off." He glanced at Major Welch and interrupted himself again. "The fact is, Major," he explained, in a somewhat lower key, " we've had to do some things a leetle out of the regular run—to git the best men we could. But if we could get a gentleman like yourself——"

" No, I'm not in politics," said Major Welch, decisively. " I've neither experience nor liking for it, and I've come for business purposes——"

" Of course, you are quite right, Major, you're just like me ; but I didn't know what your opinion was. Well, you've come to the right place for business, Major," he said, in so changed a voice that he seemed to be two persons speaking. " It's the garden spot of the world—the money's jest layin' round to waste on the ground, if the folks jist had the sense to see it. All it wants is a little more capital. Colonel Leech and them's been talkin' about runnin' a railroad through this region. You know after all's said and done, Colonel, I ain't nothin' but a plain farmer. I talks about railroads, but, fact is, I'd ruther see cotton and corn grow 'n the finest railroad's ever run. My son Wash, the Doctor, he's got education, and he's got city ways and wants a railroad, and I says to him, that's all right, Wash, you have yer railroad and enjoy it, but jist let yer old pappy set on his porch and see the crops grow. I've made ten thousand dollars a year clear money on this place, and that's good enough for me, I says. That may sound like foolishness to you, Major, but that's my raisin', and a man can't git over his raisin'."

This was a philosophic fact which the Major had often been struck with, and it appeared to him now that he had a most excellent example of it before him.

As Major Welch was desirous to get settled as soon as possible, he and Ruth rode over that afternoon to take a look at the place Still had spoken of. A detour of a mile or so brought them around to a small farm-house with peaked roof and dormer windows, amid big locust-trees, on top of a hill. Behind it, at a little distance, rose the line of timbered spurs that were visible through the hall-door at Red Rock, and in front a sudden bend brought the river in view, with an old mill on its nearer bank, and the comb of water flashing over the dam. Ruth gave an exclamation of delight. She sketched rapidly just what they could do with the place. Still observed her silently, and when Major Welch inquired what price was asked for the place, told him that he could not exactly say that it was for sale. The Major looked so surprised at this, however, that he explained himself.

"It is this way," he said, "it is for sale and it ain't."

"Well, that's a way I do not understand. Whose is it?" said Major Welch, so stiffly that the other changed his tone.

"Well, the fact is, Colonel, to be honest about it," he said, "this here place belongs to me ; but I was born on this here place, not exactly in this house, but on the place, an' I always thought 't if anything was to happen—if my son Wash, the Doctor, was to git married or anything, and take a notion to set up at Red Rock, I might come back here and live—you see?"

The Major was mollified. He had not given the man credit for so much sentiment.

"Of course, if you really wants it—?" began Still, but the Major said, no, he would not insist on one's making such a sacrifice; that such a feeling did him credit.

So the matter ended in Still's proposing to lease the place to the Major, which was accepted, Major Welch agreeing to the first price he named, only saying he supposed it was the customary figure, which Still assured him was the case. He pointed out to him that the land was unusually rich.

"What's the name of the place?" asked Ruth.

"Well, 'tain't got any special name. We call it Stamper's," Still said.

"Stamper—Stamper?" repeated the Major. "Where have I heard that name?"

"You might 'a heard of him in connection with the riot 't took place near here a few years ago, when a dozen or so soldiers was murdered. 'Twas up here they hatched the plot and from here they started. They moved away from here, and I bought it."

It was not in this connection that the Major recalled the name.

"What was ever done about it?" he asked.

"Nothin'. What could you do?" demanded Still, tragically.

"Why arrest them and hang them, or send them to prison."

Still gave an ejaculation.

"You don't know 'em, Major! But we are gittin' 'em straight now," he added.

On their return to Red Rock they found that Still's son, the Doctor, had arrived. He was a tall, dark, and, at a distance, a rather handsome young man; but on nearer view this impression vanished. His eyes were small and too close together, like his father's, but instead of the good-humored expression which these sometimes had, his had a suspicious and ill-contented look. He dressed showily and evidently took great pride in his personal appearance. He had some education and was fond of making quotations, especially in his father's presence, toward whom his attitude was one of censoriousness and ill-humor.

His manner to the Major was always polite, and to Ruth it was especially so; but to the servants it was arrogant, and to his father it was little short of contemptuous. The Major heard him that evening berating someone in so angry a tone that he thought it was a dog he was scolding, until he heard Hiram Still's voice in mild expostulation; and again at the table that evening Dr. Still spoke to his father so sharply for some little breach of table etiquette that the Major's blood boiled. The meekness with which the father took his son's rebuke did more to secure for him the Major's friendship than anything else that occurred during their stay with him.

CHAPTER XXVII

HIRAM STILL GETS A LEGAL OPINION AND CAPTAIN ALLEN CLIMBS FOR CHERRIES

As Major Welch was anxious to be independent, he declined Still's invitation to stay with him, and within a week he and Ruth were "camping out" at the Stamper place, which he had rented, preparing it for the arrival of Mrs. Welch and their furniture.

As it happened, no one had called on the Welches while they remained at Still's; but they were no sooner in their own house than all the neighbors round began to come to see them.

Ruth found herself treated as if she were an old friend, and feeling as if she had known these visitors all her life. One came in an old wagon and brought two or three chairs, which were left until Ruth's should come; another sent over a mahogany table; a third came with a quarter of lamb; all accompanied by some message of apology or friendliness which made the kindness appear rather done to the senders than by them.

In the contribution which the Carys brought, Ruth found the two old cups she had admired. She packed them up and returned them to Blair with the sweetest note she knew how to write.

As soon as he was settled, Major Welch went to the Court-house to examine the records. He had intended to go alone and had made arrangements, the afternoon before, with a negro near by to furnish him a horse next day; that evening, however, Still, who appeared to know every·

thing that was going on, rode over and asked if he could not take him down in his buggy. He had to go there on some business, he explained, and Colonel Leech would be there and had told him he wanted to see the Major and talk over some matters, and wanted him to be there too.

The Major would have preferred to go first without Still. However, there was nothing else to do but to accept the offer he made of his company ; and the next morning Still drove over, and they set out together, Ruth saying that she had plenty to occupy her until her father's return.

They had not been gone very long and Ruth was busying herself, out in the yard, trimming the old rose-bushes into some sort of shape, when she heard a step, and looking up saw coming across the grass, the small man they had met in the road, who had told them the way to Dr. Cary's.

He wasn't "so very busy just then," he said, and had come to see if they "mightn't like to have a little hauling done when their furniture came."

Ruth thought that her father had arranged with Mr. Still to have it done.

"I ain't particularly busy jest now, and I'd take feed along—I jest thought I'd like to be neighborly," repeated the man. "Hiram, I s'pect, he's chargin' you some'n ?"

Ruth supposed so.

"Well, if he ain't directly, he will some way. The best way to pay Hiram is to pay him right down."

He asked Ruth if she would mind his going in and looking at the house, and, when she assented, he walked around silently, looking at the two rooms which she showed him : their sitting-room and her father's room ; then asked if he could not look into the other room also. This was Ruth's chamber, and for a second she hesitated to gratify curiosity carried so far; but reflecting that he was a plain countryman, and might possibly misunderstand her refusal and be wounded, she nodded her assent, and stepped forward to open the door. He opened it himself, however, and walked in, stepping on tip-toe. He stopped in the middle of the room and looked about him, his gaze resting presently on a nail driven into a strip in the wall just beside the bed.

"I was born in this here room," he said, as much to himself as to her ; then, after a pause : "right in that thar cornder—and my father was born in it before me and his father befo' him, and to think that Hiram owns it! Hiram Still! Well—well—things do turn out strange—don't they? Thar's the very nail my father used to hang his big silver watch on. I b'lieve I'd give Hiram a hoss for that nail, ef I knowed where I could get another one to plough my crop." He walked up and put his hand on the nail, feeling it softly. Then walked out.

"Thankee, miss. Will you tell yo' pa, Sergeant Stamper'd be glad to do what he could for him, and ef he wants him jist to let him know?" He had gone but a few steps, when he turned back : "And will you tell him I say he's got to watch out for Hiram?"

The next moment he was gone, leaving Ruth with a sinking feeling about her heart. What could he mean?

She had not long to think of it, however, for just then she heard the sound of wheels grinding along outside, and she looked out of the door just as a rickety little wagon drew up to the door. She recognized the driver as Miss Cary and walked out to meet her. Beside Blair in the wagon sat, wrapped up in shawls, though the day was warm, an elderly lady with a faded face, but with very pleasant eyes, looking down at Ruth from under a brown veil. Ruth at first supposed that she was Blair's mother, but Blair introduced her as "Cousin Thomasia." As they helped the lady out of the vehicle, Ruth was amused at the preparation she made. Every step she took she gave some explanation or exclamation, talking to herself, it appeared, rather than to either of the girls.

"My dear Blair, for heaven's sake don't let his head go. Take care, my dear, don't let this drop." (This to Ruth, about a package wrapped in paper.)

When at length she was down on the ground, she asked Blair if her bonnet was on straight : "Because, my dear" —and Ruth could not for her life tell to whom she was speaking—"nothing characterizes a woman more than her bonnet."

Then having been assured that this mark of character was all right, she turned to Ruth, and said, with the greatest graciousness :

"How do you do, my dear? You must allow me to kiss you. I am Cousin Thomasia."

Ruth's surprised look as she greeted her, perhaps, made her add, "I am everybody's Cousin Thomasia."

It was indeed as she said, she was everybody's Cousin Thomasia, and before she had been in the house ten minutes, Ruth felt as if she were, at least, hers. She accepted the arm-chair offered her, with the graciousness of a queen, and spread out her faded skirts with an air which Ruth noted and forthwith determined to copy. Then she produced her knitting, and began to knit so quietly that it was almost as if the yarn and needles had appeared at her bidding. The next instant she began a search for something—began it casually, so casually that she knit betweentimes, but the search quickened and the knitting ceased.

"Blair? —— !"

"You brought them with you, Cousin Thomasia."

"No, my dear, I left them, I'm sure I left them——" (searching all the time) "right on—Where can they be?"

"I saw you have them in the wagon."

"Then I've dropped them—Oh, dear! dear! What shall I do?"

"What is it?" asked Ruth.

"My eyes, my dear—and I cannot read a word without them. Blair, we must go right back and hunt for them."

But Blair was up and searching, not on the floor or in the road; but in the folds of Miss Thomasia's dress; in the wrappings of the little parcel which she still held in her lap.

"Here they are, Cousin Thomasia," she exclaimed,

triumphantly drawing them out of the paper.   "Right where you put them."

Miss Thomasia gave a laugh as fresh as a girl's.

"Why, so I did! How stupid of me !" She seated herself again, adjusted her glasses and began to unwrap her parcel.

"Here, my dear, is a little cutting I have fetched you from a rose which my dear mother brought from Kenilworth Castle, when she accompanied my dear father to England. I was afraid you might not have any flowers now, and nothing is such a panacea for loneliness as the care of a rose-bush. I can speak from experience. The old one used to grow just over my window at my old home and I took a cutting with me when we went away —General Legaie obtained the privilege of doing so— and you have no idea how much company it has been to me. I will show you how to set it out."

The glasses were on now, and she was examining the sprig of green in the little pot with profound interest, while her needles flew.

"Where was your old home?" Ruth asked, softly.

"Here, my dear—not this place, but all around you. This was Mrs. Stamper's—one of our poor neighbors. But we lived at Red Rock."

"Oh !" said Ruth, shocked at having asked the question.

"No matter, my dear," the old lady went on. "Since we moved we have lived at a little place right on the road. You must come over and let me show you my roses there. But I don't think they will ever be equal to the old ones— or what the old ones were, for I hear they are nearly all gone now—I have never been back since I left. I do not think I could stand seeing that—person in possession of my father's and my brother's estate." She sighed for the first time, and for the first time the needles, as she leant back, stopped.

"I wrapped up my glasses to keep from seeing it as we drove up the hill. I wish they might let me lie there

when I die, but I know they will not." Her gaze was out
of the open door. In the silence which followed her words
the sound of a horse's hoofs was heard.

" There is someone outside, my dear," she said, placidly.
Both Ruth and Blair looked out.

" Why, it is the General," said Blair, and Ruth wondered who the General was, and wondered yet more to detect
something very much like a flutter in Miss Thomasia's
manner. Her hand went to her bonnet ; to her throat ; she
smoothed her already smooth skirts, and glanced around—
ending in a little appealing look to Blair. It was almost as
if a white dove, represented in some sacred mystery, had
suddenly lost tranquillity. When, however, the new visitor
reached the door, Miss Thomasia was quietude itself.

He stepped up to the door and gave a tap with the butt
of his riding-switch before he was aware of the presence of
the three ladies ; then he took off his hat.

"Ladies," he said, with quite a grand bow. At the
same moment, both of the ladies who knew him, spoke,
but Ruth heard only Miss Thomasia's words :

" My dear, this is General Legaie, of whom you have
often heard, our old and valued friend." Ruth had never
heard of him, but she was struck by him. He was not
over five feet three inches high : not as tall by several inches
as Ruth herself ; but his head, with curling white hair,
was so set on his shoulders, his form was so straight and
vigorous, and his countenance, with its blue eyes and fine
mouth, so handsome and self-contained, that Ruth thought
she had never seen a more martial figure. She thought
instinctively of a portrait she had once seen of a French
Marshal ; and when the General made his sweeping bow
and addressed her with his placid voice in old-fashioned
phrase as, " Madam," the illusion was complete. Why, he
was absolutely stately. Then he addressed Miss Thomasia
and Blair, making each of them a bow and a compliment
with such an old-fashioned courtesy that Ruth felt as if
she were reading a novel.

He had hoped to call and pay his respects before, he told Ruth, when he had finished his greetings; but had been unavoidably delayed, and it was a cause of sincere regret that he should be so unfortunate as to miss her father. He had learned of his absence several miles below, but he would not delay longer paying his devoirs to her; so had come on. "And you see the triple reward I receive," he said, with a glance which included all three ladies, and a little laugh of pleasantry over himself.

"See what an adept he is," said Blair: "he compliments us all in one breath."

The General looked at Miss Thomasia as if he were going to speak directly to her, but she was picking up a stitch, so he shifted his glance to Blair, and, catching her eye, laughed heartily.

"Well? Why didn't you say it?"

Miss Thomasia knitted placidly.

He shrugged his shoulders, laughed again, and changed his bantering tone.

"Have you seen Jacquelin?" asked Miss Thomasia, who had calmly ignored the preceding conversation.

"Yes, he's all right—he came back yesterday and has gone in with Steve Allen. They'll get along. He's just the sort of man Steve needed; he'll be his heavy artillery. He is looking into the matter of the bonds."

Miss Thomasia sighed.

"Two young gentlemen of the County who are great friends of ours, Miss Welch," explained the General.

Meanwhile, Major Welch and Mr. Still had reached the county seat. During their ride, Still had given Major Welch an account of affairs in the County, and of most of those with whom he would come in contact. Steve Allen he described as a terrible character. It had been a dreadful struggle that he himself and other Union men had had to wage, he said. Leech was the leading Northern man in the County, and was going to be Governor. But he was disposed to caution Major Welch somewhat against even him. Leech did not exactly understand things; he did not rely enough on his white friends. He would have turned out all the white officials and filled their places with negroes. But Still had insisted on keeping, at least, Mr. Dockett, the Clerk, in; because he had charge of all the records. But Mr. Dockett had not acted exactly right, he said, and he was afraid at the next election "they'd have to let him go." He had been "getting mighty unreasonable." Some people wanted his son, Wash, the Doctor, to run, but he "didn't know about it?" he said, with an interrogation in his voice.

Major Welch had supposed that the Doctor would find his profession more profitable, or at least that it would take up all his time if he proposed to follow it; but Still explained that there was not a great deal of practice, and that the clerk's place was a "paying office."

When they arrived at Leech's house Major Welch found it a big, modern affair with a mansard roof, set in the middle of a treeless lot. To Major Welch's surprise, Leech was not at home. Still appeared much disconcerted.

As they crossed the yard, the Major observed a sign over a door: "ALLEN AND GRAY. LAW OFFICE."

"If necessary we could secure their services," he said, indicating the sign.

Still drew up to his side, and lowered his voice, looking around: They were the lawyers he had told him of, he said. That was "that fellow Allen, the leader in all the trouble that went on."

"Who's Gray?" The Major was still scanning the sign.

Still gave a curious little laugh.

"He's the one as used to own my place—Mr. Gray's son. He's a bad one, too. He's just come back and set up as a lawyer. Fact is, I believe he's set up as one, more to devil me than anything else."

Major Welch said, dryly, that he did not see why his setting up as a lawyer should bedevil him. Still hesitated.

"Well, if he thinks he could scare me—— "

"I don't see how he could scare you. I would not let him scare me," said Major Welch, dryly.

"You don't know 'em, Colonel," said Still. "You don't know what we Union men have had to go through. They won't let us buy land, and they won't let us sell it. They hate you because you come from the North, and they hate me because I don' hate you. I tell you all the truth, Colonel, and you don't believe it—but you don't know what we go through down here. We've got to stand together. You'll see." The man's voice was so earnest, and his face so sincere that Major Welch could not help being impressed.

"Well, I'll show him and everyone else pretty quickly that that is not the way to come at me," said Major Welch, gravely. "When I get ready to buy, I'll buy where I please, and irrespective of anyone else's views except the seller's." And he walked up to the door, without seeing the look on Still's face.

The only occupants of the clerk's office were two men ; one was an old man, evidently the clerk, with a bushy beard and keen eyes gleaming through a pair of silver spectacles. The other was a young man and a very handsome one, with a broad brow, a strongly chiselled chin, and a very grave and somewhat melancholy face. He was seated in a chair directly facing the door, examining a bundle of old chancery papers which were spread out on his knee and on a chair beside him, and as the visitors entered the door he glanced up. Major Welch was struck by his fine eyes, and the changed look that suddenly came into them. Still gave his arm a convulsive clutch, and Major Welch knew by instinct that this was the man of whom Still had just spoken.

If Jacquelin Gray was really the sort of man Still had described him to be, and held the opinions Still had attributed to him, he played the hypocrite very well, for he not only bowed to Major Welch very civiliy, if distantly, but to do so even rose from his seat at some little inconvenience to himself, as he had to gather up the papers spread on his knee. It is true that he took not the least notice of Still, who included him as well as the clerk in his greeting, the only evidence he gave of being aware of the presence of his former manager, being contained in a certain quiver of the nostrils, as Still passed him.

Major Welch was introduced by Still to the clerk, and stated his errand, wondering at the change in his companion's voice.

"He's afraid of that young man," he thought to himself, and he stiffened a little as the idea occurred to him ; and at the first opportunity he glanced again at Jacquelin, who was once more busy with his bundle of papers, in which he appeared completely absorbed. Still was following the clerk, who, with his spectacles on the tip of his long nose, was looking into the files of his deed-books ; but Major Welch saw that Still was not attending to him ; his eyes were turned and were fastened on the young lawyer, quite on the other side of the room. As the Major looked he was astonished to see Still start and put out his hand as though to support himself. Following Still's gaze he glanced across at Jacquelin. He had taken several long, narrow slips of paper out of the bundle, and was at the instant examining them curiously, oblivious of everything else. Major Welch looked back at Still, and he was as white as a ghost. Before he could take it in, Still muttered something and turned to the door. As he walked out he tottered so that Major Welch, thinking he was ill, followed him.

Outside, the air revived Still somewhat, and a drink of whiskey which he got at the tavern bar, and told the barkeeper to make "stiff," set him up a good deal. He had been feeling badly for some time, he said ; thought he was a little bilious.

Just as they came out of the bar, they saw young Gray cross the court-green and go over to his office.

They returned to the clerk's office, and Major Welch was soon running through the deeds, while Still, after looking over his shoulder for a moment or two, took a seat near Mr. Dockett and began to talk to him. He appeared much interested in the old fellow, his family, and all that belonged to him, and Major Welch was a little amused at the old man's short replies.

His attention was attracted by Still's saying casually that he'd like to see the papers in that old suit of his against the Gray estate, if he could lay his hands on them, and the clerk's dry answer that he could lay his hands on any paper in the office, and that the papers in question were in the "ended-causes" case. "Mr. Jacquelin Gray was just looking over them as you came in," he said, as he rose to get them.

"Well, let him look," Still growled, with a sudden change of tone. "He can look all he wants, and he won't git around them bonds."

"Oh, no! I don't say as he will," the old officer answered.

"I'd like to take 'em home with me—" Still began; but the clerk cut him short.

"I can't let you do that. You'll have to look at 'em here in the office."

"Why, they're nothin' but—I want Colonel Welch here to look at 'em—they'll show him how the lands come to me—I'll bring 'em back——"

"I can't let you take 'em out of the office." His tone was as dry as ever.

"Well, I'd like to know why not? They don't concern nobody but me, and they're all ended."

"That's the very reason you can't take 'em out; they're part of the records of this office——"

"Well, I can take the bonds out, anyway," Still persisted; "they is mine, anyhow."

"No, you can't take them, either."

Still did not often lose his temper, or show it, if he did; but this time he lost it.

"Well, I'll show you if I can't, before the year is out,

Mr. Dockett. **I'll** show you who I am !" He rose **with** much feeling.

"I know who you are." The old fellow turned and shot a piercing glance at him over his spectacles, and Major Welch watched complacently to see how it would end.

"Well, if you don't, I mean to make you know it. I'll show you you don't own this County. I'll show you who is the bigger man, you or the people of this County. You think because you been left in this office that you own it; but I'll——"

"No, I don't," the old man said, firmly; "I know you've got negroes enough to turn me out if you choose; but I want to tell you that until you do I'm in charge here, and I run the office according to what I think is my duty, and the only way to change it is to turn me out. Do you want to see the papers or not ? You can look at 'em here just as everybody else does."

" That's right," said Major Welch, meaning to explain that it was the law. Still took it in a different sense, however, and quieted down. He would look at them, he said, sulkily, and, taking the bundle, he picked out the same slips which young Gray had been examining.

" You're so particular about your old papers," he said, as he held up one of the slips, " I wonder you don't keep 'em a little better. You got a whole lot o' red ink smeared on this bond."

" I didn't get it on it." The clerk got up and walked across the room to look at the paper indicated, adjusting his spectacles as he did so. One glance sufficed for him.

" That ain't ink, and if 'tis, it didn't get on it in this office. That stain was on that bond when Leech filed it. I remember it particularly."

" I don't know anything about that—I know it wa'n't on it when I give it to him, and I don't remember of ever having seen it before," Still persisted.

" Well, I remember it well—I remember speaking of **it**

to him, because we thought 'twas finger-marks, and he said 'twas on it when you gave it to him."

" Well, I know 'twant," Still repeated, hotly.   " If 'twas on thar when he brought it here he got 't on it himself, and I'll take my oath to it.   Well, that don't make any difference in the bond, I s'pose ?   It's just as good with that on it as if 'twant ? "

" Oh, yes ; that's so," said Mr. Dockett.   " If it's all right every other way, that won't hurt it."

Still looked at him sharply.

As they drove home, Still, after a long period of silence, suddenly asked Major Welch, within what time after a case was ended a man could bring a suit to upset it.

" Well, I don't know what the statutes of this State are, but he can generally bring it without limit, on the ground of fraud," said the Major, " unless he is estopped by laches."

" What's that ? " asked Still, somewhat huskily, and the Major started to explain ; but Still was taken with another of his ill turns.

That same afternoon, a little before Major Welch's return, Ruth was walking about the yard, looking, every now and then, across the hill, in the direction of Red Rock, from which her father should soon be coming, when, as she passed near a cherry-tree, she observed that some of the fruit was already ripe.   One or two branches were not very high.   She had been feeling a little lonely, and it occurred to her that it would be great fun to climb the tree.   She had once been a good climber, and she remembered the scoldings she had received for it from her mother, who regarded it as " essentially frivolous," and had once, as a punishment, set her to learn all the names of all the branches of a tree which hung on the nursery wall, and represented, allegorically, all the virtues and vices, together with a perfect network of subsidiary qualities.   She could remember many of them now—" Faith, Hope, Temperance," and so on.

" Dear mamma," she thought, with a pang of homesickness, " I wish she were here now." This reflection only made her more lonely, and to overcome the feeling she turned to the more material and attractive tree.

" I could climb that tree easily enough," she said, " and there's no one to know anything about it. Even mamma would not mind that much. Besides, I could see papa from a greater distance and I'll get him some cherries for his tea."

These last two considerations were sufficient to counterbalance the idea of maternal disapproval. So Ruth turned up the skirt of her dress, pinned it so that it would not be stained, and five minutes later was scrambling up the tree. Higher and higher she went up, feeling the old exhilaration of childhood as she climbed. What a fine view there was from her perch ! the rolling hills, the green low-grounds, the winding river, the blue mountains behind and, away to the eastward, the level of the tide-water country almost as blue at the horizon as the mountains to the westward. How still it was too ! Every sound was distinct : the lowing of a cow far away toward Red Rock, the notes of a thrush in a thicket, and the chirp of a sparrow in an old tree. Ruth wished she could have described it as she saw it, or, rather, as she felt it, for it was more feeling than seeing, she thought. But the best cherries were out toward the ends of the limbs, so she secured a safe position and set to work, gathering them. She was so engrossed in this occupation that she forgot everything else until she heard the trampling of a horse's feet somewhere. It was quite in a different direction from that in which she expected her father, but supposing that it was he, Ruth gave a little yodel, with which she often greeted him when at a distance, and climbed out on a limb that she might look down and see him. How astonished and amused he would be, she thought. Yes, there he was, coming around the slope just below her, but how was he going to get across the ditch ? If only that bough were not in the way! Ah! now she had the bough and could pull it aside. Heavens! it was a stranger, and he was near enough for her to see that he was a young man. What should she do? Suppose he should have heard her! At the moment she looked he was putting his horse at the ditch—a splendid jump it was. She let the bough go and edged in toward the body of the tree, listening and half seeing the rider below through the leaves as he galloped up into the yard. Perhaps he had not seen her? She crouched down. It was a vain hope, for the next instant he turned his horse's head toward the tree and drew him in almost under her.

"I say—Is anyone at home?" he asked. The voice was a very deep and pleasant one. Although Ruth was sure he was speaking to her, she did not answer.

"I say, little girl, are Colonel Welch and his daughter at home?"

This time he looked up. So Ruth answered. No, they were not at home. Her voice sounded curiously quavering.

"Ah! I'm very sorry. When will they be at home? Can you tell me?"

"Ah! ur—not exactly," quavered Ruth, crouching still closer to the tree-trunk and gathering in her skirts.

"You have some fine cherries up there!"

Oh, heavens! why didn't he go away!

To this she made no answer, hoping he would go. He caught hold of a bough, she thought, to pull some cherries; wrapped his reins around it, and the next moment stood up in his saddle, seized a limb above him and swung himself up. In her astonishment Ruth almost stopped breathing.

"I believe I'll try a few—for old times' sake," he said to himself, or to her, she could not tell which. and swung himself higher. "I don't suppose Colonel Welch would object."

The next swing brought him up to the limb immediately below Ruth, and he turned and looked up at her where she sat in the fork of the limb. Her face had been burning ever since she had been discovered, and was burning now ; but she could not help being amused at the expression which came into the stranger's eyes as he looked at her. Astonishment, chagrin, and amusement were all stamped there, mingled together.

"What on earth !—I beg your pardon—" he began, his eyes wide open with surprise, gazing straight into hers. The next instant he burst out laughing, a peal so full of real mirth that Ruth joined in and laughed with all her might too.

"I'm Captain Allen, Steve Allen—and you are—— ? "

" Miss Welch—when I'm at home."

He pulled himself up to the limb on which Ruth sat and coolly seated himself near her.

"I hope you will be at home—Miss Welch ; for I am. I used to be very much at home in this tree in old times, which is my excuse for being here now, though I confess I never found quite such fruit on it as it seems to bear to-day."

The twinkle in his gray eyes and a something in his lazy voice reminded Ruth of Reely Thurston. The last part of his speech to her sounded partly as if he meant it, but partly as if he were half poking fun at her and wished to see how she would take it. She tried to meet him on his own ground.

"If you had not made yourself somewhat at home you would not have found it now." She was very demure.

Steve lifted his eyes to her quickly, and she was rather nettled to see that he looked much amused at her speech.

" Exactly. You would not have had me act otherwise, I hope ? We always wish our guests to make themselves at home. You Yankees don't want to be behind us."

She saw his eyes twinkle, and felt that he had said it to draw her fire, but she could not forbear firing back.

" No, but sometimes it does not seem necessary, as you *Rebels* appear inclined to make yourselves at home—some-

times even without an invitation." Her chin went up a
point.

Steve burst out laughing.

"A good square shot. I surrender, Miss Welch."

"What! so easily? I thought you Rebels were better
fighters? I have heard so."

Steve only laughed.

"'He that fights and runs away,' you know. I can't
run, so I surrender. May I get you some cherries? The
best are out on the end of the limbs, and I am afraid you
might fall." His voice had lost the tone of badinage and
was full of deference and protection.

Ruth said she believed that she had all the cherries she
wanted. She had, perhaps, a dozen—. She was wondering
how she should get down, and was in a panic lest her father
should appear and find her up in the tree with this strange
young man.

In reply to her refusal, however, Steve looked at her
quizzically.

"You want to get down." This in assertion rather
than in question.

"Yes." Defiantly.

"And you can't get down unless I let you?"

"N—n—" She caught herself quickly, "I thought you
had surrendered?"

"Can't a prisoner capture his captor?"

"Not if he has given his parole and is a gentleman."

Steve whistled softly. His eyes never left her face.

"Will you invite me in?"

"No."

"Why?"

"Because——"

"I see." Steve nodded.

"Because my father is not at home."

"Oh! All the more reason for your having a pro-
tector."

"No. And I will make no terms with a prisoner."

With a laugh Steve let himself down to the limb below.
Then he stopped and turning looked up at her.

"May I help you down?" The tone was almost humble.

"No, I thank you, I can get down." Very firmly.

"I must order your father to remain at home," he
smiled.

"My father is not one to take orders; he gives them,"
she said, proudly.

Captain Allen looked up at her, the expression of admiration in his eyes deepened. "I think it likely," he said
with a nod. "Well, I don't always take them so meekly
myself. Good-by. Do you require your prisoner to report at all?" He held out his hand.

"Good-by—I—don't know: No."

He smiled up at her. "You don't know all your privileges. Good-by. I always heard you Yankees were cruel
to prisoners."

It was said in such a way that Ruth did not mind it, and
did not even wish to fire back. The next minute Steve was
on his horse, cantering away without looking back, and
curiously, Ruth, still seated on her leafy perch, was conscious of a feeling of blankness.

"I hate that man," she said to herself, "he has been
doing nothing but make fun of me. But he is amusing—
and awfully handsome. And what a splendid rider! I
wonder if he will have the audacity to come back?"

As she reached the ground she saw her father far across
the field, coming up the same road along which her visitor
was going away. When the two men met they stopped and
had a little talk, during which Ruth watched with curiosity
to see if Captain Allen would return. He did not, however. It was only a moment and then he cantered on,
leaving Ruth with a half disappointed feeling, and wondering if he had told her father of their meeting.

When Major Welch arrived, Ruth waited with some impatience to discover if he had been told. He mentioned

that he had met Mr. Allen and thought him a striking-looking and rather nice fellow ; had invited him to return, but he said he could not, that he had seen her, and would call again.

" He is a gentlemanly fellow, but is said to be one of the most uncontrolled men about here, the leader in all the lawlessness that goes on."

Ruth thought of what the old mammy at Dr. Cary's had told her.   She wished to change the subject.

" Did he say where we met ? " she asked, laughing and blushing.

" No, only said he had met you."

" He caught me up in a cherry-tree."

" What !   Well, he's a nice fellow," said her father, and Ruth had begun to think so too.

CHAPTER XXVIII

MRS. WELCH ARRIVES AND GIVES HER FIRST LESSON IN
ENTERPRISE

THE next day, Still called to see Major Welch and made him a proposition to sell him a part of the Red Rock place. On thinking it over, he said, he believed he'd rather have the Major as a near neighbor than to have him farther off, and he also believed that the Major would find it safer to buy from him a place he had got under decree of court, and had already held quietly for some time, than to buy a place about which there might be a question and where he'd be sure to incur the enmity of the old owners.

This reason, to judge from Major Welch's expression, did not make much impression on him. He did not wish to incur anyone's enmity, he said. But if he bought honestly, and became the lawful owner of a place, he should not mind what others thought.

Still shook his head. Major Welch did not know these people, he said. "And to be honest with you, Major, I feel as if having you right here by me was a sort of protection. They daresn't touch a gentleman who's been in the Union army, and who's got big friends. And that's one reason I'd like to have you right close to me."

His manner had something so sincere in it that it was almost pathetic. So, as he made Major Welch what appeared to be really a very reasonable proposal, not only as to the Stamper place, but also as to several hundred acres of the Red Rock land adjoining, the Major agreed to take it under advisement, and intimated that if the title should

320

prove all right, and Mrs. Welch should like the idea when she arrived he would probably purchase.

Within a week or two following Major Welch's trip to the county seat, and Still's offer to sell him the Stamper place and a part of Red Rock, Mrs. Welch arrived. Mrs. Welch, in her impatience, could not wait for the day she had set and arrived before she was expected. The telegram she had sent had miscarried, and when she reached the station there was no one present to meet her.

A country station is a sad place at best to one who has just left the bustle and life of a city; but to be deposited, bag and baggage, in a strange land and left alone without anyone to meet you, and without knowing a soul, is forlorn to the last degree.

Strong as she was, Mrs. Welch, when the train whirled away and no one came to her, felt a sense of her isolation strike her to the heart. A two-horse carriage, the only one in sight, stood near a fence at some little distance, and for a short while she thought it might have come for her, and she waited for some moments; but presently a tall colored man and a colored woman got into it. The man was glittering with a shining silk-hat and a long broad-cloth coat; and the woman was in a brand-new silk, and wore a vivid bonnet. Even then, it occurred to Mrs. Welch that, perhaps, the man was the coachman, and, for a moment, she was buoyed by hope, but she was doomed to disappointment. The man was talking loudly, and apparently talked to be heard by all around him. Mrs. Welch could hear something of what he said.

" We're all right. We've got 'em down, and we mean to keep 'em down, too, by —— ! " A shout followed this. " Yes, the bottom rail is on top, and we mean to keep it so till the fence rots down, by —— ! " Another burst of laughter. " You jest stick to me and Leech, and we'll bring you to the promised land. Yas, we're in the saddle, and we mean to stay there. We've got the Gov'ment behind us, and we'll put a gun in every colored man's hand

and give him, not a mule, but a horse to ride, and we'll dress his wife in silk and give her a carriage to ride in, same's my wife's got."

"Ummh! heah dat! Yes, Lord! Dat's what I want," cried an old woman, jumping up and down in her ecstasy, to the amusement of the others.

"A *mule's* good 'nough for me—I b'lieve I ruther have mule 'n hoss, I'se fotched up wid mules," called out some-one, which raised a great laugh, and some discussion.

"Well, all right; you shall have your ruther. Every-one shall take his pick. We'll do the ridin' now."

Mrs. Welch was listening with keen interest. The speaker, who was Nicholas Ash, the member from Red Rock, gathered up the reins. As he did so, someone called:

"You better watch out for de K. K.'s," at which there was a roar of laughter.

"They's the one's I'm lookin' for. I'm just fixed for 'em, by —— !" shouted the statesman.

"Dee ain' gwine meddle wid him," said someone in the crowd, admiringly.

"Don' know. I wouldn' drive roun' heah and talk 'bout 'um like he does, not for dat mule he gwine gi' me." The laughter that greeted this showed that others besides the speaker held the same views.

As the carriage drove off, Mrs. Welch's heart sank. Her last hope was gone. She was relieved somewhat by the approach of the station-agent, who up to that time had been engaged about his duties, and who now, seeing a lady standing outside, came up to her. Mrs. Welch told who she was. He had heard that Mrs. Welch was expected, but did not know the day. No telegrams, such as she spoke of, had passed through his office, and it was an all-day's ride up to Red Rock when the roads were bad. He invited her to remain as his guest. "People right often did so when they came, unexpected-like."

Mrs. Welch thanked him, but thought she would prefer

to go on, if she could get a conveyance, even if she could go that night only as far as Brutusville.

" Can't I get some sort of wagon ? " she inquired.

The agent gazed at her with a serenity that was in strong contrast with her growing decisiveness. He did not know as she could, the mail-wagon went over in the morning after the early train ; people generally went by that. Dill Herrick had a sort of a wagon, and folks sometimes took it if they got there too late for the mail-wagon and were in too big a hurry to wait till next day. But Dill was away that day. The wagon was there, but Dill had gone away on his horse and would not be back till next day.

All this was told in the most matter-of-fact way, as if it was quite as much a thing of course as any other order of nature. Mrs. Welch was on her metal. She would for once give this sleepy rustic an illustration of energy ; she would open his eyes.

" Well, is that the *only* horse anywhere about here ? " Her tone was energetic, perhaps even exasperated. The agent was unmoved.

" No'm ; Al Turley's got a *sort* of a horse, but he don't work very well. And Al ain't got any wagon."

This was too much for Mrs. Welch.

" Don't you think we might get a horse of one man and the wagon and harness of the other, and put them together ? " she laughed.

The agent was not so sure. Al might be going to use his horse, and he " didn't work so well, any.... ."

" But he does work ? " Mrs. Welch persisted.

" Oh, yes'm—*some*. Al ploughs with him."

" Well, now, let's see what a little enterprise will do. I'll pay well for both horse and wagon."

The agent went off, and after a time came back. Al would see what he could do. But again he renewed his invitation to her to wait until to-morrow. He was almost urgent ; he painted the difficulties of the journey in the

gloomiest colors. Mrs. Welch now, however, had set her
mind on carrying out her plans. It had become a matter
of principle with her. She had come down here to snow
what energy would accomplish, and she might as well
begin now.

While she waited, she passed her time watching the negroes who were congregated about a small building which
seemed to be part store, part bar-room, though from her
observation the latter was its principal office.

They were a loud and slovenly set, but appeared to be
good-humored, and rather like children engaged in rough
horse-play; and when their voices sounded most like quarrelling they would suddenly break out in loud guffaws of
laughter.

They were so boisterous at times that Mrs. Welch was
glad when the station-agent returned and asked if she
wouldn't go over and sit in his house till Al came. She
would have done so, but, as he evidently intended to
remain in the office, she thought it would be a good opportunity to learn something about the negroes, and perhaps
also to teach him a little on her part.

Were the negroes not improving? she asked. Her
companion's whole manner changed. She was surprised to
see what a keen glance was suddenly shot at her from under his light brows.

"Not as I can see—You can see 'em yonder for yourself."

"Do they ever give you trouble?"

"Me?—No'm; don't never give *me* trouble," he answered, negligently. "Don' give nobody as much trouble
as they did."

Mrs. Welch was just thinking this corroborative of her
own views when he, with his back to her, stooped for
something, and the butt of a pistol gleamed in his trousers
pocket. Mrs. Welch froze up. She could hardly refrain
from speaking of it. She understood now the signifi-
cance of his speech. Just then there was quite a roar
outside, followed by the rattle of wheels, and the next in-

stant Mrs. Welch's vehicle drew up to the door. For a
moment Mrs. Welch's heart failed her, and she regretted
the enterprise which had committed her to such a combination. In the shafts of a rickety little wagon — the
wheels of which wobbled in every direction and made
four distinct tracks — was a rickety little yellow horse
which at that moment, to the great diversion of the crowd
of negroes outside, was apparently attempting to back
the wagon through a fence. One instant he sat down in
the shafts, and the next reared and plunged and tried to
go any way but the right way. Two negroes were holding
on to him while the others were shouting with laughter
and delight. The driver was a spare, dingy-looking
countryman past middle age, and was sitting in the wagon,
the only creature in sight that appeared to be unmoved by
the excitement. Mrs. Welch's heart sank, and even after
the plunging little animal was quieted she would have declined to go; but it was too late now. She had never put
her hand to the plough and turned back.

"I can manage him," said the driver serenely, seeing
her hesitation. And as there were many assurances that
he was "all right now," and everyone was expecting her
to get in, she summoned the courage and climbed in.

It was a wearying drive. The roads were the worst
Mrs. Welch had ever seen, but, in one way, there was excitement enough. The tedium was relieved by the occa-
sional breaking of the harness and the frequent necessity
of dismounting to walk up the hill when the horse balked.

The day before had been very warm, and Mrs. Welch's
journey had not been a comfortable one, and this last
catastrophe capped the climax. But she did not complain—she considered querulousness a sin—it was a sign
of weakness. Perhaps, she even found a certain satisfaction in her discomfort. She had not come for comfort.
But when the harness broke for the half-dozenth time, she
asked :

"Why don't you keep your harness in good order ?"

The somewhat apathetic look in the driver's face changed.

" 'Tain't my harness."

" Well, whosever it is, why don't he keep it in order ? "

" You'll have to ask Dill that," he said, dryly.

When, a few minutes later, they came to their next stand she began again :

" Why don't you keep your roads repaired and rebuild your fences ? "

" I don't live about here." This time the tone was a little shorter.

" Well, it's the same all the way. It's been just as bad from the start. What is the reason ? " she persisted.

" Indeed, ma'am I don't know," he drawled, "some says it's the Yankee carpet-baggers steals all the money—"

" Well, I don't believe it—I believe it's that the people are just shiftless," Mrs. Welch fired back.

The man, for answer, only jerked his horse : " Git up ! "

" A dull fellow," thought Mrs. Welch, and presently she essayed again :

" The Yankees are thrifty enough. In all the North there is not such a road as this. I wish you could see their villages, how snug and trig and shipshape they are: houses painted, fences kept up, everything nice and neat."

" Maybe, that's where they puts the money they steals down here," said the driver, more dryly than before.

Mrs. Welch grew hot, but she could not help being amused too.

" It must be an accident, but I'll write that home," thought she. She, however, had not much time to think. For just then they were descending a steep hill and the breeching gave way, the wagon ran down on the horse, and, without a second's warning, the little steed, like the Gadarine swine, ran violently down the steep hill, and on up the road. The driver, who was swinging to him for life, was in the act of assuring Mrs. Welch that she need not be scared as he could hold him, when the rein broke and he went out suddenly backward over the wheel, and Mrs. Welch herself must soon have followed him, had not a horseman unexpectedly dashed up from behind and, spurring his fleet horse beside the tearing little beast in the wagon, seized the runaway by the bridle and brought it to a stand-still.

The transition from the expectation of immediate injury, if not death, to absolute security is itself a shock, and even after the vehicle was quite still, Mrs. Welch, who had been holding on to its sides with all her might, could hardly realize her escape. Her first thought was for the driver.

"Oh! I'm afraid that poor man is killed!" she exclaimed.

"Oh! he's all right. I hope you are not hurt, madam?" said her rescuer, solicitously. "I think I'd better hold the horse, or I would come and take you out."

Mrs. Welch assured him that she was not at all hurt, and she sprang out and declared that she would go back at once and look after the driver. Just then, however, the driver appeared, covered with dust, but not otherwise injured.

"Well, I was just sayin' I'd saved Al, anyhow," he said as he came up. "And I'm glad to find, Cap'n, you saved the others."

"What are you going to do now?" Mrs. Welch asked when the driver had finished talking to the gentleman, and begun to work at the harness.

"I'm going to take you to the Cote-house. I told you I'd do it."

"Behind that horse!"

"Ain't nothin' the matter with the hoss—it's the gear."

"I think I'd better take her," the young man who had rescued her said, though with a little hesitation. "I can take her behind me, and get her there by the through way."

"What! On that horse? I can't ride that creature," declared Mrs. Welch with wide-open eyes, looking at his handsome horse which was still prancing from excitement.

"Why, he's as quiet as a lamb—he's carried double many a time, and several ladies have ridden him. I could get you there much quicker than you can drive. All you have to do is to hold on to me. Whoa, boy!"

"I know that sort of lamb," declared Mrs. Welch. "What shall I do with my trunk?"

The young man's confidence was telling on her and she was beginning to yield. The choice was between the two horses and she had had experience with one.

"Oh! your trunk's all right. I'll carry your trunk on," agreed the driver. He had finished his mending and was gathering up his reins.

"Do you mean that you are going to get in there and try to drive that horse again?"

"That's what I'm agoin' to do 'm."

"Then I'll get in, too," declared Mrs. Welch, firmly. Her face was pale, but there was a light in her eyes that made her suddenly handsome. The two men looked at her and both began to expostulate.

"I made him come, and I don't mean that he shall risk his neck for me alone," she declared, firmly, gathering up her skirts. But the horseman suddenly interfered.

"I couldn't let you be run away with again under my very eyes," he said, smiling, "I might be held accountable by your dau—— by your fam—— your Government."

Mrs. Welch was not accustomed to being talked to in this way; but she liked him none the less for it. However, she would not yield.

It was finally agreed that a trial should be made first without her, and then, if the horse went all right, she could get in. Both men insisted on this, and as they explained that the driver could manage the horse better without her, she temporized. Indeed she was obliged to do so, for the young man who had rescued her told her plainly, though

"I COULDN'T LET YOU BE RUN AWAY WITH AGAIN UNDER MY VERY
EYES," HE SAID.

politely, that he would not allow her to get in the wagon again until the experiment had been made.

After a little time, as the horse appeared to have been sobered by his unwonted exertion, she was allowed to mount once more, and so proceeded, the young gentleman riding close beside the horse, to prevent any further trouble.

Mrs. Welch at last had time to look at her deliverer. He was a tall, fine-looking young fellow, with the face and address of a gentleman. A slouch hat, much weather-stained, and a suit of clothes by no means new, at first sight made his dress appear negligent, but his voice was as refined as any Mrs. Welch had ever heard ; his manner was a mixture of deference and protection, and his face, with clear, gray eyes, firm mouth, and pleasant smile, gave him an air of distinction and was one of the most attractive she had ever seen.

He had introduced himself to her when he first spoke ; Captain Somebody, he said, but as she had been rather agitated at that moment she had not caught the name, and she waited until he should mention it again or she should get a chance to ask the driver. When she did ask him, she understood him to say Captain Naline.

After a time, as the horse was now quiet and there were no more bad hills, the gentleman said he had an engagement, and would have to ride on. So, as Mrs. Welch declared herself now entirely easy in her mind, he bade her good-evening and galloped on, and soon afterward Mrs. Welch was met by her husband on his way over to the station with a carriage.

CHAPTER XXIX

MRS. WELCH had not been in the County forty-eight hours before she was quite satisfied that this was the field for her work, and that she was the very laborer for this field.

In three days the signs of her occupation and energy were unmistakable. Every room in the little cottage was scoured afresh, and things were changed within the old house, and were undergoing a change without, which would have astonished the departed Stampers.

A gang of darkies, of all ages and sizes, was engaged by her or collected somehow (perhaps, no one knew just how, unless Hiram, who distributed the contents of the boxes, knew), who, Andy Stamper said, looked like harvesters and got harvest-wages. The rooms were turned inside out, the yard was cleared up, the fences repaired and white-washed, and the chambers were papered or painted of a dark maroon or other rich color, then the fashion, by Doan, whom Hiram Still sent over for the purpose—Mrs. Welch not only superintending actively, but showing, with real skill, how it ought to be done; for one of the lady's maxims was, "What your hands find to do, do with all your might." Ruth, during the repairs, took occasion to pull out carefully the nail on which Andy had told her his father used to hang his watch, and sent it wrapt in a neat little parcel to Andy, with a note saying how much pleasure she had in sending it. She did not dream that by this little act she was making one of the best friends of her life. Sergeant Stamper drove the nail in a strip beside his own bed. And as he struck the last blow he turned to his wife, who with sympathetic eyes was standing by, and said :

"Delia, if I ever fail to do what that young lady asks me, I hope God will drive the nails in my coffin next day."

On the arrival of Mrs. Welch, there was a repetition of those visits of mingled friendliness and curiosity which had been paid Major Welch and Miss Ruth. And as Major Welch and Ruth formed their opinions, so now, Mrs. Welch formed hers. She prided herself on her reasoning faculty. She repudiated the idea that woman's intuition was a substitute for man's reason. She was not going to hang on any such wretched makeshift. She judged men and things precisely as men did, she said, and the only difference was that she was quicker than most men.

Dr. Cary and Mrs. Cary called with Miss Thomasia and Blair ; and General Legaie and Jacquelin Gray and Steve Allen rode up together one afternoon. The two former paid only a short visit, but Captain Allen stayed to tea. Steve treated her with that mingled deference and freedom which, in just the right proportion, make—at least, in a young and handsome man—the most charming manners. He even dared to tease Mrs. Welch on the serious sentiments she expressed, and on her appearance that day in the wagon, a liberty that neither Ruth nor Major Welch ever ventured to take ; and to Ruth's exceeding surprise, her mother, so far from resenting it, actually appeared to like it. As for Ruth, her mother surprised a look of real delight in her eyes.

It gave her food for thought. "That young man talked to me ; but he looked at Ruth. What does it mean ? It might mean one thing—yes, it might mean that ? But it is impossible !" She put the idea aside as too absurd to consider. However, she determined to be on her guard.

Mrs. Welch had no time to spend in the sort of hospitality practised by her neighbors. The idea of going over to a neighbor's to "spend the day," as most of the invitations

she received ran, or of having them come and "spend the
day" with her as they did with others, was intolerable.　It
might have done, she held, for an archaic state of society,
but it was just this terrible waste of time that made the
people about her what she saw them: indolent, and shiftless and poor.　She had " work to do," and she " meant to
do it."　So, having called formally at Dr. Cary's, Miss
Gray's, and the other places, the ladies from which had
called on her, she declined further invitations and began
her "work."　She wrote to her Society back at home, that
as she looked around her spirit groaned within her.　The harvest was ripe—already too ripe, and the over-ripened wheat
was falling, day by day, to the earth and being trampled
in the ground.　She wrote also her impressions of her new
neighbors.　She was charmed with Miss Thomasia and the
General.　The former reminded her of her grandmother,
whom she remembered as a white-haired old lady knitting
in her armchair, and the General was an old French field-
marshal, of the time of Bayard or Sidney, who had strayed
into this century, and who would not surprise her by appearing in armor with a sleeve around his helmet, " funny,
dear, old fossil that he is."　She was pleased with Miss
Cary and the Doctor, though the former appeared to have
rather too antiquated views of life, and the Doctor was un-
practical to the last degree.　They were all densely pre-
judiced ; but that she did not in the least mind ; they were
also universally shiftless, but she had hope.　They must
be enlightened and aided (Mrs. Welch was conscious of a
feeling of virtuous charitableness when she penned this.　It
was going farther than she had ever deemed it possible she
could go).　When it came to the question of the poor blacks,
the whites were all alike.　They had not the least idea
of their duty to them : even those she had mentioned as the
most enlightened, regarded them yet as only so many chat-
tels, as still slaves.　Finally, she wrote, she could not but
admit that nothing but kindness had been shown to themselves since their arrival.　One could not but appreciate such

cordiality, even if it were the result of mere impulse rather than of steady principle. But Mr. Still, the Union man of whom the Society knew, had intimated that it was only a concerted effort to blind them to the true state of affairs, and that if they exhibited any independence it would soon change. As to this she should be watchful. And she appealed for help.

Such was the substance of the first letter that Mrs. Welch wrote back to her old Reform and Help Society at home, which was regarded by some of her friends as a roseate-colored statement of the case. It was even intimated that it contained evidence that Mrs. Welch was already succumbing to the very influence she repudiated.

"But they all do it. I never knew anyone go down there who did not at once abandon all principles and fall a victim to the influences of those people," declared Mrs. Bolter, who, now that Mrs. Welch had left, represented the earnest and most active wing of the society.

"May not that prove that perhaps there is something on their side that we do not understand?" hazarded one of the young ladies of the society, Mrs. Clough, who, as a daughter of Senator Rockfield, was privileged to express views.

"Not at all," declared Mrs. Bolter. "I knew that Major Welch and Ruth were both hopelessly weak; but I confess I did think better things of Mrs. Welch."

"Do you know, now that she has gone, I confess that I always did think Ruth Welch had more sense—more practical sense I mean, than her mother," said Mrs. Clough.

"Of course, you do," replied the older lady. Mrs. Clough colored.

"And my husband thinks so, too."

"Oh! if your husband thinks so—of course!" Mrs. Bolter looked sympathetic and superior. "I supposed *he* thought so." The younger lady colored deeply.

"And my sister thinks so," she added, with dignity.

"Oh! indeed! I knew she thought some of the younger

members of the connection very attractive," said Mrs. Bolter.

Mrs. Clough rose, and, with a bow, left the assembly.

She was comforted that evening by hearing her husband not only commend her views warmly, but abuse Mrs. Bolter as a "stuck-up and ill-bred woman, as vain and vulgar as Bolter himself," whom he would not trust around the corner.

"If she is that now, what will she be after she marries her daughter to Captain Middleton?" Mrs. Clough said. "She's had him in tow ever since he came home a week ago. I do think it is vulgar, the way some women run after men for their daughters nowadays. She has not given that poor man an hour's rest since he landed."

"I don't believe there's anything in that. Larry would not marry one of that family. He knows Bolter too well. I always thought he would end by marrying Ruth Welch, and he told me to-day at the club he was going South."

"Oh! all you men always were silly about Ruth Welch. You all thought she was the most beautiful creature in the world," said little Mrs. Clough, with an air not wholly reconcilable with her attitude at the Aid Society meeting just recorded.

"No, I know one man who made one exception," said her husband leaning over and kissing her, and thereupon, as is the way with lovers, began "new matter."

"Captain Middleton is not going South," said Mrs. Clough, suddenly. "That is, he's going south; but not to the South."

"He is not! Why, he told me he was."

"Well, he's not. He's going to Washington." She spoke oracularly.

"What's he going there about? About that old affair? You seem to know his plans better than he does. I see by the papers it's up again. Or about that railroad scheme Bolter's working at? He's down there now. Larry said he had to see the Senator."

" No, about a new affair—Larry Middleton is in love
with Alice," said Mrs. Clough, with entire unconscious-
ness of the singularity of her sudden and unexpected
bouleversement. Her husband turned round on her in
blank amazement.

" Wha-at ! " He strung the word out in his surprise.

" Yes—you men are so blind. He's in love with Alice ;
was with her abroad and came home to see her." She
was suddenly interested in a very small baby-garment she
was sewing on.

" Why, you just said he was in love with Ruth
Welch ! "

" Did I ? " she asked, quietly, as calm as a May morning, and apparently with perfect indifference.

" —And you said Mrs. Bolter would catch him for her
loud, sporty daughter ! "

" Oh ! I believe I did." She was turning a hem.
" One, two, three," she counted. " Well, she won't get
him." She was interested only in the baby-garment.

" Are they engaged ? "

" Not yet—quite—but almost— Will be in a week.
Isn't that a darling ? " She held up the garment, and
spanned it with her pink fingers.

" Well, you women are curious," said her husband, almost with a gasp. " Here you have been abusing Ruth
Welch and Mrs. Bolter and every woman Larry Middleton
knew in the world, and all the time he was dead in love
with your own sister ! "

" Umhm ! " She looked up and nodded brightly, then
broke into a laugh. " And you think that's curious ? "

" Well, I'm glad of it. Larry's a good fellow. Now I
see it all. I thought he was uncommonly glad to see me
to-day, and when I undertook to chaff him a little about
Ruth Welch, looked rather red and silly."

" You didn't ! " said his wife, aghast. " What in the
world——! "

" Oh ! I'll make it all right the next time I see him.

How was I to know ? I'll write to Alice and congratulate her."

"Indeed, you'll not. Not a word. You'll ruin everything ! "

" Why ? "

" Why, he hasn't spoken yet——"

" Why, you just said— " He lapsed into reflection.

" Oh ! You men are so stupid ! " sighed Mrs. Clough. " But come, promise me."

And he promised—as we all do—always.

Having despatched her appeal, Mrs. Welch did not waste time waiting for a response, but was as good as her word and, like an energetic soul, without waiting a day, sickle in hand, entered the field alone. Her first step was what she termed " informing herself." She always " informed herself" about things ; it was one of the secrets of her success, she said.

Her first visit on this tour of inspection was to the Bend. She selected this as the primary object of her visitation, because she understood it was the worst place in the community, and she proposed to go at once to the very bottom. Dr. Cary had spoken of it as " a festering spot "; General Legaie had referred to it as " a den of iniquity." Well, if it were a festering sore it ought to be treated ; if it were a den it ought to be opened to the light, she declared. She found it worse than she had expected ; but this did not deter her. She forthwith set to work to build a school-house near the Bend, and sent for a woman to come down and take charge of it.

She was no little surprised one day when she called at a cabin where she had been told a woman was ill, to have the door opened by Mrs. Cary. Mrs. Cary invited her in and thanked her for calling, quite as if she owned the house. Mrs. Welch had her first gleam of doubt as to whether she had stated the case to her Society with entire correctness. She observed that the woman's sheets were old and patched, and she said she would have her Society make new ones. How could she know that Maria's old mistress had just brought her these and that she and Blair had mended them with their own hands ?

It does not require an earthquake to start talk in a rural community—and Mrs. Welch had not been in her new home a month, or, for that matter, a week, before she was the most talked-of woman in the County.

Notwithstanding Hiram Still's desire to keep secret the fact that he was trying to sell a part of Red Rock to Major Welch, it was soon rumored around that Major Welch was to buy the Stamper place and a considerable part of the old Gray estate. Leech, it was reported, had come up from town, given a clean title and prepared a deed which was to be delivered on a certain day. Allowing for exaggerations, it is astonishing how accurate the bureau of advanced rumor often is.

Steve Allen and Jacquelin Gray held sundry conferences in the clerk's office, with the papers in Still's old suit before them, and it got abroad that they were not going to permit the sale.

The day before that set by this exact agency for the final consummation of the purchase, a letter was brought for Major Welch. The messenger who brought it was a handsome, spirited-looking boy of seventeen or eighteen, evidently a gentleman's son. Major Welch was away from home; but Ruth happened to be in the yard when the boy rode up. He was mounted on a handsome bay with white feet, which Ruth recognized as that which Captain Allen rode. Ruth loved a fine horse, and she went up to him. As she approached, the boy sprang to the ground and took off his hat with a manner so like Captain Allen's that Ruth smiled to herself.

"Is—is Major Welch at home ?" he asked. He had pulled a paper from his pocket and was blushing with a boy's embarrassment.

Ruth said her father was not at home, but explained that

22

she would take any letter for him—or—would not he tie his horse and come in and wait for her father ?

This invitation quite overthrew the little structure of assurance the boy had built up, and he was thrown into such a state of confusion that Ruth's heart went out to him.

He thanked her ; but he was afraid his horse would not stand tied. He was stuffing the paper back in his pocket, hardly aware of what he was doing.

Ruth was sure the horse would stand ; she had seen him tied ; but she respected the boy's confusion, and offered again to take the letter for her father. He gave it to her apparently with reluctance. His cousin, Steve Allen, had told him to give it to Major Welch himself, he half stammered.

" Well, I am his daughter, Miss Welch," Ruth said, " and you can tell Captain Allen that I said I would certainly deliver it to my father. Won't you tell me who you are ? " she asked, smiling.

" I'm Rupert Gray, Jacquelin Gray's brother."

" Oh ! You have been off at school ? "

" Yes'm. Jacquelin would make me go, but I've come back for good, now. He says I needn't go any more. He hasn't got anything to send me any more, anyhow." This in a very cheery tone. He was partly recovering from his embarrassment. " Steve wanted to send me to college, but I won't go."

" You won't ? Why not ? "

" Steve hasn't got any money to send me to college. Besides, they just want to get me away from here—I know 'em—and I won't go." (With a boy's confidingness.) " They're afraid I'll get—" He stopped short.—" But I'm not afraid. Just let 'em try." He paused, his face flushed with excitement, and looked straight at her. He evidently wanted to say something else to her, and she smiled encouragingly.

" You tell your father not to have anything to do with

that Still and that man Leech." His tone was a mixture
of sincerity and persuasiveness.

"Why?" Ruth smiled.

"Because—one's a carpetbagger and t'other a scala-
wag."

"Why, we are carpetbaggers, too."

"Well—yes—but—. Steve he says so, too. And he
don't want you to get mixed up with 'em. That's the reason." His embarrassment returned for a moment.

"Oh! Captain Allen says so? I'm very much obliged
to him, I'm sure." Ruth laughed, but her form straightened and her color deepened.

"No, no, not that way. Steve is a dandy. And so is
Jacquelin. He's just as good as Steve. Never was anybody like Jacquelin. You ought to know him. That
fellow Leech imprisoned him. But I knocked him down
—I could die for Jacquelin—at least, I think I could.
That's the reason I hate 'em so!" he broke out, vehemently. "And I don't want you to get mixed up with
'em. You aren't like them. You are more like us."

Ruth smiled at the ingenuousness of this compliment.

"And you tell your father, won't you?" he repeated.
"Good-evening." He held out his hand, shook hers,
sprang on his horse, and, making her a flourishing bow,
galloped away, evidently very proud of his horsemanship.

He left Ruth with a pleasant feeling round her heart,
which she could scarcely have accounted for. She wondered what it was that his brother and Captain Allen were
afraid the boy would do.

As for Rupert, when he returned to Captain Allen he
was so full of Miss Welch that Steve declared he was in
love with her, and guilefully drew him on to talk of her
and tell, over and over, every detail of his interview. The
charge of being in love the boy denied, of course, but from
that time Ruth, without knowing it, had the truest blessing a girl can have—the ingenuous devotion of a young
boy's heart.

When her father came home the current of Ruth's thoughts was changed.

The letter Rupert had brought contained a paper, or rather two papers, addressed to Major Welch. One was a formal notice to him that the title by which Still held Red Rock was fraudulent and invalid, and that he would buy at his peril, as a suit would be brought to rip up the whole matter and set aside the deed under which Still held. The paper was signed by Jacquelin Gray and witnessed by Stevenson Allen as counsel, in whose handwriting it was. In addition to the formal notice, .here was a note to Major Welch from Captain Allen, in which he stated that having heard the rumor that Major Welch was contemplating buying the place in question, he felt it his duty to let him know at once that such a step would involve him in a lawsuit, and that possibly it might be very unpleasant for him.

This letter was a bombshell.

Mrs. Welch took it not as a legal notice, but as a declaration of war, and when that gage was flung down she was ready to accept it. She came of a stock equally prompt to be martyrs or fighters. She urged Major Welch to reply plainly at once. It was just a part of the persecution all loyal people had to go through. Let them see that they were not afraid. Major Welch was for moving a little deliberately. He should certainly not be bullied into receding from his purchase by anything of this kind, but he would act prudently. He would look again into the matter and see if there was any foundation for the charge.

Ruth rallied to the side of her mother and father, and felt as angry with Mr. Allen and everyone else concerned in the matter as it was in the nature of her kind heart to be.

Major Welch's investigation did not proceed exactly on the lines on which he would have acted at home. He had to rely on the men he employed. Both Still and Leech insisted that the notice given was merely an attempt to bully him. They further furnished him an abstract of the title, which showed it to be perfectly clear and regular, and when Major Welch applied in person to the old clerk, he corroborated this and certified that at that time no cloud was on the title.

He was, however, by no means as gracious toward Major Welch as he had been the first time he saw him—was, on the contrary, rather short in his manner, and, that gentleman thought, almost regretted to have to give the certificate.

" Yes, it's all clear to date as far as the records show," he said, with careful limitation, in reply to a request from Major Welch for a certificate, " but if you'll take my advice——"

Still, who was sitting near, wriggled slightly in his chair.

Major Welch had been a little exasperated. " My dear sir, I should be very glad to take your advice generally, but this is a matter of private business between this gentle ——between Mr. Still and myself, and I must be allowed to act on my own judgment. What I want is not advice, but a certificate of the state of those titles."

A change came over the old clerk's countenance. He bowed stiffly. " All right, sir ; I reckon you know your own business," he said, dryly, and he made out the certificate and handed it to Major Welch almost grimly.

Major Welch glanced at it and turned to Still.

" You can have your deeds prepared, Mr. Still. I am going to town to-morrow and shall be ready to pay over the money on my return." He spoke in a tone for the clerk to hear and intended to show his resolution.

Still followed him out and suggested that he'd as lieve give him the deeds to put to record then, and he could pay him when he came back. He was always willing to take a gentleman's word. This, however, Major Welch would not consent to.

Still stayed with Major Welch all the rest of the day and

returned home with him: a fellowship which, though some·
what irksome to the Major, he tolerated, because Still,
half-jestingly, half-seriously, explained that somehow he
"felt sort of safer" when he was with the Major.

Two or three days afterward Major Welch, having returned from the capital, paid Still the money and took his
deed ; and it was duly recorded.

The interview in the clerk's office, in which Major
Welch had declined to hear the old clerk's advice, was reported by Mr. Dockett to Steve Allen and Jacquelin Gray
that same evening. The only way to save the place, they
agreed, was to institute their proceedings and file a notice
of a pending suit, or, as the lawyers call it, a *lis pendens*.

"He'll hardly be big enough fool to fly in the face of
that," said Mr. Dockett.

So the very next day a suit was docketed and a *lis pendens* filed, giving notice that the title to the lands was in
question.

The summonses were delivered to the sheriff, Mr. James
Sherwood ; but this was the day Major Welch spent in the
city, and when the sheriff handed the summons to Still
and showed the one he had for Major Welch, Still took it
from him, saying he would serve it for him.

Thus it happened that when Major Welch paid down
the money he was in ignorance that two suits had already
been instituted to declare the title in Still fraudulent.

Meantime, copies of Mrs. Welch's letter to her friends had
come back to the County, and the effect was instantaneous.

When Mrs. Welch wrote the letter describing her new
home and surroundings, she gave, as has been said, what
she considered a very favorable account of her neighbors.
She had not written the letter for publication, yet, when
the zeal of her friends gave it to the public, she was sensible of a feeling of gratified pride. There were in it a
number of phrases which, as she looked at them in cold
print, she would in a milder mood have softened ; but she
consoled herself with the reflection that the individuals

referred to in the letter would never see it. Alas ! for the
vain trust of those who rely on their obscurity to hide their
indiscretions. The *Censor* was as well known, even if not
so extensively known, in the old County as in Mrs. Welch's
former home. It had long been known as Leech's organ,
and was taken by more than one of the Red Rock residents.

When the issue containing Mrs. Welch's letter first appeared it raised a breeze. The neighborhood was deeply
stirred and, what appeared most curious to Mrs. Welch was,
that what gave most offence, was her reference to individuals which she had intended to be rather complimentary.
She made up her mind to face boldly the commotion she
had raised and to bear with fortitude whatever it might
bring. She did not know that it was her patronizing attitude that gave the most serious offence.

"I don't mind her attack on us, but blame her impudent, patronizing air," declared the little General—" General Fossil," as Steve called him—"and to think that I
should have put myself out to be especially civil to her !
Steve, you are so fond of Northern cherries, I shall let you
do the civilities for us both hereafter." To the General's
surprise, Steve actually reddened.

The next time Mrs. Welch met her neighbors she was
conscious of the difference in their bearing toward her. It
was at old St. Ann's. When she had been there before,
the whole congregation had thronged about her with warm
greetings and friendly words. Now there was a marked
change. Though Steve Allen and Rupert and Blair, and
a few others came up and spoke to her, the rest of the
congregation contented themselves with returning her
bows coldly from a distance, and several ladies, she was
sure, studiously avoided her greeting.

"Well, sir, I knew she was a oner as soon as I lay my
eye 'pon her," said Andy Stamper to a group of his friends
in the court-yard at the county seat the next court day,
"but I didn't know she was goin' to take that tack. She's
done fixed up the place till you wouldn't know it from a

town place. She has painted them old rooms so black that Doan had to git a candle to see how to do it, and I was born in one of 'em. I told her I never heard o' paintin' nothin' that black befo' but a coffin, but she said it was her favorite color."

"'Pears like that's so too, Sergeant," laughed someone. "Is Hiram there much?"

"Oh! he goes there; but you know I don't think she likes him; and it's my opinion that Hiram he's afeard of her as he is of Jacquelin Gray. He talks that soft way o' hisn aroun' her which he uses when he's afeared o' anyone. She's gin them niggers the best clo'es you ever see—coats better then me or you or anyone aroun' heah has seen since the war. What's curious to me is that though she don't seem to like niggers and git along with 'em easy-like and nat'ral as we all do, in another way she seems to kind o' want to like 'em. It reminds me of takin' physic: she takes 'em with a sort o' gulp, but wants to take 'em and wants to make everybody else do it.

"Now she's been over yonder to the Bend and got 'em all stirred up, diggin' dreens and whitewashin' and cuttin' poles for crosslay."

"She'll be tryin' to whitewash them," said one of his auditors.

"Well, by Jingo! if she sets her mind to it she'll make it stick," said Andy. "What gits me is the way she ain't got some'n better to work on."

Report said that Jacquelin was blossoming into a fine young lawyer. Steve Allen declared that his practice was doubling under Jacquelin's devotion to the work—which was very well, as Steve, whether from contrariness or some other motive, was becoming a somewhat frequent visitor at Major Welch's, these days.

The General asserted that if Jacquelin stuck to his office and studied as assiduously as he was doing, he would be the most learned lawyer in the State. "But he'll kill

himself if he does not stop it. Why, I can see the difference in him already," he declared to Miss Thomasia, solicitously. Miss Thomasia herself had seen the change in
Jacquelin's appearance since his return home. He was
growing thin again, and, if not pale, was at least losing that
ruddy hue of health which he had had on his arrival, and
she expostulated with him, and tried even to get Blair to do
the same ; for Blair always had great influence with him,
she told her. Blair, however, pooh-poohed the matter and
said, indifferently, that she could not see any difference
in him and thought he looked very well. Miss Thomasia
shook her head. Blair did not use to be so hard-hearted.

But, however this was, Jacquelin did not alter his
course. The negroes had become so unruly, that, as Rupert was often away from home, and his aunt was left
alone, he came home every night, though it was often late
before he arrived ; but early in the morning he returned
to the Court-house and spent the day there in his office,
rarely accepting an invitation or taking any holiday.

When he and Blair met, which they did sometimes unavoidably, there was a return of the old constraint that
had existed before he went away, and even with Steve he
appeared to be growing silent and self-absorbed.

Blair had become the mainstay of her family. Uncon-
sciously she had slipped into the position where she was
the prop on which both her father and mother leaned.
She taught her little colored school, and at home was always busy about something. She vied with Mrs. Andy
Stamper in raising chickens, and with Miss Thomasia in
raising violets. Under her skilful management, the little
cottage amid its wilderness of fruit-trees, in which old Mr.
and Mrs. Bellows had lived, became a rose-bower, and the
fruit-trees became an orchard with its feet buried in clover.
Her father said of her that she was a perpetual reproduction
of the miracle of the creation—that she created the sun
and followed it with all the plants and herbs after their kind.

Yet, with all these duties, Blair found time to run over

to see Miss Thomasia almost every day or two ; at first shyly and at rare intervals, but, after she found that Jacquelin was always at his office, oftener and more freely. She
always declared that a visit to Miss Thomasia was like
reading one of Scott's novels ; that she got back to a land
of chivalry and drank at the springs of pure romance ;
while Miss Thomasia asserted that Blair was a breath of May.

Jacquelin, after a time, came to recognize the traces of
Blair's visits, in the little touches of change and improvement about the house : a pruned rosebush here, a fold of
white curtain there, and he often had to hear her praises
sung by Miss Thomasia's guileless tongue, and listen to the
good lady's lament because Blair and Steve did not proceed
a little more satisfactorily with their affairs. Miss Thomasia
had an idea that it was on account of Steve's former reputation for wildness. "It would have such a good influence on
Steve," she declared, "would be just what he needed. I
quite approve of a young lady being coy and maidenly, but,
of course, I know there is an understanding between them,
and I must say, I think Blair is carrying it too far." She
bridled as she always did at the thought of anyone opposing
Steve. "I know that a man is sometimes driven by a young
lady's cruelty—apparent cruelty—for I am sure Blair would
not wittingly injure anyone—into courses very sad and in-
jurious to him." Miss Thomasia heaved a sigh and gazed
out of the window, and a moment later resumed her knitting.

"Do you see anything of that—young lady, Miss
Welch ?" she asked Jacquelin, suddenly.

Jacquelin said he had not seen her for some time, except
at church, and once or twice in the village, at a distance.

"I did not suppose you had," said Miss Thomasia. "She
is a very nice, refined girl—has always been very sweet to
me when I have met her—but of course—." Her lips
closed firmly and she began to knit vigorously, leaving
Jacquelin to wonder what she meant.

"I only wanted to know," she said, presently, and that
was the only explanation she gave.

CHAPTER XXX

THE difference in the attitude of their neighbors toward them was felt deeply by Major and Mrs. Welch.
Even Dr. Cary's wonted cordiality had given place, when he
met Mrs. Welch, to grave and formal courtesy. Toward
Major Welch the formality was less marked, while toward
Ruth there was almost the same warmth and friendliness
that had existed before Mrs. Welch's letters were seen.
Ruth received quite as many invitations as before, and
when she met her neighbors they were as cordial to her as
ever. She was conscious that this difference in her case
was intentional, that the old warmth toward her was
studied, and that they meant her to feel that the change
in their attitude did not extend to her. Ruth, however,
was far too loyal to her own to accept such attentions ; so
far from accepting, she resented the overtures made her,
and was not slow in letting it be understood. There
were one or two exceptions to this general attitude. For
Blair Cary her liking deepened. Blair was sweeter than
ever to her, and though Ruth felt that this was to make
up to her for the coolness of others, there were a real
warmth and a true sympathy in Blair, and a delicacy and
charm about her manner of showing them that touched
Ruth, and she was conscious that day by day she became
drawn more and more closely to her. She felt that Blair
understood her and sympathized with her, and that, if
she ever chose to speak, she had in her a friend on whose
bosom she could fling herself and find consolement. Such

friendships are rare. The friend with whom one does **not** have to make explanations is God-given.

With her other neighbors Ruth stood on her dignity, in armed guardfulness. She carried her head higher than she had ever done in her life, and responded to their advances with a coldness that soon gained her a reputation for as much pride as she could have desired, if not for a good deal of temper. Mrs. Dockett attempted a sympathetic manner with her, and if subsequent rumors were any indication, that redoubted champion did not come off wholly unscathed.

"The little minx has got her mother's tongue," sniffed the offended lady. "Why, she actually snubbed me— *me!* Think of her daring to tell me, when I was giving her to understand that we knew she was not responsible for any of the insulting things that had been said about us, that she always agreed with her mother and father in everything !—Which I'll wager she doesn't, unless she's different from all the other girls I know ! And away she marched with her little mouth pursed up and her head held as high as Captain Allen's. She'll know when I try to be civil to her again ! She's getting her head turned because Captain Allen said she had some pretension to good looks."

It must be said, though, on behalf of Mrs. Dockett, that after the first smart of the rebuff she had received was over, she liked Ruth none the less, and after a little while used to tell the story of Ruth's snubbing her, with a very humorous take-off of Miss Welch's air and of her own confusion. And long afterward she admitted that the first time she really liked Ruth Welch was when she resented her condescension. "It takes a good woman—or man either—to stand up to me, you know !" she said, with a twinkle of pride and amusement in her bright eyes.

Mrs. Dockett was not by any means the only one to whom the young lady showed her resentment. Ruth felt her isolation keenly, though she did not show this generally, except in a new hauteur. She not only gave up visiting, and immersed herself in the home duties which devolved upon her in consequence of her mother's absorption in her philanthropical work, but she suddenly began to take a much deeper interest than ever before in that work itself, riding about and visiting the poor negroes in whom her mother was interested, and extending her visits to the poorer whites as well. She was surprised at the frequency with which she met Mrs. Cary and Blair, or, if she did not meet them, heard of their visits to the people she was attending. Once or twice she met Miss Thomasia, also, accompanied by old Peggy as her escort. "I heard that the fence was going to be put up between us and old Mrs. Granger," explained Miss Thomasia, "and I am such a poor hand at climbing fences, I am trying to see her as often as I can before it is done. I do hope the old woman will die before it is put up." She saw the astonished look on Ruth's face and laughed heartily. "You know what I mean, my dear, I am always getting things wrong. But, are you alone, my dear?"

Ruth said she was alone.

"I don't think it quite right," said Miss Thomasia, shaking her head. "Steve, I am sure, would be very glad to accompany you on any of your visitations, and so would Jacquelin." She was perfectly innocent, but Ruth was incensed to find herself blushing violently.

It happened that on these visitations, more than once, Ruth fell in with Captain Allen. She treated him with marked coldness—with actual savageness, Steve declared afterward, but at the time, it must be said, it appeared to have little apparent effect upon that gentleman. Indeed, it appeared simply to amuse him. He was "riding about on business," he explained to her. He seemed to have a great deal of business "to ride about on" of late. Ruth always declined, with much coolness, his request to be allowed to escort her, but her refusal did not seem to offend him, and he would turn up unexpectedly the next time she rode out

alone, cheerful and amused. (One singular thing was
that she rarely saw him when she was accompanied by her
father.) Still she did not stop riding. She did not see
why she should give up her visits of philanthropy, simply
because Captain Allen also happened to have business to
attend to. She began to be conscious that sometimes she
even felt disappointed if on her rides she did not see him
somewhere, and she hated herself for this, and took to dis-
ciplining herself for it by riding on unfrequented. roads.
Yet even here, now and then, Captain Allen passed her,
and she began to feel as if he were in some sort doing it
to protect her. On one occasion when he found her on a
somewhat lonely road, he took her to task for riding so
much alone, and told her that she ought not to do it. She
was secretly pleased, but fired up at his manner.

"Why?" She looked him defiantly in the eyes.

He appeared confused.

"Why—because— Suppose you should lose your way,
what would you do?" She saw that this was not his
reason.

"I should ask someone," she answered, coolly.

"But whom would you ask? There is no one—except
one old woman, my old Mammy Peggy who lives down in
this direction—who lives anywhere between the old road
that is now stopped up and the creek, and farther back is
a through-cut to the Bend, which you crossed, along which
some of the worst characters in the County travel. They
do not come this side of the creek, for they are afraid ;
I assure you that it is not safe for you to be riding about
through the woods in this way at this time of the evening,
by yourself."

"Why, I see this path—someone must travel it?" Ruth
said. She knew that somewhere down in that direction
was the old hospital-place, which the negroes said was
haunted, and which was rumored to be the meeting-place
of the Ku Klux. Steve looked a little confused.

"Yes——"

"And if no one is down here, there cannot any harm come to me." She enjoyed her triumph.

"Yet—but you don't understand. People pass this way going backwards and forwards from—from the Bend—and elsewhere, and—" He broke off. "You must trust me and take my word for it," he said, firmly. "It is not right for you; it is not safe." He was so earnest that Ruth could not help feeling the force of what he said, and she was at heart secretly pleased, yet she resented his attitude.

"Whom should I be afraid of? Of the Ku Klux?" She was pleased to see him flush. But when he answered her he spoke seriously:

"Miss Welch, there are no Ku Klux here—there never were any—except once for a little while," he corrected himself, "and there is not one in the County or in the South who would do you an injury, or with whom, if you were thrown, you would not be as safe as if you were guarded by a regiment."

Ruth felt that he was telling the truth, and she was conscious of the effect he had on her. Yet she rebelled, and she could not resist firing a shot at him.

"Thank you," she said, mockingly. "I am relieved to know they will not murder ladies." Steve flushed hotly, and, before he could answer, she pressed her advantage with delight.

"Could you not persuade them to extend their clemency to other poor defenceless creatures? Poor negroes, for example? You say there never were any Ku Klux in this County; how about that night when the State militia were raided and their arms taken from them, and when poor defenceless women were frightened to death. Were the men who did that really ghosts?"

She looked at Steve and was struck with a pang that she should have allowed herself to be carried so far. She had meant only to sting him and revenge herself, but she had struck deeper than she had intended. The look on

Steve's face really awed her, and when he spoke the tone in his voice was different from any she had ever heard in it.

"Miss Welch, I did not say there had never been any Ku Klux in this County—you misunderstood me. I said there had never been any but once. I myself organized a band of Ku Klux regulators—' a den,' as we called it, in this County—and we made one raid—the raid you speak of, when we took the arms from the negroes. I led that raid. I organized it and led it, because I deemed it absolutely necessary for our protection at the time—for our salvation. No one was seriously hurt—no women were frightened to death, as you say. It is true that some women were frightened, and, no doubt, frightened badly, at the pranks played that night. We meant to frighten the men; if necessary we should have killed them—the leaders—but never to frighten the women. Under the excitement of such an occasion, where there were hundreds of young men, some full of fun, others wild and reckless, some unauthorized acts were committed. It had been attempted to guard against them, but some men overstepped the bounds and there were undoubtedly unjustifiable acts committed under cover of the disguise adopted. But no lives were taken and no great violence was done. The reports you have heard of it were untrue. I give you my word of honor as to this. That is the only time there has been a raid by Ku Klux in this County—and the only time there will be one. We accomplished our purpose, and we proved what we could do. The effect was salutary. But I found that the blackguards and sneaks could take advantage of the disguise, and under the disguise wreak their private spite, and by common consent the den was disbanded soon after that night. There have been ruffianly acts committed since that time by men disguised as Ku Klux; but not one of the men who were in that raid, so far as I know, was concerned in them or has ever worn the disguise since then. They have sworn solemnly not to do so. At least only one—I am not sure as to one," he said, almost in reverie ; " but he is an outsider. The place where they met is the old plantation down here on the river ; this path leads to it, and at the top of the next hill I can show you the house. It is only a ruin, and was selected by me because the stories connected with it protected it from the curiosity of the negroes, and in case of invasion the woods around, with their paths, furnished a ready means of escape.

" I have told you the whole story and told you the truth absolutely, and I hope you will do me the honor to believe me." His manner and voice were so grave that Ruth had long lost all her resentment.

" I do," she said, "and I beg your pardon for what I said."

He bowed. They had reached the crest of the hill.

"There is the house." He held a bough aside and indicated a large rambling mansion below them, almost concealed on one side by the dense growth, while the other side appeared to be simply a ruin. It lay in a cleft between two wooded hills around the base of which ran the river, and seemed as desolate a place as Ruth had ever seen.

" My showing it to you is a proof that ' the den' is broken up. Now we will go back."

" I did not need it," she said, "and I will never tell anyone that I have ever seen it."

To this Captain Allen made no response.

" I must see you safely back to the main road," he said, gravely.

Ruth felt that she had struck him deeply, and as they rode along she cast about in her mind for some way to lead up to an explanation. It did not come, however, and at the main road, when her gate was in sight, Captain Allen pulled in his horse and lifted his hat.

" Good-by."

" Good-evening. I will think of what you said," she began, meaning what he had said about her riding out alone.

23

"I would at least like you to think of me as a gentle-man." He bowed gravely, and lifting his hat again, turned and rode slowly away.

Ruth rode home, her mind filled with conflicting emotions. Among them was anger, first with herself and afterward with Captain Allen.

Miss Welch, on her arrival at home that evening, was in a singular frame of mind, and was as nearly at war with everyone as it is possible for a really sweet-tempered girl to be. Dr. Washington Still had called in her absence and proffered his professional services for any of her patients. She broke out against him vehemently, and when her mother, who was in a mollified state of mind toward the young man, undertook to defend him, Ruth attacked the whole Still family—and connections—except Virgy, whom she admitted to be a poor little kind-hearted thing, and shocked her mother by denouncing warmly the stories of the Ku Klux outrages and declaring openly that she did not believe there had ever been any Ku Klux in the County, except on the one occasion when they had disarmed the negro militia—and that she thought they had done exactly right, and just what she would have had them do.

Mrs. Welch was too much shocked to do anything but gasp.

"Oh! Ruth, Ruth," she groaned. "That ever my daughter should say such things!" But Miss Ruth was too excited for control just then. She launched out yet more warmly and shocked her mother by yet more heretical views, until suddenly, moved by her mother's real pain, she flung herself into her arms in a passion of remorse and tears, and declared that she did not mean half of what she had said, but was a wicked, bad girl who did not appreciate the best and kindest of mothers.

A few days afterward, the man known as the trick-doctor, who called himself "Doctor Moses," came to Major Welch's and told a pitiful story of an old woman's poverty.

Mrs. Welch gave him some sugar, coffee, and other things for her, but he asked the ladies to go and see her. She lived "all by herself, mostly, and hones to see the good white folks," he said.

"Ef my young Mistis would be so kind as to go and see her some evenin' I will show her de way." He looked at Ruth, with a low bow and that smile and uneasy look which always reminded her of a hyena in a cage.

They promised to go immediately, and he undertook to describe the road to them.

It was too bad to drive a carriage over—you had to ride on horseback ; but his young Mistress would find it, she was such a good rider.

Ruth could never bear the sight of the negro ; he was the most repulsive creature to her that she had ever seen. Yet it happened, that from his description of the place where the old woman lived and of the road that led there, she was sure it was the same old woman whom Captain Allen had mentioned to her, that afternoon, as having been his mammy, and as the one person who lived on the deserted plantation. And this, or some other reason—for the writer by no means wishes to be positive in assigning a woman's reason—determined Ruth to go and see her. She had expected her father to accompany her, as he frequently did so, but it happened that day that he was called away from home, and as her mother received another urgent call that morning to go and see a sick child, Ruth had either to postpone her visit or go alone. She chose the latter alternative, and as soon as the afternoon had cooled a little, she started off on horseback.

Ever since her interview with Captain Allen, she had been chafing under the sense of obeying his command that she should not ride through the woods alone. It was less a request than a command he had given her. She had not ridden out alone since that evening—at least, she had not ridden through the wood-roads; she had stuck to the highways, and she felt a sense of resentment that she had done so. What right had Captain Allen to issue orders to her ? She would now show him that they had no effect on her. She would not only go against his wishes, but would go to the very place he had especially cautioned her against. She would see that old woman who had once belonged to him, and perhaps the old woman would some time tell him she had been there.

Ruth had no difficulty in finding her way. She knew the road well as far as the point where the disused road led off from the highway, and she had a good idea of direction. There she turned into the track that took her down toward the abandoned plantation, and crossed the zigzag path that she knew cut through the pines and led down to the Bend. She remembered Captain Allen's pointing it out to her that afternoon, and as she approached the path she galloped her horse rapidly, conscious of a feeling of exhilaration as she neared it. A quarter of a mile farther on, the thought occurred to her that it was cowardice to ride rapidly. Why should she do so ? And though there was a cloud rising in the west, she pulled her horse down to a walk. The woods were beautiful and were filled with the odors of grape-blossoms ; the path was descending, which assured her that she was on the right track. A little farther on, as it had been described to her, it should cross a stream ; so she was pleased to see below her, at the bottom of a little ravine, the thicket through which the stream ran. She rode down into the ravine and to the stream. To her surprise the path appeared suddenly to stop at the water's edge. There was no outlet on the other side ; simply a wall of bushes. Suddenly her horse threw up his head and started violently. At the same moment a slight noise behind her attracted Ruth's attention. She turned, and in the path behind her stood the negro, Moses.

The blood deserted Ruth's face. He had always made her flesh creep, as if he had been a reptile. She had often found him on the side of the road as she passed along, or had turned and seen him come out of the woods behind

her, but she had never been so close to him before when
alone. And now to find herself face to face with him in
that lonely place made her heart almost stop. After regarding her for a moment silently, the negro began to
move slowly forward, bowing and halting with that peculiar
limp which always reminded Ruth of a species of worm.
She would have fled ; but she saw in an instant that there
was no way of escape. The bushes on either side were like
a wall. The same idea must have passed through the man's
mind. A curious smirk was on his evil face.

" My Mistis," he said, with a grin that showed his yellow teeth and horrid gums.

" The path seems to end here," said Ruth, with an effort
commanding her voice.

" Yes, my Mistis ; but I will show you de way. Old
Moses will show you de way. He-he-he." His voice had
a singular feline quality in it. It made Ruth's blood run
cold.

" No—thank you—I can find it—I shall go back up here
and look for it." She urged her horse back up the path to
pass him. But the negro stepped before the horse and
blocked the way.

" Nor'm—dat ain't de way. I'll show you de way. Jes'
let Doctor Moses show you." He gave his snicker again,
moved closer and put his hand on her bridle.

This act changed the girl's fear to anger. " Let go my
bridle, instantly ! " Her voice rose suddenly. The tone
of command took the negro by surprise and he dropped his
hand ; the next second, however, he caught her bridle
again, so roughly that her horse reared and started back,
and if Ruth had not been a good rider she would have
fallen from the saddle.

" I'm *gwine* to show you." His tone was now different.
He clung to the bridle of the frightened horse. His countenance had changed.

Raising her riding-whip, Ruth struck him with all her
might across the face.

"Let go my bridle!" she cried.

He gave a snarl of rage and sprang at her like a wild beast; but her horse whirled and slung him from his feet and he missed her, only tearing her skirt. It seemed to Ruth at that moment that she heard the sound of a horse galloping somewhere, and she gave a scream. It was answered instantly by a shout back over the hill on the path along which she had come, and the next moment was heard the swift rush of a horse tearing along on the muffled wood-path back in the woods.

The negro caught the sound, as he turned to seize Ruth's bridle again, stopped short and listened intently, then, suddenly wheeling, plunged into the bushes and went crashing away. That same instant, the horseman dashed over the crest of the hill and came rushing down the path, scattering the stones before him. And before Ruth could take it in, Steve Allen, his face whiter than she had ever seen it, was at her side.

"What is it? Who was it?" he asked.

"Nothing. Oh! He frightened me so," she panted.

"Who?" His voice was imperious.

"That negro."

"What negro?"

"The one they call Moses—Doctor Moses."

The look that came into Steve's face was for a second almost terrifying. The next moment, with an effort, he controlled himself.

"Oh! it was nothing," he said, lightly. "He is an impudent dog, and must be taught manners; but don't be frightened. No one shall hurt you." His voice had suddenly grown gentle and soothing, and he led Ruth from the subject, talking lightly, and calming her.

"I told you not to come here alone, you know?" he said, lightly.

His manner reassured Ruth, and she almost smiled as she said:

"I thought that was a woman's revenge."

" I did not mean it for revenge ; but I want you to promise me now you will never do it again. Or if you will not promise me, I want you to promise yourself."

" I will promise you," said Ruth. She went on to explain why she came.

" The old woman you speak of wants nothing," he said, " and you have passed the path that leads to her house. That negro misled—you did not take the right road to reach her place. You should have turned off, some distance back. It was a mere chance—simple Providence, that I came this way and saw your track and followed you. If you wish to see my old Mammy I will show you the way. It is the nearest house, and the only one we can reach before that storm comes, and we shall have to hurry even to get there."

Ruth looked over her shoulder, and was frightened at the blackness of the cloud that had gathered. There was a dense stillness, and the air was murky and hot. Almost at the moment she looked, a streak of flame darted from the cloud and a terrific peal of thunder followed immediately, showing that the storm was close on them.

" Come," he said, and, catching her bridle, Captain Allen headed her horse up the hill. " Mind the bushes. Keep him well in hand ; but put him out."

Ruth urged the horse, and gave him the rein, and they dashed up the hill, Steve close at her horse's flank. It was to be a close graze, even if they escaped at all ; for the rising wind, coming in a strong blast, was beginning to rush through the woods, making the trees bend and creak. The bushes swept past her, and dragged Ruth's hat from her head. " Keep on ! I'll get it !" called Steve, and leaning from his saddle he picked it from the ground, and in a moment was up with her again. The thunder was beginning to crash just above their heads, and as they dashed along, the air was filled with flying leaves and small boughs, and big drops were beginning to spatter on them as if driven from a gun. Ruth heard Steve's voice, but could

not, in the roar of the wind, tell what he said. The next
instant he was beside her, his hand outstretched to steady
her horse. She could not distinguish his words; but saw
that he meant her to pull in, and she did so. The next
second they were at a path which led off at an angle from
that they were on. Steve turned her horse into it, and a
moment later there appeared a small clearing, on the other
side of which was an old cabin. That instant, however,
the cloud burst upon them, and the rain came in a sheet.
Before Ruth could stop her horse at the door, Steve was on
the ground and had lifted her down as if she had been a
child.

"Run in," he said, and it never occurred to her to op-
pose him. Holding both horses with one hand, Steve
reached across and pushed open the door, and put her in.
An old negro woman, the only occupant, was facing her,
just as she had risen from her chair by the fire, her small
black eyes wide with surprise at the unexpected entrance.
The next moment she advanced toward Ruth.

"Come in, Mistis. Is you wet?" she asked.

"Thank you—why, yes—I am rather—But——" Ruth
turned to the door. She was thinking of her companion,
who was still out in the storm that was driving against the
house.

"Yes, to be sho' you is. I'll shet de do'." The old negress moved to push it closer to.

"No, don't!" cried Ruth. "He is out there."

"Who? Don't you go out dyah, Mistis."

She restrained Ruth, who was about to go out again.
But the door was pushed open from the outside, and Steve,
dripping wet, with a pile of broken pieces of old rails in
his arms and Ruth's saddle in his hand, came in.

"Marse Steve! My chile! Fo de L—d!" exclaimed the
old woman. "Ain't you mighty wet?" She had left Ruth,
and was feeling Steve's arms and back.

"Wet? No, I'm as dry as a bone," laughed Steve.
"Here—make up a good fire." He threw the wood on the

hearth and began to pile it on the fire, which had been almost extinguished by the rain that came down the big
chimney. "Dry that young lady. I've got to go out!"
He turned to the door again.

"No—please! You must not go out!" cried Ruth,
taking a step toward him.

"I have to go to see after the horses. I must fasten
them."

"Please don't. They are all right. I don't want you to
go!" She faced him boldly. "Please don't, for my sake!"
she pleaded.

Steve hesitated, and looked about him.

"I shall be wretched if you go out." Her face and voice
proved the truth of her assertion.

"I must go. I am already soaking wet; but I'll come
back directly." His voice was cheerful, and before Ruth
could beg him again, with a sign to the old woman he was
gone, and had pulled the door close to behind him.

"Heah, he say I is to dry you," said the old Mammy,
and she set a chair before the fire and gently but firmly
put Ruth in it, and proceeded to feel her shoes and clothing.
"Dat's my young master—my chile," she said, with pride,
and in answer to Ruth's expostulations. "You're 'bliged
to do what he say, you know. He'll be back torectly."

Ruth felt that the only way to induce Captain Allen to
come in out of the storm was to get dried as quickly as possible; so she set to work to help the old woman. Steve did
not come back directly, however, nor for some time, and
not until Ruth sent him word that she was dry, and he
must come in or she would go out. Then he entered, laughing at the idea that a rain meant anything to him.

"Why, I am an old soldier. I have slept in such a rain
as that, night after night, and as soundly as a baby. I enjoy it." His face, as he looked at Ruth sitting before the
fire, showed that he enjoyed something. And as the girl sat
there, her long hair down, her eyes filled with solicitude,
and the bright firelight from the blazing, resinous pine

shining on her and lighting up the dingy little room, she made a picture to enjoy.

Old Peggy, bending over her and ministering to her with pleased officiousness, caught something of the feeling. A gleam of shrewdness had come into her sharp, black eyes.

"Marse Steve, is dis your lady?" she asked, suddenly, with an admiring look at Ruth, whose cheeks flamed.

"No—not—" Steve did not finish the sentence. "What made you think so?" He looked very pleased.

"She so consarned about you. She certainly is pretty," she said, simply.

Ruth was blushing violently, and Steve said:

"I'm not good enough, Mammy, for any lady."

"Go 'way, Marse Steve! You know you good 'nough for anybody. Don't you b'lieve him, young Mistis. I helt him in dese arms when he wa' n't so big;" she measured a length hardly above a span, "and I knows."

Ruth thought so too just then, but she did not know what to say. Fortunately Steve came to her rescue.

"Mammy, you're the only woman in the world that thinks that."

"I know better 'n dat!" declared the old woman, emphatically. "You does too, don't you, my Mistis?" At which Ruth stammered, "Why, yes," and only blushed the more. She looked so really distressed that Steve said:

"Come, Mammy, you mustn't embarrass your young Mistress."

"Nor, indeed—dat I won't. But you see dyah, you done call her *my* young Mistis!" laughed the old woman, enjoying hugely the confusion of both her visitors.

It was time to go, Steve said. So as the storm had passed, they came out and he saddled Ruth's horse and handed her into the saddle. He spoke a few words to the old woman, to which she gave a quick affirmative reply. As they rode off, she said, "You mus' come again," which both of them promised and doubtless intended to do.

The woods were sparkling with the raindrops, and the

sky was as if it had just been newly washed and burnished, and the earth was covered with water which shone in the light of the setting sun, like pools of crystal.

Steve bade Miss Welch good-by at her gate.   He had scarcely gotten out of sight of her when he changed his easy canter to a long gallop, and a look of grim determination deepened on his face.   At the first byway he turned off from the main-road and made his way by bridle-paths back to the point where he had rescued Miss Welch. Here he tied his horse and began to examine the bushes carefully.   He was able at first to follow the track that the negro had made in his flight ; but after a little distance it became more difficult.   The storm had obliterated the traces.   So Steve returned to the point where he had left his horse, remounted and rode away.   He visited Andy Stamper's and several other plantations, at all of which he stopped, but only for a few moments to speak a word or two to the men at each, and then galloped on to the next, his face still grim and his voice intense with determination.

That night a small band of horsemen rode through the Bend, visiting house after house.   They asked for Moses, the trick-doctor.   But Moses was not there.   He had left early the morning before, their informants said, and had not been back since.   There was no doubt as to the truth of this.   There was something about that body of horsemen, small though it was, riding in pairs, that impressed whomever they accosted, and it was evident that their informants meant to tell the truth.   If, on the first summons at a door, the inmates peered out curious and loud-mouthed, they quieted down at the first glance at the silent horsemen outside.

"What you want with him ?" asked one of the men, inquisitively.   Almost instantly, as if by machinery, two horsemen moved silently in behind him and cut him out from the group behind.   "You know where he is ? Come along."   Their hands were on his collar.

"Nor, suh, b'fo' Gord I don't, gentmens," protested the

negro, almost paralyzed with fright. "I didn't mean nuttin' in the worl', gentmens."

At a sign from the leader he was released, and was glad to slip back into obscurity behind the rest of the awestruck group, till the horsemen rode on.

It was, no doubt, well for the trick-doctor that his shrewdness had kept him from his accustomed haunts that night. He visited the Bend secretly a night or two later ; but only for a short time, and before morning broke he was far away, following the woodland paths, moving at his swift, halting pace, which hour by hour was placing miles between him and the danger he had discovered. Thus the County for a time, at least, was rid of his presence, and both white and blacks breathed freer.

CHAPTER XXXI

THE bill in Jacquelin's suit against Mr. Still was not filed
for some time after the notice was sent and the suit instituted. But this period was utilized by Steve and Jacquelin in hunting up evidence ; and by Mr. Still in holding conferences with Leech and the officers of the court. Meanwhile Steve Allen had met the Welches several times, and
although there was a perceptible coolness in their manner
to him, yet civilities were kept up. As for Steve himself, he
went on just as he had done before, ignoring the change
and apparently perfectly oblivious of the chilliness with
which he was received.

Yet Steve appeared to have changed. His old cheerful-
ness and joviality seemed to have gone, and he was often
in a state bordering on gloom. As, however, most of those
in that part of the world were at this time in a state of
actual gloom, Steve's condition was set down to the general cause. Occasionally it occurred to Jacquelin that
some trouble with Blair Cary might have a part in it. His
Aunt Thomasia's words had stuck in his memory. Steve
did not go to Dr. Cary's as often as he used to go ; and
when he did go, on his return to the Court-house he was
almost always in one of his fits of depression. Jacquelin
set it down to another exhibition of Blair's habitual capri-
ciousness. It was that Yankee Captain that stood in the
way. And Jacquelin hardened his heart, and vowed to
himself that he would not see Blair again.

At length the bill in Jacquelin's suit was ready.

It was at the end of a hard day's work that Jacquelin had put the finishing touches to it, and as he completed the copy from a draft that Steve had made, he handed it across to Steve to read over. It was a bill to reopen, on the ground of fraud, the old suit in which Still had become the purchaser of Red Rock, and to set aside the conveyance to him and the subsequent conveyance of a part of his purchase to Major Welch. It went somewhat into a history of the confidential relation that Still had borne to Jacquelin's and Rupert's father; charged that Still's possession of the bonds was fraudulent, and that even, if not so, the bonds had been discharged by proceeds of the estate that had come to the steward's hands. It charged Still with gross fraud in his accounts, as well as in the possession of the bonds. It ended by making Major Welch a party, as a subsequent purchaser, and charged constructive knowledge on his part of Still's fraud. Actual knowledge of this by him was expressly disclaimed, but it was stated that he had knowledge of facts which should have put him on inquiry. It was alleged that a formal notice had been served on Major Welch before he became the purchaser, and it asked that "an issue out of chancery," as the lawyers term it, might be awarded to try the question of fraud.

When Steve finished reading the paper, he laid it on his desk and leaned back in his chair, his eyes fixed on the ceiling, in deep thought. Jacquelin did not disturb him; but watched him in silence as the expression on his face deepened into one almost of gloom. Presently Steve stirred.

"Well, is that all?" asked Jacquelin.

"Yes." He actually sighed.

"You don't think it will hold?"

"No. I am sure we shall show fraud—on that rascal's part—at least, so far as his accounts are concerned. We have followed up some of his rascality, and I am equally sure that his possession of the big bond was fraudulent.

Your father never owed him all that money, in the world ; but how did he get hold of it ? The man in the South in whose name it was made out is dead, and all his papers burned. Still turns up with the bond assigned to him, and says it was given him for negroes he sold. Now, how shall we meet it ? We know he made money negro-trading. Rupert's story of hearing the conversation with your father is too vague. He can't explain what your father meant by his reference to the Indian-killer, and his threats against Hiram will weaken his testimony. Hiram's afraid of him, though, and he'd better be. We'll have to send him away. He's with McRaffle too much."

Jacquelin's face sobered, and he sighed. The thought of Rupert cost him many sighs these days.

" I am not sure that we have been specific enough in our charges," Steve continued, " and I am sure the judge will be against us. He has never gotten over the peeling I gave him when he first turned Rad, and he and Hiram are as thick as thieves."

" Yes ; but, as you say, we'll get at something, and it is all we can do. I am willing to take the risk for Rupert, if not for myself. Will you sign as counsel ? And I'll go over to the office and file it. Mr. Dockett said he'd wait for us."

Steve took the pen and dipped it in the ink ; then again leaned back in his chair, and then, after a second's thought, sat up and signed the paper rapidly, and Jacquelin took it and went out. In a few minutes he returned.

" Well, the Rubicon is crossed," he said, gayly.

Steve did not answer. He was again leaning back in his chair, deep in thought, his eyes on the ceiling, his face graver than before.

" Steve, don't bother about the thing any more. We've done the best we could, and if we fail we fail, that's all."

But the other did not respond in the same vein.

" Yes, we've crossed the Rubicon," he said, with something between a sigh and a yawn.

"Steve, what's the matter?"

"Oh, nothing."

"Yes, there is—tell me."

"Nothing—I assure you, there's not."

"And I know better. Confound it! can't I see something is going on that I don't understand? You couldn't be gloomier if you had broken with—with your sweetheart."

"Well, I have." Steve turned and looked out of the window to where the light in the clerk's office shone through the trees.

"What!" Jacquelin was on his feet in a second.

"Jack, I'm in love."

"I know that. But what do you mean by—by—that you have broken with——?"

"That I'm in love with Ruth Welch." He spoke quietly.

"What—what do you mean?" Jacquelin's voice faltered.

"What I say—that I've been in love with her ever since I met her." He was still looking out of the window.

"Steve!" Jacquelin's tone had changed and was full of deep reproach. As Steve was not looking at him and did not answer, he went on: "Steve, I don't understand. Does she know?" His throat was dry and his voice hard.

"I don't know——"

"Steve Allen!" The tone was such that Steve turned to look at him.

"What's the matter with you?"

"That's what I have to ask you," said Jacquelin, sternly. "Are you crazy?"

"I don't know whether I am or not," Steve said, half bitterly. "But that's the fact, anyhow."

Jacquelin's face had paled, and his form was tense.

"Steve, if anyone else had told me this of you, he'd not have stood to complete his sentence. I thought you were a gentleman," he sneered.

"Jacquelin Gray!" Steve sprang to his feet, and the two young men stood facing each other, their faces white and their eyes blazing. Jacquelin spoke first.

"As Blair Cary has no brother to protect her, I will do it. I never thought it would have to be against you."

"Blair Cary? Protect her against me? In God's name, what do you mean?"

"You know."

"I swear I do not!"

Jacquelin turned from him with a gesture of contempt; but Steve seized him roughly.

"By Heaven! you shall tell me. I feel as if the earth were giving way before me."

Jacquelin shook him off, but faced him, his whole expression full of scorn.

"Haven't you been engaged to—engaged to—or as good as engaged to—or, at least, in love with Blair Cary for years?"

Steve gazed at him for a moment with a puzzled look on his face, which gave place the next instant to one of inexpressible amusement, and then, with a shove which sent Jacquelin spinning across the room, flung himself into his chair and burst into a ringing laugh.

"You fool! you blamed fool!" he exclaimed. "But I'm a fool, too," he said, standing and facing Jacquelin.

"I think you are." Jacquelin was still grave.

"Why, Blair knows it."

"Knows what?"

"Knows that I'm in love with Ruth Welch. She divined it long ago and has been my confidante."

"What!—Steve!—" The expression on Jacquelin's face underwent a dozen changes in as many seconds. Astonishment, incredulity, memory, reflection, regret, hope —all were there, chasing each other and tumbling over one another in wild confusion. "Steve," he began again in hopeless amazement, with a tone almost of entreaty, but stopped short.

24

"You double-dyed, blind idiot!" exclaimed Steve, "Don't you know that Blair Cary don't care a button for me? never has cared and never will care but for one man——?"

"Middleton!" Jacquelin turned away with a fierce gesture.

"No, you jealous fool!"

"Then, in Heaven's name, who is it?" Jacquelin again faced him.

"A blind idiot."

The effect was not what Steve had anticipated. Jacquelin made a wild gesture of dissent, turned his back, and, walking to the window, put his forearm against the sash, and leaned his forehead on it.

"You don't know what you're talking about," he said, bitterly. "She hates me. She treats me like——She has always done it since that cursed Middleton——"

"I don't say she hasn't. I simply say she——" Steve broke off. "She ought to have treated you badly. You made a fool of yourself, and have been a fool ever since. But I know she cared for you—before that, and if you had gone about it in the right way, you'd have won her." (Jacquelin groaned.) "Instead of that, you must get on a high horse and put on your high and mighty airs and try to hector a spirited girl like Blair Cary." (A groan from the window.) "Why, if I were to treat my horse as you did her, he'd break my neck."

"Oh, Steve!"

"And then after she had tried to prove it to you, for you to go and put it on another's account, of course she kicked —and she ought to have done so, and has treated you coldly ever since."

Jacquelin faced him.

"Steve, I loved her so. I have loved her ever since I was a boy—ever since that day I made her jump off the barn. It was what kept me alive in prison many a time when otherwise I'd have gone. And when I came home, ready to go down on my knees to her—to die for her, to find her given to another, or, if not——" He stopped and turned away again.

"Then why didn't you tell her so, instead of outraging her feelings ? " demanded Steve.

"Because—because I thought you loved her and she loved you, and I would not——!" He turned off and walked to the window.

Steve rose and went up to him.

"Jacquelin," he said, putting his hand on his shoulder, and speaking with a new tenderness, "I never knew it—I never dreamed it. You have been blind, boy. And I have been worse. I was never in love with her and she knew it. At first, I simply meant to bedevil you, and—Middleton—and then afterward, used to tease her to see her let out about you ; but that was all. She has known ever since Ruth Welch came here that I liked her, and now—that I have become a fool like the rest of you." He turned away.

Jacquelin stood for a moment looking at him, a light dawning on his face.

"Steve, I beg your pardon for what I said." He stood lost in thought. The next second he rushed out of the door. In a moment he was back, and held the bill he had just filed, in his hand. Steve rose as he entered.

"What have you done ? "

"I may be a fool—but—" He held up the bill and glancing at it, caught hold of the last sheet and began to tear it. Steve made a spring, but was too late ; Jacquelin had torn the signature from the paper.

"I'm not such a selfish dog as to let you do it and bar your chance of happiness. I did not know. Do you suppose Miss Welch would ever marry you if you signed that bill ? "

"No. But do you suppose I will not tell her of my part in bringing the suit ?"

"Of course you will—but she'll forgive you for that."

It was late in the night before their disagreement was settled.

Steve insisted that he would sign the bill; he had brought the suit and he would assume the responsibility for it. But he had met his match. Jacquelin was firm, and finally declared that if Steve still held to his decision he would not press the suit at all. Steve urged Rupert's interest. Jacquelin said Rupert would still have six months after he came of age, in which to save his rights. In this unexpected turn of the case, Steve was forced to yield; and Jacquelin recopied the whole bill in his own hand and filed it the next morning. It was signed by Jacquelin and Rupert personally, and by General Legaie as counsel.

It created a sensation in at least two households in the County.

When Still read the bill, he almost dropped to the floor. The attack was made on the ground of fraud, and Major Welch had said the statute of limitations did not apply. After a conference, however, with Leech, who happened to be at home, he felt better. Leech assured him that the bill would not hold good against his possession of the bonds.

"They'll hold against all creation," said that counsellor, "if they weren't stolen and ain't been paid."

This declaration did not seem to relieve Still much.

"And they've got to prove both of 'em," added Major Leech, "and prove 'em before our judge."

Still's face cleared up.

"Well, Welch is obliged to stand by us. We'll go and see him."   ˙

So, that evening they took a copy of the bill to Major Welch. Mrs. Welch and Miss Ruth both were in a state of great excitement and indignation. The idea of fraud being charged against Major Welch was an outrage that they could not tolerate.

Major Welch alone was calm and unmoved. It was, after

all, expressly stated that no actual fraud was attributed to
him, and though, of course, he felt keenly having his name
mixed up with such a matter, he had no anxiety as to the
result.   He could readily prove that he had had no knowledge whatever of anything to arouse the slightest suspicion.
He should, of course, have to employ counsel.   He began
to canvass their names.

"Papa, why don't you get Mr. Allen to represent you ?
They say he is the best lawyer in this part of the country,"
said Ruth.   She was conscious that her color came as Still
quickly looked at her.

"He's the one that started the whole matter, ma'am."

"Why, I don't see his name to the bill !" the Major
said.

"Ain't it ?   Well, anyhow he's the main one.   If it
hadn't been for him the suit never would 'a' been brought.
Colonel Leech saw a copy of the bill in his hand-writing in
his office this morning, didn' you, Colonel ?"

Leech declared that he had seen the copy, and corroborated his client in his statement that Captain Allen had
inspired the suit.

Mrs. Welch gave an exclamation of indignation.

"Well, I did not think he would have played the
sneak !"

Ruth's face flamed and turned white by turns.

"You don't know him yet," said Still, plaintively,
"Does she, Colonel ?"

"No—he's a bad man," said Leech, unctuously.

"He is that," said Still.   He dropped his voice.   "You
look out for him, Major.   He's after you.   If I was you
I'd carry a pistol pretty handy."   Major Welch gave a
gesture of impatience.

Ruth's eyes flashed a sudden gleam, and her face flamed
again.   She rose, walked to the window, and pressed deep
in between the curtains.   Still addressed himself to Major
Welch.

"The Colonel says 'tain't goin' to be any trouble to beat

the suit; that he can git it dismissed on demurrer--if that's the word? You know I ain't any book-learnin'— I'm nothin' but a plain farmer. And he says the judge is sure to——"

"Yes—that's it," said Leech, quickly, with a glance of warning at him. "I don't cross a bridge till I get to it; I've got several in this case, but, as Mr. Bagby says, I believe in making every defence."

"That may be so; but I'm going to fight this case on its merits," declared Major Welch, firmly. "I don't propose, when a question of fraud is raised, to shelter myself behind any technicalities. I mean to make it as clear as day that I had no connection with any fraud. I spoke to Mr. Bagby when the rumor of a suit was first started, and told him so." Though he spoke quietly his voice had a ring in it and his face a light on it which made both Mrs. Welch and Ruth proud of him, and Ruth squeezed her mother's arm, in her joy. How different he looked from those other men!

Meantime the change in Steve Allen was perceptible to many who had no idea of the true reason it was so.

Jacquelin set it down to the wrong cause. Miss Thomasia, like Jacquelin, laid Steve's despondency at Blair's door, and the good lady cast about in her mind how she might draw Blair into a discussion of the subject and give her some affectionate advice. But as often as she touched on the subject of love, even in the most distant way, bringing in Jacquelin as a sort of introduction, Blair shied off from it, so that Miss Thomasia found it more difficult to accomplish than she had anticipated.

Steve, however, was working on his own lines. His present situation was intolerable to him. The fact that his name had not appeared on Jacquelin's bill stuck in his memory like a thorn. He was lying on the grass under a tree in the court-green one afternoon reading a book, not a law-book either, when the sound of horses' feet caught his ear. He looked up lazily as it came nearer, and soon in view appeared two riders, a girl and a young man. They cantered easily along the little street, their laughter coming across to Steve where he lay, his book neglected on the ground beside him. Steve stretched, and picking up his book dived once more into the "Idylls of the King." But the spell was broken. A line from Dante flashed through his mind. Launcelot and Guinevere ; Tristram and Isolt ; Geraint and Enid, interested him no more. The reality had passed before him. Resting his head against the tree, he tried to go to sleep ; but the minute denizens about in the grass bothered him, the droning of bees in the locust boughs above failed to lull him.

" ' I am half sick of shadows,' " he murmured to himself, and he sat up and, resting against the tree, thought deeply. Another line came to him :

"On burnished hooves his war-horse trode."

He suddenly sprang to his feet and walked straight to his office, his face resolute and his step determined. He was not a girl to be caught in a mesh ! He would be the other. Jacquelin was at his desk, deep in a big law-book. Steve shut the door behind him and stood with his back against it looking down at his partner.

" Jacquelin, I am going to marry Ruth Welch."

" What !" Jacquelin looked up in blank amazement. " Oh !" he laughed. " I thought you meant you had asked her."

" You misunderstand me. It is not conceit. It is determination. I have no idea she will accept me now ; but she will in the end. She shall, I will win her." He was grave, and though his words spoke conceit, his voice and face had not a trace of it. Jacquelin too became grave.

" I believe you can win her if you try, Steve—unless someone else is in the way ; but it is a long chase, I warn you." Steve's brow clouded for a second, but the shadow disappeared as quickly as it came.

" You don't think there's anything in that story about

Wash Still ? " His tone had a certain fiery contempt in it. " I tell you there isn't. I'll stake my salvation on that. An eagle does not mate with a weasel ! "

" No—I do not believe she would, but how about her mother ? You know what she thinks of us, and what they say of her missionary ideas, and Wash Still has been playing assiduously on that string of late. He is visiting all her sick, free—he says. Besides they have not the same ideas that we have about family and so on, and they don't know the Stills as we do."

" Not pride of family ! You don't know her. She's one of the proudest people in the United States, of her family. I tell you she could give General Legaie six in the game and beat him. By Jove ! I wish one could do the old-fashioned way. I'd just ride up and storm the stronghold and carry her off ! " burst out Steve, straightening up and stretching out his arms, half in jest, half in earnest, his eyes flashing and his color rising at the thought.

" Now you have to storm the stronghold all the same, without carrying her off," Jacquelin laughed.

" No, I'll carry her away some day," asseverated Steve, confidently. " It's worth all my worthless life and a good deal more too."

" I think if you get into that spirit you may win her ; but I'm afraid they'll hardly recognize you in the rôle of humility. I doubt if they have heard much of you in that character. How are you going about it ? You have not seen her since the suit was brought, and I doubt if she will speak to you."

" She will not ? I'll make her. Whether she speaks or not, I'll win her."

" There goes your robe of humility. You have to win her parents first—for you have to ask their permission."

Steve relapsed into thought for a moment, during which Jacquelin watched him closely.

" Do you think that's necessary ? " he asked, doubtfully, as if almost to himself.

STEVE STRETCHED, AND, PICKING UP HIS BOOK, DIVED ONCE MORE INTO THE "IDYLLS OF THE KING."

"I do, under the circumstances—for you ; not for Wash Still."

"The gorgon will refuse me——"

"Probably—All the same, you have to do it."

Suddenly, with a sigh, Steve came out of his reverie as if he were emerging from a cloud. His countenance cleared up and he spoke with decision.

"You are right. I knew you were right all the time. But I did not want to do it. I will, though. I'll do it if I lose her." He turned to go out.

"When are you going to do it ? "

"Right now." In the presence of contest Steve's face had got back all its fire, his voice all its ring.

"I believe you'll win her," said Jacquelin.

"I know I shall, some day," said Steve. And a little later Jacquelin heard him in his room, whistling " Bonny Dundee," and calling to Jerry to saddle his horse.

Major Welch was sitting on his veranda that afternoon about sunset when a rider came out of the woods far below, at a gallop, and continued to gallop all the way up the hill. There was something about a rapid gallop up hill and down that always bore Major Welch's mind back to the war. As the horseman came nearer, Major Welch recognized Captain Allen. He remembered the advice Still had recently given him, always to have a pistol handy when he met Allen. He put the thought away from him with almost a flush of shame that it should even have crossed his mind. Should he meet a man at his own door, with a weapon ? Not if he was shot down for it. So, as the rider approached, Major Welch walked down to meet him at the gate, just as Steve, dismounting, tied his horse.

The young man's face was pale, his manner constrained, and he was manifestly laboring under more emotion than he usually showed. Wondering what could be the object of his call, Major Welch met him gravely. Steve held out his hand and the Major took it formally. At any rate the mission was peaceful.

"Major Welch, I have come to see you—" he began hesitatingly, his hat in his hand, and his face flushed.

"Won't you walk up on the veranda and sit down ? " The Major did not mean to be outdone in civility.

"Not until I have stated the object of my visit. Then, if you choose to invite me, I shall be very glad to accept." He had recovered his composure.

The Major was more mystified.

"I have come this evening for a purpose which, perhaps, will—no doubt will—surprise you." The Major looked affirmative, and wondered more and more what it could mean.

"I have come to ask your permission to pay my addresses to your daughter."

If the Major was expecting to be surprised, he was more than surprised ; he was dazed—he almost gasped.

"What ? "

"I am not surprised that you are astonished." The younger man, now that the ice was broken, was regaining his composure. "It is, however, no sudden impulse on my part." How melodious his deep voice had grown ! Major Welch was sensible of the charm growing upon him that he had seen exercised in the case of others.

"I have loved your daughter "—(his voice suddenly sank to a pitch as full of reverence as of softness)—"a long time ; perhaps not long in duration, but ever since I knew her. From that evening that I first met her here, I have loved her." His glance stole toward the tree in which he had found Ruth that afternoon. "If I can obtain your consent, and shall find favor in her eyes, I shall be the happiest and most blessed of men." He gave a deep sigh of relief. He stood suddenly before Major Welch a different being—modest and manly, not without recognition of his power, and yet not for a second presuming on it. Major Welch could not help being impressed by him. A wave of the old liking that he had had for him when he first met him came over him,

"Does my daughter know of this?" he asked.

"I hardly know. I have never said anything of it to her directly, but I do not know how much a girl's instinct can read. My manner has seemed to myself always that of a suitor, and at times I have wondered how she could help reading the thoughts of my heart; they have seemed to me almost audible. Others have known it for some time; at least one other has. I thought your daughter knew it. Yet now I cannot tell. She has never given me the slightest encouragement."

"I thought you were in love with—with someone else; with your cousin, and her accepted lover? Rumor has so stated it?" The older gentleman's manner cooled again as the thought recurred to him.

Steve smiled.

"Blair Cary? I do love her—dearly—but only as an admirer and older brother might. I am aware of the impression that has existed, but her heart has long been given to another who has loved her from his boyhood. From certain causes, which I need not trouble you with and which occurred before you arrived, differences grew up between them, and they became estranged; but the affection remains. Jacquelin does not know it, but in time he will succeed, and it is one of my most cherished hopes that some time he will realize that great happiness in store for him. Meantime, I feel sure that you will consider what I have said of this as confidential. I have, perhaps, said more than I should have done."

Major Welch bowed. "Of course I will. And now I wish to say that I am so much taken by surprise by what you have told me that I scarcely know just what answer to give you at this time. I appreciate the step you have taken. But it is so strange—so unexpected—that I must have time for reflection. I must consult my wife, who is my best adviser and our daughter's best guardian. And I can only say that we wish for nothing but our child's best and most lasting happiness. I cannot, of course, under

the circumstances renew my invitation to you to come in."
He paused and reflected. "Nor can I hold out to you
any hope. And I think I must ask you not to speak to
my daughter on the subject until I have given my consent."

"I promise you that," said Steve. "I should not have
come to you at all unless I had been prepared to give that
promise."

The young man evidently had something more that he
wished to say ; he hesitated a moment and then began
again.

"One other thing I should tell you. I brought the
suit for Jacquelin and Rupert Gray. Although my name
was not signed to the bill, I brought the suit, and have the
responsibility."

Major Welch could not help a graver look coming into
his face—he felt almost grim, but he tried to choke down
the sensation.

"I was aware of that."

"There is one word more I would like to say, but—not
now—I should possibly be misunderstood. Perhaps the
day may come— May I say in the meantime that I am
not one who changes or is easily disheartened ? I know
that even if I should secure your consent I should have to
make the fight of my life to win your daughter—but I
should do it. I think the prize well worth all, and far
more than all I could give."

He stood diffidently, as though not knowing whether
Major Welch would take his hand if offered. The Major,
however, made the advance and the two men shook hands
ceremoniously and Steve mounted his horse and without
looking back rode off, while Major Welch returned slowly
to the house. The only glance Steve gave was one up
toward the old cherry-tree in the yard.

Mrs. Welch had seen Steve ride up and had watched
with curiosity and some anxiety the conference that had
taken place at the gate. When the Major stated to her

the object of Mr. Allen's visit she was too much surprised to speak. She, however, received the announcement somewhat differently from the way the Major had expected. She was deeply offended. Without an instant's hesitation she was for despatching an immediate and indignant refusal.

"Of course, you at once refused him and told him what you thought of his effrontery?" she said.

"Well—no, I did not," said Major Welch. In fact, though the Major had been astonished by Steve's proposal and had supposed that it would be rejected, it had not occurred to him that his wife would take it in just this way.

"You did not! Oh, you men! I wish he had spoken to me! It was an opportunity I should not have lost. But he would not have dared to face me with his insulting proposal."

"Well, I don't think he intended it as an insult, and without intention it cannot be an insult. I think if you had seen him you would have felt this."

"Do you think I would entrust my daughter's happiness to a desperado and a midnight assassin?"

"No, I cannot say that I thought you would—nor would I. But I am not prepared to say I think him either an assassin or a desperado."

"Well, I am," asserted Mrs. Welch. "I was deceived in him once and I will not give him a chance again."

"I simply told him that I would confer with you and give him our answer."

"He will take that as encouragement," declared Mrs. Welch, "and will be pursuing Ruth and persecuting her."

"No, he will not. He gave me his word that he would not speak to her without my—without our consent——"

"He will not keep it." Mrs. Welch's words were not as positive as her manner.

"Yes, he will. I will stand sponsor." Major Welch was thinking of the young man as he had just stood before him.

"Well, I am glad you extracted that much of a pledge from him. He will not get my consent in this life, I can assure him."

"Nor mine without yours and Ruth's," said Major Welch, gravely. "I will write him and tell him what you say. Shall I mention it to Ruth?"

"No, of course not."

Major Welch did not see why it should be "of course"; but he considered that his wife knew more of such things than he did, and he accordingly accepted her opinion without question.

"Where is Ruth?" he asked.

"She went with Dr. Still to see a sick woman he wanted me to see. I was not able to go this afternoon when he called, so I sent her. I don't think there is much the matter with her."

Major Welch sat for a moment in deep reflection. He was evidently puzzled. Suddenly he broke the silence.

"Prudence, you don't mean that you wish that—that you think that young fellow is a suitable—ah—companion for our daughter?" That was not the word Major Welch meant.

"William!" exclaimed Mrs. Welch. She said no more, and it was not necessary. Major Welch felt that he had committed a great mistake—a terrible blunder. A moment before, he had had the best of the situation, and he had been conscious of a feeling of somewhat exalted virtue; now he had thrown it away. He felt very foolish, and though he hoped he did not show it, he did show it plainly. He began to defend himself: a further blunder.

"Well, my dear, how could I know? That young fellow has been coming over here day after day, with his horses and buggies, on one pretext or another—tagging after—not after you or me certainly—and you are as civil to him as if he were the—the President himself, and actually send the child off with him——"

"William! Send the child off with him!—I!"

" Well, no—not exactly that, of course," said her husband, rather embarrassed, " but permitting her to go, and thus giving him an opportunity to declare himself, which he would be a stick not to avail himself of."

"I am glad you retracted that, William," said Mrs. Welch, with the air of one deeply aggrieved. " Of course, I am civil to the young man. I hope I am civil to everyone. But you little know a mother's heart. I have always said that no man can understand a woman."

" I believe that's so," said her husband, smiling. " I know I have often heard your Royal Highness say so. But did it ever occur to you that it may be because men are somewhat direct and downright ? "

" Now don't go and insult my sex to cover the density of yours," said Mrs. Welch. " Confine your attack to one. If you think that I would allow my daughter to marry that—that young upstart, you don't know me as well as you did the first day we met."

" Oh, yes I do ! I know you well enough to know you are the best and most devoted wife and mother and friend in the world," declared her husband. " But, you see, I misunderstood you. I reason simply from the plain facts that lie right before my eyes——"

" And you always will misunderstand, my dear. Your sex always will misunderstand until they learn that woman is a more complex and finer organism than their clumsy, primary machine, moved by more delicate and complicated motives."

" Well, I agree to that," said her husband. " And I am very glad to find you agree with me—that I agree with you—" he corrected, with a twinkle in his eye, "as to that young man."

Mrs. Welch accepted his surrender with graciousness and left the room, and the Major sat down and wrote his reply to Captain Allen.

He expressed his unfeigned appreciation of the honor done, but gave him to understand that after conference

with Mrs. Welch they felt it their duty to state to him
that his suit for their daughter would not be acceptable to
them, and he requested him to consider the matter closed.

As soon as he had finished the letter the Major despatched it to Mr. Allen by a messenger.

He had hardly sent it off when Mrs. Welch returned.
Her first question was whether the answer had gone. She
was manifestly disappointed to learn that it had been sent.

" I wish you had let me see it," she said.

" Oh ! I made it positive enough," declared the Major.

" Yes, I was not thinking of that," Mrs. Welch said,
thoughtfully. " I was afraid you would be too—Men are
so hasty—so up and down—they don't know how to deal
with such matters as a woman would."

Major Welch turned on her in blank amazement—a
little humor lighting up his face. Mrs. Welch answered
as if he had made a charge.

" You men will never understand us."

" I believe that's so. You women are curious, especially
where your daughters are concerned. I set the young man
down pretty hard, just as you wished me to do."

Mrs. Welch made a gesture of dissent.

" Not at all—I have reflected on what you said about—
about his not intending to be insulting, and I think you
are right. I no more wish to accept his proposal now than
before ; all I want is to—?" She made a gesture—"Oh !
you understand."

" Yes, I think I do," laughed her husband. " Why
cannot women let a man go ? "

CHAPTER XXXII

A CUT DIRECT AND A REJECTED ADDRESS

THE revelation that Steve made to Jacquelin in their law-office the night the bill was filed, seemed suddenly to have opened life again to Jacquelin. Looking back over the past, he could now see how foolish he had been. Incidents which he had construed one way now, in the light of Steve's disclosure, took on a new complexion. He appeared to have sprung suddenly into a new and rarer atmosphere. Hope was easily worth everything else in Pandora's box. When he began to visit at Dr. Cary's again, it must be said, that he could discern no change in Blair. Easy and charming as she always was to others, to him she was as constrained as formerly. She treated him with the same coldness that she had always shown him since that fatal evening when he had taken her to task about Middleton, and then had alleged that it was on Steve's account. However, he was not to be cast down now. With the key which Steve had given him he could afford to wait and was willing to serve for his mistake, and he set down her treatment of him simply to a woman's caprice. He would bide his time until the occasion came and then he would win her. According to Steve, she had no idea that he was still in love with her, and according to the same expert authority, this was what she waited for. He had first to prove his love, and then he should find that he had hers. So through the long summer months he served faithfully. Each time that he saw Blair he found himself more deeply in love than before ; and each time he feared more to tell her of it, lest Steve's diagnosis should possibly prove wrong.

He knew that the next time he opened the subject it must be final. He even stood seeing McRaffle visiting Dr. Cary's, though he fumed and smouldered internally over a man like McRaffle being in Blair's presence, however smooth he was. Steve declared that McRaffle was in love with Miss Welch, but Jacquelin knew better. Steve was such a jealous creature that he thought everyone was in love with Miss Welch—even that Wash Still was, whom Miss Welch would not so much as look at. No, McRaffle was in love with Blair. Jacquelin knew it—just as he knew that Middleton was. She could not bear McRaffle, of course; but the thought of Middleton often crossed Jacquelin's mind, and discomposed him. He had heard of the honors Middleton had won in the Northwest and of his retirement from the service. Blair had told him of it with undue enthusiasm. Confound him! When that Indian bullet hit him most men would have died. Then as his thought ran this way Jacquelin would haul himself up short, with a feeling of hot shame that such an ignoble idea could even enter his mind, and next time he saw Blair would speak of Middleton with unmeasured admiration.

At length he could wait no longer. He would tell her how he had always loved her. Steve was his confidant, as he was Steve's, and Steve agreed that this was the thing to do.

Alas! for masculine wisdom! The way of a serpent on a rock is not harder than that of a maid with a man. An opportunity presented itself one afternoon in which everything appeared so propitious that Jacquelin felt as though the time were made for his occasion. He and Blair had been to ride. The summer woods had been heavenly in their peacefulness and charm. Blair had insensibly fallen into a softer mood than she usually showed him, and, as they had talked of old times, she had seemed sweeter to him than ever before. He had spoken to her of Rupert, and of his anxiety about the boy; of his association with McRaffle, and of the influence McRaffle seemed to have obtained over him ; and Blair had responded with a warmth which had set his heart to bounding. Mr. McRaffle was a dangerous, bad man, she declared, and she was doing all she could to counteract his evil influence over Rupert. Her sweetness to Jacquelin was such that he had hardly been able to restrain himself from opening his heart to her then and there, and asking her to let the past be bygones and accept his love. But he had waited until they should reach home, and now they were at the door. She invited him to stay to tea. Her voice thrilled him. Jacquelin suddenly began to speak to her of what was in his heart. She dropped her eyes and he was conscious that she was trembling. In his constraint he referred to the past, and faltered something about Steve having set him right. She looked up quickly. He did not heed it, but went on and said all he had so often rehearsed, with a good deal more than he had planned to say. Perhaps he gathered confidence as he went on— perhaps he showed it a little too much ; for he became conscious somehow that she was not as responsive as she had been just before.

When he was quite through, he waited. She also waited a moment, and then began.

She did not care for him, except as a relative, and she never expected to marry at all. She was not looking at him, and was evidently speaking under strong feeling.

Jacquelin's hopes were all dashed to the ground. His throat felt parched, and when he tried to speak again his lips did not frame his words easily.

" May I ask if you care for anyone else ? " he demanded, in a constrained voice.

She did not know that he had any right to ask her such a question. She had already told him that she never expected to marry anyone." She had grown more formal.

Jacquelin was sure now that she cared for Middleton, and she had simply misled Steve.

" What did you tell Steve ? " he asked.

She faced him, her figure quite straight and strong, her flashing eyes fastened searchingly on his face.

" So that's the reason you have come ! Steve told you to come, and you have come to say what he told you to say. Well, go back to him and tell him I say he was mistaken." Her lip curled as she turned on her heel.

" No—no—Blair—wait one moment ! " But she had walked slowly into the house, and Jacquelin saw her climb the stair.

A moment later he mounted his horse, and came slowly away down the road he knew so well, the road to Vain regret, beyond which, somewhere, lies Despair.

He knew now it was Middleton who had barred his way, and that to keep her secret, Blair had misled Steve. He might have forgiven her all else, but he could not forgive that.

When Jacquelin announced the result of his proposal to Steve, that wise counsellor laughed at him. He could make it up in ten minutes, he declared, and he rode up to see Blair next day. His interview lasted somewhat longer than he had expected, and most of the time he had been defending himself against Blair's scathing attack. When he left, it was with a feeling that he had done both Blair and Jacquelin an injury, and when he saw Jacquelin, he summed up his position briefly: " Well, Jack, I give it up. I thought I knew something of men and women ; but I give up women."

After his interview with Major Welch, Captain Allen had appeared to be in better spirits than he had been in for some time. Even the letter he received from that gentleman did not wholly dash his hopes, and though they occasionally sank, they as often rallied again. We know from the greatest of novelists that when a man is cudgelling his brains for other rhymes to " sorrow " besides " borrow " and " to-morrow," he is nearer light than he thinks. Steve found this safety-scape.

Jacquelin did not write poetry or even " poems " on

the subject of his disappointment; but his cheek-bones began to show more, and his chin began to take on a firmer set.

But Captain Allen was soon plunged as deep in the abyss as Jacquelin.

He was sitting in his office looking out of the window one afternoon, a habit that had grown on him of late, when a pair of riders, a lady and her escort, rode up the street, in plain view of where he sat. At sight of the trim figure sitting her horse so jauntily, Steve's heart gave a bound and a light came into his eyes. The next instant a cloud followed as he recognized Miss Welch's companion as Dr. Washington Still. Rumor had reported that Dr. Still was with her a good deal of late. Miss Thomasia and Blair had met them one evening visiting a poor woman together. McRaffle had taken the trouble to state that he had frequently met them.

Steve could not believe that such a girl as Ruth Welch could be accepting the addresses of such a man as young Dr. Still. She could not know him. He followed the girl, with his eyes, as long as she was in view. For some moments afterward he sat with a dogged resolution on his face; but it gradually faded away, and he rose and went out, passing down to the street. He had not seen Ruth Welch face to face since the filing of Jacquelin's suit. But she had never been absent from his thoughts for a moment. He had heard that both she and Mrs. Welch had a great deal of feeling about the suit, and that both had spoken bitterly of him; but Major Welch had received him civilly, even though he had denied his request to be allowed to offer himself as Ruth's suitor.

With a combination of emotions, rather than with any single idea in his mind, Steve strode into the village and up the street. He wanted to get away, and he wanted to be near her and have a look in her face; but he had no definite intention of letting her see him, none, at least, of meeting her. But as he turned a corner into a shady street they were coming back and Steve saw that even at a distance Ruth Welch knew him. He could not turn back; so kept on, and as they passed him he raised his hat. Miss Welch's escort, with a supercilious look on his face, raised his hat; but the girl looked Steve full in the eyes and cut him dead. The blood sprang into Steve's face. For any sign she gave, except a sudden whitening, and a contraction of the mouth, she might never have seen him before in all her life. The next second Steve heard her voice starting apparently a very animated conversation with her escort, and heard him reply:

"Hurrah! for you, that will settle him ; " and break into a loud laugh.

Steve did not return to his office that evening. He spent the night wandering about in blind and hopeless gloom. But had Mr. Allen known what occurred during the remainder of that ride he might have found in it some consolation.

Miss Ruth had hardly gotten out of hearing of Captain Allen, and her escort had scarcely had time to turn over in his mind his enjoyment of his rival's discomfiture and his own triumph, when the young lady inexplicably changed and turned on him so viciously and with so biting a sarcasm that he was almost dumfounded. The occasion for her change was so slight that Wash Still was completely mystified. It was only some slighting little speech he made about the man she had just cut dead.

" Why don't you say that to Captain Allen? " she asked, with a sudden flush on her face and a flash in her eyes. "You, at least, have not the excuse of not speaking to him."

Women have this in common with the Deity, that their ways are past finding out. The young doctor was completely mystified; but he could not comprehend how Miss Welch could have cut Captain Allen without it, in some way, redounding to his own advantage, and, notwithstanding her fierceness and coldness toward him, he believed it was a favorable time for him

The ride home through the woods in the soft summer afternoon presented an opportunity he had been seeking for some time, and the attitude Ruth had shown toward his rival appeared to him to indicate that everything was propitious. Even her attack he construed as only a flash of feminine caprice. After her little explosion, Miss Welch had lapsed into silence, and rode with her eyes on her horse's mane and her lips firmly closed. The young man took it for remorse for her conduct, and drawing up to her side, began to talk of himself and of his affairs. Ruth listened in silence—so silently, indeed, that she scarcely seemed to be listening at all—and the young doctor was moved to enlarge somewhat eloquently on his prospects as the owner of both Birdwood and Red Rock, the handsomest places in the County. Presently, however, he changed, and as they reached a shady place in the road, began to address her. He stated that he thought she had given him reason to hope he might be successful. The change in Ruth was electric. She gave suddenly a vehement gesture of wild dissent :

"Oh ! No ! no ! Don't !" she cried, and drew her horse to a stand, turning in the road and facing the young man. "No ! no ! You have misunderstood me ! How could you think so? I have never done it ! I never dreamed of it ! It is impossible !" The deep color sprang to her face, but the next moment she controlled herself by a strong effort, and faced the young man again. "Dr. Still," she said, calmly and with deep earnestness, "I am sure that, wittingly, I never gave you the least warrant to think—to suppose that I could—that you might say to me what you have said. My conscience tells me this ; but if I have ever done or said anything that appeared to you to be a ground to build a hope on, I am deeply sorry, and humbly beg your pardon. I beg you to believe me, I never intended it. I do not wish to appear hard or—cruel, but I must tell you now that there is not the slightest hope for ʸʸu, and never will be. I do not love you, I never could

love, and I will never marry, you, never." She could not
have spoken more strongly.

The young man's face, which had begun by being pale,
had now turned crimson, and he broke out, almost violently
—reiterating that she had given him ground to think himself favored. He cited the rides she had taken with him.
Ruth's eyes opened wide and her form straightened :

" I do not wish to discuss this further. I have told you
the simple truth. I should prefer that you go on ahead of
me—I prefer to ride home alone."

" Why did you cut Steve Allen this evening? " Dr. Still
persisted, angrily.

Ruth's face hardened.

" Certainly not on your account," she said, coldly, " or
for any reason that you will understand. Go ; I will ride
home alone."

" I used to think you were in love with him, and so did
everybody else," persisted he ; " but it can't be him. Is
it that young jackanapes, Rupert Gray ? He's in love
with you, but I didn't suppose you to be in love with a
boy like that."

Ruth's face flamed with indignation.

" By what right do you question me as to such things ?
Go, I will ride home alone." She drew her horse back
and away from him. The young man hesitated for a
moment, but Ruth was inexorable.

" If you please—go ! " she said, coldly, pointing down
the road.

" Well, I will go," he burst out, angrily. " But Rupert
Gray and the whole set of 'em had better look out for
me," and with a growl of rage, he struck his horse and
galloped away.

Miss Welch rode on alone, her heart moved by conflicting emotions—indignation, apprehension—and yet others,
deeper than these. What right had this man to treat her
so ? She flushed again with indignation as she thought
of his insolence. It seemed to her almost an insult to

have been addressed by him. She went over in her mind her conduct toward him. There never was one thing of which he could have a right to complain. Of this she was sure. It could not be otherwise, for she had never for a moment been free from a consciousness of antipathy to him. Then she went over her present situation, the situation of her father and mother, now so lonely and cut off from everyone. The cool, still woods, the deserted road, the far-reaching silence, were such as to inspire loneliness and sadness, and Ruth was on the verge of tears when the gallop of a horse came to her from ahead. She wondered if it could be Wash Still returning, and a momentary wave of apprehension swept over her. The next instant Rupert Gray cantered in sight. Ruth's first thought was one of relief, the next was that she ought to be cool to him. But as the boy galloped up to her, his young face glowing with pleasure, and reined in his horse, all her intended formality disappeared, and she returned his greeting cordially.

"Well, I am in luck," he exclaimed. "Mayn't I ride home with you?" He had assumed her consent, and turned his horse without waiting for it.

"I am afraid you may be going somewhere and I may detain you."

"No, indeed; I am my own master," he said, with a toss of his head. "Besides, I don't like you to be riding so late all by yourself."

The imitation of Steve Allen's protecting manner was so unmistakable that Ruth could not help smiling.

"Oh! I'm not afraid. No one would interfere with me."

"They'd better not! If they did, they'd soon hear from me," declared the boy, warmly, with that mannish toss of the head which boys have. "I'd soon show 'em who Rupert Gray is. Oh! I say! I met Washy Still up the road yonder, a little way back, looking as sour as vinegar, and you ought to have seen the way I cut him. I passed him just like this" (giving an imitation of his stare), "and you just ought to have seen the way he looked. He looked as if he'd have liked to shoot me." He burst into a clear, merry laugh.

The boy's description of himself was so exactly like the way Ruth had treated Steve, that she could not forbear smiling. The smile died away, however, and an expression of seriousness took its place.

"Rupert, I don't think it well to make enemies of people——"

"Who? Of Washy Still? Pshaw! He knows I hate him—and he hates me. I don't care. I want him to hate me. I'll make him hate me worse before I'm done." It was the braggadocio of a boy.

Ruth thought of the gleam of hate that had come into the man's eyes. "He might do you an injury."

"Who? Washy Still? Let him try it. I'm a better man than he is, any day. But he'd never try it. He's afraid to look me in the eyes. You don't like him, do you?" he asked with sudden earnestness.

"No, but I think you underestimate him."

"Pshaw! He can't hurt you—not unless you took his physic—no other way. I asked if you liked him, because —because some people thought you did, and I said you didn't—I knew you didn't. I say, I want to ask you something. I wish you wouldn't let him come to see you."

"Why?"

"Why, because he is not a man you ought to associate with—he is not a gentleman. He's a sneak, and his father's a thief. He stole our place—just stole it—besides everything else he's stolen."

"Why, you say we—my father had something to do with that," said Ruth, quietly.

"What! You! Your father?—I said he stole!" He reined up his horse, in his amazement.

"In your suit or bill, or whatever you call it." Ruth felt that it was cruel in her to strike him such a blow, yet she enjoyed it.

"I never did—we never did—you are mistaken," stammered the boy. "Why, I wouldn't have done it for the whole of Red Rock—no more would Steve. Let me explain. I know all about it."

Ruth looked acquiescent, and as they walked their horses along under the trees the boy tried to explain the matter. He was not very lucid, for he was often confused ; but he made clear the desire they had had to keep Major Welch out of the matter, and the sincerity of their motive in giving him the notice before he should buy, and the anxiety they had had and the care they had taken to make it clear in their suit that no charge of personal knowledge by him was intended. He also informed Ruth of Steve's action in the matter, and of the episode in the office that night when the bill was signed, or, at least, of as much of it as he had heard.

"But why did he do that ?" asked Ruth.

"Don't you know ?"

"N—o." Very doubtfully and shyly.

"Steve's in love with you !"

"What ? Oh, no ! You are mistaken." Ruth was conscious that her reply was silly and weak, and that she was blushing violently.

"Yes, he is—dead in love. Why, everybody knows it —at least Jack does, and Blair does, and I do. And I am, too," he added, warmly. The boy's ingenuous declaration steadied Ruth and soothed her. She looked at him with a pleased and gratified light on her face.

"I am—I am dead in love with you, too. I think you are the prettiest and sweetest and kindest young lady in the whole world—just as nice as Blair, every bit ; and I just wish I was older—I just wish you could marry me." He was blushing and turning white by turns, and the expression on his young face was so ingenuous and sweet and modest, and the light in his eyes so adoring, that the girl's heart went out to him. She drew her horse over to his side, and put her hand softly on his arm.

"Rupert, you are a dear, sweet boy, and, at least, you will let me be your best friend, and you will be mine," she said, sweetly.

"Yes, I will, and I think you are just as good as you can be, and I'll be just like your own brother, if you will let me."

"Indeed, I will, and we will always be sister and brother to each other."

"Thank you," he said, simply. A moment later he said, reining in his horse, "I say, if you think that suit means anything against your father, I'll have it stopped."

"No, no, Rupert; I am satisfied," Ruth protested, with a smile.

"Because I can do it; Jack and Steve would do anything for me, and I would do anything for you. It was mainly on my account, anyhow, that they brought it, I believe," he added. "They said I was a minor; but, you know, I'll soon be of age—I'm seventeen now. I don't know why boys have to be boys, anyhow! I don't see why they can't be men at once."

"I think I know," Ruth smiled, gazing at him pleasantly.

"And, I say, I want to tell you one thing about Steve. He isn't what people take him to be. You know?—Just clever and dashing and wild and reckless. He's the best and kindest fellow in the world. You ask Aunt Thomasia and Blair and Aunt Peggy and Uncle Waverley and old Mrs. Turley, and all the poor people about the County. And he's as brave as Julius Cæsar. I want to tell you that of him, and you know I wouldn't tell you if 'twa'n't so."

"I know," said Ruth, looking at him more pleasantly than ever.

They were at the gate now, and Ruth invited him in; but Rupert said he had an engagement.

"There is one thing I want to ask you to do," said Ruth, rather doubtfully.

"What is it ?" he asked, brightening ; and then, as she hesitated : "Anything ! I'll do it. I'll do anything for you, Miss Ruth ; indeed, I will."

"No ; it is not for me, but for yourself," said Ruth, who was thinking of a report that Rupert had been associating lately with some very wild young men, and she had it in her mind to ask him not to do so any more. "But, no ; I'll ask you next time I see you, maybe," she added, after a pause.

"All right ; I promise you I'll do it."

He said good-by, and galloped away through the dusk.

Ruth stood for some time looking after him, and then turned and entered the house, and went softly to her room.

Ruth did not think it necessary to tell her mother or father of the incidents of her ride, except that Rupert had ridden home with her. She shrank instinctively from speaking even to her mother of what had occurred on the ride. She felt a certain humiliation in the fact that Dr. Still had ventured to address her. Her only consolation was that she knew she had never given him any right to speak so to her. She had never gone anywhere with him except from a sense of duty, and had never been anything but coldly polite to him. She was relieved to hear a few days later that Dr. Still had left the County, and, rumor said, had gone to the city to practise his profession. Anyhow, he was gone, and Ruth felt much relieved, and buried her uncomfortable secret in her own bosom.

CHAPTER XXXIII

A NEW cause of grievance against Mrs. Welch had arisen in the County in her conduct of her school near the Bend. Colored schools were not a novelty in the County. Blair Cary had for two years or more taught the colored school near her home. But Mrs. Welch had made a new departure. The other school had been talked over and deliberated on until it was in some sense the outcome of the concert of the neighborhood. Dr. Cary gave the land and the timber. " Whether it will amount to anything else, I cannot say ; but it will amount to this, sir," said the Doctor to General Legaie, " I shall have done the best I could for my old servants." And on this, General Legaie, who had been the most violent opponent of it all, had sent his ox-team to haul the stocks to the mill. " Not because I believe it will accomplish any good, sir ; but because a gentleman can do no less than sustain other gentlemen who have assumed obligations."

Thus Miss Blair's school was regarded in part as representative of the old system. When, however, Mrs. Welch started her school, she consulted no one and asked no assistance—at least, of the county people. The aid she sought was only from her friends at the North, and when she received it, she set in, chose her place and built her school, giving out at the same time that it was to be used for sewing classes, debating societies, and other public purposes. Thus this school came to be considered as a foreign institution, conducted on foreign principles, and in opposition to the school already established by the neighborhood. Mrs. Welch not only built a much larger and handsomer structure than any other school-house in that section, but she planted vines to cover the porch, and introduced a system of prizes and rewards so far beyond anything heretofore known in the County, that shortly not only most of the scholars who had attended Blair's school left, but those from other schools much farther off began to flock to Mrs. Welch's seminary.

The first teacher Mrs. Welch secured to take charge of the institution was a slender, delicate young woman with deep eyes, thin cheeks, and a worn face, who by her too assiduous devotion to what she deemed her duty and an entire disregard of all prudence, soon reduced herself to such a low condition of health that Dr. Cary, who was called in, insisted that she should be sent back to her old home. The next teacher, Miss Slipley, was one who had testimonials high enough to justify the idea that she was qualified to teach in Tübingen.

She was a young woman of about thirty, with somewhat pronounced views and a very pronounced manner ; her face was plain, but she had a good figure, of which Mrs. Welch, who herself had a fine figure, thought she was much too vain, and as her views relating to the conduct of the school by no means coincided with those of Mrs. Welch, matters were shortly not as harmonious between the two as they might have been. She soon began to complain of the discomforts of her situation and her lack of association. Mrs. Welch deplored this, but thought that Miss Slipley should find her true reward in the sense of duty performed, and told her so plainly. This, Miss Slipley said, was well enough when one had a husband and family to support her, but she had had no idea that she was to live in a wilderness, where her only associates were negroes, and where not a man ever spoke to her, except to bow distantly. So after a little time, she had thrown up her position and gone home, and shortly afterward had married. This, to Mrs. Welch, explained all her high airs. Just then Mrs.

Welch received a letter from a young woman she knew, asking her to look out for a position for her. During the war this applicant had been a nurse in a hospital, where Mrs. Welch had learned something of her efficiency. So when Miss Slipley left, Mrs. Welch wrote Miss Bush to come.

"She, at least, will not have Miss Slipley's very objectionable drawbacks—for, if I remember aright, Miss Bush has no figure at all," said Mrs. Welch. "Heaven save me from women with figures! When an ugly woman has nothing else, she is always showing her figure or her feet."

When Miss Bush arrived Mrs. Welch found her impressions verified. She was a homely little body, yet with kind eyes and a pleasant mouth. She acceded cheerfully to all Mrs. Welch's views. She was perfectly willing to live with the woman at whose house it had been arranged that she should board ; she wished, she said, to live unobtrusively. She was in deep mourning and wore a heavy veil.

Miss Bush had not been in her position long before Mrs. Welch felt that at last she had found the very person for the place. She was as quiet as a mouse, and not afraid of any work whatever. She not only taught, but wholly effaced herself, and, in fact, proved a perfect treasure.

By the negroes she was called Miss May (a contraction for Mary), which went abroad as her family name.

Miss May proved to be a strict disciplinarian, and a firm believer in the somewhat obsolete, but not less wise doctrine, that to spare the rod is to spoil the child, and as this came to be known, it had the effect of establishing her in the good esteem of the neighborhood. Thus, though no one visited her, Miss May received on all hands a respectful regard. This was suddenly jeopardized at the opening of the new campaign, by a report that the school-house, in addition to its purposes as a school-building, was being used as a public hall by negroes for their Union-league meetings. Leech, whose headquarters were now in the city, had come up to take charge of the canvass, and had boasted that he would make it hot for his opponents —a boast he appeared likely to make good. He attended the meetings at the new school-house, and it was reported that he had made a speech in which he said that the whites owed the negroes everything ; that the time had come for payment, and that matches were only five cents a box, and if barns were burned they belonged to them. The report of this speech was carried through the County next day. One night shortly afterward Andy Stamper's store was burned to the ground, and this was followed by the burning of several barns throughout Red Rock and the adjoining counties.

The reappearance of the masked order that had almost disappeared followed immediately in some places. A meeting was held in Brutusville, denouncing the outrage of such speeches as those of Leech, at which Dr. Cary presided, and Steve Allen and General Legaie, Jacquelin Gray and Captain McRaffle spoke, but there was no reappearance in this County of the masked men. McRaffle denounced the patrons and teacher of the new school with so much heat that Steve Allen declared he was as incendiary as Leech.

McRaffle sneered that Steve appeared to have become very suddenly a champion of the carpet-bagger, Welch ; and Steve retorted that at least he did not try to borrow from people and then vilify them, but that Captain McRaffle could find another cause to quarrel with him if he wished it. For a long time there had been bad blood between Steve and McRaffle. Among other causes was McRaffle's evil influence over Rupert.

Rupert Gray had been growing of late more and more independent, associating with McRaffle and a number of the wildest fellows in the County, and showing a tendency to recklessness which had caused all his friends much concern. Jacquelin tried to counsel and control him, but the boy was wayward and heedless. Rupert thought it was hard that he was to be under direction at an age when Jacquelin had already won laurels as a soldier.

26

When his brother took him to task for going off with some of the wilder young men in their escapades, Rupert only laughed at him.

"Why, Jack, it's you I am emulating. As Cousin John Cary would say, ' The trophies of Miltiades will not let me sleep.' " And when Captain Allen tried to counsel him seriously, he floored that gentleman by saying that he had learned both to drink and to play poker from him. He was, however, devoted to Blair, and she appeared to have much influence with him ; so Steve and Jacquelin tried to keep him with her as much as possible.

One evening shortly after the public meeting at which Steve and McRaffle had had their quarrel, Rupert appeared to be somewhat restless. Blair had learned the signs and knew that in such cases it was likely to be due to Rupert's having heard that some mischief was on foot, and she used to devise all sorts of schemes to keep the boy occupied. She soon discovered now what was the matter. Rupert had heard a rumor that a movement was about to be directed against Miss May's school. None of the men he was intimate with knew much about it. It was only a rumor. Steve and Jacquelin were both away from the County attending Court in another county. Blair was much disturbed.

"Why, they are going to do it on your account," said Rupert. "They say this school was started to break up your school."

"Nonsense ! Do they think that's the way to help me? The teacher is a woman," urged Blair. Rupert's countenance fell.

"They aren't going to trouble her—are just going to scare the negroes so there won't be any more meetings held there. Some say she's kin to Leech—or something."

"She is nothing of the kind," asserted Blair. "Ruth Welch told me she had never seen Mr. Leech, and declined positively to see him. When is it to be ?"

"To-night."

Blair lamented the absence of Jacquelin and Steve.   If they were but at home they would, she knew, prevent this outrage.

"Oh ! Jacquelin and Steve !   They are nothing but old fogies," laughed Rupert.   "McRaffle, he's the man !" With a toss of his head he broke into a snatch of Bonny Dundee.

Blair watched him gravely for a moment.

"Rupert," she said, "Captain McRaffle is nothing but a gambler and an adventurer.   He is not worthy to be named in the same breath with—with Steve and—your brother any more than he is to be named with my father. This is the proof of it, that he is going to try to interfere with a woman.   Why does he not go after Colonel Leech, who made the speech there ?" Rupert's face grew grave. Blair pressed her advantage.

"He is a coward ; for he would never dare to under- take such a thing if your brother and Steve were at home. He takes advantage of their absence to do this, when he knows that Miss May has no defender."

Rupert's eye flashed.

"By George ! I never thought of that," he burst out. "She has got a defender.   I'll go there and stand guard myself.   You needn't have any fear, Blair, if I'm there." He hitched his coat around in such a way as to display the butt of a huge pistol.   Blair could not help smiling.   But this was not what she wanted.   She was afraid to send Rupert to guard the place.   He had not judgment enough. If what the boy had heard were true, something might happen to him if he went there.   She knew that he would defend it with his life ; but she was afraid of the conse- quences.   So she set to work to put Rupert on another tack. She wanted him to go down to the county seat and learn what he could of the plans, and try to keep the men from coming at all.   This scheme was by no means as agreeable to Rupert as the other, but he finally yielded, and set out. Blair watched him ride away through the orchard, the evening light falling softly around him as he cantered off. She sat still for a little while thinking. Suddenly she rose, and going into the house found her mother and held a short consultation with her. A few moments later she came out with her hat on, and disappeared among the apple-trees, walking rapidly in the same direction Rupert had taken. Her last act as she left the house was to call softly to her mother :

"When Rupert comes back send him after me. I will wait for him at Mr. Stamper's."

It had occurred to her that Andy Stamper would do what she was afraid to have a rash boy like Rupert attempt. Andy hated Leech, to whom he charged the burning of his store ; but he was devoted to Miss Welch. And he had told Blair of seeing Miss May once pull down her veil to keep from looking at Leech.

When, however, Blair arrived at the Stampers's Mr. Stamper was absent. But she found an heroic enough ally in his representative, Mrs. Delia, to make up for all other deficiencies. The idea of the possibility of an injury to one of her sex fired that vigorous soul with a flame not to be quenched.

"I jest wish my Andy was here," she lamented. "He'd soon straighten 'em out. Not as I cares, Miss Blair, about the school, or the teacher," she said, with careful limitation ; "for I don't like none of 'em, and I'd be glad if they'd all go back where they come from. The old school was good enough for me, and them as can't find enough in white folks to work on, outdoes me. But—a man as can't git a man to have a fuss with and has to go after a woman, Delia Stamper jist wants to git hold of him. I never did like that Cap'n McRaffler, anyhow. He owes Andy a hundred and twenty-nine dollars, and if I hadn't stopt Andy from givin' him things—that's what I call it— jest *givin'* 'em to him—sellin' on credit, he'd a owed us five hundred. He knows better th'n to fool with me." She gave a belligerent shake of her head. "I'll tell you

what, Miss Blair," she suddenly broke out. " Our men
folks are all away. If they are comin' after women, let's
give 'em some women to meet as know how to deal with 'em.
I wants to meet Captain McRaffler, anyhow." Another
shake of the head was given, this time up and down, and
her black eyes began to sparkle. Blair looked at her with
new satisfaction.

" That is what I wish. That is why I came, " she said.
" Can you leave your children ?"

" They are all right," said Mrs. Stamper, with kindling
eyes. " I ain't been on such an expedition not since the
war. I'll leave word for Andy to come as soon as he gits
home."

As they sallied forth, Mrs. Stamper put into her pocket
a big pistol and her knitting. " One gives me courage to
take the other," she said.

It was a mile or two through the woods to the school-
house, and the novel guards arrived at their post none too
soon. As they emerged from the woods into the little
clearing on one side of which stood the church and on the
other the new school-house, the waning moon was just
rising above the tree-tops, casting a ghostly light through
the trees and deepening the shadows. The school-house
was considerably larger than any other in the neighborhood, and over one end of the porch Miss May had trained
a Virginia creeper. The two guards took their seats in
the shadow of the vine. They were both somewhat awed
by the situation, but from different causes. Blair's feeling was due to the strangeness of her situation out
there, surrounded by dark woods filled with the cries of
night insects and the mournful call of the whip-poor-
will. Mrs. Stamper confessed that the graves amid the
weeds around the church were what disquieted her. For
she boasted that she " was not afeared of that man living."
But she admitted mournfully, " I am certainly afeared of
ghosts."

The two sentinels had but a short time to wait. They

had not been there long before the tramp of horses was heard, and in a little while from the woods opposite them emerged a cavalcade of, perhaps, a dozen horsemen. Mrs. Stamper clutched Blair with a grip of terror, for men and horses were heavily shrouded and looked ghostly enough. Blair was trembling, but not from fear, only from excitement. The presence of the enemy suddenly strung her up, and she put her hand on her companion encouragingly. Just then one of the men burst into a loud laugh. Mrs. Delia's grip relaxed.

" I know that laugh," she said, with a sigh of deep relief. " Jest let him ride up here and try some of his shenanigin ! " She began to pull at her pistol, but Blair seized her.

" For heaven's sake, don't," she whispered ; and Mrs. Stamper let the pistol go, and they squeezed back into the shadow. Just then the men rode up to the school-house door. They were discussing what they should do. " Burn the house down," declared the leader. " Drive the old hag away." But this met with fierce opposition.

" I didn't come out here to burn any house down," said one of the men, " and I'm not going to do it. You can put your notice up and come along."

" Ah ! you're afraid," sneered the other.

There was a movement among the horsemen, and the man so charged rode up to the head of the column and pulled his horse in front of the leader. There was a gleam of steel in the light of the moon.

" Take that back, or I'll make you prove it," he said, angrily. " Ride out there and draw your pistol ; we'll let Jim here give the word, and we'll see who's afraid."

Their companions crowded around them to make peace. The leader apologized. The sentiment of the crowd was evidently against him.

" Now get down and fix up your notice to Leech, and let's be going," said one of the peacemakers.

The leader dismounted and started up to the door. As he did so, one of the two young women stepped forward.

SHE GAVE A STEP FORWARD AND WITH A QUICK MOVEMENT PULLED THE
MASK FROM HIS FACE

"What do you want?" asked Mrs. Stamper. The man positively staggered from surprise, and a murmur of astonishment broke from the horsemen. Mrs. Stamper did not give them time to recover. With true soldierly instinct she pressed her advantage. "I know what you want," she said, with scorn. "You want to scare a poor woman who ain't got anybody to defend her. You ain't so much against niggers and carpet-baggers as you make out. I know you."

"You know nothing of the kind," growled the man, angrily, in a deep voice. He had recovered himself. "What business have you here? Go home, wherever that may be, and leave the Invisible Empire to execute its dread decrees."

"Dread fiddlesticks!" exclaimed Mrs. Stamper. "I don't know you, don't I?" She gave a step forward and, with a quick movement, caught and pulled the mask from his face. "I don't know you, Captain McRaffle? And you don't know me, do you?" With an oath the man made a grab for his mask, and, snatching it from her, hastily replaced it. She laughed triumphantly. "No, I didn't know you, Captain McRaffle. I've got cause to know you. And you ought to be ashamed of yourself coming out here to harm a poor woman. So ought all of you; and you are, I know, every mother's son of you. If you want to do anything, why don't you do it to men, and openly, like Andy Stamper and Capt'n Allen?"

"It hasn't been so long since they were in the order," sneered McRaffle.

"Yes, and, when they were, there were gentlemen in it," fired back Mrs. Stamper; "and they went after men, not women."

"We didn't come to trouble any woman; we came to give notice that no more night-meetings and speeches about burning houses were to be held here," growled Mc-Raffle.

"Yes; so you set an example by wanting to burn down

houses yourself ? That's the way you wanted to give notice, if it hadn't been for those gentlemen there."

"She's too much for you, Captain," laughed his comrades.

"We're trying to help out our own people, and to keep
the carpet-baggers from breaking up Miss Cary's school,"
said McRaffle, trying to defend himself.

"No doubt Miss Cary will be much obliged to you."

"No doubt she will. I have good reason to know she
will," affirmed McRaffle ; "and you'll do well not to be
interfering with our work." There was a movement in
the corner behind Mrs. Stamper.

"Ah ! Well, I'll let her thank you in person," said
Mrs. Stamper, falling back with a low bow, as Miss Cary
herself advanced from the shadow. The astonishment of
the men was not less than it had been when Mrs. Stamper
first confronted them.

Blair spoke in a clear, quiet voice that at once enforced
attention. She disclaimed indignantly the charge that
had just been made by the leader, and seconded all that
Mrs. Stamper had said. Her friends, if she had any in the
party, could not, she declared, do her a worse service than
to interfere with this school. She knew that its patrons
had reprobated the advantage that had been taken of their
action in allowing the building to be used as a public hall.

When she was through, several of the riders asked leave
to accompany her and Mrs. Stamper home, assuring her
that the school-house would not be interfered with.

This offer, however, they declined. They were "not
afraid," they said.

"We don't think you need tell us that," laughed several of the men.

Just then there was the sound of horses galloping at
top speed, and in a second Rupert Gray and Andy Stamper
dashed up breathless.

Mrs. Stamper and Miss Cary explained the situation.
Hearing from Mrs. Stamper what McRaffle had said about

Blair, Rupert flashed out that he would settle with Captain McRaffle about it later.

For a moment or two it looked as if there might be a serious misunderstanding. But Blair, seconded by the men who had offered to conduct them home and by Mrs. Stamper, quieted matters; and the cavalcade of masked men rode away in one direction, whilst Andy and Rupert rode off in the other with the two young women behind them, leaving the little school-house as peaceful in the moonlight as if there had never been a sound except the cicalas' cry and the whip-poor-wills call within a hundred miles.

The incident had some far-reaching consequences. Only a day or two later Captain McRaffle went to town; and a short time after there was quite a sensation in the county over a notice in Leech's organ, announcing that Colonel McRaffle, long disgusted with the brutal methods of the outlaws who disgraced the State, had severed his connection with the party that employed such methods; that, indeed, he had long since done so, but had refrained from making public his decision in order that he might obtain information as to the organization, and thus render his country higher service than he could otherwise do.

The next issue of the paper announced the appointment of "the able counsellor, Colonel McRaffle," to the office of Commissioner of the Court, in which position, it stated, his experience and skill would prove of inestimable benefit to the country!

It was, perhaps, well for the new commissioner that his office was in the city.

CHAPTER XXXIV

LEECH AND STILL MAKE A MOVE, AND TWO WOMEN
CHECK THEM

THE departure of Leech and Still from the County was followed by the quieting down which always signalized their absence. The County breathed the freer and enjoyed the calm, knowing that when they returned there would be a renewed girding of loins for the struggle which the approaching campaign would inevitably bring. It was not even disquieted over the rumors of some unusual move which, it was reported, the Government, on the application of Leech and Still, would make to strengthen their hands. These rumors had been going on so long that they were hardly heeded now. It would be time enough to meet the storm when it came, as it had met others; meanwhile, the people of Red Rock would enjoy the calm that had befallen. The calm would be broken when Leech and Still returned for the trial of the Red Rock case at the approaching term of court. Steve Allen and Jacquelin, meanwhile, were applying all their energies to preparation for the trial. Rupert, filled with the desire to do his part, was riding up and down the County notifying their witnesses, and, it must be said, talking with a boy's imprudence of what they were going to do at the trial. "They were going to show that Still was a thief, and were going to run him and Leech out of the County," etc.

Rupert left home one morning to go to the railway, promising to return that evening. Jacquelin sat up for him, ut he did not come; and as he did not appear next morn-

410

ing, and no word had come from him, Jacquelin rode
down in the evening to see about him. At the station he
learned that Rupert had been there, but had left a little
before dark, the evening before, to return home. He had
fallen in with three or four men who had just come from
the city on the train, and were making inquiries concern-
ing the various places and residents in the upper end of
the County, something about all of which they had appeared to know. They said they were interested in timber
lands and had a good deal of law business they wished attended to, and they wanted advice as to who were the best
lawyers of the County ; and Rupert said he could tell them
all about the lawyers : that General Legaie and Mr. Bagby
were the best old lawyers, and his brother and Steve Allen
were the best young lawyers. They asked him about
Leech and McRaffle.

Leech wasn't anything. Yes, he was—he was a thief,
and so was Still. Still had stolen his father's bonds ; but
wait until he himself got on the stand, he'd show him up !
McRaffle was a turncoat hound, who had stolen money
from a woman and then tried to run her out of the
County.

One of the men who lived about the station told Jacquelin that he had gone up and tried to get Rupert away from
the strangers, and urged him to go home, but that the boy
was too excited by this time to know what he was doing.

"He was talking pretty wildly," he said, "and was
abusing Leech and Still and pretty much all the Rads. I
didn't mind that so much, but he was blowing about that
old affair when the negro soldiers were shot, and about
the K.K.'s and the capture of the arms, and was telling
what he did about it. You know how a boy will do !
And I put in to stop him, but he wouldn't be hearsaid.
He said these men were friends of his and had come up to
employ you all in a lawsuit, and knew Leech and Still
were a parcel of rascals. So I let him alone, and he went
off with 'em, along with a wagon they'd hired, saying he

was going to show them the country, and I supposed he was safe home."

By midnight the whole population of that part of the County was out, white and black, and the latter were as much interested as the former. All sorts of speculation was indulged in, and all sorts of rumors started. Some thought he had been murdered, and others believed he and his companion had gotten on a spree and had probably gone off together to some adjoining county, or even had turned at some point and gone to the city; but the search continued. Meantime, unknown to the searchers, an unexpected ally had entered the field.

That evening Ruth Welch was sitting at home quietly reading when a servant brought a message that a man was at the door asking to see Major Welch. It happened that Major Welch was absent in town, and Mrs. Welch had driven over that afternoon to see a sick woman. So Ruth went out to see the man. He was a stranger, and Ruth was at once struck by something peculiar about him. He was a little unsteady on his feet, his voice was thick, and, at first, he did not appear to quite take in what Ruth told him. He had been sent, he repeated several times, to tell "Mazhur Welth" that they had taken his advice and had made the first arrest, and bagged the man who had given the information that started that riot, and had gotten evidence enough from him to hang him and to haul in the others too.

"But I don't understand," said the girl. "What is all this about? Who's been arrested, and who is to be hung? My father has never advised the arrest of anyone."

"Tha's all I know, miss," said the man. "At least, tha's all I was to tell. I was told to bring him that message, and I guess it's so, 'cause they've got the young fellow shut up in a jail since last night and as drunk as a monkey, and don't anybody know he's there—tha's a good joke, ain't it?—and to-morrow mornin' they'll take him to the city and lodge him in the jail there, and 't 'll go pretty hard with him. Don't anybody know he's there, and they're huntin' everywheres for him." He appeared to think this a great joke.

"But I don't understand at all whom you mean ?"

"The young one. They bagged him, and they're after the two older ones too," he said, confidentially. He was so repulsive that Ruth shrank back.

"The one they calls Rupert ; but they're after the two head devils—his brother and that Allen one. Them's the ones the colonel and your friend over there want to jug." He jerked his thumb in the direction of Red Rock.

It all flashed on the girl in a moment.

"Oh ! They have arrested Mr. Rupert Gray, and they want Mr. Jacquelin Gray and Captain Allen ? Who has arrested him ?"

"The d—tectives. But them's the ones had it done— Major Leech and Mist' Still." He winked elaborately, in a way that caused Ruth to stiffen with indignation.

"What was it for ?" she asked, coldly.

"For murder—killin' them men three or four years back. They've got the dead wood on 'em now—since the young one told all about it."

"Has he confessed ? What did he say ?"

"Enough to hang him and them too, I heard. You see they tanked him up and led him on till he put his head in the noose. Oh ! they're pretty slick ones, them detectives is. They got him to pilot 'em most to the jail door, and then they slipped him in there, to keep him till they take him to the city to-morrow. He was so drunk— don't nobody know who he was, and he didn't know himself. And they huntin' all over the country for him !" He laughed till he had to support himself against the door.

The expression on Ruth's face was such that the man noticed it.

"Oh ! don't you mind it, miss. I don't think they're after the young one. They're after the two elder ones, and if he gives it away so they ever get them they'll be easy on him."

Ruth uttered an exclamation of disgust.

"He'll never give it away——" She checked herself.

"Don't know—a man'll do a heap to save his own neck." He made a gesture, drawing his hand across his throat significantly.

"I know that young man, and I say he'll die before he'd betray anyone—much less his cousin and brother."

"Well, maybe so."

Just as the messenger turned away Ruth caught sight of someone standing in the shrubbery, and as the man went out of the gate the person came forward. It was Virgy Still. She appeared to be in a state of great agitation, and began to tell Ruth a story in which her father and Rupert Gray and Major Leech were all mixed up so incoherently that, but that Ruth had just heard the facts, she could never have been able to unravel it. At length Ruth was able to calm her and to get her account. She had sent a man over to tell Ruth, but she was so afraid he had not come that she had followed him. "They want to get rid of Mr. Rupert. It has something to do with the case against pa and your father. They are afraid Mr. Rupert will give evidence against them, and they mean to put him in jail and keep him from doing it. Do you know what it is ?"

Ruth shook her head.

"I do not either. I heard them talking about it, but I did not understand what it was. They ain't after Mr. Rupert ; they're after Mr. Jacquelin and Captain Allen."

She suddenly burst into tears.

"Oh, Miss Ruth," she sobbed, "you don't know—you don't know——"

"I don't know what ?" asked Ruth, gently.

"He is the only one that was always kind to me."

"Who ?"

"Mr. Jacquelin. He was always good to me ; when I

was a little bit of girl he was always kind to me. And now
he hates me, and I never wanted the place !"

"Oh, I don't think he does," said Ruth, consolingly.

"Yes, he does; I know he does," sobbed the girl.
"And I never wanted the place. I have been miserable
ever since I went there."

Ruth looked at her with new sympathy. The idea that
the poor girl was in love with Jacquelin had never crossed
her mind. She felt an unspeakable pity for her.

"And now they want me to marry Mr. Leech," moaned
the girl, "and I hate him—I hate him ! Oh, I wish we
never had had the place. I know he would not want to
marry me if pa did not have it, and could not help him
get the governorship. And I hate him. I hope we'll lose
the case."

"I would not marry anyone I did not want to marry,"
said Ruth.

"Oh, you don't know," said Virgy. "You don't know
Wash. And pa wants me to marry him too ; he says he'll
be Governor. Pa loves me, but he won't hear to my not
marrying. And I'll have to do it—unless we lose the
case," she added.

She rose and went away, leaving Ruth with a new idea
in her mind.

Ruth sat still for a few moments in deep thought. Suddenly she sprang up, and, calling a servant, ordered her
horse. While it was being got she seized a pencil and
scribbled a few lines on a piece of paper, which she put
in her pocket.

She blushed to find what an interest she took in the
matter, and how warmly her feeling was enlisted on the
side opposed to that which she felt she ought to espouse.
And she hated herself to recognize the cause. She tried
to think that it was on account of the poor wild boy, or on
account of Blair Cary and Miss Thomasia; but no, she
knew it was not on their account—at least, not mainly so—
but on account of another.

When her horse came, Ruth muttered something to the servant about telling her mother that she would be back in a little while ; sprang into the saddle and galloped away, leaving the negro gazing after her with wonderment, and mumbling over the message she had given him.

Blair Cary was one of the best horsewomen in the State, and it was fortunate for Ruth Welch's project that night that, emulating her friend, she also had become a capital horsewoman, self-possessed and perfectly fearless ; else she could not have managed the high-mettled, spirited horse she rode.

Ruth knew her road well, and as soon as she turned into the highway that led to the county seat she let her horse out, and they fairly flew. She passed a number of men, riding all of them toward the court-house, but she dashed by them too rapidly for them to speak to her or to recognize her in the dark. As she came near the village the riders increased in numbers, so she drew in her horse and turned into a by-lane which skirted the back of the court-green and led near the lawyers' offices. Jumping her horse over the low fence, she tied him to a swinging limb of a tree where he would be in the shadow, and, with a pat or two to quiet him and keep him from whinnying, she made her way on foot into the court-green. There were a number of lights and many men moving about over across the street that ran between the tavern and the court-green ; but not a light was visible in any of the offices. Ruth walked down as far as she dared, keeping close beside the fence, and tried to recognize some of the men who were moving about on the tavern veranda or in the road before it ; but there was not one that she knew. While she was listening the sound of a horse galloping rapidly came from the direction of the road that led to the railway, and the next minute the rider dashed up. Ruth's heart gave a bound as she recognized Captain Allen. His coming seemed to give her a sense of security and protection. She felt reassured and certain that now everything would be all right. As Steve sprang from his horse, he was surrounded by the crowd with eager questions. His first words, however, damped Ruth's hopes.

No, no trace had been found of Rupert. Jacquelin and many others were still searching for him, and would keep it up. No, he felt sure he had not been murdered by any negro—that he had not been murdered at all. He would be found in time, etc. All this in answer to questions.

Suddenly he singled out one man and drew him away from the crowd, and to Ruth's horror they came across the road straight toward where she stood. She gave herself up for lost. She turned and would have fled, but she could not. Instead, she simply dropped down on the ground and cowered beside the fence. They came and leant against the fence within ten feet of her, on the other side, and began to talk. The other person was a stranger to Ruth ; but his voice was that of an educated man, and Steve Allen called him Helford, which Ruth remembered to have heard somewhere before.

"Well, where is he ?" the stranger asked Steve, as soon as they were out of earshot of the crowd.

"Somewhere, shut up—hidden," said Allen.

"Drunk ?"

"Yes, and that's not the worst of it."

"What do you mean ? He'll turn up all right."

"You think so ! He'll turn up in jail, and you and I shall too, if we don't mind. He's been trapped and spirited away—by detectives, sent up here on purpose."

"What ! Oh, nonsense ! You're daft about the boy. Many another young fellow's gone off and disappeared, to turn up with nothing worse than a splitting head and somewhat damaged morals. You yourself, for instance, when you were not much older than he——"

"Never mind about that," interrupted Steve ; "wait until I tell you all, and you'll see. I'm not given to being scary, I think."

He went on to tell of Rupert's falling in with the men

27

at the station, and of his disappearance, including all that his friends had learned of him both before and after he left. The man gave a low whistle of amazement and dismay.

"The little fool! What makes you think they were detectives?" He was groping for a shred of encouragement.

"I know it," said Steve; and he gave his reasons.

Ruth was astonished to see how closely his reasoning followed and unravelled the facts as she knew them.

"Well, where is he now? Back in the city?"

"No. They haven't got him there yet. They have hid him somewhere and are keeping him drunk, and will try taking him off by night."

"Well, what are you going to do?"

"Find him and take him away from them," said Steve. "If Leech or Still were in the County I'd find him in an hour; but they're both in the city—been away a fortnight hatching this thing."

"All right, I'm with you. But where'll we look? You say Leech and Still are both away in the city, and you don't think he's at either of their places? Where can he be?"

"I don't know, but I'll find out if he's above ground," said Steve, "and some day I'll call Jonadab Leech and Hiram Still to a settling."

"I'll tell you, Allen, where you may find him, or, at any rate, find a trace of him. At that new carpet-bagger's, Mr. Welch's."

"Nonsense! Why don't you look in my office?"

"You may say so; but I'll tell you you'd better look. You all over here think he's different from the rest: but I tell you he isn't. When it comes to these questions, they're all tarred with the same stick, and a d——d black stick it is."

Ruth stirred with indignation. She wished she could have sprung up and faced him.

"We won't discuss that," said Steve, coldly. "Major Welch certainly differs widely from you and me on all political questions—perhaps on many other questions. But he is a gentleman, and I'll stake my life on his being ignorant of anything like this. Gentlemen are the same the world over in matters of honor."

"Well, maybe so—if you think so," said the other, impressed by Steve's seriousness. "But I don't see why you should think he's so different from all the rest of them. You didn't use to find one Yankee so much better than another."

Steve declared haughtily that he did not wish to discuss that question further, and that he would have his horse fed and go to his office to make out a few notices and be ready to start off again in an hour.

"The roads are all picketed, and if they get him to the city it will be by a route they won't want to take themselves," he said grimly, as he turned away.

"Suppose he's already in jail somewhere?" asked his friend.

"We'll take him out," said Steve, stopping short. "There isn't a jail in this commonwealth that will hold him, if I discover where he is."

"All right, we'll be with you, old fellow," said his friend, his good-humor restored; "and if we could get a pull at some of your carpet-bag friends at the same time so much the better. You are not the only one who holds a due-bill of McRaffle's, and has a score against Leech. He arrested my father and kept him in jail a week." His voice had suddenly grown bitter.

When they moved off, Ruth rose and crept hurriedly away, stealing along by the fence until she was in the shadow of the offices. She knew she had not a moment to lose. She went up to the offices and scanned the doors. Fortunately, by even the faint glimmer of the stars she could make out the big names on the signs. She tried the door on which was the name of "Allen and Gray," and, finding it locked, slipped her envelope under it and crept quickly away.

She was just in time, for she heard steps behind her and caught sight of a tall figure striding across the green toward the door she had just left. She found and mounted her horse and rode away, keeping well in the shadow of the trees. As she turned into the road at a sharp canter she almost ran over an old negro who was walking rapidly toward the village. It was so close that she could not avoid calling out to him; but she was not quite in time, for her horse touched him enough to topple him over. Ruth pulled in instantly and, turning around, went back to the man, who was scrambling to his feet grumbling and mumbling to himself:

"Who d'name o' King dat ridin' over me ?"

Ruth recognized old Waverley.

"Oh! Are you hurt, uncle ? I hope not. I'm so sorry. It was so dark I couldn't see you," she said, solicitously. The tone removed the old man's irritation immediately.

"Yes'm—'tis mighty dark, sho nough. Nor'm, I ain hut none—jes kind o' skeered, dat's all. I did'n hut yo' hoss, did I ? Ken you tell me, is dee done heah anything o' my young marster ? I jes hurryin' down heah to git de lates' wud 'bout him."

Ruth told him that his young master had not been seen yet; but that he would certainly be found within the next twenty-four hours, and that she was sure he would be discovered to be all right.

"Well, I certney is glad to heah you say dat, mistis," said the old fellow, "'cause my mistis is almost distracted, and so is he mammy and all de fam'ly. I done walked down heah three times to-day to git de news, an' I know I ain' gwine shet my eyes till he found. Hits all de wuck of dat Cun'l Leech an' dat debble, Hiram Still, an' he son. I knows 'em," he broke out, fiercely, "and I'll git at de bottom of it yit." He came near and gazed up at Ruth

with a look of such keen scrutiny, that to get away from
him Ruth made her horse start. "I shall have to let him
go," she said, and at a touch of her heel her horse bounded
away.

"I knows your hoss and I knows you too, now," said
the old man, looking after her as she dashed away in the
darkness. "Well, well!" and he went on into the village.

When Ruth reached home, to her relief she found that
her mother had not yet returned. A message had come
that Miss Bush was ill and she would be detained until
very late, but would certainly be back by bed-time.

CHAPTER XXXV

CAPTAIN ALLEN FINDS RUPERT AND BREAKS THE LAW

WHEN Steve Allen stepped across his threshold he caught the gleam of something white lying on the floor just inside the door-sill. He picked up the slip of paper and, striking a light, looked at it. The writing on it was in a cramped backhand that Steve did not know and could hardly read. At last, however, he made it out:

"Your friend is in jail here on charge of murder. Will be taken to city to-night for trial." It had been signed, "A Friend," but this had been much scratched over and was almost illegible. Steve read the words again and again. Suddenly he left his office and walked quickly around the back part of the court-green, looking in all the corners and dark places. It had occurred to him that he had heard someone retreating as he approached his office. Everything, however was quiet, and the only sound he heard was that of a horse galloping on the road some distance away. As he stood still to listen again it died away. In a few minutes he had called his friend Helford into his office and laid before him his information. Helford received it coldly—thought it might be a trick to throw them off the track and obtain delay. He argued that even if it would have been possible for Rupert Gray to be put in jail right under their noses, he could not have been kept there all day without its being discovered. Steve was of a different opinion. Perdue, the jailer, was a creature of Leech's and Still's. Something assured him that the information was true, and he laid his plans accordingly. The men who were at the county seat were requested to wait, without being told what was the reason;

riders were sent off to call in the searchers who were still engaged, a rendezvous near the village being appointed. Steve, leaving the men present under charge of Helford, rode off as if to continue the search ; but a short distance down the road he turned, and, riding back by another way, tied his horse and returned to the court-green. He entered at the rear, walked up to the jail and rang the bell. After some delay a man peeped at him through the wicket and asked who it was. Steve gave his name, and said he wanted to see the prisoner who had been brought in the night before. The man hesitated a second, then said there was no such prisoner there. He took a half step backward to close the shutter, but Steve was too quick for him. He was sure from the jailer's manner that he was lying to him. The next second there was a scraping sound on the grating and the man found a pistol-barrel gleaming at him through the bars, right under his nose.

"Stir, and you are a dead man," said Steve. "Open the door."

"I ain't got the keys."

"Call for them. Don't stir ! I'll give you till I count five : one—two—three——"

"Here they are, sir." The pistol-barrel was shining right in his face, and Steve's eyes were piercing him through the bars. He unlocked the door, and Steve stepped in.

"Take me to Mr. Gray's cell instantly, and remember a single word from you means your death." Steve expected to be taken to one of the front rooms in which the prisoners of better condition were usually kept ; but his guide went on, and at length stopped at the door of one of the worst cells in the place, where the most abandoned criminals were usually confined. Two negro prisoners, in another cell, seeing Captain Allen, howled at him in glee through their bars.

"You don't mean to say that you've put him in here ?" Steve asked, sternly.

"That's orders," said the man, and added, explanatorily, as he fumbled at the lock. "You see, he was pretty wild when they brought him here."

"Don't defend it," said Steve, in a voice which brought the turnkey up shaking.

"No, suh—no, suh—I ain' defendin' it. I jest tellin' you." He unlocked the door.

"Walk in," said Steve, and, pushing the other ahead, he stepped in behind him and took his light. It was so dark that he could not at first make out anything inside ; but after a moment a yet darker spot in the general gloom became dimly discernible.

"Rupert?" Steve called. At the voice the dark shadow stirred. "Rupert Gray?"

There was a cry from the dark corner.

"Steve ! Oh, Steve ! Steve !"

"Come here," said Steve, who was keeping close beside the jailer.

"I can't. Oh, Steve !"

"Why not ?—Over there !" he said, with a motion to the jailer, to walk before him.

"I'm chained."

"What !" The young man turned and caught the jailer by the shoulder, and with a single twist of his powerful arm sent him before him spinning into the corner of the room. Stooping, Steve felt the boy and the chain by which he was bound to a great ring in the wall. The next second he faced the keeper.

"Dog !"

For a moment the man thought he was as good as dead. Steve's eyes blazed like coals of fire, and he looked like a lion about to spring. The man began to protest his innocence, swearing with a hundred oaths that he had nothing to do with it; that it was all Leech's doings—his orders and other men's work. He himself had tried to prevent it.

Steve cut him short.

"Liar, save yourself the trouble.   What are their names ?   Where are they ? "

"I don't know.   They've gone, I don't know where. They went away this mornin' before light."

"Get the key and unlock that chain."

The man swore that he did not have it—the men had taken it with them.

Steve reflected a moment.   He had no time to lose.

"Oh, Steve ! never mind me," broke in Rupert, his self-possession recovered.   "Go—I'm not worth saving.   Oh, Steve ! if you only knew ! I have done you an irreparable injury.   I don't mind myself, but——" His voice failed him and his words ended in a sob.   "I'm not crying because I'm here or am afraid," he said, presently.   "But if you only knew——"

Steve Allen leant down over him and, throwing his arm around him, kissed him as if he had been a child.

"That's all right," he said, tenderly, and whispered something which made the boy exclaim :

"Oh, Steve ! Steve !"   The next moment he said, solemnly, "I promise you that I will never touch another drop of liquor again as long as I live."

"Never mind about that now," said Steve.

"But I want to promise.   I want to make you that promise.   It would help me, Steve.   I have never broken my word."

"Wait until you are free," said Steve, indulgently.   He turned to the keeper, who still stood cowering in the corner.

"Come—walk before me."   As they left the cell he said to him : "In a half-hour two hundred men will be here. These doors will go like paper.   If they find that boy chained and you are here, your life will not be worth a button.   Nothing but God Almighty could save you."   He left him at the front door and went out.   A number of men were already assembling about the jail.   It transpired afterward that old Waverley had seen Steve enter the jail, and, fearing that he might not get out again, had told

Andy Stamper, who had just arrived. As Steve came out of the door Andy stepped up to him.

" We were going in after you," he said.

. Steve took him aside and had a talk with him, telling him the state of the case and putting him in charge until his return.

" If Perdue wants to come out, let him do so," he said, as he left him. As he walked across the green he fell in with Waverley, who gave an exclamation of joy.

" I sutney is glad to see you. I was mighty feared dee'd keep you in dyah." He was very full of something he wanted to tell him. Steve did not have time to listen then, but said he wanted him, and took him along.

" Well, jes' tell me dis, Marse Steve ; is you foun' my young marster ? "

" Yes, we have."

" Well, thank Gord for dat ! " exclaimed old Waverley. " Whar is he ? "

Steve pointed back to the jail. " In there."

The old man gave an outcry.

" In dyah ! My young marster ? My marster and mistis' son ! Go way, Marse Steve—you jokin' ; don't fool me 'bout dat."

" He's in there, and in chains ; and I want you to cut them off him," said Steve.

The old man broke out into a tirade. He ended :

" Dat I will ! De's a blacksmiff shop yonder. I'll git a hammer and cole chisel d'rectly." He started off. When he arrived, the shop had already been levied on for sledges and other implements.

The crowd was beginning to be excited. Steve took charge at once. He spoke a few words in a calm, level, assured tone ; stated the fact of Rupert Gray's arrest by Leech's order, not for his own offence, but more for that of others, of his imprisonment in irons in the jail, and of his own intention to take him out. And he declared his belief that it was the desire of those assembled, that he should command them, and expressed his readiness to do so.

The response they gave showed their assent.

Then they must obey his orders.

They would, they said.

"The first is—absolute silence."

"Yes, that's right," came from all sides.

"The second is, that we will release our friend, but take no other step—commit no other violence than that of breaking the doors and taking him out."

"Oh, h—l! We'll hang every d——d nigger and dog in the place," broke in a voice near him. Steve wheeled around and faced the speaker. He was a man named Bushman, a turbulent fellow. As quick as thought the pistol that had been shining under Perdue's nose a little before was gleaming before this man's eyes.

"Step out and go home!" Steve pointed up the road.

The man began to growl.

"Go," said Steve, imperiously, and the crowd applauded.

"That's right, send him off." They opened a path through which the ruffian slunk, growling, away.

"Now, men, fall in."

They fell in like soldiers, and Steve marched them off to the spot he had appointed as the place for others to join them.

The rendezvous was in a pine forest a little off the road, and only a quarter of a mile or so back of the village. Near the road the pines were thick, having sprung up since the war ; but here, in a space of some hundreds of yards each way, the trees, the remnants of a former growth, were larger and less crowded, leaving the ground open and covered with a thick matting of "tags," on which the feet fell as noiselessly as on a thick carpet, and where even the tramp of horses made hardly a sound. It was an impressive body assembled there in the darkness, silent and grim, the stillness broken only by the muffled stamping and tramping of a restless horse, by an almost inau-

dible murmur, or an order given in a low, quiet tone.
By a sort of soldierly instinct the line had fallen into almost regimental form, and, from time to time, as new
recruits came up, directed by the pickets on the roads outside, they, too, fell into order.

Just as they were about to move, a horseman galloped
up, and a murmur went through the ranks.

" Dr. Cary !"

Whether it was surprise, pleasure, or regret, one at first
could scarcely have told.

" Where is Captain Allen ? " asked the Doctor, and
pushed his way to the head of the line. A colloquy took
place between him and Steve in subdued but earnest tones,
the Doctor urging something, Steve replying, while the
men waited, interested, but patient. The older man was
evidently protesting, the other defending. At length Dr.
Cary said :

" Well, let me speak a word to them."

" Certainly," assented Steve, and turned to the men.

" Dr. Cary disagrees with us as to the propriety of
the step we are about to take and urges its abandonment.
He desires to present his views. You will hear him with
the respect due to the best and wisest among us." He
drew back his horse, and the Doctor rode forward and began to speak.

" First, I wish you to know that I am with you, heart
and soul—for better, for worse ; flesh of your flesh, and
bone of your bone. Next to my God and my wife and
child, I love my relatives and neighbors. Of all my relatives, perhaps, I love best that boy lying in yonder jail,
and I would give my life to save him. But I could not
kneel to my God to-night if I did not declare to you my
belief—my profound conviction—that this is not the way
to go about it. I know that the wrongs we are suffering cry to God, but I urge you to unite with me in
trying to remedy them by law, and not by violence. Let us
unite and make an appeal to the enlightened sense of the

American people, of the world, which they will be forced to hear. Violence on our side is the only ground which they can urge for their justification. It is a terrible weapon we are furnishing them, and with it, not only can they defeat us now, but they can injure us for years to come."

He went on for ten or fifteen minutes, urging his views with impressive force. Never was a stronger appeal made. But it fell on stony ears. The crowd was touched by him, but remained unchanged. It had resolved, and its decision was unaltered. When he ended, there was, for a moment, a low murmur all through the ranks, which died down, and they looked to their captain. Steve did not hesitate. In a firm, calm voice he said :

" For the first time in my life almost, I find myself unable to agree in a matter of principle with the man you have just heard. At the same time, this may be only my personal feeling, and, recognizing the force of what he has said, I wish all who may think as he does to fall out of line. The rest will remain as they are. If all shall leave, feeling as I do I shall still undertake to rescue Rupert Gray. Those who disagree with me will ride forward."

There was a rustle and movement all down the ranks, but not a man stirred from his place. As the men looked along the line and took in the fact, there went up a low, suppressed sound of gratification and exultation.

"Silence, men," said the captain. He turned his horse to face Dr. Cary.

" Dr. Cary, I beg you to believe that we all recognize the wisdom of your views and their unselfishness, and we promise you that no violence shall be offered a soul beyond forcing the doors and liberating the boy."

A murmur of assent came from the ranks. Dr. Cary bowed.

" I shall wait at the tavern," he said, "to see if my services may be of any use."

Steve detailed two men to conduct him through the guards, and he rode slowly away.

A few minutes later Captain Allen gave the order, and, wheeling, the column marched off through the dusk.

Steve had made the men disguise themselves by tying strips of cotton across their faces. He himself wore no mask. When he arrived at the jail he learned from Andy Stamper that Perdue had taken advantage of the hint given him and had escaped.

"I had hard work at first to git him out," said Andy. "I had to go up to the door and talk to him; but when he found what was comin', he was glad enough to go. I let him slip by, and last I seen of him, he was cuttin' for the woods like a fox with the pack right on him. If he kept up that lick he's about ten miles off by this time."

The breaking into the jail was not a difficult matter. It meant only a few minutes' work bursting open the outer door with a heavy sledge-hammer, and a little more in battering down the iron inner doors. During the whole time the crowd without was as quiet as the grave, the silence broken only by the orders given and the ringing blows of the iron hammers. But it was very different inside. The two or three negroes confined within were wild with terror. They all thought that the mob was after them, and that their last hour was come; and they who an hour before had hooted at the visitor, yelled and prayed and besought mercy in agonies of abject terror. When the squad detailed by Steve passed on to the cell in which Rupert was confined and began to break down the door, these creatures quieted a little, but even then they prayed earnestly, their faces, ashy with fear in the glare of the torches, pressed to the bars and their eyeballs almost starting from their sockets. When the door gave way the low cry that came up from the party sent them flying and trembling back into the darkness of their cells.

It took a considerable time to cut the irons that bound the prisoner, who, under the excitement of the rescuing party's entrance, had been overjoyed, but a moment later had keeled over into Andy Stamper's arms. Under the

steady blows of the old blacksmith's hammer, even that was
at length accomplished, and the rescuers moved out bearing Rupert with them.   As they emerged from the building with the boy in their arms, the long-pent-up feeling of
the crowd outside burst forth in one wild cheer, which
rang through the village and was heard miles away on the
roads.   It was quickly hushed ; the crowd withdrew into
the woods, and in a few minutes the jail was left in the
darkness as silent as the desert.

The news of the assault on the jail and the liberation of
the prisoner thrilled through the County next morning,
and the thrill extended far beyond the confines of the section immediately interested.   The party of detectives who
were waiting to take their prisoner to the city made their
way by night through the country to a distant station, to
take the cars ; and Leech and McRaffle, who had come on
the morning train to meet them, deemed it prudent to
catch it on its way back and return to the city.

Ruth, the morning after her visit to the court-house and
the rescue of Rupert, was in a state of great unrest.
Finally she mounted her horse and paid a visit to Blair
Cary.   They were all in intense excitement.   Ruth herself was sensible of constraint ; but she had an object in
view which made it necessary to overcome it.   So she
chatted on easily, almost gayly.   At length she made an
excuse to get Blair off by herself.   In the seclusion of
Blair's room the secret came out.   Ruth, on her part,
learned that Rupert was to be sent off ; Blair did not know
where.   One difficulty was the want of means to send
him.   This Ruth had divined.   With a burning face, she
told Blair she had a great favor to ask of her ; and when
Blair wonderingly assented, she took from her pocket a roll
of money—what seemed to Blair an almost vast amount.
It was her own, she said ; and the favor was : that Blair
would help her to get that money to Rupert without anyone knowing where it came from.   She wanted Rupert to
go out to the West and join Reely Thurston there.   Blair

demurred at this. Captain Thurston was an army officer, and Rupert was——. She paused. Ruth flushed.
She would be guaranty that Thurston would stand his
friend.

There was also another thing which Blair discovered,
though she did not tell Ruth that she had done so. She
simply rose and kissed her. This discovery decided her to
accept Ruth's offer. It seemed to draw Ruth nearer to
her and to make her one with themselves. So she told
Ruth where Rupert was. He was at that time at the
house of Steve's old mammy, Peggy. He was to be conducted out of the County that night. Whether he could
be persuaded to go to Captain Thurston, Blair did not
know ; but she promised to aid Ruth so far as to suggest
it, and try to persuade him to do so. There were two
difficulties. One was that she might be watched, and it
might lead to Rupert's re-arrest. She did not state what
the other was. But Ruth knew. She, too, could divine
things without their being explained. If, however, Blair
could not meet Jacquelin Gray, there was no reason
why Ruth herself could not. And she determined to
go. Suddenly Blair changed. She, too, would go. She
could not let Ruth go alone.

That evening, toward dusk, old Peggy was " turning
about " in her little yard, when the sound of horses' feet
caught her ear. As quick as thought the old woman ran
to her door and spoke a few words to some one inside, and
the next moment the back door opened and a figure
sprang across the small cleared space that divided the
cabin from the woods, and disappeared among the trees.
In a little while the riders appeared in sight, and when
the old negress turned, to her surprise, they were two
ladies. When they took off their veils, to old Peggy's
still greater astonishment, they were Miss Blair and the
young lady who had visited her with her young master
the evening of the rain-storm.

The old woman greeted them pleasantly, but when they

said they wanted to see Rupert Gray, her suspicions returned again.

"He ain't heah," she said, shortly. "What you want wid him?" Her eyes gleamed with shrewdness.

"We want to see him."

"Well, you won' see him heah."

They began to cajole.

"Can't you trust me?" asked Blair.

But old Peggy was firm.

"I don' trus' nobody. I ain' got nothin' 't all to do wid it. Why n't you go ax Marse Steve?" she asked Ruth, suddenly. Ruth's face flushed.

The dilemma was unexpectedly relieved by the appearance of Rupert himself. From his covert he had recognized the visitors, and could not resist the temptation to join them. Old Peggy was in a great state of excitement at his appearance. She began to scold him soundly for his imprudence. But the boy only laughed at her.

Blair and Ruth took him aside and began to broach the object of their visit. At first he was obstinate. He would not hear of the plan they proposed. In fact, he was not going away at all, he declared. He would not be run out of the County. He would stay and fight it out, and let them try him, if they wished to get all they wanted. He showed the butt of a pistol, with boyish pride.

In this state of the case, Ruth began to plead with him on his brother's account, and Blair, as her argument, took Steve. They said he was bound in honor to go, if they wished it. Ruth deftly put in a word about Thurston, and the opportunity the trip would give Rupert to see the world. He could join in the campaigns against the Indians out there, if he wished; and, finally, she begged him to go and join Thurston, as a favor to her.

These arguments at length prevailed, and Rupert said he would go.

As his friends were soon to come for him, the girls had to leave, which they did after binding old Peggy over

28

with many solemn promises not to breathe to a single soul
a word of their visit. "If she does," said Rupert, "I'll
come back here and make her think the Ku Klux are
after her." The old woman laughed at the threat.

"Go 'way from heah, boy! What you know 'bout Ku
Klux? You done told too much 'bout 'em now."

This home-thrust shut Rupert up. Blair put into his
hand the package that Ruth had given her and kissed him
good-by, and he turned to Ruth.

Ruth said, as she took his hand, "Rupert, I am going to
ask you to grant me that favor you once promised me you
would grant."

The boy's eyes lit up.

"I will do it."

"I want you to promise me you will not drink any
more."

"I promise," he said, softly, and bent over and kissed
her hand. As he stood up, the girl leant forward and
kissed him. He turned to Blair and, throwing his arms
around her neck, suddenly burst into tears.

"Oh, Blair, Blair," he sobbed, "I can't go."

The girls soothed him, and when they left a little later
he was calm and firm.

Within a little time other detectives came, and some
who were not known as detectives performed the functions
of that office. But no trace of the rescued boy was found.
The nearest approach to a clew was a report that Andy
Stamper and old Waverley, a short time after the breaking
into the jail, took a long journey with Andy's covered
wagon into another State, "selling things," and that Steve
Allen and several other men were about the same time in
the same region, and even rode with the wagon for some
days.

However, this was not traced up. And it illustrates the
times, that two accounts of the affair of the rescue were
published and given circulation: one that the prisoner
was rescued by his friends, the other that he was taken

from the jail by a band of Ku Klux outlaws and murdered, because he had confessed to having taken part in some of their outrages and had given information as to his accomplices. This was the story that was most widely circulated in some parts of the country and was finally accepted.

CHAPTER XXXVI

MR. STILL OFFERS A COMPROMISE, AND A BLUFF

THE term approached at which the Red Rock suit was to be tried, and both parties made preparations for it. A number of the prominent members of the Bar had volunteered as Jacquelin's counsel. They knew the character of the new judge, Bail, and they considered Jacquelin's cause that of every man in the State. Leech, on his side, had associated with him as counsel for Still several lawyers of well-known ability, if of less recognized integrity; and Major Welch had retained old Mr. Bagby to represent his interest. As the term drew near, Still applied to Mr. Bagby to represent him too. The old lawyer declined. The interest of his client, Major Welch, might in some way conflict, though he could not see how; in a way he already represented Still, since to protect his client he had to look after Still's title also. "Besides, Still already had lawyers enough to ruin his case," he said, "and he would charge him a big fee." But these reasons were not sufficient for Still. He wished Mr. Bagby to represent him. He told him Leech had employed those others; but he wanted a man he knew. "There wasn't a man in the State could carry a jury like Mr. Bagby, and he did not mind the fee."

Flattery is a key that fits many locks. So the old lawyer consented, after consulting Major Welch, and notifying Still that if at any time or at any point in the case he found his interest conflicting with Major Welch's he would give him up. Still grew more anxious and sought so many interviews with the old counsellor that finally his patience wore out, and he gave his new client to understand that he had other business, and if he wanted so much of his time he must increase his fees. Still consented even to this, with the effect of arousing suspicion on the old lawyer's part that there must be something in his client's case which he did not understand. "Something in it he has not let out," reflected the old lawyer. "I must get at it."

Not very long after this arrangement, Still asked Mr. Bagby to come and see him at his home on business of great importance, alleging as a reason for his not going to see Mr. Bagby that he was too unwell to travel. The note for some reason offended Mr. Bagby. However, as he had to go to Major Welch's that night, he rode by Red Rock to see Still. He found him in a state of great anxiety and nervousness. Still went over the same ground that he had been over with him already several times ; wanted to know what he thought of the bill, and of the Grays' chances of success. The old lawyer frowned. Up to the time of beginning a suit he was ready to be doubtful, prudent, cautious, even anxious, in advising ; but the fight once begun he was in it to the end ; doubt disappeared ; defeat was not among the possibilities. It was an intellectual contest and he rejoiced in it ; put into it every nerve and every power he possessed, and was ready to trample down every adversary from the sheriff who served the writ, to the Supreme Court itself. So now, when Still, almost at the entrance of the term, was whimpering as to his chances, the old lawyer answered him with scant courtesy.

"The bill ? I think the same of it I thought when you asked me before ; that it is a good bill in certain respects and a poor one in others ;—good as to your accounts showing rents and profits, and too general as to the bonds. It's a good thing you got hold of so much of Gray's paper. I knew he was a free liver and a careless man ; but I had no idea he owed so much money." He was speaking rather to himself.

"What do you mean?" faltered Still, his face flushing and then growing pale.

"That if they can prove what they allege about the crops in the years just before and after the war, they'll sweep you for rents and profits, and you'll need the bonds." He reflected for a minute, then looked at Still.

"Mr. Still, tell me exactly how you came by that big bond." He shut his eyes to listen, so did not see the change that came over his client's face.

"What'd you think of a compromise?" asked Still, suddenly.

"Have they offered one?"

"Well, not exactly," said Still, who was lying; "but I know they'd like to make one. What'd you think of our kind of broaching the subject?"

"What! You? After that bill aspersing your character!" He looked at Still keenly. "Do as you please! But Major Welch will offer no compromise." He rose and walked off from Still for a moment, formulating in his mind some sentence that would relieve him from his relation of counsel to him. It was the first time he had been in the house since Still's occupancy; and as he paced across the hall, the pictures lining the walls arrested his attention, and he began to examine them. He stopped in front of the "Indian-killer," and gazed at it attentively.

"Astonishingly like him!" he muttered, musingly; and then after another look he asked, "Do you know whether there really was a cabinet behind that picture or not?" Still did not answer, but his face turned a sudden white. The old lawyer had his back to him. He stepped up nearer the picture and began to examine the frame more closely. "I believe there is," he said, musingly. "Yes, that red paint goes under." He took out a large pocket-knife. "Those nails are loose. I believe I'll see." He inserted the blade of his knife and began to prize at the frame.

"My G—d ! don't do that ! " exclaimed Still ; and, giving a bound, he seized the old lawyer's arm.

The latter turned on him in blank amazement.   Still's face was as white as death.

"What in the d—l is the matter with you ?" demanded Mr. Bagby.

"Don't ! for God's sake !" stammered Still, and staggered into a chair, the perspiration standing out on his forehead.

"What's the matter with you, man ? " Mr. Bagby poured out a glass of whiskey from a decanter on the table and gave it to him.   The liquor revived him, and in a moment he began to talk.

It was nothing, he said, with a ghastly attempt at a smile.   He had of late been having a sort of spells ; had not been sleeping well—his son was giving him some physic for it ; 'twas a sort of nervousness, and he supposed he just had one, and couldn't help thinking of that story of the picture coming down always meaning bad luck, and the story of the old fellow being seen on horseback at night. Some of the niggers had been saying that he had been seen at night once or twice lately riding around, and he supposed that had got in his mind.   But of course he didn't believe any such lies as that.

"I hope not," sniffed the old lawyer.   He rose and took up his hat and saddlebags.   Still urged him to stay ; he had had his horse put in the stable and fed ; but Mr. Bagby said he must go, he wished to see Major Welch.   He had made up his mind that he would not remain in the case as Still's counsel.   He could not get over the feeling that there was something in Still's case which Still had not confided to him, or the idea of his wishing to compromise after a charge of fraud ; and the rough way in which Still had seized his arm and had spoken to him had offended him.   So he would not be his guest.   He told Still that he felt that he could not act further as his counsel, in association with his other counsel.   Again Still's face blanched.

He offered to throw them all over—except Leech. He was obliged to keep Leech; but the others he would let go. This, however, Mr. Bagby would not hear of.

As it was late, and the servants had retired, Still walked with Mr. Bagby to the stable to get his horse. He continued to urge him to remain in the suit as his counsel. But the old lawyer was firm.

As they approached the stables there came to them from the field over beyond the gardens and toward Major Welch's the distant neigh of a horse. Still clutched Mr. Bagby's arm.

"My G—d! did you hear that?"

"What? Yes—one of your horses over in your pasture?"

"No, there ain't no horses over in that field, or in a field between here and Stamper's house. It's all in crop. That's over toward the graveyard."

"Oh! the d——l!" the old man exclaimed, impatiently. But Still seized him.

"Look! Look yonder!" he gasped. The lawyer looked, and at the moment the outline of a man on horseback was clearly defined against the skyline on the crest of a hill. How far away it was he could not tell; but apparently it was just behind the dark clump of trees where lay the old Gray burying-ground. The next second the moon was shrouded and the horseman faded out.

When Mr. Bagby reached Major Welch's, the latter came out to meet him: he had sat up for him.

"I thought you had come a half-hour ago. I fancied I heard your horse neigh," he said.

As he went to call a servant, he picked up from a small side-porch a parcel wrapped around with paper. He took it in to the light. It was a large bunch of jonquils, addressed to Ruth.

"Ah!" thought the old lawyer, with a chuckle, "that is what our ghostly horseman was doing."

The next morning, when Major Welch and his guest

came to breakfast, the table was already decorated with jonquils, which were lighting it up with their golden glow; and one or two of them were pinned on Miss Ruth's dainty white dress.

Both Major Welch and the guest remarked on the beauty of the flowers, and the Major mentioned his surprise that Ruth should have left them out on the porch overnight. The remark was quite casual, and the Major was not looking at Ruth at the moment; but the old lawyer was looking, and his eyes twinkled as he noticed the deep color that rushed up into the girl's cheeks. No age is too great to be stirred by the sight of a romance, and the old fellow's countenance softened as he looked at the young girl.

"Lucky dog," he thought, "that night rider! I wonder who he is? I'd give my fee in this case to be able to call up that blush. I remember doing that same thing once—forty odd years ago. The flowers faded, and the girl—My dear, will you give me one of those jonquils?" he broke off, suddenly, addressing Ruth. Ruth, with a smile, pinned it on him, and the old man wore it with as proud a mien as he had ever had after a successful verdict."

The apparition was too much for Hiram Still. A few days after his interview with Mr. Bagby, Still, without consulting any of his counsel, took the step on his own account which he had suggested to the lawyer. If it went through, he could put it on the ground of friendship for Jacquelin's father. He selected his opportunity.

Steve Allen was away that day and Jacquelin Gray was sitting in his office alone, when there was a heavy, slow step outside and, after a moment's interval, a knock at the door. "Come in," Jacquelin called; and the door opened slowly and Hiram Still walked half-way in and stopped doubtfully. He was pale, and a simper was on his face. Jacquelin did not stir. His face flushed slightly.

"Good-mornin', Mr. Jacquelin," said the visitor, in his most insinuating tone.

"What do you want?" Jacquelin asked, coldly.

"Mr. Jacquelin, I thought I'd come and see you when you was by yourself like, and see if me and you couldn't come to a understandin' about our suit."

Jacquelin was so taken by surprise that he did not try to answer immediately, and Still took it for assent and moved a step farther into the room.

"I don't want no lawyers between us; we're old friends. I ain't got nothin' against you, and you ain't got nothin' against me; and I don't want no trouble or nothin'. Your father was the best friend I ever had; and I jist thought I'd come like a friend, and see if we couldn't settle things like old friends—kind of compromise, kind o'——?" He waved his hands expressively.

Jacquelin found his voice.

"Get out," he said, quietly, with a sudden paling of his face. Still's jaw dropped. Jacquelin rose to his feet, a gleam in his eyes.

"Get out." There was a ring in his voice, and he took a step toward Still. But Still did not wait. He turned quickly and rushed out of the room, never stopping until he had got out of the court-green.

He went to the bar of the tavern and ordered two drinks in rapid succession.

"D—n him!" he said, as he drained off his glass the second time. "If he had touched me I'd have shot him."

"You're lookin' sort o' puny these days. Been sick?" the man at the bar asked.

"Yes—no—I don' know," said Still, gruffly. He went up and looked at himself in a small fly-speckled, tin-like mirror on the wall. "I ain't been so mighty well."

"Been ridin' pretty hard lately 'bout your suit, I reckon?" said the bar-keeper.

"I don' know. I ain't afeared 'bout it. If they choose to ding away money tryin' to beat me out o' my property, I've got about as much as they have, I reckon."

"I reckon you have." The man's manner was so dry

that Still cut his eye at him. "Why don't you try him with a compromise?" Still looked at him sharply; but he was washing a glass, and his face was as impassive as a mask.

"D—n him! I wouldn't compromise with him to save his life," said Still. "D' you think I'd compromise with a man as is aspersed my character?"

"I d'n' know. I hear there's to be a jury; and I always heard, if there's one thing the L—d don' know, it's how a jury's goin' to decide."

"I ain't afeared of *that* jury," said Still, on whom the whiskey was working. "I've got——" He caught a look of sharpness on the man's face and changed. "I ain't afeared o' no jury—that jury or no other. And I ain't afeared o' Jacquelin Gray nor Mr. Steve Allen neither. I ain't afeared o' no man as walks.'"

"How about them as rides?" asked the bar-keeper, dryly.

The effect was electric.

"What d'you know about them as rides?" asked Still, surlily, his face pale.

"Nothin' but what I hear. I hear they's been a rider seen roun' Red Rock of nights, once or twice lately, ain't nobody caught up with."

"Some o' these scoundrels been a tryin' to skeer me," said Still, with an affectation of indifference. "But they don't know me. I'll try how a bullet 'll act on 'em next time I see one of 'em."

"I would," said the bar-keeper. "You'se seen him, then? I heard you had."

Hiram saw that he had been trapped into an admission. Before he could answer, the man went on:

"They say down this away it means something's goin' to happen. How's that old picture been standing of late?"

Still burst out in a rage, declaring that it had been standing all right, and would continue to stand till every man against him was in the hottest region his imagination could picture. It seemed to him, he said, that everybody in the

County was in league against him. The bar-keeper heard
him unmoved; but, when his customer left, he closed his
door and sauntered over to the office of Allen and Gray.

When Steve returned next day, Jacquelin told him of the
interview with Still. Steve's eyes lit up.

"By Jove ! It means there's something we don't know !
What did you do ? "

"Threatened to kick him out of the room."

"I supposed so. But, do you know, Jack," he said, after
a moment's reflection, "I am not sure you did right ?
As a man I feel just as you did ; but as a lawyer I think
we should try and compromise. The case as it stands is a
doubtful one on the law ; but what show do we stand before his new judge. You know he is hand in glove with
them, and they say was appointed to try this very case.
Remember, there is Rupert."

"I tell you what I will do," said Jacquelin, "and it is
the only compromise I will make. You can go to him and
say I will agree to dismiss the case. If he will give Rupert
the full half of the place, including the house, and me the
graveyard and Birdwood, with three hundred acres of land,
I will dismiss the suit. You can go to him and say so. It
will still leave him more than the value of Birdwood."

"Birdwood ! What do you want with Bird——? " asked
Steve, in amazement ; but at the moment his eye rested
on Jacquelin's face. Jacquelin was blushing. "Oho ! "
he exclaimed. "I see."

"Not at all ! " said Jacquelin. "I have no hope whatever. Everything has gone wrong with me. I feel as if
as soon as I am interested, the very laws of nature become
reversed ! "

"Nonsense ! The laws of nature are never reversed ! "
exclaimed Steve. "It's nothing but our infernal stupidity or weakness. Have you ever said anything to her
since ? "

"No, I am done. She's an iceberg."

"Iceberg ? When I saw her she was a volcano. Besides,

ice melts," said Steve, sententiously.   "I'm engaged in the
process myself."

Jacquelin could not talk lightly of Blair, and he rose
and quietly walked out of the office.   As his footsteps died
away, Steve sat back in his chair and fell into a reverie,
induced by Jacquelin's words and his reply.

Jacquelin had just left the office when there was a step
outside, and a knock so timid that Steve felt sure that it
must be a woman.   He called to the person to come in ;
the knock, however, was repeated ; so Steve called out
more loudly.   The door opened slowly, and a young colored woman put her head in and surveyed the office carefully.   "Is dat you, Marse Steve ?" she asked, and inserted her whole body.   Then turning her back on Steve,
she shut the door.

Steve waited with interest, for his visitor was Martha,
Jerry's wife, who was a maid at Major Welch's.   It was not
the first time Martha had consulted him.   Now, however,
Steve was puzzled, for on former occasions when she
came to see him, Jerry had been on a spree ; but Steve
had seen Jerry only the evening before, and he was sober.
Steve motioned the girl to a seat and waited.

She was so embarrassed, however, that all she could do
was to tug at something which she held securely tied up
in her apron.   Steve tried to help her out.

"Jerry drunk again ?   I thought I had given him a
lesson last time that would last him longer."

"Nor, suh, he ain' drunk—yit.   But I thought I'd
come to 'sult you."   Again she paused, and looked timidly around the room.

"Well, what is it ?   Has he threatened to beat you ? "
he asked, a shade gathering on his brow.   "He knows
what he'll get if he tries that again."

"Nor, suh," said Martha, quickly ; "I ain' feared o'
dat.   He know better 'n dat now—sence you an' my gran'-
mother got hold o' him ; but"—her knot came untied,
and suddenly she gained courage—"what I want to 'sult

you about is dis : I want to ax you,—is Mr. Spickit—'lowed to write ' whiskey' down in my sto'-book ? " She clutched her book, and gazed at Steve as if the fate of the universe depended on the answer.

Steve took the book and glanced over it. It was a small, greasy account-book, such as was kept by persons who dealt at the little country-stores about the County. Many of the items were simply " Mdse.," but on the last two or three pages, the item " Whiskey" appeared with somewhat undue frequency.

" What do you mean ? " asked Steve.

" Well, you see, it's disaway. Jerry, he gits his whiskey at Mr. Spickit's—*some* o' it—an' he say Mr. Spickit *shell* write hit down on de book dat way, an——"

" Oh ! You don't want him to have it ? " said Steve, a light breaking on him.

" Nor, suh—dat ain't it. I don' mine he havin' de *whiskey*—I don' mine he gittin' all he want—cuz I know he gwine *drink* it. But I don' want him to have it put down dat away on de *book*. I is a member o' de chutch, and I don' want whiskey writ all over my book—dat's hit ! "

" Oh ! " Steve smiled acquiescingly.

" An' I done tell Jerry so ; an' I done tell Mr. Spickit so, an' ax him not to do it."

" Well, what do you want ? "

" I wants him to put it down ' merchandise,' dat's all ; an' I come to ax you, can't you meck Jerry do it dat away."

" Ah ! I see. Why, certainly I can."

" An' I want to ax you dis : Jerry say, ef I don' stop meddlin' wid he business, he won' let me have no sto'-book, an' he gwine lef' me ; dat he'll meck you git a divo'ce from me—an' I want to ax you ef he ken lef' me jes cuz I want him to mark it merchandise ? Kin he git a divorce jes for dat ? " She was far too serious for Steve to laugh now. Her face was filled with anxiety.

" Of course, he cannot."

" Well, will you write me dat down, so I ken show it to him ? "

Steve gravely wrote a few lines, which, after reading to her, he folded with great solemnity and handed her.

They read as follows :

" LEGAL OPINION.

"I am of opinion that it is not a cause for divorce, either *a vinculo matrimonii* or *a mensâ et thoro*, when a woman insists that the whiskey which her husband drinks, and which she pays for, shall be entered on her account-book as *Mdse*. Given under my hand this —— day of ——, 18—.

" STEVENSON ALLEN,
" *Attorney and Counsellor-at-Law*."

The young woman received the paper with the greatest reverence and relief.

" Thankee, Marse Steve," she said, with repeated bows and courtesies. " Dis will fix him. I knowed dat if I come to you, you'd tell me de law. Jerry talk like he know all de law in de wull ! " Armed with her weapon, her courage was returning. " But I'll straighten him out wid dis." She tied her letter up in her apron with elaborate care. Suddenly her face grew grave again.

" 'Spose Jerry say he'll trick me cuz I come to you ? "

" Trick you—— ! " began Steve, in a tone of contempt.

" Not he himself ; but dat he'll git Doct' Moses to do it ? " Her face had grown quite pale.

" If he says he'll trick you, tell him I'll lick him. You come to me."

" Yes, suh." She was evidently much relieved, but not wholly so. " I cert'ny is feared o' him," she said, plaintively. " He done tricked Jane—Sherrod's wife—and a whole lot o' urrs," she said. Steve knew from her face that the matter was too serious to be laughed at.

"You tell Jerry that if he dares to try it, or even threatens you with it, I'll lick the life out of him and discharge him. And as for Moses——" His face darkened.

"I don't want you to do that," she said, quickly.

"Well, you tell him so, anyhow. And if I get hold of Moses, he won't trouble you."

"Yas, suh, I'll tell him ef he try to trick me. 'Cus I cert'ny is feared o' dat man." She was going out, when Steve called her back.

"Ah! Martha? How are they all at Major Welch's?"

"Dee's all right well, thankee, suh," said Martha. "Sept Miss Ruth—she ain been so mighty well lately." Steve's face brightened.

"Ah! What is the matter with her?" His voice was divided between solicitude and feigned indifference.

"I don' know, indeed, suh. She's jes sort o' puny—jes heah lately. She don't eat nuttin'. Dee talk 'bout sen'in' her 'way."

"Indeed!" Steve was conscious of a sudden sinking of the heart.

"I think she ride 'bout too much in de hot sun," explained Martha, with the air of an authority.

"I have no doubt of it," said Steve.

"She come home tother evenin' right down sick, and had to go to bed," continued Martha.

"Ah! when was that? Why don't they send for a doctor?—Dr. Still?" asked Steve, guilefully.

"Go 'way, Marse Steve, you know dee ain gwine let dat man practus on Miss Ruth. Dat's what de matter wid her now. He come dyah all de time teckin' her out ridin'——"

"Why, he's away from the County," declared Steve, who appeared to have a surprising knowledge of the young Doctor's movement.

"Yas, suh; but I talkin' 'bout b'fo' he went way. He was wid her dat evenin'. Least, he went way wid her, but he didn't come back wid her." Her tone was so significant that again the light came into Captain Allen's eyes.

" And he hasn't been back since ? "

" Nor, suh, an' he ain't comin' back nurr."

" And you don't know where Miss Welch is going, or when ? "

" Nor, suh, she ain' goin' at all. I heah her say she wa'n't gwine ; but she cert'ny look mighty thin, heah lately." The conversation had ended. Steve was in a reverie, and Martha moved toward the door.

" Well, good-by, Marse Steve. I cert'ny is obliged to you, an' I gwine send you some eggs soon as my hens begins to lay again."

But Captain Allen told her she did not owe him anything.

" Come again, Martha, whenever you want to know about anything—anything at all."

When Martha went out she heard him singing.

The story of Still's offer of a compromise to Jacquelin got abroad, and, notwithstanding the wise doctrine of the law that an offer of compromise shall not be taken as evidence in any case, this particular offer was so taken. Still found himself roundly abused by his counsel for being such a fool as to propose it. All sorts of rumors began to fly about. It was said that Mr. Bagby had declined to act as his counsel. To meet these reports it was necessary to do something, and Still's counsel held a consultation. It was decided that he should give an entertainment.

It would show his indifference to the claims of the Grays to his plantation, and would prove his position in the County. Leech thought that this would be a good thing to do ; it would anger the Grays, if it did nothing else. He could invite Judge Bail up to it.

" Make it a fine one when you do have it," said the counsellor. " I've found champagne make its way to a man's heart when you couldn't get at it through his pocket."

Dr. Still also was eager to have such an entertainment. He, too, appreciated the fineness of the stroke that, on the

29

eve of battle, would show their contempt for the other
side.   Besides which, the young physician had another
motive.   Soon after his removal from the County to the
city Dr. Still had become an admirer of Governor Krafton's daughter.   She was the Governor's only child, and
even the Governor's bitterest enemies admitted that he was
a devoted father ; and in the press that was opposed to
him, often side by side with the bitterest attacks cɔ the
Governor, was some admiring mention of his handsome
and accomplished daughter.   He would have given her the
moon, someone said to General Legaie.   " Yes, even if he
had to steal it to do so," said the General.   Miss Krafton
had had the best education that the country could afford.
This she had finished off with a year or two of travel
abroad.   She had just returned home.   She idolized her
father, and perhaps the Governor had not been sorry to
have her out of the country where half the press was daily
filled with the most direct and vehement accusations against
him.   The Governor's apologists declared that his most
questionable acts were from the desire to build up a fortune
for his daughter.   It was for her that he had bought the
old Haskelton place, one of the handsomest in the city, and,
pulling down the fine old colonial mansion, had erected on
its site one of the costliest and most bewildering structures
in the State.

It is often the case that the very magnitude of the efforts
made to accomplish a design frustrates it ; and Governor
Krafton, with all his eagerness to be very rich, and his absolute indifference as to the means employed, was always
involved pecuniarily, while the men with whom he worked
appeared to be immensely successful.   Until he fell out
with Leech and Still, he had gone in with them in their
railroad and land schemes ; but while everything that they
touched appeared to turn to gold (at least, it was so with
Still ; for there were rumors respecting Leech), the Governor was always hard pushed to meet his expenditures.

Still's explanation to his son was that he let others climb

the trees and do the shaking, and he stayed on the ground
and gathered the apples. "Krafton and Leech has both
made more money than I have," he said, shrewdly ; "but
they have to pay it out to keep their offices, while I——"
He completed the sentence by a significant buttoning of
his pocket. "They think that because they get a bigger
sheer generally than I do, they do better. But—it ain't
the water that falls on the land that makes the crops ;
it's what sinks in. This thing's got to stop some time, my
son—ground gets worked out—and when the crops are
gethered I know who mine's for." He gazed at his son,
with mingled shrewdness and affection. The young Doctor
also looked pleased. His father's sharpness at times made
up to him for his ignorance and want of education. Dr.
Still was not lacking in smartness himself, and had been
quick enough to see which way Miss Krafton's tastes lay.
He had discovered that she was both proud and ambitious
—Not politically. She said she detested politics ; that her
father never allowed politics to be talked before her ; and
when he gave a "political dinner," she did not even come
downstairs. She was ambitious socially. Dr. Still promptly began to play on this chord. He had prevailed on his
father to set him up a handsome establishment in the
city, and he became deeply literary. He began to talk of
his family—the Stills had originally been Steels, he said,
and were the same family to which Sir Richard Steel belonged—and to speak of his " old place " and his " old
pictures." He described them with so much eloquence
that Miss Krafton said she wished she could see them.
This gave Dr. Still an idea, and he forthwith began to plan
an entertainment. As it happened, it was at the very time
that Leech had suggested the same thing to Hiram Still ;
and as his son and Leech rarely agreed about anything
these days, Still was impressed, and the entertainment was
determined on. It was to be the " finest party " that had
ever been given at Red Rock. On this all were united.
Even Hiram yielded to the general pressure, and admitted

that if you were " going to send for a man's turn of corn it
was no good to send a boy to mill after it."

He entrusted the arrangements to the young Doctor,
who laid himself out on them. A florist and a band were
to be brought up from the city, and the decorations and supper were to surpass everything that had ever been seen.
A large company was invited, including many guests from
the city, for whom a special train was furnished, and Still,
" to show his good feeling," extended the invitation to
many of his neighbors. Major and Mrs. Welch and Ruth
were invited. Still remembered that Major Welch had
been to one entertainment in that house, and he wished to
show him that he could excel even the Grays. Dr. Still
was at first determined that Miss Welch should not come ;
but it was suggested that it would be a greater triumph to
invite her, and more mature reflection decided him that
this was so. He would show her Miss Krafton, and this
would be a greater victory than to omit her from the list.
He could not but believe that she would be jealous.

On the evening of the entertainment Major Welch and
Mrs. Welch attended. But Miss Ruth did not accompany
them. She was not very well, Mrs. Welch said in reply to Virgy, who, under Dr. Still's wing, was "receiving " in a stiff, white satin dress, and looking unfeignedly
scared as she held her great bouquet, like an explosive that
might " go off " at any time. Miss Virgy's face, however,
on seeing Mrs. Welch's familiar countenance, lit up, and
she greeted her with real pleasure, and expressed regret
that Ruth had not come, with a sincerity that made Mrs.
Welch warm toward her. Mrs. Welch liked her better
than she did Miss Krafton, whom she had met casually and
thought a handsome and intelligent, but rather conceited
girl.

It was a curious company that Major and Mrs. Welch
found assembled. The strangers from the city included
the judge, who was a dark-looking man with a strong face,
a heavy mouth, and a lowering gray eye ; a number of

people of various conditions, whom Mrs. Welch recognized
as men whose names she had heard as connected with
Leech; and a number of others whom she had never heard
of. But there was not a soul whom she had ever met before
socially. Not a member of the St. Ann congregation was
present. Both the Stills were in an ill-humor, and Virgy,
though she was kind and cordial, looked wretchedly unhappy. Mrs. Welch was glad that, for once, she had not
permitted her principles to override her instincts, and had
left Ruth at home. As she glanced about her, her gaze
rested on her host. Hiram Still was talking to one of his
guests, a small, stumpy, red-headed man with a twinkling
eye and a bristly red mustache, whom Mrs. Welch recognized as an office-holder who had come down from one of
the Northern States.

Still was talking in a high, complaining voice.

"Yes," he said, evidently in answer to a speech by his
guest, "it is a fine party—the finest ever given in this
County. It ought to be; I've spent enough money on it to
buy a plantation, and to show my friendliness I invited
my neighbors. Some of 'em I didn't have no call to invite,
—and yet just look around you. I've got a lot of folks
from the city I don't know, and some from the County
I know too well; but not one of my old neighbors has
come—not one gentleman has put his foot here this
night."

His guest glanced round the hall, and ended with a
quizzical look up in Still's face. "Of course, what did
you expect? Do you suppose, Still, if I were a gentleman
I'd have come to your party? I'd have seen you d—d
first. Let's go and have some more champagne."

It was the first time the fact had struck Mrs. Welch. It
was true—there was not a gentleman there except her husband.

When Mrs. Welch left, shortly afterward, Still and his
guest had evidently got more champagne. Still was vowing
that it was the finest party ever given in Red Rock, even if

there wasn't a gentleman present ; and his guest was laughing and egging him on. As Major and Mrs. Welch waited for their carriage, Leech passed with Miss Krafton on his arm. Mrs. Welch drove home in silence. There were things she did not wholly understand.

CHAPTER XXXVII

WHEN the Court met, at which the trial of Jacquelin's
suit against Hiram Still was set, all other matters, even
politics, were driven from mind.

It will not be needful to go in detail into the trial of the
case. The examination of the plaintiffs' witnesses occupied
two days. In the contest the defendant, to use the phrase-
ology of another arena, was acknowledged to have " drawn
first blood." On the morning of the trial the two sides,
with their counsel, witnesses, and friends, thronged the
court-house. The counsel, an imposing array, were ranged
along the bar, fronting the bench and the jury-box which
was off to one side, and in which sat seven solemn-looking
negroes and five scarcely less solemn white men. Major
Welch sat beside Mr. Bagby, and during a part of the time
Mrs. Welch and Ruth had chairs behind them. By the
time they were all settled it was announced that the Judge
was coming.

It had been the practice in the County, when the Judge
entered, for the Bar to rise and remain standing until he
had mounted the bench, bowed to them, and taken his seat,
when they bowed and resumed their places. It was a custom brought from the Supreme Court, before which Mr.
Bagby, General Legaie, and others of that bar had practised in old times.

Now, when the Judge entered he was announced by
Sherwood, the Sheriff, and came in preceded by Leech and
McRaffle. And not a man rose. The Judge walked up

the steps to his arm-chair, faced the crowd, and for a second stood still, as if waiting. Not a lawyer stirred, and
the Judge took his seat. A half scowl was on his brow,
but he banished it and ordered Court to be opened. The
case was called, the parties announced themselves ready,
the jury was impanelled, and the trial was begun. General Legaie was to open the case. It was the custom for
a chair to be placed inside the bar, just at the feet of the
jurors. This chair was usually occupied by one of the
older members of the bar. And as the General had been
growing a little deaf, he had been taking it of late. He
had prepared himself with great care, and was dressed with
the utmost scrupulousness—a black frock coat, white
trousers, a high stock, and immaculate linen—and when
the case was called he stood up. He presented a striking
figure. The gravity of the occasion spoke in every line of
his weather-beaten, high-bred face. To his mind it was
not a mere question of title to property he was to argue ;
it was the question between the old and the new—it was a
civilization that was on trial. He took the papers in his
hand, glanced with some curiosity along the lines of the
jury, and faced the judge.

"If the Court please——" he began, in a calm, well-
modulated voice that brought an instant hush over the
whole court-room.

His words appeared to wake the judge from a lethargy.
He, however, took no notice whatever of the General, but
addressed the sheriff.

"Put that man behind the bar."

The Sheriff was mystified, and looked first around him
and then at the judge, in a puzzled way, to see whom he
referred to.

"Suh ?"

"Make that man get behind the bar." He simply glanced
at the General. This time the negro took in what he
meant, and he approached the General doubtfully. The
General had not caught all the words, but he had heard a

part of it, and he also looked around. But seeing no one to be removed, and not understanding the cause of the order, he was just beginning again : " If the Court please——" when the negro came up to him. The General stopped and looked at him inquiringly.

" De Cote say you is to git behine de bar," said the Sheriff. The General leaned forward, his hollowed hand raised to his ear.

" De Cote say you is to git behine de bar."

The General turned sharply to the bench and shot one piercing look at the Judge ; then, seeming to recollect himself, wheeled about, walked across to Steve and laid the papers of the suit on the bar before him, took up his hat, turned his back squarely on the Court, and faced the Bar :

" Good-morning, *gentlemen*." He made them a low bow, clapped his hat on his head, and marched out of the courtroom.

It made a sensation. Steve Allen rose and asked the Court to postpone the case until after dinner, the hour for which was approaching. General Legaie, he said, was the leading counsel on their side.

" Proceed with the case," said the judge.

It was conceded that the action of General Legaie was a loss to the plaintiffs' side, but every one on that side sustained him. They did not see how a gentleman could have done otherwise.

The case proceeded without him.

It was attempted to show that Mr. Gray could not have owed all the money Still claimed, and that, if he did owe it, before Still brought suit he must have received from Red Rock crops enough to reduce the amount largely, if not to discharge it.

The investigation was fought at every point by Still's counsel, and the Judge almost uniformly ruled in favor of their objections, so that Steve Allen had hard work to maintain his composure. His eyes flashed and a cloud lowered on his brow as he noted exception after exception.

At length the Court began to head him off from even this
protection, by ruling, whenever Captain Allen rose, that
he was out of order.   When Court adjourned the second
day it was felt that except for the suspicious fact that Still
had not endorsed any credit on the bonds, no fraud had
been shown in his title to them.   Witnesses who had been
put on the stand to show facts tending to prove that he
could not have had any such amount of money had been
ruled out.   It was conceded that under the Court's ruling no sufficient ground had been established to upset
Still's title.   The defendant's counsel were jubilant, and
that night debated whether they should put any witnesses
on the stand at all.   Leech was against it.   The Judge
was with them, he maintained.   Mr. Bagby was acquiescent, but Major Welch insisted that, at least, he should
go on the stand to state his connection with the case.
He did not intend that it should appear of record that his
name had been connected with a charge of fraud, and
that, when he had had the opportunity to go on the stand
and deny it, he had failed to do so.   Mr. Bagby's eyes lit
up with a gleam of satisfaction as he listened to him, partly
because of pride in his client, and partly, perhaps, because
of the discomfiture of Leech and his client.   The old lawyer was content either way, for he did not see how he could
possibly be hurt, whatever might happen.   So, next morning, the defence began to take evidence, and after they
began to introduce witnesses it was necessary to go fully
into the case.   It was, however, plain sailing : wind and
tide, in shape of the sympathy of the Court, were with
them, and as often as Captain Allen interposed objections
they were ruled out.   Witnesses were put up to show that
Still had always been a keen business man, and had at various times lent money to his neighbors, including Mr.
Gray.   Mr. Gray's confidence in him was proved, and it
was shown that he had relied on him so far as to send him
South as his agent.   Still was ostentatiously offered by
Leech as a witness to prove everything, but was objected

to on the ground that the other party to the transaction was
dead, and was necessarily held incompetent. All the merit,
however, of what he might prove was secured. An undisputed bond of Mr. Gray's was put in proof. It was dated
at the outbreak of the war, and was the bond given for
money to help equip the Red Rock Company. This bond
was taken from the bundle of papers in the old suit
which Still had brought, and whilst it was being examined
the other papers in the file were left spread out on the
bar before Leech, with the big bond lying by itself until
it should be offered in evidence. In this way a presump-
tion was raised as to Still's means and ability to lend
money. Just then it became necessary to show the time
when Still went South, in order to connect the large bond
with that visit. An attempt was made to do this, but the
witnesses put on the stand to prove it got confused on
cross-examination and differed among themselves by several years. It was now night, and Leech was anxious to
close the case. Things had been going so smoothly that
he was impatient. He glanced around the court-room.

"Is there no one here who was present when you went
or came back?" he asked Still, with a frown. Still looked
about him.

"Yes, there's a nigger. He was there both when I
went away and when I came back. He used to work
about the house." He pointed to Doan, who stood behind the bar in the throng of spectators. "But I don't
want to put him on," he whispered. "I don't like him."

"Oh! nonsense! It's only a single fact, and if we can
prove it by one witness, it's as good as by a hundred."
He turned and spoke to Doan from his seat.

"Come around and be sworn." Doan came to the
clerk's desk and was sworn. He was told by Leech that
he need not sit down, as there was only one question to be
asked. So he stood just in front of the bar, where the
papers were spread on it, looking self-conscious and sheepish, but very self-important. Leech put his question.

"Do you know when Mr. Still was sent South by Mr. Gray?"

"Yes, suh. Cose I does. I was right dyah. See him de night he come back."

"Well, tell those gentlemen when it was," said Leech. A shade of impatience crossed his face as Doan looked puzzled. "What year it was?" He leaned over and touched the big bond lying on the bar before him, preparatory to putting it in evidence. The act seemed to arouse the negro's intellect.

"Well, I don' know nothin' 'bout what year 'twuz," he said, "but I knows *when* 'twuz."

"Well, *when* was it? And how do you know when it was?" Leech asked, sharply.

"'Twuz when de big picture o' de ghos' in de gret hall fall down the lass' time, jes b'fo' de war. Mr. Still had jes come back from de Souf de day befo', an' him and marster wuz in the gret hall togerr talkin' 'bout things, and Mr. Still had jes ontie he picket-book an' gin marster back de papers, when de win' blow 'em on de flo' an' de picture come down out de frame 'quebang, most 'pon top my haid."

"Stop him! For God's sake! stop him," muttered Still, clutching at Leech's arm. The lawyer did not catch his words, and turned to him. Still was deadly pale. "Stop him!" he murmured. A stillness had fallen on the court-room, and the crowd was listening. Leech saw that something had happened.

"Hold on. Stop! How do you know this?" His tone was suddenly combative.

"Hi! I wuz right dyah onder it, and it leetle mo' fall 'pon top my haid." Doan gave a nod of satisfaction as he recalled his escape. "Yes, suh, I thought he had got me dat time sho'!" he chuckled, with a comical glance at the negroes before him, who roused up at the reminiscence and laughed at his whimsical look. "'Twuz in de spring, and I wuz paintin' de hearth wid red paint, and marster an' de overseer was talkin' togerr at de secretary by de winder 'bout de new plantation down Souf; an' I wuz doin' mo' lis'nin 'n paintin', cuz when I heah Mr. Still say he hadn' buyed all de lan' an' niggers marster 'spected him to buy and had done bring he barn back, I wuz wonderin' what that wuz an' ef dee'd sen' any o' our blackfolks down Souf; and thunderstorm come up right sudden, an' b'fo' dee pull de winder down, blowed dem papers, what Mr. Still bring back an' teck out he pocket an' gi' to marster, off de secretary down on de flo', and slam de do' so hard de old Ingin-killer fall right out de frame mos' 'pon top my haid. Yas, suh, I wuz dyah sho'!" He was telling the incident of the picture and not of the papers, and the crowd was deeply interested. Even the Judge was amused. Still, with white face, was clutching Leech's arm, making him signals to stop the witness; and Leech, not yet wholly comprehending, was waiting for a pause to do so, without its being too marked. But Doan was too well launched to stop. He flowed on easily: " I holp Mr. Still to put de picture back in the frame an' nail 't up after marster had done put de paper what he call he 'barn,' in de hole behine it, an' I tell you I didn't like it much nohow. An' Mr. Still didn' like it much nurr."

"Stop him!" whispered Still, agonizingly.

"Here, this is all nonsense," broke in Leech, angrily. "You don't know what Mr. Still thought. You know that he came back from the South some year that there was a thunderstorm, and a picture was blown out of a frame or fell down. And that's all you know. You don't know what Mr. Still thought or anything else." But Doan was by this time at his ease, enjoying the taste of publicity.

"Yas, suh, I does, cuz I hear him say so. I holp him nail de picture back after marster had done put dem very papers Mr. Still gi' him back in de hole behine it. An' I hear Mr. Still tell marster 't ef it wuz him he'd be skeered, cuz dee say 'twuz bad luck to anybody in de house ef de

picture fall ; and marster say he wa'n't skeered, dat ef anything happen to him he could trust Mr. Still, an' he'd put
de papers in de hole behine de picture, so ef anyone ever
fine 'em dee'd see what a faithful man he had ; he had
trus' him wid he barn for thousan's o' dollars, an' he
brung it back, an' he gwine nail de picture up now so
'twon' come down no mo'."

" Oh ! Your master said he felt he could trust Mr.
Still ? " said Leech, brightening, catching this crumb of
comfort.

" Yas, suh."

" And what did Mr. Still say ? "

" He say he could too." The crowd laughed.

" And he nailed the picture up securely ? "

" Yas, suh. I holped him. Marster sont me to teck
Marse Rupert out, cuz he wuz dabblin' he little byah
foots in de paint on de hearth, trackin' up de flo', an' had
done step'pon one o' de barns whar blow' down, an' mark
it up ; an' he tell me when I come back to bring hammer
an' nails to nail de picture up, an' so I done."

Still was again squeezing his counsel's arm painfully,
whispering him to stop the witness. But Leech had to ask
one more question.

" You brought the nails and nailed it up ? "

" Yes, suh, me an' Mr. Still. An' Marse Rupert he
come back, and Mr. Jack dyah wid him, an' say he gwine
help too. He wuz always pesterin' roun', dem days."
This in pleasant reminiscence to the crowd.

" You can stand aside," said Leech, contemptuously.
He gave a sigh of relief, and Doan was turning slowly to
go.

" Hold on." Steve's deep voice broke in. Jacquelin was
whispering to him eagerly. A new light had come into
his eyes, and he was scanning Still's white face, on which
the beads of sweat had stood during the whole examination. Steve, still listening to Jacquelin's rapid speech,
rose slowly to get the bond lying on the bar. Before he

could reach it however, McRaffle, one of the counsel associated with Leech, partly resenting the neglect of himself and wishing to earn his fee, leant forward.   He would,
at least, ask one question.

"You nailed it up securely, and that was the last time
it fell."   He spoke rather in affirmation than question.

"Nor, suh ; it done fall down two or three times since
den.   Hit fall de day marster wuz kilt, an' hit fall de evenin' Mr. Still dyah got de papers out de hole agin.   Dat's
de evenin' Mr. Leech dyah 'rest Marse Jack.   Mr. Leech
know 'bout dat."

Suddenly a voice rang through the court-room.

"It's a lie !   It's all a d—d lie !"   It was Hiram Still,
and he had sprung to his feet in uncontrollable agitation,
his face livid.   Every eye was turned on him, and Leech
caught him and pulled him down forcibly into his seat,
rising in his place and addressing the Court.

"If your honor please," he said, "all of this is irrel-
evant.   I have no idea what it is all about ; but it has no
bearing whatever on this case : a lot of stuff about a picture falling down.   I shall ask you to exclude it all from
the jury——"

"But I will show whether or not it is relevant," asserted
Steve.   He had picked up the bond from the bar and held
it firmly.   His voice had a new ring in it.

Leech turned on him angrily, but caught his eye and
quieted down.   He addressed the Court again.

"I will show how impossible it is for it to be accepted.
Can you read or write ?" he demanded of Doan, who stood
much puzzled by what was going on.

"Nor, suh."

"And you cannot tell one paper from another, can
you ?"

"Nor, suh.   But ef de paper Mr. Still got out from behine de picture dat evenin' I see him git up in de hole
after you brung Marse Jack away, is de one I see him gi'
marster an' see him put in dyah, hit's got Marse Rupert's

foot-track 'pon it—least his toe-tracks—whar he'd been dabblin' in de fresh paint on de hearth ; cuz dat's de reason marster meck me cyar him out, cuz he step 'pon de barn whar blown down on de hall-flo' wid red paint, an' track up de flo' runnin' after it." (Here Steve, with a bow, handed the bond across to Major Welch.) "I see marster when he put de paper in de bundle an' Mr. Still put it up in de hole behine de picture, an' I see Mr. Still when he git up in de hole an' teck it out de evenin' de picture fall down after mistis an' all de white folks come 'way to de cote-house after Marse Jack. Ef it's de same barn hit's got he toe-marks on hit in red paint, cuz I can show you de tracks on de hall flo' now. Hit's dim, but hit's dyah on de flo' still. Ef you go dyah wid me I can show 't to you."

At this moment Major Welch, who had been holding the bond in his hand and had studied it carefully, leaned forward and held it out to the negro.

Still, with a gasp, made a grab for Leech, and Leech reached for the paper; but Major Welch put him aside without even looking at him.

"Did you ever see that paper before ?" he asked Doan. Doan's face lit up, and he gave an ejaculation of surprise and pleasure.

"Yas, suh, dat's de very paper I'se talkin' 'bout." He took it and held it triumphantly, turning it so it could be seen. "Dyah's Marse Rupert's little toe-marks 'pon hit now, jes' like I tell you." And as the paper was viewed, there, without doubt, were the prints—incontestably the marks of five little toes, as the exclamation of the spectators certified. Doan was delighted at his justification. "I knowed he teck it out, cuz I see him when he cut de string up dyah an' put it in he pocket, an' I see de string when I put it back," he said, confidentially, to the crowd. "I see him, an' Unc' Tarquin see him too, cuz he had jes' come over to see 'bout Marse Jack ; an he ax me afterwards what Mr. Still wuz doin' in de hole up dyah rummagin' papers."

STILL SPRUNG TO HIS FEET IN UNCONTROLLABLE AGITATION, HIS FACE
LIVID.

"That's so!" exclaimed a deep voice back in the crowd. "I saw him in the hole, and I saw him take some papers out and put them in his pocket." It was old Tarquin, standing still and solemn in the front row of the negroes behind the bar.

The Judge roared for silence, and Leech rose and renewed his motion. He denounced the whole story as nonsensical and absurd.

Steve Allen started to contest the motion ; but the Judge sustained it, and ruled out Doan's testimony, to which Steve excepted. Then Leech calmly offered the bond in evidence, and announced that they were through and wanted no argument.

Steve Allen offered to put Doan on the stand as his witness, but Leech objected ; the plaintiffs had closed their case, he said. And so the Court ruled. Steve Allen claimed the right to put the witness on the stand, asserting that it was in rebuttal. But the Court was firm. The Judge declined "to hear ghost stories." Steve insisted, and the Court ordered him to take his seat. He was "out of order." The case was closed, and he wanted to hear no argument. In such a case the verdict of a jury was not obligatory on the Court, it was only to instruct the mind of the chancellor. He had heard all that the jury had heard, and his mind was clear. He would instruct them to bring in a verdict that no fraud had been shown, and the defendants would prepare a decree accordingly.

On this Steve suddenly flamed out. He would like to know, he said, when he had been in order in that court. It was an outrage on decency ; the rulings of the Court were a cover for fraud.

He was certainly out of order now. The Judge was angry, but he was not afraid.

"Take your seat, sir," he shouted. "I will commit you for contempt." The anger of the Judge cooled Steve's.

"If you do, it will certainly be for *contempt*," he said,

80

recovering his composure. He was looking the Judge
squarely in the eyes.

"I will put you in jail, sir!"

"It has no terrors for me. It is more honorable than
your court."

"I will disbar you!" roared the Judge.

"You have substantially done it in this case," said
Steve.

The Judge was foaming. He turned to the clerk and
commanded him to enter an order immediately striking
Steve's name from the roll of attorneys practising in that
court, and ordered the Sheriff to take him into custody.
The excitement was intense. Instinctively a number of
men, Andy Stamper among them, moved up close to Steve
and stood about him. The colored Sheriff, who had
started, paused and looked at the Judge inquiringly. The
Judge was just beginning to speak again to the Sheriff, but
his attention was arrested.

At this moment Jacquelin rose. His calm manner and
assured voice quieted the hubbub; and the Judge looked at
him and waited. As his counsel was disbarred, Jacquelin
said, he should ask the Court to allow him to represent
himself at this juncture, and also his brother, who was still
a minor. He calmly stated the series of events that had
prevented their knowing before the facts that had just then
been disclosed, and which made everything clear; and he
asked leave to amend their bill, or to file a new one, on the
ground of after-discovered evidence. With the new light
thrown on the case, he traced Still's action step by step,
and suddenly wound up with a charge that Still had arrested his brother to get him out of the way and destroy
the danger of his testimony. A roar of applause burst
from the white men present, in whom a ray of hope began
to shine once more. Jacquelin sat down.

Of all the people in the court-room the Judge was the
most calm. He was as motionless as a sphinx. As Jacquelin took his seat there was a brief pause of deathly still-

ness. The Judge looked at Leech and waited. The latter caught the signal and his face lit up. He put his hand on the bar, and leant forward preparatory to rising to his feet. Before he could make another motion Major Welch rose. Every eye was turned on him. Old Mr. Bagby gazed up at him, his lips slightly parted, his eyes filled with wonderment. Leech, with his hand resting on the bar and his body bent forward, waited. The Judge turned his gaze to Major Welch. The silence became almost palpable. Major Welch's face was pale, and the lines, as seen in the dim light, appeared to have deepened in it. His form was erect.

"If your honor please," he began, "I am a defendant in this case, and hold as a purchaser under the other defendant a considerable part of the property sought to be recovered by the plaintiffs. I bought it honestly and paid for it, believing that it was the land of the man from whom I bought, and I still hold it. There have been a number of things since that I have not been able to understand until now. I have observed closely all that has gone on here to-day, and have heard all that has just been said. I wish to say that, as far as I am concerned—so far as relates to the part of the property formerly belonging to Mr. Jacquelin Gray and his brother now held by me—I am satisfied. It will not be necessary for the plaintiffs to take the step that has just been proposed, of filing a new bill. From certain facts within my own knowledge, and which I did not understand before, but on which, what has just taken place has thrown a full light, I am quite satisfied. And if the complainants will prepare a proper deed reconveying the land—my part of the land —to them, I will execute it without further delay, and will make such restitution as I can. I have lost what I put into it, which is a considerable part of all I possessed in the world. But "—he paused for a second—" there is one thing I have not lost, and I do not propose to lose it. I am not willing to hold another man's property which he lost by fraud." (For the first time he turned and faced the bar. His voice which, if firm, had been grave and low, suddenly became strong and full, with a ring in it of pride.) "I shall expect them to make a declaration of record that every transaction, so far as I at least was concerned, was free from any taint of suspicion." He sat down, amid a deathly silence. The next moment, from all through the court-room, there was a cheer that almost took the roof off. The Judge scowled and rapped, but it was beyond him ; and in spite of his efforts to restore order, the tumult went on wildly, cheer after cheer, not only for the act, but for the man.

Ruth, who all through the scene had been sitting beside her mother, holding her arm tightly, her face as white as her handkerchief, in a fit of uncontrollable emotion burst into tears and threw herself into her mother's arms ; and Mrs. Welch's eyes were glistening and her face was lit by a glow which she did not always permit to rest there.

Old Mr. Bagby had sat half-dazed by his client's action— wonder, dissatisfaction, and pride all contending in his countenance for mastery. Before his client was through, pride conquered, and as Major Welch took his seat the old lawyer leant forward, placed his hand on the back of Major Welch's and closed it firmly. That was all.

As Major Welch sat down Jacquelin sprang to his feet. His face was almost as white as Major Welch's.

"If the Court please——" he began. But it was in vain that he strove to speak. Cheers for Major Welch were ringing, and the Judge, his face livid with wrath, was rapping. Jacquelin was waving his hand to quiet the crowd. "If the Court please," he repeated, "I wish to make a statement."

"Sit down," said the Judge, shouting angrily to the Sheriff to restore order. Jacquelin sat down, and the cheers began to subside.

Leech and his associates had been struck dumb with astonishment. They gazed on Still in blank dismay, and, as Jacquelin resumed his seat, Leech leaned over and spoke to Still. Still sat motionless, his face ashy, his cheeks twitching, his eyes dull. Just at that moment there was a crash outside close to the window. A restive horse had broken loose. There was a shrill neigh and the sudden trample of feet as he dashed away through the darkness. Hiram Still sank forward and rolled from his chair in a heap on the floor.

The Court adjourned for the night, and the crowd poured from the court-room.

As Ruth and her mother came out, the darkened green was full of groups of men all eagerly discussing the occurrence and its probable effect on the case. Major Welch's name was on every lip.

"Danged if I believe he's a Yankee, anyway!" said a voice in the darkness as Ruth and Mrs. Welch passed by— a theory which gained this much credit: that several admitted that, "He certainly was more like our people than like Yankees." One, after reflection, said:

"Well, maybe there's some of 'em better than them we know about."

The ladies passed on in the darkness.

Hiram Still was taken over to the tavern, and Dr. Cary worked over him for hours; and later in the night the report was current that it was only a fit he had had, and that he was recovering.

Meantime Leech and Still's other counsel held a consultation, and after that Leech was closeted with the Judge in his room for an hour; and when he left, having learned that Major Welch had gone home, he mounted his horse and rode away in the darkness in the direction of Red Rock.

The next morning the Judge adjourned his court for the term. The illness of Still, the chief party in the cause, was the ground assigned.

It soon became known that Still was not going to give up the suit. It was authoritatively announced by Leech. What Major Welch chose to do had nothing to do with Still.

"If Major Welch was fool enough," Leech said, "to turn tail at a nigger's lies, which he had been bribed to tell, and fling away a good plantation, it was none of their business. But they were going to fight and win their case."

The Judge left the County, and Still, having recovered sufficiently, was moved to his home.

The day after the scene in the court-room Jacquelin Gray, Steve, and the General had a conference with old Mr. Bagby, and then together they called on Major Welch. They stated that, while they appreciated his action, they did not wish him to take such a step as he had proposed under the excitement of an impulse, and they would prefer to bring the proof and lay it before him to establish the facts they alleged as beyond question.

"It was this that I wished to say last night," said Jacquelin ; and then added that he was quite ready to make the entry of record at once that the Major's holding of the lands was entirely innocent.

Major Welch heard his visitors through, then said he preferred not to wait ; he was quite satisfied.

"It might have been an impulse last night, gentlemen, but it is not an impulse now. I have reflected very deeply, you may be sure; but I am only confirmed in my intention, and my act now is that of mature deliberation. I only wish to say one thing more : that if I were capable of holding on to this land, my wife would not permit me to do so."

He did not tell the visitors that, the night before, he had been followed home by Leech, who had just come from an interview with the Judge, and who urged him, on every ground that he could think of, to reconsider his action and retract his promise ; assured him of the absolute certainty of success, and gave him finally the assurance of the Judge himself, who had promised to dismiss the suit and enter the decree.

Nor did he tell Jacquelin that the interview with Leech

had come suddenly to an end by his telling Leech of what he knew personally, and that he considered him a proper counsel for Still, and the Judge a proper judge for him to try his case before.

This he did not mention, and they did not learn it until long afterward.

CHAPTER XXXVIII

IN WHICH MR. LEECH SPRINGS A TRAP WITH MUCH SUC-CESS

THE developments of the trial decided Jacquelin to offer immediately an amended bill, setting up all the facts that had come out. Steve Allen went South to follow up the fresh clew and obtain new evidence, and on his return it was rumored that he had been successful. Meantime Still had recovered sufficiently to be taken to a watering-place—for his health, it was said—and Leech was engaged in other parts of the State looking after his prospective canvass for the Governorship. Leech's candidacy and the final issue of the Red Rock case had become closely associated. It was charged that Leech had been engaged with Still in the attempt to perpetrate a fraud ; and it was intimated that, if the Red Rock case should be won by the Grays, it would be followed by the prosecution of Still and possibly of Leech. Captain Allen's connection with the case, together with the part he had taken in public matters, had brought him forward as the leader of the opposition to Leech, not only in the County, but throughout the State. Dr. Still was absent, dutifully looking after his father, and, rumor said, also looking after his own prospects in another field. Whether these reports were all true or not, the three men were all absent from the County, and the County breathed more freely by reason thereof. It was an unquestioned fact that when they were absent, peace re- turned.

It was, however, but the calm before the storm.

In the interval that came, Jacquelin once more brought

his suit. It was based on the disclosure made at the first
trial, and the bill was this time against Still alone. Major
Welch, as stated, had insisted on reconveying his part of
the land to Jacquelin. He said he could not sleep with
that land in his possession. So Jacquelin and Rupert were
the owners of it, and Major Welch took it on a lease.

The suit matured, and once more the term of court approached. The people of the County were in better spirits.
The evidence that Steve had secured in the South was believed to fill the broken links. On the decision depended
everything. It was recognized on both sides that it was
not now a mere property question, but a fight for suprem-
acy. The old citizens were making a stand against the
new powers. There was talk of Rupert's coming home.
He had been in the West with Captain Thurston, acting
as a volunteer scout, and had distinguished himself for
his bravery. One particular act of gallantry, indeed, had
attracted much attention. In a fight with the Indians, a
negro trooper belonging to one of the companies had been
wounded and during a check had fallen from his horse.
Rupert had heard his cries, and had gone back under a
heavy fire and, lifting him on his horse, had brought him off.
The first that was heard of it in the County was through a
letter of Captain Thurston's to Miss Welch. When Rupert
was written to about it, he said he could not let Steve and
Jack have all the honors : " And the fact is," he added,
" when I heard the negro boy calling, I could not leave
him to save my life."

Within a month after the reinstitution of the suit, Captain Thurston's company had come back from the West,
and there was talk of efforts being made to have the old
prosecution against Rupert dismissed. It was reported
that he would come home and testify at the trial. Since
his memory had been refreshed he recollected perfectly
the incident of stepping on the paper.

Rumors of what might follow the trial were increasing
daily. It was even said that Leech was trying to make up

with Governor Krafton, and that negotiations were pending between them by which one of them would become Governor and the other Senator.

Steve Allen asserted boldly that it was much more likely that one of them would be in the penitentiary, unless the other pardoned him. This speech was repeated to Leech, who blinked uneasily. He went North that night.

In view of these facts, the old County was in better spirits than it had enjoyed for some time.

Dr. Washington Still's attentions to his father, after the father's "attack" at the trial of the Red Rock case, were, however, not so filial as they were reported to be. Had the truth been known, he was not so attentive to his father's interest as he was to that of another member of the Still family. While the trial and its strange *denouement* had affected the elder Still to the point of bringing on a slight attack of paralysis, it affected Dr. Still also very seriously, though in a different way.

After the entertainment at Red Rock, Dr. Still fancied that he saw much improvement in his chances with Miss Krafton. He had expected to impress her with Red Rock, and she had been impressed. The pictures had particularly struck her. He had told her of as many of the portraits as he could remember, inventing names and histories for most of them. He had not thought it necessary to go into any elaborate explanation, consequently he had not mentioned the fact that they were the ancestors of the man who was suing for the recovery of the place. Miss Krafton had heard of the suit and referred to it casually. Dr. Still scouted the idea of his title being questioned. His grandfather had lived there, and his father had been born on the place. He did not mention the house in which his father was born. He only intimated that in some way they had been straitened in their circumstances before the war, at some period which he made vaguely distant; and he spoke of their later success somewhat as of a recovery of their estate. The suit, he asserted, had been instigated purely by spite. It was simply one of the customary attempts to annoy Union men and Northern settlers—it was really brought more against Major Welch than his father. Miss Krafton had met Major Welch, and had declared that she adored him. Dr. Still's eyes blinked complacently.

Miss Krafton was manifestly interested, and the Doctor after this began to have more hopes of his success than he had ever had. He allowed himself to fall really in love with her.

His father's connection with the bonds of his former employer suddenly threatened to overthrow the whole structure that Dr. Still was so carefully building. The story of the bonds was told, with all its accessories, in such newspapers as were conducted by the old residents ; and although Miss Krafton might never have heard of it from them, as she had never seen a copy of such a journal in her life, the papers that were on her father's side undertook to answer the story. It was an elaborate answer—a complete answer—if true. It ought to have been complete, for Dr. Washington Still inspired it, if he did not write it. The trouble was, it was too complete. It was not content with answering, it attacked ; and it by innuendo attacked Major Welch. Miss Krafton might not have believed the story, if it had been confined to Mr. Gray and Mr. Still ; but when Major Welch had accepted the story, and, as was stated, had even reconveyed his property to Mr. Gray, it was a different matter.

Miss Krafton had conceived a high opinion of Major Welch. He was so different from all others whom she had seen at the entertainment at Red Rock or had met at her father's table. She knew of the Welches' high social standing. She had met Miss Welch, and had been delighted with her also. The partial similarity of their situations had drawn her to Ruth, and Ruth's sweetness had charmed her. When the story of the Red Rock suit came out, Miss Krafton's curiosity was aroused. She wrote to Miss Welch and asked her about it.

Dr. Still had now begun to press his suit in earnest. He too had schemes which a union with Governor Krafton would further. Leech was becoming too constant a visitor at the governor's mansion to suit the young physician, and the latter was planning to forestall him.

When Dr. Still called on Miss Krafton next, after she had made her inquiry of Miss Welch, as he waited in her drawing-room his eye fell on a letter lying open on a table. He thought he recognized the handwriting as that of Miss Welch; and as he looked at it to verify this, he caught the name " Red Rock." He could not resist the temptation to read what she had said, and, picking up the letter, he glanced at the first page. It began with a formal regret that she could not accept Miss Krafton's invitation to visit her, and then continued :

" As to your request to tell you the true story of Mr. Hiram Still's connection with the Red Rock case, which the papers have been so full of, I feel——" What it was that she felt, Dr. Still did not discover, for at this point the page ended, and just then there was a rustle of skirts outside the door. Dr. Still replaced the letter only in time to turn and meet Miss Krafton as she entered. He had never seen her so handsome; but there was something in her manner to him which he had never felt before. She was cold, he thought—almost contemptuous. He wondered if she could have seen him through the door reading her letter. Partly to sound her as to this, and partly to meet the statements which he feared Miss Welch had made, he turned the conversation to the Welches. He began to praise them mildly, at the same time speaking of their impracticability and prejudices, and incidentally hinting that Major Welch had sold out to the Grays. To this Miss Krafton replied so warmly that the young man began to try another tack. Miss Krafton, however, did not unbend. She launched out in such eulogy of Major Welch, of Mrs. Welch, and of Miss Welch that Dr. Still was quite overwhelmed. He mentioned the account that had appeared in

her father's organ. Miss Krafton declared that she did
not believe a word of it. Major Welch had stated that it
was wholly untrue. She asserted with spirit, that if she
were a man, she would rather starve than have a dollar
that was not gotten honestly ; and if ever she married, it
would be to a man like Major Welch. Her color had risen
and her eyes were flashing.

Dr. Still gazed at her in a half-dazed way, and a curious expression came over his face. It was no time for him
to push matters to an extreme.

Well, some women are innocent, he thought, as he came
down the steps. And his eyes had an ugly look in them.

When he reached home his father was waiting for him.
The young man attacked him so furiously that he was
overwhelmed. He began to try to defend himself. He
had done nothing, he declared feebly ; but whatever he
had done, had been for his sake. His voice was almost a
whimper.

His son broke out in a fury :

"For my sake ! That's your plea ! And a pretty mess
you've made of it ! Just as I was about to succeed—to
make me the talk of the State !—to make me appear the
son of a—thief ! You've stood in my way all my life.
But for you, I might have been anything. I am ashamed
of you—I've always been ashamed of you. But I did not
think you'd have been such a—fool !" He walked up
and down the room, wringing his hands and clutching the
air.

"Washy—Washy—hear me," pleaded the father, rising
totteringly from his arm-chair, and with outstretched hands
trying to follow his son.

Wash Still made a gesture, half of contempt and half of
rage, and burst out of the door.

As his son slammed the door behind him, Hiram Still
stood for a moment, turned unsteadily to his chair, threw
up his hands, and, tottering, fell full length on the floor.

The newspaper of which McRaffle was one of the editors

stated a day or two later that "our fellow-citizens will be glad to learn that the honored Colonel Hiram Still is rapidly recovering from his paralytic stroke, owing to the devoted attentions and skill of his son, the eminent young physician, Dr. Washington Still, for whom we are prepared to predict a remarkable career." It "further congratulated all honest men that Colonel Still would be well in time to attend the trial of the so-called suit, instituted against him by his political enemies, which suit, to the editor's *own personal knowledge,* was neither more nor less than a malicious persecution."

How much Dr. Still paid for this notice was known only to two men, unless Leech also knew ; for Leech and McRaffle were becoming very intimate.

It had been supposed that Mr. Hiram Still's illness would put off the trial of the Red Rock case ; but Mr. Leech, who had just returned from the North, declared publicly that the trial would come off as already scheduled, at the next term. He further intimated that those who were setting traps for him would learn that he could set a few traps himself. This declaration set at rest the fears that had been entertained that the Red Rock case would be postponed.

Leech made good his word, and when it was least anticipated sprang the trap he had prepared. It was a complete surprise and almost a complete success ; and when Leech counted up his game, he had, with a single exception, bagged every man in the County from whom he had received an affront, or against whom he cherished a grudge.

One Sunday morning, about daylight, as Jerry was returning to Brutusville from some nocturnal excursion, when only a mile or two from the village, he was startled to come on a body of cavalry, on the march. They were headed toward Brutusville, and with them were Colonel Leech and Captain McRaffle. A shrewd guess satisfied Jerry that it must mean some mischief to Captain Allen. Curiosity and interest prompted him to fall in

with them ; but the men he addressed knew nothing,
and were grumbling at having to take a long night-ride.
Jerry pressed on to the head of the column, where he
saw Leech. He touched his hat, and passed on as if he
were in a great hurry. Leech, however, called him, and
began to question him, but soon discovered that he was
drunk — too drunk to be wholly intelligent, but, fortunately, sober enough to give a good deal of valuable information. Leech gathered from him that no one had the
slightest idea that troops were coming to Brutusville, unless Captain Allen had. The Captain, Jerry said, had left
Brutusville the evening before, and had gone to a friend's
in the upper end of the County to spend Sunday. Jerry
knew this, because the Captain had told him to meet him
there with his horse in time for church ; but Jerry was not
going. He "had had enough of that man," he said. He
was not going to work for him any more. The Captain
had threatened to beat him. Here Jerry, at the memory
of his wrongs, fell into a consuming rage, and cursed Captain Allen so heartily that he almost propitiated Leech.
It was a matter of regret to Leech that Steve Allen was
not in Brutusville, and so could not be arrested at once.
This, however, could be remedied if a part of the company
were detailed to catch him before he learned of their arrival. Leech would himself go with the men who were to
undertake this. He wished to be present, or almost so,
when Captain Allen was arrested. He would have taken
Jerry with him, but Jerry was suddenly so drunk that he
could hardly stand. So, having directed that the negro
should not be allowed to go until after all the contemplated arrests had been made, Colonel Leech, with a pla-
toon, took a road that led to the place where, according to
Jerry, he should find Captain Allen preparing to attend
church.

It was just daybreak when the remainder of the company
reached the outskirts of the county seat, and, in accordance
with the instructions that had been received, began to post

pickets to surround the village.   This was done under the
immediate supervision of Captain McRaffle.   Jerry remained with one of the pickets.   The morning air appeared
to have revived him astonishingly, and in a little while he
had ingratiated himself with the picket by telling a number of funny stories of Leech, who did not appear to be at
all popular with the men.   He presently insinuated that
he knew where the best whiskey in town was to be secured,
and offered to go and get some for the picket before the
officers took possession.   He could slip in and come right
out again without anyone knowing it.   On this, and with
a threat of what would be done to him if he failed to return,
he was allowed by the picket to go in.   He started off like
a deer.   It was surprising how straight he could go when
he moved rapidly !

As soon as he reached the village he struck straight for
the court-green.   Jacquelin had spent the night at the
court-house with Steve, and was about to start for home in
the first light of the morning, and, just as Jerry flung himself over the fence, Jacquelin came down from the rooms
that he and Steve occupied.   Jerry rushed up to him and
began to tell him the story of Leech's return with the soldiers.   He had come to arrest the Captain, Jerry declared.

At first Jacquelin thought that Jerry was merely drunk ;
but his anxiety on Captain Allen's account, and the clever-
ness of his ruse by which he had outwitted Leech, satisfied
him ; and Jerry's account of Leech's eagerness (for he did
not stick at telling the most egregious lies as to what
Leech had told him) aroused Jacquelin's anxiety for Steve.
Jacquelin, therefore, took instant alarm and sent Jerry to
saddle Steve's horse, while he himself hurried back to
Steve's room and roused him out of bed.   At first, Steve
was wholly incredulous.   Jerry was just drunk, he declared,
sleepily.   But when Jerry appeared, though certainly he
was not sober, he told a story which made Steve grave
enough.   The whole expedition was, according to his account, to capture Steve.   Leech and Captain McRaffle and

the captain of the troop had all said so. Steve's horse was
saddled at the door. Steve still demurred. He'd be condemned if he'd run away; he'd stay, and, if what Jerry said
was true, would settle with Leech, the whole score then
and there. He went back into his room and put his pistol
in his pocket. This Jacquelin declared was madness. It
would only bring down vengeance on the whole County.
What could Steve do against Government troops? Jerry
added another argument: "Colonel Leech ain' gwine to
meet him. He done gone off with some other soldiers,"
he asserted.

Steve turned to Jacquelin. "How can I leave you,
Jack? I'm not a dog."

"Why, what can they do with me?" laughed Jacquelin.
"They are after you about the Ku Klux, and I was not
even in the country." He was still hurrying him.

Thus urged, Steve consented to go, and mounting his
horse rode out a back way. To his surprise, he found the
lane already picketed. He turned to take another road.
As he wheeled into it he saw a squadron of troops at either
end riding into the village toward him. He was shut in
between them, with a high fence on either side. The only
chance of escaping was across the fields. He acted quickly.
Breasting his horse at the fence, he cleared it, and, dashing
across the court-green, cleared that on the other side, and
so made his way out of the village, taking the fences as he
came to them.

Ten minutes later Jacquelin was arrested on a warrant
sworn out before McRaffle as a commissioner of the court,
and so, during the morning, was nearly every other man
in the village.

Jacquelin no sooner looked at Leech, than he knew that
it was not only Steve that he had come for. As Leech
gazed on him his eyes watered, if his mouth did not; and
he spoke in a sympathetic whine.

Dr. Cary heard of the raid and of the arrest of his friends
that morning as he came home from Miss Bush's sick bed-

31

side, by which he had spent the night. He was tired and
fagged; but he said he must go down to the court-house
and see about the matter. Mrs. Cary and Blair tried to
dissuade him. He needed rest, they urged. And, indeed,
he looked it. His face was worn, and his eyes glowed
deep under his brows.

"My dear, I must go. I hear they have made a clean
sweep, and arrested nearly every man in the place."

"They may arrest you, if you go."

"They cannot possibly have anything against me," he
said. "But if they should, it would make no difference.
I must go and see about my friends." The ladies admitted this.

So he rode off. Mrs. Cary and Blair looked wistfully
after him as he passed slowly down the road through the
apple-trees. He rode more slowly now than he used to do,
and not so erect in the saddle.

He was about half-way to the village when he met Andy
Stamper riding hard, who stopped to give him the news.
They had arrested nearly every man in the village, Andy
said, and were now sending out parties to make arrests in
the country. General Legaie, and Jacquelin Gray, and
Mr. Dockett, and even Mr. Langstaff had been arrested.
Leech had come with them, and the prisoners were being
taken up to Leech's house, where they were to be tried before McRaffle, the commissioner. Captain Steve had got
away, and had tried to meet Leech; but Leech was too
smart for that.

"And they are after you and me too, Doctor," said
Andy. "Where are you going?"

Dr. Cary told him. Andy tried to dissuade him. "What's
the use? You can't do any good. They'll just arrest you
too. My wife made me come away. I tell you, Doctor,
it's worse than the war," said Andy. "I never would
have surrendered, if I'd thought it ud 'a come to this."
There was a sudden flash of wrath in his blue eyes. "I've
often been tempted to git even with that Still and that

Leech, and I've shut my ears and turned away; but if I'd known 't 'ud come to this, d—d if I wouldn't have done it!"

Dr. Cary soothed him with his calm assurance, and as the Doctor started to go, Andy turned.

"If you're goin', I'm goin' with you," he said. "But first I must go by and tell Delia Dove."

The Doctor tried to assure him that it was not necessary for him to surrender himself; but Andy was firm. "It might have been all right," he said, if he had not met the Doctor; but Delia Dove would never forgive him if he let the Doctor go into a trouble by himself and he stayed out —'twould be too much like running away. "I tell you, Doctor," said Andy, "if Delia Dove had been where I was, she'd never 'a surrendered. If there'd been her and a few more like her, there wouldn't 'a been any surrender."

The Doctor smiled, and, leaving him to go by and make his peace with Mrs. Stamper, rode slowly on to town.

He found the roads picketed as in time of war; but the pickets let him through. He had scarcely entered the village when he met Leech. He was bustling about with a bundle of books under his thin arm. The Doctor greeted him coldly, and Leech returned the greeting almost warmly. He was really pleased to see the Doctor.

The Doctor expressed his astonishment and indignation at the step that had been taken. Leech was deprecatory.

"I have heard that I am wanted also, Colonel Leech," said the Doctor, calmly. "I am present to answer any charge that can be brought against me."

Leech smiled almost sadly. He had no doubt in the world that the Doctor could do so. Really, he himself had very little knowledge of the matter, and none at all as to the Doctor's case. The Doctor could probably find out by applying to the officer in command. He passed on, leaving the old gentleman in doubt if he could know what was going on. Within ten minutes Dr. Cary was arrested by an officer accompanied by a file of soldiers. When he

reached Leech's house, he found more of his old friends
assembled there than he could have found anywhere else in
the County that day. It was with mingled feelings that
they met each other. In one way they were deeply incensed; in another, it was so grotesque that they were
amused as one after another they were brought in, without the slightest idea of the cause of their arrest.

However, it soon ceased to be matter for hilarity. The
soldiers who were their guards were simply coldly indifferent, and ordered them about as they would have done any
other criminals. But Leech was feline. He oozed with
satisfaction and complacency. Andy Stamper was one of
the last to appear, and when he was brought in he was a
sorry sight. He had not been given the privilege of surren-
dering himself. As he was taking leave of his wife a posse
had appeared, with Perdue the jailer at their head, with a
warrant for him. Andy had insisted that he would go and
surrender himself, but would not be arrested. A fight
had ensued, in which though, as Perdue's broken head
testified, Andy had borne himself valorously. Andy had
been overpowered; and he was brought to jail, fastened on
his mule, with a trace-chain about his body and a bag
over his head. The prisoners were first marched to Leech's
big house, and were called out one by one and taken into a
wing room, where they were arraigned before McRaffle, as
a commissioner, on the charge of treason and rebellion.
The specific act was the attack on the jail that night. The
witnesses were the jailer, Perdue; a negro who had been in
the jail that night, and Bushman, the man whom Steve Allen had ordered out of the ranks for insubordination and
threats against the prisoners. Leech himself was present,
and was the inspiration and director of each prosecution.
He sat beside the Commissioner and instructed him in
every case. Toward Jacquelin he was particularly attentive. He purred around him.

When Dr. Cary's turn came, neither he nor anyone else
had any doubt that he would be at once discharged. He

was one of the last to be called. He had taken no part
whatever in the attack on the jail ; all that he had done had
been to try and dissuade from it those who made the assault,
and, failing in that, he had waited, in case anyone should be
injured, to render what professional aid might be necessary.
When he was brought before Leech he was sensible at once
of some sort of change in the man. Always somewhat furtive in his manner, the carpet-bagger now had something
feline about him. He had evidently prepared to act a part.
He was dressed in a long black coat, with a white tie
which gave him a quasi-clerical touch, and his expression
had taken on a sympathetic regretfulness. A light almost
tender, if it had not been so joyous, beamed from his mild
blue eyes, and when he spoke his voice had a singular whine
of apparent self-abnegation. The Doctor was instantly
conscious of the change in him.

"The tiger is loose in this man," he said to himself.
Leech called the Commissioner's attention to the Doctor's
presence, and greeted him sadly. The Doctor acknowledged the salute gravely, and stated to the Commissioner
his views as to the error that had led to his arrest. Before
he was through, however, he was addressing Leech. A
glint shone in Leech's eyes for a second.

"Yes, it would seem so," he said, reflectively, with a
slight twang in his voice. "I should think that all that
would be necessary would be for you to mention it to the
Court." He looked at the Commissioner as if for cor-
roboration. McRaffle's sallow face actually flushed ; but
he kept his eyes on his paper.

"Why, you are the real power," said the Doctor ; "you
are the one who has authority."

Leech smiled almost wanly.

"Oh, no, my dear sir, you do me too much honor.
I am but the humble instrument of the law. I bind and
loose only as it is given me, my dear sir." His voice had
grown more nasal and his blue eyes beamed. He laid his
hand tenderly on the Doctor's shoulder and smiled half-

sadly. The Doctor moved a step farther off, his thin nostrils quivering slightly.

"Very well. I am not afraid. Only don't my-dear-sir me, if you please. I shall state frankly all I know about the matter, and expect to be discharged now and at once."

"Yes, that's right. No doubt of it. I shall be glad to do what I can to further your wishes. I will speak to the Commissioner." He smiled blandly.

He did so, holding a long whispered conversation with McRaffle, and the Doctor's case was taken up. The Doctor made his statement, and made it fully and frankly, and it was taken down. When, however, it was finished, he was not discharged. He was asked to give the names of those who were in the crowd that night, and refused. Leech approached, and tenderly and solicitously urged him to do so. "My dear sir, don't you see how impossible it will be for me to assist you if you persist in what is really a contempt of court?"

"Do you suppose I would tell you to save my life?" said Dr. Cary.

Leech shook his head sadly. He was really grieved.

"Perhaps your Commissioner might supply you names," snapped General Legaie. McRaffle looked up at him and tried to face his gaze; but it was in vain. His eyes dropped before the General's withering scorn.

The Doctor was held "on his own confession," the commissioner said. Old Mr. Langstaff was sent on in the same way; and by nightfall the entire party were in jail, sent on to the next term of the court to be held at the capital.

It was late in the afternoon when the prisoners were conducted to prison. Leech himself headed the procession, walking with impressive solemnity a little in advance of the guard. Quite a large crowd had assembled, mostly negroes; though there were some white men on the edges, looking on with grim faces and glowing eyes, their hats drawn down and their speech low, hardly articulate mut-

terings. All day long, since the news of the arrival of
the soldiery and their work, the negroes had been coming
into the village, and they now lined the roadside and
packed the court-green near the jail. As the procession
made its way they followed it with shouts of derision.
"Awe, my Lawd ! Ef dee ain gwine put 'em into de
jail!" cried out a young slattern, shrilly ; at which there
was a shout of laughter.

"Amy, come heah, and look at *dis* one," shrieked another. "Look at dat ole one. Don't I hope dee'll hang
de ole deble ! "

"Shut your mouth, you black huzzy," said a tall old
negro, sternly, in solemn rebuke. The girl gave a shrill,
nervous laugh, and, pulling her friend by the hand, pushed
her way nearer the prisoners.

"Dese heah young gals is too free wid dee mouîs ! "
complained another old negro to the taller one. Old
Tarquin vouchsafed no answer. His burning eyes were
fastened on his master's tall form as the Doctor marched
to the black door before him.

On the edge of the throng, though sufficiently disguised not to be recognized casually, was another form,
also with burning eyes, which were, however, fastened not
on Dr. Cary, but on Colonel Leech. Steve Allen had
come back that day, determined if he met Leech to offer
him a pistol and settle the questions between them, on the
spot.

As Dr. Cary passed into the jail, he involuntarily stooped.
As the heavy door closed behind the prisoners, there was
such a wild shout of triumph from the ragged crowd that
surged about the space outside that the dull, indifferent
soldiers in line before the door looked up and scowled,
with side glances and muttered speeches to each other ;
while on the outskirts the white men gathered together
in groups and talked in low tones, their faces dark with
impotent rage, but none the less dangerous because they,
too, were bound by shackles.

Excitement was hardly the name for the extraordinary sensation the arrests had caused. It was a bolt from a clear sky. By some curious law, whenever a step was taken against the whites the negroes became excited ; and the arrest of so many of the leading men of the County had thrown them into a condition of the wildest commotion. They came flocking into the village, forming and marching in a sort of order, with shouts and yells of triumph. They held meetings about the court-green, preached and prayed and sang hymns, shouting derisively about the jail, and yelling insults against the whites. Had anyone seen the throng, he would never have believed that the wild mob that hooted and yelled about the village were the quiet, orderly, and amiable people who but the day before tilled the fields or laughed about their cabins. It needed all the power of the troops stationed at the court-house to restrain them.

It, however, was not only the negroes who were excited. The news had spread rapidly. The whites also were aroused, and men from every direction were riding toward the county seat, their faces stern and grim. By nightfall the village was overflowing, and they were still arriving. As always, their presence awed and quieted the negroes. Many of them stopped outside the town. The presence of regular soldiers meant the presence of a force they were compelled to recognize. The two words heard were " the Government " and " Leech." Suddenly the two had become one. Leech was the Government, and the Government was Leech : no longer merely the State—the Carpet-bag Government—but *the* Government. He represented and was represented by the blue-coated, silent, impassive men who were quartered in the court-house and moved indifferently among the citizens—disliked, but careless whether it were so or not. The carpet-bagger had suddenly ceased to be a mere individual—he had become a power. For the first time he was not only hated, but feared. Men who had braved his militia, which had outnumbered them twenty to one, who had outscowled him face to face a hundred times, now glanced at him furtively and sank their voices as he passed. Leech was quick to note the difference, and his heart swelled with pride. He walked backward and forward through the throng many times, his long coat flapping behind him, his mild eyes peering through his spectacles, his wan smile flickering about his mouth, his book, "The Statutes of the United States," clasped under his arm, his brow bent as if in meditation. He felt that he was feared, and it was unction to his spirit. He had bided his time and had triumphed. Waiting till they least expected it, he had at one blow struck down every enemy. He, Jonadab Leech, had done it ; and they were under his feet. They knew it, and they feared him. He meant them to know it and fear him. For this reason he had sat by the Commissioner all day and instructed him ; for this reason he had led the march to the jail.

But had he struck all down ? No. One had escaped. At the thought, Leech's smile died away, and a dark, threatening look took its place, His chief enemy, the one he most hated and feared, had escaped. Those he had caught were well enough, but it was Steve Allen whom he was after chiefly—Steve Allen, who had scouted and braved and defied him so often, who had derided him and thwarted him and stung him. He had planned the whole affair mainly for Steve, and now the enemy had slipped through his fingers. It turned all the rest of his success into failure. His triumph changed to dust and ashes on his lips. He was enraged. He would catch him. One moment he denounced his escape as treachery, the next he boasted that he would find him and bring him in alive or dead. A rumor came to him that night that Captain Allen was not far off. Indeed, he was not, but Leech slept at the hotel, guarded by soldiers.

Leech headed, next day, a squad—not a small one —and visited every house in the neighborhood that Steve frequented, searching the houses and proclaiming his de-

termination to have him, alive or dead. He had the pleasure of searching once more the cottage where Miss
Thomasia lived. Miss Thomasia received him at the door.
She was white with apprehension and indignation. Her
apprehension, however, was not for herself, but for Steve,
who had only just ridden over the hill, and who had
left a message for Leech that he was looking for him,
too. Leech assured her sympathetically that she need not
be disturbed. He had to do his duty—a painful duty, but
it was necessary to execute the law. " ' They who take the
sword shall perish by the sword,' " he said, with a mournful smile and a shake of the head, and a side look at Miss
Thomasia.

" Yes, I have heard that, and I commend it to you, sir,"
Miss Thomasia declared, with unexpected spirit. " God
is the avenger of the guiltless, and He sometimes employs
those who are persecuted as His instruments."

Leech left there and went to Dr. Cary's. Here, too,
however, he was doomed to disappointment. Mrs. Cary
and Miss Blair had gone down to the court-house to look
after the Doctor, and the family was represented by
Mammy Krenda, whose dark looks and hostile attitude implied too much for Leech to try her. He contented himself with announcing to her that he was hunting for Steve
Allen, and had a warrant for his arrest.

" Yes, I heah you' huntin' for him," said the old woman,
quietly. " Well, you better mine some day he don't go
huntin' for you. When he ready, I reckon you'll fine
him."

" I mean to have him, alive or dead," said Leech. " It
don't make any difference to me," he laughed.

" No, I heah say you say dat," replied the old woman,
placidly. " Well, 'twould meck right smart difference to
him, I spec' ; an' when you push folks dat fur, you'se got
to have mighty sho stan'in' place."

This piece of philosophy did not strike home to Leech
at the time ; but a little later it came back to him, and re-

mained with him so much that it worried him. He returned to the court-house without having accomplished
his mission. He made up his mind that the old woman
knew where Captain Allen had gone ; but he had too vivid
a recollection of his last contest with her to try her again.
On his arrival at the court-house that evening, however,
he found that Tarquin was there, having accompanied
his mistresses, and he sent a file of soldiers to bring the
old man before him. When Tarquin was brought in, he
looked so stately and showed so much dignity that Leech
for a moment had a feeling that, perhaps, he had made a
mistake. McRaffle was present, sitting with that inscrutable look on his dark face. The Commissioner had already
gained a reputation for as much severity in his new office
as rumor had connected with his name in a less authorized
capacity. And Leech had expected the old servant to be
frightened. Instead, his head was so erect and his mouth
so calm that Leech instinctively thought of Dr. Cary.

However, he began to question the old servant. He
stated that he knew where Captain Allen was, and that
Tarquin had just as well tell. He did not wish to be
severe with him, he said, but it was his duty, as a representative of the Government, to ascertain ; and while on
one side was the penalty of the law, on the other was a
high reward. The old fellow listened so silently that
Leech, as he proceeded, began to think he had made an
impression, and a gleam of satisfaction lit up his eyes.
When he was through, there was an expression very like
scorn on old Tarquin's face.

"I don't know where he is, Colonel Leech," he said.
"But do you suppose I would tell you if I did ? If I
betrayed a gentleman, I couldn' look my master in the
face." Leech was taken aback.

"Here, that's all nonsense," he snarled. "I'm the
Government, and I'll make you tell." But Tarquin was
unmoved.

"You can't terrify me with your threats, Colonel

Leech," he said, calmly. "I served with my master through the war."

"If you don't tell, I'll send you to jail; that's what I'll do."

"You have already sent better gentlemen there," said the old servant, quietly, and with a dignity that floored the other completely. Leech remembered suddenly Hiram Still's warning to him long ago, "With these quality niggers, you can't do nothin' that way."

He suddenly tried another course, and began to argue with Tarquin. It was his duty to the Government which had set him free, and would pay handsomely. Tarquin met him again.

"Colonel Leech, my master offered me my freedom before the war, and I wouldn't take it. You may get some poor creatures to betray with such a bribe, but no gentleman will sell himself." He bowed. Leech could not help enjoying the scowl that came on McRaffle's face. But the old man was oblivious of it.

"I have voted with the Government since we were free, because I thought it my duty; but I tell you now, suh, what you are doin' to-day will hurt you mo' than 'twill help you. What you sow, you've got to reap."

"Ah, pshaw!" sneered Leech, "I don't believe you know where Captain Allen is?"

"I told you I did not," said the old man, with unruffled dignity.

Leech saw that it was useless to try him further in that direction, and, thinking that he might have gone too far, he took out his pocket-book.

"Here; I was just testing you," he said, with a well-feigned smile. He extracted a dollar note and held it out.

"Nor, suh; I don't want your money," said Tarquin, calmly. He bowed coldly, and, turning slowly, walked out.

Leech sat for some time in deep reflection. He was wondering what the secret was that controlled these people without threats or bribery. Here he was, almost on the

point of attaining his highest ambition, and he was beginning to find that he was afraid of the instruments he
employed. He had never seen a negro insolent to one of
the old residents except under the instigation of himself
or someone else like him, and yet to him they were so insolent that at times even he could hardly tolerate it. A
strange feeling came to him, as if he were in a cage with
some wild animal whose keeper he had driven away, and
which he had petted and fed until it had gotten beyond
him. He could control it only by continually feeding it,
and it was steadily demanding more and more. Would
the supply from which he had drawn give out ? And
then what would happen ? He was aroused from his
thoughts by McRaffle. He gave a short laugh.

"Called your hand, rather, didn't he ?"

Leech tried hard to look composed.

"Why didn't you turn him over to me ? I'd have got
it out of him. Trouble about you is, you don't know the
game. You are all right when your hand's full, but you
haven't got the courage to bet on your hand if it's weak.
You either bluster till a child would know you were bluff-
ing, or else you funk and lay your hand down. I told you
you couldn't do anything with these old fellows that have
held on. If they'd been going to come over, they'd have
done so long ago. But if you can't get them, you can
others. You leave it to me, and I'll find out where your
friend Allen is."

"Well, go on and do it, and don't talk so much about
it," snarled Leech, angrily. "I mean to have him, alive
or dead."

"And I rather think you'd prefer the latter," sneered
McRaffle, darkly.

"No ; vengeance belongeth unto God." His tone was
unctuous.

"Look here, Leech," said the other, with cold contempt,
"you make me sick. I've done many things, but I'm
blanked if I ever quoted Scripture to cover my meanness.

You're thinking of Still ; I'm not him. You move heaven and earth to take your vengeance, and then talk about it belonging to God. You think you are a God, but you are a mighty small one. And you can't fool Steve Allen, I tell you. If you give me a thousand dollars, I'll get him for you, alive or dead."

" You said you'd get him for two hundred, and I have offered that reward," said Leech.

" The price has risen," said McRaffle, coolly. " You haven't got him, have you ? If Allen runs across you, you'll wish you had paid me five thousand ; and you better look out that he don't." He rose and lounged toward the door.

" Well, you get him, and we'll talk about the price," said Leech.

" We'll talk of it before that, Colonel," said McRaffle, slowly to himself.

Leech had some compensation next day when he super-intended the arrangements for the transfer of his prison-ers to the city. His office was besieged all day with the friends and relatives of the prisoners, offering bail and begging their release, or, at least, that he would allow them to remain in the County until the time for the term of court to begin. To all he returned the same answer—he was " only a humble minister of the law ; the law must take its course." He found this answer satisfactory. It implied that he could if he would, and at the same time left an impression of the inscrutable character of the pun-ishment to come. He had begun to feel very virtuous. From being a humble instrument of Providence, he had come to feel as if he were a part of Providence itself. The thought made his bosom swell. It was so sweet to find himself in this position, that he determined to lengthen out the pleasure ; so, instead of sending all his prisoners down to the city at once, he divided them into two lots and shipped only half of them at first, keeping the others in jail in the County until another day. What his reason was no one knew at the time. It was charged around the County that he wanted to keep Jacquelin Gray until he could secure Steve Allen, so that he might march them down handcuffed together, and that he kept Andy Stamper and some of the others, so that he might hector them personally. However that was, he kept these in jail at Brutusville; and the others were marched down to the station handcuffed, under guard of the soldiers, and with a crowd of yelling, hooting negroes running beside them, screaming and laughing at them, until one of the officers drove them to a respectful distance. They were shipped to the city in a closed box-car, Leech superintending the shipment personally. Just before starting he approached Dr. Cary and General Legaie, and said that in consideration of their age he would have them sent down to the station in his carriage.

"Thank you. We wish no exemptions made in our cases different from those accorded our neighbors," said Dr. Cary, grimly. The General said nothing; he only looked away.

"Now, my dear sirs, this is not Christian," urged Leech. " I beg that you will allow me the pleasure——."

The little General turned on him so suddenly and with such a blaze in his eyes, that Leech sprang back, and his sentence was never finished.

"Dog !" was the only word that reached him.

So Dr. Cary and General Legaie went along with the rest, though they were not handcuffed. Old Mr. Langstaff was released on his recognizance, Leech kindly offering the Commissioner to go his bail himself.

On Leech's return from the railroad that night, he requested the officer in command to go through the jail with him, and gave him, in a high key, especial orders as to guarding it securely.

"It will be guarded securely enough," said the Captain, gruffly. He was beginning to find Leech intolerable. The last few days' work had sickened him.

" I'll soon have another prisoner," said Leech as he passed the door where Jacquelin was confined.—He raised his voice so that it might be heard by those within the cells.—" And then we shall relieve you."

" Well, I wish you'd do it quick, for I'm blanked tired of this business, I can tell you ! " snapped the Captain.

" Oh, it won't be long now. A day or two at most. We'll have Allen, dead or alive. I had information to-day that will secure him. And the court will sit immediately to try them."

The Captain made no answer, except a grunt. Leech puffed out his bosom.

" A soldier's duty is to obey orders, Captain," he said, sententiously.

The Captain turned on him suddenly, his red face redder than ever. " Look here, you bully these men down here who haven't anybody to speak up for them ; but don't you be trying to teach me my duty, Mister Leech, or I'll break your crooked neck, you hear ? "

He looked so large and threatening that Leech fell back. In order to appease the ruffled officer and satisfy him that he was not a coward, Leech, just as he was leaving, said that he did not care for him to send guards up to his house that night, as he had been doing.

" All right."

" Of course, I mean until toward bedtime, Captain. I think it still better to keep them there until I leave. I have important documents there. You don't know these people as I do. I shall go to the city to-morrow or next day. I have business there, and I have the utmost confidence in your ability to manage things. I shall report your zeal to our friends in Washington."

" All right," grunted the Captain. And Leech went off.

Leech started toward his house. " I'll have him recalled and get somebody else in his place," he muttered.

He stopped, and, going to his office, lit a lamp and wrote a letter to the authorities urging a transfer of the present company, on the ground that the Captain did not appear very well adapted for managing the negroes, and that he feared it was giving encouragement to those they were trying to suppress.

When he had written his letter, he sat back and began to think. He had heard a name that day that had disquieted him. It was the name of the teacher at Mrs. Welch's school. He had always supposed her name was Miss May, but it seemed that her name was Miss Bush.

One thing that had worried him in the past more than he had ever admitted even to himself had like the others, under the influence of his fortunate star, passed wholly away. He had married early in life. As his ambition rose, his wife had been a clog to him. He had tried to get a divorce; but this she resisted, and he had failed. She had, however, consented to a separation. And he had persuaded her to give up his name and resume her own, Miss Bush. He had not heard anything of her in a long time, and he was quietly moving to get a divorce on the ground of abandonment—of her having abandoned him. When this was done, why should he not marry again? Miss Krafton was a handsome girl. It would make Krafton his friend and ally instead of his enemy, and together they could own the State.

Just then there was a knock at the door. A servant entered. A lady wanted to see him. Who was it? The servant did not know. She wanted to see him at once. Curiosity prevailed. "Show her in," said Leech. She entered a moment later. Leech turned deadly white. It was Miss Bush. The next moment his fear gave way to rage. He sprang to his feet. "What are you doing here? Where did you come from?" he snarled.

She seated herself on a chair near the door.

"Don't be angry with me, John," she said, quietly.

"I am angry. Why shouldn't I be angry with you? You have lied to me."

"That I have not." She spoke firmly.

32

" You have. What do you call it ? Did you not promise never to bother me again ? "

" I have not bothered you. I came here to try and protect you."

" You have. You gave me your word never to come near me again. What do you want ? "

" I want to talk to you."

" Well, talk quick. I have no time to waste on you. I am busy."

" I know you are, and I shall not bother you long. I want you to stop prosecuting Dr. Cary and Mr. Gray and Captain Allen."

" What do you know about them ? " asked Leech, in unfeigned astonishment.

" They are friends of friends of mine. Dr. Cary saved my life not long ago."

"I wish he'd let you— I'll see you first where I wish they were now—in blank."

" There is no use in speaking that way, John," she said, quietly.

" I don't want you to ' John ' me," he snarled. " I tell you I want you to go away."

"I am going," she said, sadly. " I will go as soon as I can. I have no money."

" Where is your money ? "

" I lent it to Captain McRaffle to invest."

" More fool you ! "

His manner changed.

" Will you go if I give you the money ? "

" Yes "—his face brightened—"as soon as I have finished my year here."

He broke out on her furiously.

" That's always the way with you. You are such a liar, there's no believing you. I wish you were dead."

"I know you do, John; and I do, too ; " she said, wearily. " But the issues of life and death belong to God."

" Oh, that's just a part of your hypocrisy.   Here, if I give you money, will you go away ? "

" Yes, as soon as I can."

" And will you promise me never to breathe my name to a soul while you are here, or let anyone know that you know me ?   Will you give me your word on that ? "

" Yes."

He looked at her keenly for a moment.

" Does anyone know that you—that you ever knew me ? "

She flushed faintly, with distress.

" Yes, one person—one only."

Leech sprang to her and seized her roughly.

" And he ?   Who is he ? "

" Dr. Cary.   I told him when I thought I was dying. He will not tell."

He gave a cry of rage.

" He !   I'd rather have had anyone else know it."   He flung her from him roughly and stood for a moment lost in thought.   His countenance cleared up.   If Dr. Cary had promised not to tell, he knew he would not do so, if his life hung on it.

When he spoke it was in a somewhat changed voice.

" Remember, you have sworn that you will never mention it again to a soul, and that you will never come near me again as long as you live ! "

" Yes."   She looked at him with pleading eyes, interlacing her fingers.   " Oh, John ! " she gasped, and then her voice failed her.

For answer, Leech opened the door and glanced out into the empty passage, then seized her by the shoulder and put her outside, and, shutting the door, locked it.

A minute later she slowly and silently went down the dark stairs and out into the night.

CHAPTER XXXIX

CAPTAIN ALLEN CLAIMS THE REWARD LEECH OFFERED

LEECH had a bad half-hour; but when he left his office his spirits were rising again. He had weathered many a storm before. It would be hard if he could not weather this little trouble. He was satisfied that his wife would keep her word not to divulge his secret to anyone, and if he could but get her away everything would go all right. He would be free to marry a handsome and wealthy woman; and this alliance would give him complete control of the State. With this, what might he not have—wealth unlimited, position, unmeasured power—there was no end to it! It all stretched before him a shining track with, at the end—it appeared before him for only one brief moment—a dazzling point: at the far end of that long track a great white house, with the broad avenues reaching in every direction. Why not? Why should he not be ——? The vision made his head swim. He wiped his hand across his mouth as though he tasted something actually material.

He returned to earth, and, locking his office-door, strolled up the hill. The village was all quiet except for the sentries pacing their beats.

As Leech walked up under the clear stars, the thought came into his mind once more; and this time he tried to follow it step by step. Yes, it was possible. He was rich, powerful, fortunate. He would be Governor. What might he not be! His enemies had fallen before him—all but one, and that one could not escape. He would find him, alive or dead; and then—wealth—power—revenge! He raised his clenched hand and brought it down in the intensity of his feeling.

"Yes, by G—d! I'll have him, alive or dead!" he exclaimed. He was almost at his gate. Two steps brought him to it; and before him in the darkness, waiting for him, tall and silent, stood the man he wanted.

"I hear you are hunting for me," said Steve Allen, quietly. "I am here."

The blood rushed back and forth in Leech's veins as cold as ice, as hot as fire. What would he not have given for his guards! Why had he been such a fool as to dismiss them! He thought of his pistol; but he knew Steve was quicker with a pistol than he. So he resorted to craft. He would keep him until the guards arrived.

"How are you, Captain? Won't you walk in?" he said, with a show of ease, though his voice quavered. He thought about offering his hand, but feared to do so. If he could only detain him!

"Thank you. I will." Steve indicated with a wave of his hand that Leech should precede him; and Leech walked before him, knowing that he was his prisoner. Still he hoped help would come. They went into his library. Steve took a seat.

"What did you want with me?"

"I was only fooling," said Leech, feebly. Steve looked so placid that he began to feel reassured. "You know there's a warrant out for your arrest; and the best thing for you to do is to surrender quietly. You can clear yourself easy enough, and it's just a form. You come with me, and I'll do all I can for you." His voice was cajoling, and he looked at Steve almost tenderly. "You know I was only fooling about what I said."

Steve looked at him with cold contempt. "You'll find it ill fooling with a desperate man. Let's drop our masks. You have made a mistake to push us so far. You have offered a reward for me, alive or dead. I am here to claim it. You are my prisoner, and you know it." He gave Leech a glance that made him shiver. "Sit there, and write what I tell you." He indicated Leech's desk. Leech, with blanched face, took his seat. As he did so he glanced furtively at the clock. Secret as the glance was, Steve saw it.

"Be quick about it, and don't waste a word. I have no time to spare. Remember, it was alive or dead you wanted me." He dictated the words of a safe-conduct :

"To the Commandant of United States troops in District No. —. Pass the bearer and companions, and render them all the aid possible. For reasons of State," added Steve, with a twinkle in his eye, as he glanced over it. "Now sign it."

Leech signed slowly. He was listening with all his ears.

"Now another." Steve dictated the following to the commanding officer in the village: "I have been called away unexpectedly on business connected with the man I want, Captain Allen. Take no steps in my absence, and credit no reports not signed by me personally." Now sign it, and add this postscript : "I have decided to pursue a more conciliatory policy toward the prisoners. Please make them entirely comfortable, and give their friends access to them." Sign that, and mark it to be delivered in the morning, and leave it on your table.

"Leave it on my table ? " Leech's face blanched.

"Yes, you are going with me."

Just then steps were heard on the walk outside, and the murmur of low voices reached them. A gleam of hope stole into Leech's face. Steve Allen heard too, and he listened intently. As he turned his eyes again on Leech, a new light appeared in the latter's eyes ; fear had suddenly changed to joy.

"Aha ! Captain Allen, our positions are reversed again. Let us drop our masks indeed ! You are my prisoner now. Those are my sentries. The house is surrounded by soldiers. Ah ! ha-ha-ha !" he laughed, leaning back in his chair, eying Steve, and rubbing his hands in glee.

Steve shifted his seat a little, displaying the butt of a revolver.

"You fool!" he said, with that coolness which was Leech's envy and despair, and which made him in a way admire Steve more than any other man he knew. "Suppose they are your men? You are going with me all the same. If they come in here, you are still my prisoner; and one word—one look from you—one bare suspicion on their part that I am not going on your invitation; that it is not voluntary on your part—and you are a dead man." He loosened his pistol, and, while he listened, sat looking at Leech with a cool assurance on his face that made Leech gasp.

There was a sharp knock at the outer door. As Steve listened his expression changed to one of amusement.

"Call to them to come in, and remember you were never in greater peril than at this moment."

Leech called, and there was the slow tramp of several men in the passageway.

"Call them in here."

Leech was becoming puzzled. But he could not keep down the hope that was dawning on his countenance. He called, and they approached the door. Steve did not even turn. He was keeping his eyes on a big gilt mirror that hung in front of him and showed both the door and Leech.

The men reached the door and knocked again; then opened it, and three men in United States uniform stood in the doorway. Steve's hand left his pistol, and the eyes in the mirror were filled with a more amused smile as he glanced from them to Leech. A radiant joy sprang into Leech's face. He gave a dive behind his desk, shouting, "Seize that man. Shoot him if he lifts his hand!"

Nothing of the kind, however, occurred. At a sign from Steve, the three men came inside the room and closed the door behind them.

"Come out, Leech. These are my men, not yours,"

said Steve. "You are too big a coward to fool with; come out. Pull him out, one of you." And the man nearest Leech caught him by the arm and dragged him up on his feet, gasping and white with returning terror as he saw the trick that had been played him.

"Did you think I was such a fool as that?" Steve asked, contemptuously. "Come, we have no more time to lose. Fetch him along, men." He turned to the door, and the next moment Leech was seized and hustled out at a trot. The sight of a pistol in the hand of one of the men kept him quiet. At the door a gag was put into his mouth, a cap was pulled down over his eyes, and his arms were pinioned to his side. He was conscious that the lamps were extinguished, and the key turned in the lock behind him. Then he was borne to his gate, set on a horse, and carried off through the darkness at a gallop. He gave a groan of terror. "Remember Andy Stamper," said one of the men, and Leech remembered well enough. How far they went the prisoner had no means of knowing. After awhile the gag was taken from his mouth; but he was told that the least outcry would mean his death. They travelled at a brisk gait all night, and he knew that he had several men in his escort; but though they at times talked together in undertones, they did not address him and were deaf to his speeches. Much of the journey was through woods, and several times they forded rivers, and toward the end they must have left all beaten tracks, for they rode through bushes so dense as almost to sweep him from his horse; then they descended a steep hill, forded a stream, and, a little later, Leech was lifted from his horse, borne, half-dead with fright and fatigue, into a house, down a flight of steps, and laid on a bed. One of the men who brought him in lighted a candle and gave him a drink of whiskey, which revived him; and Leech found that he was in a large room with stone walls, furnished simply, like a bedroom, and ventilated from the top.

The man who was left with him was a stranger to him,

and, as he turned to go, Leech asked him to tell him where he was and what they were going to do with him. He felt that it was his last chance.

" Maybe keep you as a hostage, maybe not."

" As a hostage ? "

" That's the Commander's idea. As a hostage for those you've arrested, and I reckon what the Capt'n says will prevail. Good-by." He shut the door and bolted it behind him, leaving Leech alone.

This, then, explained what Steve Allen meant by what he said. He was a prisoner, to be held as a hostage for those he had arrested. There was a bed in the room ; and Leech was so fatigued that he fell asleep, and slept until he was awakened by the guard bringing him something to eat. This man, like the others, was masked, and he refused to talk at all.

" What will they do with me ? " asked Leech.

" Depends on what orders you've given about those you've arrested," said the man in a voice which Leech knew was feigned. He was going. Leech determined to make one more effort.

" Wait, please. I'm rich. No, I'm not rich ; but I have friends who are who would pay well if you—if I were to get back to them." His voice had grown confidential.

" Shouldn't be surprised." The tone was rather dry ; but that might have been due to the fact that the voice was disguised. And as he appeared acquiescent, Leech took courage. He moved a little nearer to him. " I could make it worth your while to let me go," he said, insinuatingly. The man waited. Leech's hopes revived. McRaffle had sold out; why not buy this man ? He was plainer. " Why not let me out ? " The guard was considering. " Help me, and help me get hold of—just help me, and I will see that you and your friends receive full pardon, and will make you rich."

The guard pulled off his mask. It was Steve Allen

himself. " Good-night ; " and he was gone, leaving Leech with his heart in his mouth.

There was great excitement in the County over the disappearance of Major Leech ; but it was suppressed excitement, and, curious as it may seem, his absence had the immediate effect of quieting the negroes. They were struck with awe at either the boldness or the mystery of his abduction, and almost within a night after he disappeared they had subsided. One who had seen them parading and yelling with defiance and delight the day that Leech led his handcuffed prisoners to the station to ship them off to prison, would not have recognized the awe-struck and civil people who now went back and forth so quietly to their work. It seemed almost a miracle.

All sorts of tales were published in the public press as to this latest outrage, and there was much denunciation ; but no action was taken immediately, and for a time, at least, the old County was once more under the rule of its own citizens.

Owing partly to the letter Leech had written just before his disappearance, and partly to the request of the Captain of the company, who was heartily tired of his work, an order had been issued transferring that officer's company to another post ; and he had left with his company before the fact of Leech's abduction became known. An appeal was made to the Governor to declare the County under martial law ; but though he talked about it loudly enough, and made many threats, he did not carry out his threats immediately. Perhaps the Governor was not too anxious to go into an investigation that might, instead of proving Leech to have been murdered, result in bringing back into the field his most formidable rival.

It, however, was deemed by the higher authorities that something must be done to vindicate the majesty of the law, and it was decided to send other troops to the County. The selection of troops, however, had been proved by the history of the County to be a matter of more than ordinary delicacy. Several different bodies had been sent there without accomplishing what had been hoped for.

It happened that Thurston's command had just returned from the Northwest and was awaiting some disposal. It was remembered that this same troop had once quieted things in the disturbed region, and had given, at least, more of a show of peace than any of their numerous successors had done. This was one view of the case. There was perhaps another view which may have influenced some. So Thurston was unexpectedly dispatched with his command to the place from which he had been ordered several years before. His appearance was a complete surprise to the old residents, and the effect was immediately apparent.

It was not known what it signified. Some thought it meant the immediate placing of the County under martial law, and the arrest of the remaining citizens. Others held differently. Whatever it meant, the excitement quieted down. The whites had had experience with this company, and felt that they could be relied on. The blacks recognized that a stronger power had come among them, and that it meant order and obedience.

When Captain Thurston dismounted from his horse on the very ground on which he had dismounted a number of years before, he had a curious feeling of mingled pleasure and dissatisfaction. There, amid the big trees, stood the old court-house, massive and imposing as it had looked that day when he had guyed old Mr. Dockett about its architecture, and told him that it was finer than anything in Athens; there, were the same great trees; there the same rows of old offices, only a little more dilapidated; there the same moody faces of the few whites, and the same crowd of idling negroes lagging about his troop. He turned and looked at the clerk's office, almost expecting to see the same rosy, girlish face looking out at him defiantly. Instead, a brawny negro in black clothes, with a beaver hat cocked on the side of his head, was lounging in the

door smoking a cigar. It gave the captain an unpleasant
shock ; and as he made arrangements about placing his
camp he wondered where old Mr. Dockett was now, and how
his pretty daughter was coming on. He had not heard
from her since his last campaign. She was probably married. The idea gave him an unpleasant sensation. He
always hated to hear of any pretty girl marrying. It
seemed to make the world lonelier. The negro in the door
sauntered across toward the camp and spoke to some of
the soldiers familiarly, his silk hat on the side of his head,
his cigar rolling in his mouth.

"What company is this, men ? "

The words reached the Captain. One of the men who
was working told him shortly.

" Who's your Captain ? "

" There he is."

Thurston had grown stouter, and the negro did not recognize him.

" That little man ? What's his name ? "

Thurston caught the speech and, before the soldier
could answer, bawled at the negro, " Come here and take
hold of these things, and don't stand there interfering with
the men." The darky looked at him in blank amazement.

"Who ? Me ? "

" Yes, you."

" Not me ; you don't know who I am ! " He reared
himself back and stuck his thumbs in his armholes.

"No, and I don't care a hang either," said the little
Captain. "Sergeant, make that man take hold of those
things and put them in place."

" I'm Senator Ash," declared the man, surlily, swelling
with importance, and turning to walk away.

" Halt, there," said the soldier, coldly.

Nicholas Ash turned at the tone, to find the sergeant
quietly taking his pistol from the holster.

" You come back here."

"I'm Senator Ash."

"Well, I don't give a ——— who you are; if you are Captain Jack himself, you catch hold there, as the Captain says, or 'twill be the worse for you. He won't stand no foolishness. I've seen him string a man up for less than you have said already." And the weather-beaten soldier looked so coldly on the senator that the latter deemed it best to go through the form of obeying, and, swallowing his rage as best he might, took hold and did his first manual labor in some years.

This was the first official act of Captain Thurston on his return, and, though it was an accident, it, perhaps, saved him trouble in the future.

The Captain availed himself of the earliest opportunity to hunt up his old friends. When he had pitched his camp and got settled, he sauntered up to Mr. Dockett's. As he walked along he noted the changes that had occurred since he went away. The yards were more uncared for, the houses more dilapidated, and the fences more broken. As he entered the Dockett yard, he was pleased to observe that it was kept in its old trim order. The breath of flowers that he remembered so well, and had always associated with the place, met him as of old. When he opened the gate he saw that there were several persons on the porch; but as he approached they all rose and disappeared in the house. There were one or two white dresses in the party. He had not long to wait. At his knock Mrs. Dockett herself appeared, and he thought he could see the firm set of her mouth and the glint in her eyes as she bore down upon him. She looked much older. She did not appear surprised to see him. She invited him in, but did not say anything about her daughter; and at length the Captain had to ask after her. She was very well, she thanked him. She had some young friends with her.

In this condition of affairs, Captain Thurston had recourse to stratagem. He adroitly turned the conversation to Rupert Gray, and began to tell of his success in the

West, and of the incident when he had showed such bravery while acting as a scout with him. He was conscious
at once of the change in the good lady's manner, and of
the increased interest she betrayed; so he dilated on it at
some length. No one ever had a warmer historian. He
made Rupert out a hero, and was congratulating himself
secretly on his success, when, with a sniff, Mrs. Dockett declared that she was not surprised at Rupert's acting so. It
was only what she should have expected from one of their
young men, and she was not surprised that the Yankees
should have been obliged to call on him to help them. But
she was surprised that Captain Thurston should have ex-
posed a boy like Rupert, hardly more than a child, to such
danger. Why had he not gone himself to rescue his men?
Thurston could not help laughing at the turn she gave his
story. This shot appeared, however, to have somewhat
cleared the atmosphere. Mrs. Dockett began to unbend.
She "would see her daughter; perhaps, she would come
in; she would like to hear of Rupert." Just then, whether
for this reason or one in which the visitor had a more personal concern, the door opened and Miss Dockett walked
in unbidden. She, too, had grown older since Thurston
went away; but the change was not to her disadvantage.
The plump little figure had developed; the round face had
in it more force; and she had become, if not a very pretty woman, at least a very comely one. She greeted the
Captain distantly, but not coldly. She began by making
war at once, and that the little officer was used to. It was
only indifference that he could not stand.

"Well, and so you have come back, and I suppose you
will expect us all to get down on our knees to you?" she
said, her chin a little elevated.

"No, not you. I'll make a treaty with you, if you
won't insist on my getting down on mine to you," he
laughed.

"To me? I supposed Miss Welch was the only one you
did that to."

This was encouraging, and the little Captain was instantly at his ease.

"Miss Welch ? Who is Miss Welch ? "

"Come, now, don't be trying that with me ; I know all about it, so you might as well tell me. Perhaps, you'll need my assistance. All the gentlemen seem to be victims to her charms. Captain Allen thinks there is no one like her. Some men, when they are discarded, take to drink, but here they seem to take to Miss Welch."

"Well, some men need one kind of stimulant, and some another ; now, I like mine with a proper mixture of spirit and sweetening." The little Captain's eyes were helping him all they could.

"I don't know what you mean, I'm sure." She looked down coyly.

"Say, a sort of peach and honey ? "

"You men have such vulgar similes." The little nose was turning up.

"Well, I'll be literary, and say 'a snow and rose-bloom maiden,'" said the Captain, who had been reading Carlyle. "I always think of you in connection with roses and snow."

The little nose came down, and the Captain's peace was made. He began to tell of Indian fights and long marches over parched or snow-swept plains, where men and horses dropped. Miss Elizabeth, like Desdemona, to hear did seriously incline, and the Captain was invited to supper.

CHAPTER XL

THE disappearance of Leech had strangely affected Miss Bush. She was much agitated by it. Her host was sure at first that Leech had gone off; then he was sure he had been murdered. Miss Bush was accustomed to investigate for herself. Among her acquaintances was old Peggy, who lived in the cabin on the abandoned place. Miss Bush, in her round among the negroes, had found the old woman, and, in the face of some coldness on the latter's part, had persisted in showing her kindness, and had finally won her gratitude, if not her friendship. Soon after Leech's disappearance she paid old Peggy a visit. Then she went to see Miss Welch. If Miss Welch would only use her influence with Captain Allen! Miss Welch had none; they did not even speak. But she made a suggestion.

So, one evening about dusk, just after the arrival of Thurston with his command, a visitor, deeply veiled, applied to the sentinel at the gate of the court-green, and asked leave to see Mr. Jacquelin Gray. The sergeant of the guard was called, and, after certain formalities, she was admitted to the clerk's office; and a few minutes later Jacquelin Gray came in. The visitor stated, with some nervousness, that she wished to see him privately, and Jacquelin, wondering what the stranger could want with him, walked with her into the inner office. Even there she appeared greatly embarrassed. She evidently did not know how to begin, and Jacquelin, to relieve her, asked her kindly what he could do for her.

"I have a great favor to ask of you," she said.

"Well, madam, I do not know what I can do for any-one, a prisoner like me," said Jacquelin, smiling half-grimly, half-sadly. "But I think I can say that whatever I can do I will do."

"I am sure you can. If you cannot, no one can. I want you to intercede for me with Captain Allen."

"With Steve! For you? Why, I do not know where he is! And I am sure if he knew you wanted anything he could grant, he would do it on your own simple request. Who are you?"

The visitor, after a moment of hesitation, put back her veil and faced him. "Don't you remember me?" she asked, timidly.

Jacquelin looked at her earnestly. For a moment he was deeply puzzled; then, as a faint smile came into her eyes, a light broke on him.

"Why, Miss Bush! What are you doing here?"

"I am teaching school. I am the school-teacher at the Bend, Miss May."

"Is it possible?" He stepped forward and took her hand warmly. "I never knew it. I have heard the name, but I never connected it with you. Why did you not let me know before? I am very glad to see you, and I can say that anything in the world I can do for you I will do."

"You must not promise too fast. It is a great favor I have to prefer," she said. "And I do not know whether, when you hear it, you will be willing to help me."

"Well, I know. I have not forgotten the hospital."

She appeared once more deterred from speaking by embarrassment.

"I want you to save Jonadab Leech," she said.

"What! What do you know of him?" asked Jacquelin, in sincere astonishment.

"I know he is alive."

"You do? What do you know of him? What is he to you?"

"He is—he was—my husband."

33

" Miss Bush ! "

" We were separated. But——" She stopped in agitation, pulled down her veil, and turned her face away.
Jacquelin watched her in silent sympathy.

" I am sure it was his fault," he said.

" Yes, I think it was," brokenly, from under her veil.
" He was not very kind to me. But I cannot forget that
-he was my husband, and the father of my child."

" I will do what I can for you," Jacquelin said, kindly.
" Tell me how you think I can help him. What do you
know of him ? "

She composed herself, and told him what she knew.
She knew where Leech was, and the conditions under
which he was held. She wanted Jacquelin to interfere
personally. This alone would save him, she believed.
The difficulty was to get Jacquelin free. Here her powers failed, and she sat looking at Jacquelin in hopeless
anxiety.

Jacquelin thought deeply. Suddenly he roused himself.

" All right, Miss Bush. I will see what I can do. You
are just in time. The order has come this evening, I hear,
for us to go to the city to-morrow. I have never asked a
favor of my keepers ; but I will do it for you, and, if you
will wait in here, I will let you know if there is any
chance."

He went out, leaving the little school-teacher in the dim
office. His first visit was to his fellow-prisoner, Mr. Stamper. It was an extraordinary request that he made of
Thurston a little later : to be allowed to leave his prison
for the night, and take Andy Stamper with him, and to be
lent two good horses. But it was granted. He promised
to be back by daylight, and Thurston knew he would be
back.

" I will be here, dead or alive," said Jacquelin ; and he
and Andy Stamper rode away in the dusk.

Leech was awakened from his slumbers that night by the
trampling of many horses outside, and footsteps and voices

in the rooms above him. He started up in terror; for though he could not catch anything that was said, he knew from the sound that there must be many men in the party, and he felt sure that his time had come.

He rose and groped around his chamber. By creeping up to the chimney and listening intently, he could after awhile distinguish a part of what was said. To his unspeakable terror he could hear his own name mentioned again and again. The men were a body of Ku Klux, and they were debating what should be done with him. Most of the voices were low, but now and then one rose. He heard one man distinctly give his vote that he should be hanged, and, judging from the muffled applause that followed, it appeared to meet with much favor. Then he heard the name of Steve Allen, and the discussion seemed to be heated. Suddenly, in the midst of it, there was a general exclamation. A door slammed; a heavy tread crossed the floor above him, and dead silence fell. It was broken by a single voice speaking in the deep tone which Leech recognized instantly as Steve Allen's. He gave himself up for lost. But he was astonished at the next words that caught his ear. Captain Allen's voice was clearer than the others, or he was speaking louder, and to the prisoner's surprise he was defending him, or, at least, was opposing the others. He was evidently angry. Leech heard him say he was surprised to find them there and to learn why they had come. There was a confused murmur at this, and Leech heard one voice calling, "Order! Order! Remember your vows."

This produced quiet, and the voice said (evidently speaking to Captain Allen):

"It is the decision of the Supreme Council. We have come to take the prisoner and deal with him according to our laws."

"And I tell you," said Captain Allen, his voice ringing out clear and perfectly audible, "that I do not recognize your laws, and that you shall not have him. He is my prisoner, and I will defend him with my life. You will not get him except over my dead body."

There was a suppressed murmur at this, but Captain Allen continued, speaking firmly and boldly. He went over the state of affairs in the County, and related his object in capturing Leech to hold him as a hostage for his friends and relatives. To do away with him would be to destroy the very object with which he had taken him prisoner, and would render himself liable for his murder. This he did not propose to allow. He should hold Leech for the present, and meantime would be responsible for him; and he would allow no one to touch a hair of his head.

Leech began to breathe again. It was a strange feeling to him to be grateful to Steve Allen ; but at that moment he could have kissed his feet. There was more talking, but too confused for Leech to catch what was said ; and whenever Allen spoke it was in the same bold tone, which showed that he remained firm ; and, at length, Leech could hear the crowd going. They came down outside the house, and Leech could hear them getting their horses, and, finally, they rode away. One thing, however, terrified the prisoner. The voices of two men talking near the wall reached him from above. One of them was grumbling that Captain Allen should have come and prevented their carrying out their plan. Who was he, he asked, that he could come in and defy the decision of the Supreme Council ? He had left the order, and declared that he did not recognize them any longer ; and the speaker did not like to have him or anyone setting himself up and claiming to be above the order.

"Oh, never mind about that," said the other ; " he won't be here all the time. We'll come back some time when he is not here, and deal with that dog as he deserves ; and then Allen will find out whether he is as big as he thinks himself."

Just then an order was given by someone, and they rode off, and left Leech with the drops of sweat standing out on his forehead. The sound of their trampling died away, and there fell a deep silence, broken for a little while by the faint sound of a distant footstep, which Leech believed to be that of his captor and guard ; and after a short time even this died out, and Leech went back to his bed, trembling with fright, and, finally, sank into a fitful slumber.

He had not been asleep a great while when there was again a sound of horses trampling. Leech sprang up once more, in an agony of terror. He heard a challenge from above—" Halt, there ! "—from some one who seemed to be a guard, and then a colloquy, in which he could distinguish his name ; and then his guard seemed to yield. After a short interval he heard the footsteps of several men coming down the stair that led to his door, and there was a short consultation outside. He heard someone say, " This is the place Steve said he is in ; I know it."

They tried the door, and then a voice called him, " Leech, Leech—Colonel Leech ! " He was afraid to answer. He was almost dead with fright. It called again ; and this time he was glad he had not answered, for he heard one of the men say, " He forgot to give me the key. We'll break in the door. Wait, I'll get an axe."

He went up the stair, and Leech could hear the other waiting outside. Leech was sure now that his last hour had come. In his terror he ran to the chimney and attempted to climb up in it. It was too narrow, however ; and all he could do was to get up in it a little way and draw up his feet. Here he stuck, wedged in, paralyzed with terror, while he heard the blows outside under which the door was giving way.

Presently the door was smashed in, and Leech could see the light of the torch, or whatever it was, flashed upon the floor, and could hear the voices of the men.

" He isn't in here," he heard one say, and his heart revived a little ; but the next second it sank, for he heard the searchers say, " There is his bed. He has been in it ;

so he must be here somewhere." They approached the chimney, and one of them held his torch up.

" Here he is," he laughed. " Come out, Colonel."

He did not wait for Leech to move, but, reaching up, caught him by the leg and pulled him down amid a cloud of dust and soot. Leech must have presented a strange appearance, for the men, who were masked, burst out laughing. Leech began to pray for his life, but the men only laughed.

" Come on, Colonel. We'll present you to your friends as you are," said one of them, the smaller. " You ought to be pleased with your looks, for you look just like one of your friends. You wouldn't know yourself from a nigger."

Leech recognized Andy Stamper, and knew he was lost. Andy had escaped. He began to beg him, and to make him all sorts of promises, which Andy cut short.

" Oh, pshaw ! Come along. Shut up. This is no time for you to be making promises. Come along, and keep your mouth shut."

They seized him, and dragged him up the steps and through a door out into the darkness. There, at a little distance, were two horses, on one of which Andy Stamper sprang, while the other man made Leech mount up behind him ; and then, springing on the other horse himself, they set off at a sharp trot. As they mounted, Leech recognized Jacquelin Gray. He nearly fell from his horse.

As they followed wood-paths he began to have a dim hope ; not much, however, for he could not think that these two men could intend him any good. Once, as they were on a road, the sound of horses' feet ahead reached them, and the two riders instantly left the road and struck into the bushes.

" If you get out of this," said Andy Stamper, "and get back safe to your friends, will you swear you'll never say a word about it to anybody ? Never a single—— ? "

" Yes, I'll swear. I swear before——" said the prisoner, so quickly that the other had not time to finish his question.

"That you will never tell anyone a word about this place, or how you got here, or how you were taken, or anything?"

"Yes, yes. I swear before G—d I never will—never a word. I swear I won't."

"Let's see. How will you swear it?" asked the other, reflectively.

"I'll swear it on the Bible. I'll swear on a stack of Bibles."

"We ain't got any Bibles," said the other, dryly.

"I'll give you my word of honor as a gentleman."

The other only grunted. He was not much impressed.

"I'll swear before——"

Mr. Stamper suddenly roused up to the necessities of the occasion.

"Here," he said, quickly. "Do you swear that, if you ever breathe a word as to how you got here, who brought you, or who took you away, or anything you saw here, or anything about the place at all, you hope G—d will strike you dead, and d—n you in h—l fire?"

"Yes. I'll swear it," said Leech, fervently. "I hope he will d—n me forever if I do."

"And strike you dead?" repeated Andy, not to admit any loophole.

"Yes."

"If that don't keep him nothin' will," said Andy, dryly, half-aloud; and then he added, for further security: "Well, you'd better keep it, for if you don't, the earth won't be big enough to hide you. You won't have another chance."

As they waited, a body of horsemen, heavily muffled, rode silently along the road they had just left, and passed out of sight into the woods behind them. It was a body of Ku Klux making their way back home, or, perhaps, back to the house from which Leech had just been taken. The two rescuers rode on and at length emerged into a field, and, crossing it, dismounted behind a clump of buildings.

The eastern sky was just beginning to redden with the

first glimmer of dawn; and the cheep of a bird announcing it was heard in the trees as the men tied their horses.

" Come on," said Andy. " In a little while you can make your promises." They led Leech between them, half-dead with fright and fatigue, and, helping him over a wall, dragged him up to a door, and, opening it, walked in.

" Who's that ? " asked a man, rising from a sofa, where he had evidently been asleep.

" Here we are ; back on time," said Jacquelin, gravely.

" Ah ! you've got back ? Wait. I'll strike a light. Who's this with you ? "

" A prisoner," said Andy, with mock solemnity ; " but whether white or black you'll have to tell."

The man struck a light, and Leech, to his astonishment, found himself in the presence of a Federal officer—of Reely Thurston.

The two men stared at each other in blank amazement. And it is probable that, if at that moment their happiness in finding their chief wish gratified could have been marred, it would have been by the fact that they owed this to each other. Perhaps something of this kind must have appeared in their faces, for Jacquelin laughed.

" Well, you two can settle matters between you. We are off—to jail," he said. " Now, Major Leech, you can make good your promises ; and it will depend on whether you see fit to do so or not, whether we have done a good act or not. Good-night." He and Andy went off.

The next day the prisoners were sent to the city under Captain Thurston's personal guard, the little Captain, for his own private reasons, deciding to take them himself, Leech accompanied them.

CHAPTER XLI

THE vows of a considerable part of the human race are said to be writ in water, but it is by no means only that sex to whom the poet has attributed this quality, which possesses it. Quite another part of the race is liable to forget vows made under conditions that have changed. And Major Leech was of this number. He no sooner found himself free and guarded by a power strong enough to protect him than he forgot the oaths he had sworn so volubly to Andy Stamper that night when he stood in the darkness of the deserted plantation ; and he applied himself with all his energy to repair his fortunes and revenge himself. His enemies were in his power. With them free he might have to undergo trial himself ; with them under indictment for offences against the Government, even if they were not convicted, he was free to push forward his plans. It was too great a temptation for him to resist, too good an opportunity for him to pass by ; and perhaps even Andy Stamper did not blame him, or even expect him to forego it.

The story the returned captive told of his wrongs was one strange enough to move hearts even less inclined to espouse his cause than those of the authorities into whose ears he poured it, and almost immediately after his arrival the machinery of the law was set in motion. His grudge against Captain Thurston was as great as that against the residents of the County—indeed greater ; for he professed some gratitude for Jacquelin Gray and Stamper, and even

521

had an offer made them of a sort of pardon, conditional on their making a full confession of their crimes. But investigation showed him that for the present he would weaken himself by attempting to attack Thurston. Thurston had secured his release. So for the time being he was content to leave the Captain alone, and apply all his energies to the prosecution of the enemies against whom he was assured of success.

In a little while he had his grand jury assembled, and the prisoners were all indicted. An early time was set for their trial. Dr. Cary was among those indicted.

In this state of the case, it appeared to the Doctor that the time had come when he could no longer with propriety refrain from applying for help to his old friend, Senator Rockfield, who had asked him to call on him. It was no longer a private matter, but a public one. It was not himself alone that was concerned, but his nearest friends and neighbors; and in such a case he could no longer stand on his pride. Already the prison was in view; and the path seemed very straight, and the way of escape seemed blocked on every side. Step by step they had been dragged along; every avenue shut off; all the old rights refused; and it looked as if they were doomed.

So Dr. Cary sat down in prison and wrote a letter to his old college-mate, setting forth the situation in which he found himself and his friends, giving him a complete statement of the case and of all the circumstances relating to it, and asked that, if in his power, the Senator would help him.

He told him that unless some action were taken promptly he saw no escape, and that he seemed doomed to a felon's cell. The Doctor told his friend that, while he had been present for a little while with the masked mob that broke into the jail, he had been so for the purpose of trying to dissuade them from any act of lawlessness; and the part he had taken could be proved by a hundred witnesses. But all those who had been arrested were indicted

with him, which would prevent their testifying for him ;
and if any others were to come forward to testify, they
would simply subject themselves to immediate arrest.

"I can give you no idea," he wrote, "of the condition
of affairs here, and shall offer no proof except my word.
Unless you and I have changed since we knew each other
man to man in that old time long ago, no other proof will
be necessary ; yet if I should attempt to give you a true
picture, I should strain your credulity.

"I think I can say, with Cicero, it is not my crimes,
but my virtues that have destroyed me.

"But if you wish to know the whole state of the case, I
would ask you to come down and see for yourself. Unfortunately I shall not be able personally to extend to you
the hospitality of my home ; but if you will go to my house,
my wife and daughter will show you every attention, and
do everything in their power to promote your comfort.

"Lying in jail as I am, under indictment for a scan-
dalous crime, with the penitentiary staring me in the face,
I perhaps should not sign myself as I do ; yet when I call
to mind the long and distinguished line of men of virtue
who have suffered the same fate, and reflect on my own
consciousness of integrity, I believe you would not have
me subscribe myself otherwise than as,

"Your old friend, JOHN CARY."

This letter reached Senator Rockfield at an auspicious
time, one evening after dinner, when he was resting
quietly at home, enjoying a good cigar, and when his
heart was mellow. It happened that certain measures
were pending just then, to secure which the Senator's influence was greatly desired. It also happened that a number of other measures of a very radical character had lately been proposed ; and the Senator had gone somewhat
deeply into the subject, with the result of unearthing an
appalling state of affairs in the whole section from which
this letter came. Moreover, Captain Middleton happened

to be at the Senator's house at that very time, and added certain details to those the Senator had learned, which stirred the Senator deeply.

The Senator's part in the release of the prisoners that shortly followed Dr. Cary's letter was not known even to Dr. Cary for some time, and was never known generally.

Senator Rockfield read Dr. Cary's letter all through twice, and then leaned back in his big chair and thought profoundly. The letter dropped from his hand to the floor, and his cigar went out. His wife, seeing that something was moving him deeply, watched him anxiously, and at length asked: " What is it? " For answer, the Senator merely picked up the letter, handed it to her across the table, and again sat back in deep thought. She read it, and looked at him more anxiously than before, her face paling somewhat. His face, which before had been soft with reminiscence, had grown stern. He was conscious that she was looking at him, and conscious of her thoughts as she was of his. Suddenly he rose to his feet.

" Where are you going ? " she asked, though in reality she knew.

" To send a telegram."

" I will call John."

" No, I am going to see Secretary ——."

He folded the letter and put it into his pocket. At the mention of the name, the light sprang into her eyes—the light of contest. She knew that it would be a crucial interview, and that her husband's future would depend on it.

" Shall I ring for the carriage ? "

" No, I will walk. I want to cool myself off a little." He stopped as he reached the door. " He was the first gentleman of our class," he said. He went out.

A half-hour later, Senator Rockfield was admitted to the study or private office of the Secretary who had the direction of matters affecting the South and who controlled everything which related to it.

He was a man of iron constitution, a tremendous

worker, and his study at his home was only a private apartment of his office in the great Government building in
which he presided. His ambition was to preside in a
greater building, over the whole Government. He gave his
life to it. Every other consideration was subordinated. It
was a proof of the Senator's influence that he was admitted
to see him at that hour. And at the instant he appeared
the Secretary was busy writing a momentous document.
As the Senator entered, however, he shot a swift, keen
glance at him, and his face lit up. He took his appearance at that hour as a proof that he had yielded, or, at
least, was yielding.

"Ah! Senator. Glad to see you," he said, with a smile
which he could make gracious. "I was just thinking of
you. I hope I may consider your visit a token of peace;
that you recognize the wisdom of our position."

He was speaking lightly, but the Senator did not respond in the same vein. His face did not relax.

"No, far from it," he said. Without noticing the chair
to which the Secretary waved him, he took Dr. Cary's letter
from his pocket and laid it on the table under the Secretary's nose. "Read that."

The Secretary's face clouded. He took up the letter and
glanced at it; then began to read it cursorily. As he did
so his face assumed another expression.

"Well, what of this?" he asked, coldly. He looked at
the Senator superciliously. His manner and the sneer on
his face were like a blow. The Senator's face flushed.

"Just this. That I say this thing has got to stop, by
G—d!" He towered above the Secretary and looked him
full in the eyes. He did not often show feeling. When he
did he was impressive. A change passed over the other's face.

"And if it don't?"

"I shall rise in my seat to-morrow morning and de-
nounce the whole administration. I shall turn the whole
influence of my paper against you, and shall fight you to
the end."

"Oh! you won't be so foolish!" sneered the Secretary.

"I will not! Wait and see!" He leant over and took up the paper. "I bid you good-evening." He put on his hat and turned to the door. Before he reached it, however, the other had reflected.

"Wait. Don't be so hasty."

The Senator paused. The Secretary had risen and was following him.

"My dear Senator, let me reason with you. I think if you give me ten minutes, I can show you the folly——"

Senator Rockfield stiffened. "Good-evening, Mr. Secretary." He turned back to the door.

"Hold on, Senator, I beg you," said the Secretary. The Senator turned, this time impatiently. "What guarantee have I that this letter is true?" asked the other, temporizing.

"My word. I was at college with the writer of that letter. He was my dearest friend."

"Oh! of course, if you know yourself that those facts are correct! Why did you not say so before? Take a seat while I read the paper over again."

The Senator seated himself without a word, while the Secretary read the letter a second time. Presently Senator Rockfield leant over and lit again the cigar he had let go out an hour before, and which he had carried all this time without being aware of it. He knew he had won his game.

When the Secretary was through, he laid the letter down and, drawing a sheet of paper toward him, began to write.

"When do you want the order issued?" he asked, presently.

"Immediately. I am going South to-night."

"It will not be necessary. I will issue an order at once that the prisoners be admitted to bail. In fact, I had intended to do so in a few days, anyhow."

The Senator looked politely acquiescent.

"But I am very glad to do it at once, at your request. You see, we are obliged to rely on the reports of our agents down there ; and they report things to be in a very bad way."

The Senator looked grimly amused.

" No doubt they are."

" I will send you a copy of the order to-morrow. I hope you will take it as a proof that we really are not quite as bad as you appear to think us." He began to write again.

The two men parted ceremoniously, and the Senator, after sending a telegram South, returned to his home.

As he entered, he found his wife anxiously awaiting him.

" I won," he said, and she threw herself into his arms.

The effect of this interview was immediately felt in the old County, and after a short time Dr. Cary and the other prisoners confined with him were admitted to bail, and eventually the prosecutions were dismissed. But this was not until after the event about to be recorded.

CHAPTER XLII

THE effect of Leech's return to power was soon visible, and the gloom in the old County was never so deep as it became after that. The failure of Steve's daring and high-handed step but intensified this. It appeared as if a complete overthrow had come at last.

As is often the case when unexpected failure has come to brilliant and promising plans, popular opinion veered suddenly; and whereas, but a little before, all were full of wonder at Steve Allen's daring coup, now that it had failed many were inclined to blame him. He ought either to have let the Ku Klux, who, it was understood, had tried to get hold of Leech, deal with him, or else have let him alone. Now he had but intensified his malice, as was shown by the rancor with which he was pushing the prosecutions. He had given Leech a national reputation, and increased his power to do harm.

Captain Allen was deeply offended by some of the things said about him by certain of the members of the secret society, and he met them with fierce denunciation of the whole order. It was, he said, no longer the old organization which, he asserted, had acted for the public good, and with a high purpose. That had ceased to exist. This was a cowardly body of cut-throats, who rode about the country under cover of darkness, perpetrating all sorts of outrages and villainies for purposes of private vengeance. He gave them to understand clearly that he was not afraid of them, and denounced and defied the whole gang.

But one thing Steve could not meet so well. He could

not meet the charge that his wild and reckless act in carrying Leech off had, in the sequel, done harm, and had intensified the hostility shown to the old County, and increased the rigor with which the citizens were treated. Even the friends who adhered stoutly to him were forced to admit that, as it turned out, his carrying Leech off was unfortunate. The downcast looks and the gloom that appeared everywhere told him how deeply the people were suffering. Another thing stuck deeper in his heart. He was at liberty and his friends in prison. Jacquelin was in prison under indictment when he had taken his place, and but for him would be a free man.

Steve had thought at times of leaving the State and going West. Rupert's career there showed what might be accomplished. But this idea passed away now in the stress of the present crisis. He would not leave the State in the hour of her darkness. He could not leave his friends. It would be desertion.

Another cause of anxiety began to make itself apparent to Captain Allen about the same time. He knew, as the reader knows, that Captain Aurelius Thurston had long been an ardent, if a somewhat intermittent, suitor of Miss Welch ; though his information was derived, not from the cold statement of the chronicler, but through those intuitions with which a lover appears to be endowed for his self-torture as well as for his security. Miss Ruth, it is true, had denied the charge, made from time to time, respecting Captain Thurston ; but we know that these denials are frequently far short of satisfying a lover's jealousy. And it must be confessed that she had never taken the trouble to state to Captain Allen the explicit and somewhat decisive conditions under which she had consented to continue the friendship.

Captain Thurston, thus cut off from his habitual occupation in that quarter, shortly after his arrival, as has been seen, went back to his old flame, Miss Elizabeth Dockett, and was soon as deeply immersed in that affair

34

as he had ever been with Miss Welch.   As Miss Elizabeth, however, treated him with unexampled rigor, and Mrs. Dockett never for an instant permitted him to forget that he was occupying the position of a tyrant, the Captain found himself obliged to seek at times the aid of a friendly ally, and turned for consolation to Miss Welch, who cheerfully rendered him in another's behalf all the service she had declined in her own.   Thus the little Captain was much more welcome at the Welches' home than he had ever been before, and rumor was kind enough to declare that his attentions were far from being unacceptable.   His duties at the court-house, as Commandant of the County, were sufficient to account for all the time he spent there, including whatever hours he passed at the old Dockett place among the trees and lilacs, while his presence at the Welches' could only be attributed to one cause.

This report reached Captain Allen, lounging on the verandas of his friends, and it did not serve to make his life as a refugee and exile more agreeable.

Matters were in this condition when the news came that the next week had been set as the time for the trial of the Red Rock prisoners.   Judge Bail had already arrived, accompanied by McRaffle.   A special jury was being selected, and the witnesses were being summoned.   They were a set to make the outlook as dark as possible—Bushman, and Perdue, and Dr. Moses, and a score of the worst negroes in the County.   Captain Allen knew that Leech had said he would rather have him than all the other prisoners put together.   And at length came a definite statement that Leech would abandon the other prosecutions if Allen would surrender himself and stand trial.   It had come through McRaffle, who claimed to have secured this concession.

Next day, Steve rode down to the court-house, and, giving his horse to a negro, with directions to send him to Dr. Cary's, walked across to Captain Thurston's camp. A number of his friends saw him, and came crowding up with wonder and curiosity in their faces. Steve spoke to them cheerily, stopped and chatted lightly for awhile, and then left them and walked quietly across the green to the camp, leaving them staring after him open-eyed and with anxious faces. He knocked at the door of the office which was the Captain's head-quarters, and, on being bid to enter, opened the door.

Perhaps there was not a man in the world whom Reely Thurston would not rather have seen at that moment than Steve Allen. He sprang to his feet as Steve entered, and stared at him in blank amazement. He had no idea why he had come, and, for an instant, perhaps, supposed it was with hostile intent. This idea, however, Steve at once dissipated by his manner.

"Good-morning, Captain Thurston." He held out his hand, and, having shaken hands with the Captain, flung himself into a seat.

"Give me a cigar. I have come to have a talk with you," he said, lightly. Thurston handed him a cigar and lit one himself, his face perplexed and a little troubled as he pondered on what could possibly have brought him this visitor. Steve saw his perplexity and smiled.

"I have come to see what terms I can make through you, Captain, before I give myself up."

"Wait. I am not authorized to make any terms. I must notify you——" Thurston was beginning very seriously. But Steve interrupted him.

"I did not say *with* you, but *through* you. I would not place you in such an embarrassing position. I suppose you would not mind seeing what terms you could make with your friend, Colonel Leech." Thurston flushed.

"He is no friend of mine," he said, hotly.

"Oh, I thought you had made up," said Steve, maliciously. "Well, he will be if you give me up to him. But I thought you might make a little better terms for me than I could for myself, as he seems to prefer the city to the country just now, and I fear a communication from me would not meet with the consideration at his hands that the closeness of our intimacy a short time since should secure for it."

"What the d—l are you driving at, Allen?" asked Thurston. "You know what I think of Leech, and how he regards me. But that does not alter the fact that I am sent here to catch—to apprehend you—and if I do my duty I should have you arrested."

"Of course, Captain Thurston, do your duty," said Steve, coolly, his face hardening a little and his upper lip curling slightly.

"No, no, Allen. I did not mean it that way. I am only trying to get at what you want. I am a little mystified."

His evident friendliness soothed Steve's feelings, which had been ruffled by his former speech.

"I want to see whether I would not be accepted as a propitiatory offering in place of my friends—of others who have done nothing, and deserve no punishment. I am the head and front of the whole business. I am responsible for all they are charged with, and they are not. And I want to get them released, and give myself up in their place."

Thurston looked deeply troubled. He shook his head thoughtfully.

"I do not want to arrest you. I must say that you are the last person in the world that I wanted to see. But if you stay here, I must arrest you. If, however, you came here with any idea that I would—I mean, that I could—make terms with you, I do not wish to take advantage of your mistake. There is a door. You can walk out of it while I go and call the sergeant of the guard."

Steve shook his head.

"No, no. I am going to give myself up, anyhow. It is the only thing I can do to help them. Perhaps, if these scoundrels get me, they may let the others off. I am the one they are after. But I want you to assist me. You are a gentleman, and can appreciate my position."

Thurston looked at him a moment, and then reached out his hand.

"Allen, I promise you I will do all I can."

The two men shook hands across the table; and Steve, settling himself comfortably, gave Thurston an account of all that had taken place between himself and Leech the night of his capture, and between himself and the band of Ku Klux the night they had come to take Leech from the place where he had confined him. He showed Thurston that he had known of the plan to rescue him.

"But why did you carry him off?" asked Thurston. "I can understand all the rest; but I do not see how a man of your sense could have supposed that you could accomplish anything by such an act."

"It was to gain time, Captain Thurston, and to tide over a crisis; and that it did. You do not know how desperate we are. Let me explain. But for that, Dr. John Cary and Jacquelin Gray would to-day be wearing convict suits. Leech had already appointed the time for that. I tided over that crisis."

He went on, and gave Thurston an account of all that had taken place in the County under Leech's régime since Thurston had left. It opened the young officer's eyes, and, when Steve was through, Thurston's face was filled with a new sympathy.

"Allen, I will do all I can for you," he said, again. And he did. He wrote to Middleton and his friends.

The news that Steve Allen had surrendered himself caused the greatest commotion not only there, but throughout the rest of the State. Even far outside the South it was regarded as a most important incident; and the newspapers declared that it was the signal of a complete collapse of the opposition to the Government. Steve was represented as every species of brigand, from the sneaking lawbreaker who entered houses under cover of night to the dashing, bold, mountain robber and desperado who held passes and fought battles with Government troops, and levied tribute on the surrounding country.

The man who profited by all this was Jonadab Leech.

He immediately took advantage of the turn in affairs to exploit himself, and to strengthen the foundation of his re-established plans. When he first heard that Steve Allen had surrendered himself, he could not believe it; but when the report was verified, he was wild with joy. He told, again and again, with many new embellishments, the story of his seizure and incarceration, and the horrors of the midnight meeting when he was tried and condemned to death without a hearing. (In his later relations there was an intimation of threats of torture having been used, and no mention of the mode of his escape.) He had visited the national capital, and he redoubled his energies in pushing the prosecutions of the Red Rock prisoners. He declared that nothing could be done until these men were punished, and the authority of the Government asserted. He contrived effectually to create fresh doubts as to the zeal of the Governor, and to supplant him as the representative of the Government. His star was once more in the ascendent. His fortunes were more promising than ever. His ambition had taken a higher leap, and he felt that now no power could keep him from the attainment of his wishes.

His whole attitude and relation to his former friends changed. Why should he handicap himself by attempting to carry the burden of Still and his tottering fortunes? He gave Still plainly to understand that he had higher aims than merely to obtain a few thousand acres of farming land. He was now a public man, and affairs of State were occupying his attention. To be sure, he continued to act as his counsel, and bled his client for ever-renewed fees in a way that made Still groan and curse. But this was all. He was engaged now in loftier aims. His name had been mentioned in the national Senate, in connection with the plans for the "pacification" of the section for which he spoke; and someone asked, "Who is Colonel Leech?"

"I will tell you who he is," said the Senator who was quoting him. "He is a man who in a short time will be your compeer on the floor of this body."

This retort was unction to Leech's soul.

Meantime the last hope of the old County was being destroyed. A black pall seemed to have covered them. The local press raved in impotent rage, and declared that open war would be better than the oppression to which they were subjected.

Just at this juncture, when Steve's surrender and Leech's triumph seemed to have put the uttermost affliction on the people, the order which Senator Rockfield had secured from the authorities came, and the prisoners named in it were released on bail. The order, however, having been issued before Captain Allen surrendered himself, did not include his name or apply to him. So when Dr. Cary, General Legaie, Jacquelin Gray, Andy Stamper, and the other residents of Red Rock were released, Captain Allen was still held, and bail was refused in his case. The issuing of that order and the discharge of the other Red Rock prisoners inspired Leech to hurry up the prosecution of Captain Allen. Thurston was working for him, and Senator Rockfield was beginning to investigate matters in the State. Bolter had written an urgent letter respecting the railway investments, and had said that Middleton was interested and had come home on Major Welch's advice to see about the matter, and was talking of coming South. So Leech could not tell when new difficulties might arise.

It was soon rumored that the Government would make a test case of the prosecution of Steve Allen, as the leader and head of the resistance to it. Leech was moving heaven and earth to secure his conviction, and was staking everything on this issue. Leech did not even deny it. He rushed forward his prosecution. If he could get Steve Allen shut up within the walls of a Government prison for a term of years, he would be free to carry out his schemes; and of this he had no doubt. Judge Bail was to try Steve, and the witnesses were being got together by McRaffle. Leech did not want to prosecute Steve for a minor offence, such as the rescue of Rupert. He wished to put him entirely out of the way. A long term only would now satisfy him. The offences with which Steve was charged were not grave enough, the penalties not heavy enough. The attack on the jail had been thrown into the background by the more recent outrages committed by the Ku Klux. Prosecution for the seizure of Leech himself would look like personal hostility, and weaken his cause ; and, besides, some awkward facts might come out in the development of the case. Thurston would be sure to tell how he had escaped, and the whole story would come out and create sympathy with the prisoner, and bring ridicule upon himself.

So Leech suddenly made a change of base. He desired to pose as a public-spirited man. He determined to drop the prosecution for the attack on the jail, and prosecute Steve Allen for the Ku Klux outrages, as to which the Government was more particularly interested. The difficulty was to establish Allen's active connection with the Ku Klux. Leech knew of his own knowledge, from Allen's statement to the assembly in the room above his prison that night, that Steve had left the order and opposed them at that time, if he had ever belonged to their organization. So he was somewhat at a loss to prove his connection with them as an active member. Accident, however, suddenly threw in his way the means to accomplish his wish, and to punish two enemies at once.

Leech had been in the upper end of the County looking after witnesses, when he met Miss Welch, who was on her way home from Dr. Cary's. She gave him a cold bow, and was passing on ; but Leech stopped her with an inquiry after her father.

"He is very well," said the girl, coldly.

"I suppose he, like all loyal men, is rejoicing over the capture at last of the head of all the trouble that has been going on down here ?" Leech's face wore a soft smile.

"I was not aware that Captain Allen was captured. I thought he surrendered." Ruth's color deepened in spite of herself.

"Well, we have him safe at last, anyhow," smiled Leech, "and I guess we'll keep him. No doubt your father is as much pleased as anyone. It puts an end to the outrages down here, and your father, of all men, should rejoice. He is too good a citizen not to."

"He is too good a man to rejoice in anyone's misfortunes," said Ruth, warmly ; "and Captain Allen has had nothing to do with the outrages you refer to. He never had anything to do with the Ku Klux except once or twice. I have his own word for it."

Leech's eyes were resting on her face.

"Ah ! You have it on good authority." His tone was most polite.

But Ruth fired up.

"I have. Captain Allen is a gentleman ; and when he says that he has never had anything to do with the Ku Klux since the first or second time they acted in this County, I am sure it is so. What he has done since then he did alone." She could not resist this shot.

Leech did not appear to mind it. His mild eyes were glowing with a sudden light, almost of joy.

"No doubt, no doubt," he murmured. And, as Ruth was moving on,

"Please remember me kindly to your father and mother."

As she rode away Leech actually slapped his thigh, and he smiled all the way home.

CHAPTER XLIII

RUTH had heard of Captain Allen's surrender the day after it took place. Mrs. Stamper, passing through from the railway on her way home from a visit to her husband in jail, had stopped and told her all about it. Ruth almost fell to the ground during Mrs. Stamper's narration. She could scarcely stand up. When Mrs. Stamper had passed on, Ruth rushed into the house and was on her way to her own room when she met her mother.

"What on earth is it, Ruth?"

"Oh, mamma!" Ruth began, but was unable to proceed, and burst into tears. Mrs. Welch also had heard the story; and she divined the cause of her agitation, and drew her into her chamber, and there Ruth opened her heart to her mother.

"I know I ought to hate him, mamma," she wept, "but I do not. I have tried to hate him, and prayed—yes, prayed to hate him; but I like him better than any man I ever met or ever shall meet, and even when I cut him on the road I liked him. I hate myself; I am humiliated to think that I should care for a man who has never said he loved me."

"But he has said so, Ruth," declared Mrs. Welch.

"What?" Ruth's eyes opened wide with a vague awaking something.

"He came to see your father, and asked his consent to pay you his addresses."

Ruth sprang to her feet as if electrified.

"Mamma!" The blood rushed to her face and back

again. She seized her mother, and poured out question after question. Her whole person seemed to change. She looked like a different being. A radiance appeared to have suddenly settled down upon her and enveloped her. Mrs. Welch was carried away by her enthusiasm, and could not help enjoying her joy. For once she let herself go, and gave herself up to the delight of thorough and complete sympathy with her daughter. She told her everything that had occurred, and Ruth in return told her mother all that she knew and thought of Steve. Thus Mrs. Welch became Ruth's confidante, and, in her sympathy with Ruth's happiness, committed herself on Ruth's side beyond hope of withdrawal.

Just then Major Welch opened the door. He stopped and looked in on the scene in wonderment. Ruth rose and flung herself into his arms.

In the conference that ensued, Ruth, however, found ground for more distress. Her father had heard the whole story of Captain Allen's surrender of himself. He had just got it from Thurston. He also knew of the telegrams Thurston had received in response to his giving notice of the surrender, and he was full of anxiety. He was by no means sure that Captain Allen, however high his motive, had done a wise act in giving himself up. He did not believe his action would be effectual to obtain the release of his friends, and he had put himself in the power of those who would move heaven and earth to secure his conviction. The dispatches that had come from the city clearly indicated this.

Under the new revelation that Major Welch had received, his interest in Captain Allen naturally increased beyond measure, and he showed it. His only hope was that proof as to Captain Allen's case might not be easy. The new laws under which the prosecutions were being pressed aimed at recent acts, and it might not be possible to prove Captain Allen's participation in these acts.

His carrying Leech off could, of course, be proved; but

while Leech would naturally push the prosecution for this, as Leech had returned, the Government might not now take that so seriously. As her father discussed Captain Allen's chances earnestly, Ruth sat and listened with bated breath, her eyes, wide with anxiety, fixed on his face, her hands tightly clasped, her color coming and going as hope and fear alternated.

It was a few days after this, that she had her brief interview with Leech.

The next day after that interview an official rode up to the door and served a summons on Ruth to appear as a witness for the prosecution in the case of the Government against Stevenson Allen. With this notice he brought also a letter to Major Welch from Leech, who wrote Major Welch that for reasons of importance to the Government he had found it necessary to request his daughter's attendance at the trial. The letter was full of expressions of regret that he should have to cause Major Welch's daughter any inconvenience. She was the only one, he said, who could prove certain facts material to the case for the Government.

As Major Welch read the letter his countenance fell. Ruth's knowledge of Captain Allen's confession of his part in the Ku Klux organization had filled out Leech's case, and Captain Allen was in graver danger than he had apprehended. The next day it was known in the County that Ruth had been summoned by Leech, and that the object of the summons was to have her prove Captain Allen's confession to her of his part in the acts of the Ku Klux. It was stated that Leech had written Major Welch to obtain the information from him, and that Major Welch had replied that his daughter would be on hand, dead or alive. The excitement in the community was intense; and the feeling against the Welches flamed forth stronger than it had ever been—stronger even than before the trial of Jacquelin's case. Intimations of this came to the Welches, and they could not ride out without encounter-

ing the hostile looks of their neighbors.   It was asserted
by some that Major Welch and his daughter had trapped
Steve, and were taking their revenge for his part in
Jacquelin's suit.   Major Welch received one or two anon-
ymous letters accusing him of this, and warning him to
leave the country without attempting to push his malice
farther.

As the Major treated these letters with the contempt
they deserved, and destroyed them without letting either
Mrs. Welch or Ruth know anything about them, they
would have given him no further concern except for the
fact that he had made up his mind to go North just then
on business.   The letters came near preventing his going ;
but as the matter was urgent, he went, and the rumor got
abroad that he had left on account of the letters.

Ruth was in a state of great distress.   She hoped she
would die before the day of the trial ; and, indeed, to have
seen her, one might have thought it not unlikely.   Dr.
Cary was sent for.   He prescribed change of air and scene.
Mrs. Welch shook her head sadly.   That was impossible
just now.   "You look as though you needed change yourself, Doctor," she said.   And well she might say so.   The
Doctor had aged years in the last weeks.   His face had
never lost the prison pallor.

"No madam—I think not," he said, calmly, his hand
resting against his breast.   Mrs. Welch did not know that
he meant that he was past that now.

"Then you must take a rest," urged Mrs. Welch.

"Yes, I think I shall take a rest before long," said he.

Ruth was out riding one afternoon just after this when
she met old Waverley.   She stopped to inquire after Miss
Thomasia who she had heard was ill.   The old man was
actually short to her.   "I don' think she'll last long now,"
he said, so significantly that it pierced the girl's breast like
a knife.   Ruth had always felt that Miss Thomasia and she
had one thing in common, and Miss Thomasia had always
been sweet and gracious to her.   Now the picture of the

old lady at home, lonely and ill from anxiety and distress, pursued her. She could not get away from it. At length she turned her horse, and rode slowly back to the little cottage amid the vines. An air of stillness that was oppressive surrounded the place. For a few moments Ruth thought of drawing back and going home. Then her courage returned. She sprang from her horse, and, tying him, walked up to the door and knocked. The knock was answered by old Peggy. The old woman's eyes darted fire at Ruth, as she answered her. She did not know whether Ruth could see Miss Thomasia or not—she thought not. Miss Thomasia was asleep. Ruth, however, persisted; she would wait until Miss Thomasia waked up. She took her seat quietly on the little veranda. The old woman looked puzzled and disappeared. Presently she returned, and said Miss Thomasia would see Ruth. Ruth went in. Miss Thomasia was sitting up in a little rocking-chair. Ruth was astounded to see the difference in her since she saw her last. She looked years older. She received Ruth civilly, but distantly, and let her do the talking. Ruth kept well away from the one subject that was uppermost in both their minds. Presently, however, in face of her impenetrable coldness, Ruth could stand it no longer. She rose to go, and bade the old lady good-by.

"Good-by, my dear," said Miss Thomasia. They were the words with which she always said her adieus. Her voice was feeble, and she spoke very low. There was something in her tone, something of resignation and forgiveness, that went to Ruth's heart, and as she turned away—a deep sigh caught her ear. She turned back. Miss Thomasia's thin hands were tightly clasped, her eyes were shut, and her lips were trembling. The next moment Ruth was down on her knees beside her, her head buried in her lap, pouring out her story.

"I must tell you," she sobbed. "I came to tell you, and I cannot go away and not tell you. I know you love him, and I know you hate me. You have a right to hate me ; they all hate me, and think I am hard and cruel.   But I am not, and neither is my father."

She went on, and, as she told her story, the other lady's hands came and rested on her head and lifted her up, and the two women wept together.

A little later Blair came in, and stopped, surprised, on the threshold.   The next moment she and Ruth were in each other's arms, weeping together ; while Miss Thomasia, with her face brighter than it had been since the news reached her of Steve's surrender, smiled on them.   Presently old Peggy opened the door, thinking perhaps Ruth had been there long enough.   She gazed on the scene in wonder for a moment, and then closed the door.   " Well, dee beats me," she muttered.   When Ruth left, Miss Thomasia looked better than she had done in days, and Ruth's own heart was lighter.   That night Blair asked old Mr. Bagby if there was no way in which a woman could avoid giving evidence against a man, if she were summoned and did not wish to testify.

" One," said the old lawyer " —two : she can die."

CHAPTER XLIV

The account of affairs in the South that Middleton had
got from Senator Rockfield had decided him to go down
there. It awakened old recollections, and recalled a time
in his life which, though there were many things in it
that he would have had otherwise, was on the whole very
pleasant to him. He had tried to do his duty under very
adverse circumstances, and, though he had not been sustained, events had justified him. He happened to be
present in the gallery during the debate in which one Senator asked, "Who is this man Leech?" and another replied, "He is a man who will soon be your compeer on this
floor." The statement had astounded Middleton. Could
it be possible that Dr. Cary, Jacquelin Gray, and General
Legaie were in jail, and that Leech was about to become a
Senator of the United States. It seemed incredible to the
young man. He had in a way kept himself informed as to
the old County, and he knew that there had been trouble
there; but he had had no idea that things had reached
this pass. That night he had the conversation with Senator Rockfield about Dr. Cary, and soon afterward he got
a letter from Thurston which finally decided him to go
South and see for himself.

His arrival at Brutusville was regarded very differently
by different people. The Welches were delighted to see
him, and so was Reely Thurston. Leech met him with a
show of much cordiality—extended his hand, and greeted
him with warmth which somehow cooled Middleton. Mid-

dleton could not for his life help having that old feeling of repulsion. He was conscious of a change in Leech. Instead of his former half-apologetic manner that was almost obsequious, Leech now was lively and assertive. His air was that of an equal—indeed, almost of a superior.

The strangest greeting, however, Middleton met with was from " Dr. Moses." Moses had returned to the County after the arrival of the troops, and had been much in evidence about the court-house, where he appeared to be in Leech's employ. The day after Middleton arrived, Moses came out of a yard just ahead of him, and advanced to meet him, hat in hand, grinning and showing his repulsive teeth and gums. It was almost a shock to Middleton to see him.

"How's Mass' Middleton ? My young master ? Glad to see you back, suh. Does you 'member Moses—ole Moses ?"

" Yes, I remember you," said Middleton, almost grimly. The negro burst out into a loud guffaw.

" Yas, suh. I knows you 'members Moses. Yaw-yaw-yaw-ee. Done lay de whup on Mose' back too good not to 'member him, yaw-yaw-yaw-ee. Dat wuz right. Now you gwine gi' me a quarter for dat." He held out his hand, his eyes oscillating, in their peculiar way.

Middleton pitched a dollar into his hand and walked on hastily, followed by the thanks and protestations of gratitude of the negro. He did not see the look that Moses shot after him as he followed him at a distance till Middleton went into Mrs. Dockett's.

As the trick-doctor turned back, he muttered, "Yas, done lay de whup 'pon Moses' back. Dollar don' pay for dat. Ain' *Cap'n* Middleton now, jes Marse Middleton. Ump !" He disappeared with his uneven gait around the rear of Leech's law-office.

When Middleton mentioned to Mrs. Welch his meeting with Moses, to his surprise she spoke of him with unmitigated detestation, and, equally to his surprise, she spoke of

Captain Allen with much less reprobation than from his knowledge of her views he had anticipated.

Most of the other friends of Middleton received him with even greater cordiality than he had expected. Mrs. Dockett invited him to come and occupy his old quarters, and made him understand distinctly that it was to be as her guest. She did not board any Yankees now—except Captain Thurston, of course, The Captain was an old friend, and she had to take him in for old times' sake ; she could not let him be starved or poisoned at that miserable hole of a hotel.

Middleton laughed as he thanked her. He knew which way the wind was setting with Thurston. He was staying with his cousins, he said. But he hoped Mrs. Dockett would be good enough to let him come to dinner some time and eat some of her fried chicken, which was the very best in all the world, as he knew by experience. Mrs. Dockett declared that he was flattering her ; but this Middleton stoutly repudiated. He had said so in every country he had visited, and there was no reason why he should not say so now. In fact, he so flattered Mrs. Dockett that the good lady declared at the table that evening—gazing hard at Captain Thurston—that Captain Middleton was quite a model now that he no longer wore that horrid blue coat, but dressed like a *gentleman.* " By Jove ! Larry," said Thurston, " you've been acting on the lessons I gave you. You've captured the brigadier first charge. Keep on, and you may capture the whole army, my boy."

" You blackguard !" said Middleton. " You yourself flatter and humbug every woman you meet, so that you think everyone else must be playing the same game."

" Have you told the Senator's daughter about the chickens in this country ? " drawled Thurston.

For reply, Middleton shied a pillow across at his friend. " Of course I have, and how about you ? "

" Oh ! I like Mrs. Dockett's chicken too."

To Middleton's surprise Thurston actually flushed a little

"Reely !"

Thurston's eyes twinkled, and he grew red.

"Well ! And she ?"

Thurston met his gaze this time.

"Larry, how could any sensible woman resist my charms ?" he laughed.

"Are you engaged ?"

"Only in a military sense—as yet."

"But she likes you ?"

"Larry, she's the most unaccountable creature."

"Of course."

"You don't know how clever she is."

"To discover your good qualities ? "

"And sweet and kind-hearted."

"To like you ?"

"Yes, such a vagabond as I am. And how charming she can be ! She's about six girls in one—one minute one thing, the next another."

"That just suits you. You need just about that many to be in love with."

"She's the only girl in the world I ever was in love with," asserted Thurston, boldly.

Middleton whistled.

"Here, you are not talking to her now, but to me. Have you told Ruth Welch that ?"

"She's my confidante."

"She is ? That accounts for it," said Middleton.

"She likes Allen," said Thurston, explanatorily.

"Oh !"

"And Miss Cary likes Gray." This with a keen look at Middleton.

"Ah ?" After a pause : "Who told you so ? "

"I have it from the best authority."

"Miss Cary, or Gray ? "

"No, Miss Elizabeth."

"Oh !" laughed Middleton. " Reely, what a humbug you are."

" No, only a diplomatist, my dear boy. It's necessary, to accomplish anything with the dear creatures."

The morning after Middleton's arrival he was driving to the county seat, when at a turn in the road he met Dr. Cary walking. It had rained the night before, and the road was muddy and heavy ; but the Doctor was trudging along with his old black saddle-pockets over his shoulder. Middleton pulled up, and sprang out and greeted him.

The Doctor returned his greeting cordially, and invited him to come and see them.

" What are you doing walking ? " asked Middleton. " Has your horse got away ? "

The Doctor smiled half-grimly. " Yes, some time ago." The smile died slowly out. " I have no horse now," he said, gravely. " I lost my horse some time ago, and have not been able to procure one since." Middleton looked so shocked that the Doctor added, " Usually my patients, who are able, send a horse for me ; but sometimes I have those who are no better off than myself." Once more the smile flitted across his worn face.

" Steve sent me his horse when he gave himself up, but Leech has taken him. He has a brand on him, and Leech claims, I believe, that he belongs to the Government, and Leech now is the Government."

" I will see if he is," said Middleton, with a sudden flush of anger. " I'll put a brand on him."

Middleton asked to be allowed to take the Doctor to his destination. The old fellow at first demurred ; but on Middleton's insisting, yielded. It was a little warm walking, he admitted.

" Why don't you borrow the money to buy a horse ? " asked Middleton, presently. " I wish you would let—— " He was going to ask the Doctor to let him lend him the money ; but the Doctor interrupted him.

" Ah ! sir, I have borrowed too much money already. I thought then I could pay, I know now I could never pay."

When they reached the place to which the Doctor was going, it was a negro cabin.

"I have to look after them, sir," explained the old fellow. "I don't know what they will do when I am gone."

The deep sincerity in his face took away any suggestion of egotism.

Middleton drove on in deep meditation, trying to unravel the tangle of his thoughts. As he drove into the village, he was passed by a carriage and pair. In the carriage sat Leech and a negro. They were both dressed in long black broad-cloth coats, and the negro wore a shiny new beaver.

That very afternoon Middleton began to negotiate for a horse that he thought would suit an old man. His intention was to buy the horse, and when he went away ask Dr. Cary to keep it for him and use it.

As he was looking at a horse, Leech came by. He stopped and looked on, a smile on his sallow face.

"If you want a good horse, don't buy that one. I've got a lot on my place, and I'll lend you one," he said.

"Thank you, I prefer to buy," said Middleton, coldly, examining the horse.

"All right, I'll sell you one—cheap. I've got the finest lot you ever saw. Some of the old Cary stock," he added.

"I've no doubt you have," said Middleton, dryly, a frown gathering on his brow.

"You used to be a better judge of a horse than that," laughed Leech.

Middleton straightened up and turned on him so angrily that Leech stepped back involuntarily. The next instant, however, he recovered himself.

"Find a good many changes since you went away, I guess?" His voice was full of insolence, and his face wore a provoking smile. Middleton was trying to control himself. Leech misinterpreted his silence.

"Some of your friends sort of gone down the hill?" He nodded his head in the direction of the jail beyond the court-green. His insolence was intolerable.

"Are you trying to be insolent to me?" demanded Middleton. He stepped up close in front of Leech. "If you are, you are making a mistake." His manner and his face, as he looked Leech in the eyes, abashed even him, and he changed his tone. He did not mean to offend him, he said; he was only "jesting when he called them his friends."

"I don't wish to be jested with," said Middleton, coldly, turning away.

As Leech went on he smiled to himself. "Ah, my young man, times are changed," he muttered to himself, softly; "and if you stay here long you'll find it out!"

Middleton concluded his purchase, and the following evening rode his new horse up to Dr. Cary's.

That day Leech called Moses into his office. "I see your friend Captain Middleton is back?" he said. Moses uttered a sound that was half a laugh, half a snarl.

"Yas—all dat comes don' go, and all dat goes don' come"; he snickered.

"You better not fool with him," said Leech. "He knows how to manage you." He made a gesture, as if he were cutting, with a whip, and laughed, tauntingly.

Moses's eyes moved swiftly. "Nor I ain' forgit; I'se done learnt some'n' sense den. He better look out."

"You think the Ku Klux would trouble him?" asked Leech.

Moses stole a swift look at him. "He better look out," he repeated.

"Have some whiskey," said Leech.

There was one man in the County besides Leech who was not overjoyed to see Middleton. When Jacquelin Gray heard of his arrival, his countenance fell. Perfect love may cast out fear, but it does not cast out jealousy; and Jacquelin was conscious of a pain in his heart. He did not know whether Blair Cary liked Middleton now very much or not, but he feared she did; and Middleton had been the cause of his rupture with her. When, therefore, he met Middleton he could not pretend that he was glad to see him.   So he greeted him distantly, though with marked civility.   Middleton was unusually cordial to him ; but this only grated on Jacquelin.   There was a smile in his eyes which Jacquelin, torturing himself as every fool under like circumstances does, interpreted as a glance of triumph, if not of positive compassion.   This was the more biting to Jacquelin because it was at Dr. Cary's that they met, and Blair was unusually gay that evening. Her cheeks, which were sometimes pale, were now flushed, Jacquelin felt, with pleasure at Middleton's presence.   She talked mainly to Middleton, to Jacquelin scarcely at all. At length Jacquelin rose and said he must go.

" Why, aren't you going to stay to tea ?   I thought you were?" Blair asked, in genuine surprise.   Her color had suddenly vanished, and she looked at him with a vague trouble in her eyes.

" Thank you, no," said Jacquelin, shortly.   " Good-evening, Captain Middleton."   He bowed ceremoniously.

" I had hoped to have the pleasure of riding back with you," said Middleton.

" I am walking," said Jacquelin, grimly.   He went out. Blair excused herself hurriedly to Middleton.   " Oh ! Jacquelin," she called, " will you take this letter for me, and mail it to-morrow morning ? "

" Can't I take it ? " asked Middleton.   " I am going by the office."

" Oh ! Jack will take it, thank you."

As she gave Jacquelin the letter she glanced up in his face inquiringly.   But Jacquelin's eyes avoided hers.   He took the letter and stalked out.   How he hated Middleton !   And how he hated himself for doing it !

He strode down the road full of bitterness, weaving himself a nettle-web that stung him at every step.   The moon was just rising above the tree-tops, and its silvery beams were struggling with the last light from the slowly fading west ; but Jacquelin was all in darkness.   All his

plans had come to naught, overthrown by this smiling outsider. He groaned in his helpless anguish. Had he not
waited ; tried to keep his ideals ever before him ; served
faithfully ; never for a moment faltered or turned aside for
anyone else ! And what had it availed him ! Here was a
lifetime of devotion flung away for the facile addresses of
this interloper.

At a point in the road, he caught, for a second, just on
top of a hill some distance before him, the outline of a
man's figure clear against the sky in the cleft between the
trees. It moved with a curious dip or limp that reminded
him for a moment of Moses the trick-doctor. The next
second the figure disappeared. When Jacquelin reached
the spot, he stopped and listened ; but there was only
silence and a momentary crackle of a piece of bark as some
night-animal moved up a tree deep within the shadows.
Jacquelin walked on once more, in the dusk of the road
and the deeper gloom of his own thoughts. He could not
go home, because he had told his aunt he would stay at Dr.
Cary's to tea, and she would wish to know why he had
not done so, and when she heard of Middleton would want
to hear all about him, and he could not talk of Middleton
then. So he wandered on.

When he reached home Miss Thomasia had retired, and
he went silently to his room, cursing his fate and Middleton.

Early next morning, Jacquelin was awakened by voices
in the yard. Someone was talking to Miss Thomasia. All
Jacquelin heard was that Captain Middleton had been
shot the night before at the fork of the road that led to
Dr. Cary's. Jacquelin lay still for a second—quite still—
and listened. Could it be a dream ! The body had been
found right at the fork by Dr. Cary as he was going home
from seeing Sherrod's wife, and he had sent for Mr.
Jacquelin.

Jacquelin's heart stopped beating. He sprang from bed
and threw open a window. Old Gideon was the speaker.

" What's that ? " asked Jacquelin.

Gideon repeated the story, with further details.

" Is he dead ? "

" Nor, suh, he ain' dead yet ; but de Doctor say he ain'
got much show. Ef he hadn't happened to git dyah
pretty soon after he was shot, he'd been dead pretty soon."

" Thank God ! "

Jacquelin had felt like a murderer. The thought of
Blair, stricken in the moment of her joy, came to him
like a stab in his heart. His heart gave a bound that he
was able to rejoice that Middleton was not dead.

Old Gideon was giving particulars.

" Some thinks 'twas dem Ku Kluxes—some dat dee wuz
after somebody else, whoever 'twuz. I don' know who
'twuz," he asserted, with manifest veracity. " But I sholy
don' 'prove of folkes' shootin' 'roun' at folks dataway, dat
I don't ! Dee done sen' for Mr. Welch and de Capt'n at
the cote-house."

When Jacquelin reached Dr. Cary's he was met by Blair,
white-faced and tearful.

He walked straight up to her and held out his hand.

" Blair." His voice had all the old tenderness. The
lover had disappeared. It was only the old, old friend—the
brother.

" Oh ! Jacquelin ! " And she burst into tears.

Dr. Cary's providential appearance on the spot where
Middleton lay had undoubtedly saved Middleton's life ;
and although at first the wound appeared very desperate,
his splendid constitution stood him in good stead, and in a
very short time he began to rally. " It is in such instances
as this," said Dr. Cary, " that a man's habits tell. Nature
conducts her campaign with less than half her forces in
action ; it is when an accident comes that the reserves tell."

One of the first things done, after it was known whether
Middleton would survive the immediate shock, was to
telegraph to Miss Rockfield.

The sudden shock appeared to have driven away all the

cloud of misunderstanding that had so long settled between Jacquelin and Blair; and although Jacquelin felt
that all was over between them, his self-abnegation
brought him a content to which he had long been a
stranger. Every moment that he could spare he was at
Blair's service; but she was most of the time at Middleton's bedside, with Ruth, and all Jacquelin could do was to
show by his silent sympathy how deeply he felt for her.

One afternoon she came and asked him to go to the
station for Miss Rockfield.

"Who is Miss Rockfield?" asked Jacquelin. "I know
she is related to Middleton; but who is she?"

"She is Captain Middleton's *fiancée*," said Blair,
quietly.

"What!" Jacquelin turned hot and cold by turns.
"Blair!"

Blair's eyes were dancing, and her mouth was trembling
with the effort to suppress the sign of her triumph.

Jacquelin positively staggered. He hitched up Middleton's horse and went for Miss Rockfield; but how he
reached the station and what happened that evening he
always vowed he could never remember. When Miss
Rockfield arrived, Middleton was already out of danger.
The strain, however, had told heavily on Dr. Cary. Still
he refused to rest.

A night or two later, the Doctor had just come home
from a round of visits. He had come by the court-house,
and had paid Steve a visit. Every effort had failed to put
off Steve's trial. Leech had brought the judge, and they
were together at Still's. The Doctor was much depressed.
He would write to Senator Rockfield, and see if he could
not make one more attempt. He looked so fagged and
worn that Mrs. Cary and Blair urged him to put off the
letter. But he said it must be done at once. The day for
the trial was approaching, and every hour was precious
now. So he wrote the letter. Then he lay down on a
lounge.

The next moment there was the clatter of horses' feet outside, and a man riding one horse and leading another dashed up in the yard at a gallop and gave a shout:

" Aw—Dr. Cary."

Mrs. Cary's countenance fell. The Doctor's face, which had just before been expressive of extreme fatigue, suddenly took on a new expression.

" You cannot go ; it is impossible," declared Mrs. Cary. The Doctor did not answer. He was listening to the conversation going on outside between the messenger and Mammy Krenda.

" Leech ! " exclaimed Mrs. Cary, and sprang to the door. " He says that Leech is dying." A light almost of joy had come into her face. The Doctor rose and passed out of the door by her.

" What's that ? What is the matter ? " he asked. His face was as calm as a statue's !

Mrs. Cary reported what she had heard : " Leech was ill—had been taken with violent cramp, and was having fit after fit. He was supposed to be dying. He was at Birdwood."

" You cannot go ; you are worn out," urged Mrs. Cary, imploringly as the Doctor straightened himself.

" I must go," said the Doctor. He turned back to get his saddle-bags.

" It is the visitation of God," murmured Mrs. Cary to herself.

" Not until all medical means have failed," said Dr. Cary, gravely. The man on the horse, thinking that the delay meant that the Doctor was not coming, said :

" They told me to tell you he'd pay you anything in the world you asked."

The Doctor turned and faced him.

" He has not money enough—the Government has not money enough—to induce me to go, if he were not ill," said he, slowly. " I am going because he is sick and I am a physician."

He leant down and kissed his wife, and walked down the path toward the horses. Mrs. Cary went out with him, and saw him mount the horse the messenger had brought and ride away in the darkness. Then she went into the house with a white face. She did not retire that night. Blair and she sat up waiting for him.

The sun was almost rising when they saw him come riding up through the orchard. As they went out to meet him, he sat up very straight. The sky was all pearl, and he seemed to be riding in the sunrise.

As he dismounted he almost fell, but recovered himself and tied the horse. A messenger would come for him, he said.

" How is he ? " asked Mrs. Cary.

" Out of danger," he said. " I am glad I went. He would have died if he had not been relieved."

Mrs. Cary said nothing. Her eyes were searching his face, which seemed to have grown thinner in one night. She threw her arm around him to support him. They walked up to the door, and he sat down on the step and passed his hand over his brow. " I am very tired. I have fought—" he began ; but did not finish the sentence. The next second he sank forward on the steps.

With a cry to Blair, Mrs. Cary caught him. She raised him up ; his eyes opened once and rested on Mrs. Cary's face, and a faint smile came into them. His lips murmured his wife's name, and then Blair's ; and then his eyes slowly closed, and, with a sigh, his head sank on Mrs. Cary's arm, and the long fight was done. John Cary, of Birdwood, had laid down his arms.

Jacquelin was absent from the County when the news of Dr. Cary's death reached him. At first he could hardly grasp it. It seemed as if it could not be true. He had never thought of Dr. Cary's dying, or of the County existing without him. All of Jacquelin's own family except Rupert and Miss Thomasia had passed away, and he was accustomed to death. Many friends had gone. Dr. Cary had sat at their bedsides and closed their eyes; but, some-how, it had never occurred to Jacquelin to think of Death striking him. He seemed to be a part of the old life—in all the County, its best and most enduring type; and, now that he had gone, Jacquelin felt as though the foundation were falling out—as though the old life had passed away with him.

The next thought was of Blair. The two had been so absolutely associated ever since he could remember. He could hardly think of her as surviving. He hurried home. As he neared the neighborhood, every man he met was talk-ing of the Doctor. They all felt like Jacquelin. They wondered what would happen, now that the Doctor had gone. At one place, where Jacquelin had to wait a lit-tle while, a group were discussing him. They were talk-ing of him as they remembered him in the war. They were all poor men; but they had all been soldiers, and they spoke of him as of a comrade. He was always at the front, they said; he could hardly have been there more if he had been the Colonel. If a man was shot, before they knew it there was Dr. Cary. He said he could save at any time those not badly wounded; those who were badly shot he could only save on the firing-line. And he was as quick to look after a wounded Yankee as after a Confederate, they asserted. "A wounded man wasn't an enemy," he had said; "he was a patient." They all had stories of his courage, his en-durance, his kindness. One told how he had sent a fresh cow over to the speaker's wife on a time when the children were sick; another mentioned how he had come around once to collect some money, but, finding that they did not have a cent, had lent them some he had just collected from Andy Stamper. A third related how he had kissed and prayed with a wounded Yankee boy, who was dying and wanted to see his mother. "He leant down by him," said the man, "and put his arm around him, and said 'Now I lay me,' just for all the world like a woman. And, next minute, after the boy got quiet, he was leaning over get-ting a ball out of a man right by him."

There was a long pause after this simple recital, which had been delivered in a quiet, monotonous tone.

"They say Leech was as good as dead when he got to him."

"I'd 'a' let him die a thousand times," swore one, with deep sincerity.

"Yes. Well, so would I. But, somehow, the Doctor, he always was different. Seemed like, big as he was, he couldn't bear any ill feelin's."

There was a silence after this.

It was broken presently by one of the auditors.

"And that was the man they put in jail," he said, bitterly.

"Yes, and murdered," responded the others.

Jacquelin rode on. He, too, felt that Dr. Cary had been murdered.

When he reached Dr. Cary's, the first person he met was Mammy Krenda. The old woman was the picture of grief. She did not utter a word, nor did the young man. She simply opened the door and stood aside while he softly entered the little room where rested the silent form of her old master. The quiet figure, the calm, upturned face, had suddenly ennobled the little apartment. The hours that had passed had smoothed out the traces of care and pain, and the Doctor lay in perfect rest. There was, perhaps, a trace of scorn of the ills he had so long faced, but Jacquelin did not note it. What he saw was only perfect peace, and a face of undisturbed nobility. Gazing down on it, his heart softened; his bitter thoughts passed away, and he sank on his knees, and thanked God for such a life.

He became conscious presently that someone was standing by him, and he rose and faced Blair. Neither spoke a word; but he took her hand and held it, and the next second she sank on her knees, and after a moment he knelt beside her.

CHAPTER XLV

DR. CARY had hardly been laid away, when the County had to face another sorrow.

The trial of Captain Allen was set for the next day, and the county seat was in a fever of expectation and apprehension. It was the final struggle between the old residents and the new invaders, and it seemed that the latter must triumph. There was no hope. It was the beginning of the complete subjugation of the people. All thoughts were centred on the little village where the battle was to be joined and fought. A dark cloud seemed to have settled like a pall over the place which even the soft afterglow of a summer evening could not lighten. The breath of flowers was on the breeze that came from the shrubbery-filled yards and rustled the trees. Yet the sounds were subdued, and the faces of the people were gloomy and grim. The Judge had arrived, and had taken his room in the old Hotel. Leech, solemn and once more self-assertive, with a face still pale from his recent attack, but a gleam of joy in his pale blue eyes, was quartered with Judge Bail in the hotel. Some said he was afraid to go to his house; some that he wanted to be near the Judge, and keep his mind filled with his insinuations. It was hinted that he was afraid Bail would offer to sell out. McRaffle had quarrelled with Leech and had made such an offer. He had also said that the Judge could be reached, if the sum tendered were large enough. At least, such was the rumor about the village. The jury was assembled and kept together. The witnesses had been brought to town and were also keeping together.   The lawyers, with grave faces, were consulting behind locked doors and closely shut windows —those who represented the Government in a room adjoining Leech's, and not far from the Judge's chamber ; and those who were for the prisoner, among them some of the ablest lawyers in the State, in Steve's old office. Mr. Bagby and General Legaie were the leading counsel, and Jerry lounged about the door like a Bashi-Bazouk. The crowd in the village was larger than it had been in a good while.   Men were assembled in groups in the suburbs or on the verandas, sullen and almost awe-struck, discussing the points in the case with the intelligence of those trained by sharp experience to know the gravity of such an occasion and to weigh the chances.   It was known that the principal evidence against Captain Allen was his own confession.   This was his chief danger.   Leech (it was noticeable that, when Leech was there, it was not the Government, whose soldiers were still quartered in the village, but Leech that was spoken of as representing the prosecution)—Leech could not prove any act of his without that. The lawyers could break down all the witnesses except one —the one to whom Captain Allen had been fool enough to talk ; her testimony they could not get around.   Mr. Bagby and General Legaie had said so.   Mr. Bagby said that a man's own confession was the hardest thing in the world to overcome ; that one was a fool ever to confess anything. Such were the observations of a group assembled on one of the street corners, out of hearing of the sentries.

This idea gave the discussion another turn.   " Was Captain Allen really in love with Miss Welch ? " someone questioned.   He had been in love with her beyond a doubt, but he had stopped visiting her.   Some thought she had led him on, to get all out of him she could ; others that he had stopped, and that she was taking her revenge. One element considered that it served him right.   Why should he have to go off after a Yankee girl, whose people were all against them, when there were plenty of their own

girls just as pretty and more attractive? Others took
Steve's part. If a man fell in love he fell in love, that
was all; and if he was in love, he had a right to do as he
chose—there was no Mason and Dixon line in love. Even
these, however, thought that Miss Welch was taking her
revenge.

Andy Stamper, who had come up and was grimly listening with unwonted silence, broke forth with a strong denunciation of such nonsense. He did not believe a word of
it. Miss Welch had been to see Miss Blair Cary and Miss
Thomasia, old Mr. Langstaff and Mr. Bagby, and had done
all she could to keep from testifying. She was "cut up
as the mischief about it," declared Andy. She had wanted
to go away, but Leech was too sharp for her; he had had
her recognized to appear. He knew he could not convict
the Captain without her. Her father, too, was awfully
troubled about it, and had been to Washington to see what
he could do. He could not bear Leech. Was he not getting ready to sue him about that railroad steal? He had
just come back from the North. They had not come to the
court-house. Perhaps he had been able to do something?

The crowd did not accept Andy's views. Some of them
thought the attitude of Major Welch was all a sham; that
his anger with Leech was just a pretence, and that he was
really in collusion with him. Had he not objected to Captain Allen's visiting at his house, and hadn't he done all he
could to trace up Leech when the Captain had him hidden.
He had made a big show of giving up when Captain Steve
and Mr. Gray proved Hiram Still's rascality; but he had
bided his time, and he was getting a pretty sweet revenge.
He had been North; but the speakers believed it was to
push the case against the Captain, not to stop it. He
could have stopped it easy enough, if he had chosen. He
was "in with the biggest of 'em."

Little Andy chewed in glum silence. Suddenly he burst
out:

"Well, I say that man don't pretend to nothin'. Whether
36

he likes the Captain or whether he don't, or whether you
like him or whether you don't, is one thing. But what
he is, he is ; and he don't pretend to nothin'. If all Yankees was like him, I wouldn't care how many they was—
unless I had to fight 'em."

This sententious speech had its effect on the crowd, and
the sergeant was proceeding to expound further his opinion. But just then the sound of wheels was heard ; and the
next moment a close carriage, with a good pair of horses,
drove quickly by them in a cloud of dust. It was recognized as Major Welch's carriage, and, though the curtains
were half-drawn, the group recognized the occupants as
Major and Mrs. Welch and their daughter, and one other
person, who was leaning back. One man thought it looked
like old Mr. Langstaff ; but, of course, it was not he. A
number of groans followed the carriage as it passed on
down the street toward the hotel. Andy's countenance
and stock both fell.

To a man like Steve Allen the sentence which appeared
to wait for him on the morrow was worse than death. He
had faced death scores of times, and would readily have
done so again, on any occasion. But he had never apprehended that a shameful sentence, however undeserved,
would be passed on him. Better, a thousand times, that
he had died in battle and lain with his comrades, who had
left honorable names. He summoned to his aid all his fortitude, and tried to soothe himself with the knowledge that
he had never committed a dishonorable act ; that the cause
of his present situation was the desire to act a noble part
and save others. But do what he might, he could not keep
from his mind the feeling that, deserved or not, a conviction and sentence to the penitentiary placed a stigma on
him never to be erased. All his high hopes would be
blighted, his future ruined ; he would have brought dis-
grace on his family ; he could never more face men as he
had done heretofore ; he would not be fit to speak to a
lady.

He was aware at intervals that this was a weakness, for he had moments when he recognized that an undeserved sentence could not degrade; but do what he might, the horror of it would come back to him. With it was another wound. The blow had been struck by her whom he loved. The girl whom he had given his whole heart to and whom he had thought the truest, bravest, highest woman in all the world, to whom he had spoken as he would not have spoken to any other man or woman, and who, he had hoped, cared for him, had turned and betrayed him. But for her he would be free to-morrow. He knew it himself, and his lawyers, in their last interview with him, just over, had told him so. They would do what they could; but the fact remained that he had confessed his part in the act for which the prosecution was brought, and they did not see how they could get around it. Some of them had suggested that they had a single chance. The witness was in a condition of high excitement; and they might, by severe cross-examination, confuse her and destroy the force of her evidence. This Steve promptly vetoed. He would not have it done. The lawyers gazed at him in dismay.

"My dear sir, it is your only chance."

"I do not care, I will not have it," said Steve, firmly. "I said it, and I will have no cross-examination on that point."

"That is Quixotic."

"Then I'll be Quixotic. I've been so before. Don Quixote was a gentleman." General Legaie's eyes sparkled suddenly as they rested on him.

They had left him, saying good-by with that solemnity which showed how forlorn their hope was. As they reached the outer door and passed across the court-green, old Mr. Bagby said, "That is really a most extraordinary young man, and to think that such a man should be in prison under indictment."

The little General breathed a deep and fervent oath.

"What a pity that he could not have married that nice

young lady, Miss Welch—such a nice young lady!" proceeded Mr. Bagby, half in soliloquy.

"Marry her! Marry that woman! The viper!" ex-
ploded the General. "I'd rather die!"

"Oh, a very nice young lady," pursued Mr. Bagby to
himself, as he walked on, feeling his way in the darkness.
He did not tell the General that he had lately had an interview which had raised Miss Ruth Welch in his esteem
and changed her, in his mind, from the viper which the
General conceived her to be, to the nice young lady of
whom he muttered in the dusk of the summer night.

This interview with his lawyers had been over an hour
ago. Steve was still in the room in which the interview
had been held; but the high stand which he had taken with
his counsel had now lost some of its loftiness as the hard-
ness of his position stood nakedly before him. After all,
had not this girl betrayed him? Why should he sacrifice
himself for her? This thought flitted before Steve,
only for an instant. He put it away from him with a gesture of bitterness. At least he would be a gentleman, whatever befell. He took from his pocket a pistol which he
wore when he surrendered, and which had not been taken
from him, and examined it attentively, with a curious expression on his face. He was thinking deeply. Suddenly
his expression changed. "Never! Cowardice!" He
flung the pistol over on the cot by the window. The reflection had come to him that it would be taken as a proof
of fear as well as of guilt. And, moreover, the thought
had come that he might still be of use.

The triumph of Leech recurred to him. He very often
thought of Leech—of Leech, who had hounded him down,
and not only him, but others a thousand times better: Dr.
Cary, the high-minded, noble gentleman, the faithful
Christian. Leech, the vampire, sucking the life-blood of
the people; the harpy, battening on the writhing body of
the prostrate State, had broken Dr. Cary's heart. Jacquelin had told Steve how the Doctor looked as he lay in his

coffin, murdered ; his face full of scars, but calm with the stamp of immortal courage—like an old knight, paladin of a lost cause, stricken through the heart in a final charge, before the light of victory could fade from his brow. Steve, thinking of this, was leaning against the bars of his open window, looking away into space through the dusk. The window was in the rear of the jail, and looked down on a vacant, weed-grown lot, back of the court-green. Steve became conscious of the presence of two men in the open space beneath. They had just moved, so as to be in the shadow of the building, and were right below his window, conversing earnestly. Suddenly their voices rose, and Steve was almost startled to recognize Leech and McRaffle. He could not help hearing what they were saying. McRaffle was insisting on something, and Leech was refusing. McRaffle broke out in a passion. He was evidently under the influence of liquor.

"You owe it to me. You said you would pay me $1,000 for him, alive or dead," he asserted. "I kept my part of the bargain ; now, blank you ! stand up to yours."

"If you had brought him dead, I might have paid ; but you did not capture him," said Leech, with a harsh laugh. "He gave himself up."

"Well, it was in consequence of the report I circulated," insisted McRaffle. "Do you suppose he'd have given himself up, if he had not heard that if he did so the others would be released ?"

Leech laughed incredulously. "More fool he !"

"And whose idea was that ?"

"My friend, there's no use to try that game on me. What good would that have done, if I had not induced Miss Welch to tell what your friend was fool enough to confide to her ? Where would we have been but for her testimony ? If anyone is entitled to claim the reward I offered, I am the man. I must protect the Government." He spoke unctuously.

"You think you are entitled to everything. I know

how you'll protect the Government!" sneered McRaffle. "Suppose your important witness won't testify?" he asked.

"She'll sleep in jail. I'll make Bail give her the apartment next her friend," said Leech, scornfully. "They'll enjoy that."

Leech never knew how close Death brushed by him that instant. Steve's pistol was lying on the bed, within a foot of him. He seized it. He would rid the country of that cursed presence, and pay his own debt at the same time. He had cocked the pistol involuntarily, when he came to himself. Oh! if he only had him face to face, in an open field, both armed, he could settle the final score! He uncocked the pistol and flung it away from him.

"Miss Welch won't refuse," Leech went on, "I am smart enough to know how to deal with women as well as men." He laughed arrogantly.

"You think so? You are sometimes too blanked smart for your own good," said McRaffle.

Leech, stung by the speech, turned on him.

"I'll put you on the stand," he threatened.

"Not much, you won't. I won't testify."

"You're getting pretty squeamish all of a sudden," sneered Leech.

McRaffle wheeled on him in a rage.

"Don't you dare sneer at me that way," he said. "If you do, I'll——"

He seized Leech by the shoulder.

"I'll tell how you deal with women—for instance, with Miss Bush, the school-teacher, *alias* Mrs. Jonadab Leech!" he hissed.

Leech seemed suddenly to shrink up.

"What do you know about—about her?"

"Put me on the stand, and I'll tell you all you want to know," said McRaffle, tauntingly. "Perhaps, you don't want me as a witness now? Well, I'll tell you what I'll do. Pay me the thousand dollars, or—I tell you—

endorse my note for a thousand, and I'll keep quiet. Otherwise, I'll have to get Dr. Still to endorse it, or maybe even the Governor," he said, meaningly.

"Well, if I do, will you swear that you will never open your mouth again about this to a single soul on earth?"

"Make it twelve hundred," said McRaffle. "The Governor'd give twice that to know of Mrs. Leech. I reckon it would be some time before you'd dine with Miss Krafton again."

Leech seized him to stop him.

The rest of the conversation was in a lower key, and they soon moved off together, leaving Steve still in darkness, literally and figuratively. But he had conquered a great temptation. This reflection, after a time, brought a feeling almost of peacefulness. He threw himself on the bed, and began to go over his life. Presently he began in humility to look to a Higher Power.

At that moment his door was opened, and a voice said:

"A visitor to see you, Capt'n. Will you come to the parlor?" The messenger was the old Sergeant, O'Meara, whom Thurston had placed in charge of the prison.

Steve, after a moment, left his cell and walked slowly through the corridor to the apartment adjoining the jailer's quarters, which was dignified by the name of parlor. It was lighted by a small lamp, the rays of which hardly reached the walls. The room was empty. But Steve could hear from the voices that there were two persons in the next room. He walked to the open window and waited, with his head resting on his arm against the bars. The same reverie from which he had been aroused returned.

The door behind him opened and closed softly.

"Captain Allen!" said a faint voice. Steve turned.

"Miss Welch!" He stood dumfounded. Before him, with her veil only half thrown back, was Ruth Welch. She stood just inside the door, motionless as though planted on the spot; and, as Steve did not move, the whole space of the room was between them. Her eyes, which she lifted for a second to Steve's face, fell.

"Captain Allen," she began, and then faltered. After a second, however, with an effort she began again.

"I have come to see you ; to see—to see if there is nothing I can do to—to help you ? "

At the words, Steve's heart hardened.

"No, thank you, there is nothing," he said. His voice was hard and unnatural. She made a movement, almost as if she shrank back. But she began again, speaking very slowly and painfully :

"I do not know what to say. But I want—I want to see if there is nothing——? " She broke off, but began again : "You don't know how deeply—how terribly— I——" Her voice failed her. She stopped and wrung her hands. "Is there nothing—nothing I can do ? "

Steve stood like stone. "No, nothing."

She broke the silence that fell.

"I thought there was—there might be. I hoped— there might be. You do not know how terribly I feel. I hoped there might be some way for me to help you, to atone for my wicked folly. I did not know——"

Her voice failed again, and she put her handkerchief quickly to her eyes.

Steve, up to this time, had not volunteered a word or stirred from where he stood. His heart began to relent, and he felt that he must say something.

"You need not reproach yourself," he said. "I have not done so. It was my folly, not yours."

"Oh, no, no ! I will not let you say that," she broke out, vehemently. "You trusted me. You have been only brave and noble. But I did not know ! I thought, when I told it, it would help you. You will believe that, will you not ? "

She came a step or two nearer in her intensity, and gazed at him earnestly.

"Yes, if you say so," said Steve.

"I do," she declared, earnestly. "I thought, when they were prosecuting you, that it would set you in the right light; and it seems that dreadful man knew how to distort it and knew— Oh ! it all seems like a dreadful nightmare ! I have done everything I could. And my father has, too. Is there no way ? Do you not know of one way in which my testimony could not be taken ?" Her voice faltered, so that Steve could scarcely catch the words.

"No, none whatsoever."

"Yes. There is one way. I have heard—I have been told there is one," she persisted, faintly.

"And what is that ?" asked Steve, coldly. Suddenly she broke down.

"How can you be so hard on me—so cruel ?" she sobbed.

Steve watched her, at first almost grimly ; but her weeping softened him.

"Miss Welch, do not distress yourself," he said, quietly. "There is no way to help me ; but it is not your fault. I believe what you have told me."

"There is one way," she said.

"And that is ?"

"To marry me."

"What !" Steve almost tottered.

"To marry me. If you marry me, I could not be made to testify against you. I have been told so." She had recovered her composure and was speaking quite calmly.

"I could not let you do that," said Steve, firmly.

"I have come to ask you to do it," she went on, speaking quite as if she were but finishing her first sentence. "And afterward, you could—get—a—a—divorce. I would go away and hide myself, and never, never trouble you again." Her composure deserted her, and she buried her face in her hands. If she could have seen Steve's face at that moment—the sudden flame which lit it up—and the gesture which he made, as though he would have caught her in his arms, and that with which he restrained himself and reasserted his self-control, she might not have wept. But she did not see it, and Steve was able to master himself, though when he spoke his voice had wholly changed.

"I could not do that," he said, gently, and with a new tone. "I could not allow you to sacrifice yourself."

"It would not be— Yes, you can," she pleaded.

"No," said Steve, almost sternly. "Do not, I beg you." He lifted his hand as though to put her from him; but suddenly clutched at his heart.

She stopped sobbing. He turned half-away.

"Go," he said. "Leave me, please."

His voice could scarcely be heard, and he put his hand to his forehead. She turned without a word, and moved slowly toward the door. As she put out her hand to open it, she suddenly sank in a heap on the floor. In a second Steve was at her side. He stooped and lifted her, as though she were a child.

"Ruth," he said; and, as she opened her eyes, "forgive me." He caught the hem of her dress and crushed it against his lips. "I could not let you do that. I could not let you sacrifice yourself."

"It is no sacrifice. Do you not see? Oh! Can you not see that—I—love——?" She could not complete the sentence. Her head drooped.

"What! Ruth!" Steve stood her up on her feet and held her at arm's length. "Ruth Welch, for God's sake do not tell me that unless it is true." His eyes were burning, and were fastened on her face with a gaze that seemed almost to scorch her.

"It is true," she said, in a low voice, and tried to turn her face away. Steve did not stir.

"Wait," he said, hoarsely. "Does your mother know of this?"

"Yes." She was looking in his eyes now quite calmly.

"Where is she?"

"In the next room."

Steve suddenly caught her in his arms.

A little later Mrs. Welch and Steve had an interview.

AND THERE, IN THE LITTLE PARLOR, STEVE AND RUTH WERE MARRIED.

Steve told her that while he had loved her daughter better than his life, ever since the day he had met her, and while the knowledge that she cared for him had changed the world for him, that very fact would not permit him to let her take the step she proposed. He would not allow her to sacrifice herself by marrying him when under a criminal charge, and with a sentence staring him in the face. Mrs. Welch adroitly met this objection with the plausible argument that it was as much on her daughter's account as on his that she desired it. She spoke for her husband as well as for herself. It would prevent the horror of her daughter's having to appear, and give testimony against him, in open court. She did not believe Ruth could stand the ordeal. She knew she would not testify, even though she should be sent to jail and kept there. This Ruth stoutly confirmed. She would die before she would answer a question.

Mrs. Welch, having come over to Steve's side, was a powerful ally ; and as Ruth resolutely maintained her position that she would die in prison before she would utter one word, there was nothing else for Steve to do but yield to their proposal. He raised the point that it was too late, as it was now midnight, and no license could be secured or clergyman be found. But Mrs. Welch was prepared to meet this objection. Captain Thurston had authority under the law to issue the license, and a preacher could be secured. Indeed, Mr. Langstaff had come down to the county seat with them.

So in a short time these preliminaries were settled. A few friends were brought in quietly : General Legaie, who knelt on one knee and lifting Ruth's hand kissed it reverently ; Mr. Bagby, whose eyes twinkled with deep satisfaction over a double victory ; Reely Thurston and Jacquelin Gray, and Andy Stamper who had got wind of the matter and asked permission to come. And there in the little dingy room, in the presence of these and of Major and Mrs. Welch, Steve Allen and Ruth Welch were married at midnight by old Mr. Langstaff.

CHAPTER XLVI

THE OLD LAWYER DECLINES TO SURPRISE THE COURT, AND SURPRISES LEECH

THE next morning the case was called, and the whole village was astir. In the little conclave held after the marriage it had been discussed whether anything should be said about it until after the jury was impanelled, when it could be sprung on Leech, and, in the surprise thus occasioned, the jury be forced to give a verdict of acquittal.

Some were for taking this course, and this was Steve's wish ; but old Mr. Bagby said, No. He had lost one case, he said, by allowing his client to act on a sentiment, and he would not risk another. Sentiment was sentiment, but law was law. He looked through his spectacles significantly at Major Welch. He believed in making every defence as you came to it. So, as Major Welch was sure he would receive the telegrams he was expecting from the North, and agreed with Mr. Bagby, this plan was adopted. It was decided to announce the marriage before the beginning of the trial, and take the postponement that would almost inevitably occur.

The secret was well kept, and, up to the last moment before the trial, there was no idea on Leech's part of what had taken place. He had put on a new and longer black coat than usual, and a carefully tied white cravat ; and, with his books and papers clasped to his breast, and his pale eyes downcast except when he lifted them covertly and cast a swift glance of conscious triumph around him, he moved about the court-green busy and noiseless. He was still haggard from his late illness, but there was an air of triumph even in the flapping of his loose coat and the line of his thin back.

But, notwithstanding Leech's ignorance, an idea had got abroad that something unusual would happen. The lawyers for Captain Allen were still grave; but they wore a more confident air than they had exhibited yesterday. Andy Stamper was chirpy and facetious, and had a look of deeper mystery than he was wont to wear except when events were about to happen. It was known that Major Welch, who had just returned from the North, had been to the railway station after midnight, and had remained there until daybreak; and it was known, further, that Mrs. Welch and Miss Welch had left the tavern, and were stay-ing at Mrs. Dockett's. So there was something in the air. It was rumored that McRaffle had been sent away by Leech.

When Captain Allen walked across the green from the jail to the court-house, he wore a look of triumph which cheered the hearts of his friends. They crowded round him, to speak to him and shake his hand; and he laughed and chatted with them like a victor, not like a prisoner. One man called to him: "We came near taking you out of yonder last night, Captain; and if you just crook your finger, we'll clean up the whole gang now. There's several of the old Company around here yet." Steve looked over at him and smiled.

"It's all right, Michael. Don't trouble yourself." And the crowd pressed after him into the court-house, which was already jammed.

The case was called, and the Court asked the usual question whether counsel were ready. Leech replied meek-ly that the Government was ready, and glanced across at the array of counsel for the prisoner. After a moment's hesitation, old Mr. Bagby slowly rose:

"If the Court please!" he said, "we are ready for the defence; but before entering on the case, there is a state-ment which I feel—which we feel—it is proper we should make, as we do not wish to surprise the Court, or to take

any advantage of a state of facts which may cause a surprise to the other side."

He turned to Leech, on whose face a look of wonder was
beginning to dawn.

"I believe I see among the list of witnesses summoned
for the prosecution the name of a witness—.." (the old lawyer took up the book containing the list of witnesses, and
scanned it as if he had not seen it before)—"of a young
lady—ah—Miss Welch—who, I believe, has been summoned
ah—who I understand has been summoned to prove—ah—
to testify to certain statements alleged to have been made
by our client, which are deemed material." He looked
across at Leech, who was staring at him in vague wonder.
"Am I correct in this, Colonel Leech?" His voice was
never so unctuous and his manner so civil as when he was
preparing a deadly thrust.

"Umph, I don't know. I believe there is a witness of
that name, to prove some of the prisoner's confessions.
There are a number of others. We are not dependent on
her at all," said Leech, with insolent indifference.

"Ah!" drawled the old lawyer. "I was misinformed."
With a bow, he took his seat. As he did so, he added,
slowly, "I understood she was a material witness—a *very*
material witness. If she is not, of course—— ?" He
looked benignantly at the jury and shut his lips. He was
apparently relieved. Leech cleared his throat nervously.
He saw he had lost whatever advantage the statement
would have given him.

"I did not mean that. I did not mean to say she is not
a material witness."

The old lawyer turned his eyes on him slowly. "A *very*
material witness?"

"Oh, well, yes; I suppose you might say so."

Mr. Bagby rose again.

"Then I will resume my statement. I am informed
that this young lady to whom I have referred is summoned
to prove certain statements of our client, respecting his

supposed connection with the secret and unlawful order for the suppression of which the law, under which this prosecution is ostensibly made, was framed. I am informed, further, that she is a very material witness—so material, indeed, that but for her testimony it is possible this prosecution, in this particular form, might not have taken place."

Leech cleared his throat ominously, and Mr. Bagby looked at him benignly.

"I am inclined to credit this report not only from facts within our own knowledge, but also because I understand that these conjectured statements, whatever they were, were made in the course of conversation of a kind peculiarly confidential, under seal of a friendship unusually close and intimate ; and I cannot believe that the learned and amiable counsel for the Government would have wished to violate wantonly such a confidence. I can only think he considered that his duty required it. And I am glad to say I have his own statement that such was his view of the case " (he took from his hat a paper and held it in his hand), "in a letter which he personally wrote to the young lady's father.

" It is under these circumstances that I feel it is due to the Court, and may lead to a different disposition of the case, to say to the Court that the young lady in question is not an eligible witness in this prosecution." (He here took from his hat another paper.) " She has been united in the bonds of matrimony to my client, and is at present the wife of the accused, Captain Stevenson Allen, and thus is not an eligible witness for or against him."

He resumed his seat slowly and sedately, amid the dead silence which had fallen on the court-room. The next moment the crowd took in the situation, and the old courtroom rang with cheer after cheer. Even the jury were moved to grin, and exchanged pleased glances and words of wonder and satisfaction.

During the tumult that went on, Leech's face was a study.

Surprise, dismay, baffled revenge, rage, fear, craftiness, dissimulation—all had their place. He looked about him at the shouting assembly, and gauged all the elements. He took in Captain Thurston's jolly face, Major Welch's look of satisfaction, and the shrewd content of old Mr. Bagby, as Major Welch handed him a batch of telegrams. He saw the other lawyers' faces light up as the telegrams were handed on to them and were eagerly scanned. He knew the wires had been well worked. He calculated all the chances. And when the judge, with sharp reprimands and angry threats, had quelled the noise and restored order, Leech rose.

It was true, he said, that the testimony of the witness mentioned was material in the aspect of the case as it stood at present, and it was true that he had summoned Miss Welch as a witness, only under the strictest sense of duty and at the greatest cost of pain to himself, as he had already stated to her father. And he was glad that they at last recognized it. He had not known that the friendship between the—ah—witness and the prisoner, had been carried so far—indeed, it seemed that this last degree of intimacy must have been of quite recent date. Had he known it, the Court would have been spared some trouble and the Government considerable expense. As it was, while he was not prepared to say that the Government could not compel the witness to testify when the disability had arisen under such circumstances (here he glanced at the judge, and read on his countenance that this view was untenable ; so he added), or could not convict without the witness, his idea of his duty to the Government was so high that he was unwilling to risk going to trial under the circumstances, until he had summoned one or two other witnesses who could prove the same facts ; and he should therefore consent to an adjournment till next day.

Mr. Bagby rose. "You will ask for it," he said, looking at Leech. "We are ready to proceed." He addressed the Court in a few words, and urged that the case proceed

or that the prosecution be dismissed.   This Leech "could
not consent to,". and the Court refused it.   Then the old
lawyer more firmly insisted that his client be admitted
to bail.

Leech was about to rise to resist this also.   At that moment, however, a dispatch was handed him.   It was from
his friends at the national capital, and stated that Major
Welch. had secured an order to admit Captain Allen to bail.
Leech turned the dispatch over carelessly, face downward,
leant back, and spoke aloud to the man who had handed it
to him.   "I'll send an answer.   Wait a little."   He rose.

This motion, he said, he should be glad to assent to,
and, indeed, was about to propose himself, as such novel
circumstances had arisen ; and he should be glad to do
anything that would please his friends, especially Major
Welch, and he hoped he might add his congratulations to
the young couple and his friend Major Welch, if it was
not too late.   This was received with bows more or less
perfunctory ; only old Mr. Bagby bowed low with mock
gratitude, and General Legaie, twirling his mustache, said
something aloud about a "shameless dog."   The bail
was quickly arranged, and Captain Allen walked out amid
the cheers of the crowd.   The delight of the multitude
about the court-green, among whom the story had rapidly
spread, knew no bounds.   There are some things that
strike chords in all hearts, and the happiness of a newly
married couple is one of them.   The negroes had responded
to it as quickly as the whites ; and when Captain Allen,
who, immediately on the announcement, had been joined
by his wife, walked from the court-room, with her at his
side blushing and pale by turns, but with her face full of
joy, the enthusiasm of the crowd knew no bounds.   Whites
and blacks crowded up to congratulate him, and to shake
his hand and say pleasant things to his wife.

Through this throng Leech had to push as he made his
way from the court-house, his bundle of papers hugged to
his chest.   His sallow cheeks were deadly white, and his

37

face was drawn and white; but the look of baffled rage in his eyes was not seen, as he kept them turned to the ground. He saw many whom he had deemed his closest followers pressing up to be seen among those who congratulated Captain Allen, and he knew by these weather-cocks that the wind had turned and the game was lost.

CHAPTER XLVII

In the old stories, the climax used to be considered attained when the young couple became engaged. Like the hero and heroine of the fairy tales of our youth, in that golden land of " Once-upon-a-time," all that was to be told after they became engaged was that " they married and lived happily ever after." In the modern stories, however, this seems to be but the beginning of new adventures. Marriage, which used to be the entrance to bliss unending, appears to be now but the " gate of the hundred sorrows ; " and the hero and heroine wed only to find that they loved someone else better, and pine to be disunited. They spend the rest of their lives trying to get unmarried. Nothing is so unconventional as to love one's own husband or wife, and nothing so tame as to live pure and true to one's vows in spirit as well as in fact.

It must be said, at once, that this is not a story of that kind. The people described in it knew nothing of that sort of existence. Any reader who chooses to go farther in this history must do so with the full knowledge that such is the case, and that the married life of the young couples will be found as archaic and pure as that of our first parents, before modern wisdom discovered that the serpent was more than the devil, and the tree of knowledge of good and evil more than a tree of knowledge. Still, when we have come so far together, it is necessary to go a little farther.

Thus, it must be briefly explained, for the benefit of those who may be interested to know, what became of those

whose story they have been following; and such as do not
care to read farther, may leave off here and content themselves with knowing that they met, if not the fates they
deserved, at least, the fates which life brought, and met
them with undaunted hearts.

The temporary adjournment of the prosecution against
Captain Allen was but preliminary to a continuance, and,
finally, the case was altogether dismissed. The prosecution of Major Welch's son-in-law was a very different thing
from that of a mere citizen of that unhappy section. But
the investigation that followed proved triumphantly that
Captain Allen's part in the movements that had taken
place had been precisely what he asserted they were, and
that he had done much to break up later the organization
of night-riders.

Not that this was the end of the troubles in the Red
Rock country, and in the section of which it formed a
part, or of the struggle that went on between the people of
that section and Leech and the other vultures who were
preying on them. The talons of those vultures were too
firmly imbedded to be easily dislodged. But in time, the
last of the harpies was put to flight.

As for Leech, there is record of one of the name who,
after holding the leadership of one party in his State, on
the overthrow of that party by the outraged white people
of the State, soon became a partisan on the victorious side.
There is also record of a Leech who, having been during
the "carpet-bagger" régime a man of large means and
political prominence, was known at last mainly on account
of an unsavory story of the manner in which he had tried
to get rid of his wife, and marry another woman. Having
been frustrated in that design through the efforts of a
former political associate, a certain Colonel McRaffle, who
attained a temporary celebrity on account of his disclos-
ures before the Commission that investigated the frauds
in the State, this Leech, it appears, fell into great want,
and was nursed through his last illness by the faithful

wife whom he had so ill-treated.   Readers may decide for
themselves whether either of these was the once supreme
"carpet-bagger" dictator of Red Rock—if, indeed, they
both were not the same person.

But to narrate all this would lead this history into wholly
other lines.

The day after her marriage, Ruth received a deed which
had just been recorded, conveying to her the part of Red
Rock which Major Welch had bought of Still and restored
to Jacquelin, and with the deed a letter from Jacquelin,
asking her, as Steve's wife, to accept it from him and
Rupert as a wedding present.   The letter said things about
Steve over which Ruth shed tears, though her radiant
face showed how happy she was.

"Dr. Moses" had a somewhat curious career.   Jacquelin's statement of what he saw the night of the attempted assassination of Middleton cast suspicion on Moses ; and
he was arrested, and arraigned before a negro magistrate.
It was shown that he had made prophecies or threats
against Middleton.   But Leech appeared as his counsel,
and at least twenty witnesses testified to the man's having been at the Bend all night.   So he was at once discharged ; and the shooting of Middleton was, in the public
press, generally charged to the bands of midnight assassins,
to whom it was the custom at that time to attribute all
outrages that were committed—at least, where the objects
were Northern men.   One journal, indeed, alleged that
Jacquelin himself was concerned in it, and charged that his
crowning infamy was the attempt to place the shooting
on "a reputable colored physician in the County—one of
the few men whose education had enabled them to enter
one of the learned professions."   The prophecies of Moses,
however, greatly increased his reputation ; his prestige
and power became tremendous, and he was, perhaps, the
person most feared in the whole County by his own race.
Finally, indeed, he became such a dread to them that
they rose, and he was run away from the Bend by his own

people. Nothing more was heard of him in the County. But some years later, in one of the adjoining States, a negro was hanged by a mob, and an account of it was published in the papers. The press of one side stated that he confessed not only the terrible crime for which he was hanged, but, in addition, several others sufficiently heinous to entitle him to be classed as one of the greatest scoundrels in the world. The other side asserted that he was a physician of standing, who had at one time enjoyed a large practice in another State, from which he had been run out by the bands of masked desperadoes who had terrorized that section. In proof, it declared that "he died calling on all present to meet him in heaven." As both sides, however, concurred in giving his name as Moses ——, and his former domicile as Red Rock, we have some ground for supposing that "Dr. Moses," as Andy Stamper said, at last came to the end of his rope.

Did our limits permit, the marriage of several other couples besides Steve and Ruth might be chronicled. But the novelist cannot tell at one time all he knows. Be this known, however, that as some citadels are captured by assault, so others capitulate only after long siege ; and this both Jacquelin and Captain Thurston discovered.

When the engagement of Captain Thurston and Miss Elizabeth Dockett was announced to Mrs. Dockett, it was by Miss Dockett herself. It must be left to the members of Mrs. Dockett's own sex to say whether Mrs. Dockett was surprised or not. But if Miss Elizabeth had struck her flag, Mrs. Dockett had not by any means struck hers. Her first pronunciamento was that she had not a word to say against Captain Thurston, who was, she admitted, a perfect gentleman ; but that she wanted him to understand that everyone who came into that house had to dance to the tune of Dixie. This the Captain professed he was prepared to do, and would only ask that he might sometimes be allowed to warble in his own room the Star-Spangled Banner.

Not long after this, the Red Rock case was to come up again. But a little time before the term of court at which it was to be tried, an offer of compromise was made to Jacquelin. It was said that Hiram Still had one night seen the "Indian Killer" standing by the red-rock, and that this influenced him to make his proposition. Later on, some said the apparition was Rupert, who had just come back from the West a stalwart youngster as tall as Jacquelin.

Under the terms of Still's offer the mansion and a part of the plantation were to become Jacquelin's and Rupert's, while the overseer's house, with something like half the estate, was to remain Mr. Still's.

Jacquelin was, at first, unwilling to make any terms with Still. He was satisfied that, with the evidence he now had, he should win his case, and that Still could be sent to the penitentiary. But Bail was to sit in the case again, and the upper court was composed of Leech's creatures; so that no one could be sure of winning his cause, whatever its merits; while Still himself was reported to be so feeble that his death was expected at any time.

There were, perhaps, other reasons that moved Jacquelin. Miss Thomasia, when she heard of Still's offer, promptly urged its rejection. She would never allow him to be lawful owner of an acre of their old place, though, she added, with a sigh, she herself would, perhaps, not live to set foot there again.

"Yes, you shall," said Jacquelin; and he wrote that night and accepted the terms proposed. His first act was the fulfilment of his pledge to his mother on her death-bed; and she was laid beside her husband in the Red Rock burying-ground, in sight of the old garden in which she had walked as a bride.

When Miss Thomasia entered the Red Rock door on the day of her return, she stopped and clasped her hands tightly. The eyes bent on her, from the walls seemed to beam on her a welcome.

" Well, thank God for all His mercies ! " she said, fervently ; and, taking her seat in an arm-chair, she spent most of the afternoon knitting silently and looking round her with softened eyes and lips that moved constantly, though they uttered no sound.　Later she went out into the garden, and looked at the remnants of the flowers that were left ; and there Steve and his wife found her when they came to take tea with her that first evening, and there, still later, Jacquelin brought Blair to tell of his new happiness.

THE END.

www.ingramcontent.com/pod-product-compliance
Lightning Source LLC
Chambersburg PA
CBHW030739030726
47497CB00001B/51